Intelligence Quotient

Eliza DeMille Robinson

Published by Colesville Fields, Inc.
contact@TJEd.org

Book and cover design by Daniel Ruesch Design
Alpine, Utah | www.danielruesch.net

ISBN 978-0-9912240-4-3

TJEd.org/Intelligence

To Mom and Dad,

For fighting for freedom together,

And inviting me to join you.

quo·tient
/ˈkwōSH(ə)nt/
noun

1. result obtained by dividing one quantity by another.

2. a degree or amount of a specified quality or characteristic.

Prologue

Darya watched with disdain as Harrison gave what would indeed be his final speech.

For years, she had sat at his side, playing the part of his wife. She had given him three children and a happy marriage. And although her role as his wife had been a facade, it had not been altogether unpleasant.

Harrison had been a good man, a generous husband and father. He had been committed to his work and passionate about his ideals, but at times he had become so consumed by his work that he forgot to be a father and a husband when he was at home. Still, she hadn't ever minded that. The more passion and excitement about his work that he shared with his wife at home, the more Darya had on him to report back to her homeland. It was nothing malicious; simply a devotion to her people.

No, those years undercover had not been unpleasant. In some ways, she had even come to enjoy the role of Harrison's wife and the mother to his children. She had experienced their first two children as more a part of her assignment than anything. But after several miscarriages and their years of longing for another child, Darya's little Valkyrie had been a miracle that touched and changed her heart.

For those three short years after her baby was born, Darya had actually found the mission intermixing with her true self. She had grown to love her older children, and even to love Harrison. Shannon, of course, had been her pride and joy, and the little angel's gentle, kind and loving spirit brought a touch of peace into Darya's life, a sense of Westerner purpose that she had never even cared to understand before.

It had been with a heavy heart that Darya heeded the call to return to her homeland. She had come to love this little family of hers, because of the spirit of Valkyrie.

Valkyrie...

Darya felt a sudden pang surrounding that nickname. She had first been the one to call her daughter that.

Shannon had been born such a kind, pure, beautiful spirit. Darya had called her Valkyrie based, in part, on those traits.

While the two-year-old Shannon tended toward those gentler qualities, she was also a protector of those in need, a light in a dark world, a defender who would rather put herself in harm's way than allow others to suffer. She was unafraid to stand up against the most treacherous of monsters and giants. To others she was a shield against pain and hurt, who took their fears and pains upon herself. She had been that light in her family—and could have been for the rest of the world as well...if Harrison hadn't twisted everything to his will.

Darya swallowed in sudden pain, remembering the night she had given her daughter the nickname. That evening Harrison and Kristen had been engaged in an intense battle of wills. Harrison had fought angrily against his thirteen-year-old daughter. Kristen generally submitted to him but on this particular day she battled him relentlessly.

Darya had kept her head down while they fought through their anger. Eric had also remained silent and stayed out of it.

Harrison's intense screams turned to curses and had ultimately gone too far; still Darya and Eric cowered and retreated, not wanting any part of it. Even when Harrison grabbed his daughter and threw her in anger against the wall, Darya and Eric had kept still.

It was then that brave, gentle little Shannon had hurried to the scene, facing her father head on. "Don't push her, Daddy!" Shannon had demanded, protectively extending her arms in front of Kristen. "Don't hurt my sister."

Harrison had stopped himself then, storming from the military base quarters—not returning until he had cooled down.

Darya's pain intensified at the memory. That tiny little child had been unafraid to stand tall against the great and terrible General himself in defense of the defenseless.

That night, as she helped her little one to sleep, Darya had told her she was proud. "You're not afraid to stand up against giants," Darya told her in awe. "You are brave and kind, a shield for those who need protection. You're my little Valkyrie."

The nickname had stuck, and Darya had used it for her often after that.

Years later, Darya learned the news that Harrison had not only destroyed that gentle little angel and turned her into a monstrous assassin, but that he had called his destroyer "The Valkyrie."

It had broken Darya's heart. Harrison had twisted even that which was so profoundly, innately good, turning it into something ugly and terrible.

Shannon was no longer the brave, beautiful light who would stand up resolutely against giants who threatened to hurt and oppress. Now, she was the Valkyrie, the Chooser of the Slain, guiding the souls of the dead to the gods. She was no longer the defender of the weak, standing up against the ice giants. Instead, she was Harrison's slave for evil.

Darya would always hate him for that.

For several years after she returned to the Motherland, Darya watched her family from afar. She watched the General as he became increasingly hard and cold. She watched as he took over his spot in the public eye, bordering on tyrannical in his behavior, but coming off more as a hero to his people.

She watched Kristen, far too young, as she bore a child, and Darya mourned the fact that she had not been there to help her daughter through those years. She even wondered how much her staged death had led to the rebellious behavior which had gotten Kristen into trouble.

She watched humble Eric as he worked away his life in the military, never really aspiring for anything great—unlike his father. The boy had always been rather ordinary, and Darya wasn't entirely sure where he had gotten that. Still, she appreciated the simple man for what he was becoming, and wished she had more of an opportunity to be a part of his simple life.

In all those years, she heard nothing of Shannon. She was certain that Harrison was punishing Darya, keeping her little angel entirely out of the public eye so that Darya would never be able to learn of how she was doing. That was a painful reality, yet she could never find herself blaming Harrison for this. She might have been vengeful, too, had their situations been reversed.

After fifteen years Darya learned the fate of her daughter through an eight-second video feed showing her little Valkyrie, now all grown up, decimating an entire warehouse of Russian agents. Darya's blood boiled.

She then called in the only favor she had ever asked for. She wanted information on her daughter, and a mole within United Intelligence provided the painful answers.

Harrison had destroyed all the angelic, gentle, sweet traits of the girl and turned her into a merciless assassin. And this: *this was unforgivable.*

It led Darya back into a field from which she had long since retired. She wanted answers, and she would find them—whatever it took.

She learned of the Intelligence Project. She learned all that Harrison was trying to do. She learned what he had done to Shannon, how he had truly destroyed all that had once been their daughter. And in that moment, she decided that he would not get away with this.

So today: *today he would die.*

Harrison Altman had always been so fond of his little plans. He already knew he was going to die. He had instructed one of his precious Zhànshì, his own grandson, to do it. But Harrison didn't know what was coming.

Poor Zhànshì Eli would have to pay the price.

Eli Altman sat slumped in a daze, the strong narcotic she'd administered affecting his mental state. He watched the entire event through foggy eyes. He would remember sitting in this position. He would remember shots being fired, a rifle in his hands. But he would wake up the next day in a safe place, a hotel room across town, having not the slightest idea how he made it there. It wasn't her problem how he dealt with the gaps in his memory.

Across the street the crowd was in pandemonium. Upon the stage the General lay in his own blood as a girl attempted to protect him. Beautiful. Really. But Darya found herself untouched by the sentiment.

Darya gritted her teeth and her eyes pulled into a disdainful glare. *"An eye for an eye, Harrison,"* she transmitted to him through the link— which she had long since procured to destroy this man and his dreams. *"A tooth for a tooth."* She set her jaw, fingering the trigger once more. *"My precious little angel, for yours."*

☆ ☆ ☆ ☆ ☆

PART ONE

Foundational Reconstruction

REDEEM CONTROL. TRUST EMOTION.
ALLOW FOR WEAKNESS.

1

Hemostasis

Eli stared at the Council members in utter disbelief.

There was no way to convince them. They had made up their minds. And they were all tainted imbeciles!

"We cannot afford to aid the Republic in the fight against one of their greatest adversaries," Councilwoman Gustaffson said. "Russia is far more valuable as a distraction for the Republic. Several battling states are far preferable to one supreme superpower."

"Prudence would suggest we back off on this one," Sorrento agreed.

"And what about our asset?" Eli asked with pointed disdain. "What about Ava? What about Harrison's plan? Are we to throw up our arms and let Russia have the greatest weapon ever created?"

"We have our mole within the mansion," Gorden offered. "For the time being, it's almost preferable to have her where we can keep an eye on her. Until we can arrange for a secure extraction without inciting all-out war with Russia."

Eli opened his mouth to object once more, but Prince Richard raised a hand to stop him and spoke before he could. "Look, none of us is saying this situation is ideal. Remember that you're the one who assured us you could control her. She slipped through your fingers. But, no matter what you threatened them with, we are not prepared to go against Russia with our armies over one person. And until we can arrange to extract her or acquire her peacefully, the asset will have to remain at Sasha's estate."

"I assured Jackson Davis that if he would not return Ava, we would send in the force of our armies." Eli's words were spoken through gritted teeth, and he hoped that someone in the room would understand the gravity of this situation.

Councilman Lopez was the one to outright huff, his finger stabbing the air as he scolded, "Perhaps next time you'll think it through before you make such an outrageous threat that you ultimately have zero control over!"

The conversation shifted, but that comment rang in Eli's ears over and over again. What exactly did these people think the title "General" meant? Eli was certain that in his entire lifetime, Harrison had never received such disrespect. Even Eric had been shown deference among his peers.

But none of these people saw Eli as an equal. The title of "General" was now just that: a mere title. They perceived that because they had appointed Eli to this position by majority votes, somehow his position here was meaningless. Was he just to be another pawn? Was he just a scapegoat to incur all the blame for wrongs done, without any real power to make the calls?

Eli swallowed hard, no longer paying attention to what was being discussed in the Council room before him. He leaned back in his seat as the realization sunk in.

The United Kingdoms were a pure aristocracy. They claimed to be a republican monarchy, but that was farcical. Lionel hadn't had any real power in his final years, nor really had Eric. And neither did Eli.

The members of this Council were a governing aristocracy. There was a class divide, even within Council, and Eli Altman was very low in the chain of command, though his bloodline should have given him some amount of power if they were being true to their aristo background.

Suddenly, Eli could not help thinking of how close things had been to changing. All the years since Harrison's death, this aristocracy had formed its deep roots. But when Ava had risen up, they had paused. They had watched. They had listened, and they had waited. Whatever story Eli had told Ava about how ridiculous her role in the government had been—Lionel and Ava had been close, *ever* so close. They had almost done it. They had almost broken through the gridlock of these bureaucratic aristos; men and women who had every intention of inheriting power, money and fame by claiming to be in the fight of their lives *for the people*—having no intention of actually doing anything.

Every single man and woman in this room would be content to live out their lives and die without seeing the world any different than it was now. The people of the United Kingdoms desperately wanted to be free and to fight for their right to do so against an enemy who would ultimately come for them. And this committee operated under the farce that they were truly fighting in the name of the people. Now, here they were, talking about the upcoming election and the new seats that needed to be filled, and who might make good candidates, when at this very moment, a greater evil than any of them understood was spreading across the expanse of this world. If General Li and the Politburo did not conquer them, then Darya and the Jiānhùrén surely would.

Nothing Eli said to these men seemed to make a difference.

But Ava, and Lionel, almost had.

Almost.

Eli breathed a heavy sigh, and his decision was made. Harrison never would have sat back and waited for these arrogant, pigheaded bureaucrats to make a decision—when clearly they had no intention of ever doing so.

No, Harrison would have done it his own way. And so, Eli would do the same.

If these carcasses didn't want to hear what Eli had to say, then he wouldn't say another word to them. He would simply do it his way.

The General stood up in the middle of Council session, and all eyes turned to him. He met no gaze and answered no question as he silently left the room.

If these politicians didn't want to get anything done, then he would do it himself.

☆ ☆ ☆ SIX WEEKS LATER ☆ ☆ ☆

To eat, or not to eat; that was his question.

Kyle stared at the pizza box for a long time, far longer than he should have. It wasn't as if he were going off the deep end. But it was day seven of this stakeout, and ordering healthy meals was getting old.

He left the box on the ottoman and went to his wall map, hoping to kick the craving by distracting himself.

Understanding the world, and the war, used to be so easy. There had been the good guys versus the bad guys; the United Kingdoms against the Republic.

Nothing was that simple anymore.

As he saw it, there were now six major powers, or six geopolitical entities vying for power.

He noted the first power written clearly on his wall map: the United Kingdoms, led by Council and, specifically, Prince Richard and General Eli Altman. Australia, having recently been liberated by the Kingdoms, was now as much a part of them as any other country within their coalition.

Second was the Republic led by the Politburo, and specifically President Kwon and General Li.

The third side consisted of Russia, led by the Russian Leadership Committee, and specifically, President Volvakov and Agent Jackson Davis.

The fourth geopolitical entity were the countries of Africa, led by their leader Sizwe and aligned with the third side.

The fifth world power was aligned with the Kingdoms, while it remained a free state—that being Brazil.

And lastly, the final geopolitical power was the new anarchist group, the Jiānhùrén, led by Darya Petrovna.

Kyle cocked his brow thoughtfully. More accurately, the Jiānhùrén were a geopolitical actor on the world's stage. To be an actual world *power*, they must hold territory, and thus far, they had none.

So, five powers and a sixth geopolitical entity.

He stared at this map most mornings, attempting to understand the global fight that was occurring and to ensure he was still doing the right thing for the United Kingdoms.

He always came back to the same answer. The five separate powers held different ideals and beliefs, but ultimately, they all wanted structure, peace and good governance. Some believed in freedom, where others cared less for it; yet they all seemed to be pursuing the same means—building world structure according to their version, their way.

The Jiānhùrén were the wild card. They had no ideals of government and peace or structured nations. They cared little for freedom and less for security. They were simply an anarchist group, bent on tearing people and governments and even the world down. They weren't fighting to help their people or their country. They were fighting to hurt and destroy those in positions of power.

From the movements Kyle had managed to track back to them, it was clear they were no respecters of one nation over the next. They hurt the Republic as much as Russia, Africa as much as the Kingdoms, and had even begun a few terrorist movements within Brazil.

They had to be stopped. And although Kyle was ultimately still in this for his people, for the United Kingdoms, he could not deny the fact that stopping the Jiānhùrén would help everyone. If they were just hurting the Republic, he might reconsider. But they were hurting the United Kingdoms and needed to be stopped.

He had to do this. It was that simple.

Kyle left the map and took a seat on his couch, both eyes on the screen that held the surveillance video, though in his peripheral vision he was still eyeing that pizza box on the ottoman before him. During his time undercover in Russia, he had partaken in many things for the sake of his cover that he had given up once he returned to his regular eating routine. But pizza...this was one craving he hadn't yet been able to kick; neither was he ready to give in to it.

The surveillance video showed a simple thug, Arman—supposedly one of Darya's main contacts. Kyle had been watching him for a week now, and so far seen nothing suspicious. But today, something seemed different. Normally the man was alone in his apartment, when he was there at all. Today, however, six other large, armed men had joined him. None had said a word about why they were all there, yet it seemed as if Arman had been expecting them.

The men had ordered a great quantity of pizza, and for an hour now they had been slowly devouring it. On a whim, in a moment of weakness, Kyle had choked and put in an order of pizza for himself. That was why it still sat unopened on his ottoman.

"It's getting close," Arman informed his crew, glancing at the watch on his wrist. "Clean up this clutter and let's get set up for the meet."

Kyle let out a breath of relief. Finally, something of use.

The men cleaned up the plastic cups and leftover pizza boxes and, once more, Kyle glanced at the box on his ottoman. Now was as good a time as any. He opened it and retrieved a single slice. Indeed, it was wonderful. He enjoyed it immensely as he watched the screen in anticipation. A lot of fit people ate pizza—most of the thugs on the screen, for one thing. In Kyle's estimation, pizza was a worthy addition to a healthy diet.

Several more minutes passed, and Kyle enjoyed every bite of his food until it seemed it was time for the meet. Arman's men hid in closets, behind couches and window curtains—apparently, they were expecting company.

Eventually, a formal knock came at the door, and Arman prepared himself with a deep intake of air, checking the room once more to ensure that none of his men were visible. He reached into his pocket as if feeling to ensure a specific item was still there. When he was satisfied with the state of things, he opened the door.

Kyle's eyes bulged and he swallowed his large bite in one gulp without chewing. He was shocked by who entered the room.

Neither Arman nor his visitor said a word until she was fully inside the room. In one glance she seemed to sum up what was going on. Kyle knew well that she had likely already scoped every threat in the room.

"Do you have the cash?" Arman asked in a gruff tone.

Valkyrie did not attempt to meet his gaze, still she glanced around the room, anywhere but at Arman. "I do," she replied. "Though I am curious as to why we didn't perform a simple wire exchange."

"Your boss doesn't pay you to be curious," Arman said. Kyle knew that the Jiānhùrén didn't like any mobile trails. They did everything in cash and would trade out this cash at the first opportunity to avoid a paper trail as well.

"My boss doesn't pay me at all," Valkyrie replied in her monotone voice.

Clearly that took Arman off guard, but he chose to ignore it. "That's not my problem. Let's see the money."

Valkyrie held a large briefcase, but from the look on her face, she had little intention of giving it to the man just yet.

Kyle leaned forward, and unconsciously, he glanced out his window. Directly across the way was Arman's apartment, and Kyle could actually see a figure on this side of the curtain, weapon drawn and ready to fire.

This looked like trouble. Kyle stood, setting the slice on the ottoman and reaching for his weapon, with one eye still on the screen as he neared the window.

"I was told we would be meeting alone," Valkyrie observed with not a hint of fear in her voice as she called the enemy's hand.

Arman gritted his teeth and signaled to his men. They immediately left their positions, training weapons directly on Valkyrie.

"And I was told you weren't the chatty type!" Arman said in annoyance. "Hand over the briefcase and let's get this over with!"

Valkyrie set the briefcase on the edge of the sofa, but still did not allow Arman near it as she raised her hand. "Just one question," she said, shocking Kyle and Arman alike: "How do you know Darya Petrovna?"

Arman instantly hissed and pulled his own weapon. "Open the case," he ordered. "Or I tell your boss how this went down."

Valkyrie was clearly frustrated, but she strangely complied. It was clear that her questions were indeed her own. Eli had not ordered this extra chattiness. A few months ago, Kyle had wondered what Valkyrie's obsession with Darya had been about. Now he knew. But it still surprised him to see such a *human* side of her.

Valkyrie complied, entering a code and opening the case. Arman stepped forward to examine the money, and Kyle found himself sighing heavily. Eli was paying them off for something. Either deliberately or because he was being blackmailed, he was helping the Jiānhùrén. And Kyle had to put a stop to it before it was too late.

Still, now was not the time to step in. He needed to follow the trail back to Darya first, or all of this would have been meaningless.

When he had examined the money and found it to his liking, Arman nodded pleasantly, taking the case and walking closer to the door. "Good," he said. "Now, as to your other question, I'll let Darya answer that one for herself."

The hand in his pocket came out, and Valkyrie must have seen what it was before Kyle did, because she reacted immediately in attempt to disarm the man. Two men tried to stop her on the way, and she disabled them both easily before it was made clear what Arman held in his hand when he used the remote-control device.

Valkyrie miraculously did not scream out in pain, but she collapsed to her knees, unable to move. Having experienced the remote device himself, Kyle knew how excruciating it was. His first instinct was to move in to protect her, but he had to stop himself. This wasn't like the old days. This could be the lead to Darya that he had been needing. He could still get Valkyrie out in the end; but perhaps this would lead him right to the enemy.

Two of Arman's men thought Valkyrie was incapacitated when they moved in, but apparently the level of pain had not been enough, because she retrieved a knife from her boot and took both of them down as soon as they neared. The men screamed out in pain, and several others aimed weapons and looked to Arman for confirmation.

"We need her alive!" he commanded, though his wide eyes made it clear he wasn't so sure.

He attempted to increase the intensity of the device, and Valkyrie hunched down farther in greater pain. All they needed to do was wait until it rendered her unconscious.

Over a minute passed, and although Valkyrie shook violently from the pain in her kneeling position, she would not go unconscious. Kyle's knuckles gripped white on his weapon. It was difficult to hold back, though he felt he must. This was his old partner. They had worked for over a year together, and although he couldn't exactly say he was close with the robot assassin, he also couldn't deny that he cared for her.

Suddenly, he found himself wondering again how Ava had managed to fry up the device and somehow use the link against the enemy. She was more powerful than he had known.

"Why isn't she out yet?" one of Arman's men asked in fear and frustration.

Arman shook his head, his wide eyes uncertain. "She shouldn't have withstood this much!" he said in confusion. "And I don't know what effect this prolonged exposure to the remote will have."

Kyle swallowed hard, considering that. If it was just about a bit of pain and uncertainty, he knew that he could allow Valkyrie to bear it for the sake of a greater cause. But if this could cause permanent damage... hadn't Valkyrie faced enough of that in her life?

He opened the window, reaching slowly for his grappling hook as he considered. A smoke bomb through the window, then he could slide in and take them all out. But then the trail would end. Unless he could manage to get the intel out of these men through bribery or, if it came to it, more extreme methods.

"Get that sedative in her!" Arman ordered. "I can't let this thing run much longer."

One of his men slowly walked toward Valkyrie, a needle in hand. They should have used a tranq gun. The second he was close enough, Valkyrie took the man down with minimal effort.

Arman cursed. Kyle held his breath as he considered.

"Blistering AI," another man hissed.

Strangely, the comment had a profound effect on Valkyrie. She stood, in spite of the heavy pain from the remote, and threw the knife across the room at the man who had spoken. He screamed out in pain and attempted to dodge, but apparently the first knife was simply a cover for the second, which landed snugly in his belly. The man screamed out in horror.

"Taint this!" Arman said, and he raised his weapon with the obvious intention of ending this for good.

Kyle acted faster than the enemy could. By eyeballing where Arman stood on the screen, he did a quick math equation and aimed through the blackout curtains as he took a single shot.

The man dropped.

The remote fell flat on the floor, still turned on and causing Valkyrie immense pain. Kyle wondered that it hadn't affected him yet. Perhaps it was set on her specifically this time. The other few men in the room went to defensive actions, and Kyle fired the smoke bomb as planned. The grappling hook was sent in, and he flew into the room, taking them down one by one with almost no difficulty. By that time, Valkyrie had managed to crawl across the room, retrieve the remote control from Arman's hands, and crush it on the floor with the butt of the man's weapon. Even after the remote was destroyed, she seemed weakened and unable to stand. By that time, Kyle was finishing up the final touches, tying up loose ends and now-empty hands.

Several of the men had been severely wounded and would need immediate care, but with Arman gone, Kyle also needed answers.

He went to the man he had observed to be second in command—the one who had called Valkyrie an AI and received a knife to his abdomen. Though intensely wounded, he would live with the right care. "I need to know how to find Darya," Kyle growled in the man's face. "Your leader is dead now. And you'll soon follow if I don't get answers."

The man gritted his teeth in hatred, and when he spoke, he spat through his teeth at Kyle. "I'd receive far worse than what you threaten if I gave you anything."

"I can get you the medical help you need—" Kyle offered.

The man shook his head in painful acceptance. Then, once more, fury. "I was dead the second you came through that door!"

He bit his teeth hard together, and a poison released into his mouth, causing the man to shake violently before dying. Kyle watched the man in horror before turning and realizing that all of the men had done the same. Not a single survivor.

"Window, not door," Valkyrie corrected, though she, too, sat watching in horror from her slump on the ground. She swallowed, "You came through the window. He said door."

Kyle watched her for a long time.

Things had gotten very serious, very quickly. This was how Darya did things. No man left to tell the tale, no leads. No trails. No loose ends. If there was even a chance of capture, these soldiers were trained to end it before they could give anything up. Kyle trembled to think what type of threat Darya offered that was great enough to cause these wretches to act so loyally, to the death in a matter of seconds.

Kyle looked around the room with a heavy heart. This was going to be much harder than he had initially anticipated.

It took him several seconds to accept the fact that he had failed this first mission before he managed to let it go and move onto the next task.

Valkyrie was struggling to stand, and Kyle went to help her. "Nice work there," she muttered, and he almost thought there was a hint of sarcasm in her tone. "Why take out your enemies when you can let them do the work for you?"

"I didn't want them...I never intended..." he trailed off when he sensed the strange understanding in her tone.

"I know," she said simply in monotone. She had been trying to make light of the heavy situation, and he appreciated her for that. But her dark humor didn't actually help right now.

"Come on," Kyle said, changing the subject. "Let's get you out of here."

✫ ✫ ✫ ✫ ✫

"Who's ready for Christmas?" Sasha asked pleasantly.

Kai's hand shot straight up. "I am! I am!"

"Not me," Viktoriya said with sudden wide eyes. "It snuck up way too fast."

"We've still got time," Zak offered, glancing at the calendar on the dining room wall.

Ava was usually silent during the meals, rearranging her food and pretending to be eating, every now and then actually taking a bite. Mostly, she was observing the others.

Sasha said there were many stages of healing. Her first week here had been spent in the "deep sadness" stage of healing, but more recently she had moved to anger. It was easier to be silently angry than to be mopey and sad all the time—and truthfully, she preferred this.

Viktoriya asked her a question or two, which Ava answered cursorily, but she didn't pursue more. While most of their meals were informal, Sasha had requested a more formal supper in the evenings. He claimed it was because so many of them got too busy with work and skipped dinner, but Ava knew it was a way to get her around the others—even if she had nothing to say.

Ava had been entirely honest with Sasha in the fact that she had no desire to pursue relationships here with anyone but him. She had her walls up, stronger and greater than ever, and she had no intention of letting anyone but her father in.

She was quiet and guarded when with the rest. Only when she was alone with Sasha did she allow herself to really open up. Viktoriya probably thought Ava was dull and uninteresting—and maybe she was—but the last thing she wanted right now was more friends for Eli to target.

Now and then, she could not help but glance at Jackson. They saw so little of each other, even living in the same mansion. A month and a half now, yet only during these meals in the evenings did she ever see him. And every once in a while, she looked just in time to catch him watching her too.

He was older now, more handsome, more fit. His beard suited him better than it used to. He looked stronger. He looked wiser. But he wasn't as outgoing or sociable as he once had been—or at least not with her there, not during these evening meals.

"What's everyone's favorite present you've ever gotten for Christmas?" Zak asked the room at large.

Viktoriya replied first, then Kai and Sasha. Ava simply observed them, still hardly touching her food. She would eat later. Being on her guard made it hard to feel hungry.

"Mine would have to be my specially engraved watch from Sasha," Jackson replied when asked directly.

"Which mysteriously disappeared some months ago," Sasha noted with a chuckle, indicating the new watch Jackson now donned. Though the slight tone of sarcasm from Sasha suggested that he knew the whereabouts of the watch.

"Hey! It helped us win out in Africa!" Jackson replied proudly. "I've never had a better gift than that!"

Ava considered the comment without any outward expression. She knew the whereabouts of the watch too. It had stunned her when, many months ago, she had noticed Jackson's watch on Valkyrie's wrist. But when she pressed Valkyrie for an explanation, all the woman would say is, "It's mine now."

Clearly there was a story behind this, one Ava was unlikely to ever learn of, since she would never speak directly to Jackson.

"What about you, Ava?"

Ava sighed inwardly. She had really hoped not to have to answer this one. Or any of their questions, really. But Viktoriya was always determined to get whatever she could out of Ava.

"What's the best Christmas gift you've ever been given?" she repeated when Ava didn't immediately reply.

The answer to that question was simple: she had none to compare. But not wanting to make a scene out of her lack of holidays spent, and knowing Sasha would reprimand her for a snarky response to Viktoriya, she searched for a close comparison.

"It's between two for me," she offered.

Jackson was often in his own thoughts during these dinner events, but strangely, whenever Viktoriya directed comments at Ava, he seemed as eager to hear her reply as anyone. Having his eyes on her now made responding a bit more difficult.

"Last year for my birthday, my brother gave me two concert tickets to see my favorite music artist, J.J. He even offered to go with me when I told him I had no one else to take." She smiled despite herself, painfully remembering how much she cared for Eli, even after everything that had happened.

"We didn't end up going," Ava explained. "He got injured and we were in the hospital at the time of the event. I guess to make up for it, this year for my birthday, he gave me my own private party and concert. All the female aristocracy came. I got to meet J.J. backstage."

"How is there any question which of those gifts was better?" Viktoriya asked with a sudden laugh on hearing how the second one compared.

Ava shrugged outwardly, though inside she felt solemn. "In reality, I think I appreciated the first gift more. It was more meaningful, even if not as elaborate, because it felt...real. And *he* felt real."

Not knowing why she had chosen to be so honest, she suddenly grew uncomfortable. She looked down at her salad and stabbed the fork into a cherry tomato, but didn't attempt to move it toward her mouth. A snarky comment would have been preferable, it turned out.

The energy at the table was sober for a time, and in order to lighten it, Viktoriya spoke happily, "Those were both birthday presents, though. What about Christmas?"

Ava managed to hide her frustration. "I don't know," she lied quickly. A look from Sasha told her the reply had sounded a bit too harsh, so she added more, "I'll have to think about it."

It was clear that Jackson and Sasha both understood.

She hoped that would be the end of it. Viktoriya enjoyed pressing Ava to her limits, which was one reason Ava tended to avoid her. Still, she wasn't clueless and hopefully could sense that there was no reason to continue this discussion.

Zak spoke then, kindly, but solemnly. "You've never gotten a Christmas present, have you?"

Ava shrugged lightly. "We didn't celebrate holidays much. I've always been provided with my needs. Everything else is just luxury."

Now understanding, Viktoriya seemed to regret pushing her. "Well, there's a first time for everything," she offered simply. In an attempt to change the subject, Viktoriya made another comment directed at Ava. "You know, I've never seen someone who can pull off any style the way you do. I once tried to dye my hair black. Let's just say, it wasn't my look. But I've now seen three different looks on you, and each time I felt like it was made for you."

"You should see her when she's not disguised," Sasha said proudly.

"In Korea, you had straight dark brown hair and an olive complexion," Viktoriya noted thoughtfully. "Then when you showed up here a few weeks back, you had longer hair, sandy blonde and wavier. Now the short, light blonde, which suits you even better. Which one is your natural color?"

Ava's eyes narrowed suspiciously as she watched Viktoriya. Why did it always seem like Viktoriya was probing Ava for something?

"This one," Sasha replied when Ava gave no response. "She's naturally a light blonde, though usually she keeps it longer."

The conversation thankfully turned away from her at that point.

Ava was silent during the remainder of the meal, and Jackson, too, seemed to disappear into his own thoughts. Unconsciously, Ava touched her shoulder length hair with her good hand, missing the length but knowing it was too hard to manage with a broken right arm.

The waitstaff removed all the salad plates and soup was brought out and laid before them.

"You're quiet tonight," Viktoriya observed to Jackson, as if reading Ava's thoughts.

"When am I not?" Jackson asked in reply, though it almost seemed like his thoughts were elsewhere.

"Don't answer that," Zak broke in quickly, and the entire table turned to stifled laughter. Jackson seemed slightly embarrassed, but he wore it well.

Sasha started asking Zak about some of the progress on his research, and Zak erupted in excitement, sharing a detailed description of his very involved scientific day. Viktoriya looked genuinely interested in every word, and Ava wondered if she actually was—or if she pretended to be for his sake.

Ava herself was highly interested in Zak's research, as it was directly related to the Intelligence Project. She held on to every new piece of information he shared at these meals, knowing that it was all she would get since she refused to speak directly with him. Apparently, they had received a drive with information containing research and development on the project, specifically centered around the flaw. With the wealth of knowledge and research, Zak was working toward a cure to the flaw.

Sasha usually filled Ava in on the details they were recovering, and she hoped that maybe, someday, it could lead to an actual cure to those who were infected—that being, everyone with the chip.

Jackson pretended to pay attention, but she could see that his thoughts were still absent. He finished his salad, having waved off the waitstaff so he could eat the remainder, and he pulled the soup close, taking his first spoonful. He didn't seem to enjoy the taste as much as Ava had. She found the soup to be quite delicious. Still, he continued to eat.

"My idea is to remove the chip completely! For those yet unaffected by the tumor, it would be a simple procedure, and I think it would have very little impact on their way of living following the surgery!" Zak seemed to grow more animated with every second.

Eventually, little Kai stopped him with a loud exclamation of, "I don't know what you're saying!"

Viktoriya clearly enjoyed that one, and in that moment, Ava thought she finally noticed the difference between her fake interest and the real thing. She would watch for that in future interactions.

Ava's thoughts were interrupted by a strange movement from Jackson, a sudden gagging sound. She almost thought he was choking on a bite of his food. He stood up abruptly and walked to the side of the room, stuffing a finger in his throat and forcing himself to gag until he vomited. She watched in confusion and concern, not having any idea what was happening. Sasha rushed to Jackson's side, and the others looked alert and disturbed.

"Poisoned," Jackson managed to croak between retches.

"Taint!" Sasha cursed. "Get the physician!" he yelled to Viktoriya, who was already on her way. "Have security round up the entire kitchen staff," he ordered Zak. "Don't let anyone out of the estate!"

Ava watched in terror, having no idea how to help. Was this really how Jackson would die? After everything?

The poor little boys sensed the tension in the room as Jackson continued vomiting into the bowl Sasha had retrieved for him, looking paler and weaker every second. Sasha stayed at his side, reminding him to breathe through it.

Little Jon started crying, and Kai yelled at him to stop. Not knowing how else to help, Ava hurried to the highchair and unbuckled the boy, trying hard not to glance again at Jackson. *Please. Please don't let him die right now. Not like this.*

She took Jon and Kai out of the dining area and into the parlor, focusing on breathing herself. "Why is Jackson sick?" Kai asked her with concern.

Ava shook her head as she sat down with them on the couch, unable to answer, but holding the two boys tightly, despite her broken arm. *Please, let him be okay.*

"Does he need medicine?" Kai asked seriously.

Ava nodded, her eyes still clamped shut, forcing herself to breathe, not wanting this to turn into a panic attack.

"I don't know how much," Viktoriya said, as she and the medic rushed past the front entrance and toward the dining room.

Ava tightened her shut eyes, her hands going numb and cold.

"Don't sleep!" Kai demanded.

"I'm not," Ava muttered.

"Your eyes are closed," he persisted, and she forced them open so he would stop complaining to her.

Jackson had to be okay. He could not die like this!

"Can we watch a show?" Kai asked, poking at her face and purposefully trying to annoy her so that she would agree to it.

"No. Just calm down," she said, though it was meant more for herself than him.

Jon pulled her hair, as he was very fond of doing, but this time it barely registered.

Just breathe. Please, Jackson, please be okay. Just breathe.

She could hear the commotion and ruckus in the house as it was put on lockdown. She sat there uselessly while Jackson was probably fighting to survive. And it all seemed so...pointless. He couldn't die from a bowl of poisoned soup!

Several minutes passed before Viktoriya entered the parlor, looking concerned but not grave. That was at least something. "Thanks for taking them," she muttered. Jon reached immediately for his mother and began crying as soon as she entered the room.

"Is he...?" Ava could not bring herself to finish.

"They're working on it," Viktoriya replied, taking the boy into her arms. "I think he'll be okay. Believe it or not, this isn't the first time people have tried to..." she did not finish. "Although, they've never made it into the mansion before."

"Why?" Ava asked, not comprehending.

"Russians don't like it when foreign agents run their government," she replied simply. "He hardly leaves the mansion anymore except with an armed escort. And even then, it's hard to get a loyal guardsman."

"That's horrible," Ava said, the horror showing in her expression.

Viktoriya sat beside Ava, taking both boys now. "No, it's not pleasant. It's the joke around here that Boris is sharing his immortality with Jackson. He's survived dozens of attempts now. It's kind of a miracle he's still here."

"I had no idea..." Ava admitted.

"It's not on local news," Viktoriya explained. "We don't really want it spreading that more Russians want him gone. Best let people think they bear that burden alone. Don't worry. We have a medic in house. You've met her." Viktoriya indicated Ava's arm. "She's one of the best. He'll be okay."

Ava nodded, wanting to believe that was true.

"Can I watch a movie?" Kai repeated, to his mother this time.

"I burned them all," she said, almost automatically before returning to Ava. "I'd better take the boys away from the craziness for a bit. Good luck."

She started to walk to the door, but then stopped, turning to face Ava again. "You want to come?"

An image of Hawkins flashed through her mind. Followed by Ame. Then Breanna. "I'm fine," Ava replied, not intending to sound as harsh as she did.

"I'm sure," Viktoriya said with a slight touch of annoyance as she left.

Ava couldn't bring herself to go near the kitchens. There was nothing she could do to help. She'd just be in the way, another problem for Sasha to deal with when she wanted him focused on caring for Jackson. So, she went to her quarters, found a dark corner, and sat there alone.

It was an hour or two before Sasha knocked at her door. She let him in, afraid to ask anything, or even to look at him for fear that his face might give away Jackson's gruesome fate.

"How are you holding up?" Sasha asked, and the lightness to his tone did not sound like that of someone grieving.

She managed to look up and face him. "Is he...?" Still, she could not finish.

"He's going to be fine," Sasha assured her, stepping farther into the room and allowing Ava to close the door behind him. "He caught it soon enough. The medic doesn't believe he'll suffer any long-term effects. A few days of flu-like symptoms, but nothing lasting."

For the first time since this whole thing started, the tightness in her chest released and she felt like she could actually breathe again.

Sasha chuckled. "Zak has suggested that it's time to treat Jackson as a monarch and hire a food tester. This is the second time...."

"He's been poisoned before?" Ava asked with exasperation.

Sasha nodded soberly. "Not in my estate. But at a government banquet some weeks back, before your arrival. He's received many death threats and attempts. Honestly, it's becoming more common by the day."

"Well, shouldn't we...? I don't know, hire him a bodyguard?"

Sasha sighed heavily as he considered that. "I didn't think we had to, within my own estate, but possibly.... He's been reluctant to the idea. Perhaps after this. Anyway, enough of that. How are you doing?"

In light of Jackson's current predicament, Ava's emotional problems seemed insignificant. "I'm fine, Sasha. You should be with Jackson!"

"Zak is with him now. Don't worry yourself about it." Sasha looked around the room with perceptive eyes. "You haven't made this place home yet," he noted.

That was true. In fact, she deliberately avoided anything that might make it feel homier. Still, she decided to challenge his assumption. "I don't have anything to make it mine with," she pointed out.

"I'd like to take you shopping—"

"No, please. I'm all right. The clothes you bought me are generous enough. I don't need any decorations or anything. This room is fine."

"Well I know you haven't touched the bookshelf. How about a television? Video games? Anything to give you something to do in here!"

"It's fine, Sasha."

"You spend several hours in here each day while I'm working. And I support your desire to be alone at times, but at the very least you should have something to do!"

Ava did not respond. She did spend hours in here alone, that was true. Much of her time was spent thinking, and the rest she spent in observation. Her connection to the Tower was so strong. She understood it all so differently now, ever since the blackouts. She could connect with and control them all simultaneously—or at least, she had been able to once.

But now.... She knew there was a physical block between her mind and the Tower, a block that she had put there herself, ever since the blackouts.

For hours every day, she sat cross-legged on the floor, observing her link, and trying to understand that block. She was here to recover and to find refuge with Sasha. That was true, but she was also here to fight.

Of course, the Committee of Russian leaders would be far from trusting her, if they even knew who she was. And it might be a long time before she really had any sway here, if ever. She would not be on the committee of those making decisions, but at the very least, she intended to be prepared when it was time to follow orders.

The block in her mind was a physical barrier that she did not understand, but she knew why it was there. She was afraid of her own power and her lack of understanding. She was afraid of the pandemonium and chaos that she had once caused, and might cause again if she tried to control the Towers. She was infuriated at herself for being afraid of her own power, but no matter how many times she tried to mute Eli's voice in her mind, showing her pictures of horrific chaos and telling her it was her fault, she could not shut him out completely.

"And now I see you're a million miles away," Sasha observed to himself.

"You can put whatever you want in here," Ava offered.

"Kind of missed the point on that one, darling. It's about making it better for you."

When Ava didn't respond, he eventually changed the subject. "I wanted to ask you...I've decided to let go of two thirds of the staff, to only keep those most trusted. I should have done it already, and after today.... Anyway, we'll be very short-staffed. I was wondering if maybe you'd be willing to take on some of the duties here?"

"What, like make food?" Ava asked with sudden surprise. She really didn't have the skills for that. An MRE around the campfire was one thing; this was quite another.

"Oh no! We'll keep Maxim. He's been with me for over a decade and I trust him. More like washing dishes...feeding horses. I don't know. Wherever we're short-staffed."

"Is this because you need the help? Or because you're worried about me?"

"Both, really."

"I told you I'm fine."

"We could use the help," he said decidedly. She didn't entirely believe him but agreed anyway.

"Of course. Since I'm not running missions for you, I've got to earn my keep somehow, right?"

"Thank you, love. You won't try and poison Jackson's food, will you?"

Ava gasped in surprise before she noted that Sasha was grinning at her.

★ ★ ★ ★ ★

"You're welcome, by the way," Kyle said pointedly as they ate at his table.

"I had it under control," she said in monotone.

Kyle chuckled. "So, what was your plan? Take them out one by one as they neared?"

"Yes."

"And when he was ready to shoot you from across the room?"

"You swooped in and shot him," Valkyrie noted.

"Well, yes. That's what happened. But what was your plan?"

"It does not seem wise to remain here in this apartment," Valkyrie observed, glancing at the window. He had closed the blinds, but still.

"I called in help from a friend of mine," Kyle explained. "He'll take care of it for us. I plan to leave tomorrow. But we're safe here until then."

Valkyrie nodded almost imperceptibly, then returned focus to her meal.

"So, if you don't mind my asking, do you know why Eli sent you on this mission?"

A brief stillness, then she replied, "I am the only agent he has who follows orders without thought or internal judgment. He does not want anyone knowing about his involvement with the Jiānhùrén."

Kyle narrowed his eyes in consideration. "And what *is* his involvement with the Jiānhùrén?"

"I do not know. I was attempting to find that out before you jumped in and ruined everything. Now there are no survivors to ask."

"What...that is *not* what happened," Kyle protested. He waited expectantly for her to respond, and then threw his arms up in aggravation, realizing it was no use to try and reason with this woman. "Fine. Whatever. But *you* ruined *my* op by being here, for the record. I had a flawless recon operation going before you showed up and got yourself into trouble. And when you get back to Eli, please: try to remind him that the Jiānhùrén have twice now gone back on their deals with him. He needs to stop before he gets in too deep. Whatever they have on him, it isn't worse than the record he's building in participating with them."

"I will not tell him this," Valkyrie stated simply.

Kyle rolled his eyes to indicate the obvious. It was lucky to get a full sentence out of Valkyrie, let alone a speech of beratement like the one Eli needed.

"He would not listen to me," she said, and took him by surprise with this statement.

Kyle breathed in carefully before speaking. "Why did that comment about you being an artificial intelligence bother you so much?" he asked as new thoughts entered his mind.

She did not look up to meet his serious gaze. She simply stared at her meal. "Because I am not one."

Fair enough. But the number of times he, and everyone, had referred to her as the "robot assassin" were too many to number, and he had to wonder if that, too, bothered her.

When she finished eating, Valkyrie stood, walking around his apartment and taking in the empty scene. Her eyes stopped on the pizza box, and she stared, but said nothing.

It was enough to cause Kyle immediate embarrassment, and he wordlessly grabbed the box, hurrying to the kitchen and nearly hurling it into the wastebasket with a nearly full pizza inside. "So when is your flight back to London?" he asked, hoping to move on quickly from her obvious judgment.

"Tomorrow morning," Valkyrie replied without emotion.

"And your arrangements for tonight?"

"I have a room at the airport."

Kyle winced. The airport rooms here were horrendous, even for Valkyrie.

"Stay here instead," he offered. "This place is outstanding. Five-star. It's the lap of luxury. Come on, I'll show you the spas and pools. It's pretty amazing."

She looked up and watched him then, once more an obvious judgment in her blank expression. "You seem to be enjoying your life after death."

Kyle smiled widely. "You could say that."

Helio took care of the entire mess quickly, quietly and efficiently. It was beneficial to have such a substantial ally, especially when Kyle could no longer turn to his own government.

Valkyrie was quiet as always, but behind that emotionless mask, something more seemed to be hiding. It was almost as if she wanted to say something, but didn't know how to form the words. It was after dark when the spa was closed and all the people had left that he finally took her down to see the luxurious resort. "It's more fun in the day," he admitted, "when you can actually swim. But I like coming out now and then and walking around the pools at night. They keep them lit up, and it has a good feel to it."

They walked for several minutes wordlessly before Valkyrie found a spot to sit at the edge of one pool, right down on the ground. Kyle hadn't really expected to linger, but clearly, she wanted to enjoy the scenery a bit longer. So he humored her, finding a place to sit and wishing he had rocks to skip across the water while he waited for her in the vast, empty silence.

"Darya Petrovna is my mother," Valkyrie said, causing Kyle's gut to tighten involuntarily.

Apparently, she didn't want empty silence after all. Of course, he already knew this, but being completely unprepared for this admission, all he could think to say was, "Oh...."

Another long silence before she continued. "I warned her, at the Russian ballet. I prepared her for our arrival. And in turn, she attempted to have me killed—and succeeded in killing many others. Once more, today, I followed orders to work kindly with Mother's people. And again, she tried to hurt me."

Still, Kyle found himself at a loss for words in his shock at how many words Valkyrie had.

"Is it normal for mothers to despise their children so much?"

Well, no, it wasn't. But then, nothing about Valkyrie's family was normal. Kyle did not give an answer, and another long silence passed.

"I believe I know why she hates me," Valkyrie eventually ventured. After what seemed like an eternity, Kyle wondered if she had any intention of telling him her thoughts. Eventually she worked up to it. "I believe it is because of what that man said today."

Kyle narrowed his eyes and glanced to the left, trying to rewind through all the conversation she'd had with Arman. Finally, it registered, and a strange pang went into his chest—for Valkyrie, surprisingly. "Because she sees you like an AI," Kyle concluded, and Valkyrie simply nodded.

"Everyone does now," Valkyrie said, and he somehow felt how deeply this affected her, despite the lack of emotion she shared. "Except for Ava."

Kyle's head lifted pensively and he stared at the lit-up pool, thinking suddenly of Ava. He remembered that last night on the naval ship, her sharing the beauty of the ocean, him missing it entirely. She probably would have pointed out the beauty here too, if she were here. Ava had always treated Valkyrie differently, and it had always seemed strange to Kyle. Now it occurred to him that possibly there had been something that Ava saw, something that Kyle missed entirely; apparently there were a lot of those.

Kyle was at a loss. He wished he could reassure her that he saw who she really was. But he didn't—or at least, he never had before. She now showed a new side to herself that was difficult for him not to see, even when she did her best to hide it.

The tense moment and the deafening silence put pressure on Kyle to think of something, some word of encouragement or reassurance. But to be perfectly honest, this was his first introduction to this line of thinking, and he hadn't prepared any good words for her yet.

Suddenly Valkyrie stood, breaking the silence. "I must rest. My flight is early."

Kyle stood and they walked wordlessly back to the apartment. His thoughts were mild and mellow, even with this new consideration. Perhaps Valkyrie was a little more human than she made herself out to be. And if so, Kyle had probably been a real jerk these past years.

☆ ☆ ☆ ☆ ☆

"Hors d'oeuvres?" Mikel asked, offering the tray to the guests as they eyed his plate. The first man passed, but his escort took one.

29

Mikel moved along, taking note of the many Councilmen and other politicians at the event. This wasn't really his idea of an invigorating mission, but he didn't have much say in the matter.

His time in Australia had been freeing. He had learned what it felt like to make decisions based on his own conscience, and not the whims of a commander.

Never before had he struggled to follow orders as he did now. He could not decide if the difficulty lay in the time on his own, or if the orders being given actually were the issue.

So far there hadn't been anything really terrible. But neither had he been ordered to do anything that seemed truly important for the greater good. For three weeks now, he had been going on daily missions to satisfy the General's ego. "Get some dirt on that Councilman, send an anonymous threat to that one." Everything seemed centered on securing Eli's place within Council.

Mikel was a purebred warrior. He had been trained since childhood to fight against a terrible, even evil, enemy. Now his skills were being put to use as a gumshoe private investigator to stroke a politician's ego. And if this was how the government was spending their people's tax dollars, then there were some serious conversations that needed to be had!

Mikel was pulled back into the present as he put eyes on the mark. The crown prince, Lionel's son Richard, joined the party with his lovely wife. The event was being held at Richard's estate, and the man lavishly flaunted his wealth to his party guests.

Eli had requested some dirt, anything that could be used against him if need be. So far Mikel had come up empty. The man had a flawless record. He was the crown prince, for pity's sake. He was born into the spotlight and his parents and their team had done very well to keep any skeletons from ever entering the closet.

Still, Eli's orders were insistent, and Mikel was told to dig deeper. It might help if Mikel had anyone left to reassure him that he was crazy, and that following orders had always been like this, but Kyle was dead, Ava had been reassigned, and Ella was on probation—she and Eli did not get along very well.

Mikel had been honestly amazed by how much the girl refrained, when he knew how deeply she hated the General. But one snide huff when Eli mentioned Ava's reassignment and he had drilled her until she said what she was thinking, "It's really no wonder Ava would ask for reassignment to get away from your suffocating presence." Eli was the General now, and he wasn't about to let anyone get away with such disrespect—least of all a Zhànshì who had shown such insolent tendencies in the past.

Mikel had other friends among the Zhànshì, but he had no contact with any of them. Either they were off in the world doing authentically important things, or Eli kept them just as busy on his humiliating tasks.

Mikel continued his rounds until he caught sight of something interesting. A young girl had a determined look on her face as she swept carefully across the room. She was probably in her early twenties, of Latin origin and quite attractive. Clearly, she meant business with the prince. Mikel wasn't here as a bodyguard, but if this scorned young woman did have malicious intentions towards Richard, perhaps Mikel could stop her from humiliating herself and making a scene, and get some dirt for Eli instead.

He stopped her a few hundred feet before she made it to her destination. "May I help you, ma'am?" he asked politely, blocking her path intentionally.

She shook her head without a word, still highly focused as she attempted to move past him.

Mikel shifted once more to block her way. Only then did she glance up to face him. "Get out of my way, please," she insisted.

"If you have trouble with our host, perhaps it would best be discussed in private?"

She gave him a sudden smug smile. "That would defeat the purpose of making a scene though, wouldn't it?"

Mikel looked her up and down more closely. "You're a reporter," he said in sudden realization.

She didn't bother to confirm his inquiry as she pushed past him. "Look, lady," Mikel said as he followed quickly behind her, "if you have some sort of dirt on him, I'd love to hear what you got."

"You're about to," she said with that smug little grin of hers.

"I mean before you spout it to the world! My employer would pay greatly for your little bit."

31

She stopped to finally regard him as more than an obstacle, turning to face him. "And who are you, again?"

Mikel gave a proud smile. "Let's just say, we run in similar lines of business."

Obviously, that was a load of taint. But honestly, at this point Mikel was desperate for any piece of gossip that might get him out of here and satisfy Eli's demand.

This time it was she who eyed him up and down. "You don't look like a typical waiter," she admitted. "But you don't look much like a reporter either."

Mikel painted on a rakish grin, hoping to win her over with his smile. "And what do I look like?"

She considered for a moment before responding. "A stuck-up jerk, if I'm being honest." Then, once more, she moved along.

Mikel laughed out loud, trailing behind her again. "Well, you're right about that much. And you look like the proud, obnoxious 'I can do it all' type."

"If that's your subtle way of calling me a feminist, then I'll take it."

"Hold on, sweetheart," Mikel requested, almost leaping forward to get in front and block her path again. "I'm telling you kindly. If you go over there right now and make a big scene, they'll cut it off before you get a full sentence out. Let's talk this through and think of a better way to get your story told without making yourself into an unhinged party crasher."

"If that's your subtle way of saying 'journalist,' then I'll take that one too."

Mikel couldn't help his sudden smirk. "I like you."

She gave him a withering side-eye before replying, "I have a boyfriend. And I'm fairly certain he could take you."

Mikel fought the urge to laugh out loud at that. Instead, he settled for a challenging, "Don't be so sure, sister."

"If you'll excuse me, I have an appointment," she attempted once more to press past him.

"You're sure I'm not going to change your mind?" he asked pleadingly.

The look she gave nipped that question in the bud. Mikel stood aside. At the very least, he'd be here to witness this little scene.

Richard's team would surely quiet any news of this outburst from a determined journalist, but Mikel would have a front row seat to take the dirt back to Eli.

The girl—Mikel had forgotten to catch her name—was a confident, determined little bee, and she made her way right to her target, nothing distracting or deterring.

She didn't care that Richard, the crown prince of England, was in the middle of talking with several other prestigious politicians. She pushed right up to him and said her piece without a pause.

"Prince Richard, what can you tell me about the untimely death of the reporter Harvey Caldwell?"

Richard paused mid-sentence, looking taken aback. Finally, he replied with that perfect, political charm when he said, "Not much."

"And what about the claims that his death was an attempt by Council to cover up a story that could condemn every member of our leading aristocracy in one fell swoop?"

Richard's eyes widened deeply. Mikel had a knack for reading people—years of training will do that—and he could tell that this man had no idea what she was talking about.

Just then, security neared to remove the trouble from the scene. Mikel was certain this woman could put up a fight if she wanted, but she was poised to go willingly. "No further questions," she said mockingly as the security kindly presented the nearest exit. "Thank you, your honor." And with a melodramatic curtsy, she was on her way.

Mikel watched as Richard attempted to shake off the disturbance, though it was clear that it had a profound effect on him.

Knowing that he had a short window to catch the girl, Mikel quit his waitstaff career forever by giving the entire tray to a guest who requested one piece, and he hurried after the girl.

He caught her just in time as she was returning to her cab. "Hey!" Mikel called out to her. "Wait! Just a moment."

She stopped halfway through getting into the car. "Can I help you?" she demanded with obvious annoyance.

"What was that all about?" he asked, moving closer to her. "What kind of brassy accusation are you throwing out there?" he said, stopping on the other side of the door. "You trying to get yourself killed?"

"If that's what it takes," she muttered, and her thoughts seemed to be somewhere else.

"You know he didn't have any idea what you were talking about?" Mikel said pointedly.

She nodded. "Yeah. I could tell. But I needed his reaction to know for sure."

"So, you just went up there, made a crazy mess and risked yourself just to get a reaction?"

She gave a smug smile. "Clearly, you're still new at this, so I'll catch you up. If this story has merit—which I'm not suggesting it does, it was just a story I was given that sounded fun to chase—if it does have merit, either he knows about it, or he's about to find out. And whatever he does next will help me put the pieces together."

"How are you supposed to know what he does next?" Mikel urged, as if she were the crazy one here. "It's not like you have a mole inside. You'd have to have the place bugged, and there's no way an amateur like yourself—"

"I need to go now," she cut in, unfazed by Mikel's criticism. "I have other engagements. Good luck with your..." she flicked a hand dismissively at his waitstaff uniform, "whatever it is that you do."

She climbed into the cab and was on her way. But one thing was clear: whoever this strange amateur was, she had resources far above her paygrade.

"Let me guess," Eli said from his office chair, not bothering to look up from his paperwork, "you have nothing to report."

"Actually," Mikel said with a proud tone in his voice, "I think I got something this time."

Eli looked up with sudden interest. "Sit down," he ordered, and Mikel did so happily. "I'm all ears."

Mikel related the story, having run into a strange little reporter and being certain she was up to something. Then, he told Eli of her claims to Richard. And there was the weird part. Mikel knew how to read people. And if Richard knew nothing of this prestigious reporter's death or this bold story, why did it look so suspiciously, even for a slight millisecond, as if General Altman did?

Mikel managed to continue on with the story without hinting at this new concern. He tucked it in the back of his mind to dig out later, when Eli's gaze wasn't so fixed on him. Still, as he finished the story, he left out how sure he was that this journalist had greater resources, and instead played it off as if she were just an amateur with no experience in the field. "And that's that. She left and I headed back—securely—to home base."

Eli nodded slowly before sitting back comfortably in his seat. "What was this reporter's name?"

Instinct kicked in, and Mikel knew without a doubt that there was something to this. He had to thank the name of the General that he hadn't ever discovered who the girl was. "I never got it," he admitted truthfully. "She wasn't like most reporters, who are upfront about themselves and their journal. She seemed to be there more for the information and the reaction than to build her name."

Eli nodded once more in deep consideration. "Well, this is definitely something. If there is any truth to her claims, I want to know about it. And I want to know who she's getting her information from. Find out who she is. I want a report and her background check on my desk by tomorrow morning."

"Yes, sir," Mikel said, standing and leaving the room quickly.

An eerie feeling in the pit of his stomach gave him pause. If Eli did have anything to do with the mysterious death of the first reporter, what was to stop him from silencing another?

2

Mental Conditioning

Kyle attempted to be polite by offering her the bedroom, saying he would happily sleep on the couch. Something about the past year of treating her like she didn't have feelings had bothered his conscience, and he would do what he could, however small, to make up for it.

"This is your room," she objected in her monotone. "I will take the couch."

"No, you'll take the bed," Kyle reiterated, attempting a charming insistence. It had worked wonders with Hailey when they were together. Not so much with Valkyrie.

She started toward the sofa and sat down. "Goodnight," she said, and Kyle sighed heavily.

"Take the bed, please, Valkyrie."

She eyed him with what could have been her version of suspicion. "For what reason do you insist on this?" she asked clinically.

Kyle shrugged, smiling slyly. "Because I'm a gentleman," he offered genuinely.

She raised one eyebrow at that comment. "No, you're not," she disagreed.

Rather than stinging, her objection struck him as funny. "Well, I can try, can't I? Just go take the bed. I'll be fine. I'm serious, Valkyrie. I'm not backing down on this one. Just go."

And in the end, she did.

Kyle made a nice bed of the sofa, and was several hours into a comfortable sleep when he was startled awake by the light turning on.

He sat up, immediately prepared for danger, but it was only Valkyrie.

"Get up," she ordered, and then Kyle was certain there was a problem.

"What? What's wrong?" he croaked, suddenly alert.

"It's halfway through the night," Valkyrie informed him. "It's your turn to take the bed."

"What? No! I'm trying to sleep. Go back to bed!" He lay back down and got comfortable once more.

"It's your turn," Valkyrie persisted.

"I don't want a turn. I'm comfortable here. Just let me sleep."

Valkyrie went to the sofa, grabbed Kyle by his arms and pulled him to a sitting position. "What the taint, Valkyrie?" he asked, genuinely confused and frustrated now.

"It is halfway through the night," Valkyrie repeated. "It's your turn to take the bed."

Kyle huffed in annoyance. She wanted to be treated like a normal human; well maybe she should try acting like one!

"I. Don't. Want. It." He spoke each word loudly and distinctly, hoping that would get through to her. And at this point, it was absolutely true. He wasn't just being noble or gentlemanly anymore. He just wanted to lay back down and close his eyes.

Valkyrie would not let him. "It's your turn," she insisted.

Kyle growled, standing up and pulling her along. He was determined now to win this, not for any sacrificial reasons, but because he was annoyed by her apparent sense of fairness. "Go back to bed," Kyle urged, pushing her along through the small hallway.

She stopped flat in the hall when it occurred to her that he was trying to send her back to the bed, rather than going there himself. Then, she tried to switch direction, back toward the couch, but Kyle put his arm out, resting his hand on the wall and blocking her path with his forearm.

She stopped, rather than running into it, and then she looked up at him in confusion.

He watched her at first with a proud confidence. She simply stared, expressionless. Eventually, Kyle smiled, realizing how good it was to be among friends again—even if that meant Valkyrie. His smile was real and touched his whole face. And almost as if in immediate reaction to seeing it, Valkyrie's face shifted ever so slightly, and only momentarily, flashed the quickest hint of a smile he had ever seen. It was gone before he could tell if it had really happened. "Wait, do that again," he ordered.

"What?"

"Smile again."

She didn't seem to understand. So, Kyle smiled once more, and as if she could not resist responding the same, she flashed that micro smile again.

"There!" he said, though it was already gone. Then, with the left arm that lay uselessly to his side, Kyle moved his hand to her mouth and turned the corners of her lips up into a smile once more.

"There. Like that." He couldn't help his chuckle then at how funny she looked as he pulled his hand away and her mouth remained awkwardly in the smile he'd formed there on her face.

Valkyrie did not move a muscle, instead following his orders and remaining as he had instructed.

"You've got it too," he told her proudly in realization.

Only then did her expression change into the slightest hint of curiosity as she asked, "What do I have?"

"The Altman smile," he explained. "It's all there. It just comes and leaves faster than most others. But it's there."

Strangely, his words caused a new expression to form on her face. He didn't understand it initially, and it too was gone so quick, he almost questioned whether it had been there at all.

Valkyrie suddenly turned her head and seemed to look for a way out. His arm still rested on the wall, blocking her exit from the hall in the direction of the couch. Having nowhere else to go, she stood there awkwardly—which was also new for her. He wasn't going to let her take the couch, and clearly that realization perplexed her.

For some reason, this made Kyle smile once more. She was strange, stranger than probably any person he had ever met, but she was kind of fun, in a weird, Valkyrie sort of way.

Her hair was down, resting long and straight over her right shoulder. He wasn't sure if he had ever seen it down before, but it suited her—very well actually. She looked up at him, when there was no way out, and met his stare.

Valkyrie, the supposed expressionless robot, gave Kyle a look he'd never experienced from a woman before: a look of curiosity and maybe even of a sudden new desire.

A strange, hazy feeling took over him then as she stood just inches away from him. He involuntarily leaned in closer, and if it had been any other woman, he would have kissed her. But then he remembered who was standing there. He turned his head suddenly at the last moment, looking away. Realizing then just how strange this all was he said aloud, "Whoa. That was weird."

Her expression changed once more. It showed more emotion than he had ever seen from her: a look of hurt. It, too, was gone in an instant.

He had said the words out loud, with an almost disgusted little shake of his head, as if the thought of kissing her was disturbing.

But it was!

Even so, when she looked at him now, in this hurt way, he instantly regretted his openness. She had been right; she was clearly capable of emotion, and she was unable to hide it from him now as she turned away and hurried back to the bedroom, closing the door behind her.

The robot assassin left him there cold, feeling like a fool, and a taint for being so unfeeling.

The next morning, Valkyrie had apparently meant to leave before he was up, but Kyle heard her quiet footsteps and stopped her at the door.

"Hey, are you sneaking out?"

"I didn't feel it was necessary to wake you," she said in a monotone voice.

Kyle sat up, feeling groggy and tired. It had not been easy to fall back asleep last night, with such strange new thoughts on his mind.

"And you won't...uh, you won't report back to them about me?" he asked hopefully, disliking how awkward the request sounded. "I mean,

I'll be long gone from this place before you return home and report. But..."

"I will not give you up," Valkyrie agreed.

"Thanks," Kyle replied simply.

Valkyrie turned again to face the door, putting her hand on the doorknob.

"Hey, Valkyrie," Kyle said, standing and walking slowly toward her. The problem was, he had no earthly clue what to say to her. He settled for the truth, without the confusion of last night's addition. "It was good to work together again."

Valkyrie turned only her head to face him, but she nodded. "Indeed, it was."

"I'll...see you around sometime?" he said hopefully.

"I'm sure our paths will cross again," she agreed.

He didn't know what else to say. But man, he wished he knew what else to add to clear the air. Instead, he said nothing, and Valkyrie opened the door and was on her way.

Kyle turned back to his apartment, attempting to get her out of his mind, having no idea how much new thoughts about Valkyrie would torment him for weeks to come.

★ ★ ★ ★ ★

Extreme. Workaholic. Overcommitted. Intense. He'd been called these things and many more in his life—and particularly in the past few months. Call it what they want. Jackson would take it. A person didn't change the world by living a "balanced" or "safe" life. They did it by being extreme. By putting in the effort. By being intensely committed to a goal, and working for it with massive effort, fighting longer and harder than anyone else. Zak had once asked him what it took to become great. Jackson was learning that for himself, it came down to one word: discipline.

Jackson's regular routine was highly regimented. He spent every minute of every waking day intentionally, in a way most people would not be willing to do, but in a way he knew he must if he was truly to become successful in his goals, in making a difference.

He was not born with anything special. There was nothing unique or particularly different about him. He wasn't the type who had been born great, as Shakespeare would have put it. But he certainly intended to achieve greatness.

Of course, these constant assassination attempts weren't making his work any easier.

After almost a week of high fever and vomiting, he was finally on the mend. He was tired of the walls of the mansion's infirmary and grateful to be independent again.

Boris remained at Jackson's side as he headed toward the kitchens for dinner. Sasha had suggested that from now on, it may be best if he ate his meals separately and after the kitchen workers had retired. The cook, Maxim, would make and serve Jackson's meals by his hands alone.

Jackson entered the dining hall and he and Boris sat down beside each other at the table. Of course, he would miss the company of the others—particularly, he would miss the only opportunities he had to see Ava—but he admitted it was for the best.

"I know you said you never wanted soup again," Maxim said, entering the dining hall with a small platter. "But this one is very good!"

Jackson smiled and thanked the man. "I'll take whatever you give me, Maxim. I'm still in awe that I don't have to cook anything for myself. This life is the lap of luxury."

"Sasha pays me well to make sure you spend your time on more important things," the large man replied happily. "That is, until you can find a wife to do it for you instead."

Jackson chose not to respond to that one, placing his focus on the soup instead.

"Kidding," Maxim said when he saw how the distasteful comment made Jackson uncomfortable.

Maxim was in his early fifties. He was tall and robust. He loved food, was passionate about culinary arts, and most of all, he enjoyed sharing his talents with others. "I promise, it's not poisoned!" he said with a sort of wicked grin when he noticed how Jackson hesitated with the platter.

Jackson chuckled. "I just didn't know where to start when I received the whole dinner at once! You've spoiled me with the many courses!"

"It's a safer bet this way," Maxim said with a shrug. "And don't worry, I'm the only one who was involved in the preparation."

"That's only reassuring if you're not the one who tried to kill me in the first place," Jackson shot back ironically.

Maxim didn't hesitate before grinning wickedly. "I'm not foolish like the amateur who tried to finish you last week. I know the best way to effectively poison someone is through trace amounts over time that can't be detected, but ultimately do the job. Now, enjoy your meal." This last part he said with an eerie sort of pride.

"Now I'm really reassured."

Maxim started to leave, and as he walked out, he spoke in an overly dark, eerie tone, "Be sure to finish every last bite."

Jackson chuckled to himself, though admittedly, he stared at his food longer than he should have, deciding whether or not it was worth the risk.

Eventually, the answer presented itself and he began his meal. If he was going to die anyway, may as well die enjoying a lovely meal rather than go of starvation.

After a few minutes, Maxim appeared once more in the room. "You sure you wouldn't like anything stronger to drink that down?"

Jackson glanced at the glass of water and shook his head. "You know I don't drink anymore. This is perfect. Thank you."

Maxim shook his head sadly. "Terrible habits you've developed. Life is meant to be enjoyed."

"I'll enjoy the good health and long life that helps me accomplish my goals."

Maxim gave him a pointed look that reminded Jackson you couldn't always control such things. Still, Jackson would do his part.

To be perfectly honest, giving up drinking had been a minimal change in his life. Probably the most difficult change had been his regimented sleep schedule. He'd always been a night owl at heart, and would sleep in on any given day if he could. But he'd also learned that his most productive hours were early in the morning. He now woke up hours before what he had once considered grueling. And if he could commit to that, he could avoid drinking.

Maxim glanced at the entryway into the kitchens as someone came to the door.

Jackson almost started when he saw Ava standing there, her hair pulled back, an ear bud in one ear and an apron covering her shirt. She, too, seemed surprised to see Jackson there at the table. For a second as she waited at the door, he almost thought she was there to talk to him. But then she looked at Maxim and spoke in a slight tone of irritation, "I finished loading the dishwasher. Now what?"

Jackson sat in stunned amazement. Was Ava some sort of kitchen staff now? From Zhànshì, to hero of the world, to the General-elect, to... Maxim's extra kitchen hand? He sensed the shame in her demeanor. She had not wanted to be seen by anyone who knew her.

"Please polish the counters, and clear the colonel's plate when he's done."

Jackson almost objected, but Ava was already headed back into the kitchens.

"She...works for you now?" Jackson asked cautiously.

"By Sasha's request," Maxim explained. "Though I must say, she's the best hand I've ever had—even with that broken arm."

Jackson cocked his head in surprise. "That is," Maxim explained, "she's become the best. I have had to teach her every task from the beginning, even the simplest of chores. And yet, as soon as I explain it once, she does better than anyone, including myself. She is very trainable."

Jackson bit his lip at the comment. The man had no idea.

"Of course, you can't teach artistry," Maxim replied further. "I don't think she'll pick up cooking anytime soon, but she's a good work hand. I best head back to the kitchens."

"Maxim, I don't want her serving me," Jackson said sternly. "I'll take care of it myself."

Maxim overtly shook his head disapprovingly and left the room, and Jackson only hoped that meant he would tell Ava not to worry about it.

Jackson found himself feeling suddenly sick at the thought of Ava as a kitchen worker, wondering why in the General's name she was here serving him now. He obviously wasn't going to allow that to happen.

He finished his meal silently and Boris did the same.

Soon Ava returned, and this time both ear buds were in. She avoided his glance, and when he mumbled a hello, it was clear she hadn't heard— or possibly that she pretended not to.

Still, she could not entirely avoid contact with him when she had been sent in specifically to clear his things. "Are you done?" she muttered, though still not making eye contact.

Jackson wanted to curse Maxim. He stood, meaning to tell her she was fine, but she took it as an indication that he was finished, and she could do her work. So, she moved past him and pulled the platter closer toward her.

"Wait, you really don't have to—" he began, but she ignored him. He was suddenly frustrated with her treatment of him, which deliberately made him look like an arrogant carcass who couldn't do anything for himself and proudly sat back while others waited on him.

"Wait," Jackson pleaded, carefully pulling the earbud from her ear so she could hear him.

She looked up at him in surprise, her eyes narrowing.

"You don't have to do that," he said, ignoring her stony expression. "You have a broken arm! I can take my own plate to the sink."

He handed her the earbud awkwardly, then put his hands on the platter, pulling it back toward himself. Before he could lift it she forcefully attempted to pull it back from him. "You're sick," she said, and that tone of hers was the first indication in this interaction that she might not actually hate him.

"I'm not sick anymore," he said reassuringly. "It's really fine, Ava."

She gulped hard, clearly not knowing how to interact with him. He was at a loss for that too right now. The last thing in the world he had wanted was to accept Ava into the estate and hand her a serving uniform.

Of course, all of the employees on the estate were of a free working class and proudly did their jobs. But it was different with Ava. She was here for refuge, not to serve Jackson.

"Can I ask what you're doing? Here with Maxim?" Jackson risked the question.

Ava finally released her grip from the platter and stepped back a few feet. Even now, she would not make eye contact with him. "Sasha asked me to help out. He had to let go of a lot of the staff. He says he needed the help. But...I think he just said that to give me something to do."

Jackson watched her in surprise. "And is this what you want to be doing?" he asked carefully.

She met his gaze then, for the first time, and her expression was difficult to interpret. "I've never been depressed before," she said in a moment of genuine honesty. "They always kept me too busy."

That sounded like all the more reason not to force her to work!

She looked away again. "I'm glad to have something to do. Sasha is right, I was sitting around too much. Can I take that for you? Maxim will get after me if you're the one who brings it to the sink."

"No," Jackson said tersely, "I'll take it. Thanks."

In his mind, he found himself thinking of Ava during the Talks, which felt like years ago now, with everything that had happened. She had assumed an air of confidence then that had been intoxicating. She had never seemed so self-assured, so confident, so...herself. The quiet demeanor and the way she avoided eye contact now pained him. He wasn't sure if her confidence was gone entirely, or if she simply had none *with him*. Either way, it was painful.

"You don't have to—"

"Thanks anyway," Jackson repeated, lifting the platter and heading toward the kitchens.

Maxim huffed at Jackson and questioned why he would never let anyone else help him. It wasn't that. He wasn't about to let Ava with her broken arm serve him hand and foot. That just wasn't going to happen.

On the way back to the dining room, Jackson stopped abruptly in the doorway when he saw Ava kneeling at the table beside Boris. Her arms were around his neck, and she hugged him tightly.

An image suddenly flashed through Jackson's mind of her holding *him* that way, but they were far from a reality in which that would happen. There was so much damage. So much pain. And still, he hadn't the faintest idea where to start in attempting to repair it.

Though he hadn't fully entered the room, she must have sensed his presence, because she let go of Boris, resumed standing, and walked toward the entrance to the kitchens.

There were so many things he wanted to say to her, but she didn't give him the chance as she walked directly past him, as if not noticing he was there, heading back to the kitchens with Maxim.

45

Boris seemed to give Jackson a mournful, knowing look. The carcass acted like it was easy to fix it—but he wasn't the one who had anything to repair!

"I don't want to hear it," Jackson muttered.

Boris almost seemed to assume an air of contempt at that.

Jackson and Boris headed toward the gym. Jackson's physical fitness had taken a beating the last week, and though he was still unable to do anything too active, he would practice martial art forms in preparation for his night routine.

He thought of Ava more than he should, but no amount of thinking about her had solved the problems or given any answers. So, for now, he must simply focus on those things within his power and control.

★ ★ ★ ★ ★

It took a bit of time and effort, but Mikel did it. He found the reporter, Hailey Ramirez. She was low-grade, junior staff. She hardly got paid enough to afford the cab that had gotten her to the gates of the party, let alone make it onto the guest list. Clearly, she had some outside help.

A great part of Mikel desired to go out and speak with her directly, find out more about this mysterious reporter and her outside support. But there was just one problem: what Mikel knew, Eli would know. Mikel was already struggling with the idea of handing this name over to Eli, let alone collecting fuel to add to the flame.

Clearly, there was an interesting story here. Unfortunately, it was not within Mikel's power to pursue it. So instead, he dropped the topic altogether.

Still, he wasn't entirely ready to hand over Hailey Ramirez to the General. Something within him said that was a bad idea. No news had left Richard's estate about the strange encounter, so Eli might not hear it from anyone else. Mikel wondered if he could put an end to this hubbub altogether.

From a different paper, Mikel picked another low-grade reporter with a similar physical description, and he pulled up her file. She was an activist in her own way, though most of her interests were strange and irregular. The report was delivered to Eli's desk the next morning as ordered, and Mikel was granted the privilege of another, ridiculous, menial mission from his grand General.

A few more weeks of this, and he might lose it altogether.

☆ ☆ ☆ ☆ ☆

Christmas Eve arrived almost without warning. Jackson had been sick the entire week leading up to it and really hadn't had much time to prepare. Luckily, he was able to throw together some thoughtful gifts for Sasha and Zak. For Viktoriya and the kids, he found some last-minute presents. He really wasn't much of a gifter; he was good at them when he tried, but it was usually the last thing on his mind. Still, he made an effort, as he knew gifting was important to the others.

Jackson had enjoyed the holidays as a child, but as an adult he had usually worked through Christmas. It wasn't until joining Sasha on the estate that it became more of an event in his life again. Sasha took the holidays quite seriously, and therefore, so did everyone else. Of course, now having children at the estate would make it that much more exciting.

The real trouble was Viktoriya's bright idea to shower Ava with gifts from each of them. It wasn't that he thought it was a bad idea. Of course Ava deserved a real Christmas—and her first one, at that! But Viktoriya had requested that each of them come up with a specific, meaningful gift to give Ava in order to make it memorable.

In the past it may have been a no-brainer. But now...he wasn't sure how to give Ava a meaningful gift, and he definitely didn't know how it would be received. Still, he picked the gift that kept coming back to his mind and gave it to Viktoriya to wrap.

"Good book," she noted when Jackson handed it to her. "But are you sure it's her style?"

Jackson gave her a look that said he didn't want to talk about this. "Fine. I'll just wrap it. No more questions."

"Thank you. I need to head back to work. Thanks for wrapping all the presents for me."

"You're welcome. I've got nothing but time!" This she said with a hint of sarcasm. "Oh, by the way! I just wrapped the gift you got for me. Love it. Well done."

Jackson chuckled as he walked away, back to the office for a meeting with the second minister of defense.

The next morning the kids were up almost as early as Jackson. He still went for his run with Boris before the sun, but when he returned home, the kids were already waiting on the stairs.

"Where are your parents?" Jackson asked, stopping at the stairs.

"Mom says we can't wake them up for another hour!" Kai moaned.

Jackson chuckled and went to the library to get some studies in before the others awoke.

Soon enough, they were gathered around the Christmas tree with the fire blazing warmly. "Where's Sasha?" Jackson asked, looking around the room as he took a seat.

"He went to get Ava," Viktoriya explained, sitting close beside Zak. "Apparently, she didn't want to come. I think he's forcing her."

After a few more minutes, Sasha entered with Ava and they took a place on one of the sofas together. Ava was in sweatpants and a long sleeve shirt, her now shoulder-length hair worn loose. She didn't necessarily look displeased to be there, but she didn't look as happy about it as the others. Her demeanor lately actually reminded him so much of the Ava of fifteen—observant, calculating, but also angry, abrasive, and frustrated with all humans in her vicinity.

Sasha started off the morning with some good thoughts, and the opening of presents began. The kids were ecstatic as always, and it was fun to see them enjoying the magic of the holiday so much.

Jackson opened his gift from Sasha and was pleased to see a watch with a special inscription to replace his old one. "Ah, Sasha, you shouldn't have."

"I'm tired of that ugly, cheap imitation you're wearing," Sasha explained with a chuckle. "Only the best for you, my friend."

"One of these days maybe I'll graduate to Sasha's favorites list and get a watch of my own," Zak commented with a sarcastically mournful tone.

Sasha laughed and indicated Kai to a specific present under the tree. "That gift is for him."

Zak happily opened the wrapping to find his very own, high-quality watch with a dedicated inscription.

At first, Ava observed the proceedings with that same, watchful attentiveness that she assumed during the meals, almost as if she was trying to figure everyone out, the dynamics and the relationships. As the morning dragged on, when she began smiling at how Kai and Jon enjoyed the magic of it all, he almost thought she was enjoying the Christmas spirit as much as the rest.

That was, of course, until Kai pulled out a present and Viktoriya directed that he give it to Ava. Her eyes widened and she looked alertly at Sasha, as if searching for an escape. He just smiled encouragingly and reminded her to accept the gift from little Kai.

"That's from me," Viktoriya said, and Ava's uncertainty increased.

"I...don't want this," Ava said, even before opening it.

Ouch.

Sasha chuckled, leaning closer to her. "Normally people just say 'thank you' and open it."

She struggled silently for several moments before finally working up to the words. "Thank you," she forced, though there was little indication of true gratitude in her demeanor. And this was just the first one!

Ava opened up the gift slowly and carefully, causing the painful silence to drag on further.

"You open gifts like my grandma," Zak teased. "We're not in a depression, Ava. You can rip the paper."

Funny, particularly since they sort of *were* in the midst of a depression.

But as he watched her ignore Zak's request, still slowly opening the gift, it occurred to Jackson that she might be taking a long time in order to gain composure and prepare herself for what she inevitably saw as a painful experience. He didn't understand why she was so cold to Viktoryia and Zak. To him, sure! It made perfect sense. But she had cut Zak out just as wholly. And it didn't matter what Viktoriya did, Ava would not let her through her shell.

After what seemed painfully, awkwardly long to everyone, the gift was finally opened. Ava stared at the box in her hand, clearly attempting to work up to some sign of gratitude.

"I didn't know what color you like," Viktoriya explained, "so I got a pack with a bunch of options."

It was a set of nail polish. And Viktoriya had made fun of *his* gift? Then again, Jackson remembered Ava's specially manicured hands during the Talks, the carefully done French tips. At least at that time, she had enjoyed the beauty of her hands.

"If you want, I can paint your nails for you some time," Viktoriya offered.

Still, Ava struggled to speak. Sasha gave her a slight, loving squeeze on her left arm which probably only Jackson noticed, and she managed to look up and swallow. "Thank you," was all she could muster. Then the box sat in her lap as if she didn't know what to do now.

The next gift was Jackson's for Viktoriya. "A pair of hiking boots!" she said, acting surprised. "How did you know?"

Jackson rolled his eyes. "You sent me the link," he replied, causing a few chuckles from the others.

Several more gifts were given around the room before Kai was instructed to hand another one to Ava. Once more, her reaction was alert, and almost terrified, like a deer in the headlights. She shook her head again and was about to object, but Sasha reminded her the correct words to say were, "Thank you."

"It's from me," Zak said. "So you know it'll be good."

Of course, when the gift was opened, and everyone stared at a strange looking sleep eye mask, no one had much to say.

Ava couldn't help looking at Zak with confusion.

"To help you sleep," Sasha offered, though he, too, seemed a bit unsure.

"No!" Zak said, as if his intentions for the gift should have been obvious. "It's for when you go shooting!"

For the first time since she had arrived, her mask of stone broke momentarily into a smile. It had been so long since Jackson had seen that smile that his heart seemed to melt in his chest, and he desperately wished he could have been the one to cause it. But of course, only Zak had that ability, to bring joy out of the pain.

Sasha laughed out loud, and Ava's smile deepened. Jackson was smiling now too. And Zak looked rather proud of himself. Only Viktoriya was left confused.

"Thank you, Zak," Ava said, that smile still on her lips, and she actually seemed to mean it.

The gift exchange continued until a third gift was handed to Ava, this time from Sasha. Either because it was from him, or because Zak had broken the ice on the subject, Ava did not look so disappointed at being given something this time.

Jackson wasn't altogether excited at having his gift be given last. He should have made sure it was closer to the front. He was already unsure about it, but at this point, there was little he could do without making a scene.

Ava opened the small, carefully wrapped box.

"Let me guess," Zak said, "a watch?"

Sasha gave him a subtle glare.

But when the box was opened, Ava's breath caught. No one could see what was in it but her and Sasha. "How did you...?" she couldn't finish the question as her voice seemed to choke up suddenly. She looked on the verge of tears, and this, too, was something that Jackson had not seen in Ava since her arrival.

Sasha's demeanor was somber. He was clearly glad she enjoyed the gift, but for some reason, it saddened him. "I was on the Politburo at the time...I was able to collect it from the box of things they left behind. I kept one for myself. The other is yours."

Finally, Ava ended the anticipation for everyone else. Clearly this moment was meant to be shared between Sasha and Ava alone, but the others observed, and could not help being curious.

She pulled from the small box a single dog tag with the chain.

"I wear her name on my chest," Sasha explained, pulling out his own dog tags with one extra tag on them. "Now you can too."

Ava's demeanor was somber, truly grateful, and full of awe, where Sasha's was quiet and soft. Jackson knew simply from Sasha's behavior what the gift meant. It was Kristen Altman's set of dog tags, collected from the Beijing Tower after her death.

Zak and Viktoriya were not quite in the loop, but sensing the heaviness of the moment, neither one pressed for answers.

Little Kai, however, was not about to let go of his curiosity. "What is it?" he asked, walking right up to Ava and grabbing her hand so he could see the tags closer.

"It's...it's my mom's," Ava explained, and then once more, she smiled, a loving smile for her mother, and Jackson looked down, finding himself suddenly feeling the weight and meaning of the moment. Kristen Altman had been a great woman, indeed. He wished he could have known her better. His few memories of her were far from doing justice to the woman.

Kai moved back to the tree and picked out another gift, but the moment between father and daughter was clearly not over, and Ava turned and hugged her father tightly as the others continued opening gifts. Jackson knew he should let them have their moment, but he struggled to look away.

It only occurred to him some minutes later how much trouble he was in, as Ava put the dog tags around her neck. His gift had to follow *that*! Part of him was tempted to sneak to the pile and steal the gift back. She wouldn't wonder that Jackson hadn't gotten her anything, would she?

He had almost decided on doing just that when Kai pulled out another gift and Zak announced that it was for Ava.

Jackson suddenly tensed in his seat. Would it look too bad if he grabbed it now? Said he had changed his mind about the gift?

The answer was certain. It was too late, but he kicked himself for not ensuring his gift was presented before Sasha's.

Once more, Ava seemed surprised, especially when Kai handed her the gift, and she noted that it said it was from Jackson.

She looked up at him in surprise, for just a moment before looking down again. So, she hadn't expected something from him. He could have gotten away without doing this!

Once more, Ava carefully opened the gift, and he could see that she worked to maintain composure before having to face the uncertainty of another present from an unlikely person. Sasha, too, watched with intense interest. Of course he wanted to know what Jackson would have chosen to give her.

When the wrapping was off, Ava stared at the book in her hands, and Jackson held his breath in anticipation.

Eventually, she opened the title page, and silently read the note he had included there for her. *"To a journey I wish I had been brave enough to start a long time ago."*

She stared at that note for a very long time before managing to turn the pages. He could see when she noticed his first note in the margins.

He had read the whole thing, and commented as if to her, just like she had once done for him with his favorite book.

"A Russian translation of *Pride and Prejudice*," Sasha noted aloud for anyone who had missed it.

Still, Ava carefully leafed through a few pages, and he could see her attempting to compose herself, or possibly deciding how she would act.

Eventually, Ava swallowed hard, closing the book. But she did not look up, and she did not manage to say the words that Sasha had forced out of her before.

Instead, she gathered the other two gifts in her hand and stood. "Thanks, everyone," she forced. "Merry Christmas—" She cut off at the end of that statement, and then it was clear she was struggling to breathe. She attempted to leave the room without making a scene, but he could see that it was everything she could do not to bolt outright.

Sasha waited only a moment before standing. "Go on without me," he urged. "Merry Christmas." He followed her out.

Jackson closed his eyes sadly. He hadn't been sure whether she would appreciate his gift, but he certainly hadn't expected her to hate it this much.

Eventually, Jackson opened his eyes to see that Zak, Viktoriya and even Kai were all watching him with awkward expressions.

"Why does she hate you?" Kai asked, causing Jackson to laugh in surprise, and Viktoriya to hush him.

"I did warn you it wasn't her type," Viktoriya said, attempting to lighten the mood. It fell flat.

"You guys suck at giving gifts," Zak said to both of them. "Nail polish?" This was *his* attempt to lighten the mood, and for whatever reason, it worked.

Jackson could not help laughing, and Viktoriya too laughed even as she put her hands up defensively. "I don't know what she likes! She won't say more than two words to me!"

"Well, at least Sasha and I got it right," Zak said with a sarcastic sigh.

"What even was your gift?" she said in exasperation. "How come you can give the dumbest things and you're a hero? Yet I put my heart and soul into what I do and always come out wrong?" Her statement was said with a great amount of love for her husband, despite her words.

She and Zak always teased one another in loving ways, but Jackson had never seen them actually fight. Zak clicked his tongue. "You put your heart and soul into a tub of nail polish?"

She jabbed him in the stomach for that one.

"Can I have the rest of Sasha's presents?" Kai asked, suddenly breaking them from the moment and causing several laughs.

Sasha followed Ava to her room immediately, knowing that her struggle for breath was the beginning of a panic attack, though not entirely understanding why Jackson's simple gift had triggered one.

Ava let him in, and after he helped her by breathing and counting before it fully took hold, they sat on the couch together in silence. He wanted to ask the question, but he had promised her once that he would not push her when it came to these attacks. He would simply be there for her, and she could share what she wanted.

Still, there were many questions on his mind, and it was difficult not to ask. Eventually, Ava glanced at the book that had been thrown onto the bed when she hurriedly entered the room, and Sasha took the moment to risk an ever so slight nudge. "I assume there's a story behind this," he offered. It wasn't even a question really, and he hoped it hadn't felt too pushy.

Ava nodded simply, and after a time, she worked up to relating it to him. "I don't want to talk about Jackson," she admitted. "But the book.... The first time I read it I enjoyed it mostly for the romance and the fun of the time period. I enjoyed it, but I didn't really notice how great it was." She swallowed hard. "It was Lionel's favorite. He made me read it again, with a different outlook. Everything was different that time through. Actually, every book he had me read and discuss with him was a search for principles of leadership, which we always found." She smiled sadly.

"He made me notice leadership principles in everything I did. He taught me *noblesse oblige*—noble obligation. He taught me that my position came with an obligation to those I serve. And I fell in love with those concepts. I fell in love with leadership. I've never wanted anything more...." Her voice trailed off for a time. "I've been afraid to pick up any of those books again, because I'm afraid to go back to that yearning for leadership when I know I'll never have the chance again."

Sasha wanted to object to that statement, but he chose to pick his battles.

"Anyway, I gave that book to Jackson during the Talks, and asked him to read it. He was going to. But then Eli bombed the science lab. Jackson left in a hurry, and he left me and that book behind at the same time." Again, she breathed in deeply. "That's all painful enough. But he doesn't know what this book means to me. This book...it was the first one I read where Lionel really opened my eyes to my duty. It was the first time I realized that I had a choice, and I wanted to be a leader. But I can't have any of that now. And I'm afraid of how much I used to want it, and of wanting it again, when I can never have it."

"Jackson doesn't know why the gift triggered such a reaction," Sasha said sadly.

"He didn't see my reaction. That's why I came here. I don't care if he thinks I'm aloof or ungrateful. As long as he doesn't see me weak like this."

And this was the battle. He could not let that comment slide. "You do realize, Ava, at least, I feel compelled to remind you that this was exactly what Eli used to do. Shut people out so they wouldn't see his weakness."

"Look, Sasha, I know all that. But it's difficult enough to open up to you, when all of my instincts cry out at me to push my weakness aside, hide it, cover it up. I made a promise to you when you took me back not to shut you out. But right now, that's as much as I can handle. The thought of Jackson seeing what a wreck I am is just too much. And after all his warnings about Eli...if he knew how bad it got...I can't see him look at me as if to say he warned me all along."

Sasha thought to himself that if Ava believed Jackson was the type to say, "I told you so," then she sorely misunderstood his character. "As long as you don't attempt to push me out too. It's true that hiding weakness is not an indication of strength, but neither is wearing weakness on your sleeve. Sharing your heart with the right people at the right times makes all the difference. I hope I can help you along the way." He nodded resolutely, leaving it at that.

"Now, about this whole reading business," he moved to the bookshelf and searched through titles. "I don't see that there's any reason for you to be afraid of reading. Let's just see if we can find the right book. How about '*Little Women*,' Alcott?"

She simply shook her head, and Sasha understood that it presented painful memories from a time with Lionel.

"*Anthem*? Ayn Rand?"

Again, she shook her head.

"*Emma*? Also by Austen?"

She smiled suddenly, memories seeming to flood her mind. "I read that one again with Lionel too. He said I reminded him a lot of Emma. I had all this potential to help people, but if I used it in selfish or immature ways, I could do a lot of damage." Then sadness overtook the smile. "And he was right. I led Katia right into a life that she can't break free of now."

Sasha turned back to the shelf. "So that one's a no. How about *The Great Gatsby*? Who am I kidding? That's a terrible book!"

"I like it," Ava replied. "Those who are your peers have great influence over you. Best not get caught up in the wrong crowd."

"I guess I missed that lesson," he replied dryly, then continued searching.

He browsed the titles and fell on one. He hesitated to even bring it up to her because of the awful state she was in, and soon decided against it.

He offered Dickens, Brontë, Steinbeck, Defoe, Twain, Hawthorne and many others. But she'd read every one—and discussed them with Lionel—and therefore they were too painful at this time.

For some reason, he kept going back to that one title. Finally, he decided to trust the feeling, though it didn't exactly make sense.

He pulled the book from the shelf and handed it to her. "What about this one?"

"*Anna Karenina*," Ava read aloud. "Jackson and I started that once," she said as if in realization. "We were only a short way in when our covers were blown in Korea. I never picked it up again. I guess I was sort of waiting to read it with him someday.... But honestly, that's probably never going to happen." She glanced once more at the book, then, seeing the author's name she related, "Leo Tolstoy. He's the one who wrote *War and Peace*." The look in her eyes was one of suspicion.

"Don't worry. It has nothing to do with war, politics or leadership," he spoke quickly, knowing of course she would find those things within if she were looking for them. "It's more about relationships, identity and self-discovery." Then his tone became serious. "I should warn you; this is not a lighthearted, wholesome read like Austen, or even *War and Peace*. It's a very...heavy book. It's heartbreaking and painful. But there is light, peace and even hope scattered in."

For some reason, that warning seemed to interest her more, and she opened the book. "I don't think I could handle a happy-go-lucky read right now," she admitted. "It would sound like nonsense with where I'm at in my life. Maybe a heartbreaker will be easier to relate to."

Sasha chuckled softly. If this was her next book, he would certainly need to mentor her through it so that it was a healing book, rather than fuel to the flame of depression and anxiety. "Open it to the first page," he suggested. "Read that first line."

"'Happy families are all alike. Every unhappy family is unhappy in its own way,'" she read aloud in Russian.

Sasha nodded as Ava considered the statement. "The entire novel is built on that one line," Sasha explained. "As you read it, I want you to compare every character, every storyline, every individual and every family to that thought. What makes a person truly happy? And what makes a person unhappy?"

He could see in her sudden new determination that he'd done right by this simple prompt. Ava was one who thrived off assignments. "I'll have the answer by page two," she said with a tone of sarcasm, though beneath it there seemed a truthful determination.

Sasha chuckled once more. "Atta girl. Now get reading. And Merry Christmas."

★ ★ ★ ★ ★

Zhànshì Six was a force to be reckoned with. He had been the one to rescue Ava from the Tower in Korea and get her safely home. He had been the one to rescue Mikel and Ella from a mob within Central America. He had taken care of Hawkins, and others who had been serious threats. He was Eli's secret weapon.

Ava was gone, and it would be a difficult task to gain her back. Kyle was dead, though he had been Eli's first choice for this job. Mikel was too strong-willed and free spirited, and Eli knew he would question him at every turn. Valkyrie was needed elsewhere—there was no one else, even among the Zhànshì, who he trusted enough in his dealings with the Jiānhùrén.

And so Zhànshì Six became Eli's closest and most trusted soldier.

He stood before Eli as they met in a darkened, secluded street well before dawn. Eli was a careful man, and in business like this, he could not risk being overheard by bugs or spies within the mansion or even United Intelligence Headquarters.

Eli passed the file to Zhànshì Six, who accepted it without word. "This is the file of a nosy reporter who's been getting a little too close to a story that cannot be told. Mere mention of the possibility of its being true could have catastrophic effects."

"Is it true?" Zhànshì Six asked gruffly. Normally, this man was not one to ask questions. Eli would let this one slide.

"Let's just say, the fate of our nation is in danger. It's my job to ensure the security of the Kingdoms. And this story puts us at risk."

Zhànshì Six nodded simply. "What do you want me to do with her?"

Eli sighed heavily. He had thought that through extensively. This was just a naive, ambitious journalist who had gotten herself in with the wrong story. That didn't mean she deserved to die. Still, he could not allow her to get in too deep with this story. If it were ever told...Council would go up in flames. And this was not the time.

Eli wasn't the greatest fan of the myriad members of Council either. At a time of peace, he might even rally for universal reelection. But the United Kingdoms could not afford such a political mess when the war was at such a serious state. Three years from now, any journalist could tell this story how they wanted. But for the time being, it could not get out.

"Having her killed would cause too much suspicion," Eli explained, "particularly after Harvey Caldwell was killed—it won't matter whether we had anything to do with it. But she needs to forget this story." Eli handed Zhànshì Six a vial, which the man would know what to do with. This wasn't their first time dealing with such matters.

"Understood, sir," Zhànshì Six said. "Consider it done."

"I do," Eli assured the man. And in truth, he had complete faith in Zhànshì Six's abilities. He hadn't let him down yet.

☆ ☆ ☆ ☆ ☆

Ava sat sideways on the couch with her back to the arm rest, reading alone in the dimly lit room. It had been several days since Christmas, and almost all she did now was read. She was lost in the book, and deeply enveloped in the characters and storyline.

Ava compared Kitty to her own story. So many young, naive girls fell into that same trap, not differentiating true, genuine love from flashy confidence. Marianne Dashwood. Natasha Rostov. Emma Woodhouse, and many more.

And so had Ava. She had chosen Eli. Maybe his love wasn't flashy, but his flame burned red, and she'd run to that rather than trusting what was right in front of her.

Still, she could not say she regretted her choice to give her brother a chance, but neither could she ever afford to run to him again.

Ava swallowed her thoughts, as just then, Jackson walked in, going straight to the fireplace and leaning against the wall above it, his eyes closed as he breathed in and out deeply several times.

Ava watched him, unsure how to react. She had the absurd urge to sneak out hoping he wouldn't notice her since eventually he would turn around and realize she was there. What kind of spy didn't check the room before entering? Eventually he seemed to sense a presence. He turned and saw, finally, that she was there.

She made a lame excuse, "I wasn't watching you," she lied quickly. "I was reading my book."

Jackson's expression remained flat and slightly mournful. He didn't respond, but walked across the room to the couch, sitting down on the other end from her, staring across at the fireplace, but saying nothing.

Ava pulled her feet closer to her chest to give him space. The silence lingered as he breathed in a focused manner until she couldn't help speaking, "Are you okay?"

He finished his next focused breath before replying, "Just stress," he explained. "I'll manage."

A thought suddenly occurred to her, and she spoke before thinking. "Have you ever had a panic attack?"

His eyes narrowed in thought. "I don't think so," he admitted, yet seeming unsure.

Ava clicked her tongue as Jackson's comment answered the question. "You would know if you had."

Jackson nodded in understanding. "What is it like?"

A silence passed as Ava wondered if she was ready to have a conversation with him. Again, she answered before she really knew what she was doing. "Maybe different for others, but for me it feels like I'm drowning. The water crushes down on my entire body, and no matter how hard I try to suck air into my lungs, it won't come. It genuinely feels like you're going to die. Your body attacks you from the inside out, and you're utterly helpless."

Jackson's expression was deeply caring and thoughtful, still, he watched the hearth. "Sounds...horrible."

Ava huffed slightly. "You could call it that."

Another silence passed. This was the time to make an excuse about why she should be going and get out of there, but for some reason, she did not move.

"I've been stressed and anxious out of my mind before," Jackson admitted. "But I've never experienced what you're talking about."

Ava found herself scowling suddenly. The thought of Jackson going through a panic attack sent a pang, even though it hadn't ever happened. She never wanted him to face that. The very thought of it pained her.

"How do you manage the stress?" Ava found herself asking, despite her plan never to speak to any of them conversationally.

"Running. Strength exercise. Any kind of physical activity that gets the stress out. I recently started meditating and breathing exercises—a friend of mine, Sizwe, recommended it. And it's helped a lot too. I think everyone deals with stress in their life. Half the time my stress is unreasonable. The other half, the weight of the impending doom in the world is on my shoulders and I'm supposed to come up with answers. Either way, the stress can become overpowering."

She decided not to voice her thought, that he reminded her of Eli. It was true. They had so many similarities, but at the end of the day, Jackson chose to be a good person. And Eli...didn't.

"It's not because of Eli, is it?" she asked with sudden concern.

"No," he spoke with a shake of his head. "I guess his bark proved bigger than his bite. He hasn't followed through on any of his threats. Perhaps Council wouldn't let him. I don't know for sure."

That, at least, was a relief. Still, Jackson was overwhelmed. "So, what is it?" Ava asked the question bluntly, genuinely having forgotten manners as of late.

Again, he was thoughtful before responding. "I guess my heart is in Africa with my brothers and sisters who are fighting. And here I am in the comfort of this mansion, safely in Russia. I'm needed here. If I leave, I think everything I've done with the Committee will go to shambles. They still need constant coddling and reminders. Every day here is a battle. I'm working with hundreds of Russian leadership, attempting at every moment to hold this all together."

"What about Sasha?" Ava objected. "Can't he help?"

Jackson hesitated. "He's stepped to a minor role on the Committee. He has other obligations, and he can't commit to the constant presence at this time. He has more pressing concerns."

"You mean me," Ava realized aloud. So, it was her fault.

Jackson smiled. Still, he hadn't once looked directly at her—not since realizing she was there. It was strange from Jackson, who was so confident and good with people. Was this purposeful?

"He's a family man first now," Jackson explained of Sasha. "And he has rightly earned it. No, there's really no one else who can do the day in and day out work with the Committee right now. I know I'm needed here, but every day my closest friends are fighting a battle in the trenches. And I sit in the comfort of this mansion." He sighed deeply, thoughtfully. "I've been thinking a lot about Thomas Jefferson lately. Working as French ambassador during the Revolutionary War. He sat safely in France while his brothers fought in the States. He was safe and out of danger, but the battle he fought was probably vicious, mangled with guilt and regret that he wasn't physically fighting beside them. The United States wouldn't have won without the work he did in France. It was just as necessary. Still, I imagine that his heart was in the trenches with his brothers in the war."

Ava looked down thoughtfully, feeling for him. "I forget, you're still an American at heart."

61

Jackson nodded softly. "I am, but it's great history either way. The United States had the longest standing freedom since the Roman Republic. Some people say they became too arrogant, and admittedly their financial instability was real in those final years. But it's my opinion that the Republic knew they couldn't get away with world domination against people who so well understood freedom. So, they removed the threat."

Ava had never thought of it like that.

"Anyway. That's where the stress arises. I know the best thing I can do for them is fight here, but it's not an easy battle. And the work here sometimes feels so...*ridiculous* in the wake of greater threats."

Ava nodded, not knowing what else to say. She wished she knew how to help, but it had been a long time since Ava knew how to comfort this man in his trials. She shifted her book awkwardly in her lap, and Jackson caught the movement.

"*Anna Karenina*," he observed. "That's a heavy read."

Ava nodded. "That's what Sasha said, but I guess he also thought I was ready for it."

"I'm sure you are," Jackson agreed quickly. After a lull he spoke again. "You and I started it together once," he said, as if to remind her.

She nodded as indication that she remembered.

He offered a half smile. "I finished it a few weeks later, when it became clear we probably wouldn't have a chance to read together again."

The expression on her face was slightly pained, though she attempted to hide it.

"How far into it are you?" Jackson asked, moving on from the comment.

She held it up to show him. "Anna just headed back home to Petersburg. But honestly, I've been more interested in Kitty and Levin's story."

He smiled at that, still watching the flames.

"Do they ever...work it out?" she asked hopefully.

Jackson shrugged nonchalantly. "You'll have to keep reading."

Ava sighed. "You never were one to give spoilers," she replied reproachfully.

Jackson looked at her then, as if wanting to see her expression. Then he smiled sweetly.

That smile, directed at her...she couldn't remember the last time... and it pained her deeply. She almost tensed, looking for an excuse to escape, but by then he was watching her thoughtfully.

Jackson didn't look away, but his expression changed and she could tell his thoughts had too. "Viktoriya has tried to reach out, a lot of times. You keep blowing her off. Why?"

Ava breathed in deeply. She couldn't seem to look him in the eyes, though he was ready. So now she was the one to watch the fire. For half a minute, she wondered if she would tell him the truth. And strangely, in the end, she did. "I've had a lot of really good friends in the past," she admitted. "People I came to love with my whole heart. And they're all gone now."

Jackson observed her thoughtfully. "You don't want to replace them?" he offered a question.

"No. It's not that. No one will ever be able to replace Breanna in my heart. Or Ame. Or Hawkins. It's just...to be honest, I don't want to get close to anyone else just to lose them. I'm tired of losing everyone. It's not worth making bonds anymore."

Jackson watched her, a sad expression on his face. Then he risked asking, "What about Sasha?"

Ava shrugged slightly. "It's too late with him. I already love him. It'll break my heart to lose him no matter what at this point. So, I may as well enjoy what time I have with him."

Jackson nodded simply in understanding. After a while he asked softly, "And what about me?"

That question shocked her so much, she couldn't help but turn to face him.

They remained there, looking into one another's somber eyes for a time. And had he remained silent long enough, she may have been forced to answer that question too. But he seemed to grow uncomfortable at the vulnerability he had just offered, and instead tried to mask it with a different meaning. "You're talking to me now," he said, his somber mood lightening. "Isn't that risky? You might start to care about me."

63

Ava stared at him, seeing right through his mask of sarcasm. He was afraid of her knowing he cared, so he covered up his vulnerability and poked fun of hers.

"You're right," Ava said, hurt by his sudden sarcastic comment in light of how genuine she had been with him. "I better go."

She moved forward, and would have stood to leave, but he stopped her. "Wait. I was joking."

"Good one," Ava replied dryly. Several beats passed in silence before she faced him once more. When she did speak, it was in a hoarse whisper. "I already lost you, remember?"

They stayed there, silent for a time, staring at each other.

This was dangerous territory. She had risked staying for a few words, and it turned to a serious confessional. Only, she didn't know how to soften it with sarcasm like he had.

Jackson eventually spoke, deeply serious this time. "I'm sorry, Ava. For everywhere I went wrong. For all the mistakes I made. For pushing you away. I'm sorry for hurting you, and taking away every option you had but to stay with Eli."

He swallowed hard, but he wasn't done. "I'm sorry I projected my fears and my issues onto you. I can never fix everything and everywhere I went wrong. I could spend my whole life trying to make up for it, and it would never be enough. I know a simple 'sorry' doesn't cut it. But I need to say the words anyway. I'm sorry for what I did to you. I'm sorry for letting you down. And I'm sorrier than you can ever know that because of that, it means I've lost you. That I don't get to be in on the jokes. That you go silent when I enter the room, and make excuses to leave when I'm there. I'm sorry that I hurt you. And I'm sorry that I lost you as a friend. Because you truly were the greatest friend I ever had."

Ava felt the truthfulness in his words. She thought of that time, years ago in Korea when the two of them had resolved weeks of bitter fighting with simple apologies.

In truth, Ava was not angry with him. She had long since forgiven Jackson. And yet, he was right, that because of the rift that had been formed between them, she didn't know how to let him in. And even now, she didn't know how to tell him that she had forgiven him.

Instead she listened silently. And when it was clear that he had finished with his apology, after another lingering silence, her hands began to go numb. She rubbed her fingers against her thumb, attempting to get feeling back into them, and Jackson glanced down, having noticed the movement. A strange anxiety suddenly took over.

She wasn't ready to let go, not fully. She may not be angry, but she wasn't ready to trust him again either. All the pain she had felt since Yuri's death seemed to rain down on her in a moment, overwhelming her.

Taint. Just moments ago she had explained to him the mechanics of an anxiety attack. Now she was having the onset of one. Because what? She couldn't handle the pain of his presence?

She managed to keep her breathing steady long enough to stand from the sofa and exit the room. Almost as soon as she was in the hall, she felt the overwhelming weight constricting her chest. She started to her room, prepared to deal with this alone.

But then she remembered another promise she had recently made to Sasha. He had begged her, "Please, bother me! I don't want you ever being alone for one of these attacks again. Promise me, you'll come to me." And she had promised him.

So, Ava went to the library, to Sasha's office. It didn't matter that the reasons for the panic were ridiculous. He wouldn't ask. It didn't matter that she had no answers. He would not press for them. He would just help her, teaching her ways to cope, assuring her that she was not alone. He would simply be there for her, and in these moments, that was all she needed.

☆ ☆ ☆ ☆ ☆

Mikel returned to his quarters at the United Intelligence base, a sick feeling in his stomach. Things had gone too far this time.

A few meaningless recon missions, being Eli's lapdog—that had been hard enough; but this time, he knew it had gone too far. And it had to stop.

He had attempted to protect Hailey from Eli, giving him a different name, and it seemed that had been the right decision.

65

A horrific train accident had left the young reporter with a severe amnesia, and Mikel knew it could not be coincidence, even though dozens more were wounded or killed in the accident.

Eli had reacted rashly. He had attempted to silence this woman and had managed to do so. Had Mikel given the right name, it would have been Hailey in the hospital with unspeakable head trauma. Instead, Mikel had naively offered up an innocent civilian, with albeit interesting habits and behaviors, and served her up on a platter for Eli.

If Mikel was Eli's little task student for the menial ops, who was doing the real dirty work for the General?

Mikel could not forgive himself for the trouble he had caused an innocent woman. In truth, he had known this was a possibility. He had suspected that Eli was somehow involved in the death of the first reporter. But it had all seemed too much, too unbelievable. Yet, Mikel had been wary enough not to give the real identity of Hailey Ramirez. So why hadn't his conscience stopped him from giving up another innocent soul?

He had to admit to himself, in part, he had purposefully done this. He had to know what Eli would do. He had to see where this was headed. He had to find out if he were crazy, or if his intuition was right about this one.

If nothing had happened, then no one would be the wiser. But something had happened. Eli had proven his hidden agenda. And Mikel felt the weight of responsibility for the casualties along the way. Heavily he felt it. He wanted to vomit, but managed to control it by swallowing down several sips of water from his bottle on the bed. This had all gone too far. He was not out of line in feeling that his orders were flawed. If the General was involved in a coverup of this magnitude, then perhaps he wasn't so worthy of the title or the power which allowed him to give Mikel such menial, dangerous orders.

A movement in the shadows of his quarters startled him, and he retrieved his weapon, shifting on the lights.

"I mean you no harm," the man said, almost before Mikel could take his measure. He was large, gruff, bulky, but his face was rather ordinary and unremarkable, the kind you would forget just minutes after seeing it.

"What are you doing in my quarters?" Mikel asked with suspicion, though not with great concern as of yet. This was United Intelligence Headquarters. The man couldn't have made it in without being an active agent himself. Besides, Mikel held the weapon, and the man across the room was at his mercy.

"I am a friend of Ava's," the man said. "And whatever Eli has told you about her, he has lied."

Mikel's eyes narrowed in consideration. What was that supposed to mean?

"Can I ask again what you're doing in my quarters?" Mikel pressed for a response.

The man nodded. He seemed strangely unafraid of Mikel and the weapon directed at his face. "I'm here because I believe you are also a friend to Ava. And I want to offer you a chance to join our side."

3

Diffidence

Jackson sat at the library table several hours before the others, trying to catch up on research and studies. His schedule looked intimidating to anyone from the outside. He got up before the sun, and he and Boris would go for a morning run to help clear his mind and prepare his body for the strain of a high-stress day ahead—as all his days were. Then he would shower, get dressed, and begin his studies. All of this took three hours every morning before anyone else began their work. He ended his studies in time for a morning briefing, then spent the eight hours of a regular workday in intense meetings with Committee members before winding down in the evening with exercise and physical training before bed.

His days were entirely filled with work, but they were productive. He was moving forward. He was working toward greatness. And he was willing to do what few others would, to put in the hours that few others wanted to.

He could have time for leisure later on, "someday," but his life wasn't meant for entertainment. That wasn't what he wanted. He wanted to be great. He wanted to change the world and that meant sacrificing his time for a greater cause.

Sasha and Ava entered the room at eight on the dot. The meeting would start in ten minutes, but Sasha liked to be sitting before it began. Zak always came at the last minute. Ava was not allowed in the Russian Leadership Committee meetings, of course. But Sasha had been bringing her to the meetings between the crew for the past week. She said very little. She still considered her place there to be rocky and unstable, and there was truth to that. Yet, it was a start.

"Morning," Sasha directed to Jackson.

"Morning," Jackson nodded in response.

He was at first unsure how to deal with Ava. After their conversation last night, he was certain he had offended her. She didn't want an apology. No amount of "sorry" could make up for what she had faced because of him. He knew that. Still, he had felt it was important to say the words anyway, no matter how she reacted to it.

He expected a cold, hostile or indifferent manner from her this morning, and he was surprised when instead, she looked directly at him and smiled.

He was so taken aback, he almost forgot to smile back at her and only did so just in time before she had looked away.

"It's cold in here," Sasha noted, seeing how Ava shirked off a shiver.

Truthfully, he had been so invested in his studies, Jackson hadn't noticed. But now that Sasha mentioned it, the room was rather chilly. Jackson glanced at his jacket, which he had left hanging on the rack by the door.

"I'm going to go turn up the heat," Sasha said. He moved to the rack and grabbed the only jacket there, without thought of whose it was, and handed it to Ava. "Here you are. Put this on. I'll be back in a minute."

Jackson pursed his lips to hide his smile and looked down again at his papers as Sasha left. He hadn't noticed the cold before, and he would be fine without a jacket now.

Ava put one sleeve over her good arm, then attempted several times to get the other sleeve to her broken one. It wasn't working. She cursed under her breath after one attempt that clearly pained her.

Maybe it was the fact that it was his difficult jacket, maybe it was the smile she had given him when she entered the room, or maybe it was just that he knew how to fix the problem and wanted to help when she looked like a dog chasing her tail. Whatever the reason, he stood from his seat and walked to the edge of the table where she stood.

"Here, let me," he offered, and she stopped, though surprised, holding still and allowing him to help. He removed the sleeve from her good arm. "I've learned that when you have an injured limb," he began, "it helps to start with that side." And so, he carefully put the right sleeve over her cast. "After that, you can more easily maneuver to grab the other side." He allowed her to do so.

"Right. You'd think after eight weeks I would have thought of that," she grumbled. "Now that I'm this close to having the cast removed." She managed to put the sleeve on, but then as she attempted to zip it up, she had several failed attempts before cursing again.

This time, he said nothing. Instead, he reached for the two bottoms of the zipper, fastening it and then slowly zipping it up for her.

He hadn't meant to be invasive of her space. He just knew how frustrating injuries could make it to accomplish even the simplest of tasks. Still, when the jacket was fully zipped, and he looked to face her, his fingers resting on the zipper atop her chest, he realized he probably should have let her do that part. He dropped his hands to his side awkwardly.

"Thanks..." Ava said, though the look she gave him said there was more than that on her mind.

Feeling suddenly embarrassed, he thought to turn and retreat back to his seat, but he held his ground for a moment longer, enough time for her to speak.

"I'm sorry I ran away last night. I wasn't mad. I'm not angry. I just... it was a lot."

"Yes. It was," he agreed. "I'm sorry."

"Don't be," she replied, seeming to mean it. "You said you could never say the word 'sorry' enough. But you don't have to. We both made mistakes. Maybe best to just let it go and move on."

Jackson nodded slowly. He still lingered there close to her, wishing he could fix the feeling of such vast distance between them, but having no idea how.

Ava unconsciously put her hand in the pocket of the sweater she wore, and something jingled inside. She pulled out the object, which Jackson already knew to be his truck keys. But as soon as she saw them, her eyes fell on the gift he had only just received on Christmas from Zak—a leather key charm with his name inscribed on it. Her face went pale.

"Oh no! This is your jacket! I thought it was Sasha's, I'm sorry!" She replaced the keys in the pocket, then quickly attempted to unzip the jacket and return it to him.

Once again, he invaded her space involuntarily, placing his hand on hers to stop her. "No, it's okay. I'm not cold. Please. Just keep it."

She still seemed unwilling, but he would not allow her to unzip the jacket, holding her hand still with his. "After all the work it took to get it on you?" he said sarcastically. That did not change her reluctance. "It's okay, Ava. I'm serious. Please just wear it, will you?"

She probably never would have agreed if it weren't for Zak breaking the moment by entering the library. Jackson pulled his hand from off of hers. And, obviously not wanting to make a scene, Ava kept the jacket on, though still clearly with great hesitation.

"Someone forgot to turn on the heat," Zak observed, taking his seat.

Sasha entered soon after, and they began.

The library door opened with a loud bang against the wall and Lieutenant Colonel Vasiliv made a loud entrance.

Jackson couldn't contain his excitement. He stood and pushed his chair back. "Vas!" he said with a broad grin. "What are you doing here? I thought you had flown in to Moscow!" He walked around the table toward his friend, and they took each other in a large bear hug.

"I'm not late for the morning meet, am I?" Vasiliv asked after they had pulled away.

"As always," Zak grumbled bitterly.

Vasiliv looked around the room, and stopped on Ava. "Who's this?" he asked the room at large.

Jackson could see that Ava was as uneasy about answering that question as he was. How was he supposed to introduce her?

"This is my daughter," Sasha replied clearly without any hesitation at all. He'd already decided it was time to claim her as his own.

The subtle look of gratitude on Ava's face could only have been noticed by those who truly knew her, but Jackson did.

"Ava," Sasha continued, using her real name to top it all off.

Vasiliv nodded approvingly. "Didn't know you had kids." Then to Ava, "I'm Vasiliv, Jackson's best friend."

Ava smiled, though deeply behind it he almost sensed regret. That had once been her title.

"He wishes," Zak muttered to himself.

Vasiliv sat next to Jackson at the large briefing table. "Jackson's pushing paid off," he explained when they had all settled in. "The president has agreed to send the Russian Elites to Africa."

"He could've told me," Jackson said with sudden annoyance.

"He's planning to announce it to the Committee beginning of next week. He asked that you and I do a check on the team before Monday, pick the five who will be sent. Sasha, he wants you in Moscow for the announcement and dealing with the Committee on the matter."

Jackson nodded thoughtfully. "That's good news."

Sasha was the first to notice Ava looking left in the dark. "The Elites are the Russian equivalent of…"

"Of Jackson," Vasiliv finished when Sasha hesitated. "Minus the 'rogue agent, take over the enemy government and use it against your own' bit."

"They're an elite squad of highly trained men and women," Zak gave the only good explanation so far. "Not agents of infiltration, but assassins, tactical specialists and warriors."

"What Jackson was supposed to be," Vasiliv offered.

"They're highly skilled soldiers," Jackson added. "They've been trained underground for the past years without the knowledge of the Republic. They're only now being put to good use and have accomplished countless feats against the enemy." More to the point, they were the Russian equivalent of the Zhànshì—though he didn't mention that in front of Vasiliv.

"Jackson has been trying to get a team of Elites sanctioned to help in Africa," Vasiliv finished.

"Are we sure we love the idea of Jackson being in the same room as a group of skilled assassins, some of whom are bound to want him dead?" Zak returned to the matter at hand.

"Oh right," Vasiliv said as if remembering. "Have you had any more assassination attempts lately?"

Jackson shrugged nonchalantly. "A few…."

"I offered to be your bodyguard," Vas said, raising his arms helplessly. "There's no one I trust more to lead the fight in Africa."

"So, who's watching *your* back?" Vasiliv asked pointedly.

"Boris, mostly," Jackson teased, looking down at where Boris sat beside him. And in truth, Jackson went almost nowhere without his friend anymore. "Anyway, I really should be there to help choose—"

"I'd like to send Ava with you," Sasha said suddenly, surprising everyone in the room, including Ava. "I can't take her with me to Moscow, but she could be of help in picking the team," Sasha explained. Then, leaning back, he added, "And in watching your back."

Vasiliv was clearly very confused as he looked Ava up and down. "So, *she's* the bodyguard?" he whispered with raised eyebrows.

"There's merit," Zak added.

Vasiliv was still watching her in confusion. "What happened to your arm?"

"Car accident," Ava replied, almost without thinking.

"I'm sorry. I'm clearly missing something," Vasiliv said, finally voicing his confusion.

Jackson had not given his thoughts either way on the subject. In truth, he didn't know what to think. The idea of her coming was strangely exciting, but that was the selfish side of him that longed for more time with her. He couldn't stand the thought of her having to protect him like a hired bodyguard, especially wounded as she was. Then again, her input on the team might prove useful.

"My daughter is a skilled specialist," Sasha explained it in layman's terms. "She has some experience in assessing skills on the topics that would be required."

Still, unconvinced, Vasiliv shrugged. "I don't really care who all comes, as long as Jackson's there."

Jackson gave his friend a look of surprise.

"You've proved your worth to me," Vasiliv said proudly. "And I value your opinion in this choice. Besides, the president requested you be involved in the decision."

"I'd certainly feel better about it if Ava was there," Zak offered.

"As would I," Sasha agreed.

Still, Jackson wasn't about to give Ava orders. He looked across the table to where she sat, and once again the sight of her in his blue jacket made him feel confoundingly pleased.

She still seemed surprised that Sasha had suggested this, yet she looked eager, excited even. "I just want to help," Ava said plainly. "Whatever I can do to be of assistance in the war efforts, I'm there."

"Great," Vasiliv said, standing suddenly. "Then it's settled. Tomorrow morning the Elites will gather at the Northeastern Tower. Jackson, let's go for a drive."

Jackson thought of all the work he had on the roster for the day, but a few hours with Vasiliv to get a firsthand account of current events in Africa beat it all.

"I just need to reschedule some meetings," Jackson said, standing and looking down at his paper schedule for the day.

"You really need to get yourself a secretary," Vasiliv pointed out. Then he glanced at Ava. "Do you need a job?"

She gave him a strange, surprised look, but Sasha spoke before she could answer. "I'll handle it," he offered.

Jackson nodded appreciatively, choosing to ignore Vasiliv's distasteful offer to Ava. He really didn't like the idea of Ava working for him, in any capacity. Boris followed Jackson as he started toward the door.

"You drive," Vasiliv said as he began opening the door. "I like your truck better."

Jackson turned to grab his jacket from the rack behind the door and suddenly hesitated when it wasn't there. Right.

He turned and looked helplessly across the room at Ava. Clearly, she had watched the exchange and was already hurriedly removing the jacket. He should have just come up with an excuse, but it was too late and Ava hurried to him, handing him the jacket with the keys still in the pocket.

"Sorry," Jackson muttered, apparently eternally using that word with her.

She shook her head at him to say it was fine, though apparently not wanting to deal with the embarrassment of anyone knowing she'd had his jacket this whole time. She moved past Vasiliv outside the library and away from everyone.

"Whoops," Sasha said awkwardly.

Not understanding the details, Vasiliv gave Jackson a suspicious look which Jackson ignored, leaving the room and heading toward his truck with Boris close behind.

"Sizwe is fierce. He's the type that you want on your side—and that you don't want against you."

Jackson laughed heartily, mentally flashing through many images of Sizwe's fierce strength in battle. "That's an understatement."

"If ever I've heard one," Vasiliv agreed with a similar hearty laugh.

There was a momentary silence before he attempted to change the subject entirely.

Jackson was mostly focused on the road. It had been a while since he was able to leave Sasha's estate, but with Vasiliv and Boris there, he risked it. He used to drive to clear his mind, similar to running. Now he wasn't able to go much beyond a ten-acre radius. Still, he was grateful for Sasha's large estate, which gave him space to roam even while confining him.

"So, what's this whole thing about Sasha's daughter?" Vasiliv asked with sudden interest.

"What about it?" Jackson deflected, not prepared to talk about this with Vasiliv.

"I don't know, all of it! The girl's a small, angry-looking thing with a broken arm, yet Zak somehow would 'feel better if she accompanied us to protect you?' I'm obviously missing something."

"She's got a long history of…I don't know, training. Talk to Sasha if you have questions."

"You've known Sasha several years. Have you ever met the girl before?" This was probably meant to catch Sasha's lie, but it wouldn't work.

"Yes. I've known her longer than I've known Sasha, actually."

Vasiliv settled in his seat, surprised. "Training? She can't be more than twenty! Sasha never seemed like the type to regulate his children's schooling to ridiculous measures. I always thought he'd be more the free-range type of parent."

Not knowing how else to respond, Jackson settled for, "Sometimes the way you mentor other people is not the same standard you hold your children to."

Vasiliv still didn't seem to buy that.

"I just don't see how she can help in our selection more than you or I."

"Maybe it's just a third opinion," Jackson offered, suddenly feeling frustrated. "I really don't want to talk about this right now. I didn't cancel my entire workday to satisfy your curiosity. Can we discuss efforts in Africa please?"

"All right. Fine." But Jackson could tell his thoughts had not yet shifted, and soon he proved that. "Why was she wearing your jacket?"

"Vasiliv, I'm serious!"

"Look, I'm your best friend. I just want to know if there's someone in your life I should know about."

"No. There's not. She's here for Sasha. Period."

"So, you won't mind if I ask her out?" Vasiliv pressed, baiting him.

"Yes! I would mind most strongly. You will not ask her out. I don't want you to look at her, let alone talk to her!" His sudden heated passion subsided and he took a breath. "Now, tell me about the battles in Biraan."

Vasiliv chuckled heartily. "At least we cleared that up." He sat back in his seat comfortably. "The battles have gone well for the most part...."

★ ★ ★ ★ ★

Kyle set up camp alone, as always. It felt just like old times with Valkyrie and Ella in Africa, except without Ella's constant attitude and Valkyrie's dry, humorless humor.

He was back to hunting down the commander, not knowing how else to find Darya. The commander was easy to detect. He was still wreaking havoc, though this time he was in southern Africa, as central Africa was involved in heated warfare with the Republic.

Kyle was camped a few miles outside of their sight, and he kept tabs on them from the bugs he had planted in their camp. He had no real quarrel with the commander anymore, but if the man could lead him back to Darya, and the ultimate purpose of the Jiānhùrén, that would be great.

As it was, he spent a lot of his days hiking, hunting, and sitting around camp. He didn't want to be noticed by the enemy, but he also missed battle and the excitement of doing something that seemed, well, *useful*. Still, he knew that while this may not feel useful, it would reap far greater rewards in the end. That is, he hoped it would.

Kyle went for a long hike, scoping out the area and getting a long-range view of the commander's campsite with his own eyes. At times like this, he really missed his Chameleon stealth suit. He could easily have gone every day into their camp with it and not been spotted. As it was, he had to be much more careful. If anything, that was his greatest regret about leaving the United Kingdoms' government service. No matter how much money he had access to between Eric's sum and Helio's vast pockets, he didn't have access to the incredible technology of the United Kingdoms, and he missed it.

Kyle stumbled back into camp close to lunchtime and suddenly regretted not having taken the time to hunt some game before returning. He'd have to consume another MRE, which really didn't sound appetizing at the moment.

Kyle stopped in his tracks when he returned from the tree line and noted a small, controlled fire had already been lit. He was certain he had not left a fire going when he had gone off earlier. Kyle didn't make such senseless mistakes.

But there it was. Chills ran down his spine as he considered what that might mean. The commander had often been several steps ahead of him. Perhaps he had discovered Kyle's campsite and was here for another creepy meet.

Kyle prepared himself and his weapon, and moved into the campsite. If the commander intended to capture him, there probably wasn't much Kyle could do at this point. May as well face this head on.

Kyle walked toward the fire and noted the cook set propped over it, with a rabbit grilling over the fire, but no one attending to it. Kyle narrowed his eyes as he looked around the camp for any sign.

Near the fire he found a set of footprints that he immediately recognized.

"Valkyrie!" Kyle said, louder than intended.

Just then, she exited the tent and walked back toward the fire, her face as expressionless as if they were still a team, and this was absolutely normal.

"I thought I would get lunch started while you checked the perimeter," she said in monotone, returning to the fire.

He was suddenly overwhelmed by an urge to run and embrace her, but he refrained, knowing it would probably not be well received. His thoughts of Valkyrie over the past weeks had tormented him relentlessly. And now, here she was.

"What are you doing here?" he said with a sudden smiling grin, stepping closer to the fire.

"I have a meet with the commander," she replied plainly.

"Eli sent you out on another meet?" Kyle said with sudden frustration. "Even after what happened last time?"

"Eli is not aware of what happened last time," Valkyrie replied, turning the roaster to get the other side of the rabbit. "The report he received was not entirely accurate."

Kyle watched her with surprise. "You lied to him. Are you crazy? The Jiānhùrén are actively trying to capture you! If you keep running into these operations, they're going to succeed one of these times."

"That is the plan," Valkyrie replied. Then she pulled out a bowl for each of them.

Kyle moved to the log he had set by the fire for sitting and took a place next to her on it. "How is that your plan, Valkyrie? I thought you had decided not to pursue your mother. You know how dangerous she is. It's not worth it."

"I am not doing it for myself," Valkyrie replied earnestly. "But how else will you find the Jiānhùrén and take them down?"

He watched her for a long time, trying to register if what she was saying was real. Eventually, he could not help but ask the question as plainly as he saw it. "You're here to help me?" He didn't mean to sound so touched by that.

After a time, she looked up to face him. "I'm here to fight with you, Kyle. The Jiānhùrén are the greatest threat to the Kingdoms since the first inklings of the Republic were formed. We cannot allow them to succeed. So, I am here to fight with you."

Kyle wasn't one to be easily overwhelmed by emotion. But he could not begin to explain, even to himself, how much those words meant to him.

"I will ultimately always have to return to Eli, and fabricate stories that he will buy into. But wherever, and whenever I can, I will be here to fight by your side." Her tone was emotionless, but the meaning behind the words was clear, powerful and filled with emotion.

All he could do was offer a simple, grateful smile.

They were silent for a time before she pulled the rabbit off the spit. Her look at the rabbit turned suddenly to dissatisfaction.

"I named him 'Fluffy.' But he's not fluffy anymore."

Kyle burst into uncontainable laughter. He had forgotten how much he missed this bizarre woman.

★ ★ ★ ★ ★

As always, Jackson enjoyed the task of driving. It had been too long since he'd been on a real trip, and it felt good to have his hands on the wheel and his foot on the pedals.

"Sorry I took the front seat," Vasiliv said from the passenger seat, speaking to Ava who was in the back.

"I don't mind," Ava reassured him again. "I prefer the back." Jackson guessed she could have changed the statement to "I prefer being farther away from Jackson."

"So how long have you been at Sasha's estate?"

"Eight weeks," Ava replied directly.

It felt painfully like the one-way conversations between Viktoriya and Ava. Viktoriya would ask a question, hoping to encourage conversation. Ava would answer as simply as she could and leave it at that.

Vasiliv clearly felt the awkwardness in the air, but he did not yield. "Jackson tells me he knew you before Sasha."

No reply.

"How did the two of you meet?"

"It's a long story," Ava said, with no indication of any plans on telling the story.

"We've got nothing but time," Vasiliv replied pleasantly, but a little too forcefully.

"Vas, don't interrogate her," Jackson urged.

"I'm not much for small talk," Ava admitted frankly, almost at the same time as Jackson.

"Me neither," Vasiliv said. "But I've found it's hard to ever get to the big talk, the real talk, until you go through a bit of the small talk."

"I'm not much of a talker at all," Ava replied, obviously hoping to end the conversation there.

Once more, Jackson knew better. She was quite a talker, but only among those with whom she was most comfortable.

Vasiliv's face tightened in annoyance. "So, tell me about your schooling?"

Jackson gave Vas a look that begged him to stop.

"Long and grueling, like most," Ava replied simply.

"Do you hold any resentment toward your father for putting you through such an extreme schooling regimen?"

"Not at all. I loved my education. I wouldn't change a thing. And I respect my father for his choices regarding it."

The look on his face said Vasiliv was unimpressed by this girl. "In my school they made a point of teaching social skills," Vasiliv said with a touch of annoyance.

"Vas!" Jackson objected in surprise.

From the rearview mirror, Jackson could see that Ava's expression hadn't changed. "Hmm," she replied flatly. "They did a great job."

The touch of sarcasm made Jackson laugh out loud, and even Vasiliv chuckled with enjoyment of her jab at him.

"All right," he said, nodding approvingly. "I just have one last question. Will you have dinner with me?"

Clearly the question was to strike a reaction from Jackson, and he managed to hide it, though he would hit Vas for that one later.

"No," Ava said once again without embellishment.

Again, Vasiliv laughed in surprise. "Well, okay then. I guess that's that."

Without a word, Ava put her earbuds in and didn't say another word the remainder of the drive. Vasiliv took the message, and soon directed conversation back to Jackson.

They talked more about their friends in Africa and some of the experiences they'd had. Every now and then Jackson saw little reactions from Ava in the rearview mirror. He suspected that the earbuds were just a way to shut Vasiliv up. Even if she was listening to something, it was obvious she could hear them talking too.

He didn't mind. In moments when he and Vasiliv would laugh together, he almost thought he saw a smile on her lips. She couldn't have understood their inside jokes and Vasiliv's strange, merciless humor. And her smile only followed Jackson's laughter. He couldn't help remembering a time when he had lived to make her smile. Now the mere sight of him laughing seemed to be enough to tempt her. He missed that as much as anything from her. But those stolen glances from the rearview mirror would have to be enough for the time being.

☆ ☆ ☆ ☆ ☆

They spent the remainder of the day scoping out the area and talking over plans, both short-term and long-term. Valkyrie was determined that this meet would lead to her capture, that Kyle would follow her to find Darya, and ultimately help Valkyrie escape. It was a good plan, though highly risky.

"I don't want them using that remote on you again," Kyle noted with distaste as they walked the perimeter, discussing their ideas.

"I can handle it," Valkyrie replied assuredly.

"We don't know that. What if it has lasting effects? I don't want to risk you really getting hurt."

"They will most certainly use it in their attempts to capture me," Valkyrie replied.

Kyle sighed, the sound of a stick cracking as the weight of his boot rested fully on the ground. "You're probably right about that, but when they do, just don't fight it for so long. Give in sooner."

Valkyrie was silent for a long time. "I do not know if I am capable of that," she admitted.

"Come on, haven't you ever gone under cover before? It's just playing a part. When they use the device on you, offer a little struggle, then let them get you, all right?"

Still, she was hesitant to reply.

"Valkyrie, this is part of the mission. If they really manage to injure you, then you won't be much help when I need you, okay?"

"When will you need me?" Valkyrie asked, changing the subject.

"I'll reach out through the link when the time comes. All right," he eventually changed the subject. "When is the meet?"

"Three days."

"Well, you're here early," he realized.

She didn't seem to want to reply to that.

"Did you just think it would take longer to find the commander?" he offered.

She gave a terse shake of her head. "I arrived early in order to ensure I could find you, and we could make our plans before the meet."

A new thought occurred to him, and he stopped walking for a brief moment as he asked, "How did you know I would come after the commander?"

She was slow to respond, as always, but eventually, she did reply. "I know you," she said plainly. "With no other leads, it was inevitable you would end up here."

Kyle nodded in understanding. "I guess that's fair."

"To fulfill your vendetta," she added.

"All right, now!" Kyle objected.

☆ ☆ ☆ ☆ ☆

Ava followed closely behind Jackson as they walked through the large room, watching the Elites hard at training.

Vasiliv and Jackson conversed together, and Ava listened. She did not know why Sasha had suggested she come. She did not feel like a valuable asset, but she watched the training men and women, searching for some way to be of use to Jackson.

Jackson took down the names of those who impressed both him and Vasiliv, narrowing them down. There would be another private training later to determine the final team that would be sent to Africa.

As she watched, Ava thought of her years in training. She caught the movement from a woman at the side of the room, focused intensely on her forms. Outwardly there was no indication that she hoped to impress, but Ava had been this woman. She knew what it was like to be in a lineup, compared to everyone around for her flashy skills and a record that had taken years to build. Oftentimes, it came down to moments like this. The five-man team that was chosen would have an opportunity to truly make a name for themselves, and every person in this room likely hoped to be chosen.

Who was Ava to be on the committee deciding the fate of these people? She had never done anything really notable. She didn't really think she deserved to be here now, as an authority over these people.

"Any thoughts?" Jackson whispered, turning to her. He was probably just trying to be polite.

Ava shook her head.

Jackson turned back to Vasiliv, and Ava continued watching the training Elites. Ava couldn't help berating herself over the thought that she had been chosen, but she had failed the mission. She had never made a name for herself, not really. She had run away before having the chance.

During lunch in the Tower, Ava still said nothing as Jackson and Vasiliv decided on who to select.

Jackson gave her every opportunity to speak, but Ava had no comment. She could sense in Vasiliv now more than ever that question, "Why is she here?"

Vasiliv left to get seconds, and Jackson continued browsing his list, hardly noticing that Vasiliv had gone.

Ava wanted to take the moment to speak, but didn't know how to break the silence. It wasn't until Jackson looked up to grab another bite that he noticed her watching him. He glanced at her untouched plate. "Are you getting enough to eat?" he asked suddenly.

"I don't know why I'm here," Ava admitted in a hoarse whisper.

Jackson looked her in the eyes then with full surprise. "Are you kidding? Ava, your opinion is invaluable to me." And the look he gave her said he really meant that. "If you notice or think of anything, however small, I want to hear about it."

Jackson's reassurance changed her confidence on the subject some.

"What do we think of Nastia?" Jackson asked when Vasiliv had returned.

"She's great, an A plus. I want her on the team."

Ava made an awkward sound in attempt to speak, but stopped herself. It was enough to get the others to look at her though, and then she had to speak.

"She is good," Ava agreed. "A bit overconfident in herself though. It's weakening her technique and will definitely weaken her leadership potential."

Vasiliv gave her a look of judgment which she managed to ignore, looking only at Jackson, who was encouragingly trusting.

"You think she'll take direction?" he asked.

"I think she'll struggle. In her performance today, there were obvious moments of disdain directed at the leadership here."

Jackson looked warily. "You mean at me?"

Ava nodded. "Still, she's good. If she'll take direction, she could be among the best."

"What do you mean about her technique?" Vasiliv asked.

Ava struggled to explain it to him. The look in his eyes made her feel anxious and insecure. She didn't deserve to be here. He knew that, and so did she. What was she even trying for?

She broke off mid-sentence after mumbling incoherently. Then she swallowed hard and held her breath. Her hands suddenly felt tingly, and she rubbed the fingers against the thumb in attempts to keep the blood flowing. Her chest felt unbearably heavy. How could she get out of here now without making a scene?

"I think I understand what you mean," Jackson said, and Vasiliv threw his hands up in the air.

"How?! She didn't say anything!"

Strangely, just having Jackson say he understood lessened the weight on her chest.

"For example, I don't think it really registered as an issue before, but during her three-point high kick, she adds an extra few inches to her lift that is showy, flashy, but unnecessary."

Ava nodded emphatically. That was exactly right! And she had many similar moves that she was clearly proud of because she was the only one who did them that way. But there was a reason people didn't! And not just because they were unable.

"I used to do that type of thing for show," Ava explained, "to get higher scores and to impress overall. But it's an expenditure of energy that I've learned in recent years you never should do in actual battle."

Jackson nodded in agreement, and Vasiliv seemed to understand.

"All right, so she likes to look cool. And she does it well. I still think she has the skill. I guess the only question is if she's willing to humble herself and take criticism. If you think her overconfidence also affects her ability to follow the chain of command, we can't choose her. I really don't want to have someone out there that won't listen to my orders."

"Agreed," Jackson replied with a nod.

"She's going to hate being corrected," Ava noted. "Especially in front of the others. But if she'll take the criticism, you know she's more apt to follow orders she doesn't like."

"And if not?" Jackson asked them both.

"Then I don't want her on my team anyway," Vasiliv offered.

They went through the remaining names. Ava offered many things she had noticed. Jackson tended to give her the benefit of the doubt, as if he was rooting for her, wanting her to be right. Vasiliv was quite the opposite, but ultimately—with each comment—he was coming around, acting less unsure about her.

Three days to spend in planning and preparation, yet they were done planning and preparing after one hour.

So, three days to kill time; with the least chatty person in the world—not that Kyle was much better.

Most of the day was spent in silence. They interacted and worked together. They hunted together. They set up fire and cooked meals together. In the past, Kyle had often allowed Valkyrie to do more than her fair share of the work. But this time around, he was attentive to the fact that she was human, and no person wanted to be treated unfairly. Least of all, Valkyrie, who was obsessed with fairness in all things.

Each had to have half the rabbit to eat, half the log to sit on, half the water, half the work, all to favor her new never-ending obsession with fairness. And, admittedly, it grew tiresome after a few hours, but after a year and a half of treating her unfairly, he decided it was necessary.

★ ★ ★ ★ ★

In the evening, they gathered in the Tower training room again, the selected eleven candidates waiting for a chance to prove themselves once more. Vasiliv related the critiques that he and Jackson had, as well as those Ava had added.

Ava and Jackson stood in the background. None of the candidates would want to be ordered by Jackson, and none of them knew Ava. Vasiliv was to be the team leader, and it was best that the comments came from him.

Eventually Nastia was called forward. Ava cringed inwardly, thinking of how painful this would be for the poor woman. All of her comrades were there observing and listening, watching. She was obviously respected and praised by her peers. It would not be easy for her to concede. But if she could manage to swallow her pride, she would be chosen for a mission that could make her career.

Nastia listened with a stone face as Vasiliv critiqued her performance. To her credit, she had an air of respect for Vasiliv. She seemed to take the criticism at first, nodding in understanding and consideration. It was not until the moment that Vasiliv's confidence broke for just a moment that everything shifted.

"And it goes…gah, I don't remember. How did you explain it?" he turned toward Jackson and Ava for clarification on his wording.

He had flawlessly spoken to all the others as if all of the critiques were his own. But, of course, it was in this moment that he struggled, probably because of how Ava had mumbled through her explanation of this one.

Still, Ava's heart sank and she knew how it would go from there.

Nastia's air of respect vanished when the question was directed at the others. So, this United Kingdoms' agent and this little girl with a broken arm were the ones criticizing her? And she was expected to listen to *them*?

It was the smallest moment before Vasiliv remembered the words and continued with the critique on his own, but it was too late.

Nastia's teeth gritted into a tight jaw. Her eyes pulled together into an all-out glare. Vasiliv finished, but only when the words were complete did he notice her change in stance and demeanor, and it surprised him.

"Did you hear me, Elite?" he raised his voice harshly.

Her eyes rose to meet his but held no respect now. "I heard you," she replied coolly.

"Then do it again, the way I said."

She did not budge.

"That's an order, Elite."

A cold silence before she replied in an icy tone, "I'm supposed to take the word of a rogue, failed United Intelligence agent for it?"

Jackson bit his lip uncomfortably.

Ava wished she could take them aside and explain where they had gone wrong. She still believed that Nastia was worth it. She still believed that this woman could overcome this weakness and be one of the best. Ava was still rooting for her. And what was more, she completely understood why Nastia was struggling now. Ava wouldn't have held much respect for these two losers either.

"You're supposed to take *my* word for it," Vasiliv replied coolly. "Do it again."

She did not move. Her pride was on the line now. All of her peers were watching. She could not concede when the criticism came from those who she considered to be a weak excuse for an enemy agent, and a useless, wounded little girl.

Ava remembered this moment in her journey, the moment when someone had outlasted her and changed her mind, the moment when she had been humbled. Ame had changed the way Ava looked at people. In truth, she had never been the same since that long training session.

"With all due respect, sir, I don't really care what the gentle United Kingdoms' tactics are. This is how we do it here."

"It's not about gentleness," Ava spoke before she knew she had. "It's about stamina. Your moves are impressive, but only to the outside observer. It won't scare away an opponent. And it will only waste your energy. A few subtle changes would make the moves downstream. Believe me, I've learned the lesson myself."

A few chuckles and whispered comments from the sidelines. Who was this little girl again? And why did she think she could tell the Elites how to fight?

Nastia noticed the comments from her peers. She stood even straighter. She could not back down with her pride on the line.

"Believe...*you*," she said challengingly. "And who are you again, sweety?"

Ava did not answer. She should not have spoken in the first place. She lowered her head and backed down.

"That's what I thought," Nastia muttered under her breath. "If any one of you wants to test me on my skills, let's do it," she said this between clenched teeth. It was mostly directed at Jackson—she really hated him—but there was a bit in it for Ava, and now even Vasiliv, too.

Ava suddenly had deja vu, thinking of the training with the Zhànshì, her and Eli being questioned and challenged to prove themselves. Now it was her and Jackson. Only, back then she had been excited and eager to do it. Now, as she looked at herself, she found that she agreed with these people who looked at her in scorn. Who was she? What did she have to offer them? It was doubtful she could beat any one of these people in her current state. She was a mess! What right did she have to criticize them? She glanced at Jackson, feeling suddenly uncomfortable.

But Jackson's gaze was strangely reassuring. He gave her that look that said, "Oh, if only these people knew." That look that didn't pity her. That look was proud. That look was encouraging. He believed in her. He thought that Ava could take this woman, even now, but he didn't know how weak Ava had become....

"There's a time and a place for questioning authority, Nastia," Vasiliv spoke gruffly. "This is not it. Take the advice or don't. Either way, you ignored a direct order. Time to move along."

Nastia snarled. Her overconfidence was one thing, but she didn't understand what she was missing out on. Vasiliv wanted her on his team, but her understandable disrespect of Jackson and Ava was going to lose the opportunity for her.

Once more Ava thought of Ame and how grateful she was for the lesson she had been taught that day—even if it had not been an easy one to learn in the moment.

Could Ava actually humble this woman in her current state? Or would she prove Nastia's point that these two were not worth listening to?

Nastia walked away in anger, back toward the others. She didn't understand what she was passing up.

"Can I fight her?" Ava asked Jackson in a whisper.

He looked at her with sudden surprise. "Sorry?"

"Can I fight her?"

"What? No. This isn't the time. You have no need to prove yourself to her. She just lost her chance."

"She has every right to doubt us," Ava said, feeling for this woman. Then thinking of how much she doubted herself, she questioned her sanity once more, but suddenly she thought of Lionel and his statement that it was always worth proving to oneself that you were capable of being strong. "And maybe it's not her I need to prove myself to," Ava admitted weakly.

His look was uncertain.

"I haven't fought anyone since Eli. I've been...afraid to even think of it. Please, Jackson. I think I need this. And I think she deserves a chance. She really could be one of the best."

He let out a breath of surprise. "Are you sure about this?" He glanced at her broken arm. "I don't feel comfortable letting you out there alone against her right now."

There it was: the pity. Her confidence wavered. His belief in her was why she had been even willing to try.

"Don't get me wrong," he whispered, sensing how she seemed to deflate at his words. "I still think you could beat her even now, but...."

"Then let me. Please?"

He seemed at a loss, but when was the last time Ava had looked up at him and begged him for anything? He shrugged. "All right. If you're sure."

Vasiliv was already working with the next candidate. Jackson waited until he finished before moving forward and surprising everyone, including Vasiliv. "Nastia, I'd like you to come forward once more."

The woman was still fuming in anger, clearly realizing she'd blown her shot, but also furious that it had been unfairly criticized by those she considered weaklings. Still, she came forward.

"You have every right to question us," Jackson admitted. "We've never proven ourselves to you, but you need to understand that there will be many people in your life who have rank on you, who don't seem like they deserve it more than you do. And it won't matter. Rank is rank, orders are orders. If you can't learn to humble yourself and follow orders—even from those who seem less deserving than you—then I have to warn you that, no matter your skills, you will be passed over for many opportunities that could have been yours. We will pick those willing to follow orders over those with talent ninety-nine percent of the time. Fortunately for you, today is an exception to the rule. You want us to prove it to you? So be it. Pick a partner. Ava and I will take you both on in hand-to-hand combat."

That surprised Ava too, but she found herself smiling subtly. He wouldn't let her fight alone.

Vasiliv looked rather excited to see this one play out.

Nastia glared at Jackson deeply. "I'd rather just crush you by myself."

Jackson smiled wide. "In fact, you'll need to pick two others to handle this one." He nodded at Ava. He was confident, that was sure, but it almost seemed he was more confident about her abilities than his own skill.

Suddenly, she regretted not eating lunch earlier. A bit of extra strength would be useful at this moment. Still, she was resolved. Jackson believed in her, far more than she believed in herself right now. She was determined to be everything he believed she was. She had to be.

Ava may not need to prove herself to any of these people, but she had many times found that she needed to be everything that Jackson saw her as and more. Because the person he seemed to think she already was… that was the person she longed to be.

Still, Nastia was frustrated, but she picked two of her peers and they joined her front and center. Jackson chose a simple, five man sparring rule. "The goal is to remain on the ten-foot mat. If any part of you touches the floor off the mat at any time, you lose a life. Three times and you are removed from the fight. This is not only a battle of intense strength and skill, but also endurance. Everyone, take your places on the mat and let's begin." Then he turned it over to Vasiliv.

Butterflies filled her stomach in anticipation. It had been so long since she'd sparred anyone. She hadn't realized how much she missed this. Ava took a place beside Jackson, on the mat, across from the three others. When she glanced at him and found him already looking at her reassuringly, her confidence endured. She didn't know why he believed in her so strongly. He had always thought more of her than she deserved.

"Don't hurt your arm or Sasha will kill me," Jackson whispered.

Ava tucked her arm in close to her stomach, and there it would remain for the entire fight. She would have only her three other limbs to accomplish this. Maybe he shouldn't have had Nastia pick a third opponent.

This felt so much like the fight with Eli and the Zhànshì. Only this time, Jackson stood at her side rather than being the main opponent across from her.

As Vasiliv was about to start the fight it occurred to Ava that she had never actually seen Jackson fight before. What if he sucked?

Kyle and Valkyrie made a fire together after dark and cooked a meal of fresh game, still mostly in silence. They had already finished talk of strategy, and neither had much else to say.

Kyle watched Valkyrie, sitting there near him on her half of the log, watching the flames. All the thoughts of the past few weeks consumed him at once.

Hailey had formally broken up with him until things settled down in the war around them, and in the last few weeks he had been grateful for that. He could not help smiling. Maybe it was all in his head. Maybe he was making things up and was preparing to shoot himself in the foot, but he felt strangely that he must at least give it a shot.

"Hey, you remember last time we were together? You had your hair down. I had never seen it like that before."

Valkyrie nodded. "I usually keep it up."

"You should take it down again," he asked hopefully, but then he felt a little foolish. It wasn't very nice to ask someone to change their appearance for his sake.

She cocked her head at him in consideration, as if wondering why. But then she reached up and pulled the elastic from her head, allowing her long hair to fall down and frame her face. She pulled it all together then, throwing it over her right shoulder.

His eyes remained on her. She looked...good, to say the least.

"Is that better?" she asked sincerely.

Kyle shrugged. "Not necessarily. It just looks different. I like both ways though."

She struggled to keep wisps of hair from blowing into her face. "It always gets in the way," she explained. "It's more practical to keep it up."

"Have you ever considered cutting it short? Like Ella?" Kyle asked curiously.

"No," Valkyrie said. "I like it like this. It's pretty."

Kyle smiled involuntarily. "Well, that we can agree on."

She cocked her head at him in curiosity.

He hadn't exactly intended anything before, but seeing how she struggled to keep the hair from blowing into her eyes, he thought he could offer a little help. Kyle scooted closer, reaching his hand to her hair and asked, "May I?"

She did not object, though her subtle nod was almost not really an answer. Kyle took it for a yes. He easily gathered the stray wisps and pieces from her face and pulled them over to the side. He was about to tell her she could go ahead and put it back up if she wanted, but he didn't have the chance.

She grabbed his arm in her hand and forcefully pushed his away. "Don't," she said, looking suddenly displeased with him.

Apparently, the nod hadn't been real. "I'm sorry," Kyle quickly apologized, holding his hands out in front of him carefully. "I didn't mean to disrespect you or make you feel uncomfortable."

She looked at him, her eyebrows pulled together, her lips parted just so, and her eyes showing that same curious look he had never seen on a woman before, the one that had almost made him kiss her last time he saw it.

"It makes it difficult to breathe regularly," she explained her predicament.

She could have said almost anything else, and he would have continued with his apology and backed away. But this...this answer made him bite his lip and, involuntarily, he moved in the littlest bit closer when he quietly gave an explanation. "It's called attraction. And don't worry, you're not the only one who feels it."

Her lips closed tightly, and she stiffened. A part of him was ready to turn away and say "well this is weird" all over again. This wasn't actually real, was it? With Valkyrie, of all people? But the way she watched him, and the memory of how his rejection had clearly hurt her last time, made him pause.

"It is hard to breathe," he agreed in almost a whisper. "But it's kind of nice too, isn't it?"

She swallowed hard, as if trying to process these emotions that she had clearly never experienced before. She gave a simple nod.

As uncomfortable as she was, he felt he should pull away, although he didn't want to. But then, of all things, she reached her hand out and touched his shoulder, holding a piece of his jacket between her fingers. Once again, it was subtle. Even at her most expressive, Valkyrie was almost unreadable. But Kyle had known her a long time, and he was starting to understand her expressions a bit more. She wanted him to lean in further, the last few inches, and just try it out.

Still, he worried she would feel violated if he moved in any closer, so he slowly started to pull back. She then gripped his jacket more firmly in her hand, as if pleading with him not to move away. Her face said whatever her grip didn't, and Kyle didn't have another thought before moving his head those last few inches toward her, and kissing her gently.

Hailey had taught him how to kiss softly and sweetly, and he had to consciously focus on doing so now, though that feeling of attraction was hard to hold back.

Valkyrie returned the kiss. She didn't seem to know what to do, and her body remained awkward and stiff throughout the exchange, but she was far better at this than she probably realized.

It all felt so good, so perfectly wonderful, that it took a moment to register what had happened when she pushed him away forcefully, shoving him back almost a foot.

"Stop," Valkyrie pleaded. "Don't ever do that again!" she demanded, and Kyle suddenly worried he had misread this entire scenario.

But one glance into her eyes and he knew he had not. She had wanted him to kiss her. She had even probably enjoyed it at first. But she now breathed in quick gasps every couple of seconds, trying to catch her breath and looking strangely afraid.

"I'm sorry," Kyle said immediately, feeling horrible for causing her what seemed like actual, physical pain.

She breathed in another quick gasp, and Kyle could see that she still struggled for breath, but was attempting to hide it from him, as if he would somehow think less of her for it for some reason.

"I'm sorry," Kyle repeated in a hoarse whisper, his eyes filled with honest apology.

She swallowed, and continued to struggle for breath.

"I'm sorry, Valkyrie. I swear, I won't do that again, okay?"

She leaned forward then, nodding, and although she had just shoved him away, she looked desperately as if she wanted him to hold her now. All the mixed signals were leaving him in a state of confusion. It was clear that he could not read Valkyrie as well as he had previously thought.

Rather than moving in uninvited once again, he simply put out his arms, an offer for her to take if she wanted, and repeated again the words, "I'm so sorry, Valkyrie. I promise, I won't do it again."

She moved slowly towards him and was soon in his arms, confusing him even more. Maybe she didn't know what she wanted any more than he did.

Kyle wrapped his arms around her as soon as she held firmly onto him. He held her closely, but tried not to hold her too tightly, so she could push him away as soon as she wanted, which was starting to seem inevitable at this point.

She remained there in his arms for several minutes as she worked to catch her breath without him knowing what was happening. When her breathing had slowed and ultimately steadied, she again pushed him away and stood.

"I'm going to bed," she explained, then walked toward the tent.

It probably wasn't best to follow her right away. "I'll...check the perimeter," Kyle said, almost to himself as she left him there alone.

★ ★ ★ ★ ★

"Go!" Vasiliv yelled to start the fight, and Ava thought of Breslin beginning the event.

Everyone was slow to move at first. No one wanted to be the first. Everyone wanted to wait and see what cards their opponents would play, but Ava wasn't in the mood to wait around. Part of this was proving to herself that she could do this. Part of it was teaching Nastia a lesson that would hopefully help her in life, a lesson Ava had learned the hard way. So, Ava made the first move, going after Nastia directly.

Nastia and her right-hand man, Pierre, fought off the attack, and Jackson and the third man went for each other. Nastia and Pierre clearly planned to get Ava out of the way right off the bat so they could fight off the real threat, the enemy agent who was running their government.

Jackson noticed the attacks on Ava as she was pushed closer to the edge of the mat, and he moved to her aid while fighting his own opponent.

Admittedly, it was far more difficult sparring two opponents without use of both arms, yet Ava was surprised by how she managed to hold her own for the time being.

Ava used mostly a rare Chinese form of martial arts during this fight, not because it was the best option to fight off her enemy's strategies, but because it primarily required the use of her legs.

Just bringing his fight closer to Ava's brought the necessary distraction Ava needed to get a good upper kick on Pierre, pushing him slightly off the mat.

"That's one," Vasiliv announced.

The other candidates watched the battle with obvious interest, reminding Ava of the Zhànshì on the sidelines.

Jackson and his opponent aimed heavy blows, and soon Jackson managed to get the man off the mat.

"One," Vasiliv said for him.

Frustrated with Ava's astonishing skill, Nastia's arrogance grew. She did her fanciful moves as if to prove to Ava she knew better and to rub it in her face. Ava took the opportunity to prove it was a mistake to be so showy, even beyond long-term performance. Nastia did an over-the-top high kick that was meant to look menacing, but Ava saw it coming from a mile away, and used her one good arm to sweep the motion and knock the woman off balance. An inch lower and Nastia would have had serious stability. Nastia hit the ground with a heavy thud. Not off the mat, but a serious blow.

Jackson went for Ava's second opponent, Pierre, leaving the door open for Ava to grapple momentarily with Nastia on the ground. This was Ava's specialty. She quickly maneuvered Nastia into a chokehold between her thighs. Once more, this was not the way to win this specific battle as Nastia remained on the mat through the entire movement, but that was not the point Ava was attempting to make. Instead, she hoped the woman would realize that her arrogance would be her undoing. It was absurd to automatically assume that she was the best in every room she entered. Ava had long since learned that, no matter her skill level, there were others who could best her, there would be off days, and there would be serious threats. And in fact, the only way to truly be safe was to always assume her enemies were serious threats.

Nastia was unable to pull free from the chokehold, and the others were too preoccupied in a two-on-one fight with Jackson to notice her need. Ava took the moment to watch Jackson fend off his enemies, and was highly surprised by his skill. Thank the General he wasn't terrible at this.

Ava let go of her chokehold before loss of consciousness would have started, and Nastia struggled back to her feet. Ava then delivered the blow that pushed the woman off the edge for the first time.

Then Ava turned to help Jackson, as he was nearing the edge of the mat. She took away one of the opponents while Nastia returned to the mat, and Jackson was able to secure himself to a safe zone once more.

She tried not to focus entirely on Jackson, but now and then she caught glimpses of the many fighting styles he used. He had adapted to different choices for each of the three opponents, based on their preferences, and she found that she would have chosen the same things he did, if her arm would have allowed her to. Apparently, his United Intelligence training had taught him some of the same things as her Zhànshì training, and his fighting quotient was excellent.

Nastia had returned to the mat with a new fire, and a desire to prove herself. She was not the type who enjoyed losing, and particularly she did not like being proven wrong. However, Ava noticed that her showy moves were kept to a minimum now as she focused instead on more practical fighting movements.

Jackson got his main opponent off for a second time, and Ava fought the other two until he returned. It seemed they had a bit of a routine down, as they worked together on the process. Either one of them would fight two, while the other knocked one off the mat, then they would return to the other's aid and go for another round.

After Pierre was knocked off a second time, apparently noticing the strategy that had the others winning, he changed his. Rather than go back to fight Jackson, who had just gotten him off, he hurried to where the other two fought Ava, and joined them almost before Jackson could.

Even the slight second of having to split focus between the three before Jackson took one had been enough to break Ava's focus, and Nastia used that moment to attack in full force. She knew her opponent's weakness, and she slammed her body directly against Ava's broken arm, causing intense pain throughout her arm, down her shoulder and her back. Before Ava could recover, one of the others pushed for her legs, knocking her off balance.

This would be her first time off the mat. It wasn't a total loss, though it felt like one.

But Ava had given up before Jackson had and he came to Ava's aid just in time. He gripped her by the belt as her body was in midair and pulled her back onto the mat before she could fall backward on the ground.

She wanted to laugh at how amazing that had been. Who was this guy, again? And how was he not a Zhànshì?

Once Ava was safely on the mat, Jackson moved for Nastia, apparently wanting to fight that fight himself for a bit, and Ava took on his previous main opponent, Pierre, while the other man moved back and forth between them, hoping to help where most needed, but honestly not making much of a difference to his team either way.

Ava managed to get him off the mat for the third time, and he was removed, turning the match from three-on-two to two-on-two.

Nastia focused still on Jackson and Pierre on Ava. He was just as brutal as Nastia, looking for every opportunity to get to Ava's weakness, and it was a challenge to keep enough distance between them that he could not get to her arm. He was fearsome and imposing, not the type you would want to mess with; but Ava had little choice on that right now.

Nastia got a good hit on Jackson that pushed him off the mat, and Ava let go of her desire to beat them without any slips. It had been a good idea, but in the end, they would still win this fight. At this point, they had to.

In some ways, the one-on-one fight was more difficult, as if the addition of a third man had been as distracting for their opponents as it had been for them. The fight seemed more challenging now than it had before. Still, Jackson managed to get Nastia off for her second time, and Ava took courage, despite her tiring body. She did feel sick, and weak, and exhausted, but for the first time in a long time, she did not feel broken. In fact...she felt strong. That was a feeling she had very much missed.

So many close calls, so many painful blows, but her opponent did not get her any closer to falling off the mat. And soon enough, Ava got a hit on him just in time to fall into the others' fight, and he lost his balance as he tripped over Nastia. Ava used the moment and got him off the mat. That was the third time for Pierre. Now, the battle had truly shifted.

Nastia and Jackson pulled away from the fight as Ava returned and everyone redoubled with the shift in the game. Nastia was alone now, and it was Jackson and Ava against her.

Jackson looked at Ava then, a thoughtful expression. "You want to finish this alone?" he asked her, even with Nastia right there to overhear.

Ava thought again of the Zhànshì fight, her and Eli being the only ones left in the ring after Ella was removed. And in that moment, she had decided to concede. She had not needed to prove herself to Eli, or to anyone. She had been confident in her abilities and was strong enough to accept that without beating Eli.

Nastia didn't need to be demolished by these two, but she did need to learn a lesson—one that would be better learned in a one-on-one battle. Ava nodded, and Jackson stepped off the mat.

A few people complained from the sidelines. Even Nastia looked frustrated. "I could have taken you both!" she said through gritted teeth.

Ava did not reply. And she allowed for the momentary pause in the battle to get her bearings.

Soon enough, Nastia's anger boiled over and she went in for the kill. The attack was fierce and painful, but Ava managed. She had not once been pushed off the mat—thanks to Jackson—and she hoped to win this fight without a slip. She had once been humbled by an unlikely mentor, and even if Nastia didn't grow to love Ava for this fight as Ava had come to love Ame, at least she would hopefully learn the necessary lesson.

The fight was brutal and long, and in the end, it did become a battle of endurance. If Ava had eaten anything recently she would have lasted easier, but if Nastia had reserved her energy rather than show off with flashy movements, perhaps she would have reserves to rely on now too. Both of them struggled. Ava was well aware that Nastia was not the type to ever give in—short of collapsing from exhaustion—nor was Ava.

After considerable time, it probably became tiresome for others, but Ava noted that Vasiliv stood watching every hit and every move, as if still awed by the skills Ava now proved to have. And Jackson, too, remained, watching every step of the way—as if cheering her on from the sidelines with his great belief in her.

She lost track of time well before it was over, and in the end, Vasiliv called it with the tiniest slip from Nastia off the mat—so close it barely seemed real. Nastia argued at first that it hadn't been. Then she turned to Ava, fuming in anger.

"I didn't see it either," Ava said, still working to catch her breath. "Let's continue."

Nastia's eyes tightened in astonishment. She had expected that Ava would be on Vasiliv's side, and eagerly claim the win. But if the win wasn't solid and agreed upon, Ava would not call it quits.

It wasn't the long, arduous fight or the many skillful moves from Ava that in the end changed Nastia's opinion. It was that one statement. Nastia stood there on the mat, working to catch her breath. Eventually, her anger dissipated, and she crossed the mat, putting her hand out to Ava.

"I trust the mediator," she said in contradiction of her previous exclamations. "You won fairly."

Ava looked out at the offered hand, but it was Nastia's right hand, and unfortunately, Ava could not offer her own as readily.

Nastia seemed to notice Ava's expression. "Oh, right." She switched hands, putting the left one out this time and Ava put her hand out to meet it.

They shook hands with strong grips, and the nod they shared was one of respect. They both had been amazed by the other's skills. Maybe

Nastia had not been entirely humbled, but if nothing else, she had changed her opinion, and that was something.

Vasiliv announced his picks for the team. Nastia's name was top of the list, followed by the main man she had picked to join the fight and three other skilled Elites. When Nastia stepped forward, Vasiliv spoke closely to her, and Ava watched his lips to understand his words.

"I'm not picking you just because of your skill," he explained. "I knew what you were capable of two hours ago, and I had already written you off. I'm picking you now because that girl says you have a potential for greatness in the field that I can't imagine. And I think I believe her. But you don't get there by being right. You get there by doing the right thing. Am I understood?"

She nodded emphatically. "Yes, sir."

"Good. Then take your place."

Ava stood once more in the background with Jackson, and he chuckled to her, pointing out the expressions of some of the others who watched them. "I think a lot of them wish they'd had the chance to fight us."

"Correction, they wish they could have fought *you*," Ava replied with a slight smile. "They still hate your guts. But I think they like me now."

Jackson grinned broadly at that. "That's because they assume you're Russian."

"Mmm, details," she replied sarcastically.

"Well, should we challenge the rest and take them on?"

Ava was silent as she considered the absurdity of that. She already felt lightheaded and on the verge of collapsing from exhaustion. "I think I might need a snack first," she said awkwardly.

Jackson chuckled. "I'm sure we can arrange that."

★ ★ ★ ★ ★

It felt a long, confusing time as Kyle walked the surrounding area, giving her some time to settle before he showed up again. It had obviously been a mistake to move forward and act on his rash feelings.

Then again, was it rash? It wasn't as if this was the first time he had ever considered kissing her. But he had been smart enough last time to realize it was a bad idea.

Still, as poorly as it had ended, it was hard to regret something that, at least for a moment, had been so...good.

His one consolation was that it would be easy for Valkyrie to move on and pretend it never happened. And, at the very least, it wouldn't wreck the partnership they currently had on missions.

After a good twenty minutes, Kyle made his way back in the direction of camp. He checked the campfire, ensuring it was fully put out, then walked slowly and unsurely toward the shelter.

Surprisingly, Valkyrie stood outside the tent, a subtle look of determination on her face. Kyle hoped her determination wasn't centered on ending him. That would be unfortunate.

Unsure if it was a bad idea, he walked in the direction of the tent, right toward Valkyrie. She had put her hair back up in a high ponytail. He realized once again that it wasn't how she did her hair that made her beautiful. She just was beautiful, one way or another.

He tried to think of a good line to say to avoid being killed by her, but he realized there wasn't anything he could say if she had already made up her mind about that.

Kyle pursed his lips into an awkward smile as he approached, waiting to see how this altercation would end.

"Do it again," Valkyrie said in a hoarse whisper when he was close enough to hear.

He knew what she meant, and immediately that same intense feeling of attraction overwhelmed him at the thought. But really, he decided he had to be sure they were talking about the same thing before he did anything so bold.

"Do what?" he asked, and she stared hopelessly at him, not wanting to say the words. "Kiss you?" he offered.

Valkyrie nodded slowly.

Kyle did not need to be told twice. He moved the final distance toward Valkyrie and, pulling her into his arms, he kissed her. Once again, he worked to hold in his feelings so as not to be overwhelming. This was still her first time kissing anyone. And it was definitely his best time so far.

Her body began to tense suddenly, and Kyle pulled away before she could shove him again. She looked still longing, and he figured it was better to stop at that point, rather than when she wanted to hurt him.

"Goodnight," Valkyrie said, swallowing and wiping her lips with the back of her hand. Then she left him standing there alone.

"I just have one question," Vasiliv said to Ava as they began their journey back to the mansion. "Are you sure you don't want to go to dinner?"

4

Belonging

The night after returning to the mansion, Jackson was heavily in practice with the dummies and punching bags. Boris was beside him fighting and seeming to work on his own battle techniques. In the beginning, when Jackson would work on his martial arts and close quarter combat techniques, Boris would just watch him with a seemingly turned up brow as if to say, "Why are you attacking that inanimate object?" But ever since they had been attacked by a rogue Russian force, Jackson captured and Boris shot, his friend seemed more willing to work on his attack skills.

Jackson glanced up when he sensed a new presence at the opened door, but he did not stop his chain punch until he had repeated his planned number of repetitions.

By that time, Ava had fully entered the room and stood beside a punching bag nearest the entrance. "Do you come in here a lot?" she asked when he had finished his reps.

"Every night," Jackson said, sweating heavily and breathing rapidly from exhaustion.

Ava stepped in, leaning her weight on the large punching bag. "So... running in the morning, and martial arts in the evening?"

"It helps me unwind," Jackson said, shrugging as he removed his protective gloves. "Jogging gets my day started. This is a natural way to end it."

"I've been avoiding this room. I've been avoiding all thoughts of anything I used to do. Anything that reminded me of Eli…."

Jackson tried not to show any surprise at how much she was talking to him, but for now, he would encourage conversation.

"Thanks for your help yesterday. You were amazing. Even with the broken arm. I'm sorry if I shouldn't have let you—"

"No!" she objected, raising her hand. "I wanted to. It felt good. Sasha says I need to reaffirm my identity, because so much of myself has been warped by Eli. He said I should try new things, and that it's okay to avoid the old things for now. But fighting yesterday…it reminded me that there are parts of me that were there before Eli—like my fighting abilities—that maybe he pushed or forced. But they're things that I don't want to give up. So, I need to learn how to make them a part of my new identity, and not just the one that he created for me."

Not only was she talking to him, she was seriously opening up to him for the first time since she had arrived. He couldn't begin to explain what that meant to him. And if he tried, he was sure he'd scare her off. So, he played nonchalant, but tried to subtly project caring.

"It was the first time I've ever actually seen you fight," Jackson admitted.

"You, too. You were great out there. I honestly didn't know you were such a skilled combatant—no offense."

Jackson shrugged. "Well, Harrison put me in an accelerated program. It better have paid off in some ways."

Ava's eyes narrowed in surprise. "Harrison?"

Jackson nodded nonchalantly, petting Boris when his friend came up to him. "Apparently he hand-picked me from the Academy. Basically put me in accelerated Zhànshì Training. I was supposed to lead the team that would take the Towers."

Ava walked forward, obviously surprised and interested. "Really? I didn't know that. I mean, I knew that you were implanted in Russia on Sasha's team, working with Kyle. Working with me. I knew you were on the team. I didn't realize you were meant to lead it."

Jackson put his hands up. "Don't ask me why he picked me instead of you or Kyle! Or heaven forbid, Sasha. I really have no clue. I mean, he gave a little explanation in my file that Sasha acquired. Harrison wasn't much for explaining. It was more like, 'These are the orders. Get to work.'"

Ava chuckled. "Yep, that pretty much sums it up. But this file...I mean, what *did* it say? If I may ask."

Boris walked to the side of the room to get a drink from his bowl, realizing he wasn't up for boring conversation, but Jackson found himself appreciating every moment that Ava remained. Even if they were talking about Harrison, of all things.

"I'll let you read it if you like. Mostly he talks about my work in the Academy and my leadership potential. He talks about my past relationship with my sister, and how it will perfectly make room for you. Nothing really new."

Ava nodded with interest. "Well, no wonder you're so good."

"I'm not that good," Jackson protested. "The only reason I won yesterday was because you were next to me."

"That's not true. You were fantastic. I mean, I saw a few things you could improve on, but I felt like I was fighting beside a fellow Zhànshì— Kyle or Mikel. Those were the elite assassins of Russia, remember. And you took out several of them on your own."

"What could I improve on?" Jackson asked with distaste, apparently forgetting the compliment and only hearing the criticism.

Ava chuckled. Then, as a new idea seemed to form in her mind, she walked onto the mat. "Come on. I'll show you."

Jackson shook his head in protestation. "No, I'm not gonna fight you, Ava."

"Come on!" she pleaded.

"You're wounded, and you'll still kick my carcass to a pulp. I'll stick with opponents closer to my level."

"Just try," she urged.

And still, so much of him wanted to say no. But there Ava was, standing but a few feet away, asking him to spend time with her. She wasn't running away, or avoiding him, or acting shy or distant. When would he ever get a chance like this again? So, at the risk of completely humiliating himself, he joined her on the mat.

Ava took on a fighting stance, but Jackson stood there stiff and uncertain.

"Come on," she urged. "My arm is fine. It's basically healed. I get the cast off in a week or so!"

That was not his concern right now. More like his pride. Jackson slowly put his hands up and took on a good form. This was not going to be fun. Not even a little bit.

At first, she seemed to be waiting for him to make a move, but when it was clear he never would, Ava moved in for a jab. He blocked it, and entirely missed the second hit that followed almost immediately.

He pulled away in pain where she had knocked the breath out of him. Still, he tried not to react overtly, and played it off with a laugh as he attempted to catch his breath. Ava did not wait for him to recover. She moved in once more.

He tried to block, and again, managed to dodge a hit here and there. She was so quick, and so...sneaky. It was difficult to predict her next movements, and inevitably, she'd always get a few good hits in—ones that hurt. This was definitely not his idea of fun. Maybe they should go back to arm wrestling!

Several more times this happened until Jackson about stepped off the mat and said he was out. Ava stood back, allowing him a moment to recover.

"Pretend you're guarding the core of the Tower. I'm a saboteur. If I get inside, if I get past you, we lose Russia. Help is on the way. They'll be here any minute. And I'm already wounded. You don't have to beat me. You just have to fend me off until backup arrives. Now fight like you mean it!"

He wasn't all that fond of games, but he could see the power in simulation. So, he got in character. He imagined himself at the Brazil Tower those years ago. The Agent Valkyrie was attempting to break in, and it was Jackson's duty to last against her until help came. He couldn't win. He already knew that much, but maybe he could survive...for a few minutes.

Now fully in character, he fought a little more seriously. She still snuck in several hits, and they hurt badly, but he stopped backing away when it hurt, and instead continued the fight as if it were real.

Even wounded, she was incredible. She practically ignored use of her right arm, but she didn't seem to need it. His training and connection to the chip couldn't hold a candle to hers. He may have brute force, but she had a dexterity and speed that he couldn't hope to match.

The Agent Valkyrie was indeed a force of nature, and Jackson Davis was far from true competition. Still, he tried. He did not risk attacking. He just focused on defense. He just had to last a few more minutes. He could do that...right?

Taint. How was she so good?

He felt himself slowly weakening with every painful blow. He just had to last a few more minutes. Almost there.

Several more blocks, several more blows. Where was that backup? This was getting more difficult. His breathing was quick, and he was sweating even more now. A painful blow to the side of his head had his ears ringing. Just a few more minutes.

"Is that all you got?" the agent asked as she threw in another fierce blow.

"Absolutely!" Jackson replied, momentarily out of character, and making himself laugh.

She did not break character, and she did not find it funny. "Well, I'm just getting started," she spoke threateningly. And apparently that was true, because she began attacking with a new fierceness and power that was difficult to keep up with.

He had almost been able to fend her off at first. But now...? There was no way he would last another few minutes.

She kneed him in the groin, and that one really hurt. On any other day, he'd be on the ground, groaning in pain. But if she made it past him...they lost the Tower. Just a few more minutes.

She had upped her power. Maybe there was a little more in him that he had been holding back too. If this really were life or death, he would fight with a bit more intensity. So, he amped it up a notch. Still, he felt like he was barely keeping up with her. But even if barely, he *was* keeping up with her.

Just a few more minutes.

The agent hit him backward a few feet, and while he grounded himself, she stepped back. The look on her face was fierce, and strangely smug. "Bad news, soldier. Word just came through your radio. The backup was overrun on the way. They're not coming. The only thing standing between me and that Tower core is you. Surviving isn't enough anymore. You have to beat me. Or you lose everything you've worked for."

Jackson gritted his teeth in anger. He couldn't beat a Zhànshì. He couldn't beat the great Agent Valkyrie. Not a chance! But he had to at least try...didn't he? Surrender was not an option in this case. And neither was losing. He had to win this fight. No matter what. This would be a good qualifier for the word "yet."

Jackson moved forward, risking his first offensive move in the fight. His opponent blocked it easily and offered a counterblow that hit him hard. The pain barely registered. That didn't matter right now. He had to win this fight, even if it broke every bone in his body to do so.

He went in for another attack, and another, and another. The agent fought just as fiercely as before, but now Jackson fought with a new intensity that he had not previously known was in him.

Blow after blow they went in for offense and blocked for defense. In the back of his mind he was still very aware that this was Ava, and he would not do anything that would truly hurt her, though she had landed a couple of blows on him that he would complain about later...to Boris.

Initially, he had barely been able to keep up with his opponent while on the defense, but now, she was breathing just as heavily. She was sweating, and her face was reddened. She was exerting herself as much as he. They were both giving their all. And surprisingly, his was actually enough to compete with hers.

Of course, it had to be. In fact, it had to be enough, not only to compete, but to win.

He fought with everything in him. As did she.

Ava tried to get him to the ground, and he knew that her grappling skills were excellent—he'd seen it yesterday. He countered those attempts aggressively. He wasn't about to hand this fight to her like that. She may be better at grappling, but he dominated in close quarters. He could handle heavy blows. He could handle intense pain. And if he could constrict her movements, he could hopefully get in enough good hits to gain an advantage.

So, while she tried to bring the fight to the ground, he worked them toward the side of the room, blocked in by dummies, punching bags and a wall a few feet from them.

Jackson got her near the wall, but she managed to force him on the ground just in time. She had almost achieved a chokehold on him using the crook of her knees, but he broke the hold before she had finished it, and he pulled back just in time. He hit the wall and was unable to move back any farther. Ava hurried forward for another go, and he could see in her eyes that she was about to finish this.

But there was far more at stake than his pride. He had to win this fight.

He ducked and raised his foot just in time, tripping her to the ground. She clearly saw this, too, as an advantage over him, and started to move to grapple with him again. But before she could gain the upper hand, he used her momentary lack of balance, grabbing her entire body and pulling her close. Her back was to his chest, the back of her head on his shoulder, and she practically sat on his lap while he leaned against the wall. She usually moved like a viper, and this time was no different, but he was getting better at predicting her next moves. And when she went to curl out and turn away, he used the movement against her, putting her neck in the crook of his arm and grabbing it with his other hand.

She knew this hold could prove deadly, and she fought fiercely to stop him, but in this moment, he held her, using the force of his weight against the wall as leverage until the chokehold was in place. Then he squeezed. Just slightly, enough to prove the chokehold as effective, though not enough to hurt her. Even then she struggled for several moments, attempting to break his hold, trying to break his strength by uppercuts to the side of his head. He did not let go.

Just a few more seconds. If he could handle the pain just a little longer, he would win this fight. He did not waver. He did not let go his hold.

Ava fought against the chokehold longer than most people would be able to—and in truth, that was fair. She was a Zhànshì. She could handle a chokehold for much longer before going unconscious, especially as she strained the muscles in her neck and fought the hold.

Over a minute passed with him leaning against the wall, holding her body there closely, suffering through every pain and every blow until finally, she stopped struggling.

He almost couldn't believe it when she relented, tapping her hand on his outer thigh twice, indicating she was done and would be unconscious in a real fight if he applied any more force to his hold.

Jackson let go immediately, and Ava stood up quickly. Almost as if facing a real opponent, she hopped back several feet, putting some distance between them before standing still. They both stayed there like that for a long time, Jackson slumped on the ground with his back to the wall, Ava leaning against the nearest dummy, both of them attempting to catch their breath.

Ava was the first to eventually do so. "The weakness of the elite squad we faced yesterday was overconfidence. They did not see us as a real threat, so they missed the threat entirely and were overcome by it. Your greatest weakness is lack of confidence. You don't believe that you have a chance to win, and so you don't even really try."

She took another breath. "Overconfidence is dangerous in a fight. If you're too arrogant to see your opponent as a serious threat, you'll be surprised when someone stronger overcomes you. But lack of confidence can be just as deadly. If you enter a fight expecting to lose, you will. When I told you simply to buy time for your team, you fought purely defensively. And you lasted well, even when I was giving my all."

Jackson tried to stop his heavy breathing, feeling foolish that it was taking him twice as long as her to recover from the fight.

"But when I told you backup wasn't coming, when I told you that you had to win, you fought in an entirely different way. Before that, you were the one holding out on me, and you didn't even realize it. As soon as you knew you had to win, you really fought. You gave it your all. And at least today, you bested me. The upper hand could go differently next time with people so evenly matched, but you won this battle. Don't ever underestimate your abilities, Jackson. You're *incredible*."

Her emphasis on this word indicated how much of a fight he had put up for her. He could hardly believe her insinuation that they were "evenly matched," even if she only had use of one arm right now. Ava was supposedly one of the greatest of the Zhànshì, and Jackson had just bested her in a fight. Was this real?

For a long while, Jackson remained sitting there against the wall, panting for breath, and Ava used the dummy for support. Eventually though, she stood up straight. "Thanks for the fight." She looked then as if she would go.

Jackson spoke first, "Wait," he pleaded. "Sit down a minute. Please?"

Ava hesitated for a long moment before agreeing, walking across the distance and moving beside him against the wall, with a few feet of space between them. Boris seemed to take their sitting together as an invitation, and he joined them by the wall.

They just sat there in silence. Jackson wished he knew what to say, how to get through to her. He had asked her to stay with him, but for what reason? It wasn't like they had anything to say to one another.

So, he let the silence linger. After a time, it seemed to overwhelm Ava, just like the other night, by the fireplace, and she was compelled to speak. "I miss you," she admitted in a quiet, breathy tone.

That sent a pang to his chest, but he hid his initial reaction, turning to her with somber eyes. "I miss you too," he said, in a barely audible whisper.

They stared at each other for nearly a minute. So much of him wanted to just move over those last few feet of distance and take her into his arms. She had just admitted to missing him. She had no clue how much he missed her.

"What if..." she started, then stopped. "What if we tried being friends again?"

He couldn't tell her how much that prospect meant to him, how much he desperately wanted it—and he could definitely not convey to her how much he wanted far more than friendship with her. Instead, he settled for a simple nod and, "I would like that."

She swallowed hard. He could sense how hesitant she was, even now. "Where...where do we start though?" she asked helplessly. "With everything that's happened...how do we pick up all the broken pieces and even begin attempting to place them back together?"

This, he did not know. It was easy enough to say, "let's try again." But where to even start? He had asked himself this very question many times, and still had no clear answer.

"Maybe...at times like this, it would be best to just start over," she offered, having no other solution when he offered none. "Start from the beginning?" Still, she seemed uncertain.

Jackson smiled, putting his hand out for her to shake. "Hi. I'm Jackson."

She gave a chuckle and slow shake of her head, causing him to laugh. Still, she took his offered hand and shook it.

"I'm twenty-seven," Jackson added, deciding perhaps he should give himself a more proper introduction. "I was born and raised in the United Kingdoms, but defected to Russia, of all places, and helped them run a revolution that broke them free from the Republic. Now I'm a member of the national security team on the Russian Leadership Committee. I know, I know. I'm throwing out the titles—you've got to start with the impressive stuff when introducing yourself."

She seemed to be on the verge of mockingly looking down her nose at him, but she listened, smiling awkwardly while he talked.

"I never knew my dad. But I loved my mom. So much that I formed my entire identity around being the type of man that she would be proud of. It's yet to be determined whether or not I've done a good job."

Silence lingered momentarily as he pondered that. He took another breath before continuing. "After years of wondering, I finally located my missing sister Maelyn a few months ago—after reliving old memories and realizing how much I still cared."

He was about to move on from that, but Ava spoke before he could. "You found your sister? Where is she? *How* is she?"

"She's in Brazil. She's been eight years clean and sober, and is attending a prestigious medical school there. I can't believe how well she's doing for herself."

"Have you talked to her?"

He sighed heavily. "Not exactly, no. She tried to find me too, but of course, according to my military and United Intelligence records, I'm dead. I haven't had the heart to reach out and tell her otherwise. She's safely there. And every day I think about reaching out, I don't, because even though I know I'm doing what I'm supposed to with my life, there's still a part of me that is ashamed of the fact that I am a traitor to my people. I don't know if I can face her and admit that. So, for the time being, I remain a coward, and let her think I'm gone."

Ava watched him with a sober understanding then, and he had to move on to avoid facing the painful feelings that her expression begged forward.

"I'm an arrogant carcass, but I'm working on humility. If it weren't for my mentors, Sasha Ivanov and Sizwe Jelani, I would be a total wretch. I struggle to trust people—especially when I know they could hurt me. And I struggle to admit that I don't know everything." He sighed heavily. "Sasha is a better man than I could ever hope to be. And yet I'm constantly running into the problem of thinking I know better. One of these days, I'll realize that I don't know anything, and that Sasha has all the answers."

Ava giggled outwardly at that. "Same."

They shared a moment of lightheartedness before he breathed in deeply, and continued. "All I really want is to be a great man. And I'm working my carcass off to that end. But I still wonder at the end of every day if I'll ever measure up. I want to change the world. I want to help bring freedom from the chaos. The world is messed up, but I'm still cocky enough to think I can help save it. And we'll see. Maybe I just will. Maybe not. But I'll spend the rest of my life trying."

Another silence before he finished. "And there you have it. That's me. That's all there is to know."

Ava smiled, leaning her head on the wall, eyeing him with a sideways glance. "Is that really how you introduce yourself to people?"

He didn't allow a beat to pass before responding, "It gets awkward at dinner parties. Sasha's told me to tone it down. But we'll see. I think I know better."

She laughed at his intentional irony, and he joined with a deep smile. Then, when the moment had passed he looked at her expectantly. "Well?"

She took a deep breath in, as if preparing for a similar speech. Then she put her hand out and said simply, "I'm Ava."

Then...nothing. That was her whole speech. "Really?" Jackson asked, laughing. "That's all you've got?"

She joined in the laughter, throwing her hands up in frustration. "That's all I could think of!" she spoke with a slight tone of embarrassment.

"Well, at least it's a start." Still, he waited, watching her, allowing her the chance to change her mind and say more if she wanted.

After a time, she breathed in again, and this time attempted more. "I'm nineteen years old. My mother's gone, but my dad is more a part of my life now than he's ever been, and I live for every day because of him. I had a brother—I *have* a brother. But things are...rough, and I don't know if it will ever get better. I used to be strong. I used to be so...great. And now I just feel...weak. All the time." She swallowed hard, and he could see how painful that was for her. "Sasha tells me that the moon goes in cycles. He says that when the cycle goes through a time of invisibility, you can't see the moon at all. You'd actually think that the light had dispersed entirely and that it will never return. But it's just a time of darkness, and someday soon, before you know it, the moon will shine again, as brightly as ever." Every word seemed painful to utter, and he could now see why she had struggled even to begin.

"I want to believe that he's right, but so much of me is worried that he isn't—that I'll never be okay again. I have regular panic attacks. I can't sleep without medication, and I constantly feel overrun, lost, depressed, or just...empty. Lionel told me that no one man could have such power over me, but what if he was wrong? I want to believe that it will get better, but what if Eli did it...?" She swallowed hard before whispering the last part of her fear, "What if he really managed to break me?" The unshed tears in her eyes were an indication of how painful that thought was to her.

"He didn't," Jackson said quietly, reassuringly, and meaning it entirely. "He didn't break you, Ava. If he had managed to break you, then you wouldn't have gotten away. But you did. You got out. And yes, things look bad. They look impossible right now, but it will get better. Because as long as you're still trying, as long as you're still breathing, there is hope."

She watched him, and he could see how much she wanted to believe that, but still, she wasn't sure.

"Sasha always knows better, remember?" Jackson offered. It was an attempt to lighten the mood, but it fell flat.

"I don't want to believe that I could have given away so much of my power to be broken this way," Ava admitted ashamedly. "And still, after everything, I can't fully believe that he is evil. I know he was misguided. I know he made mistakes. Sasha has helped me realize the 'manipulation' and 'emotionally abusive tactics' and whatever else they call it. And I see that. I do. But I don't think he was really trying to hurt me. I still can't believe that. And no matter how hard I try, no matter what step it is in the healing process, I can't bring myself to hate him."

Jackson nodded somberly. After a moment to let her words sink in, he replied. "I don't hate Eli either. Not anymore. I used to. You know that very well. But the more I'm learning of the world, the more I humble myself and let go of my pride, the more I realize that Eli isn't the great evil in the world. Eli isn't the bad guy. The real evil is corruption. The real evil is a higher power of bad that is enemy to good. Zhang, the Politburo, General Altman, the members of Council—these are just men and women. The real evil is the corruption that overpowers good men and turns their hearts cold and unfeeling. We're all just people, trying to do our best. And some of us get lost along the way. But Eli isn't the real evil in this world, and neither is General Li. They are just men. The enemy we have to fight is a whole lot bigger than that."

Ava watched him with a deep interest, trying to comprehend his meaning, and the changes in him since the last time they had really conversed. "How do you know all this?"

He considered for a time before replying, suddenly thinking of Sizwe. "I've lived an entire life that was not my own," he said in almost a whisper, looking away from her and out at the room ahead of him. "I've seen the world from an entirely different culture in Africa, with different spirituality and different meaning. I lived a life in the United Kingdoms. Now I'm seeing the world through Russia's eyes. And I lived an entire life in Africa from the perspective of my friend. When I put the three lives together, I feel like I understand the world in a higher way than I ever did before.

"I am just a man. I have been tempted by power. I have fallen into the traps of corruption. I can't tell you how many times I have been compared to Harrison Altman to my face—and not just the good qualities. But he was just a man. And I see how he fell into the traps that he did. If it weren't for the things I learned in the life of my friend, I would still be on that path, leading to a never-ending road of seizing power, control, tyranny and corruption. But I have seen truly great men. I have witnessed their humility, even with the utmost power and following. I know what greatness looks like now. And I know what it isn't. And knowing what I do now, I could never fall into the trap of corruption without deliberately choosing it."

He unconsciously chewed his lip as a new thought occurred to him. "I don't think Eli is truly evil, because he was never really shown another way. He was never presented with a real opportunity to be great. Still, he could have done better. He *should* have done better. But he fell into the place that was laid out for him. And he wasn't given many other options, or many better examples. But knowing what I do now, having seen what I have, if I chose what Eli did, it would be in direct violation of the truths that I know and understand. And that would make me evil." He nodded for emphasis, realizing this for the first time. "Even so, I'm just a man. And the enemy that is evil is a lot bigger than that. But then, so is the greater power of goodness—of *greatness*."

Jackson finally looked back at Ava, having been staring off into the distance until now as he contemplated. Her expression was deeply thoughtful as she watched him. "You've changed," she said, clearly not knowing how else to describe it. "You're so...wise."

He gave a half smile. "You've changed too," he offered, but the way it affected her so poorly, he wondered if that had been exactly the wrong thing to say.

"I wish I hadn't," she said weakly, looking on the brink of tears. "The person I was during the Talks, the person I was when I was helping lead the Kingdoms and being mentored by Lionel...she was so...so confident, so hungry for more, so unbreakable, so...strong. I was the best me I've ever been, during that time. Now...I'm the weakest."

"No," Jackson disagreed strongly. "You're wrong about that. The person you were during the Talks was strong and confident, that's true. But that person hadn't faced what you have. That person hadn't lived through what you have. And that person hadn't survived what you did. Sasha is right, Ava. You're going to conquer this. You're going to make it through this. And when you do, you'll be stronger than ever, because you faced greater obstacles than any version of yourself ever has before, and you overcame them. I can't wait to see how strong you are then. I can't wait to see you when you're unstoppable. When you're truly unbreakable. And the person you are right now, the person you are today, she's the one who's going to get you there. You're stronger now than you ever have been. This version of yourself is facing the challenges of a lifetime and overcoming them. You already are unbreakable."

A tear fell down her cheek, and he was surprised when she didn't immediately shy away from him in attempts to hide it. Indeed, she had changed.

"You're the best friend I've ever had, Jackson," she said in a soft whisper. "Thank you."

"We're going to win this, Ava," Jackson said in a passionate, confident tone, believing those words to the core. "We're going to win this fight. And the world will never be the same because of it."

She watched him, trying to decide whether or not she believed him. In the end, it seemed she did. "And Eli?" she asked hopefully.

He considered for a long time. "Maybe he'll change," he offered. "Maybe he'll choose another path, and attempt to redeem himself. But certain things he can never make up for. You can never risk getting close to him again—not that it's my choice." He added the last part to assure her he was not trying to control her decisions. And he could see from the way she nodded at his words that she knew it was right. "He's lost you. And he's given up his freedoms by usurping that of others, even if he does decide to be better—which I hope he will."

Ava shook her head, wiping away at another tear with her sleeve. "I wish it were that simple. But I think you're wrong about Eli."

He raised his eyebrows, causing her to chuckle.

"I know," she said in response to his reaction. "I've been telling you that for, how many years now? In the past it was in his defense. But this time.... You said he isn't really evil, because he was never given a chance to choose good, that he never had anyone who showed him another way. But that's not true. A lot of us did. Me, Lionel, Katia, Sasha, my mom, even Eric was doing his best. And of course, there was your example, which I think only fueled his anger, realizing what he could be. Time and again we showed him. He saw the difference between good and evil. He knew it. And yet, he chose to do wrong, time and again. So, maybe I've been wrong about him too. Maybe he really did want to break me. Maybe I should hate him. Still...I'm not there yet."

He watched her for a long time, realizing how wise she, too, had become.

117

Another long silence passed as neither of them knew what to say. Eventually, Ava laughed and was the one to break the silence. "Well, I've never introduced myself to someone like that before."

Jackson chuckled. "Really? You should start. It saves so much time!"

She giggled at that, and he couldn't help the urge he felt once more to reach over and pull her into his arms. He did manage to refrain though.

"So, friends?" Jackson asked, putting his hand out again for her to shake.

She accepted. "Friends," Ava agreed.

Still, that wasn't the half of what he wanted with Ava.

But it was a start.

★ ★ ★ ★ ★

The next morning, Kyle and Valkyrie said nothing about what had happened. They got to work and focused on the regular tasks of the day, with a bit of time for rehashing their strategy. But when they had finished working and returned to camp, they sat once more around the fire.

As much as Valkyrie had opened up to him several weeks before, Kyle felt a need to be open with her too. He told her some about his fears and struggles. Her expression was subtle, but he was starting to see past the mask of no emotion, and she was starting to lose that mask with him.

Then, just like the night before, as soon as the conversation had mostly concluded, Kyle kissed her. And when she was done, she said goodnight, and they left it there.

The entire three days passed in the same way. Kyle felt it the greatest accomplishment in his life when, on the third night, he made a silly comment, and Valkyrie laughed. Right there, right then, for him to see. He watched her, a sudden longing beginning. Not just to kiss her, but to have her as his own, and to be hers too.

He had never imagined something like this happening, with Valkyrie least of all. But one day at a time, one bonding evening at a time, he found himself beginning to care for her, deeply.

The fourth day, they awoke and prepared for the meet. It was difficult to say goodbye after three perfect days, but they managed to do so and focus on the next mission at hand.

But nothing happened. The meet was simple. Valkyrie made the drop, and they let her go, without any sort of altercation.

Their plan was foiled, and Kyle could not help being frustrated. They would have to find another way to Darya, which was a tiresome realization. But when Valkyrie returned to camp with him, he could not find any more room for disappointment. They had one more day together, and that was something he could only cherish.

They set up a long-range communicator between them. If Valkyrie was sent in to meet with the Jiānhùrén again, she would give Kyle enough time and warning to make it there. And if he found any leads, he would contact her. For the moment, that was as good as it got.

The fourth evening together was best of all, because it had been unexpected, a very pleasant surprise. And Kyle was surprised when it was Valkyrie who started the conversation that night, wondering if she could show him something she had never before shared with anyone. All Kyle could think was, "Haven't you already?"

Valkyrie unlaced her right bootlaces and pulled from the lining a small bag. She placed it on the log between them, opened the pouch, then poured the contents out for him to see.

She showed him every trinket, where she had gotten it from, and what it meant to her. A pin from her mother, a watch from her father, shoelaces from Ava—shoelaces from a lot of other people. A dagger from Jackson, and many other small little mementos of her past.

Kyle watched her, a smile on his lips as he listened to her passionately—in her Valkyrie, monotone way—explain why each trinket mattered. A feeling of awe overtook him as he listened. He could have listened to this woman talk forever.

She eventually finished and slowly started packing the items up. "Wait," Kyle said.

He reached into a cargo pocket and found a small marking pen. Then in another pocket he found a coin. Using the marker, he drew a smiley face on the coin, then handed it to her.

"This is my memento," Kyle explained. "So that you can think about me every time you see it."

Valkyrie watched him carefully, a thought beginning to form that he knew would come to her lips if he waited just a moment more. And soon enough, it did.

"I don't need a coin to think about you."

Kyle's expression tightened, his heart clenched in a good way, a feeling he had never felt before. He smiled.

And so did Valkyrie, but not the micro-version of a smile. He could see how she carefully worked to slow the movement down, and she stopped at the exact right time, holding her lips still when they had formed a smile.

Kyle was not ready for the night to be over, but the feelings of overwhelm were astounding. He leaned in and kissed her softly. Not enough to have her want to push him away. Just enough to show her how much he cared about her, and for her to offer the same.

His feelings in this moment, his feelings for Valkyrie, were unlike anything he had ever felt before. And he dreaded the fact that she would have to leave him in the morning.

On the fifth day, Valkyrie woke up first, as she always did, and it was quite a while before she shuffled into the tent and woke Kyle. "I cleaned up half of camp," she explained.

Kyle couldn't help his chuckle as he rolled over, not yet wanting to get up.

"Now I have to be on my way. Goodbye." She stood and started out of the tent.

Kyle hopped to his feet and hurried outside. "Wait," he said as she tried to hurry away.

She stopped and turned to face him. "What?"

"You can't just go like that," Kyle explained. "Not after the week we just had."

Valkyrie watched him, a blank expression on her face. "Then how should I go?" she asked, a touch of genuine curiosity in her tone.

Kyle smiled deeply, holding his arms out, but standing still.

She hardly hesitated a moment before coming back and hugging him tightly. He enveloped her in his arms, his lips resting on the side of her head, where he kissed her softly.

"Until next time, my Valkyrie," he whispered gently.

"Until next time, my Kyle," Valkyrie repeated in a similar whisper.

The word "my" before his name caused as much elation as any time kissing her had. And he knew in truth that he was hers. He hoped she was really his too.

He squeezed her arm lovingly, not wanting to let go, but knowing he must.

She was the one strong enough to pull away, yet as she lingered there, staring at him with that look in her eyes, he knew without a doubt that his intense feelings for her were not one-sided.

And with that, she was on her way, once more leaving Kyle there to deal with these new thoughts and feelings alone.

The next few weeks were entirely different between Ava and Jackson. One day to the next, they rekindled a friendship. The night after they had made their truce, Viktoriya and Zak asked Jackson to join them for a game night. He agreed, and found Ava and Sasha to offer a similar invite. "Want to come play games?" he asked, directing his comment to Ava.

Sasha was clearly taken by surprise. He almost declined the invitation, until he realized who the comment was directed toward. Ava worked to decide whether or not she was ready for that. Eventually, she nodded. Sasha was in obvious shock, but he, too, agreed and joined the party.

Ava still sat on the edge, only next to Sasha, but just the fact that she was there in the first place—that was huge. It was as if, in accepting Jackson back into her life, she had decided to make room for Viktoriya and Zak too.

Not only was she warm, friendly and receptive to conversation, she even started it. She asked Viktoriya a few questions, getting to know the woman for a change.

The entire room was in shock, wondering how and when the abrupt shift had taken place. Jackson found himself happier than he could say, seeing Ava as she once had been, seeing Ava as she had been when she was his.

Still, a pang remained in his stomach. This was a step toward healing, but it would be a long time if ever, until she could really be his again.

Zak wanted to play the new card game he had received for Christmas, wherein everyone gave answers to certain questions secretly. Then the answers would be read out loud, and they had to guess who had put in what—with a complicated point system that Jackson didn't care for.

It wasn't the game itself that got to him. In truth, he had never before actually liked this kind of game, but when a question was read out loud, "What's your favorite song," and the answer was very strange, most of the group was sure it was the fake—an answer that was from the game itself, having nothing to do with any of the players responses. At that time, Ava said, almost to herself, "It's Jackson."

None of the others heard her, but Jackson did, and though he worked to agree with the group in order to win the point, he recognized that she knew him. The rest of the team voted, and when it got to her, Ava shook her head. "It's Jackson," she said, but she didn't offer explanation or compelling argument—she was not yet comfortable enough in this group for that. None of the others changed their votes, but Ava was right, and they were all surprised by the reply.

Several times things like that happened, moments where either Jackson or Ava would prove how well they knew each other—even the things that no one else knew about them. By the end of the game, Jackson had changed his mind, and decided that this was now his favorite game to play—as long as Ava was there playing with him.

He had almost forgotten how much history they had. He had almost forgotten how well they knew each other. They had both changed, that was true, but the memories they shared were not lost, even now, even after everything.

Ever since that first night, Ava had started joining him every evening in the gym. They sparred each other each night. And every time, his confidence grew, even when she beat him. Still, he knew she was better than he was. He only beat her four in ten times sparring, but even that was a victory. When her cast was removed, she was still supposed to be careful with the arm, but just the fact of having the cast gone made her better.

She taught him things he had never paid attention to before. In his training, they had taught him to predict the movements of his enemy, but he had not known then that the chip enhanced one's ability to do that—or even that he had the chip. As she taught him how to really focus in, and tap into the power of the chip, he could sense this ability and his "fighting quotient," as she called it, growing stronger every day.

★ ★ ★ ★ ★

"You're getting better," Ava teased as they entered the downstairs hallway nearing both of their rooms. "Eventually you might be able to beat me when I'm not half incapacitated." She held up her still weakened arm.

Jackson clicked his tongue discontentedly. "Careful, kid," he teased, "maybe I was going easy on you too. What's that make, eight to nineteen?"

"Eight to twenty," she corrected. "You keep not counting the one where Boris joined in."

"All right, that one was not a fair battle! And what made him choose your side anyway?" He opened the door to his apartment and invited Boris to go in, but the dog remained with Ava. Jackson scoffed. "Want to come in for a drink?" he asked Ava in an attempt to keep his dog.

She chuckled, glancing inside the opened door. "Sure. I don't have a full kitchen in my room like some people."

"Just a small one," Jackson teased as the three entered the room. "You can sit down. I'll pour us some drinks."

Ava sat on the sofa in the little sitting room, taking in the large suite around them. "How come people always give you the best rooms? This place is like a grand suite! My room is like a closet comparatively."

Jackson smiled as he poured a glass of water over extra ice for her. "I don't know. I guess people just see me as a sort of princess."

"Assassination attempts included," Ava teased.

He crossed the room and handed her the glass before taking a seat. "Come on now. You say that like no one's ever tried to kill you before. I only moved into this room a few months back, when the attempts on my life were becoming more...frequent. Viktoriya wanted the kids next to her anyway, so Sasha had me moved down here. It has its own washroom and a small kitchenette, so I really could stick here for days as a recluse if needed.

And, of course, there's direct access to the safe room." He pointed to the large metal door in the middle of the west wall.

The last comment caused her to take in the rest of the large apartment, and soon her eyes stopped on the mantle above the fireplace where one book sat alone. She recognized it immediately, and a strange rush passed through her. It was the book she had left him, *Les Misérables,* with her notes in the margins. Of course, glancing at it, she immediately noticed the mangled and burnt sections. She narrowed her eyes into a silent question.

Jackson turned to see what she was looking at, and when he realized what it was, he suddenly looked embarrassed. Leaving his drink on the middle table, he stood and walked to the fireplace, picking up the book from the mantle.

"It's not normally the centerpiece of the room," he said defensively. "I actually just pulled it off the shelf recently and..." he trailed off as Ava smiled, kind of enjoying the slight flush of his cheeks as he was clearly fighting off embarrassment.

Ava stood and walked to where he was. "I didn't think anything of it," she replied comfortingly. "It is your favorite book, after all."

"Yeah, yeah it is," he affirmed, but the sentimental way he said it almost made it seem like he meant more than just the book *Les Misérables* itself, as if specifically this copy, mangled, warped and burnt as it was.

Ava thought better than to ask what had caused the current state of the book, and instead she reached out and asked, "May I?"

He handed it to her, and she began flipping the pages. It was indeed the copy she had given him, with all her notes and comments. Jackson stood there close by the fireplace, saying nothing as she went through it all slowly. Eventually, she ended on the cover page, and as it flipped open, she found the picture of her and Jackson sitting by the sofa in Korea reading. The photo had been taped inside with obvious care.

Ava stared at that photo for a long time before looking up at Jackson, who stood there watching, still looking slightly flushed. The obvious difference between the boy in the photo, and the man standing before her now was almost startling. And, apparently, he was noticing the same thing about her as he stared at the photo and then took in the picture of the woman standing before him.

"Things were a lot simpler then," he noted.

Ava offered a half smile, glancing once more at the photo, and then again at Jackson. "Yeah, they really were. *We* were a lot simpler then too."

He chuckled once in agreement.

"I never thought of myself as young or naive at the time," Ava explained. "But looking back now..." she trailed off.

Still, Jackson said nothing, looking very thoughtful. Feeling uncomfortable with the lingering silence, Ava found herself trying to fill it again. "You're different now. And it's not just the beard."

At least that got a smile out of him.

"You just look...older, more grown up now."

"Well, if growing up means constantly walking around feeling confused and uncertain, then sure."

Ava giggled with him.

"It was all so much...easier back then," Jackson admitted.

"We just did what we were told," Ava agreed. "Followed orders. And that's a far cry easier than being the one who has to come up with them, as you do now."

Jackson, still smiling, nodded in agreement.

After another long silence, Ava closed the book, but as she moved to return it to the mantle, she found another surprise sitting there. Ava let out a startled huff. "So he *did* give it to you." She set the book down, retrieving the note she had written for him. "I expected him to toss it in the trash the first chance he got."

"Uh, no, actually," Jackson corrected. "Yuri never gave it to me. After he died, his wife delivered the letter."

Ava breathed out sadly, holding the note in her hands, though not attempting to open it. "A lot has changed since then too," she said softly.

"I never...actually read it," Jackson admitted.

She looked up in surprise.

"It was delivered at a vulnerable time," he explained. "And it's never felt like the right time since."

Ava gulped, then laughed awkwardly. "Well, let's save ourselves the embarrassment then!" she said, attempting to stuff it in her side pocket.

He reached out as if to stop her, but held back before making contact. "I...if you don't mind, I would still like to, eventually."

Ava watched him for a long time, not sure how to respond. So much of her wanted to rip it in half and toss it in the fire right then and there so he would never set eyes on the vulnerable words. Still, another part of her was hurt that he had never taken the time to read the thoughts and feelings of her heart and soul in the first place.

"It's...not really worth reading," Ava said weakly, though she handed it back to him. "But it is yours."

He smiled thankfully. "Don't worry, I'm not asking for you to return all of my old letters either," Jackson said as if to comfort her. "Even if I am embarrassed by how juvenile I may have been. I won't assume anything as I read it. I know it was written a long time ago."

Ava turned, walking slowly back toward the sofa. "Actually, I don't have your letters anymore. Eli took them, and destroyed them as a punishment. He said it was to help me move on after the ballet, but he was angry at me, and he knew it would hurt me."

Jackson, clearly not having any idea how to reply to that, stood there in silence.

When she had returned to the couch, she retrieved her water and faced him again. "It's not a big deal. He took everything and everyone. He said it was to teach me a lesson, but Sasha believes he was trying to cut all my ties to other people so I would only have him left." Ava unconsciously reached for her dog tags for comfort, remembering what else he had stolen from her.

Still, Jackson stood in silence, not knowing how to respond.

"Sorry," Ava said, suddenly realizing how uncomfortable she had made things. "Didn't mean to go all dark on you."

He stepped forward comfortingly. "No, I mean, if it helps to talk about it, then of course you should. I want you to open up to me."

She shrugged. "Just don't...judge me, when you read it. I was naive and silly and probably misread everything as I have in most of my relationships with people."

He looked down at the letter in his hands, and she sensed a curiosity in him. If he hadn't wanted to read it before, he certainly would now.

"And just make sure to burn it when you're done," she laughed as she stood, "so I don't have to deal with the embarrassment of anyone else laying eyes on it. I'm gonna head to my room now. G'night."

He seemed to want to stop her, but let her go as he sensed her discomfort. The last thing she wanted was to ruin their friendship by his reading the note now and thinking of her as a starry-eyed schoolgirl. If he ever asked her, she would assure him that things had changed. He would laugh as he read about her reasons for choosing Eli. But as far as her feelings for Jackson, she still meant every word of that letter as if she had written it yesterday.

Ava rubbed her arms with a slight touch of regret. Her right arm had lost so much muscle within the cast, and it looked weak, pale and limp. It would take far longer than she liked to admit to rebuild what she had lost, but she would gladly have given up that and much more to get away from Eli.

She shrugged aside the disappointment and turned to the tray that Maxim had filled with lemonade for everyone.

"Sasha requests that you join them," he said as she walked through the kitchen door. "I don't have any more work for you now."

She offered a thank you and made her way through the mansion and to the back door. The others claimed it was a beautiful, warm day, that they must take advantage of the good weather. But Ava found it to be quite brisk. The only redeeming quality was the sunshine melting the little patches of snow. It didn't really seem like a lemonade-yard-type-of-day. Then again, in this part of Russia, this was often as good as could be hoped for.

Ava found Sasha where he sat at the little picnic table, and she set the tray down on the table before him. Sasha looked up to meet her glance. "Well thank you, dear!" he said delightedly.

"It's from Maxim," Ava explained.

"Ah. Well, I'd like you to sit down and join me. No need for you to work away this lovely day."

Ava sat down across from her father, looking off into the distance where the kids played on the new playground, which had been Sasha's generous Christmas gift to Kai and Jon.

Sasha was similarly looking off into the distance, but not at the playground. It took Ava a moment to find the object of his attention. Jackson was always busy with work, but he hadn't wanted to miss out on this "perfect" day, so he sat on a lawn chair with his laptop. He was just as distracted by people-watching.

Ava watched Sasha watching Jackson watching the others, and she tried to imagine what was on each of their minds. It didn't take long to see what was on Jackson's mind. Zak was playing with the boys, and Viktoriya enjoyed the playground swings. They looked like the picture-perfect family—the white picket fence family Jackson had always wanted. There was a sort of painful longing in the way Jackson watched his best friend live out his own dreams while he worked his life away.

Ava couldn't help the pang of sadness for Jackson, wishing she knew a way to give him everything he wanted, but also knowing that was impossible.

Sasha turned to face her, and Ava regarded him in return. They shared a long, knowing glance, both thinking about Jackson. Eventually Sasha broke the silence. "Do you think you would ever want a family?" he asked softly.

She managed to hide her immediate embarrassment, instead masking it with a quiet, forced laugh. Never before had the thought crossed her mind. Not until sitting there, seeing Jackson and wishing she could make his dreams come true.

"Not in this lifetime," Ava said tersely, and she could tell she had been convincing. "Maybe in another life. No, I don't think I will ever have a family."

He nodded, looking slightly disappointed.

Jackson had turned back to his work, but neither Sasha nor Ava could forget that moment, that look on his face that hinted at all that he was missing.

Sasha sighed, finally picking up a cup of the lemonade and taking a sip. "Sometimes I wish Jackson and Viktoriya had just been married instead."

Ava was so startled by the serious statement that she could not respond. Fortunately, Sasha didn't expect her to. "Zak would have been fine! He's sociable and had hundreds of options in Russia. Jackson and Viktoriya could have lived a lovely, simple life here at the mansion. They both could have had everything they wanted. Jackson would be free to pursue his mission, and he would have been a wonderful father to those boys. It could have been his baby that Viktoriya carried now."

Sasha couldn't possibly know how much that idea pained Ava, and he looked so set, so serious as he related this wish, it was clear he really meant it. "I just think it all would have been better that way." He sighed once more as if in regret. "But sometimes things just don't go as they should."

He looked up finally, and Ava hid whatever emotion his comments gave rise to, smiling instead. "It sure would have been easier," she attempted to agree with him. "Wouldn't it?"

Sasha nodded sadly. "People need to be able to make their own decisions," he replied. "But from the outside looking in, sometimes I wish I had more sway than I do. I wish my boy could have been happy." After a long silence as Sasha watched "his boy," he eventually smiled. "Then again, there is always time," he said with more optimism now. "Jackson is young. Still, I think as long as this war continues, as long as he remains in Russia, there is no chance for him having what he wants. Not when every father's daughter wants him dead. It would have been easier. That's all."

Zak broke the conversation up when he noticed the lemonade, and he and the boys made a beeline for the table. He was such a good dad for those boys, but hard as she tried, Ava couldn't get Sasha's words out of her mind as she imagined it being Jackson there instead, playing and being a goof with his children, with his gorgeous, pregnant wife watching and laughing from the swing.

Perhaps it would have been better after all.

"She's in the training field," Sergeant Breslin spoke in a hushed tone. "The General has his way of breaking Zhànshì like broncs."

"I am well aware," the large man said with a sort of reverent understanding.

"I know you know what he did to Fourteen in Brazil," Breslin admitted as they walked through the dimly lit halls. "And that was only a part of his work on her. I wish I had been aware. I would have put a stop to everything. I would never have let him get away with it...but the newer trainers, they support him fully. He's slowly removing and replacing anyone who opposes him. The only reason I'm not gone yet is because of the king's request that I remain."

"Unfortunately, you might not have King Lionel's support for much longer," the man replied soberly.

Breslin gave a pained half-smile. "I have heard his condition is worsening. I only pray we can find a miracle before it's too late. Council's corruption...Hawkins' silencing...I'm afraid we're in a losing battle."

The large man stopped, and Breslin had to do the same. "There are dark forces awakening, it is true. But while there may be darkness, there is still light. That is why I'm here."

Breslin nodded gravely and they continued in silence until they made it to the outer doors that led to the training field. Zhànshì Nineteen was outside, slogging through the mud as she made another round of the intensive obstacle course.

"I'll take it from here," Breslin relieved the trainer on duty and the trainer left wordlessly.

From there, the quiet man left his spot in the shadows as he moved to approach Nineteen. Before he left Breslin behind, he stopped one last time. "There is a place for you on the new third side, Breslin, when you're ready. I suggest that when the king passes, you find your way to us before the General has his way with you."

Breslin considered that invitation for a long time before he shook his head. "No, I'm afraid my place is here. Colonel Altman left me with the charge of helping these young Zhànshì. As long as there is breath in my lungs, I will remain and fight to help them where she cannot."

The man nodded in understanding. "You have done the Colonel proud, Breslin." He started to walk away once more, but Breslin called out to him in a hushed tone.

"Take care of Fourteen. Take care of all of them."

The man smiled. "I always do."

With that, he continued forward. Breslin watched as the man made contact with Zhànshì Nineteen. "Who are you?" the girl asked, standing from the mud to face him.

The large man gave her a caring look. "Hello, Ella. I'm a friend of Ava's."

Truer words had never been spoken.

5

Adaption

The alarms in the mansion started seconds after Jackson's personal alarms. He hurriedly got to his laptop and made sure that the surrounding cities were notified and sought shelter. Simultaneously, Sasha would ensure the rest of the mansion made it safely into the underground cellar. The whole system was streamlined at this point and there was really nothing to be too concerned about, so long as everyone did their jobs.

Jackson worked almost to the last minute before closing his laptop and heading out with Boris. "Don't worry, bud," Jackson comforted his friend, "we've done this before. Just another routine air raid. We'll be fine."

He stopped briefly in the hallway, staring at Ava's room and considering whether or not to go by, just to check if she had already left. He thought of the letter, words she had written months past, things he had only the night before laid eyes on. He wished he had read it sooner. Maybe things would've been different.

Jackson shook himself from the thought as the alarms continued with the flashing lights. She would have woken from the alarms and left for the cellar nearly fifteen minutes ago. There was no reason to go to her room when he would find her safely with the rest of the mansion's occupants.

Still, the thought tugged at him as he and Boris made their way up and out the back door of the mansion. He kicked himself for being so worried. She would be with the rest, and it wasn't his job to keep tabs on her; she would probably dislike him doing so. Still, he could not fully leave to the cellar until he knew for sure. He put an earpiece in his ear and reached out to the others, lingering at the back door.

"How we doing?" Zak asked Jackson as they connected over the communicator.

"The surrounding cities have begun defensive measures. Towers are ready. Everything should be in place," Jackson offered, hesitating and not sure how to ask the question on his mind.

"Good. You're sure cutting it close," Zak noted. "They're less than three minutes out."

"I had a lot to do," Jackson replied with a slight chuckle. "And I enjoy living on the edge." Still, he struggled to ask about Ava, as if it was admitting how he felt for her.

"As does our furry friend," Zak said, mentioning Boris. "You two were made for each other."

"Jackson!" Sasha's voice came over the line. "I haven't had a moment of downtime, but I haven't stopped worrying about you either. Would you guys get in here already?"

"Yeah, I'm on my way. I just wanted to check, is everyone present and accounted for?"

"You mean besides you two and Boris?" Sasha reprimanded.

Jackson's eyes narrowed in confusion at the statement. "You *two* and Boris?" He stopped on the steps leading into the darkened night, but could not move forward. Finally, he felt the urgency and the need to ask the question. "Is Ava there?"

A momentary silence. "What do you mean?" Sasha asked, sounding suddenly terrified. "You're on the same floor! I assumed she was with you!"

Jackson cursed. "Let Boris inside. I'm going after her!" He rushed back toward the mansion and was grateful Boris followed his command, heading in the opposite direction. Jackson did not think; he reacted. He bolted inside and back down the stairs.

"Jackson!" Sasha reached out through the earpiece.

"Don't try and stop me, Sasha! I have to—"

"I know that! It's my daughter! Just take her to the safe room. There's not enough time now to make it back!"

Further empowered by Sasha's approval, Jackson jumped down the stairs several steps at a time and shot down the hallway toward her room. "Ava!" he said, banging on her door. No response. He tried for the handle, but the door was locked. He stepped back to get some momentum before kicking it in. Then he bolted inside, expecting the worst.

She was just...sitting there on the bed, half dressed with her eyes closed.

"Ava," he said, rushing to her, "what the taint are you doing?" He carefully held her at both shoulders, wondering if this was some sort of panic attack, but she did not exactly look panicked, simply... concentrated. "Ava, we need to get out of here! You hear those alarms? You see the flashing lights? They'll be here any minute!"

"I'm trying," Ava whispered, almost more to herself than to him. "I can't connect. Something's blocking. I'm trying. I swear I'm trying! I can't seem to stop it."

"I'm not asking you to stop it!" Jackson clarified, attempting to tug her forward, though she fought back with her strength and would not budge from her spot as she pushed him away. "We need to get out of here!" Jackson explained. "Do you hear me? Let's go!"

"Boris is safely inside!" Zak's voice sounded through the communicator. "Do you have Ava?"

"They'll hurt so many people," Ava muttered. "I have to stop them. Or it will all be my fault." It almost seemed as if she were half asleep, like sleepwalking or in some sort of dream state.

"Ava!" he said, trying to shake her out of it, but that didn't work either. "We need to move!" he declared, emphasizing each word sternly. "Let's go!" He moved in to grab her again but she pushed him away just as forcefully as before.

"Something's blocking it. I'm trying. I swear, I'm trying!"

"We need to move!" he repeated, attempting to pull her once more.

She reacted swiftly by pushing him back several feet. Still, her eyes remained closed.

"Jackson," Sasha's voice now. "They're on us! Is my daughter safe?"

A quick realization that there was no other way to reach her caused him to search for access to the link, and he found it surprisingly quickly. "*Ava*," he said through the link this time, moving in close again and grabbing her shoulders once more, "*you need to wake up! Now!*"

Her eyes shot open and for a split second he thought it had been him that woke her. That was until she forcefully knocked him to the ground, holding his ears and covering his head as the windows shattered and the room filled with flames.

"Jackson!" Sasha's terrified voice once more sounded through Jackson's ringing ears.

Ava blocked the heat for a brief moment before he realized what had happened. Then he rolled, pulling her under so that it was now him blocking her from the flames until the room cleared from the initial blast.

He stood quickly and helped her to her feet. Holding on to her hand he pulled her with him as they left the room and went into the hall. Thankfully, she seemed fully awake now and ran just as urgently. She tried to continue past the hall and up the stairs, but he stopped her. "It's too late," he urged. "Come on."

His fingerprint and retinal scan opened the saferoom door and they entered it quickly as further explosions sounded in the wave above them.

The door was closed and locked before Jackson turned to face Ava, who was panting and attempting to catch her breath.

"Jackson!" Zak this time.

"We're good," he replied through the earpiece. "Just in time. Suggest radio silence until end of raid."

"I'm sorry," Ava said, seeming guilty and ashamed for whatever reason. "I tried! I promise, I tried to connect. I couldn't get past the block! I don't know what's wrong with me. Something is in the way! I tried to stop them. I didn't mean to let this happen."

Jackson watched her in confusion for some time before stepping forward. "Listen to me, Ava. It isn't your job to stop them. We never asked you to use your abilities to protect us. Unlike the United Kingdoms, we haven't based our entire survival on the abilities of one person. Russia has systems in place. They've built underground bunkers at every few miles in every city! By now the whole nation should be safely underground."

She looked up in shock. "I don't understand. I thought...I thought they would...I thought I had to...."

"Well you don't," Jackson interrupted. "Not here. You don't have to feel responsible for the safety of this people. We would never put all that pressure on you. All right? Everything's fine. You and I are probably the only ones who were that close to obliteration." He meant it sarcastically, but she took it hard.

"I'm sorry," she muttered. "I didn't mean to put your life in danger." She put her hands to her head as if trying to understand what was happening.

"I don't blame you," he replied assuredly. "Honestly, I'm not sure you were fully awake."

It seemed that much they agreed on.

She stood there in silence for a long time, looking pale, tired and confused. "So much for those sleeping pills," she muttered. "Thank you, for saving my life."

"Of course!" Jackson said, and immediately regretted how emotional that had sounded. "I would have done it for anyone," he said to clarify, and immediately regretted how unfeeling that one came out.

"I know that," Ava shot back.

An awkward silence followed before Ava looked around the small safe room, taking in her surroundings. "How many times have you survived these attacks?" she asked when the moment had calmed and she regained normal breathing.

"This is the fifth time," Jackson replied, checking the security of the door once more before letting down his guard. "For a minute there, we had help from the United Kingdoms. But obviously we're on our own now."

Ava offered a half smile. "I'm sorry," she said earnestly. "I put my heart and soul into that treaty."

Jackson let out a subtle laugh of self-mockery. "And I'm the one who ended it. You don't have to apologize for that."

Ava's expression touched with sadness. "You know I didn't have anything to do with Yuri's death, don't you? I was there, I was following orders, and I regret that now. I didn't know what Eli had planned.

When he gives an order, you obey it. You can't imagine what he put me through after that, even just for questioning him. But if I had known he was going to kill Yuri, I never would've obeyed. Yuri was a friend and a mentor in a way. He taught me so much in our short time together."

Jackson offered a pained smile. "Me too." The wound of Yuri's loss was apparently still deeply rooted. Not wanting to continue with the unsettling conversation, he walked toward the dresser and pulled out spare clothing. "I'm gonna hit the showers. Maybe get some sleep after that. I'll take the pullout bed."

She was clearly about to object, to say that she couldn't sleep anyway and didn't need the nicer bed. He didn't give her the chance as he entered the washroom and closed the door.

He took his time, hoping she'd have a chance to get settled and fall asleep while he was gone, but she was awake and reading on the bed when he returned.

He eyed the large book curiously but couldn't make out the title from where she held it in her lap. "Light 2 a.m. reading?"

She smiled, holding up the large book for him to see.

"The *Complete Works of Jane Austen*," he read aloud. "Which one has captured your attention tonight?"

"*Persuasion*," Ava said simply. She placed a loose paper in the book to save her space, then got up and grabbed a stack of clothing she had collected. "I'm going to shower too. Night."

He prepped the pullout bed and got comfortable.

★ ★ ★ ★ ★

Ava stared in the mirror in frustration. Ella was right; time after time, people had to sacrifice to save Ava. She was weak and useless in the fight—at least when it mattered. And she was tired of it. She was tired of being rescued like a dainty little damsel. She was tired of being the broken Cinderella that J.J. talked about. This was it. This was the last time she would let it happen. From now on, she would be strong enough. She would rescue herself, or she would be the one to die trying.

Jackson was asleep when Ava reentered, so she returned to the bed and to her book, raking through her tangled wet hair with her fingers.

She had cut it to her shoulders after the surgery on her arm, but even at this length it had been difficult to handle. Her arm was healed now, however, which made life much easier in every aspect.

She began reading and was soon lost in the words of the novel again. It must have been an hour or so before Jackson sat up abruptly, as if waking startled from a noise, though she hadn't heard anything. Ava observed him as he looked around, getting his bearings. It almost seemed that in his sleep, he had forgotten where they were. When he knew the answer to that unspoken question, he rubbed the sleep from his eyes and moved to sit up on the pullout bed.

"Morning," Ava offered.

Jackson sarcastically glanced at the large clock on the wall. "I think you mean goodnight."

Ava smiled and focused on the book.

A minute or so passed before Jackson spoke again. "So," he asked, clearing his gruff throat. "How does *Persuasion* compare to *Pride and Prejudice?*"

She met his glance, a sudden desire to passionately tell him why she loved this one, but she restrained herself. "It compares well," she replied instead.

He made a funny face. "That was a non-committal answer."

"I guess you'll have to read it," she replied mysteriously. It seemed a sort of callback to Jackson's invitation for Ava to start reading those years ago, and it was clear that both of them thought of the comparison.

"Fair enough," Jackson replied. "Give me a tagline or something though. Why should I read this one?"

She thought about all the ways to answer that. How much this book reminded her of them, though she didn't want to admit that one out loud. "Best love story ever," she said instead.

"Better than *Pride and Prejudice?*"

"For me, yes."

"Better than *Bendigo Shafter?*"

"One hundred percent."

"Better than *War and Peace?*"

"I relate to it more," she offered with a shrug.

That seemed to interest him. "How's that?"

Once more, the desire to jump in excitedly and tell him all the comparisons was overwhelming. Instead, she flipped back to one of the earliest pages and read the marked passage aloud, "'Now they were as strangers; nay, worse than strangers, for they could never become acquainted. It was a perpetual estrangement.'"

His eyes narrowed as he considered that, but he said nothing.

"It's worth reading someday," she offered carefully.

"Read another quote," he requested, pushing the blanket off him as the room seemed to grow warmer.

Ava smiled. It took her longer to find the next one, as she hadn't gotten there yet this read, but she knew where to look for it. "In the final note from Wentworth to Anne," Ava gave an explanation of the quote, then read it aloud, "'You pierce my soul. I am half agony, half hope. Tell me not that I am too late, that such precious feelings are gone forever. I offer myself to you again with a heart even more your own, than when you almost broke it eight years and a half ago.'"

A momentary silence lingered as she stared at the page and felt that same thrill she always did when reading the confession of love here. Eventually she looked up at Jackson, who was watching her.

"Wow," Jackson said with a serious expression on his face. "That's good," he admitted with a genuine appreciation for the poetic words.

"It's Jane Austen," Ava replied pointedly. "Of course it is."

He smiled at that. "I've only read the one from her. Maybe someday when I have more time...."

Ava nodded agreement. "It's worth the read."

Jackson's expression became more thoughtful. "Well, we have a few hours before morning. Think we could read it in that time?"

Her stomach did a summersault. So many emotions, it was hard to interpret. She stared at him for a long time before standing and walking to the counter at the corner of the room. She was not ready to go there again. Not today.

In an exaggerated upbeat tone she replied, "I think we should play cards."

"Cards?" he asked in confusion.

She retrieved them from the cupboard she had previously explored and held them up pointedly. Then she walked toward the pullout bed where he sat, but at the last second shifted and took a seat flat on the floor. "Friends play cards," she replied teasingly.

"Friends can read together too," he objected.

Ava scoffed as she shuffled the deck. "Say what you want, but I would never read Jane Austen late into the night with Zak."

That got a smile out of Jackson, but it was soon replaced with a look of sadness. "You know," he said, in hardly more than a whisper, "we didn't get everything wrong the first time."

Ava stared at him helplessly. "No, we didn't," she agreed, matching his somber tone. "But no matter how many times I look back and try, I cannot tell the difference between the times we got it right and the moments we drove ourselves voluntarily off a cliff. And for that reason..." she trailed off momentarily, then smiled, and once more in exaggerated optimism she finished the sentence, "I would like to play cards."

She saw how that hurt him. It hurt her too. He could have no idea how much she longed to read late into the night with him, to discuss her ideas and her feelings without reservation, to go back to the way it once was. But Ava had fallen in love with Jackson reading together in a similar way. Perhaps not everything in their relationship had been wrong, but the moment she fell in love with him, it all went downhill from there. She could not allow herself to make that mistake this time around.

"Okay," Jackson said, choosing to set aside the pain and match her enthusiasm. He joined her on the floor.

"Now," Ava said, handing the shuffled deck to Jackson. "Teach me your favorite game, and I'll crush you in it by round two."

★ ★ ★ ★ ★

Usually Ava followed through on her competitive threats, but this speed game was one he happened to excel at, and she didn't get the hang of it so quickly.

By the tenth round, she was angry, and he was hungry, so he raided the small pantry for snacks to refuel as she worked on her strategy. No luck for her, as he kicked her carcass again.

They enjoyed much laughter—that is, he laughed a lot, and she mostly growled in frustration. Now and then though, between rounds, they would share a few snacks and a few teasing comments, and then she would take the time to laugh or smile rather than growl.

It must have been another hour or two before she finally won a round, and feeling very pleased with herself, she grabbed the entire deck of cards and threw it in the air in celebration.

"There!" she said happily. "Now we never have to play that game again!"

"We're about a billion to one at this point," Jackson argued through a fit of laughter, mumbling through a cracker in his mouth. "Don't you want to beat me in the all-arounds?"

"Heck no!" she replied, walking around the room to stretch her legs and seeming to flaunt her victory in the very way she moved. "I won the last game. And that's all that matters."

"All right, get over here!" Jackson said challengingly, gathering the cards from around the room. "We're not done yet!"

She giggled, but ignored the challenge, taking a seat on the pullout bed above him. She let out a serious breath as her mood changed. "I'm sorry, by the way, for getting you into this mess. I honestly don't know what happened out there. I vaguely remember my attempts to connect with the Tower and drop the ships. But honestly, it's all a bit foggy until I opened my eyes and saw you standing before me in my room and the humming of the approaching aircraft in the distance."

He stopped gathering the cards, turning slightly to face her and looked at her just as seriously. "I lied earlier, when I said I would have done it for anyone. I mean, I sort of would have. We would have sent someone. And in the past, it might have been me. But I've long since stopped being the main one to rush into the field, and even if I tried to, the others wouldn't let me."

She watched him thoughtfully. "Then why did you come for me?"

"Because it was you." He shrugged. "I didn't exactly think about it. I heard you were still inside, and I bolted. And rather than attempt to stop me, Sasha offered suggestions on how to help, either because he was just as concerned for you, or because he knew he couldn't stop me if he tried."

Ava gave a half smile, but didn't seem to know how to answer.

"All right, loser, get over here and let's see if that win was a fluke or not."

She scoffed but obeyed, rejoining him on the floor.

And when Jackson won, *he* apparently flaunted it just a little too much, because the entire deck was thrown directly at his face this time.

As he laughed the surprise away, the door to the safe room opened, and they both flinched suddenly.

Standing outside were Sasha and Zak.

Jackson stood up quickly, noticing the strange look Sasha had on his face. "It's over?" Jackson asked.

Zak nodded. "It's over. But we've never taken fire on the mansion before. It'll take a lot to rebuild. And it's not pretty."

The mansion was chaos, and the next several days were spent in cleaning up and rebuilding. Sasha had been quiet and awkward around Jackson all that time, so when Jackson found the man working alone, picking up shattered remains in one of the upper bedrooms, he took the chance to help him and talk together.

"You're not mad at me, are you? For going after Ava?"

"Of course not!" Sasha shot back. "How could you think that? She's my little girl. I'm grateful you saved her."

"Then why the silent treatment?"

Sasha was quiet for a time before responding. "I suppose it's more the state I found you in when it was all over. I admit, it wasn't what I was expecting. You didn't even have your earpiece in so we could get a hold of you. And the two of you staying up all night together as if on holiday and not in the middle of a dangerous attack—"

"I was worried she'd have a panic attack or something," Jackson explained. "I knew she wouldn't be able to sleep, and I wasn't going to leave her alone while I dozed off without a care in the world."

"I understand that. It's just...it's just the way I saw you with her when I entered. I don't know exactly...."

"If you're asking about my intentions with your daughter," Jackson cut in with a touch of amusement, "I assure you, my intentions are pure."

Jackson expected Sasha to join in the sarcasm, but his expression became even more serious and he waited until Jackson stopped working to look at him before replying, "It's not Ava that I'm worried about."

Jackson gave no reply and Sasha was forced to explain. "The last thing that Ava needs right now is romance, and she knows that. She is entirely focused on her healing and recovery, and I believe a part of that is repairing the rift between you two. But my worry is that, while she is entirely and innocently focused on renewing friendship with you, your heart might get involved. You've always been headstrong. You've always been a romantic. Ava is not. Most of her friends have been men, with nothing of the sort involved. I'm not worried that you'll hurt my daughter. I'm worried that you're hurting yourself. I don't want you to get your heart broken by this girl again, and certainly not when it's the furthest thing from her mind."

Jackson could not answer for a long time. He wanted to argue with that, to say that Sasha hadn't been there and didn't know that Ava had been just as involved in the romance all this time. But all he could think, over and over again, was, "Let's play cards. Friends play cards." Maybe it was all his fault. Maybe it had never been what Ava wanted, even the first time, and perhaps he had invented this all in his mind.

Maybe. But Jackson didn't think so. There were moments with Ava, moments that he knew were real. Moments that he was certain she felt the same. Perhaps she was not ready to move forward with that now, but that didn't mean that all they had shared hadn't been real either. If Sasha had read that letter from Ava….

And yet, she had taken pains to assure him that the letter had been "written a long time ago" when things were "different."

Eventually, Jackson stood from his crouching position, grabbing the now-full garbage sack and throwing it over his shoulder. "What do you want me to do?" Jackson asked genuinely. "Do you want me to back off?"

"I don't want you to pull away, not by any means," Sasha clarified, "I still believe your friendship should continue for her sake. Just…don't let your heart get too involved. I don't want you to get hurt."

Jackson slowly nodded in consideration. Eventually, he spoke seriously, "If you're asking me to step back for Ava's sake, then I will. You're right, the last thing she needs right now is some man trying to pursue her. So I won't. But if you really are trying to protect me, if you're trying to warn me away before I get in too deep and fall in love with your daughter..." Jackson inhaled slowly as he considered, then spoke more honestly about this than ever, "I think it's a bit late for that."

Not exactly prepared to hear any reply from Sasha at this point, Jackson left the room, and hoped to leave the conversation there forever too.

☆ ☆ ☆ ☆ ☆

"Can I ask you a question?" Ava inquired as they sat around a table in the town restaurant. Only Jackson had not joined, as it was too dangerous for him to leave the mansion. Besides, he was extremely busy with his work during the days.

It was little Kai's birthday, and he had requested to go outside the mansion for ice cream, after the chaos of rebuilding in the past weeks.

"Go for it," Viktoriya said, licking her spoon.

Ava hadn't wanted any ice cream, or any treat at all really, so Sasha had gotten her a simple iced tea—but she had hardly touched that either. She couldn't help thinking of that last week in the Kingdoms, with Eli constantly pressing her about her weight and that she should eat more. She had always taken good care of herself, and he had no right to drill her about her weight. Now at every meal, she couldn't help hearing his voice, telling her she wasn't eating enough. Only, now it was the truth.

"What compelled you to choose them over your past?" Ava said, not wanting to spell out in detail the fact that Viktoriya had once been an agent.

Viktoriya looked at Zak, then at Sasha, and back to Ava. "To be honest, I didn't choose these people initially because I bought into their freedom movement, or because I thought they were better than where I came from. But my loyalties changed the moment I had my little guy." She rubbed the birthday boy's head lovingly. "I was never trained for that type of mission. My government just took advantage of the opportunity I was given. Still, this kiddo changed me for good. I picked him, and when Sasha, Jackson and Zak talked about freedom for Russia, I bought in. Not because I love this place more than my homeland. And not really because I wanted to be in on some big movement. Only because I knew they were going to really do it, and that this would ultimately be a safe place, and a free place, to raise my children. Then I found Zak, and he really messed me up!"

Zak made a melodramatic love-struck face at his wife, and Ava couldn't help smiling. "And how did *that* happen?" Ava couldn't help adding the next question that had been heavy on her mind since she had arrived—and particularly since Sasha had voiced his desire for a different outcome.

"I swept her off her feet," Zak said with a shrug. "What else is there?"

"But didn't you have a history with...?" Ava trailed off, unsure if she should say it with possible listening ears in public that hated his very name.

Viktoriya simply nodded. "But he and I both realized that was over some time before Zak and I got together."

"They actually went on several outings together," Sasha noted for all to hear. "She and our friend. I thought they might go for each other."

Zak glared suddenly. "If you had, I would have had to challenge him for you." Obviously, it was meant as a joke, but after several weeks of fighting Jackson every evening, Ava knew how skilled he was. There were probably very few people who could easily overcome him in a fight.

"Please. You didn't even notice me at the time," Viktoriya disagreed.

"Only because he kind of had dibs."

Ava scoffed at that use of the word in reference to a human being, but Zak hadn't meant anything by it.

"Even back then, I noticed you. It was you who didn't notice me."

Ava found herself strangely hovering over the word "outings" in her mind. She couldn't help wondering what an "outing" with Jackson would be like. Of course, he wasn't really able to get "out" anymore.

"Personally, I think you two are a much better fit," Sasha noted kindly, which caused Ava to raise her eyebrow. Was he being nice? Or did he mean that comment, and his statement from before had been the exaggeration?

"Besides," Zak interjected with an air of added drama, "Jackson only has one love, and it's his mission."

Sasha was the one to scoff this time. "Love is the great equalizer, my friend. And not even the strongest of us are immune."

"How did you meet your wife, Sasha?" Viktoriya asked, and suddenly Ava wondered if Viktoriya knew who Sasha's wife, and Ava's mother, was.

Sasha offered a pained smile, the one he always assumed when anyone mentioned Kristen. "Perhaps a story for another day," Sasha offered simply, and it was clear it was painful to talk about.

"He was her S.O.," Ava related, almost before she knew what she had said. She immediately realized how inappropriate it was to continue the personal conversation when he had attempted to shut it down, and she was about to apologize verbally, but the pleasantly surprised look he gave her stopped her suddenly.

"How did you know that? Did she tell you our story?"

Ava shook her head. "I don't remember her ever telling me anything about her history. But after her brother died, he left me everything of his, and that included several of her old journals. I read them cover to cover, several times. I felt like I really got to know her for the first time."

Sasha's smile was no longer pained, but truly happy. "What did she say about me?"

Ava chuckled, thinking back to them. "She hated you in the beginning! She said you were stuck up, proud, and full of yourself. But when you met her son for the first time, that's when she softened to you."

Sasha's expression changed again. It was a deep sadness that Ava could not explain. It wasn't his normal sad expression about Kristen, and she almost thought that this new expression was for Eli.

He gulped painfully. "I think I had better get a drink to swallow down this ice cream. It's very rich today!" With that, he stood and walked to the front of the restaurant. Ava watched him with concern as he left.

"She was my hero, you know," Viktoriya said in a slightly reverent, hushed tone. "Your mother. I wanted nothing more than to be just like her. For a long time in my career, I lived by her example. Whenever hard moments came along, I always asked myself how she would react in my situation. I know, it's a bit cheesy, but she was my idol, my inspiration."

Well, that answered that question. Viktoriya definitely knew who Kristen was to them.

"It broke my heart when she died. You asked why I chose these guys. That was the first time I chose a different path than I think she would have. I had to pick my kids."

"My mother did too," Ava said in sudden defense of her mother. People always denigrated Kristen's memory for the kind of mother she had been. And in truth, Ava had many times too. But she had long since changed her opinion on that. "She stopped journaling a few years after I was born. But there wasn't an entry where she didn't mention her love for me and my brother. She was faced with so much manipulation, so many ultimatums, and she had very little control over where she spent her time in life. But all the control she did have, she devoted to making the world a better place, for her children, and everyone else's. Over and over again, she made that vow. And the world wouldn't be what it is today, for me, or for them," Ava nodded at Viktoriya's boys, "if it weren't for what she did."

Sasha reappeared then, and not wanting to pain him further, Zak was the one who quickly changed the subject. Still, Ava could not help noticing how Viktoriya observed her just a little longer than normal, as if still deeply contemplating Ava's words and their application in her own life.

They focused more on Kai after that and made the occasion special for him. Still, there was a new sort of understanding between all of them, a way the reverence of Kristen's memory had shifted things.

Soon enough, Sasha suggested they return back to the mansion and go horseback riding, which Kai immediately endorsed.

The others cleaned up, and Ava took her almost untouched tea to the trash before heading to the washroom.

As she washed her hands, she couldn't help being grateful again that her cast had been removed. Her arm still ached at times, but she was over the clunky arm and difficult-to-maneuver cast. Still, Jackson's advice about how to dress with a wounded limb had been invaluable during that time.

She caught a glimpse of a woman as she exited one of the washroom stalls and came to the sink to Ava's right. Ava avoided looking at her to skip unnecessary conversation.

Her still wet hands went immediately to her temples when a sudden, intensified pain pushed on her chip.

She glanced then at the washroom door as it opened, still holding her throbbing head, with the sound of the running water from the sink playing in the background. Three soldiers pushed inside, and two of them were not women. The three soldiers barred the door closed, and the woman beside her joined them as they came at Ava almost all at once.

The others were outside, not a few hundred feet from her, but Sasha and Viktoriya currently had no access to the link, and there was no one else. She thought about screaming out, but then an image of a scornful Ella popped into her head, accusing Ava of being weak and always needing to be rescued.

The headache weakened her immensely and she worried that if it was the same thing that had been used on her in the Brazil Tower those torturous weeks, she would go unconscious any moment.

Ava gritted her teeth. Ella was wrong. Ava was not weak. Never again. She had promised herself, and it was time to prove it.

Still, to be safe, she screamed out loudly. Then she fought back. Her practice with Jackson every night prepared her to fight without much use of her still weakened arm. But these four people were highly skilled, and Ava was in excruciating pain, which seemed clearly focused on pushing her into unconsciousness.

Ava kicked the first woman with a fierceness that pushed her back against the washroom stalls, which pained her, and infuriated her further.

The other three moved in at her again and Ava did her best to keep them off, attempting to fight with heavy kicks, but finding the small space too constricting. She used her right arm in a blow to the side of the head of a man as he moved in, and she could tell how much the blow hurt him when he flinched and moved back. Still, she almost wondered if it had hurt her more as she screamed out in pain from her yet sub-par arm.

The others were back, close up and on her in seconds. Jackson was much better at close quarter combat. She wished she had the strength he did to handle heavy blows, and to deal them. She attempted to do so, but she could hardly think, let alone handle the intense pain.

She fought relentlessly for some time, her hazy mind wondering if these were Eli's men, Darya's, or even the Republic's.

Soon enough, the four of them accomplished their task, holding her tightly at every limb and her head, so she could barely move. They were attempting to get control of Ava until she lost consciousness, to simply hold her still. The hold they had on her was difficult to break, but she managed a close, sharp elbow into one of the men's sides, and he huffed in pain, breaking hold enough for her to turn her head and bite him fiercely on the side of the arm. He screamed out, and the others held even tighter. Ava struggled to break away. She screamed out loudly again.

"No use, lovely," one of the men whispered. "No one's going to rescue you today."

He spoke in English, no hint of a Middle Eastern accent to match his ethnicity. He was from Eli. There had to be something significant in this news, but she couldn't place what her intuition was attempting to tell her.

"Who are you?" Ava said, and found her words sounded muffled and stuttered. She tried to search for an energy signature from one of the remote-control devices, but she could not get past her mental block.

"What, you don't recognize us?" the first girl from the washroom said in an exaggeratedly injured tone.

"We're not from her generation," another man explained.

"I trained with her," the other girl said, and Ava attempted to turn to see who it was, but was forced to remain still. "I remember her forceful little will," the girl said harshly. "She always thought she was the best."

"Any time now, lovely," the man urged her to go unconscious.

Not a chance.

Ava glanced at the furthest mirror on the wall and was able to get a glimpse of the girl who had supposedly trained with her. It was Zhànshì Ten. They were all Zhànshì, all much older, having gone into the field before Ava's prime in training.

"What did Eli tell you?" Ava said through gritted teeth, and still, her words sounded dull, as if her tongue had gone numb.

"He said you went bonkers, tried to join the enemy. We're here to rescue you and take you home to your dear ol' brother."

"He's lying," Ava urged. "Eli isn't who he used to be. You have to believe me."

"We're just doing our jobs, Altman," the other man said simply. "You can take it up with the General."

The fog in her mind increased. She found herself suddenly wishing Remington were still there to watch over her.

Ava gulped suddenly, ashamed of that thought. Ella was right. Ava had become weak and reliant on bodyguards. She had once been the highest scoring Zhànshì in training. She had beat all of these people's scores, by a longshot. She had taken on many worthy opponents, and she was not about to give up now. She had promised herself, never again.

The lights in the room flickered for a moment, as Ava's connection with the Tower in her desperation grew strong. And that was when it hit her, what her intuition had been trying to scream out at her. These were Zhànshì! And if there was one thing in common they shared, it was the chip.

So, Ava pushed. Although she had felt a serious block in her connection with the Tower since her arrival, she felt no block in connecting with their chips, and when she pushed, they reacted. Subtly at first, as their holds on her wavered.

Ava pushed harder, thinking of Darya and the remote, how much she had needed to push to change the course of that interaction. She pushed with every ounce of energy left within her.

All four of the Zhànshì let go, pulling back as they held their heads and screamed out in pain. It seemed they could not handle what they were serving.

Still, it wasn't enough, and they started pressing through it. Ava pushed harder, but her wavering strength was failing her. Nothing she did when she pushed felt like enough.

A pounding sound against the door surprised Ava, and she heard Sasha screaming her name from the other side. They were coming to rescue her.

If Ava didn't stop these Zhànshì first, this could turn into a bloodbath. None of these Zhànshì deserved to die for following orders, but Ava would not lose Sasha, or anyone else, for attempting to protect her.

She pushed harder. Still, it was not good enough.

Suddenly, Ava thought of Breanna, of that final image, of swimming with the current, rather than pushing against the train.

She closed her eyes. She searched for the current, the immense power of its strain. And rather than pushing against it, Ava climbed on board the train, and swam with the current.

The four Zhànshì didn't even scream as they all went immediately unconscious on the floor of the washroom.

The pain did not stop for Ava, even after her enemies were down, and she was certain there was still some sort of device pressing against her chip.

It took another minute and loud slamming against the door before it was broken in. Sasha and Zak entered with weapons drawn. Ava was hunched in a slump on the floor by the sink, but she was conscious.

Sasha and Zak took in the sight of the four unconscious Zhànshì. Sasha ran up to her and took her into his arms, muttering questions of "what happened?" and "are you okay?"

"Rem—remote-control," she managed to mutter the words.

Looking confused, Sasha asked for more, but Zak was already searching the unconscious Zhànshì. "You mean this?" he asked, holding up a remote-control device that he'd found in one of their pockets.

"Give that to me!" Sasha said in a grunt.

Zak immediately obeyed, and after exploring the buttons momentarily, Sasha discovered how to turn it off.

Ava breathed out in immediate relief.

"What is this thing?" Sasha hissed in anger.

All Ava could think was of Eli. In her weakened, foggy state, she found herself wanting to fight back. From halfway around the world, she found his signal.

"Nice try, Eli," she said weakly. *"But you won't beat me that easily."*

There was a long silence until he responded. *"We'll see."*

☆ ☆ ☆ ☆ ☆

"Well done, Ava," the physical therapist said encouragingly. "I think that's enough for today."

Jackson had only just entered the gym, curious how the therapy was going in rebuilding her muscles, now that the cast was gone.

"You heard him," Sasha said when Ava continued with the next rep, lifting the heavy weight with her mended arm and trembling slightly from the pain.

"I'm not done," Ava grunted.

"Yes, you are," the physical therapist disagreed. "You've done enough for the day. Please stop."

She went in for another rep, and Jackson cringed, not liking what he had just walked into, but not exactly sure if he should go either. Ava looked angry and determined and even a bit rebellious, which never went over well against Sasha.

"Ava," Sasha said sternly, "you heard the man. It is time to be done for the day."

"He barely pushed me. At this rate I won't be back to optimum strength for months."

"Yes," the therapist said in a sort of demeaning tone, "healing a bone takes a bit of time."

"I broke my femur in three places," Ava shot back, "along with four ribs, my arm and several skull fractures. I don't need you to tell me what it takes to heal! I just need you to help me do it or leave and let me do it myself!"

Though seeming a bit taken aback by her response, the man was determined to have his way here. "You've lost quite a bit of muscle over the past weeks. It will take time to recover that. If you do too much too quickly, you will do more harm than good. Now, I am telling you to stop."

"I know the mechanics of healing," she pressed, "and not just scientifically, like you. I've been through it. I know what I'm doing."

"Well, you're not the one with the degree and job title, are you?" he shot back challengingly.

She growled then, but set the weight down. Jackson held his breath, hoping that would be the end of it, but Ava walked determinedly to the pullup bar.

"Don't even think about it!" the physical therapist snarled.

"Ava!" Sasha said in surprise. "You are done! Stop!"

"If he won't push me, I'll push myself! Please, trust me on this, Sasha. I know my limits, far better than either of you. "

"And I know how to do my job!" the therapist said with sudden frustration. "You're going to hurt yourself and set back your healing."

"You're going easy on me," Ava disagreed through clenched teeth, using both arms to perform a standard pullup.

"If you're trying to prove some point," Sasha said in obvious anger, "then you're doing a poor job. I want you to stop. Now!"

"You all think I'm weak!" Ava insisted. Then she let go of the bar with her left hand, now using only the just barely uncasted arm to pull herself all the way up and down again.

"I think you're an idiot!" the physical therapist disagreed harshly.

Sasha gave the man a look to shush him, and still Jackson stood hidden at the doorway of the gym, now staying more out of interest than because he thought he could help in any way.

"I can do far more than you think, doctor," Ava replied, obviously attempting to remain calm and reasonable. "My body was at optimum health at the time of the arm breaking. I want to get back to that as soon as possible. I'll do whatever it takes. You can push me harder than you have."

"Well I'm not going to," the therapist said in frustration. "And at this point I'm considering giving you up as a patient altogether. I don't have time for people who will not follow my regimen."

"Your regimen is weak!" Ava growled, dropping from the bar and standing in what looked to be an attack stance. "And so are both of you!"

Jackson widened his eyes in surprise at the harshness. In truth, he had never seen Ava look so...well, terrifying.

Sasha's stern anger softened after a time. "Is that you talking, Ava? Or is it Eli?"

She ground her teeth together, remaining there for a time, sweating from the exertion of the exercise and breathing a bit faster than normal. Still, her intensity remained as she stared the man down.

Eventually, she turned away from him, storming toward the exit... toward Jackson. He moved out of her way, when it was clear she had no desire to sit around and chat with him, and her anger continued to flare as she left them there.

Jackson was not the only one to let out a breath of relief. That had been intense, to say the least.

"Your daughter is a real charmer, Sasha," the physical therapist said. "I see why you've kept her hidden all these years."

Sasha shook his head in exasperation. Finally, Jackson walked fully into the room.

"So..." Jackson said in a conversational tone, "trouble in paradise?"

"I'm assuming you saw that?" Sasha said, still looking a bit lost in his confusion.

"Yup."

Sasha let out a heavy sigh. Then threw his hands up helplessly and groaned.

"I'm out for the day," the physical therapist said. "Call me if you feel there's any reason for my continuing this case."

"Come back tomorrow," Sasha replied with a stern glare.

"Mm-hmm. Call me." After the man had left, Sasha turned to Jackson as if for answers.

"Don't look at me," Jackson said with a shrug. "I was hiding. She's a bit scary when she's mad."

"I don't understand! One moment she's depressed and wants to be coddled. The next she's mad at me for not pushing her and acting like it's my fault that she's fallen so far behind in the first place!"

Jackson moved to the pullup bar and began a few reps. "It's hard to go from having every moment of your life controlled to being personally responsible for your own well-being," Jackson offered. "It's possible she feels a sense of guilt for the lack of motivation she's felt the last weeks, for backsliding so much. Feeling as helpless as she did against those Zhànshì probably made her realize she's been going too easy on herself."

Sasha considered that for a time. "I suppose. It's just, I have been fully prepared and ready to handle the pain and sorrow from her. The anger is a bit harder to swallow."

Jackson smiled, pulling himself up again. "Congratulations. Now, you're a real dad! Honestly, I'm just glad she's mad at someone besides me!"

Sasha scoffed. "Well, are you going to help me?"

Jackson dropped to the floor. "Sorry—me?"

"Yes, you. Talk some sense into her? Like you said, you're not the one she's mad at."

Jackson winced.

She was in the kitchens, working hard, seeming to take out her anger on her work. It was obvious she knew he was there, but clearing his throat didn't get her attention. She did not want to talk, and Jackson was close to giving it up as a hopeless cause. Still, he remained, coughing uncomfortably, which she ignored just as completely.

"Can you stop doing the dishes so violently?" Jackson requested.

She threw another plate into the dish water before whirling around to face him.

Jackson smiled awkwardly, his hand raised in a weak greeting. "H-hi."

"What do you want? Sasha sent you here to convince me I was wrong, right? Well, I don't want to hear it. He thinks I'm weak. They both do! They're going easy on me. It's ridiculous! They had me do a couple of stretches, then three sets of only five reps with one weight and called it a day! For the first sixteen years of my life, I trained for ten straight hours a day! I don't need to be treated like a little girl. I need to get back my strength so I can fight!"

Jackson paused as he considered how to respond. Five reps did seem a bit small-time, especially for a Zhànshì. "Look, Ava. If Sasha is going easy on you, it's probably because he's worried about pushing you too far the other way. All you've ever known is people who pushed you too hard and too far. He wants to be a place of peace and refuge. Not another screaming General. Would you really want him to treat you the way Eli, or even Harrison, did?"

After a moment, she swallowed, as if his words made at least a bit of sense. Still, her anger did not fully subside.

Jackson took a new approach, that of sarcasm. "Something tells me my words of wisdom haven't magically solved this for you."

"He thinks I'm weak," she shot back immediately.

"That's not true, Ava. Sasha is just wary—"

"Not Sasha. The P.T." Suddenly, looking helpless with that divulgence, she sank to the floor. Although he didn't enjoy hardwood floors for sitting as much as Ava did, he felt it was best to be on her level and so he joined her there, crouching.

"You and Sasha both have my past to compare, and even if I seem weak now, at least you can remember what I used to be. But all this man has seen is this." She held up her weak arm as if in explanation.

"He's seen a lot of broken arms before," Jackson objected. "He helped me through my recovery after I was kidnapped and tortured by a Russian extremist. Besides, who cares what he thinks?"

Ava narrowed her eyes incredulously, and gave a look as if to say he were dumb. "My recovery is determined directly by what he thinks."

"Ah. I guess there is that."

"He's right. I am weak. I've never been so weak in my life."

"Yeah, but you've never been so strong either," Jackson offered that same little trope again. "Tap into that inner drive and prove him wrong."

"What do you think I was trying to do? He sees me as helpless, says the word and Sasha shuts it down."

Jackson nodded in understanding.

"I'm so tired of this. I'm tired of being weak. I'm tired of the panic attacks. I'm tired of all of this!"

"Hey. You know what they say, breaking is the easy part. Rebuilding isn't so easy. This is it; this is recovery. And it's not pretty, and it's not fun, and in fact it sucks. But this, kid, this is where the rubber hits the road. This is where the heroes are set apart from the lackeys. I know it sucks. But I also know you have what it takes to succeed. If you need to change Sasha's mind, then I suggest you do it rationally—with words, rather than anger. Yeah?"

She sighed heavily, but ultimately, she nodded in agreement.

☆ ☆ ☆ ☆ ☆

I know I haven't been treating you fairly," Ava admitted, as they sat together on Sasha's small office sofa. "You've done everything for me, and my behavior has made me seem ungrateful. I am far from that, Sasha. It's just that...I understand why the P.T. thinks I'm weak, but when you take his word so firmly over mine and the limits I know I have, it makes me think you see me that way too. And I guess I've been feeling that if you of all people see me as weak, then I really have lost myself."

Sasha observed her for a time, considering. There were so many routes he could take in dealing with her fears. He could attempt to reassure her, as he knew Jackson did—and as Jackson well should, in his relationship with Ava. But Sasha could see that there was something Ava needed besides reassurance: validation.

Sasha unconsciously scratched his head as he leaned back in his seat. He attempted to look comfortable as he prepared to open up to his daughter, but given the topic he would now broach, he was far from it.

"When I met your mother, she appeared to me to be the strongest woman in the world. There was a sort of confidence, pride and grace that she had about her that just made her seem that way. And for a long time,

I believed it to be so. As I came to know her better, and as she allowed me further into her life, I began to question that assumption. She opened up about her shattered youth, about losing her mother and her father retreating into his work. I remember thinking then, as I learned about this painful past, that there was no way this poor woman could ever recover from it and that it would surely shape the rest of her future."

Sasha inhaled a long breath and watched Ava as she listened intently.

"As we became closer still, soon Kristen opened up about Eli, her little boy, and about her horrific first marriage. She was in her mid-teens when she had her baby and when her father made her marry. That alone has been the breaking of many women. Add to that the abuse from her husband, and once more, as your mother opened up to me, I remember thinking that there was only so much that one woman could bear, and that truly she had reached the limit. I grew close to your mother, I fell in love with her, all the while assuming that she must assuredly be broken by this history.

"We were just months away from being married when Harrison took Eli away for the Zhànshì Training Program. Kristen said she supported him, but deep down I knew she felt she'd had her child stolen from her. And this, too, has been the breaking of many women.

"My work ultimately led me to the Republic, and our long-distance marriage was a painful reality that we both had to bear. I wasn't there to help her when she lost her sister. I wasn't there when she found out she was pregnant again, despite her vow that we would not bring another child into the world only to be given to Harrison again.

"And once more, she claimed she supported the General, but I knew how much it broke her heart to give her little girl to him. I wasn't there when her daughter was kidnapped nine years later, and when the General himself gave up pursuit of his granddaughter in favor of his experiments. I didn't see the agony your mother went through in trying to get you back, but when I heard of it, I wondered how she had been strong enough to make it through that fight entirely alone.

"I was there when we learned that the General had turned you against us. All the years, all the pain and suffering she went through, if ever there was a moment when she was close to breaking, that was it. Somehow though, she didn't. She made it through.

"She was forced into the role of leader and an image for the people, forced to mask her fears, her pains and her feelings with fake smiles and forced strength, and that has been the breaking of many women. But all of these she bore with dignity and grace.

"She lost her father and nearly her daughter to an assassin in the same day, and she went through the pain and fear alone.

"And when she was faced with death, in her final moments, she proved to us all once more that none of these had been enough to break her. And indeed, that nothing ever could.

"All those years, I wondered every time she was faced with another challenge, how she continued forward with that same dignity, confidence and grace when any one of those things on her list of obstacles would have broken most people. If there's anything I learned from your mother, it's that when painful challenges come, we can either break, or we can adapt.

"They say that what doesn't kill you makes you stronger, and I've always hated that because it assumes that time really heals all wounds. It doesn't. And it doesn't account for the scars left behind. This pain you feel, it will never really go away completely. You will never fully heal from the wounds that have been inflicted. These scars will remain for you to carry throughout your life. But the immense pain you feel now will subside, the gaping wound will heal into a scar. It will become easier to live your life again. Like this once broken arm of yours, the bone will mend, and in time, you may even regain the muscle and the strength you lost. But the scars from within, and without," he pointed to the scar on her arm from the surgery, "these will remain."

Ava held onto Kristen's dog tags as she responded. "Jackson keeps saying that I'm stronger now than I've ever been," she said, allowing the emotion to sound through her voice, "and I appreciate him for saying it, and for meaning it as he does, but Daddy, he's wrong! I've never been weaker. I've never felt more broken. I've never been this lost. And I want to believe I'll come out of it. I just want to be strong again!"

"You will, my love," Sasha promised. "In time, you will. You have faced your own list of obstacles that would have been enough to break many people. But you have adapted, you have grown, you have overcome. Things may look dire now, but this will be no different. You will continue to grow, to overcome, and to adapt. Just like your mother did."

☆ ☆ ☆ ☆ ☆

6

Desertion

"Are we sure they're Zhànshì?" Zak asked suspiciously from the briefing room table.

"I recognized the faces," Sasha said, "though I couldn't place them exactly."

"Why haven't we asked Ava?" Zak said with a sudden shrug. "She would know, wouldn't she?"

Jackson and Sasha shared a look. "It's not that simple," Sasha admitted. "The Russian Leadership Committee is hesitant enough as it is to have her here at all. Jackson has convinced them that it's worth the risk. And I've attempted to promise I can handle things…" he trailed off.

"The Committee has agreed to her remaining," Jackson explained, "only under the condition that she is strictly removed from any involvement with the war and workings of the government. And of course, they really don't know what all she is capable of, or they never would have agreed at all."

Zak sighed heavily. "They were pretty carced about her involvement in choosing the Elite team, weren't they?"

Jackson smiled sadly his confirmation. "Eli sending in a team of four Zhànshì to extract her hasn't helped either. They killed two people in their escape from one of the most secure prison facilities in Russia. Needless to say, I agreed that we would keep her out of the politics."

"Which is why she hasn't come back to the meetings," Sasha explained. "I told her the situation, and she understands. Still, her involvement in this case would be helpful. Can you show me the picture again?"

Jackson agreed, pulling it up on screen. He studied the faces, one by one, as did the others. "I don't know the old Korean man at all," Jackson said. "Actually, I don't know either of the men, but the girl looks vaguely familiar."

"She would have been several years younger when you met her," Sasha noted, hoping it would be proved somehow.

"Puberty," Jackson muttered in annoyance. "I don't know. I couldn't say for sure."

The first photo had been taken at the Russian border fence, with the three strange people standing on the outside of the border. Then, for a matter of less than a minute, there had been a strange fluctuation in the Tower which caused a disruption in the security monitors and defenses. Less than half a minute—yet, when it was back to normal, the three of them had somehow ended up on the other side of the gates, and the second photo showed them miraculously within Russia.

"How else would they have made it through the gate defenses?" Zak said, staring at the images.

"As far as we know," Sasha objected, "Ava is the only person capable of disrupting Tower defenses."

Silence lingered for longer than Jackson liked as they considered that. "You don't think...?" Zak could not finish the question.

"She hasn't been able to connect with the Towers since she arrived," Jackson disagreed, though he was not naive enough to think that people—including Ava—were incapable of lying. Still, he didn't like the look of questioning on Zak's, and even Sasha's face.

"I'm going to see if it caught any footage," Jackson said, wanting to shift the focus away from Ava. He pulled out his laptop and logged into the system. He was on the Russian Defense Committee and received alerts almost as soon as anyone. He had been alerted ten minutes previously about a strange disruption at the fence, and on seeing the images, he had immediately been concerned that this problem was bigger than illegal immigrants, hence calling for an emergency meeting.

"White girl, black young man, and Korean old man," Zak noted. "Doesn't sound like your run-of-the-mill immigrants from the Republic. Isn't that one too old to be a Zhànshì, though?"

"Yes, he is," Sasha agreed.

Jackson focused on the system and finally pulled up a video recording. There were heavy defenses and cameras all along the gates that surrounded the borders of Russia, and they were motion activated to trigger on at the slightest movements. "Here we go," Jackson said, broadcasting the video onto the larger screen.

The strange, three-man team neared the gates, staring up at the height and looking somewhat intimidated. That is, the older man looked intimidated. The girl looked annoyed, and the boy seemed eerily confident.

"Can you pull on sound?" Zak asked.

Jackson struggled through the system momentarily before Zak urged, "Let me." In a matter of seconds he had sound on.

"I assume you have a way out of this one too?" the girl asked with a slight tone of mockery.

"Trust him," the old man tried to calm her. "We've made it this far, haven't we?"

"Miracle," she replied dryly, "that you survived this long without me shooting you."

The younger man chuckled wryly but mostly seemed to be ignoring the others as he stared at the wall, his thoughts seeming distant. His eyes closed momentarily, and when they opened again, he grinned widely. "There it is."

The connection cut off. And the next video was of them walking away from the wall, now safely on the other side.

"Who else has seen that look before?" Sasha asked his friends.

Jackson knew exactly what he meant. "Ava," he said, nodding in agreement. That distant look, the way she seemed to be talking to or conversing with another world entirely while connecting with the Tower.

"I had thought she was the only one who could control the Towers," Sasha muttered in great surprise. "But, even if briefly...he must have."

"Well, things just got real," Zak noted with a deeply heavy voice.

"You think they're here to extract her?" Jackson asked, not wanting to believe it.

"What else?" Sasha replied.

"So, what now?" Zak asked in concern. "How do we deal with this level of threat? I mean, a drone strike could—"

"Hold on," Sasha objected. "Before we blow them from existence, I think it's worth finding out if we're right."

Jackson was silent for a long time as he considered. He was not the type to go straight to attack mode, but this type of threat was not to be taken lightly. "I'm not so sure we can take the risk, Sasha," Jackson said in a weighty tone. "This is a threat level that I don't even really know how to describe to the Committee. If they had any clue what we're dealing with…there would not be a question. There's a reason we didn't give them a full memo on Ava either."

"You face threats at the borders near us every day," Sasha objected, "and don't report them to the upper Committee."

"I'm not the only one who's seeing this footage, Sasha! However much they may trust me, the Committee still keeps heavy tabs on my activity. Not reporting this could be the thing that proves to them I am an enemy of the state after all. I don't think it's worth the risk."

"There was a time when we decided that Ava wasn't worth the risk either. Taint, there was a time when Russia wasn't sure if *you* were worth the risk. I'm not saying if this goes south that we can't return to that option. But suppose…" he put his arms in the air uncertainly. "I don't know. Do they look like the sort of team Eli would send to extract Ava?"

Jackson looked once more at the paused video, his eyes narrowing.

"Not even close," Zak admitted. "They're too conspicuous, too noticeable. Wherever they go, they'll raise eyebrows. Besides, he clearly has other ways of sneaking his people through the border without sending them to the gates."

Jackson nodded, suddenly kicking himself for not noticing that fact sooner. It wasn't that he wouldn't have ultimately come around, but Sasha always thought of these things first. He had years of experience recognizing details, and even Jackson's years of advanced training could not account for Sasha's firsthand experience. Still, "He tried sending a normal team," Jackson noted. "That didn't go well. Maybe this is another attempt."

"I'm not saying it couldn't be, but Eli does everything in a calculated, careful manner. This is all too messy. We have to consider the possibility that it isn't him."

"So, we take a team," Jackson offered, "we confront them directly, try and get some idea of why they're here. We keep a drone on site, in case it's needed."

"Can you really get away without telling the Committee about this?" Zak asked worriedly.

Sasha still seemed eager to do so. "Sometimes it's better to ask forgiveness than permission," he quoted with a slight hint of sarcasm, yet also seeming to mean it.

Jackson considered before shaking his head. "No. If things did go wrong...there's too much at stake. There's no way that we're the first ones to hear about this. I'll call a meeting right away." Jackson stood, preparing to get to work.

"And if they don't agree with your plan?" Zak asked pointedly.

Jackson looked at him and smiled. "Then I'll convince them."

☆ ☆ ☆ ☆ ☆

Jackson seemed hesitant when he confronted Ava in Sasha's office. He had asked for a meeting with her, and it all seemed very formal and official. They had become close friends in the last two months, and his professional demeanor took her off guard. Still, she was in a good mood and had to work to act serious when it was clearly what he wanted.

"Are you finally going to offer me that job as your assistant?" Ava teased, sitting across from Jackson in the office. "I'm not sure Maxim will ever let me go. How much is the pay? I get free food—really good food—at the other job, so you have to understand I'm not in a great hurry to leave."

Despite his serious mood, he cracked a smile. "I'm not asking to have you work for me," Jackson clarified.

She sat back in exaggerated nonchalance. "Ah, well, your loss."

He smiled further. "I have a feeling you're right about that. However, this is kind of a separate, important matter."

Noting once more how serious he was, she tried to stop being playful. "What's up?"

"I understand if you want nothing to do with this. You've been through a lot, and this is risky, and dangerous, but..." he pulled a photo from a file and handed it to her. "Do you recognize any of these people?"

Ava's eyes widened in surprise. "Yes," she said in sudden shock. "Mikel and Ella. I don't know him," this pointing to the older, Asian man. From the picture, this man seemed small, frail and physically weak. But there was an inner strength in his steely gaze that could not be denied, even in a photo. She looked up to face Jackson. "Are they in Russia?"

Jackson nodded. "It's possible that they're here for another attempt at an extraction."

Ava didn't mean to react so outwardly, but his statement caused her to laugh out loud. She was definitely having too much fun for a serious meeting, and she'd try to tone it down.

"No," she said, when Jackson seemed confused. "No, there's no way that Eli sent them in to get me. Ella's relationship with him is unstable at best. He would never trust her with something so important. Mikel is too cocky for his own good. And I have no idea who that guy is— definitely not a Zhànshì. No, there's no way he sent them."

Something in Jackson's expression made her pause. She looked down thoughtfully before facing him again and saying what was clearly on his mind. "Of course, it's possible he sent these two because of their closeness to me," Ava noted soberly. "He's always known how to get to me. Maybe he sent them because he knew I would trust them sooner than anyone else. Except that guy."

Jackson nodded seriously. "That's my concern as well. Eli always has an intricate plan that accounts for the details. Then again, they could just as well be here to plant a few bombs and wreak the havoc he threatened to send me."

Ava breathed in heavily, sitting back in her seat. "What are you going to do?" she asked, not sure she was ready for an answer.

Jackson licked his lips as he considered, then he confided in her. "We can't always assume that everything that happens in the world is part of Eli's plans. If we do, we'll create our own doom, like a self-fulfilling prophecy. At the same time, we can't be too wary. Still, the oddity of this group piques my interest, and Sasha has convinced me to give them a chance to explain themselves."

A sudden hope filled her. "You're not just going to kill them?"

"Only if they leave me no other choice. Twenty minutes ago, our locator drone found them and cornered them in a large crevice. They have been instructed to wait there. We have them on surveillance. They're less than an hour from our current location. They obviously knew where to find you."

Ava's eyes narrowed thoughtfully.

"I've convinced the Committee to let me take a small crew to confront the Zhànshì directly. So far, they have been completely obedient to all orders that have been relayed. I'm hopeful that we can work this out peaceably."

"Did they say what they wanted?"

He nodded. "They said they need to see Ava Altman. Once again, the oddity in the whole scenario gives me hope that maybe it isn't Eli. It's doubtful he would announce it openly like that. Still, we can't be certain. I have convinced the Committee to let me go and meet them."

He paused, feeling his way to the point. "I've also convinced them to let you go."

Ava stared at him in shock. "Isn't that the worst possible idea?" she blurted in surprise, though in truth, she really wanted to go. Ava had healed from the physical wound of her broken arm and wasn't worried about her ability to fight. In fact, lately she felt more herself than ever. The panic attacks were minimal, she could sleep fine without meds, and her friendships with the others were pleasant and rewarding. She felt truly like herself, like the fun, easy-going Ava from the Talks again, and she loved that. "This is me trying to be strategic, not that I'm afraid or don't want to go—but if they are here to take me back, is it wise to take me right to them?"

"Probably not," Jackson admitted. "But they say they won't deal with anyone but Ava Altman. I don't think you're all that much safer within the mansion, seeing that Eli knows exactly where to find us. Beyond that, I think the boy, Mikel, might have managed to access the Tower briefly. We may need your abilities if they do turn out to be a real threat. What you did with Eli's first team...no one else can handle it that way.

And honestly, if we have any chance of working through this peaceably, I think it's with your help. That being said, I completely understand if—"

"Then I'm there!" Ava interrupted excitedly. "Of course I'm there! When do we leave?"

Jackson stood quickly. "As soon as possible. Sasha's preparing to leave as we speak."

☆ ☆ ☆ ☆ ☆

Ava, Sasha and Jackson drove in the same truck on their way toward the Zhànshì, and the conversation was pleasant and enjoyable. They talked and laughed, and Ava herself was the main source of the comedy. In the past month, her confidence seemed to have returned. She seemed genuinely happy again, genuinely herself once more. If, as Sasha said, the moon went in stages, this was a stage of light and joy, and Jackson cherished every moment of it.

Jackson observed as Ava sat close to Sasha, leaning her head on his shoulder often, always in close contact with her father. She had always been fond of hugging. There had been a time when Jackson was the one she held closely to. Admittedly, he missed that more than almost anything in the world. Their friendship had healed in so many ways, but physical contact—outside of their usual sparring—was no longer a part of it.

At one point, Sasha must have caught Jackson staring and realized what his thoughtful expression meant. He gave Jackson a sort of knowing, pained look, yet also managed to warn him off at the same time.

Jackson's men arrived on scene and the team filed from the trucks to surround the large crevice. Ava and Sasha followed Jackson's lead to the top of the mountain where they could look down at the scene below. When Jackson and the others made it to the top of the hill, they noted the Zhànshì within. They stood in the chasm, surrounded from every angle.

"Think you can talk them down enough for us to round them up without a firefight?" Jackson asked.

Strangely, Ava hesitated. He could sense that she was considering her next moves, and hadn't decided yet what to do. What was she thinking?

"I'll see what I can do," she offered.

Jackson's men had surrounded the cliff line, and the lieutenant yelled down at the two Zhànshì to put their hands up. They seemed overly bothered, but slowly they followed Mikel's lead.

"Does this look un-menacing?" the young girl, Ella, asked loudly. "I don't know what I'm doing."

Jackson chuckled, thinking of a young Zhànshì Ava and finding a similar comparison with the rough edges. He signaled to Ava, indicating she could stand and talk to them.

Slowly, she rose to a crouching position, and immediately the Zhànshì turned to face her. "Thank the General," Mikel uttered when he saw Ava standing there.

"Is that her?" the old man asked.

"Unfortunately," Ella grumbled with a look of contempt.

"What are you doing here?" Ava asked loudly, apparently not knowing how else to start. "Did Eli send you to recapture me?"

"Nice to see you too, Ava," Mikel said, pretending to be hurt by her harsh tone. "Been a while. Haven't seen you since Kyle's memorial. How are things?"

Surprised, Jackson looked up at Ava, at first in disbelief, but her pained expression affirmed the question. Kyle...dead? Why hadn't Ava ever mentioned that? He felt himself suddenly deeply saddened by the news. He had liked Kyle and respected him greatly.

"Don't play games, Mikel," Ava shot back. "Tell me why you're here."

"Why do you think?" Ella snarled.

The old man raised a hand to quiet her, as if signaling that Mikel had the floor to speak, and not she.

"You're supposedly a traitor," Mikel retorted, "and a crazy one at that. Of course, Eli is attempting to cover that up with lies about reassignment. Your car accident was all over the news, then erased within minutes. When you dig deeper, they're saying the reason you were removed as General was because of your mental state."

"I'm not a traitor, Mikel," Ava shot back through gritted teeth. "Eli's the traitor. He betrayed everything we were taught to believe in. Council is corrupt. They've effectively dethroned Lionel and removed the last vestiges of good that were left within our government."

"I notice you didn't defend your mental state," Ella sneered. She clearly had something against Ava.

"Don't get me wrong, Ava," Mikel spoke as if Ella hadn't. "I didn't believe a word of what I discovered. And I didn't believe a word of what Eli told me, or the rest of the Kingdoms."

"Then why are you here?" Ava persisted. "You know he's a liar. If you knew half the things he's done, you would not follow him blindly—"

"We're not," Mikel interrupted. "We're not here for Eli. We're here to join you."

A look of hope crossed her face, and Jackson almost cringed. He wanted to believe it too, but she could not fall for them that easily with no real proof. As if she had read his mind, her expression changed, and she asked pointedly, "How do I know this isn't a ploy from Eli?"

Ella was the one to speak this time, responding in anger, struggling to keep her arms up. "Taint it, Ava! You know how much I hate you. But that only started because of your relationship with *him*. I detest Eli Altman, and the second I heard there might be another option, I was on board."

Ava seemed to accept the girl's answer, and once again, that concerned Jackson. She then turned her attention to Mikel. He shrugged. "I mean, I've been anti-Altman since Eric. Not you, of course. If you had been made real General, I would have followed you till the day I died, but working for Eli these past months...well, let's just say that I was just as happy to find another option."

"Who are you?" Ava asked the old Korean man.

"My name is Damian Cho. I am Mikel's right arm. And I am in favor of freedom for all, not just the Kingdoms. I believe this new, third side is the best possible way to achieve that."

"So what do you want then?" Ava asked, seeming to buy their responses. Jackson was still highly skeptical, and concerned that she took it so easily.

Mikel shrugged. For a Zhànshì he was very...chill, far more like Zak than Kyle. "We were thinking maybe you'd take us back with you. Show us your plans, see how we can help and all of that."

"We can't do that, Ava," Jackson whispered sternly from the ground to her right side.

She nodded in understanding. "Unfortunately, that's not an option," Ava said politically.

"Carcass, Ava!" Ella shouted in sudden anger, seemingly out of nowhere. "I have never held my hands up in surrender in my life! Now I'm going on two minutes. Doesn't that tell you *anything*? I'm willing to humble myself for the greater cause. Could you try to do the same?"

"So, what? You want to join Russia?" Ava asked to clarify.

The two Zhànshì shared a look and Mikel was the one to answer. "We were thinking more along the lines of *you* leading us. Of joining *you*. If that means dealing with Russia, then fine."

Ava seemed surprised. She considered, watching them. Then she slowly turned to look at Sasha and Jackson all at once. "We can't take them right to the mansion," Jackson reiterated. "*Maybe* we could take them to the Tower. Under armed guard. Even that is dangerous if Mikel really did break through our defenses remotely, but it's probably our best bet."

Ava looked disappointed by this reply. She turned to face them again, and once more, her look of deep consideration concerned Jackson. "I can't take you back," Ava explained.

"Then come with us," Ella said grouchily.

"Eli has done far worse than manipulating a few Zhànshì," Ava replied. "How do I know you're not still working for him?"

Ella looked bothered, but Mikel took on a serious expression—for the first time that Jackson had seen. "We didn't come here because of Eli. We were sent by Remington. Short of that, all I can say is I guess you're just going to have to trust us."

She observed them for a long time. Then, she seemed to agree with him, and she nodded deeply. Her eyes became resolute, decided. Before this very moment, he had been so sure that he could trust her on this op. It was only then that Jackson knew for sure he had made a mistake in letting her talk to them; in bringing her at all.

How could she be so naive? What cause did she have to really trust them? How could she act so swiftly, so recklessly?

She stood up from her crouching position and started over the cliff edge.

Jackson hurriedly indicated Sasha to do something, not knowing what to do himself. "Wait! Ava!" Sasha shouted quickly.

She stopped, turning to face him.

"Don't go!"

She looked helplessly past Jackson and to Sasha. "I have to, Sasha. The Zhànshì who broke out caused enough damage, and from what that video showed, Mikel is too dangerous. I'll lead them out of Russia. We won't bother you again. You can let us go."

"It's not that simple!" Jackson shot back.

"No, you don't have to go," Sasha said, almost at the same time. "Stay with us."

"You said they can't come as friends—only as prisoners. Well, then I'm going with them."

"I can't let you do that either," Jackson spoke up, hating the fact that he had to do this. How could she be so...clueless?

She looked at him then, slight annoyance showing now. "I didn't take any information while I was there. I'm not going to give up any grand plans, because I don't know anything! Even if I did, I never betrayed you to Eli. And I'm not going to now."

"It's not just about that!" Sasha countered, though in reality it was exactly what Jackson had been referring to. "Ava, we can do this together!"

"I didn't come here just to be nursed from my wounds, Sasha. I appreciate everything you've done for me, but I came here to beat Eli. I can't do that with a group of people who don't trust me or my friends. I have a much greater chance with them."

"I trust you, Ava!" Sasha assured her, pleading now, laying his weapon on the ground as he held his hands up in front of him carefully. He looked as if he was trying to talk her off a ledge. In a way, he was.

Ava smiled sadly at her father. "I know you do, Sasha, but with all due respect, you're not the leader of Russia." She glanced slightly at Jackson, enough that only the three of them close together would've noticed. "You don't command your people. Right now, I have no chance of making a difference with you."

She started to move farther. His instincts took over and, though he did not point his own weapon at her, he signaled to his closest men that she was a threat, and they reacted in turn. "I can't let you go, Ava," the warrior in Jackson took over all else.

Her stern, angry eyes hardened on him. When she spoke, she sounded as gruff as Ella, and far angrier as her tone rose with every word. "The Zhànshì have taken on more than some thirty soldiers. I could take you all myself! I will disable your drone and your weapons. And I'll have their help!" Pointing to the Zhànshì at the bottom of the rock cliff. Her next words were said loud enough that probably anyone in the area would have heard. "I know where every one of your men is and how well-equipped they are. I can relay intel to my people through the link. Don't make this a battle between us!"

"Jackson!" Sasha said pointedly, worriedly. Jackson knew what he meant, but it was hard to obey. They would never beat Ava in a physical battle—Jackson had a four in ten chance of beating her one-on-one, but by then, her Zhànshì friends would have taken out the rest of his men. Even if she was bluffing about her ability to connect with the Tower now and disable the drone, there was still too much risk that Mikel could do it.

He had to reach her another way.

"Don't go, Ava," Jackson earnestly pleaded. "Not right when I'm finally starting to..." he trailed off.

Her eyes softened and her words were quieted. "When you're finally starting to believe maybe I won't betray you to Eli? You're finally *starting* to trust me again?"

Jackson didn't respond, so Ava did. "I haven't really earned your trust, have I, Jackson? I've only earned your hope. I can do much more with them. And then maybe you'll finally really believe I was telling the truth all along."

She started walking forward again, and probably on a command from the link, the Zhànshì below separated from their location in the middle, each in preparation for a good vantage point to fight.

"Jackson!" Sasha repeated, more sternly this time.

He didn't know how to stop her. He knew they couldn't lose her—especially if these Zhànshì were just taking her back to Eli. "What if they're lying?" he asked her desperately. "What if they're still loyal to Eli?"

She seemed to take this as an opportunity to prove the mistake he'd made with her. Turning again to face him she said somberly, "Then I'll deal with it as I come to it. But I'm going to take a chance on them."

The unspoken words "like you should have taken a chance on me before" pained him deeply.

That was it. Jackson was convinced now that she had decided to follow them specifically because of the words Mikel used. "You're just going to have to trust us." That had been exactly what he needed to say to get through to Ava, and it was specifically because of the mistake Jackson had made in not being willing to trust her all those times before.

So much for all of the healing of these past months. So much for the reconciliation between them. The wounds of the past were still too deep, still too painful, and Jackson cursed these Zhànshì for coming too soon, before they could really mend things between them.

If he would have just given her a chance to prove herself sooner.

"Ava, please," he pleaded, sounding as desperate as Sasha had. More, even. "Don't leave me again." He whispered the last words, hardly able to utter them and certainly not wanting anyone else to hear it.

At first her expression became questioning. Had she heard him right? Had he really said it that way? Had he pleaded with her, not just to remain with *them*, but with *him* specifically?

Then, seeming to take in the bigger picture now, her eyes became angrier than ever and her jaw tightened. "Don't say that to me," she said in a whisper. Then her voice rose even louder so that all could hear again. "Don't say that to me with your men pointing weapons at my face!" She vehemently gestured to his officers. Her next words were a literal scream. He had never seen her so angry before, and as she spoke, she must have connected with the Tower enough to turn off the drone, because it fell uselessly to the ground, powerless. "You sound just like him!"

That stung like a knife wound to his gut.

She shook her head in disdain. "These people aren't lying and manipulating me, Jackson. *You* are! You're just like him."

The pain in her voice was overwhelming.

"No, Ava," he said, setting his weapon down in the dirt and signaling his men to turn away from her. He felt more defenseless than ever. It wasn't because he didn't have a weapon to defend himself. It was that he didn't have the words.

"I'm not lying, I promise. I swear, I'm not manipulating you. I'm just...I'm just a carcass, okay? I do care about you, more than you can possibly know, but I won't make this personal." He had to step back from his feelings, because every time he shared them, she looked firmer than ever in her decision to fight him.

It was just like that night by the fireplace. He had borne his heart, said he was sorry, and she had run away without a word. She didn't want to hear about his feelings right now. She needed pure logic to win her over. He put his hands out in front of him carefully. "You said you came here to have the best chance of beating Eli. We are still most effective if we stick together."

She shook her head. "I'm not leaving them."

"Fine! Then bring them," he said, and though strategically it sounded like a terrible plan, he meant it. "You said you're ready to take a chance on them. Well, I'll take a chance on *you*. Please. We have a better hope of winning this war together." He slowly walked closer to her, trying to avoid being threatening as he did so.

She looked down again at the others and for the first time seemed to be considering his words.

"I'll trust you," Jackson pleaded. "All the way. I'll let you in on greater plans. I'll try. And I'll try with them too. Please."

This better be the right call. If the Zhànshì were lying, they had a real threat on their hands. But the potential gain if they were telling the truth was immeasurable. Three Zhànshì. They needed this. And, most importantly, he wasn't ready to give up on Ava. Not anymore. Not ever again.

"You'll trust us?" she asked hopefully.

"I will trust *you*," Jackson offered. "I honestly can't promise any more than that right now."

After a long consideration, Ava relaxed. She turned to the Zhànshì. "Put your weapons down. We're going together."

They awkwardly gathered at the trucks. If the Zhànshì wanted, they could drop every one of Jackson's men in less than a minute. So, in reality, it wasn't all that bad to put their weapons away, but it was hard for them to feel powerless, as it had been for him.

"We'll head to the Northeastern Tower," Jackson spoke carefully to Ava.

She narrowed her eyes, but he held up a hand to pause her. "I'm trusting. I am. But we also have to think logically. Suppose we *are* wrong about them. Are you prepared to put the kids in danger? Kai and Jon? Zak's unborn baby?"

That stopped her in her objection.

"I just want to be cautious," he reassured her. "That's all."

Ava agreed. "Fine. But I don't want them feeling like prisoners. There's no telling how they'd react to that."

"Understood. We'll do our best to make them comfortable."

"I'll go with them," Ava added. And though it made sense, it strangely hurt that she was the one to suggest—no, to demand it.

Still, he wordlessly assented. He stood less than a foot from her, beside the trucks. She seemed to accept his act of faith. It was risky to let her travel with them. They could recapture her and take her back to Eli. So many things could go wrong, but he promised he'd take a chance on them, for her.

She turned to leave but he caught her hand, causing her to turn and face him again. "I'm sorry, Ava, for what I said." His words were hushed once more as he struggled to get them out. "I promise, I wasn't trying to—"

She shrugged it off, though he could tell it still hurt her. "Let's just forget about it."

Forget about it. That was always her solution. Forget their first kiss. Forget every fight. Forget their entire past and start fresh. Forget the fact that he had been this close to telling her how he felt, and her anger had shut him up. Yeah, best forget it.

With that, she headed to drive with the other Zhànshì.

Jackson stood there alone for a long minute before Sasha joined him silently. Eventually, he spoke. "I know you don't want to talk about it. I just wanted to say, you did well. Swallowing your pride. You did the right thing, whatever was necessary, and you did it well. Still, I hope you see that her feelings for you are different. I don't want you to get hurt, son, though perhaps it's too late for that too."

Jackson didn't respond. Normally this was where he would shut Sasha up. But right now... he almost wished his friend would say more.

"You were right," Jackson managed, his dry throat causing it to sound croaky. "She sees me like him. Maybe I am..." he trailed off.

"You're not Eli," Sasha replied in a gentle tone. "But it is easier than you may think to become so. Do not allow yourself to grow cold and unfeeling. Do not shut those out who should be the closest. And never choose your pride over your conscience. Today, I watched you swallow that pride. You did whatever you must for the sake of the greater cause, and although I can see how much it hurt you, I am prouder than you could possibly know."

Jackson didn't have the words to respond, but he didn't have the chance either as one of the soldiers neared, reporting that they were all loaded up.

"See you at the Tower," Sasha said, then headed to join Ava and the Zhànshì in their truck.

☆ ☆ ☆ ☆ ☆

The first meeting in the Tower went as well as could be expected. The Zhànshì had remained well-behaved. As they discussed the details of the escape they had made, Ava followed how Jackson watched their every move and gesture and listened to the very tone of their voices. She hadn't really understood it at the time, but he had watched her this same way when he interviewed Eli and accepted the declaration of war.

It was almost as if he was reading them. Every detail, every movement, every tone, helped him decide the truthfulness in their words. Watching him observing them, Ava was now certain that this was exactly what he was doing, though she had no idea where he had learned to read people so minutely.

Mikel was his ever-charming, over-confident self. Ella was her ever-abrasive, angry self. And Damian was unexpectedly wise, deep and well-informed. Not only that, he truly did seem to be Mikel's right arm, as if an extension of Mikel's very being. Damian kept Mikel grounded in a way that Mikel had desperately needed his entire life, and already Ava had to admit Mikel was better for it. In the same way Sasha had been a mentor for Jackson and Ava, this man was a strengthening, counseling, grounding presence for Mikel.

The meeting concluded, and Mikel found Ava by the door, putting his arms around her from behind and hugging her tightly. "It's good to be back together again, isn't it?" he said pleasantly.

Ava, smiling, agreed. Mikel had always been overtly physical in his interactions with others, but he was so good at it, so tasteful, and she trusted him enough that it did not bother her as it would with most people. Come to think of it, Mikel could get away with a lot of things that most people could not.

"Come stay in the apartment with us!" Mikel suggested. "It's huge! And there's more than enough space for you."

"Only if you room with the guys," Ella rebutted, coming to stand with them. "I will not be sharing a room with her."

"We're chill," Mikel added. "You don't have to sleep there. Just come on over, and let's catch up."

"Absolutely," Ava agreed, not bothering to remove Mikel's arms from around her, even now. "I can come with you now. I have nothing else to do here."

Ava found herself glad that the Zhànshì had come now, and not a month or two previously when she was at her worst. These days, she could smile, and laugh, and truly feel happy and joyful again. She was grateful they had not arrived in the thick of her painful healing.

"Look at you two lovebirds, blossoming together like old times," Ella spoke disgustedly, and though Ava rarely knew what Ella was talking about, that comment was obviously false. So false in fact, that she did not bother to correct it.

It wasn't until Ava glanced across the room where Jackson stood, gathering his things, observing the scene with a sideways glance that she grew uncomfortable. It was clear he had heard. It was clear he had seen how Mikel continued to embrace Ava for seemingly no reason, but to be close to her.

Mikel's behavior and Ella's comment had not bothered her, but the way Jackson would perceive them...that ever so slight pained look on his face as he packed his things and pretended to be in his own thoughts? *That* did bother her.

Ava gently removed Mikel's arms from around her, putting a few feet of distance between them. But of course, Ella couldn't shut up, not when there was a chance to drag Ava through the mud. "As much as I don't like you with anyone, I prefer this pairing to poor Kyle being stuck with you. He's lucky to be free of it now."

Just then, Jackson joined the group, a disheartened look on his face. "I wonder if I might obtain some report on that from one of you," he said to the group at large. "I hadn't heard that he was deceased."

He strangely avoided looking at Ava, and she almost wondered if he was angry with her for not telling him.

"Did you know Kyle?" Mikel asked.

Jackson nodded, a shadow on his countenance. "We worked together in Russia, and in Africa. He was a good kid."

Ella immediately objected with Ava's past tagline. "Kyle was not a kid."

Ava found herself smiling at Jackson, and expected him to look her way too, sharing the past memories regarding that word. But he did not look at her, and his somber expression did not change as he nodded and replied, "Right. He was a good man. I'm sorry to hear of his passing."

"He was in love with Ava," Ella said, as if knowing how much Ava didn't want her to speak.

"Ella," Ava spoke up harshly, hoping to quiet the girl, but Ella didn't listen to anyone, least of all to Ava.

"Obsessed with her, more like. And it got him killed."

"At least we know he died doing what he loved," Mikel offered with a caring tone. "Protecting his girl."

"It wasn't like that!" Ava objected. "None of it was like that. And he's not..." she cut herself off, not wanting to get into this debate again.

"It's a crying shame how many people have died to save her," Ella blustered, as if excited to share her loud opinion with a new victim. Ava gritted her teeth angrily.

"Some people are worth dying for," Jackson offered, surprising Ava. It was clear that he was not happy with her for some reason. Yet even now, he defended her.

"Maybe," Ella huffed. "But I seriously doubt she's one of them."

Ava swallowed a hard, painful lump in her throat, wishing she knew how to defend herself against this little terror. Why could she never stop? Why couldn't she leave it alone?

"You must not know her the way I do," Jackson said pleasantly to Ella. And Ava couldn't explain what that comment meant to her—especially if he was mad at her right now.

Jackson turned to face the group as a whole. "We'll meet tomorrow morning at the same time. Until then, I have work to do with the Committee. He nodded, and excused himself, still avoiding Ava's glance, though she desperately hoped he would look her way. He never did.

"Funny how we're supposedly here as friends, yet we're not allowed to eat in the commissary with everyone else," Ella growled.

"I told them we would prefer to eat privately," Ava explained. "If you want, I can tell them you'd like to eat there with the Tower workers and officers instead."

Ella did not respond, instead choosing to glare at Ava and let that answer suffice.

Catching up with her friends was nice, but Ava could not get Jackson out of her mind. "I should have invited him to join us," she said out loud, not even meaning to be heard.

"What? That self-righteous, arrogant carchead?" Ella huffed. "I don't want him here."

"I like him," Damian objected. "He seems to be a wise and virtuous young man. I believe we're in good hands with this one."

"Did you hear how he called Kyle 'kid' as if he's some wise old sage? He can't be more than, what? Six years older than Kyle?"

"Seven," Ava corrected.

"But he's more mature than any of us," Mikel replied. Then, glancing at Damian, he shifted his stance, "Well, more than most of us, that is."

"He didn't seem all that impressive to me," Ella said stubbornly. "Just cocky and full of himself."

"It's why he and I get along so well," Mikel replied proudly. "I think he's great."

"You would," Ella scowled.

Ava wanted to be here with them. At least, she wanted to want to.... But all she could think about was Jackson. Still, she remained, paying her dues to her friends, knowing that they needed her far more than he did right now.

When it was late, and everyone was ready to prepare for sleep, Ava left, going down to the gym and hoping to find Jackson there. She was disappointed to find it completely empty. And not having any idea where his room was, she gave in for the time being.

Ava went again to the gym early the next morning, but he didn't join her then either. After the morning meeting, Jackson left quickly when Ava committed herself to spend the day with her friends.

She let it go. They would find time to talk eventually. And right now, the Zhànshì needed her help in transitioning.

Ava didn't go to the gym that night in search of him. She just wanted to practice. At least, that was what she told herself. Tonight, however, she heard the guttural sounds of clamor and exertion from within. She knew even before she entered that he would be there. What she didn't know was how intense, how angry, how involved in his routine he would look when she arrived.

She watched him for a time. She knew he had sensed her presence when she entered, but he did not turn to face her. His gritted teeth and angry grunts as he hit the punching bag with each new blow were proof of the aggression he was working to get out.

For a split second, she almost thought to leave him there alone, but she did not know when she would run into him alone again in this vast Tower, and she would not miss this chance.

She tried to pretend she didn't sense the tension in the room when she went right up beside him and spoke pleasantly. "Want to try getting those moves out on an enemy with arms to hit you back?"

He did not reply, and another grunt and heavy blow to the bag showed he was not in the mood for sparring—verbal or otherwise. "Come on. I need to get some energy out too! Let's go!"

"I don't want to do this right now, Ava," he responded curtly, waving her away and moving to another dummy across the room.

"Do what?" Ava asked, her hurt suddenly showing in full force when she said, "Why are you mad at me?"

He turned quickly to face her, a look of stunned anger on his face, as if to convey that she should know exactly why. "How can I be mad?" Jackson said, but the tone was one of snide sarcasm. "I'm not allowed to be mad at you."

"What's that supposed to mean?"

He shook his head in annoyance, trying to form his thoughts or to collect his anger before facing her again. Eventually, he did so. "I don't get to be mad at you. I can't be hurt by you, because the mistakes I made with you were so vast that I can never repair the damage. I can't make up for the cost of what I did. I was a carcass. I played God. Not only did I cut you out of my life in a violent and sickening way, I practically forbade your own father to have anything to do with you! I took away all other options you had left, so you had nothing but Eli. And like I said, it doesn't matter how many times I say the words, 'I'm sorry,' I'll never be able to make up for what he did to you. And I blame myself for that every day. So, no, I don't get to be mad at you for stupid little things. Because I have no right to be angry at you after what I did to you."

"It doesn't work that way," Ava objected.

"No," Jackson agreed, a harshness to his tone that made her uneasy. "No, it doesn't, unfortunately. And I'm still carced out of my mind."

"Why?" Ava pleaded, taking a step forward, toward him.

He swallowed hard, as if trying to gulp down his anger. Then he shook his head several times, as if trying to recover from a blow to the jaw. Neither movement made his expression any softer. "I told you, I don't want to do this, okay?"

"Just tell me why you're mad," Ava pleaded, a sudden emotion coloring her words. She could not stand the thought of him being angry with her.

Once more, he swallowed hard, then turned to face her square on. "I'm not like you, Ava. I don't forgive people in the blink of an eye. I don't trust people despite every warning I have that tells me to be wary. I get that you are a miraculous force of nature that somehow, against all odds, can withstand abuse and hurt and still come out trusting, loving and kind. Well, the rest of us can't be perfect the way you are."

"I don't know what you're talking about," Ava said, tears filling her eyes as she took another step forward, trying to close the distance between them in whatever way she could manage.

"I understand that I shouldn't have any right to be angry," he said, still confusing her with these riddles. Why wouldn't he just explain in simple terms what the taint was wrong with him? "I understand that how I feel will never redeem me from the damage I caused. But I don't understand you. I don't get how you looked me in the eyes two and a half years ago, and told me that you weren't like my mother and my sister, that you would never betray me the way they did, and then the second you had the chance, you abandoned me just like they did."

If that had been everything, it still would have broken her heart. But he wasn't finished yet.

"I don't understand how you could tell me that you loved me like family one day. Then a few days later, you told me to my face that if you ever had to pick, you would drop me to the curb and pick your 'real' family every time. And the thought of it hurt badly enough. But then you had to prove it to me, over and over again, when you chose Eric and Eli, repeatedly, over me."

Again, the pain in her chest overwhelmed her to nearly a breaking point. But she held strong and still, waiting and allowing him to say all that he felt.

"When you came back, you told Sasha, and you told me in that letter, that it was because of Eli. You said that you had to pick him, because he needed you, and you couldn't bring yourself to leave him. And like a fool, I believed that!"

She stepped forward once more, about to object and tell him that this was the truth, but he didn't give her the chance to speak.

"But then, the second these people from your past show up, you didn't even blink before throwing everything you had with me away and choosing them. Two months ago, you shook my hand and said you wanted to be my friend. Then, two days ago, I had to beg you to stay with me over a couple of acquaintances from your past—one of whom hates your guts. And I made an utter fool of myself in front of my men and Sasha, begging you on my knees to pick me." He gritted his teeth, a new intensity to his anger that pained her with the truthfulness of his words.

"I made myself a fool. And still, you turned me into the bad guy. You compared me to Eli. You said I was manipulating you. And even I believed you in that moment. But the more time I think about it, the more I can't stand how angry I am at you. Because you promised me that you would never leave me like my family did. You swore that you would choose me. And then, at every single opportunity, you jump at every chance to pick anyone in the tainted world *but* me!"

Ava swallowed hard, her unshed tears blurring her vision of the man before her.

"So, yes, I know. I know that I have no right to be angry. I realize that my pain is miniscule and meaningless when compared to the grand scheme of things and the horrors you faced from Eli because of me. I realize that I will never be able to repair the damage. I know that I messed up. And I will regret it every day for the rest of my life." This time, he was the one to step forward, and rather than anger, his tone seemed for the first time truly pained. "But, Ava, can you possibly conceive, even for a moment, the slight possibility that you might have hurt me too?"

Ava breathed in heavily. Her only consolation was that her blurry eyes made facing him a little easier. Still, she did not know how to reply. It seemed Jackson had nothing else to say.

When she didn't respond, eventually he ran his hand through his hair and turned away from her to face the dummies again.

A long silence passed. When he eventually turned around, he had softened. The anger was gone, but still there was a deep sadness in his eyes. "I'm sorry," he said.

Those words, again. Those two words that he would apparently never be able to say to her enough. Those two words that she hadn't even thought of saying to him.

"I'm sorry," he repeated, not knowing what else to say. "I shouldn't have said anything." He cursed to himself.

Ava still stood there, not having the slightest idea how to fix things.

Jackson kicked the nearest bench in frustration. "I'm sorry, okay?" he repeated once more, and she desperately wished he would stop saying those words to her. Each time felt like a blow to the gut. He was right. She had never even considered that she might have genuinely hurt him too. She had never even entertained the thought.

Jackson sighed deeply, and she could sense that he now felt as helpless as she did. "Let's just forget I said anything, okay?" But this, too, seemed like a pointed comment, as if alluding to another hurt he had never opened up about before, and one she had entirely missed.

Still, he watched her helplessly, and she stood motionless. Finally, he stepped forward and put his hands on her forearms. "Let's just call it a night, yeah? I shouldn't have yelled at you. I'm sorry, Ava."

"Stop saying that," she muttered, barely audible.

"What?" he asked, apparently not having heard her.

She did not repeat herself, and after a time, he removed his hands from her arms. "I'll walk you back to your room, all right? Let's just move on."

He tried to do so, walking toward the door and apparently hoping she would follow. She did not. And after a moment, he must have realized she wasn't going to. "I'll call Sasha," he offered, apparently not knowing what else to do with her at this point.

He went to his bag and reached for his mobile. Only when he had it in hand and was standing again, having prepared to call Sasha did she finally utter the first words of explanation to his hurt.

"You never needed me," she said weakly.

He looked up to face her. She could see from the look in his eyes that he had heard her. For a long time though, he said nothing.

Eventually, she tried to explain herself further. "You and Sasha, you had each other. And you were both so strong. I knew you would be fine. But Eli had nothing. He had no one. He needed me. And so I picked him. And when these Zhànshì showed up, I didn't pick them to get away from you. You're stronger now than ever. You're better now than ever. You don't need me. But these Zhànshì have nothing. They needed me. You never did."

His expression turned to a deeper sadness, and he allowed his hand, holding the mobile to sink lower. When he spoke, it was barely audible, coming out in a hoarse whisper. "Maybe you're wrong about that too."

That pained her more than anything. But it wasn't true. Jackson didn't need her. He never had. He was perfectly fine on his own. But if he had needed her like Eli had, like the Zhànshì did, nothing in the world could have stopped her from choosing him.

A long silence lingered. She did not know how to reply. She did not know how to ever make up for how much she had hurt him.

"There she is!" came a loud exclamation from Mikel as he and the others entered the room. Ava had never disliked them more.

Jackson turned away, again toward his bag, as if not wanting to be seen by them. She wished she could sink far away from the watchful eyes as Mikel, Ella and Damian surrounded her. "Let's get some training in!" Mikel said pleasantly. "Why didn't you tell me this was where you disappeared to last night? We'd have been right there with you! Jackson, want to go for a round of sparring?"

"I was actually just heading out," Jackson replied, pulling his bag over his shoulder and facing them. There was no indication of the deep hurt he had shared with Ava, yet he seemed mentally and physically exhausted as though their encounter had worn him out.

"Perhaps *we* should be the ones to leave," Damian suggested, having seen the social cues better than either of these two supposed "friends" of hers.

"Nah, come on! I'm here to party! You and me then?" Mikel asked Ava.

She shook her head. "I think I'm tired."

Mikel shrugged. "I haven't finished telling you about our boss moves in Australia. Let's head back to the room."

She nodded despite herself, trying to get a glimpse, anything from Jackson. He looked once more at her as he neared the door, but then walked through alone when she made no move to go with him.

Once more, he gave her the chance. Ava loathed herself when, even then, she picked them.

Jackson was still waiting at the lift when they arrived. Desperately, she wished for another chance to talk, but she didn't know how to politely ditch Mikel and his crowd.

"What floor?" the lift officer asked as they all entered.

"Eighteen," Mikel replied when neither Ava nor Jackson spoke.

"And twenty," Jackson replied next.

Floor twenty, Ava thought. How many rooms could there be on that floor? Maybe she could find him later.

The lift ride was uncomfortable. She stood beside Mikel, Damian and Ella, with Jackson behind and the lift officer farther still in the back. She was aware of Jackson's eyes on her. There was so much to say, but not with the others there. She had to get him alone. There had to be a chance for this later.

After what felt like an eternity, the lift doors opened and Mikel, Damian and Ella walked out directly. Ava moved more slowly, not wanting to leave Jackson now when there was so much to say, but having no good excuse for staying.

She exited the lift, then turned to face Jackson for the brief seconds until the doors closed. One look between them seemed to convey the longing both of them felt for the old times, when it was so easy to be alone, to talk and open up without anyone else there to stop them.

The door closed.

Suddenly, Ava's eyes squinted in confusion.

She had seen something.

There was something she had noticed in the briefest moments before the doors fully closed. She knew it was important, though she couldn't place yet what it was.

It came to her suddenly, and in an urgent panic she pressed the button to reopen the lift, but it was too late to reopen it. The lift officer's movement, the placement of his hand from behind Jackson in the lift. He had tensed ever so slightly, preparing for the moment when he would have Jackson alone.

"What?" Ella asked in a mocking tone. "Didn't get a kiss goodbye?"

Ava connected to the Tower quickly, and didn't bother to ponder on why the block seemed suddenly gone. It was a mental block, and apparently this risk was enough to break it.

She reopened the doors through a command to the Tower and before they were even fully open she moved in.

Jackson stood tense and careful as the knife at his neck moved in an effort to slit his throat. Ava jumped forward, gripping the lift officer's armed hand and forcing it toward her, away from Jackson.

He moved out of the line of danger and Ava pressed the enemy to the wall of the lift. She forced the armed hand against the wall and disarmed him in a swift motion. Then she moved to a grip on his shoulders and banged the man's head forcefully against the wall, causing him to go immediately unconscious.

"What the taint!" Mikel said, almost at the same instant that it all happened.

Jackson gripped his bleeding neck from the side of the lift, a look of terror on his face. That knife had intended a kill; a second or two more and he would have been dead.

"How did you see that?" Ella asked from outside, seeming just as relieved and surprised.

Mikel moved inside and took hold of the unconscious foe, and Ava went to Jackson, inspecting the wound at his neck.

"It's deep," she said in serious concern. "We need to get you to the infirmary." Her hands felt the wound, and only after a moment was she aware of Jackson looking seriously at her.

"Thank you," he said soberly. She had not many times seen Jackson afraid, but she saw the look of fear in his eyes now. It had been so close. Her rescue had happened in just seconds, and she could have easily missed it.

"Get on!" Ava ordered Ella and Damian, not looking away from Jackson, her hands applying pressure at his neck in an attempt to staunch the flow of blood. "We're taking him to the infirmary."

They did as ordered, and Mikel restrained the lift officer. "He must be one of Eli's spies," Mikel muttered.

"No," Jackson corrected, wincing slightly from the pain. "Just a concerned Russian citizen attempting to protect his homeland."

Mikel looked up with sudden horror. "You mean one of your own people tried to kill you?"

"Not my people," Jackson replied pointedly. "Even with granted citizenship, they'll never accept me as one of them. He's just one of many Russians who wants me dead."

Mikel cursed audibly.

"That was quick movement," Ella said to Ava, and it almost sounded a compliment until she continued. "Too bad you didn't have such a cool head when fighting beside our friends. Maybe they'd still be alive now."

Ava ignored the comment as she generally did Ella's jabs. She remained close to Jackson, holding his neck with one hand, the other resting on his chest protectively. She would have stayed there forever, but the look Jackson gave her begged her to move away. "I got it now," he said softly, yet assuredly.

She knew he was angry with her, but it didn't seem like that was why he wanted space. More as if he felt uncomfortable with the closeness for some reason. She stepped back on his command, and he held his bleeding neck.

Mikel grunted at the wound before Jackson covered it. "Well, that guy wasn't messing around. He wanted to put you down. Did he say anything?"

Jackson shook his head, then flinched from the pain and held still. "As soon as the doors were closed, he moved from behind and there was a knife at my neck. I didn't have a chance to react before the doors opened and Ava had him."

"She was always the quickest in training," Mikel replied as if proud. "She broke all of Eli's records for quick response time."

"Didn't help Kyle much," Ella muttered.

They quickly got him to the infirmary, and when he was sitting on a hospital bed with a nurse working on the wound, he assured the Zhànshì he would be fine now. "You can head back. It's late. Don't stay up on my account."

"Jackson," Ava objected.

He met her eyes. She felt it again, that same longing for what couldn't be. All she wanted was to stay there with him, and she could see he wanted that too, but with the others right there watching, she had no idea how to explain why she wanted to stay.

"It's okay," Jackson said in a somber tone, "go with your friends."

She felt the jab like a knife wound, whether he intended it or not. Her "friends," as if to say he was not one of them.

"What the taint happened?" Sasha asked, hurrying into the room and to Jackson's side. He cursed again when he saw the wound that was now being stitched back together. "I don't care what you say, I'm getting you a security detail, some of my most trusted officers. I know you enjoy the freedom to roam, but at some point, we need to think about your safety."

Mikel, Damian and Ella had already started toward the exit. "Coming?" Mikel asked pointedly.

Having still no excuse not to, Ava followed, though it felt like it would crush her to do it. Why couldn't the fact that she *wanted* to stay be enough? Why did she have to have a good reason? Sadly, for a group of purebred soldiers who had been raised to follow orders to the T, acting purely on emotion just wasn't a good enough reason for anything.

As they walked, Ava stared unconsciously at her hands, drenched red with Jackson's blood.

"I can't imagine that," Mikel said seriously as they walked back to the lift. "The guy sacrifices everything for these people, helps free them, and they're still trying to kill him? Seems like everyone in the world wants him dead. How does a guy like that trust anyone?"

"Who cares?" Ella huffed. "Add me to the list of who wants him gone! Now can we just get to our room in silence?"

"The meeting with the Committee didn't go as we had hoped," Jackson admitted to the room of Zhànshì.

Ava stared at the bandage on his neck, remembering how close a call last night had been. She had predicted as much as Jackson said. The fact that they were now meeting in the apartments rather than one of the briefing rooms was proof in and of itself.

"I can't tell you how much work it took to get them to accept even just Ava a few weeks ago. But this is perceived as too high a threat level. And unfortunately, there is nowhere in the country of Russia that the Committee is willing to risk the presence of three powerful Zhànshì. The only way the Committee is willing to let you stay is in a medically induced coma."

"To taint with that," Ella replied with wide eyes.

Mikel nodded in obvious agreement.

"Of course, they don't have any reason to suspect your abilities with the Tower. But to them, three trained elite assassins can't be risked, after what happened with the last group." Jackson sighed heavily. He still avoided her gaze, and it hurt her. He didn't seem angry anymore. If anything, in regard to her, he just seemed pained. "It's too bad really," he admitted to the room at large. "From everything I've witnessed, I have every reason to trust you. And I was even coming to like...some of you." This he directed at Ella, as if to say she was the exception.

Ella glowered. Ava couldn't help chuckling. She had never met anyone who didn't like Jackson. And she had never met anyone who bothered Ella more than she herself did, but Ella clearly disliked Jackson—though he was more amused by her—and it was fun to witness.

"Well, I guess that's it then," Mikel said, putting his hands in the air. "Back to plan A, as in: Ava comes with us, we leave Russia for good, and you never have to worry about hearing from us again.'"

A deep pang touched her heart. She looked mournfully at Jackson. There was no easy way out of this one. She was being forced to pick. And she had already promised loyalty to the Zhànshì.

For the first time that morning, Jackson turned his eyes to her. They watched each other, a deep sadness in both of their eyes. She almost wondered if he was waiting for her to pick him this time. She hoped he could see how much she wanted to.

The Zhànshì needed her. But then...what if Jackson had been telling the truth last night? What if he truly needed her too? Was there anyone in the world that she would rather pick than him?

Jackson was the first to look away, apparently deciding that Ava had not made up her mind. She hadn't, but it wasn't like that.

"Actually, I have another idea," Jackson replied hesitantly. "If you're willing to take a risk, I may have a much greater opportunity for you even than within Russia."

"I like risk," Mikel replied with a casual shrug. "What's the catch?"

Jackson was slow to speak. It was clear that he was uncertain about this option, but ultimately, there weren't many other choices right now. "The Republic has almost entirely abandoned the war with Russia to focus efforts on the rebellions in Africa. They consider us as good as gone, but they still hope they can ultimately reconquer and subjugate Africa. The leader of the rebellion there, Sizwe, is a friend. I've told him about you, and he has agreed to take you on—with only a simple screening process to ensure your trustworthiness."

Mikel and Ella shared a look, and Ava watched Jackson, trying to comprehend what this meant for her.

"If I'm being honest, your abilities will be of much greater use in Africa than they ever could here," Jackson continued. "For the time being, Russia is stable. Africa is where the fight is. Beyond that, you never would really have had a place here. I hardly even do. You saw what happened last night, with the attempt on my life. I face several of them a month. Although the leadership of Russia has accepted my value to their current needs, the people of Russia are far from accepting of an enemy agent in the high ranks of Russian leadership. And you wouldn't even have the full support of the leadership. You would be heavily watched and regulated. You would never truly be in on the higher decisions and committees—and that's assuming I convinced them not to drug you into a coma."

Mikel and Ava shared a look now, resonating with the truthfulness and honesty of that comment. "And should we expect anything different in Africa?" Mikel asked pointedly.

Jackson nodded confidently. "Absolutely. Sizwe is not like the political leaders we're used to. If he deems you trustworthy, you will be as a brother to him. I've gone through the process myself. I assure you, it's nothing like you've ever faced or likely will ever again. But it is worth the initiation. And when it is done, he will trust you as he does his closest men. I have explained the value that the four of you can bring to this fight. And he is willing to accept you in as major leaders in the war. If we win in Africa, the blow to the Republic and the advantage we'll gain over the Kingdoms will be immeasurable. You four will be among the greatest warriors who accomplish that victory."

"Do we all have to go?" Ava asked, and she had to work to ignore the looks from Mikel and Ella. It was clear they thought she was selfishly asking if she could stay. Maybe she was.

Still, the slight look of hope in Jackson's eyes was worth the touch of betrayal from the others. And yet, ultimately, he looked down for some time before facing her and responding. "Unfortunately, there is no longer a place for any of the Zhànshì within Russia. The threat has been decided to be too great."

"Don't worry, love," Sasha piped in from where he stood on the outer edge of the room. She had almost forgotten he was there. "Where you go, I go, at least for the foreseeable future."

She gave him a thankful smile, but behind that smile was a deep pain that she could barely manage to mask. She loved Sasha, and she was grateful that she would not lose him. But what about Jackson?

"So, what's all this about some 'screening process?'" Ella asked. "I'm not all that fond of interrogations."

"Like I said, I've been through it myself. I assure you, it's entirely..." he trailed off, searching for the right word.

"Painless?" Mikel offered.

"Safe?" Damian added when Jackson still said nothing.

Jackson bit his lip. "Worth it," he settled for.

"Well, that's reassuring," Mikel said dryly.

Ella put her face in her hands, muttering curses about how much she disliked Jackson.

"And I'm not asking you to go it alone either," Jackson spoke reassuringly. "My ultimate duties lie in Russia for the time being, but Sizwe has asked that I accompany you to him and participate in the screening process. I've done it before, and I go willingly again."

Mikel seemed uncertain, but ultimately turned to Ava for an answer. "Well, fearless leader? What's the call?"

Ava didn't want to be their leader. At some point, maybe she should hand that title right back to Mikel, but for today at least, she would accept their appointment. "I don't see any better options," Ava offered. "If we can help free Africa, we'll have a huge edge in the greater war. And, maybe, eventually, we can prove to the leaders of Russia that we're trustworthy."

"I was never in this for Russia," Mikel clarified. "I just want to dethrone the King—that being Eli. I'm still entirely and completely loyal to my homeland."

"As am I," Ava agreed.

Ella rolled her eyes, her signature move. "I don't care. I just want Eli to pay."

"Then let's win in Africa!" Damian spoke excitedly. "That sounds like a victory for the Kingdoms, especially if Eli has nothing to do with it."

"True enough," Jackson replied with a nod. "Council will not be pleased that he wasn't involved in getting leverage within Africa when he could have before now. It won't be enough to have him removed, but it's a start."

"When do we leave?" Mikel asked for everyone.

Jackson looked at his watch. "Honestly? As soon as we possibly can. The Committee is getting antsy about this situation. I'm sorry to say that the rest of your stay will not be as pleasant as it previously has been. There are some extra precautions being taken."

Mikel stood, and Ella and Damian followed. Who were they kidding? Ava wasn't their leader. Mikel had earned that title, and he deserved to keep it. "We're ready now," Mikel said.

Jackson stared blankly for a moment before standing. "Okay. I'll set up our ride."

He started toward the door and left the room.

"I better pack some things," Sasha noted, and followed Jackson out.

Ava panicked suddenly, wanting desperately to tell Jackson how sorry she was, and knowing that she was running out of time.

She hurried to the door, but was unable to pass. "You are to remain in the apartments until accompanied by the colonel," the armed guard replied. "It will be locked from the outside."

"Wait, I just need to say one thing!" she objected, but he was already starting to close the door.

Down the hall, she could see Jackson, standing and talking to his new male assistant.

"Wait," she pleaded once more, but the guard closed the door in her face.

Ava stood there feeling like a fool. She didn't want to turn around and face the other Zhànshì, who she knew would be passing judgment with their stares. And for just a moment, she found herself resenting them for ever showing up and ruining everything.

The door reopened, and the guard apologized. "You may pass, ma'am," he said, clearing the way.

There were twelve armed men outside the door, prepared in case of a struggle with the Zhànshì. She doubted that would be enough, but she had no intention of fighting these men.

Jackson still stood there by his assistant, not having moved but watching. Obviously, he was the one to have given the order for her passage.

All eyes were on her. This wasn't the kind of apology she had envisioned. The guard hadn't even closed the door again, so the tainted Zhànshì could see her just as clearly.

"Do they need more time?" Jackson asked.

It occurred to her as she stood motionless, this wasn't exactly the right time or place for what she wanted to say. He would accompany them to Africa. Maybe there would be another chance to find him alone, but the weight of the words she still had not fully said had been crushing down on her all night. She honestly did not know if she could handle another night like that.

But then...she remembered the embarrassment in his anger when Jackson had spoken of how she made a fool of him in front of his men. She glanced at the filled hall, and she once again felt a crushing pain and her own sort of embarrassment. So, she turned to go back into the room, having said nothing.

The Zhànshì watched her in confusion. Everyone did. She had already made a scene. She had already made a fool of herself. She may as well get some relief out of it.

So, she turned again and walked quickly through the door, toward Jackson. The intensity of her movement apparently concerned many of the guards, who drew weapons and attempted to stop her, but Jackson signaled them to stop.

She thought of that time, during the Talks, the two of them walking alone through the halls, feeling miles apart. She had hugged him tightly, in hopes of repairing the damage between them. And it had helped. It had made a difference. Maybe that could be enough now too?

She went directly to him, put her arms around his neck and, avoiding his wound, held him tightly. Despite the stack of papers in his hands, he put his arms around her waist and held her just as tightly.

"Forgive me," Ava whispered, clinging to him. "I never meant to hurt you. I'm sorry." She let go, knowing all the eyes that were on her, knowing that the guards suspected she had a knife to stab him in the back.

His face was surprised as she pulled away. It was clear that he had not expected such a strange, public display from her, with both of their people watching. Still, she hoped the words and her regret had gotten through to him.

Ava awkwardly turned away and made her way back to the room. The door was closed and locked behind her.

"And here we go again," Ella grumbled, breaking Ava from her painful thoughts. "Typical. Ava can't leave without making sure she's left behind another lover. Give me a break."

Ava chose to ignore the comment and pretend it didn't hurt her like every other time, but someone else stood up for her this time.

"Hush, child," Damian chided. "You've no idea what you're talking about."

Gratefully, Ava smiled at the old man before leaving the main room for one of the bedrooms, in hopes of freeing herself from the judgmental eyes.

★ ★ ★ ★ ★

"Hello, dear," Sasha greeted his daughter as she approached his seat on the plane. Most everyone was asleep at this point, though obviously not her.

"What's all this?" she asked about the many piles of papers surrounding him. He moved a stack off the seat next to him and gestured for her to sit down.

"Just some loose ends I need to tie up in Russia so I can start a new life." He spoke pleasantly, but his words caused a deep scowl from her.

"I don't want you to have to give up everything you've built there just for me."

Sasha chuckled. "Well, *I* do. Don't worry, love, I am more than ready to leave this all behind. And it is in better hands than my own."

"You've put your life into this," Ava declared. "You should have the opportunity to see it through."

"I have. Russia is free. They are an independent land working toward freedom from oppression for the rest of the Republic. What more could I do?"

"You could stay with Jackson. I'll have Mikel and Ella."

"I'm not leaving you, Ava," Sasha spoke with a tone of finality. "I have sacrificed close to thirty years of my life in the service of my country and of Russia. It's time I retired and focused on my family."

She had a perplexed expression on her face, and Sasha could tell she was deep in thought. "What if I don't want you to stay with me?" she asked seriously. "What if I want you to go back with Jackson?"

Sasha observed her for several seconds until it was clear she meant her statement. "Then I would tell you that it's not your choice," Sasha replied caringly. "I'm going to remain with you. Jackson is a big boy. He can handle himself."

"And all the people who want him dead?"

"You've seen our fortress in the mansion. He'll have Zak and Viktoriya. He'll even have Boris," this he said with a touch of sarcasm, but Ava did not laugh. "He'll be safe there."

"In the place where he almost died from being poisoned?" Ava replied in a quiet challenge.

Again, Sasha watched her, attempting to understand where this was all coming from. "I worry for him too, love. But my place is with you."

She closed her eyes sadly. It was obvious that her objections went deeper than where Sasha should live. Soon, she gave him greater understanding. "I wish this hadn't happened. I know, you've said it's pointless to wish things like that, but I do. Everything was so...good, for just a minute there. I mean, it was horrible at the same time. But it was getting better. You and I were close, I was working through my issues. And Jackson and I were finally becoming friends again." She trailed off in thought. "I'm glad that Mikel and Ella have found their greater calling and all. I'm glad that Remington believed in me enough to lead them here. But a part of me..." her voice hushed to a whisper as she stared at her hands, "a part of me resents them for coming, and even resents Remington for sending them."

Sasha watched her caringly, attempting to understand so that he could comfort her. "It was a time of refuge," he offered, "but times like that cannot last forever. At some point, we must move forward, there must be progression, and there must be change."

"I know that!" she shot back, then her eyes closed sadly. "But it feels like I'm losing him all over again."

Sasha's eyes narrowed as he considered the implications. He had been so certain before about Ava's friend-like feelings toward Jackson, but the pain she bore now suggested possibly something more. "Ava," Sasha offered in a similar quiet tone to hers, "I know in the past we have spoken about an imaginary, parallel world where you would marry and have a family. Hypothetically speaking, in another world, do you think you would ever be romantically involved with him? With Jackson, that is?"

Her eyes finally opened, and when she turned to face him, he caught the glimmer of unshed tears. She did not respond audibly but instead offered a nod as answer.

Sasha nearly caught his breath as he considered that. Ava was so young, so focused on her mission, and Sasha had always assumed from her responses to him that she had no ideas of romance. Jackson, on the other hand, had a mature love for Ava that Sasha had assumed was unrequited. Only now did it occur to Sasha that Ava might possibly have been even more closed off about her feelings than Jackson ever had. All those times that Sasha pressed for answers, and she gave stony responses in the negative, perhaps that was just her guard and not her childlike innocence as to romance.

"And in this world?" Sasha asked softly.

Her expression became one of helplessness. "I don't know how!" she whispered with a deep pain. "And I'm afraid he'll never forgive me."

Sasha felt the answer like a kick in the gut. If he had been wrong, then he had caused Jackson meaningless pain and worry with his warnings. "Are you suggesting," Sasha asked, needing it to be said plainly so there could be no confusion, "that you have feelings...that is, that you have romantic feelings for Jackson?"

She hesitated long as the shimmering in her eyes continued. Then she simply nodded sadly.

Sasha let out a breath of surprise. "My goodness, Ava, do you love him?"

Ava had no chance to respond, since the man in question approached to their side. "Well," Jackson said cluelessly, having no idea what he had walked into, "shall I put on a pot to brew? Everyone else is asleep. I guess we're still the night owls." He sat on the bench parallel to them. Only as he looked at their expressions did he realize it was a bad time. "Sorry, did I interrupt something?"

"No," Ava replied cheerily. Just like that, her emotion and pain had disappeared, and the mask of sweet innocence had returned. She was better than he had realized. "It turns out Sasha is as much a workaholic as you, though."

Jackson smiled deeply. "I learned from the best."

"The real question is, who did *you* learn it from?" This Ava directed at Sasha.

Despite himself, he put his questions aside and matched their playful mood. "Some of us are just born this way."

"How's your neck?" Ava asked Jackson, changing the subject.

Jackson's hand went involuntarily to the bandage. "Sore, but I'm sure I'll be fine. They say it'll scar, so I'll have a constant reminder every time I look in the mirror of how you saved my life."

"We saved each other," Ava replied almost automatically. From Jackson's response, it was clear this was a shared statement between them, but all Sasha could think in that moment was about the romantic implications. How could he have misread his own daughter so entirely?

Apparently, Ava noticed Sasha's serious thoughts about the matter, because she grew suddenly tense. "I'm gonna get some water. Maybe I'll close my eyes for a bit." With that, she excused herself.

Sasha remained silent for a time.

Jackson stood and took the seat that Ava had left vacant. He glanced at the documents in Sasha's hands and around him, then offered a feeble smile. "Is this your way of telling me you're leaving me?"

"I, uh, I assumed you knew," Sasha replied, missing Jackson's sarcasm until it was too late.

"Doesn't mean the blow doesn't hurt when it finally lands. Yes, I knew, and I agree you should stay with her. I think in our years together you've taught me well. I should be able to handle things all right. That is, as long as we video call at least twice a day when I mess everything up."

Sasha smiled at that. "I wouldn't miss it for the world."

Jackson seemed almost as though he would go then, but Sasha stopped him. "Jackson, I wanted to say...I never should have gotten involved in your relationship with Ava."

Jackson's eyes narrowed in surprise, but he came back with more sarcasm. "I would be worried if you missed getting involved in any area of my life, Sasha."

"I realize, I may have been wrong...about...well, about all of it. I should not have asserted myself as I did."

Again, Jackson was taken off guard by the comment, though he made no reply.

"I was worried at the time about you getting hurt, because I believed your feelings were one-sided."

Silence. Almost a full minute. Then, "Did she say something to you?" Jackson asked with a scowl.

"All I mean to say is that I may have been wrong. I shouldn't have gotten involved, and I'm sorry I did."

"What did she say?" Jackson asked. His interest was pained, almost as if he was scared to hear the answer.

"I would no more betray her confidence than your own," Sasha replied. "I just wanted to say that, should you wish to pursue your interest in my daughter, you have my blessing."

For whatever reason, Jackson did not look pleased by the invitation. Perhaps his anger was based on the fact that it was a bit late for pursuit when they would be separated by thousands of miles. Perhaps he was just tired of Sasha getting involved. Or maybe he was simply taken by surprise, and it came off as anger. Whatever it was, he gave no reply. After several moments of silence, he stood and left Sasha there alone to regret his meddling.

7

Dream Hemorrhage

As everyone entered the parlor, Sizwe took a special interest in Mikel. "Are you of African heritage?" Sizwe asked, noting his ebony skin.

"Actually, Australian Aboriginal," Mikel corrected with a wink.

"Ah," Sizwe replied. "My mistake." He turned to the others in the room then and spoke to them all as if one. "You may be seated."

They did as ordered. Jackson sat in the middle of the room to the far left of the largest sofa. To his right sat Sasha, Ava beside him. To his left, on the smaller sofa, Mikel and Ella sat together. Each of the others had an ally, while Jackson sat alone. He had Sizwe, and he did not feel uncomfortable, as the others did in this place. For him, it felt strangely like home.

"I sense a great amount of discord in this room," Sizwe said, looking around at the group of five. Damian was allergic to all medicinal teas and could not participate. So, remaining in the room were Jackson, Sasha, Ava, Mikel and Ella. It was the same little sitting room that he and Zak had been shuttled into the first time around.

The members of the group looked around at each other. Jackson first met Ella's glare, and she was the one to respond. "Yeah, I'd say so."

"I think she's the only problem, if I'm being honest," Jackson replied casually, causing her to huff in annoyance.

Truthfully, he didn't have a problem with Ella. If he had met her when he met Ava, they probably could have been good friends, but she had a beef with Ava, and she automatically picked sides for people. And to be fair, if he had to choose between the two of them, there really was no question. Still, it was fun to tease her.

"Jackson said we're wasting our time by lying to you," Mikel spoke earnestly. "So, I'll speak my mind. I have some questions about the integrity of some of them." He nodded to Sasha and Jackson, each in their turn. "I like them as people, but I don't know if I can ever really respect anyone who seriously betrays their people for the enemy."

"And you, Ava?" Sizwe asked, turning to her.

Ava was in a cheerful mood today and seemed to be in awe of their surroundings. "How do you know my name?" she asked pleasantly.

Sizwe smiled. "I have seen your face before. In the dreams of my brother." He nodded toward Jackson.

"It wasn't like that," Jackson objected, not liking how he made it sound. "He means my memories."

Sasha and Mikel both stifled smiles.

Ava wore her cheerful attitude proudly. "The people in this group are some of my most treasured friends," Ava responded to the earlier question. "I have no ill feelings toward any of them."

"Yet some of them have ill feelings toward you," Sizwe replied, and though most of them would assume he meant Ella, it was Jackson who he nodded at.

Ava looked up to face Jackson, an expression of pain, even shame on her face. "Oh...I guess they do," she admitted, suddenly seeming embarrassed. Jackson wanted to assure her he was no longer angry, that he had indeed forgiven her, but Sizwe moved along too soon.

"And you?" Sizwe asked Sasha.

"I know very little of them," Sasha explained about Mikel and Ella, "but these two I love as my own children."

Mikel overtly laughed at that, causing the others to look at him. When he had everyone's attention, he shrugged exaggeratedly. "I don't know. I just don't remember you coming around much while Ava was growing up. She has serious daddy issues. And the fact that you were on another continent her whole childhood didn't help that."

"Mikel," Ava urged, attempting to silence him. "My supposed 'daddy issues' are none of your business, and it's not his fault."

It was indeed a sore spot for Sasha, who looked down and breathed heavily.

"Discord, indeed," Sizwe repeated.

The door opened and Talice entered, a platter of teacups in her hands. She walked to Sizwe, offering him the first cup as a sign of respect. Next, she went to Jackson, who accepted the cup. From there, she simply went in line, not knowing the proper order of recognition for the rest.

Jackson gulped it down, no hesitation. All of the others regarded their cups suspiciously.

"Ugh," Ella grumbled. "Clearly, you don't know the threat of being poisoned," she said, with a disgusted grunt.

"Twice," Jackson replied calmly when the tea was gone. "Almost didn't make it past the first one."

"And is it any wonder when you drink things down without a second thought?" she replied pointedly.

He took on a sarcastically awe-struck expression. "I hadn't thought of that!"

Ava at least appreciated his playful comment. Apparently, she was the only one in the mood for humor today.

Sasha was the next to drink it. He had in the past received a report about what was to occur. This was completely new to the rest of them. Ava followed suit with a sort of optimistic acceptance. "If we die, we die among friends," she said pleasantly.

Again, Ella growled. "Speak for yourself."

Mikel followed Ava in taking the drink. Ella waited until the others had finished their tea entirely before even taking a sip.

"Really?" Mikel asked her with an annoyed expression.

"If you all die, the fight must go on. I won't rest until that tyrant is destroyed."

Ava could not seem to keep from scoffing at that comment. She did not like it when people attacked Eli—Jackson knew that first-hand.

In an attempt to lighten the mood, Jackson spoke. "No wonder she's so grouchy," he said to no one in particular. "You haven't slept in, ...how long?"

"Normally, we prefer to do these dreamwalks on a one-on-one basis," Sizwe spoke to the room as a whole. "In a group setting there is possibility for negative consequences—loss of agency and feeling of violation—but the special circumstances led us to, conflictedly, make an exception in this case.

"For the purposes of this experience, we will not pick any specific path. With as many minds and memories as we have in attendance, we will use this room as a sort of returning point." He took the neural pathway devices and placed them on his own temples, then a set for Jackson, then the rest in the same order as they had consumed the tea.

"Close your eyes," he said, taking a seat in his armchair. "Try to remember every detail of this room. What did you notice when you entered? What were the decorations that caught your eye? What was the color of the wall? The rug on the floor? What were the patterns on the seat you chose? What were the colors, designs and descriptions that stood out to you?"

The dreamlike daze started to overcome Jackson's mind, just like the last time. He knew that the hypnosis was beginning. As Sizwe continued speaking, they were entering the dream.

Sizwe continued to walk them through the details of the room, though their eyes remained closed. When he eventually told them to reopen their eyes, they were sitting in the same room as before, but it felt different. A gray hue was in every detail that had previously been colorful and bright. He felt a little foggy of mind and knew it was an effect of the herbally-induced hypnosis. It would not be easy to have a wandering mind in this place. Instead, they would all follow where Sizwe led them.

"Look around the room. Let your eyes drift past the furniture and instead notice each other. Take in each person, each face, every feature. Whether you have feelings of love or malice for these people, notice them. What in their features is to be admired? What could be improved?"

"Mikel's zit sure stands out to me," Ella said, breaking the tone of the room.

"Jerk," Mikel shot back in annoyance. He did not seem to like having his imperfections pointed out.

"Look deeper now," Sizwe said, unfazed by the immaturity in the room. "Choose one face. What do you see? Who do you see? Beyond the surface, the good and bad?"

Jackson found himself looking at Sasha, his mentor and friend.

Sasha was almost twice his age. He was a healthy, fit man. He was the type you wanted to age into. Jackson had watched him while Sizwe said to notice the surface, but then he was told to look deeper, and Jackson did.

Sasha was a strong man. He had faced things that Jackson could not imagine. Grief and pain beyond compare. Joy and love like no other. He had faced betrayal. He had faced abandonment. He had faced shame and regret. But he was still standing. Every day, he got up, and he fought again. He never quit. He never stopped. He never for a moment wavered, and that was a strength that Jackson desired more than anything.

Jackson broke for only a moment and noticed that Mikel had been studying *his* face, while he studied Sasha. Ava watched Ella, who looked at Mikel. And Sasha was looking at his daughter. It seemed strange that every person noticed another, no one was left out, no repeats. It almost felt like a strange design from the person guiding them, and Jackson wondered if somehow Sizwe had managed to guide them softly into even this smallest of choices.

"In the past, I have led a dreamwalk with guided questions that take me to the most intimate of answers. However, in this case, with the feelings of tension from each of you, I have a feeling there may be a better way to arrive at the truth I desire. You will be the ones to ask the questions. One after the other, you'll ask another the thing you most want to know, pinpointing the discord you feel toward them. Now, who will begin?"

Sizwe looked around the room, waiting.

Jackson tried to remember his last dreamwalk. He couldn't seem to recall any details, any of the questions or answers or memories, though usually he remembered the entire event vividly. Strange effects of the hypnotism. He was so focused on trying to remember, that he could not think of a question for any of the others.

"How about...what's your favorite memory?" Ava offered hopefully.

Sizwe smiled at the sweet comment. "Not quite our focus, child. Anyone else?"

Fortunately, Sasha came up with one, directed at Mikel. "You certainly seem to think you're the king of the world," Sasha said, and Jackson was surprised by the obvious venom in his words. He hadn't known how strongly Sasha disliked Mikel—none of them had, until now. "Who made you the best? What makes you think you're above the rest of the world?"

Another effect of the dreamlike state, one had little control of their usual abilities to hide emotions. All would be out in the open, for better or worse.

Mikel grinned, and looked like he was about to answer with a quick comeback, but before he could, the room around them changed.

Jackson vaguely remembered watching from the side of the room as they wandered his memories last time, but that was not how it occurred this time. Instead, he became Mikel. He could see through the boy's eyes. He felt what Mikel felt, thought what he thought.

Mikel sat in his testing chair. This was it, the big day he had been waiting for. This was his chance to prove himself.

He glanced up at the clear glass that showed in the upper wall, through to the viewing room, where the General himself sat with the head trainer, Kristen, observing.

The *General* was here, watching *Mikel!* Witnessing *his* test. And when Mikel's test showed how great he was, the General would no doubt congratulate him.

Eventually Eric finished the test, but he didn't tell Mikel the results. Instead, he told him to wait there while he went up and spoke with the others. Eric left to the viewing room. Mikel witnessed the moment when the General's shoulders slumped in defeat. "Another failure!" he cursed.

Mikel had become incredible at reading lips. All the Zhànshì were trained to do it, but he was the best.

"What am I doing?" the General asked the room, but it seemed more directed at himself. "What the taint am I still doing this for?"

"Mikel's a good kid," Kristen spoke up.

Mikel liked Kristen, more than all the rest of the trainers combined. She was the only one who really got to know the Zhànshì individually. She had a relationship with every single one. She didn't just see them as Zhànshì. She almost treated them like a sort of mother. And of course, it was clear to everyone that she loved Ava best of all, which was fair, since Ava actually was her daughter. Still, Mikel was certain that Kristen had his back, even against the General.

"I'm not trying to raise some 'good kids!'" the General shot back in sudden anger. "I'm trying to create a weapon! And none of them comes close to what we need! Taint. If you hadn't screwed up Valkyrie—" This he directed at Eric.

"*Me?*" Eric shot back, looking ready for a fight. "*I* screwed her up?"

Kristen raised her hand, stopping her brother and pushing him back.

"I'm tired of these failed experiments," Harrison muttered.

"Mikel has some incredible talents that I think you'll find valuable, sir," Kristen urged, and Mikel found himself more grateful than he knew how to express.

Harrison stood, towering over his daughter, and raised his hand as emphasis when he seethed his next words. "Don't talk to me about their talents. You make me a weapon to destroy the enemy, and *then* we'll talk!"

He started away, and Kristen, looking defeated, replied, "Yes, sir," though he was no longer there to hear it.

The General passed right by Mikel without a word, without a glance, without anything. Mikel was not worth the General's time. That much was clear.

The vision shifted to later that night. Training had concluded, and all the other Zhànshì had started toward the doors, but Mikel stayed sitting there, by the firing range, watching Kristen while she worked with the other trainers, discussing the day's exercises.

After a time, she turned and noticed him. She gave a half smile and walked to where Mikel stood. "It's time for bed, Mikel," she reminded him, though her tone was gentle and kind.

"I'm not valuable to the General," Mikel muttered sadly. "I'm a failed experiment."

Her eyes touched with surprise. "You watched us through the glass," she realized, and he replied with a simple nod. Kristen wasted no time before crouching down to Mikel's level. He was tall for his age at ten years old, but not as tall as she.

"Mikel, I would never disrespect the General, and I assure you, that's not what I'm doing now. But sometimes he gets these ideas in his mind of exactly what a person should be. And if they don't live up to that depiction perfectly, then in his mind, that's a 'failed experiment,'" she used her hands to make quotation symbols. "So, no, your test didn't score exactly the thing he wanted it to, but it honestly doesn't matter. You are an incredible Zhànshì. You have strengths that no one can compare with. If you want to excel at something, anything, then it doesn't matter what some score on a test says. You put your mind to it, and your heart into it, I know without a doubt that you can accomplish anything. Literally, anything."

Somehow, he believed her when she said it.

"Besides," she added with a casual shrug. "Being on the General's radar is overrated. You can do a whole lot more when he's deemed you useless. Believe me, the best thing that ever happened to you was 'failing' that test. Now you can do whatever the living taint you want. And believe me, Mikel, when you do it, you're going to be the best in the world."

His sadness soon shifted into a deep grin. "I can do *anything* I want?" he asked once more to be sure.

She nodded with a proud smile. "Anything."

He didn't tell her this, but he decided, then and there, that his "anything" would be the very thing the General had hoped for. So, maybe he would do it under the radar, but he would do it. And the General would never know what hit him when Mikel rose up and became the best—whatever that even meant.

"Then I'm going to do it, Kristen," he told her confidently. "I'm going to be the best."

She smiled, and the look in her eyes said she believed him entirely. All he needed was her belief in him. That was enough. "I know you will, Mikel. And when you go out and change the world with your version of best, just know, wherever I am in the world, I'm still your biggest fan."

She put her fist out for him, and he met it with his. "Yes, ma'am," he said with beaming pride.

The memories shifted from moments in training, moments in the field, until, finally, a moment in a small, cold prison cell, staring at a flickering light. And Mikel did it. He defied all odds.

The memories shifted through events in Australia, and Mikel's immense leadership with Damian by his side, guiding him and grounding him with his inspiring, dedicated strength. Then, he was returned to work with Eli, put in to do the work of the lowest of agents, but even then, he always knew where he was headed, he still knew he would make the Colonel proud.

Remington came, and offered Mikel another option and he would not leave without Ella, and particularly Damian, to join him. He had the beginnings of a team, and he intended to see them through to the end.

With his mind and heart in it, he had done what should have been physically impossible, and soon enough, he would earn the title of "the best in the world."

The memories faded until the group sat around the small sitting room again. Mikel had a sort of awed look to his face, as if going through those memories had sparked things that even he had forgotten.

Sasha was the person who had asked the initial question, and now his expression had really changed. He had been humbled and in the look he now gave Mikel, it was clear to Jackson that Sasha was as in awe of this strange new force of nature as Jackson now was.

None of them had known he had learned how to control the Towers fully, not even Ava it appeared, from the look of shock she, too, wore toward her friend. They had known that, to a small degree, he could influence the power, but his abilities went far beyond that—to the point of truly rivaling Ava's—and most especially because it should have been impossible for him to do so.

"Wow," Ava said, audibly speaking what all of them felt. "You really are the best, Mikel," she said approvingly.

Jackson nodded as if to agree with Ava's words of praise.

He sat back in his chair confidently. "Oh, I know I am, love." And though his overly arrogant tone of defiance bespoke a lack of maturity, none of them could deny the truthfulness of his words.

A silence passed until Sizwe brought them back in. "Who is next?" he urged.

"My question is for Jackson," Mikel was the next to speak. "I want to know how in the General's name you ever found it within your perfect moral compass to defect and join the enemy? How do you still call yourself a patriot?"

"First of all, I don't—" was all he could reply with until the memories came.

Jackson's entire journey flashed before his friends, and they lived through it as if they were him. He lived through it again, for the third time. Moments within the Kingdoms when he noticed the problems. Reading classic history books that showed the discrepancies. His call to make a difference. The journey of his work, each and every moment that had ultimately led to his decision—no matter how small, no matter how big.

Natasha. Agent Altman. The bombshell that the United Kingdoms implanted their agents with life-threatening chips without their knowledge or consent. Russia's reaction to Kristen Altman's death. The Brazil Tower Massacre. Being abandoned by his people to the fate of President Zhang. Being rescued by Sasha. Seeing the good of the Russians. Seeing the potential of such a highly educated people who truly knew how to think independently. So many moments, so many intricacies. And finally, a decision. He could not change the United Kingdoms from the inside. The corruption of the government was unfortunately a battle he could not win from another continent, where they had placed him—particularly when they had effectively turned him over to the enemy to do whatever they wanted with him.

United Intelligence didn't even attempt to rescue him or contact him, and that was fair. He would be discovered if they did, and might die anyway while putting more lives in jeopardy. They hadn't been upfront about the fact that they must disavow him since he was under suspicion, but he had understood the unspoken message clearly.

In the end, it came down to so many small details, one could only understand his decision by living through it themselves. And they did.

They had thought he no longer loved his country. That was not true. He loved the United Kingdoms. He just loved the cause of freedom more.

When they returned to Sizwe's study, no one had anything to say to Jackson, but Jackson wondered if that look on Mikel's face meant he had changed his mind. Ella, too, looked strangely different in her expression toward him.

Finally, Jackson glanced at Ava, wondering if there would ever be a world in which she could really, truly understand him. Apparently, there was. She nodded approvingly at him, a caring smile as if to say, "I finally get it." She didn't know how much that response meant to him.

After another long silence, Sizwe asked the question again. "Who would like to ask another question?"

For a while, no one responded. Eventually, it was Ava who spoke. "Why do you hate the world so much, Ella? Why do you hate everyone and everything?"

Ella glared deeply, and then the memories started.

All the other Zhànshì spoke of Kristen as their favorite trainer, but Ella was too young to remember much of the time before Kristen had been moved to the spotlight of the Kingdoms. There was one trainer though, who she loved more than the rest. Ame was always there, and she paid a special interest to Ella. She was kind, and although they didn't see each other out of training, Ella could almost feel Ame's overwhelming love for her.

Ella roomed with many different Zhànshì, but it was during her time rooming with Breanna that Ella learned some really special tricks. Breanna could do anything, sneak into anywhere, hack into anything, and she taught Ella to do the same.

"Tell me what you want to do," Breanna said, "and we'll make it happen."

Ella didn't really have any desire to do anything she shouldn't. At six years old, she actually liked the rules of the Zhànshì, but Breanna was mischievous and had run out of sneaky things to do. "Name it," she urged. "Whatever you want to do."

"We could...get extra fruit from the commissary?" Ella offered.

Breanna huffed. "You can't tell me that's the best you can come up with. I'm talking really pushing the limits. Really breaking the rules. Crossing the line now and then. There's no better way to live."

Ella didn't know if that was true, but she felt pressured at this moment to take Breanna's word for it.

"We could...sneak into the trainer's apartments?" Ella said.

Breanna eyed her suspiciously. "And...?" she pressed for more.

"And I could talk to Ame and ask why she always comes with me when I'm transferred."

Breanna considered for a moment. "Huh. That is odd. I hadn't noticed that before. But we can't do that. She'll probably turn us in."

"I'll convince her not to," Ella replied hopefully, liking the sound of visiting Ame more and more.

"How could you do that?"

"I heard her arguing with another trainer the other day. She cursed the General's name and said she hated him."

Breanna's eyes widened with sudden excitement. "That could get her fired. Or worse. It'll be enough to shut her up. And I'm curious about her strange stalking. Let's go."

"Thanks for being my friend," Ella said. Breanna was the first Zhànshì who had ever taken any real interest in her. The others were all obsessed with scores and training, but Breanna just seemed to want to have fun.

"My usual partner in crime is Ava," Breanna explained. "But you'll do, when she and I are in different stations."

Breanna did the work and trained Ella on each detail. After discovering which one Ame was stationed in, they snuck into the apartments. "You'll do the talking," Breanna encouraged. "And remember, I have nothing to do with this. I'll hide in the back. Don't mention my name, or I'll hack into your scores and turn you into the weak link of the Zhànshì."

She disappeared into the shadows, leaving Ella alone to do the dirty work. Ella typed in the universal code Breanna had taught her, and Ame's door opened. Ella walked inside.

Ame sat there alone in the small room. Trainers' quarters looked just like Zhànshì quarters. Ame's roommate was there, fast asleep, but Ame sat awake, staring at her scanner when Ella entered.

"Ella!" Ame whispered in surprise. "What are you—?" she cut off, glancing at where the other trainer slept. Then she hurried off her bed and ushered Ella back into the hallway. "What are you doing in here?" she whispered, closing the door behind her.

"I came to ask you why you always follow my transfers," Ella gave her explanation.

"I...um...it's complicated." She glanced down both sides of the hallway, worried someone would see them. "You need to get back to your room! We'll both get in trouble if they find you here."

"My roommate is sleeping too," Ella lied. "I want to talk. Will you take me back?"

Ame hesitated for a long moment. In the end, she accepted.

That was just the beginning. From then on, Ella would inevitably show up at Ame's door each night and would not leave until Ame took her home. The walks were always wary, and Ame was overly careful in the beginning. But when she came to expect it, things grew less tense. Ella would ask her questions, and Ame would reply. Soon, they began to connect over small similarities.

It was several years later before Ella put the pieces together of all the answered questions. "You're my mother, aren't you?" she asked one evening on their walk back to Ella's room.

Ame hesitated for a long time before admitting, "Yes, Ella, I am."

And though nothing really changed, everything felt different from then on. The only other Zhànshì who knew their parents were the Altmans. Most of them had no idea of their backgrounds, but now, Ella had a connection to her past. She had her mother, even if their relationship didn't look like most mothers and daughters.

Ella learned to be as manipulative and mischievous as her friend and teacher Breanna. None of her Zhànshì roommates ever turned her in for her late-night excursions, because Ella knew how to threaten them where it hurt—with scoring. And she claimed to have an in with one of the trainers who would cover for her if they ever did try and tell the truth. She knew it wasn't kind, or good behavior, but she would have done that and more for even a few minutes with her mother each night.

Ella cared about training as much as the next Zhànshì, but her identity felt greater than most of her comrades, because for most of them, all they had was their training. But Ella, she had her mother.

It wasn't until Eli showed up for evaluations that everything changed.

Ame was in tears when Ella came to her that night. "We can't see each other anymore, Ella," she explained, a deep sadness consuming her. "And I might not be transferred with you anymore."

"It's Eli, isn't it?" Ella asked, concern for her mother in her eyes. "He's taking you away from me?"

Ella saw how her mother worked to hide her anger, but ultimately, it consumed her. "I hate them! All of them! Those sick, twisted Altmans! They're all the same! Harrison took everything away from me because of one mistake. And he has tortured my entire life by 'letting' me have the smallest of places in yours. Eric is no better. He hurt my best friend, destroyed her. He's sick. And I think he means to hurt you too. And Eli... he used to be my friend. He used to be so good. But he's just like them now. I hate him!"

"What about Ava?" Ella asked, wondering if she should hate the girl who had once been her friend too. She already now hated the rest for her mother's sake.

Ame's face softened. "She's a good girl." Then she scoffed. "But then, Eli was good once too. She'll probably turn out just like them! Harrison's evil clutches have distorted the beauty in everything. He's a cruel tyrant, and the generations that followed are just like him."

Ella was silent for a time before offering comfort. "We'll find a way to be together. Eventually, we'll work it out."

Ame looked up hopefully. "I want to believe that, Ella. I really do, but you don't know the power of the Altmans. Eli threatened me today, and he means to go through with it. Mark my words, he will find a way to separate us, no matter what it takes."

The next day, a helo crashed in enemy territory. Ella was forced at the age of ten years old to take two lives in order to survive, only to stumble upon the crash site, and wish she hadn't survived.

She stared at the body of her mother, whom she had barely even gotten to know in this life, and all she kept thinking over and over was,

He did this. He found a way. He caused this. She was right. You'll never be together again. Because of Eli. Because of the Altmans.

Kyle made her snap out of it. He made her help him save Ava. She was still a good girl. Maybe she would never turn bad, at least that was what she told herself in that moment.

Kyle was there for Ella, truly there for her then. He was the only one besides Breanna and Ame who ever had been.

When she took her anger out on the men who questioned her, Kyle stopped her and let her hurt him instead. Eventually, she stopped hitting him, and cried, being held in his arms. He was a good friend, and in that moment, she knew he was worth trusting; worth loving.

Ella was put back in training. She was supposed to forget about what she had been through. Other than Kyle, no Zhànshì had faced killing someone before finishing training. And they put her right back into her old system, without offering real help of any kind. She wasn't supposed to have known that Ame was her mother, so why would that death affect her so deeply?

Only Breanna offered any sympathy, when they were transferred back together. "I need to tell you something," Breanna admitted one night, when Ella said she wasn't in the mood to talk about her feelings. "I think I'm in trouble, Ella. I've gotten into something that could be really dangerous. You know me, always walking on a very thin line. But if the trainers find out...I might be in serious taint."

"What did you do?" Ella asked suspiciously.

Breanna's look was one of love, one Ella did not understand. "I found my Ame. And even if it gets me killed, it will have been worth knowing him. Who knew that our stories would be so similar?"

Ella didn't have the heart to tell her then that what she suggested wasn't how the Altmans worked. They wouldn't have Breanna killed. They still needed her. No, they would kill Toby, and Breanna would spend the rest of her life regretting her little "moments" with her father that had ultimately cost him his life.

And it turned out, Ella was right. They didn't physically kill him, but they took away the man that Breanna had come to know.

"I hate him!" Breanna cursed. "I hate Eric! And I'll kill him myself if I ever have the chance!"

"They're all the same," Ella muttered.

Breanna didn't even hear her behind her fury. "They've suspended me. They're going to put me on probation. I don't give a carc! I'll run away. I'll find out what that carcass loves most, and I'll rip it away from him! I swear I'll do it!"

That night, Breanna was suspended and transferred away, and Ella never saw her again.

When she learned of Breanna's death, she begged for any details. "I don't know much," the trainer said. "But I heard from one of the U.I. agents that Ava had the chance to save her. She chose herself instead—for the good of the plan."

And that was when Ella decided. Ava was no longer that "good girl" her mother had spoken of. She was just like them. Just like Harrison, who had ripped everything from Ame. Just like Eric, who had ripped everything from Breanna. Just like Eli, who had ripped everything from Ella. Ava was no better.

Yet, Kyle was still obsessed with protecting her. Kyle, the one person Ella had left in the world. And all he cared about was Ava. It infuriated her. She knew how this would end, and it wasn't well. She tried to change him, tried to break him free of his obsession, but it didn't matter what she said or did, nothing would change Kyle's mind. And in the end, it cost him his life.

What hurt most of all was that Ella *had* reached him. They had become so close that he had asked for her to be the one to give his eulogy. Then, of course, that honor as well as all others was offered to Ava, someone who didn't even know or care about Kyle. She was selfish and prideful and all she wanted was the sympathy of her supposed loss, and the glory of handling it like a champ.

The Altmans were all the same. Ame would have fought back if she had ever been given the chance, but she was dead now. Breanna had sworn she would make Eric pay, if ever she could, but she was dead now.

So, it was left to Ella alone to rid the world of these wretches. She would hurt Eric, make him pay—even if from the grave, by tarnishing his name and legacy. She would hurt Eli, cost him everything in this life. And if that little twerp got in the way, Ella would hurt Ava just the same.

The memories faded; they were all brought back to the room.

The past two memories had brought a sort of respect, an understanding, and peace to the room. This time was different. They had felt her fury. They had felt her pain, but there was no healing. There was no closure. No resolution. She was still just as angry, just as bitter. And if it was the last thing she did, she would hurt the Altmans.

Sizwe was the only one who could seem to speak after that. "I am sorry for what you have faced in such a short time," he told her, a look of genuine understanding on his face. "When we have finished with the others, I have a friend I would wish for you to meet. I think you would benefit from her story, and she from yours. Until then, we must continue."

The tension in the room was greater than ever, and yet, they were supposed to move on.

In her anger, Ella could easily speak. "Why are you so *weak*?" she hissed at Ava. "Why can't you fend for yourself? And why is it that everyone else has to keep dying for you?"

Up until this moment, Ava had been pleasant and cheery. But with that question came a look of horror—not at the accusation. Jackson could see her sudden fear, her sudden hesitation as she muttered the word, "No," helplessly. She did not want to enter these memories. And she certainly didn't want the others to witness them with her. But it was too late. Her happy, awed attitude shifted to terror as the memories started.

"Three weeks, she hasn't spoken one word," the one named Fyodor said to the Russian lieutenant general. Fyodor was the one who spoke English. The lieutenant general had strangely never learned. Ava wondered why a man of such high rank was bothered by a captured child anyway, but perhaps the circumstances around the capture piqued his interest.

They spoke before her now in Russian, assuming she could not understand, having no idea that Russian was her first language.

She had spent hours on end over the past weeks with this cruel man yelling in her face, taking all comforts away as a means to punish her for her silence.

But she would not break. One thought pressed her forward. *Mom and Dad will come and get me.* She knew this to be true. She just had to survive until they arrived. Her mom used to tell her that no matter what happened to her in life, she had control over one thing—her attitude. And so, she tried to be happy and hopeful through the pain, through all her fears, through the many lonely, terrifying nights. She tried to smile, like her mother would have, even when she was most afraid. And so, in this moment, she smiled awkwardly through her fear.

The lieutenant general was highly annoyed and huffed, "Fine. I don't have time for her anyway. Sell her to a brothel. They won't mind her silence there."

A moment of weakness caused her to squeak in sudden fear. She regretted it immediately, and tried to mask it as a hiccup, but the lieutenant general had noticed, and he saw right through her.

What good was her training if she could not act through her fear? But she was terrified. She held her breath, praying repeatedly for her parents to come sooner, trying to smile through her fear and looking strangely insane as she did it.

The lieutenant general crossed the room and crouched down on the floor in front of her, leaning in until his face was inches from hers. "You understand me," he spoke, still in Russian, as if testing her.

She managed to feign a lack of understanding, but her moment of weakness had already ruined her. The lieutenant general reached into his belt loop for a serrated fixed blade, eight inches long. He grabbed her hand and placed the blade on one of her small fingers.

"Let me put it this way," he growled. "You tell me your name, or I slice away your pretty little finger."

Her first thought was that she could handle the pain—or at the very least, she would learn to handle it. But it wasn't just the physical pain that this wound would cause. If he took her finger, she could never go undercover. Scars were bad enough, but a missing limb?

She had to last until her parents came, but if she didn't give him something, then her future career was done for.

"One," the lieutenant general counted in Russian. "Two. Three—"

Just as he put pressure from the blade on her finger, she replied quickly, "Diana!"

The lieutenant general stopped, pulling the blade from her finger. The small slice that he had inflicted before she responded was painful, and the wound began bleeding immediately, but it could have been much worse.

"Diana," he said, a look of satisfaction on his face. Then he looked up at the man standing by the door, who in three weeks had failed to do what the lieutenant general had done in a matter of seconds. "Consider your resignation accepted, Fyodor. I never want to see your face again."

Then he turned back to face Ava, holding the blade up threateningly to her cheek. "Make no mistake, little Diana, I can make this place much worse than a brothel. I suggest you cooperate, if you want to save yourself."

And he proved it to be true over the following weeks. He made her life a living hell. He and his men were violent, cruel and sick, and she was a sort of hobby to them.

She tried to smile through the fear and pain, but it grew harder and harder to manage.

One thought kept her going. *Mom and Dad will come soon. They will come any day. I just need to survive a little longer.*

Another month passed.

No one came. She couldn't say exactly when she realized that no one was coming. Eventually, it occurred to her that she was alone. If she wanted freedom, she needed to escape.

So, she tried.

She made it from the building and five miles from the property, slogging in the snow with nothing but her simple sackcloth dress to keep her warm. When they found her, she was frostbitten, and barely alive. They brought her back to their lair, nursed her back to health, then transferred her to the cells within the Moscow Tower.

In some ways, this place was safer. The lieutenant general was now the only one who had direct access to her. Still, that was bad enough. She received regular meals here, and proper medical treatment, but she had no way to escape. The Tower was impenetrable. Still, she managed to smile through the pain and fear.

Something bothered her; Liam kept talking to her. Breanna said that Liam wasn't real. She said that Ava had an imaginary friend, and Ava had come to accept that. Not wanting to be childish, she had come to ignore his voice. It had been almost a year since he had tried to talk to her, but for the past months, he had been trying to get through to her.

Eventually, there was no one else to talk to, and she was tired of feeling alone.

"Help is coming," Liam assured her. *"Harrison finally found word about you with the lieutenant general. He is working on a peaceful negotiation. You will be freed."*

"I tried to escape, and they locked me in the Tower!" Ava replied mournfully. *"Now there's no hope of getting out."*

"You're in the Tower?" Liam asked with a sudden, strange excitement.

"Yes."

A long silence passed. Hours. When he finally responded, she was defeated by his words. *"Harrison says the mission has changed. He will still work toward peaceful return. But as long as you're in the Tower, you are safe."*

She didn't buy that for a second. They had no idea how bad the lieutenant general was. *"So...no one's coming?"* she asked.

Another long silence. *"I'm sorry, Ava, but it might be a bit longer."*

Tears streamed down her weary face. So many more nights, when even one felt like it would break her. But through her tears, she managed to turn up her lips, and smile.

Weeks passed. Then months. The lieutenant general lost interest, and handed her off to some of his men. They were just as bad, some of them worse.

She tried for a long time to smile, but slowly her smile faded, until she had nothing left to give.

"Your mother wants you to keep fighting," Liam said after another week or two. *"She wants you to know how much she loves you. Harrison won't let her come. She tried to come and rescue you, and he had her locked up. She wants you to know that she'll find a way to tell your father.*

And when she does, he'll come and save you. She told me that Harrison will pay for this. And she wants you to know that she loves you. Your dad will be there soon."

"*I've been waiting four months, Liam,*" Ava sent back, surprised by how unfeeling it sounded. She had very little emotion left to give at all—either good or bad. "*How long am I supposed to wait?*"

A silence lingered before he replied. "*As long as it takes.*"

"*Is my mother with you? Right now?*"

"*No, but I'm able to talk to her. She hasn't rested one day since you were taken. She's doing everything she can to save you. You just have to believe that you're going to make it out. You have to believe that help is coming.*"

"*Where is my father?*" Ava asked helplessly.

"*Closer than you think, Ava.*"

"*And can you talk to him?*"

"*No,*" Liam admitted. "*Your father shut off his access to the link many months back. He thinks it's safer for him this way.*"

Ava stared out at the cell ahead, not really understanding what any of this meant. "*And because of that, I'm gonna die here.*"

"*No. You're going to make it. Harrison is working toward a peaceful negotiation for your return. But even if that falls through, your father will come. You just need to last a little longer.*"

"*And if I don't?*" she replied, tears coming to her eyes. "*You don't know what they're like, Liam. You don't know what they—*"

"*I know, Ava. I know.*"

Another silence, and she wiped at her tears. "*I want to get out of here, Liam. I have to get out of here.*"

"*There is...one way,*" he offered. "*But it's dangerous.*"

"*Just tell me. I will do anything!*"

"*If you could just communicate with the Tower. If you could ask it to help you—*"

"*I'm not stupid, Liam! Stop wasting my time!*"

"*I'm sorry. I shouldn't have said anything. Help will come.*"

But for several more weeks, it didn't. The headaches were unbearable. She felt sick every day. She could hardly sit up, let alone continue training in that tiny cell.

One day, her new keeper apparently decided there was no room for her in the Tower cells. "Time to find a new home, little one," the man grumbled as the guards pulled her out of there.

Her next prison was only a mile out of the Tower. The headaches continued. Eventually, they became so painful that she could hardly speak a full sentence without drawling and muttering.

Her captors thought she was losing it. Luckily, there wasn't much more they wanted from her but good sport, and constant drugs in her system kept her well enough for that.

At some point, when she had long since lost track of time, Ava wondered if she hadn't stabbed herself in the back with that little squeak. Life in a brothel would have been better than this.

Long after her rescue, the nightmares persisted. Harrison performed treatments on her to help, and little did she, or anyone but him know, that he manipulated this opportunity to his will, turning her heart toward him and away from her parents.

She grew to resent them. She grew to adore Harrison. He was the only one in the world who was there for her. When the nightmares came, he was always there to comfort her and to help her through. He was everything to her.

And when he died, a piece of her went with him—the strength she had to carry on through the fear. Now, she was truly alone in the world to deal with nightmares that she didn't understand.

Night after night, she would wake up screaming or panting for breath. Her roommates grew frustrated—except when she was lucky enough to have Breanna. She would leave and wander the halls to catch her breath, but her trainers would find her there, and she would be ordered back to bed.

She had no understanding or explanation for these nightmares. She didn't know why or where they came from. And she certainly didn't know how to handle them. Yet she was forced to, alone.

When evaluations came up, she would hesitantly speak of her fears. It almost seemed as if her evaluators didn't take her seriously. They ignored her when she said she worried the nightmares might be rooted in truth. They claimed she had just seen a scary movie once, and it had stuck with her. But the nightmares came, night after night, week after week, month after month, year after year. Eventually, somewhere along the line, she came to accept that these weren't memories from a bad movie. This was her past.

She stopped bringing it up in evaluations. They didn't believe her, and it probably only marked her as crazy to keep speaking of it. She would deal with the pain herself.

More waking up panting. Her Zhànshì roommates grumbling and telling her to shut up. Wandering the halls, being forced back to her room by frustrated trainers. This was her life.

The only thing that kept her going was making Harrison proud, getting high scores. She had to live up to the Altman name. It was all she had.

Kyle was connected to her fears, but Harrison had erased that part of her past. She hated Kyle. He was rude to her. He fought her. He pushed her. And he felt sickening to be around.

Her life was a written routine. Win in training. Wake up terrified. Be yelled at to go back to bed. Start over the next day. That was her entire life, until a stranger showed up.

Jackson wasn't like anyone she had ever known. He was annoying, and overly confident, and entirely strange. But when he got permission to take her off base, she found herself strangely interested.

And when he left, she knew she would not soon forget him.

Ame died. Ava was sent to heal. Ame had jumped because of Ava, and she knew she would always blame herself for that.

Event after event, they watched the story of her life play out.

Ava did all she could to save her friend, but in the end, Breanna died, and Ava knew she would always blame herself.

Remington and several dozen United Intelligence agents gave their lives for Ava. And she had to accept that their deaths were her fault.

Ava was presented with an option to join Jackson and Sasha, but she wasn't ready to give up on the United Kingdoms just yet. She went back, and her voice was truly heard.

She made a difference, with Lionel, her mentor, her true friend.

But not for long.

The Jiānhùrén attacked. Ava had nearly been killed. She took out the Tower grid. Eli showed her the countless deaths that were her fault. She was stripped of everything, turned to a slave once more, turned to do Eli's bidding, while he inherited all that had once been hers. But even then, she managed to turn up her lips and smile.

Eli's manipulation was relentless, painful, crippling.

Then Yuri's death. Ava fought Darya, but Eli had made a deal. Yuri's death broke Ava's heart.

She blamed Eli. And he punished her. Severely.

Lionel and Hawkins brought her back. She learned to smile again.

Kyle died. This, too, was supposedly her fault, but it did not affect her in the same way as the others. She could not believe, after the conversation and the healing from that night, that he was really gone.

Eli manipulated.

Hawkins died.

Ava fought Eli. She left, breaking her own arm to do so.

Remington was there. He led her to hope.

She begged Sasha to take her back. And he did.

Still, the weight of every death weighed heavily on her. Eli's voice continually ringing in her ears, "You did this. This is your fault. You caused this." She fought daily to overcome that voice. But every time Ella said the words again, all Ava could think was, *You're right. They're all dead because of me. Never again. I will never let anyone sacrifice for me again. It's all my fault. Too many are dead already. No more.*

The memories ended; they were all pulled back to the room.

Jackson struggled now to look across the room at Ava, not knowing if she wanted to be seen right now. It seemed he was right. Her face was in her hands, and she shied away from the rest of them—a painful comparison to her cheery state before.

She blamed herself. She was ashamed. But it was more than the deaths. It was all the abuse from Eli. She blamed herself for that too. For falling for it. For allowing it to happen to her. Even the memories from childhood she blamed herself for. She was ashamed and embarrassed.

These were her deepest wounds, her deepest hurts, and now they were out in the open for all to see.

No one knew how or what to say after that. It seemed, not even Sizwe was inclined to break the silence. Ava would not look up from her buried face in her hands. She could not handle the thought of being seen by any of them right now.

"It is...difficult to put a measure on pain," Sizwe said after almost an entire minute. "But some people are forced to face in their lifetime more than anyone should have to. I am afraid, that all of those seated before me are among that type."

Still, Mikel and Jackson shared a look as if to say, "I'm glad we went first." Their pains and struggles seemed insignificant now, having seen what the others had gone through.

Ella seemed deep in thought in the aftermath, though she would not look up to face the others any more than Ava would right now.

"I have seen a sufficient amount for most of you," Sizwe said. "But there is still one who has yet to share. Does anyone have a specific question?"

Mikel was the one to shift in his seat, and raised his hand—which was not in his usual, assertive character.

Jackson could not help but look once more at Ava. Still, she hid her face from the others, looking down and away from them though she had finally removed her hands. He didn't know why she felt the need to hide. None of what he had seen caused him to think less of her. If anything, he was more in awe of her than ever. Did she not realize how strong she was? Did she not understand how incredible she was for overcoming what she had?

"Yes," Sizwe asked Mikel, who had waited patiently to be called on.

Mikel hesitated to look up across the room at Sasha, but when he did, his eyes were sad. No longer accusatory, but clearly bitter. "Where were you? In all of that? Why weren't you there for her? You were hardly even in her story until the end. What kind of father—?"

"That will do," Sizwe stopped him, and by then the memories had begun to shift the room.

"We're never having kids," Kristen stated, though it sounded more like a plea.

"We already have a kid," Jacob pointed out the picture frame on the wall of the two of them, and an eight-year-old Eli.

"You know what I mean," she grumbled. "I won't do it, Jacob. I won't give another child to him."

"Then say no," Jacob replied sternly. "Eventually, you need to learn how to say no to that man!"

"Not with this," she said, shaking her head vigorously. "You don't know him like I do. He'll find a way. He'll find a way to take my baby. And I won't do it again."

"He's still our son," Jacob said in a hoarse whisper. "Why can't we just fight to have him back?"

"I signed him away before I was even legally an adult," she said, tears in her eyes. "He didn't have a father. And he barely had me."

"Well, things are different now," Jacob urged. "He does have us."

She shook her head again. "It's five years too late for that. He has the chip. We have to let him be raised with the others. I don't know what will happen to him if we don't."

"And we don't know what will happen if we do," Jacob countered.

He could sense how painful this was for her. He just wanted her to understand that together, they were stronger, even than Harrison.

"We're not legally his guardians. Technically, he is a child of the government Zhànshì Training Program."

"And the second you say you want to," Jacob whispered for only her to hear, even if the place was bugged, "we take him and run. I will ensure that Harrison never finds us."

He could see how tempting the thought was to her. But ultimately, she changed her mind. "And Shannon? I can't leave my little sister."

"Then we take her too."

"And Ame and the rest? I won't do it, Jacob. I won't leave them, not one of them. As long as I'm involved, I can ensure they're taken care of."

"And what about when they finish training?" Jacob argued.

"Then they'll be adults, like you and me, fighting for their country, just like we do. We all make sacrifices in this war, don't we?"

The memories shifted. The same apartment, but both of them were older now.

"Tell me you didn't?" Jacob pleaded. "Tell me you didn't do what I think you did?" He already knew what the answer would be.

Her eyes filled with tears. "Council showed me the research. Being born of two parents with the link increases the odds of being in range by over thirty percent!"

"Then tell them to do it themselves!" he seethed.

"I signed the papers, Jacob."

"Taint it, Kristen!" he screamed, knocking down a vase and shattering it on the floor. He had never used this intensity with her before. "That is my child too!"

"You didn't even know about it until now."

"But I had a right to be a part of this decision!"

"You're not legally a citizen of this country. You're an insert. And you don't even exist in the Kingdoms!"

"I'm not talking about legality here, Kristen. I'm talking about morality. How dare you make this decision without me?"

"And what if I had waited? What would that have changed? You are an agent whose work is irreplaceable. I'm an asset of the government who doesn't get to leave even if I want to. What kind of alternative life were you hoping to give this baby? At least this way, I get to be the one who raises it."

"You're thinking only short term again. You are talking about turning our *baby* into another government agent!"

"And what else would it be, born from the two of us? Jacob, I told you I never wanted to have kids again. We weren't supposed to. But it happened. And there weren't many better alternatives here. I still can't leave Eli. I still won't abandon the other Zhànshì. The only way to do it all is for this child to be a Zhànshì too. Don't you see that?"

Jacob sat on the bed, putting his head in his hands. "Council is twisted. They're all as bad as Harrison. This country, this whole world is tainted. And we're right in the thick of it."

Kristen allowed the silence to sink in before she sat beside him and responded. "And what if this baby is it? What if our child turns out to be the hero who saves us all? Wouldn't that be worth it?"

He looked up to face her. He wanted to be angry. How was it that she always chose Harrison's plan? Even when Jacob had convinced her of Harrison's weaknesses? Even when he had pointed out the plan's flaws? Even when she knew that Harrison had gone too far in so many ways? She still always followed him, and that broke Jacob's heart more than he could convey.

"You still believe in his plan. Even after everything."

"Of course I do!" Kristen replied. "Maybe Eli's not the one. But he's still a fighter. Maybe Shannon's not it. But she could have been if it weren't for the accident. I am committed to this fight, Jacob. We have to win the war. We have to win for freedom."

"Even if it means sacrificing the lives of our children?"

She watched him for a time before replying. "There was never a war in history, for good or bad, that did not cost the sacrifice of the children. What makes us any better than the whole of history? I'll sacrifice myself willingly. And ultimately, our child will have her own choice. But it is our duty to give her every possible advantage. I don't see any better way than this."

Despite the anger, despite the pain, a look of hope entered Jacob's eyes. "Her?"

Kristen smiled. "We're going to have a little girl."

The memories shifted, several years after Ava was born.

Jacob made it back home every chance he got, though of course, his position in Russia made that rarer than he wished.

Still, he treasured every opportunity to see little Ava. Eli was in his teen years now and far too focused on his training to care for visits with his stepdad. Still, Jacob tried.

Ava adored him, and he loved her more than he knew was possible, his little girl.

Indeed, seeing her only twice a year was agonizing. There was not a day that passed that he did not think of her and that he did not miss her. But this was the sacrifice.

Of course, it may have been easier if they had never had a child in the first place, as they had planned. But God had His own plans, and Jacob had come to accept it for what it was.

Still, there were moments when he wanted to run away, leave behind the mission, and take his family away to safety. That was the selfish side of him, and he knew that he could not do it, but he could also not forget about the temptation either.

What would it have been like, to have a normal family? To be a normal stepfather? To have a normal relationship with his wife? To be a normal dad for his little girl? He didn't want to be a deadbeat dad. He wanted more than anything to be there, with them. Yet his calling had him elsewhere.

Still, it didn't make sense to him. Why would God send him a child that he could not have a hand in truly raising? He trusted Kristen with Ava. And from what he had seen of Zhànshì training, there was little to be afraid of there. But Jacob was far from trusting of Harrison, and he worried constantly about what that man would ultimately do to his family.

Memories shifted, years again into the future.

Sasha had been accepted as a member of the Politburo. No agent in the history of the Kingdoms had ever made it this high into enemy ranks. His nearly twenty-year placement had paid off.

The background checks were extensive. He was heavily watched for over a year. When it had all begun, he had urged a shut off in the link, not knowing what resources the Politburo would have to surveil him and not wanting to take any chances. There was no communication with his people, not in over a year.

Still, every day, he thought of his little family back home. Kristen, working her tail off to raise, not only her own children, but all of the Zhànshì in her care, acting as a sort of mother to them. Eli, now the age of twenty, was one of the top agents in the field, and Jacob couldn't have been prouder of him.

Ava had been getting into trouble with her friend Breanna, and Kristen had worried about it greatly, but Jacob could only smile. She was still a child, even in the most intensive military training program of the United Kingdoms. He was glad she had a friend to get her into trouble now and then.

All was well on his mission, and he was *this close* to claiming the prize of a title on the Politburo. So, it was a great surprise when, out for a bite to eat with friends from the leadership of Russia, Jacob saw a face he recognized from across the pub. Remington.

He should not be here. He might ruin everything. He had warned them—no contact, whatsoever. Why had they sent in an agent for a meet?

Remington's expression was grave. And ultimately, Jacob knew he would not be here unless something was seriously wrong.

"I'm going to relieve myself," Jacob told his friends. "Save my seat."

He could not risk speaking directly with Remington. He knew there were spies even now watching him, but if he could turn on the link, even for a brief period, he could get answers.

He went into the restroom and locked the door. Leaning against the wall, he closed his eyes, trying to access the link. It was a mental switch to turn off or on, but it could only be done by the individual, only for oneself, and it was not an easy mental process. He tried to find the link, scanning through every avenue of his mind, searching for a thread, anything to lead him to the front door. It took longer than he would have liked, but eventually, he found it, and managed to access the link.

"*Remington, what are you doing here?*" he asked urgently, not wanting the link to remain for any longer than it had to.

"*I'm sorry, Jacob. You know I wouldn't be here if it wasn't necessary.*"

"*Why are you here? What does Harrison want?*"

"*Not Harrison. Your wife.*"

Jacob shook his head in confusion.

"*I'm sorry, Jacob. I wish I had come sooner. And I'm afraid that what I'm about to tell you might cost your seat on the Politburo.*"

The memories went on, through the horrors of rescuing Ava. She was a mess, she was no longer herself, but she would recover. She had to make it through.

Jacob hadn't thought twice before giving up his seat. He confided what he could to Andre Volvakov, and his friend promised he would do his best to cover it all up for him. Remington had done his part to help Sasha lose the tails, but even a brief time without that watch would be enough to ensure he lost the seat. He didn't care about that anymore. None of that mattered now.

He rescued his little girl. He took her to safety in Brazil, and he would help her recover. He assured Kristen through Liam that Ava was safe now, but he could not risk telling her where they were. Still, she would be next. He would break her from Harrison's grasp, and they would never return to that man's dominion. He would protect his family above all else. That was the mission now.

Weeks passed. All Ava could talk about was getting back to training. She spoke of her test, that she was ten years old now, and she needed to go back. It was past due.

He had not told her yet that her old life was gone and that she could never have it back. It was best for her recovery to have that hope to hold onto.

She suffered from nightmares and panic attacks that he had no idea how to help with. At moments, she terrified him with the weight of her screams and terror. He started to wonder if he could ever really help her, if he could ever fix what had happened to her. No amount of therapy could ever truly remove the memory of what she had faced—the details of which he didn't know the half of.

Only Remington knew where he was, and he sometimes stopped in to check on things. He came once, in the middle of one of Ava's attacks, and Jacob was at a loss. She was inconsolable. She was erratic. She couldn't seem to tell the difference between her dream and reality. He struggled to admit the word, but she was even...dangerous. If Remington had not been there...Jacob honestly wasn't sure if he would have survived her crazed frenzy.

Remington tranquilized her. Even though it seemed so cruel to do to a ten-year-old, Jacob had been worried she would hurt them, as well as herself. Remington and Jacob sat there, Jacob holding his unconscious daughter in his lap, not wanting to admit the truth.

"She's not fine," Remington pointed out the obvious. "And I hate to be the one to say it, but I don't know if you can do enough for her on your own."

Jacob swallowed hard, not wanting to believe it.

"How often does she...?"

"Almost every night," Jacob replied, swallowing the pain. "And it's getting worse. She's not herself. What they did to her...."

Remington closed his eyes, deeply saddened. "There are ways," he said. "There are methods."

"Don't you dare try and convince me to take her back to him!" Jacob hissed through gritted teeth.

Remington looked up to face his friend, a look of genuine caring on his face. "Do you want to save her, Jacob? Or do you want to be with her? I'm sorry, friend, but I don't think they equate to the same thing right now."

Jacob shook his head angrily. "There has to be another way. Isn't there anyone else with the same technology to help her?"

Remington simply shook his head. "Not with anywhere the success that they've had. And I fear, the severity of her mental trauma...she needs far more than simple therapy."

"I'm not doing this, Remington. Not tonight." His sudden sharp tone warned his friend to change the subject.

"Then I won't press it," Remington replied soberly. "But I'm afraid you might not want to face another night like that. Perhaps you should attempt to drug her before she sleeps."

"I'm trying to wean her off all the drugs."

"Might not be the best time to face withdrawal, on top of the trauma."

"So, I should just drug her up for the rest of her life?"

Remington looked at Jacob pointedly, as if to remind Jacob that there was a better option.

"He left her there," Jacob said in a hoarse whisper. "I will never forgive him for that. And I will never again trust him with her safety."

"You don't have to," Remington replied confidently. "I was placed as her bodyguard. If you send her back, I'll never leave her side again. And I'll never let him hurt her again."

Jacob shook his head. "No, Remington, I'm not leaving her."

Remington's face touched suddenly with deep emotion. "I spoke with the Russian informant you asked me to find. The president has managed to save your spot on the Politburo. There was footage of the raid we did to save her. He released it to the Politburo, told them you had a bastard daughter and you received word she was in danger. With all her captors dead, and no log of what actually transpired, there's no one to disagree with the story the president spun. Word is the girl did not survive. You're recovering from the grief. Your place is secure."

Sasha's stomach dropped, but he sent a challenge in his voice, not wanting to accept what that might mean. "And that's supposed to tempt me?"

Remington's look was not uncaring, yet he saw right through Jacob's harsh statement. "We need this victory, Sasha. You've been working toward this end for two decades. I wish it had been me. I wish you could have stayed and been the family man like you wanted. But you had your call, and you accepted it."

Jacob's eyes flooded with tears. "Calls change."

"But yours hasn't, has it?"

Why must his friend turn his mission on him in this way? Why was Remington here, if just to ruin Jacob's chances of protecting his daughter?

"You should have saved her sooner," Jacob replied through gritted teeth, speaking the final truth that he had been holding onto for the past month.

Remington's look was one of shame. "I know that now. And I will regret it for the rest of my life. But I promise you this, Jacob, I will take that regret, and I will fuel it into a passion to protect your daughter that even you could not compete with. Give me that chance. This is my call, and I will accept it fully. But you must return and fulfill yours."

The words rang true, but it still did not make sense to him. Why did God send him a child if it was not his to raise? Why was it that he constantly seemed to be pulled toward his work, when all he wanted was to drop everything and be this girl's father?

Why did Remington get to be there for her now, like Jacob should have always been able? He had been told many times that "life was not fair." But never had it seemed so intensely cruel as it did now.

Memories shifted, only days had passed, but Sasha had made up his mind, though it was the hardest decision he'd ever made.

"I get to go back to training now?" Ava asked excitedly. "I get to see Mom? And take my test?"

The private plane was already in the air, with only the two of them in the cabin. He watched his girl with heavy eyes, wanting nothing more than to abandon all else and be there with her.

"I hope I make everyone proud!"

"You will, love," Jacob said, his heart still heavy. "I know you will."

A new thought seemed to occur to Ava, and she faced him, her eyes serious. "Are you going to stay this time, Daddy?"

Emotion choked him, and he struggled for words. It was a long time before he replied. "I want to, Ava, more than anything in the world, I want to." He paused, wishing for another way, knowing there was none. "Ava, the world we live in, it's not safe, and it's not fair for a lot of people. There are whole countries of people who don't get to be with their families. There are kids even younger than you who are rounded up and sent into the battlefield. There are people who have never tasted freedom and who don't even have any concept of what it is."

She was too young to fully comprehend what he was saying, but the depth in her eyes showed that she was trying.

"Ava, what you went through, what you lived through, there are little kids who face that kind of thing every day." The tears flooded even more fully, spilling over onto his cheeks, and seeing her tough daddy cry caused tears to enter her little eyes too. "But, kiddo, I have an opportunity to really help with that. I want nothing more than to go and be with you, your brother and your mommy. I promise you that. But Ava, there are people who need to be saved, there is a world that needs to know freedom, and Daddy has a chance that he can help that happen. I know that you're too young to fully understand what I'm saying. And you shouldn't have to answer this kind of question, not for a lot of years. But I need to ask you anyway, because whether either of us likes it or not, you're already on the path to becoming just like me.

"So even though you're too young to have to think of something this heavy, I'm going to ask you the question that no one else has given you the opportunity to answer. Your mommy and I, we have a mission to help bring freedom to the world. And Ava, we can't do it alone. So, I need to ask you, I need to ask you this question—though you shouldn't have to answer it for so much longer." The tears streamed heavily down his face, and her cheeks were almost just as tear-streaked. "Ava, will you fight for freedom with me? Will you help Mommy and Daddy in our calls? And will you answer your very own when you're old enough to receive it?"

Even as young and innocent as she was, she understood the weight of the sacrifice he was asking her to make. And it took her a time to consider before she looked up again to face him, her expression proud and confident. Then she nodded. "I will, Dad. I promise. I'll do whatever I need to do. I'll fight with you and Mom. I'll do whatever it takes."

He closed his eyes painfully, and the tears began to collect at his jawline and dampen his collar. Neither of them had any idea how much he was really asking of her. And he still believed it was unfair that someone so young should have to be asked that question; but that was the world they lived in, and that very fact was what he hoped to change.

Maybe, if he did his work well enough, if Kristen fully committed to whatever was next for her, and if Ava could make her own sacrifices in her time, then maybe *her* children would be offered a better world than the one he had to offer his little girl.

He still could not understand why God would send him a baby, then practically forbid him a chance to raise it. But he prayed that God's plan included a hopeful future for Ava, and every other innocent child like her.

It was another eight months before Jacob was able to return and check in. By then, everything had changed.

Ava was cold and unfeeling toward him when he met her on the training ground. He didn't know what to make of it. She would not even allow him a word.

Kristen broke down into tears when he finally got her alone, away from the spotlight. She was not the type to cry easily. It was clear that she had been dealing with a deep pain for a long time, and doing so alone, and he cursed that he had not been able to be there for her.

"He took her, Jacob," she said, barely audible through the tears. "He took our little girl away. He changed her. I don't know what he did. I think he warped her memories. I don't know! But he changed her." She was inconsolable and he couldn't get any straight answers from her. "It's all my fault," she cried. "It's all my fault."

All he could do was hold her through the tears, but when she was finally herself again, Jacob prepared to find answers, whatever it took.

"What are you going to do?" she asked warily. "Jacob, he'll never let you close to him. If you do anything, his people will kill you. Don't do this!"

"I'm just going to ask him a few questions," he spoke comfortingly, but if the opportunity presented itself, he would not hesitate to fire a bullet in that man's brain.

"I'm coming with you," she insisted.

"No!" he objected.

"Yes. I know you. You'll get yourself killed over this. I'm coming too."

He knew he could not stop her, and, unfortunately, he was less likely to attempt killing the General if it risked her too.

The General was out on the training ground. He finally had a prize in these kids worth his time, and that prize was Jacob's daughter.

Kristen had been right, all those years ago, before Ava was born. "What if it's our baby? What if our child is the hero? Wouldn't that be worth it?"

Jacob knew the answer to that question now. It was not worth it. Not even close.

"You're ahead by an eighth of a second," Harrison spoke pridefully to Ava as she completed another loop around the track.

He noticed Kristen and Jacob nearing the field. "Ah, Ava. Why don't you go join the others for a while? I need to have a little talk with your parents."

Ava looked up and saw what Harrison had seen. The look of disdain she gave Kristen and Jacob broke his heart. That wasn't his little girl. It was Harrison's lapdog.

Harrison signaled his bodyguards to enter in closer as Jacob and Kristen neared him. Jacob held Kristen's hand, and he could sense that she was trembling. She was terrified to face Harrison. This man could take everything from her in an instant, and he would not hesitate to do so. Every time she had ever confronted him in the past, on urging from Jacob, Harrison had pushed back, punishing her in great backlash, causing her to immediately regret it. This time was no different, as it led to him removing her as head trainer and placing her into the role of a figurehead instead.

Still, she knew there was no stopping Jacob from this confrontation, and she also knew that it was much more likely to end up with him dead if she did not go.

"Jacob, good to have you back!" Harrison spoke conversationally. "How are things on the top?"

Jacob let go of Kristen, continuing forward until Harrison's men physically stopped him. "That's close enough," Harrison said. "I really don't want to end the day with a knife in my back."

"I would aim for the heart," Jacob seethed between gritted teeth. "Tell me what you did to her, you blistering carcass!"

"Oh, well, that's not very nice. As I recall, it was you who asked me to help her. Both of you. I did the initial treatments when she first arrived, but that wasn't enough, was it? And Kristen, you asked me to perform more. You had to know there were potential side-effects."

"Don't play games with me!" Jacob yelled.

Harrison's guards reached for Jacob's gun and pulled it away from him. He could still find a way to kill Harrison without that.

"You two should be proud," Harrison spoke arrogantly. "Your daughter is the answer to all our hopes and dreams."

"What did you do to my little girl?" Jacob screamed, and the harshness of his tone surprised Harrison, though he managed to feign control.

Suddenly, Harrison's expression became serious, even mournful. "I did what was necessary," he admitted, and Jacob saw that he believed that lie. "Her feelings of anger and pain were immense. It was not something we could erase entirely. A little nudge in a different direction was necessary."

Jacob let out a breath of surprise. Harrison's men no longer physically held him back, but they blocked the path to the General, and he had two more guards close by him for added protection.

"You made her hate *us*?"

"Not exactly," Harrison played with words again. "I made her love me. What else happened, where else her feelings turned, that was out of my control."

"I don't believe you!" Jacob hissed.

"How could you do this to me?" This time, Kristen was the one to speak, and her tone was one of deep horror.

Harrison looked up to face her, and his sad expression was genuine. "I never intended to hurt you, Kristen, but sacrifices needed to be made. Ava is the key, the missing piece. I need her loyalty. I had no intention of taking her from you. But I had to ensure she would remain loyal to me, above all else. As I said, whatever side-effects may have occurred were out of my control."

"I'll kill you for this," Jacob muttered, and the guards moved to hold him again. Jacob did not attempt to fight them off. "I swear, Harrison, you will pay for this!"

Harrison faced Jacob head on. Still, that look of regret was surprisingly genuine. "I already am. Every day I pay for the choices that I have been forced to make. But that's the world we live in. We were handed a broken machine and asked to fix it. Sacrifices must be made. Your daughter is a minimal one on the list, I assure you."

"I'll never forgive you for this, Harrison," Kristen cried, stepping up closer and being stopped by another guard. "I will never forgive you. And I will never trust you again."

The look he gave her was deeply sorrowful. Jacob could see that Harrison regretted it. So then, why couldn't he just choose to be better, if he always regretted the choices he made?

Still, despite his sorrowful look, his words were painful and pointed. "I don't need your trust, Kristen. Or your love." Then he smiled, a pained, regretful smile that said he was even now suffering over his choices. "I have Ava's."

The memories faded. They were back in the study. All eyes slowly turned to Sasha, who looked deeply pained. It could not have been easy to relive those memories in full color, with every bit of emotion. And of course, to share it with five other people.

Jackson noticed as Ava's hand slowly moved to Sasha's forearm, which was resting in his lap, and she held on tightly as if to offer comfort. Jackson was glad to see that she no longer hid her face from the rest of them. All he wanted was to take her in his arms and tell her she had nothing to be ashamed of. But of course, now was not a time for that.

"The wounds of the past make the scars of today," Sizwe said, pulling the attention of the group back to him. "The men and women in this room carry deep scars of painful wounds. But the scars you carry cannot be seen by the physical eye alone. Today, you had no choice but to vulnerably share your deepest wounds with friends, with strangers and with enemies alike. This one event may not have been enough to heal the rifts in the relationships in this room. But to witness another's wounds, and to share your own in a way that allows you to experience each other's pains as your own...it is not something that can be done lightly. It is my hope that you will recognize what you have been through together this day and work to repair what you can."

Sizwe looked at each of them individually. "I am proud to call you friends. And although it is not necessary at this time for you to become my brothers and sisters, as Jackson has, there may be a time for that in the future. What I have learned this day has been enough. And I hope that you will leave with similar enlightenment.

"A dreamwalking exercise where you experience so many others' lives can be even more exhausting than most. And for a day, I would bid you simply rest. Soon enough, we will talk of the war and of your place in the fight beside my people. Until then, rest."

The room went dark as the dream faded into sleep.

8

Virulent Complexity

Jackson was the first to awaken. He had been through this before and he had been the first to drink, so it made sense that his daze would wear off first. The others all looked so peaceful there, sleeping.

He felt a strange new bond with these people as he looked at each one of them in turn. It wasn't the same as with Sizwe. With these, he had only seen fragments, whereas with Sizwe, he had practically lived an entire other life. Still, he understood each of these people in a new way. He cared for them more than he previously had—even Sasha and Ava, whom he had already cared for deeply.

Sasha was the next to open his eyes. He noticed how Ava now leaned on his chest, asleep, his arm around her shoulder, and he smiled. Jackson could imagine the years of pain surrounding Ava—he had felt so much of it firsthand through the dreams. Yet now he was able to fully commit himself to his daughter, like he had always wanted.

"I have you to thank for this," Sasha whispered, surprising Jackson with how he seemed to read his thoughts. "What you've done in Russia. The revolution. Everything we've accomplished. And ultimately, you taking my place as a greater emissary there...I don't need to be there anymore, not like I used to. I can be here now. And I have you to thank for that."

Jackson offered a smile, but inside he found himself wondering if that meant he would spend the next twenty to thirty years sacrificing for the cause before he could ever enjoy the fruit of his labor.

Then again, that was the price to be one of the greats, wasn't it? Jackson chose it again, in that moment, just as he did with every passing day. It was worth it. No matter how difficult. It was worth it.

Sasha moved, leaving Ava there on the sofa asleep. "Would you mind?" Sasha said, as if asking him to stand and walk to the other side of the room with him. "It will be best if she wakes up without us too near."

Jackson stood up quickly. "Of course!"

Ava was the next to awaken. At first, she looked confused, but she soon sat up straight with understanding. And then, she must have remembered again what she had just faced, because her face became grave, and she once more bowed her head in embarrassment.

As soon as the others were fully awake, Sizwe reentered the room, saying nothing at first, but walking to his armchair and taking a seat. "You have been asleep for a long time, but I believe that more rest would do you well. Please, make your way to the rooms provided and you may sleep."

Everyone went, one by one, slowly making their way to the door. Ava left first, not speaking to anyone. Sasha followed behind her, though he stopped at the door long enough to greet both Mikel and Ella as they neared. None of them said anything, but Sasha put his hand out to each of them, and Jackson witnessed the exchange, knowing that there were some things far beyond words. And when he made it to the door, he shared similar moments with both Mikel and Ella.

It occurred to Jackson as he left the room toward his personal quarters, that he was supposed to return home to Russia in the morning, but that was the last thing he wanted. There was so much to be done here. And this...this was home.

Still, he thought of Sasha, the decades of service, and he swallowed his desires. He would go where he was called, however painful. The price of greatness was high indeed. But he would pay it again and again, no matter the cost. He could only pray it would all truly be worth it in the end.

Jackson was exhausted, but for whatever reason, his mind was too busy to sleep. Thoughts of his departure had him too agitated to rest.

He walked from his private quarters and down the hall, taking in the familiarity of this place, which he had only ever physically been to once before. Yet, he held countless shared memories in these halls, talking to friends, working toward the freedom of a people.

The door was open to the sitting room, and Jackson wondered if he would find Sizwe inside. He would like to have a good talk with his brother. But it was not Sizwe who he found within; somehow, he always found himself drawn to wherever she was.

Ava sat in the corner of the room, on the floor against the wall, reading a book. "Ava," Jackson murmured. "What are you doing in here?"

She looked up at him, and he saw the exhaustion in her face. "I'm reading," she replied plainly.

"In a room full of couches...you're on the floor...reading...in the middle of the night."

"Yes."

"Why?"

The look she gave him was hard to interpret—almost like a snide, disappointed embarrassment. "Do you even have to ask?"

Understanding touched him. Nearing her, he crouched down and sat on the floor in front of her. "Nightmares," he replied quietly.

"They gave me a room with Sasha. It was nice of them. With shared rooms...there's no one I'd rather be with. Sasha's fast asleep. But I can't...."

"You can't sleep with other people in the room," Jackson offered.

And for some reason, her jaw tightened in what looked like anger. It soon melted into something else entirely. "Was I the only one who was humiliated by that thing today?"

Jackson's eyebrows pulled together. The thought had never even crossed his mind. "Humiliated? Why on earth would you be?"

She shook her head with seeming disdain. "Okay, fine. We saw the heartbreaks of Ella's past. We saw your reasons for defecting. We saw why Mikel is so cool, and why Sasha wasn't there in my life. But what about my little vision?"

"I understand," Jackson offered. "I'm sure it was hard to live through all that again."

"It's not that," she said quickly, proving he had truly no idea what she was referring to. "I live through those things every single night! But to have all of you see it...?" She said it like it was the worst thing in the world. "It was humiliating."

"What exactly are you ashamed of?" he asked her, truly not understanding why she felt this way. "Kyle's death? How Eli manipulated you?"

She looked away, shrugging her shoulders, and he could see in every movement how embarrassed she was. "All of it. But mostly...the nightmares."

The nightmares. That was how she referred to her memories of her time in Russia, the horrors that she faced.

"What about it?" Jackson prompted. He did not want to make her think he didn't care about her feelings. Of course he did. But she was wrong about this!

She struggled to look at him, though eventually she managed. "I didn't want anyone to ever see that. It's horrible enough facing it on my own. But now, all of you know exactly what terrifies me...everything that happened in that time...." There was so much shame in her eyes, and it broke his heart.

"Ava, listen to me," Jackson pleaded softly, holding her attention. "Believe me when I tell you that you have absolutely nothing to be ashamed of."

She gulped hard, unable to hold his gaze. "I don't think any of you will ever look at me the same," she muttered, and he could see how much that thought pained her. "I'm broken. And I've had to carry that with me all these years. But I could always at least choose to be strong, or pretend to be strong. Now...now all of you know the truth. And yes, it's humiliating."

"Ava," Jackson whispered, feeling the depth of her pain and not having the slightest idea how to help her. "You're right. I'll never see you the same. Just like I'll never see Ella, Mikel or even Sasha like I used to.

But it's not because I think you're weak. It's because now I know how strong you are."

She swallowed her pain, then turned to face him. He didn't know if his words had gotten through to her, but he desperately hoped they did. She closed her eyes, breathing deeply. "I was finally starting to be myself again...now I feel worse, more broken than ever."

When she eventually opened her eyes again, her look was plaintive, and she confided in a helpless whisper, "I'm...so...tired."

"I'll ask Sizwe for a private room for you—" he started.

"No! Please. I don't need to ask for favors. That's just more proof...."

"Listen," Jackson said caringly. "You have to stop doing this to yourself. It isn't weak to ask for the things you need."

She shook her head. "I don't want to ask for anything, Jackson. I just..." her eyes tightened, and she looked almost like she would break when she admitted, "I just want to go home with you."

His heart clenched within his chest, and he wanted nothing more than to give her everything she wanted. But the Committee would never let her back. It wasn't an option anymore, and they both knew that.

Still, he couldn't begin to explain how much those words meant to him. He moved closer to her, putting his hands on her arms and leaning in. He closed his eyes and kissed her forehead softly, then remained there, lowering his head enough to rest his forehead on hers.

"I don't want you to leave," she said weakly. And he had never wanted anything more than to stay there with her now.

And now, he knew he was facing the cost. It couldn't be as easy as fighting off homesickness. No, it had to be as painful as leaving Ava here, when all he wanted was to stay there with her.

He didn't know how to tell her that he couldn't stay. Fortunately, he didn't have to.

"I know you have to go," Ava whispered, and he felt her breath on his lips. He could not seem to move away. "But...I want to be with you. I would choose you, Jackson, if I could, right now. I promise, I would choose you."

His stomach burned with a desire he had not felt in so long, a real desire to kiss her, to hold her in his arms, to have her right there with him. He fought the urge. It was the last thing she needed right now, to be kissed by a man when being haunted by her nightmares.

"I would choose you too," Jackson whispered. He felt her hand go to his arm, holding on tightly, and he flexed involuntarily. "I promise, I would."

They remained like that for a long time. Jackson fought the pain in his knees as they started falling asleep from the awkward tension. He didn't mind the pain. He didn't want to move, and neither did she. Her hand moved from his arm, then rested on his chest. It was everything he could do not to kiss her. Both of their eyes were already closed, and they were so close.... But it wasn't what she needed right now, even if both of them wanted it desperately.

Eventually, after a long time, his knees gave in, and he was forced to move. Ava pulled away then too, as if thinking he had for some reason regretted being so close. He hadn't. He would have stayed there forever if his tainted knees hadn't failed him.

When they were both seated again, and space had been put between them, he took in her pale skin and baggy eyes. "You look exhausted," Jackson noted, still in a soft whisper. "We should get you to bed."

"I can't—" she started to object, but he stopped her.

"I was given private quarters. You can take mine. I'll room with Sasha."

She started to object further, but he wouldn't hear of it. He stood and offered his hand to help her up. She retrieved her book, *Pride and Prejudice*, the Russian translation, the one he had given her. "Did you bring that on our trip to find the Zhànshì?" Jackson asked, helping her to her feet.

She gave an awkward half smile, not wanting to answer it.

"Good," he said simply. "I hope you like my notes."

"I already cherish every one," she said seriously.

He gave her a long, deeply loving look. "You have no idea how many times I've read the version of *Les Misérables* you gave me, how much I cherish that."

Her smile was genuine when she looked up at him as they stood there, neither of them really wanting this moment to be over, for he was going back to Russia far too soon. "Thank you," she said hoarsely.

"For what?"

She breathed out before replying. "For never looking at me like I'm broken, even when you know I am."

He could have argued once more that she was not broken. Instead, he nodded genuinely, hoping the look he gave now conveyed how deeply he cared about her. "You're welcome."

Ava was settled in her new room, and Jackson left her there, following her instructions to her previous shared quarters. He entered the room and quietly made his way to the empty bed across from Sasha's. Jackson lay down, appreciating how the pillow smelled like Ava. He could not help smiling, breathing in deeply, thinking of Ava, longing for more time.

He had only barely closed his eyes when a grumpy, tired voice noted with suspicion, "You're not my daughter."

The group sat around the commissary, sharing one table. Only Ava had not joined them yet. The air in the room was so different from what it had been before. The new respectful understanding that they shared for one another seemed to have built a deeper closeness than Jackson had anticipated for such a short session.

They sat talking, teasing and laughing as if they were old friends. Even Ella looked startlingly different. She was still grumpy, as had become her nature, but she was less bitter towards these specific individuals.

"She avoids any foods where you can feel the seeds," Mikel teased his friend.

"The texture is gross!" Ella explained. "I don't like food in the first place. I only eat it to survive. I don't want anything that's chewy or mushy."

"Is there any part of life that you *do* find pleasure in?" Sasha asked, but he said it so lovingly, and with that kind smile of his, it was impossible to be offended by it—even for Ella.

"Yes!" she replied swiftly. Then she struggled to think up an answer for a long time. "I take pleasure in pointing out other people's flaws," she concluded.

"This much we knew," Jackson said with a chuckle. "By the way, Mikel, how's that zit of yours doing today?"

"Shut *up*," Mikel pleaded, glaring at Jackson.

Sasha and Jackson enjoyed a bout of laughter. Even Ella was smiling widely. And although Mikel was glaring, it was clear that he enjoyed the comment and the caring jabs from his new friend.

Mikel was first to break from the moment, glancing past Sasha and Jackson to the entrance of the large commissary. "There's our girl," he noted pleasantly, then raised a hand to wave her over.

The room was filled with so many unfamiliar faces—at least, to her—and Jackson could sense Ava's hesitation when he looked at her, though she managed a smile.

They all knew what that meant.

Jackson stood from the table and went to meet her by the door. "Good morning," he said pleasantly.

That look of overt embarrassment still emanated in her demeanor. He wondered how long she had waited by the door, working up the courage to enter before finally coming in.

"How did you sleep?" he asked as he led her to the table, hoping the change of topic would help her forget her concerns.

"I slept well. Thank you. For the room and everything."

"Of course," he nodded caringly as they arrived at the table. When they were close enough that the others could hear, Jackson spoke again. "It's no wonder you couldn't sleep in the same room as Sasha. He snores like a jet plane."

Sasha chuckled, as did the others, before greeting Ava. "Good morning, love!" Sasha said happily.

Ava sat on the bench, between Jackson and Sasha. Still, Jackson could sense her hesitation, that stiffness of every movement while she attempted to act cheerful. She was afraid to face these people, with all they now knew about her. But she had nothing to be afraid of.

Jackson placed his hand on her knee and squeezed gently, hoping to comfort her. It was meant as an encouraging gesture, and he hadn't really considered the romantic connotations until he saw how Sasha noticed the movement and watched with a sideways glance.

Ava looked up at Jackson too, with momentary surprise, but grateful for the support. Strangely, even knowing what Sasha must be thinking, and even considering how Ava was likely to take this new gesture, he did not remove his hand from her knee, and, if anything, he squeezed tighter.

"Crazy day, yesterday," Ella spoke directly to Ava. Though her words were far from a real apology, everyone there sensed the meaning, the offered olive branch, and Ava took it.

"Yes. It was," she agreed, looking at Ella with a comprehending expression.

"I, for one," Mikel broke in with a light touch of humor, "will never forget those highlights about that Mikel guy. I mean, wow!"

The surprising comment had everyone at the table laughing. Jackson decided that Mikel had that same ability that Zak possessed, to lighten even the heaviest of loads with his sometimes tasteful, and sometimes extremely distasteful, humor.

"When do you leave?" Ava asked Jackson, when the laughter had settled down some.

He smiled down at her, thinking of those quiet moments he had shared with her last night, and wishing for so many more. "I'm actually not sure anymore," Jackson admitted happily. "Sizwe requested that I stay and help with negotiations for a few more days. The Committee agreed."

"For what?" she asked with surprise.

The energy at the table went tense as everyone else considered what she did not yet know. Sasha was ultimately the one to answer. "Eli is here," he admitted carefully. "Council has decided that it's important to help Africa win a few victories against the Republic. They want to deal with Sizwe directly and discuss terms for a short-term alliance."

"Oh," was all she could seem to say.

"Sizwe has no interest in any sort of serious alliance with the Kingdoms," Jackson explained. "But in the short-term, he could really use the help. If they're going to survive at all, this negotiation is vital. He knows I've dealt with the General in the past. He's hoping I can help him with a careful agreement now."

"Don't worry," Ella cut in as if to comfort Ava, "I've been assured that this will ultimately help us to defeat Eli. It's just a short-term move to gain more power in Africa. And when we're in a better position here, we'll be more prepared to take him down."

Jackson was relieved to hear the girl speak the words they had spent some hours explaining to Ella. It seemed they had at some point in their long conversation this morning convinced her of the wisdom of this move, even if it seemed like a step backward to her.

Ava nodded in understanding. "Okay," she replied, and though she smiled, it was clear there was much she held inside.

He lovingly rubbed his thumb along the side of her knee, hoping to offer support. Surprising both Jackson and Sasha—who still watched with a sideways glance—Ava moved her hand to meet Jackson's where it rested on her knee, and she gripped it tightly in her own.

"A-anyway," Jackson said, suddenly struggling to speak with the intensity of his emotions in that moment. "It gives me a few more days here," he offered, stroking the side of her hand now as he held it tightly. "And I'm grateful for that much."

"Me too," she admitted softly.

"Is Ava here?" Eli asked, ignoring the beginning request Sizwe had given.

Jackson opened his mouth to respond in the negative, but Sizwe answered before he could. "Yes," he replied plainly.

Jackson gritted his teeth in frustration. Sizwe had never spoken untruth, and he was not about to start now, but he could have kept his mouth shut and allowed Jackson to tell the lie instead.

Eli nodded, a somber look on his face. Jackson couldn't help the sudden flash that went through his mind—a memory of Sasha confronting the General, and Harrison's deep remorse as he pondered on what he considered to be "a necessary evil." Eli's expression now looked just the same.

"How is she?" he begged for more.

Jackson was not about to fuel the abuser on news of the victim. Eli had lost the right to know anything about his sister. "I'd like to discuss your garrison," Jackson changed the subject. "We understand that your army is on the doorstep, prepared to aid Africa."

"Come on, Jackson," Eli pleaded. "You won't give me anything?"

"Not about that," Jackson replied sternly. "But regarding the terms of this agreement, I'm all ears, and would be happy to discuss it further."

Eli watched Jackson with obvious frustration. "You have no idea the pressure I was under to keep her in check," Eli spoke somberly. "If I had not done what I did, the Ava we know would have been erased."

"Africa has been acquiring large sums of money, and they are prepared to pay you in straight cash for the aid you offer," Jackson said, though it was a struggle not to confront Eli on this. The man should have found another way.

Eli shook his head with sudden scorn, but he managed to control his anger within moments, returning to a look of sadness when he spoke. "You have no concept of what I'm up against, Davis."

"I have some idea," Jackson replied quickly, and immediately regretted his fast words. He would not indulge Eli. He could not let these negotiations turn to a discussion about Ava.

"I have been protecting Ava longer than you've known her," Eli said, still somehow managing to keep his tone emotionless, though Jackson knew there was hatred behind it.

"Africa is prepared to make a generous payment," Jackson said, turning to Sizwe and signaling.

Sizwe slid a piece of paper across to the General.

Eli didn't even look down. Instead, he met Jackson's stare and held it. "I don't want your money," he said in a low voice.

"I think you'll find that the sum is more than generous," Sizwe objected.

Eli did not break his gaze from Jackson. "I don't care about your riches. With the Republic weakening, the United Kingdoms are close to securing the title of wealthiest conglomerate in the world. I *don't* want your money."

"There are, of course, other options we would be willing to consider," Sizwe began.

Still, Eli didn't deign to look at the noble statesman, and the fact prompted Jackson to reciprocate the steely gaze. Eli still saw the fight in Africa as a tiny, meaningless rebellion. He still thought of Sizwe as nothing. He was only here to face Jackson.

"Council had their own agenda when it came to the threats I made to you," Eli said in a harsh tone. "And unfortunately, I was not permitted to demolish your nation like I could have in an instant. However, Council has no control over the decision I make here today. I don't want anything trivial you have to offer me. I just want to see Ava."

Sizwe huffed in surprise. "You'll send an entire army to fight our battle if we simply allow you a moment with one girl?" he asked, practically in horror.

"Never going to happen," Jackson replied, holding the strong glare of his opponent, unwavering.

Eli leaned in toward Jackson, attempting to be more menacing. "I don't want to hurt her, Jackson. This isn't an attempt to take her back. I just want to see her."

Jackson held that stare for a long time more. He could see Sizwe out of the corner of his eyes, looking dumfounded and at a loss. He did not know the mercurial, melodramatic Eli like Jackson did.

He just wanted to see her, did he?

Jackson eventually broke his gaze, reaching for his mobile and finding a picture with Ava in it. Sasha had one of the servers take a picture of the mansion occupants on Zak's birthday. Jackson zoomed in to Ava in the picture, then slid it across the table for Eli. "There. Now, let's talk about the garrison."

Eli surprisingly did seem to enjoy the photo, despite his immediate anger. In these moments, it was clear to Jackson that Eli truly did love his sister. But his sick, twisted manner of loving her was unacceptable.

"How's her arm doing?" he asked with genuine concern.

"Good as new," Jackson answered simply.

Eventually, after studying it for some time, Eli slid the mobile back to Jackson, and looked up to face him sternly. "Five minutes with Ava, and the garrison is yours. No other payment necessary."

"No," Jackson objected.

Eli stood, and pushed his chair back. "Take it or leave it." He made his way out of the meeting room, joining his men outside and returning to his camp.

Jackson cursed to himself in frustration. There was no getting through to that man. No matter how strong Jackson was, no matter how much he tried, there was no reasoning with Eli. He either had his way, or he left them cold.

Jackson eventually looked up to face Sizwe. Only when he saw the look of deep concern on his brother's face did it occur to him how trivial this seemed. They were talking about the lives of millions of innocent people, the freedoms of nations that had been nearly twenty years subjugated. The countless lives of Sizwe's friends, brothers and sisters for this cause was just a grain of sand in a vast desert of sacrifices that would be required. This garrison could be a major turning point. And all it would require was for a girl to spend five minutes with her brother?

Sizwe eventually met Jackson's gaze. "I understand what she has been through," Sizwe said helplessly. And it was true. He had lived through much of it as if it were his own memories. "And in truth, I feel genuine remorse for reopening those wounds in such a painful way, humiliating her in the group session, when she should have been afforded a private dreamwalking experience. For the rest of you I believe it was a healing experience, though in her case it brought out all the negative aspects that I initially worried about. She has been through a great deal of trauma surrounding her brother. I understand why you hesitate. But...."

Jackson looked down, remembering countless faces, countless people in Africa who had sacrificed far more than what they were talking about.

"Is there no other way to reason with him?" Sizwe asked, sensing Jackson's deep dilemma.

Jackson once more searched for answers, for anything. But eventually, he came to that same realization. "No. There isn't. If we don't give him what he wants, he will never send the garrison."

"And if we did concede. Would he remain true to his word?"

Jackson sighed heavily, strangely wishing that this answer was different too. "Yes. He will. He will honor his word, if we do as he asks."

Sizwe nodded, a deep sadness in his eyes. He knew what Jackson was struggling against. But Jackson also knew what Sizwe was thinking. He thought of his own child, his brothers and sisters, his own parents, and innumerable more. He imagined each of their sacrifices. What was being asked of Ava could not hold a candle to what was being considered now. Yet...Sizwe could not ask Jackson to see the bigger picture. He could not ask him to make this sacrifice.

"We should return to the base," Sizwe said, not pressing Jackson. Still, Jackson knew the thoughts behind the words he left unspoken.

Jackson could not say anything to Sizwe on their return to the base. He could hardly meet the man's gaze. In the vastness of the war they were facing, his problem here was so trivial. But when he thought of asking Ava to do this.... He couldn't do it.

And yet...how could he not?

Confiding in Sasha was difficult. As a father, which had become his principal role now, Sasha would never allow it, never even think of it. "He has his own motives," Sasha spoke assuredly. "I don't know what he'll do. But I know him—he has become Harrison. Every time you trust that man, he twists the knife in your back and bends it to his will. He will plant a tracker on her, or do something to the chip, or...I don't know! He'll take advantage of the opportunity one way or another. Harrison's entire plan centers on Ava. You think they're just going to let you keep her?"

"I know that, Sasha, but you have to understand what—"

"I can't believe you're even considering this!" Sasha said in a heated tone. "After what you saw...how can you even think of subjecting her to his will again?"

"I know, Sasha, but—"

"No! You saw a glimpse of what she and I have faced at the hand of the Generals. And that should have been enough! If you had experienced the half of what I've seen by their hand—"

"And *you* haven't seen what *I've* seen!" Jackson shouted. Then, controlling himself, he said carefully, "You haven't seen what Africa has been through. This could be a turning point for them."

Sasha looked up to face him somberly. Then with deep sadness he asked, "Hasn't she been through enough?"

★ ★ ★ ★ ★

Ava sat in her new favorite corner of the small study, reading a book of African legends that she had found on the shelf. Now that she had finished the only book she had brought with her—twice—she would have to get creative. She did not speak the language, and had to use a mobile translation for every new sentence, but it was an interesting sort of study, and one she enjoyed.

The door creaked open, and Ava looked up, expecting Jackson. She was surprised when Sizwe was the one who came inside.

He glanced around the room, noticed her sitting there on the floor, and his eyes furrowed in surprise. "I see you've made my study into your little nook," he noted.

Ava hopped to her feet, feeling suddenly embarrassed. She set the book back on its shelf and started toward the door. "I'm sorry! I won't come in here again."

"I did not ask you to go," he responded.

She took that as a command to stay, stopping abruptly in front of the door, not knowing what to do.

Sizwe was intimidating. He was quiet and hard to read. He was the leader of the African rebellions, and an estimable man. She felt altogether...*inadequate* in his presence.

"You may sit a while," he offered. "The couches are quite comfortable." This he said pointedly, noting how she had strangely been sitting on the floor.

Not knowing what else to do, she obeyed, taking a seat on one of the sofas. Sizwe crossed the room to his chair and sat down, closing his eyes and breathing deeply. She watched him do this for several minutes before breaking the silence by noting, "You're meditating."

A smile came to his lips, though his eyes remained shut. "I was attempting to."

"Jackson says you taught him how."

"He did learn from me. In a way."

"He says it helps him with stress."

Sizwe gave a simple nod of his head.

"How do you do it?" she asked, the thought not even occurring to her that talking to him might be interrupting his meditation.

Sizwe opened his eyes, then watched her. After a time, he spoke, "You are weak." The words felt like an instant jab to the stomach, though he wasn't done. "And you desire to be strong again."

He hadn't meant to insult her. He was simply stating the truth. Ava nodded, not knowing how to respond verbally.

"You have faced much trauma and pain," Sizwe noted. "Yet I have known many who faced more and managed to remain intact."

Ava swallowed painfully. Once again, she worked to remind herself that he wasn't trying to offend her. He just spoke the truth, whether it hurt or not. "So how did they do it?" she asked, attempting to mask her vexation with a question.

He leaned forward, steepling two fingers on his lips as he considered. "There are many ways to remain strong," he said thoughtfully. "Ultimately, it connects back to one thing: inner peace. If you truly understand yourself, you can withstand anything."

"I had a friend who told me that once," Ava said suddenly, thinking of Lionel. "Actually, he said you can withstand 'anyone,' but I think he meant the same thing."

Sizwe gave one simple nod of his head. "Do you believe you know who you are, Ava Altman?"

She breathed out heavily, considering. She wanted the answer to be yes. She wanted to say she had herself totally figured out, and that Lionel's one statement to her had been enough. But after months of healing, in one day it had crumbled apart and become clear again that she was a mess. She was falling apart, and she hadn't the slightest idea how to put herself back together, let alone what "back together" even meant.

"No. Unfortunately, I don't think I do," she admitted somberly.

"No," Sizwe agreed. "I think not."

She waited for him to give her some grand answer, but he left it hanging there. "So, what do I do to find inner peace?" Ava asked hopefully. "How do I come to truly know myself?"

A slight smile came to the corner of his lips. "That is the age-old question," he said proudly. "And once you know enough to ask the question, well, then you're well on the path to finding the answer."

Ava's eyes furrowed in confusion. "That doesn't really give me an answer," she noted with distaste.

"No, it does not," Sizwe agreed. "But you have begun to ask the question."

Ava sighed heavily. This conversation was not going as she had hoped it would. "How did Jackson find inner peace?" she asked, as a new thought occurred to her. "He's different now. He seems like he's really...found himself. How did he do it?"

"Perhaps you should ask him that question yourself," Sizwe suggested, vexing her even further. Still, he gave something of an answer. "From what I observed of him, he changed after his first time dreamwalking. He saw his life journey, where he had been. He thought of his goals, and where he wanted to end. He then witnessed a life that was not his own. And then...he made a decision. He found himself, and he chose himself—that is, he decided what he wanted to be. And he has not wavered since then, from what I see."

Ava nodded in deep consideration, thinking of her conversation with Jackson about how he had gained his wisdom. "My experience dreamwalking wasn't so pleasant," Ava admitted bitterly.

Sizwe nodded and there was a touch of regret in his expression. "You faced the loss of agency and the feelings of violation that I mentioned was a danger for a group session. I am sorry that your experience was so unfortunate."

"Maybe it would have been different if the others hadn't been there. But as it is...all I got from it was more fear and more shame."

Sizwe scowled. "Then you weren't paying attention."

Again, she was provoked by his bluntness. "Pretty sure I was," she replied coolly, sounding more like Ella, or her old self, than she would have liked.

He shook his head. "No. You were not."

Ava glared at him, suddenly disliking this man.

"If you had been paying attention, you would have seen what I did."

"Oh yeah? And what's that?" The defiance in her tone was now unveiled, and it caused him to smile.

"I witnessed the hero's journey," he replied earnestly. "At every stage."

Ava's eyes tightened as she considered. "The hero's journey..." she muttered.

He nodded simply. "Your friend Mikel. Jackson. Sasha. Even Ella, though she is still very young and her journey will require a great amount of healing."

"So, the guys are fine, but Ella and I are messed up. Is that it?"

"No," he objected. "But you have not found your inner peace. Not like the others have. You are both younger than the men. There is still time."

"And what if there isn't?" Ava objected. "I've been weak long enough, haven't I? This war is raging in full force. The abilities I have could make a real difference. I don't have time to sit around, moping my life away until I find this inner peace you speak of."

He smiled gently. "The hero's journey is different for everyone, but certain points look the same for all. Hopes and dreams. Trials. Overcoming. And great victories. As well as terrible losses."

"I've been stuck in the trials for a lot of years now," Ava sulked bitterly.

"The journey is not one straight line. The landmarks come in ebbs and flows. You will face victories, as you have in your life, and you will face more obstacles, which you will have to overcome before you experience great victory once more."

She considered that for a time, remembering the so-called "journey of her life" and trying to see this pattern he spoke of. "I was best when I was with Lionel," she observed, almost to herself. "When he was teaching me to lead the Kingdoms."

"That was a time of great victory, yes," he agreed.

"And now...I'm stuck again."

"Now," he disagreed, "you are facing the greatest obstacle you have ever had to overcome—your own mind. You will not win this battle, not until you discover your inner peace."

Ava sighed in frustration. "And you don't have any tips on how to do that?" she asked in discouragement.

"I have many," Sizwe replied, surprising her.

"Oh... Well, can you tell me some?"

Sizwe smiled. "Perhaps, in time."

"I thought we just established that I don't have time!"

"You have heard the saying by Lao Tzu, 'When the student is ready the teacher will appear.'"

"Yeah, so? I'm ready! Are we gonna do this, or what?"

Sizwe chuckled softly to himself. "When the student is ready."

"I'm ready, okay?" she pleaded. "What do I have to do to convince you?"

"Be ready, and I will be convinced."

Ava huffed in annoyance. "Why does Jackson like you so much, again?"

Sizwe chuckled once more. "It is clear why he likes you. Your impatience is...entertaining."

"Well, thanks for all the tips and tricks, old man."

He nodded, as if to say, "you're welcome," deliberately ignoring the sarcasm in her tone. Then, he closed his eyes, leaned back in his seat, and began to meditate once more.

Only then did it occur to her that he hadn't even bothered to answer the simple question she had asked in the first place. That entire chat, and she still didn't even know how to meditate.

☆ ☆ ☆ ☆ ☆

Jackson struggled for words when the group sat around the table. He should ask her privately, give her a chance to object without embarrassment, but Sasha had told him simply, "If you ask her, she will say yes, no matter who else is there. Let the others give their two cents."

Still, it didn't sit right.

"So, what does he want?" Mikel urged Jackson to explain the strange negotiations that had occurred.

Jackson looked at Ava, across from him in the sitting room, wishing for all others to be gone right now. If only he could explain to her why he was asking this. If only he could help her understand why he was even considering this.

"He wants to meet with Ava," Sasha spoke somberly, when it became clear that Jackson could not utter the words.

Ella sat back in her seat, grunting and throwing her hands in the air. "Here we go again! We all know how this ends. He either wins her over, or he somehow convinces her to join him. Then we're all screwed, and she goes back to being his slave."

"It's not gonna go down that way," Jackson said with a stern shake of his head.

"You mean you're actually wanting to go through with it?" Mikel asked, surprised.

Jackson turned to face Ava. "We haven't agreed. We wanted to give you the chance to speak your thoughts. Ava, this could be a turning point for Africa. This could gain the advantage that will help them win this war."

She nodded deeply, considering his words. "Of course I will," she said seriously. "If you think we need this, then of course I'll do it."

"I don't want to ask this of you," Jackson said in a sorrowful tone.

She bowed her head in deep thought, and no one spoke as she considered. Eventually, she looked up to face him. "I want to be strong," Ava said, almost to him alone.

"Sometimes strength is learning when to say no," Damian argued. And he was right. Jackson had been the first to tell Ava that he believed she should have no interaction with Eli again, and she had agreed. But a lot more was at stake here than any of them understood.

"Eli is a viper. He'll find a way to use this against us," Mikel spoke with concern. "This is a bad idea."

"I said a similar thing," Sasha spoke quietly.

"But?" Ella asked pointedly.

Neither Sasha nor Jackson could seem to form a reply.

"But…" Ava eventually offered. "This is one of those times when the sacrifice for the greater good is more important, right?"

Still, neither of them replied.

"I think it's a *bad* idea," Mikel argued.

"Me too," Ella seconded.

"As do I," Damian agreed.

Ava looked at Jackson, and the searching in her expression said that his opinion was all that mattered. The difficulty was, he agreed with them. Eli always had ulterior motives. What if he turned this against them? They were sure to regret doing this in the end.

"I think you should go," Sasha was the one to speak, and it surprised everyone.

Ava turned to face him, and Jackson looked at him in surprise.

"We'll take whatever precautions we can. There is a great risk involved, but there is an advantage that is hard to weigh it against."

Sasha met Jackson's gaze, and Jackson gave a thankful nod. Still, it was clear that Sasha had come to this conclusion too. But having to ask this of her was proving impossible for Jackson.

"Then I'll go," Ava said simply.

"Have I mentioned this is a mistake?" Mikel chimed in once more. "But if we're doing this, we better be dang careful."

"Did he mention anything about us?" Ella asked as the thought occurred to her.

Jackson replied in the negative.

"He probably has no idea that we'd go to Ava," Mikel offered. "He probably thinks we're back in Australia. That's a good thing."

"And we can use it to our advantage now," Sasha agreed. "You both could serve as backup, if anything does go wrong."

"Eli may be one of the best," Ella offered. "But he's no match for all of us."

Jackson believed that to be true, but there was more to it than just that. Eli always had a plan. Jackson only hoped it wouldn't win out this time.

☆ ☆ ☆ ☆ ☆

Jackson assured Ava that she would not be alone, for even a second. "No matter what he says, that's non-negotiable."

She was grateful for that, but she sensed that there was still more on his mind. "I'll be fine," she assured him with a genuine smile. "I've faced him many times before. And I was going to have to face him again eventually. I'll be okay. I'm just glad that our interaction will be worth something to Africa."

"I hate to ask this of you," he lamented as they sat alone in the meeting room, awaiting Eli's arrival. It was a secure building some miles out from the base, in the center of the village.

"The very fact that you and Sasha are asking is why I know it's so important," she assured him. "It will be okay."

Jackson nodded, though his expression was still heavy with guilt.

The door opened and Eli was led inside.

Ava's chest tightened. Her entire body stiffened. She couldn't remember ever really being afraid of Eli, but for some reason, she found herself terrified as he stepped inside the room.

He looked well. He looked himself, dressed again in military garb as the General in the field.

A strange desire to go to him, to hug him and to ask how everything was, overwhelmed her. Her conflicting feelings were overwhelming. A part of her was terrified and begged to get away. The other part simply loved this man, her brother, and wanted to connect as they once had.

When the guards left the room, Eli took in his surroundings. It was a stark contrast to Sasha's memory of Harrison, who had eight armed guards to protect him against one man, whereas Eli the General came alone. He was a Zhànshì, after all.

His eyes scanned the room, ultimately rested on Ava, and he smiled. His real smile. She knew he meant that. He was happy to see her. And she could not help but smiling back at him. The urge to run to his arms consumed her to the point of having to grab hold of the chair that stood in front of her so she would not move, even as she struggled to breathe for immense fear of him.

He stared at her for a moment, noting her uncasted arm, her shorter hair done in two braids, her skin gone paler during time in Russia, her white knuckled grip against the chair—he seemed bothered by that part.

Eli looked up then to face Jackson. "Alone, please," he said in a cool tone.

"Not for a second," Jackson replied from where he stood, resting his back against the wall in the corner of the room and with his arms folded, appearing more at ease than Ava knew him to be.

"Then I'll take my garrison and go—"

"Sit down, Eli," Jackson urged. "This is the best you will ever get. Take it or leave it."

Eli considered for a moment, a challenge in his eye. But eventually, he seemed to concede, realizing that Jackson would not change his mind.

He stepped up to the table and sat down.

Ava slowly pulled the chair in front of her out from under the table and took a seat, across from her brother.

"You look good, Ava," Eli said, smiling. "But...I can tell you've lost a lot of weight. Are you taking care of yourself?"

Ava tsked suddenly. "I asked you not to comment on my weight again."

"I'm worried about your health," he said in his truly caring tone, and it was clear he meant that. "You've lost a lot of weight, and muscle—"

"Drop it, Eli! Or I leave of my own free will."

Eli watched her for a time, then looked up to Jackson, and there seemed to be a pleading in his expression, to Jackson of all people, as if in concern about Ava's health.

"You just said I look well," she argued pointedly, wanting to break the moment between the other two.

"That was more of a pleasant greeting than truth..." he admitted.

"Fine, just say it. I've never looked worse! I guess you were right, I can't live without you." This she said in a dramatically sarcastic tone.

Eli chuckled. "Okay, that might have been a bit steep. But at the time, I really didn't know if you could."

"Thanks for the vote of confidence, brother," she replied dryly, though she could not help the smile that came to her lips.

Was it really so bad? Was she really supposed to cut him from her life completely? There was still so much love, so much good between them. She honestly couldn't remember now, why she had been so afraid to face him. Then again, even now, her constricted chest struggled to raise up and down in normal breathing.

"How's Katia?" Ava asked.

Eli smiled deeply. "We're engaged."

A sudden pang hit her. These were the lives of some of her best friends, and she was missing them entirely. "What? How? When?"

In one moment, she found herself regretting everything. She never should have left him. Why did everyone say he was evil and manipulative? This Eli, this was her Eli, her brother, her friend.

"We haven't set a date yet, but I'll make sure to send an invite."

Jackson shuffled in the corner, and Ava involuntarily turned to face him. He stood looking wary, and his expression was one of deep concern. Yet he said nothing.

When Ava looked back at Eli, she tried to be more wary. There were real reasons she had left. She couldn't remember most of them right now, when all she wanted was to be close with her brother again, but she could remember one.

Hawkins, she repeated to herself, over and over. *Hawkins.*

"Heard anything from Kyle?" Ava said, changing the subject when it became clear that the relationship between Katia and Eli was too much for her to handle right now.

Eli huffed in annoyance. "No, Ava. Still dead."

"Hmph," Ava replied discontentedly.

"There is one thing though, that you should know." His expression became sorrowful. "Lionel...."

Another pang. She didn't want him to finish. "What is it?" she pleaded, despite her fears. "Please, tell me he's getting better?"

Eli gave a simple shake of his head. "He passed away a week ago."

Her throat felt suddenly dry and clammy, and her heart sank. She had known when she left that she probably would never see him again. But it hurt worse than she had imagined.

"I hadn't heard..." she whispered painfully.

"They haven't announced it officially yet," Eli explained. "Richard wanted to tie up some loose ends that Lionel left behind before it was made public."

Ava didn't like the sound of that, but it was out of her control now. "Did he...die peacefully?"

Eli sighed. "Not exactly."

Ava nodded sadly. "I'm glad his suffering is over now."

"And you'll be glad to know he never forgot you. Not until the end. He remembered his wife, but he had no memories of any of his children or grandchildren. Yet one name that he would not stop asking for until his dying breath was, 'Ava.'"

Tears filled her eyes at the thought. Lionel was gone, and she hadn't even been there to say goodbye.

Eli reached across the table and offered a comforting hand.

"Don't touch her," Jackson ordered, and in that moment, she thought maybe he was overreacting just a little bit.

But then, she had to remind herself, she could not trust her own emotions when it came to Eli. That was a part of the problem. She wanted to believe in him, she always would. That was why there must be distance between them.

"Come on," Eli objected, not obeying Jackson's demand.

"Remove your hand," Jackson spoke sternly. "Or get out now."

Eli glared at Jackson steeply, but ultimately, he pulled his hand away.

"Why did you want to see me?" Ava's comment was meant to break the glare between them. It took a while, but it worked.

He turned to look at her, and she could sense his regret. "Ava, I made a lot of mistakes. I know you'll never believe me, but I want you to know that I had nothing to do with Hawkins—"

"Don't!" Ava objected, raising her hand. "Don't go there, Eli. You may convince me of a lot of things. But I will never believe this one. Please, just don't."

He swallowed hard, and eventually agreed. "Understood." He changed the subject to talk of her arm and the healing process she'd been through. He spoke of her hair, that he liked it this length and that it suited her better than the long hair—though she disagreed about that.

"How has your link been?" he asked in seeming, wary concern. "Has anything felt...off?"

"All right, time's up," Jackson said, stepping forward.

"Why?" Eli said, seeming to wonder where he had erred.

Jackson pointed to his watch. "Because it's been five minutes. That was what we agreed to. That's what you got. We're done here. Guards!"

Several men entered the room in order to peacefully escort Eli away. Eli hesitantly stood, and started to follow them, but he stopped at the door. "Just...don't go near the Towers," he warned. "Whatever you do. Stay away from the Towers of the Republic."

"What are you talking about?" Ava asked in confusion.

"Please," Eli muttered as the guards continued to press him through the door. "Just trust me. All right?"

The fear in his eyes was real, fear and concern for her. Not knowing what else to do, she nodded.

And then Eli was gone.

Jackson suggested that they must wait a good few minutes before leaving themselves.

Ava didn't have the heart to talk. She stayed there in her seat, thinking over every detail of their conversation, every smile, every gesture, remembering it over and over, wishing it had been longer. She wanted to be able to trust him again. But she couldn't trust herself with him, which meant she could not allow herself to be in his life. At least not until she found her "inner peace," and maybe not even then. The thought pained her deeply.

"We can go now," Jackson offered.

She stood and silently followed him out of the meeting room, but she stopped in the small entry room, not yet prepared to leave this building and start the trek home with many watchful eyes.

"Can I...can I just take a minute here?" she asked, leaning against the wall in the small, five-foot-long entry room.

He watched her warily at first. "Of course. Eli is back at his camp. I'll wait just outside."

Ava nodded thankfully. She waited until he was gone before she collapsed against the wall, breaking down in tears. Kristen had once told her that there was no real shame in crying, if the reason was good enough. Ava couldn't think of any greater reason right now than the loss of her brother.

Lionel was really gone. And he had not forgotten her, though she had effectively abandoned him. Eli was engaged to Katia. And she had no part in their relationship. She would not be able to attend their wedding. She would not be there to hold their firstborn baby. She had no part in Eli's life anymore, and that pained her more than she thought possible.

She knew he loved her. She could see it in the way he looked at her. She knew he truly cared about her, and worried about her. Why did everything have to become so tainted between them? And why was there no hope for real reparation in the future?

She was so caught up in her thoughts, that she hardly noticed when Jackson entered the room, having only just barely left. He walked right to her and took her in his arms without a word. Neither of them said anything for several minutes as she cried.

There had always been something special about Sasha being there for Ava's panic attacks, but even then, she felt embarrassed to be so weak for her father, and it was a struggle to open up. But strangely, she did not feel embarrassed as Jackson held her. She did not feel uncomfortable. There was no inner voice telling her to run as fast and as far as she could. Instead, she clung to his presence. She felt at peace. She even felt...safe.

Eventually, one of Sizwe's men entered and explained that they were requested back on base. Jackson thanked the man and said they would be out soon. Still, he waited, not pushing her, until she had recovered.

"I'll be fine," Ava eventually said. "It hurts so much right now...I miss him so much. But I'll be fine. Someday...someday I'll be fine. I just need to find my inner peace."

It was clear he didn't understand every word she said between scattered breaths, but he pretended to and nodded agreement, which was sweet of him.

Eventually, she wiped her tears for the last time and pulled from his embrace. "I'm good now. Thank you. Let's go."

It had been an emotional decision, made on a whim. He had just wanted to see Ava, and nothing else mattered. Of course they could have used the money! The United Kingdoms were in as much trouble as the Republic at this point. But Council was not here to make that call, and he was done relying on them. When it came to the war, to the things he could control, he was not about to turn to them for support. He had taken matters into his own hands.

And despite all the reasons he should regret his rash decision and how it had all gone down, he could not.

"So, what do we do, sir?" the captain of the garrison asked when the two of them sat alone in their leadership tent.

Eli looked up and faced him with tightened eyebrows as if it were obvious. "We send the garrison! Prepare your men. We're going to help Africa win back Torro Niqa. Let's go!"

"Yes, sir!" his commander agreed, leaving the tent quickly.

No games, no ulterior motives this time around. He had just wanted some time with Ava, and though he wished it had been longer, and though he hated Jackson for how the man had hovered and controlled every moment of it, he still found that those five minutes had been well worth it.

Perhaps they would learn to trust him with this act of goodwill. Perhaps they would stop assigning such blame to Eli, and realize that oftentimes, that all the time, he had Ava's best interest in mind and was doing all that he could to protect *her*.

He hadn't been entirely truthful about things with Katia. Their relationship had grown complicated and messy, but he had said what he knew Ava wanted to hear. He hadn't had the chance to smooth over the topic of Hawkins, but he just wanted Ava to be happy.

He could tell by how horrendous she looked that she had not been taking care of herself, and none of those idiots seemed to care! He hoped his concern for Ava's well-being had gotten through to Jackson and that the man would take steps to ensure Ava's health.

He hoped more than anything that Ava would accept his last piece of advice and avoid the Towers. He could not stand the thought of her being killed like the other agents in a meaningless, quick death. Counter Intelligence was becoming more aggressive every day. Hundreds of agents were dead. He hoped in the General's name Ava would not be added to that list, but there was little Eli could do to protect her now.

Perhaps, in time, they would realize that he had always been looking out for her and still hoped to do so. Perhaps someday, Ava would forgive him and accept his promises that he had not really been responsible for Hawkins's death. The woman herself had made it vital. His decision to have Hawkins killed had been necessary, and if Ava truly understood, he had no doubt that she would be on his side in the matter.

The tent flap reopened, "We're ready, sir. You can contact Colonel Davis and make arrangements."

Eli sat back in his seat, feeling overwhelmed and even heavy. "You make the contact. I have other concerns."

His captain seemed surprised, but agreed. "Yes, sir. Of course." With that he was gone.

The tent soon opened again, and Eli was about to berate his captain to leave him alone, but it was Zhànshì Six who entered. "I did the recon you requested, sir."

"Good. What did you discover?"

Zhànshì Six sat down, which was not usual for him. Clearly, there was a lot to be said. "I think you'll like my findings, General Altman."

"Well?" Eli pressed pointedly.

"As you suspected, Colonel Davis took added precautions during your meet. There were other observers on the outskirts, prepared to join if necessary. It seems Ava was not the only Zhànshì who fled to Russia."

☆ ☆ ☆ ☆ ☆

"Do you want to talk about it?" Jackson ventured carefully. They were alone within the back of a truck, headed for the base and it seemed like the time to offer a listening ear, before they were surrounded by their friends again.

Ava was hesitant at first and he was about to tell her she didn't have to when she spoke, "I don't know what to say," she admitted. "I guess I just feel like a walking contradiction." She shifted in her seat beside him and he was conscious of her hand where it was placed on her knee, near to him.

"A contradiction?" he asked when she gave no immediate explanation.

She licked her lips before nodding. "I hate him so much." Her words showed how passionately she meant that and, truthfully, Jackson was surprised. The last she'd said about it, she could not bring herself to hate Eli. Yet it was undeniable now.

"But I love him *so* much," she continued further and this time he could see just as clearly how much that statement was true. "I can't help still loving him. And it's not just a trauma bond—at least, I don't think it is."

Jackson offered a pained smile, having no answer for her either way.

"I am terrified of him," Ava continued, the fear showing in her eyes clearly. "But I miss him like crazy. He hurt me so much. But he was so good to me too. And I know you're going to say it's all a part of the abuse and that he just did what he needed to on any given day to control me—"

"I wasn't going to say that," Jackson disagreed.

She gave him a challenging look as she evidently did not buy it. Still, she began explaining herself before he could prove himself. "I don't understand these competing emotions, and it's all so confusing because

I don't know how to define it at all. I can't just explain it to make sense to you or myself or anyone."

Jackson nodded in pained understanding. "You want to make it make sense," he offered. "You want to look back at your past and draw a line in the sand that says, 'This moment marks the time he stopped being your loving brother and instead became the abusive tyrant.' But it doesn't work that way. There is no clear line. Sometimes there's no clear moment in time that marks the change. It's all so much more complicated than that."

Ava watched him as if trying to understand how he knew what she was going through as he clearly did. "Your mother," she said in sudden realization. "And your sister."

His tight smile was his only response before he went in deeper. "My entire relationship with my mom was a series of ups and downs. There were some really good days, and some really bad days. But mostly there were a whole lot of days with a whole lot of both." He visibly winced at a sudden, painful memory. "The same day she told me I was the best man she had ever met, that she had never been prouder and that she would give up her vices to be better for me and Mae, that was the same day she got wasted and screamed at me that she wished I had never been born because I ruined her life by entering this world." He let out a pained breath and Ava offered a caring expression.

"The same day we made nests out of cut grass after mowing the lawn and we stayed outside in them for hours...that was the same day she sat back and watched as her boyfriend beat the taint out of me for not being ready to go back to school because I couldn't read a simple chapter book." He huffed, wishing that carcass could see how far he had come—certainly no thanks to his supposedly "motivational" abuse.

Ava's hand moved to his to offer comfort and he accepted gratefully, wishing he'd been brave enough to do it first. "I'm sorry, Jackson," she said softly. "I went through a lot with Eli, but nothing like that—"

"Didn't you?" Jackson asked, indicating her arm with a glance.

"I broke it myself," she explained. "I started that whole fight—"

"Or is that his gaslighting telling you it was your fault?" Jackson asked genuinely. "He's twice your size, Ava. And just as well trained in hand-to-hand combat. Don't try and convince me he couldn't have found a way to contain you without hurting you back. And when he had you in an arm lock and you moved against it, he could have let go. He could have removed the pressure when he realized what you were doing. He was stubborn and angry and wouldn't let you go. He was just as involved as you were and far more to blame. He used his strength as an advantage to hurt and control you. And I'm tainted grateful you made it away from him, but it could so easily have gone another way."

She swallowed hard, pulling her hand back and looking out the truck, away from him, uncomfortably. Several beats passed as tension filled the air. He was not usually so brutal in assessing Eli anymore, yet for all these months she'd been defending Eli and claiming he never really physically hurt her. In all that time, no one had ever explained that truth to her the way that all of them saw it. For some reason, he felt he needed to now.

"Anyway," he offered carefully, more softly this time, "that's not the point you were trying to make. I guess the thing I've learned about toxic relationships—and I don't just mean people who offend us or make our lives difficult, I'm talking about genuinely toxic relationships—the thing I've learned is that just like every other thing in the world, it's complicated. People want it to be all black and white—either we're good guys or bad guys—but it's not that simple."

She was still pulled away from him thanks to his bold assessment of Eli's physical abuse, and Jackson attempted to ease the air with his softened tone.

"People are complex," he explained further when she was looking at him once more. "Eli can be an abusive tyrant *and* a caring brother. My mother could be a loving mom and a terrible parent at the same time. Emotions are just as complicated. You can love the parts of Eli that were good while still hating the things that made him bad. You can appreciate him for the moments when he was kind to you while still abhorring the times that he hurt you. It's okay to have conflicting emotions because people are complex, and just like one label doesn't fully sum up a human being, one emotion doesn't fit every aspect regarding them either."

"You're right," Ava said, nodding in agreement. "All these months in recovery, I've been trying to explain it as the old Eli and the new one. But it's not true. Even before it got really bad, it wasn't always good. And even when it was really bad, there were moments that were good."

"I loved my mother," Jackson offered. "And I'll remember her fondly for the rest of my life. And yet, if I ever have kids, I won't let myself be anything like her. If you decide to forgive him, that doesn't make what he did okay or mean you were wrong to leave. And remembering the good times doesn't mean you ever have to justify the bad."

"I love Eli too," Ava offered. "I don't know yet if I'll forgive him. But either way I won't let his lust for power taint this world. I'll fight him if I have to."

Jackson offered a half smile. "People are complex. Emotions are complex. But I will say, relationships don't have to be that hard—only the toxic ones are that rough. It can be so much better than that."

The look she gave him was filled with hope and he could not look away from those green eyes if he tried. "I hope that's true," she said softly.

He thought suddenly of all those months of pain with her when things got so tainted up. There had been a time he thought he would never have the privilege of being close to her again. Now here she was. He was well aware of the fact that they were needed on the base, yet he did not want this moment to ever end. "Can I hug you, Ava?" he asked in sudden desperation.

She watched him with a touch of confusion. The only indication of an explanation he offered was the look of panic on his face. All of this would end too soon, and he resented the fact that he had to go back to meet with the others—let alone returning to Russia for work. She said nothing as she moved in and held him tightly.

Neither of them said a word, yet it seemed clear to both of them that this time it was her comforting him. "Was I wrong?" she asked softly, in a way that showed how much she cared for him. "Have you needed me this whole time?"

He breathed out in a moment of overwhelming pain, having no verbal response to that. Soon, she accepted that he could give no answer. She simply held him and he clung to her in return. "I'm here now," she whispered.

Jackson prayed silently that they would never lose one another again, though it seemed an impending doom that all too soon they would be parted. "What if I stay?" Jackson whispered as she lingered there in his arms. "What if I find someone else to take my spot and I stay here?"

She gave no response and eventually he realized it was a useless question. If he did stay...then he would have stayed. What was she supposed to say to that?

"I would love that," Ava eventually offered, though hesitantly. "I would cherish every moment with you. But don't you need to go and hold the alliance together?"

Of course he did. And yet, in this moment he had to wonder if there were other things in life that were allowed to matter to him as much as his work did. What if Ava was one of those things for him?

Someone banged on the truck door, informing them that they had arrived and that it was time to get out—since they clearly weren't planning to on their own. Ava pulled away quickly, obviously not wanting to be found so close with Jackson if the door was opened. "I guess we should get back?" she said, though it sounded more like a question.

"Yeah," Jackson replied helplessly, thinking back to that first night after the library with her and how she'd been rushed to head back to her trainers then. How different everything was now. How much more he cared for this woman all these years later. How much harder it was to let her get out of that vehicle and head toward reality, when all he wanted was to stay in that moment with her forever.

She waited outside the truck for him for several long moments before looking inside. "You coming?"

He nodded dismally before hesitantly exiting the vehicle and following her back into the base, back to reality.

☆ ☆ ☆ ☆ ☆

Eli sent his garrison as promised. The simple battle was successful, and the Republic retreated when the combined forces moved into the city of Torro Niqa.

Sizwe asked Jackson to remain, to help with any further negotiations for the next few days as they moved forces in to hold the city, and the

Russian Leadership Committee agreed. Jackson was greatly relieved by the possibility of more time. He wasn't ready to leave Ava yet.

"Dude," Jackson said as he sat with Sizwe, Sasha and Vasiliv in the study, "living here is so easy. It's been a whole week with no assassination attempts."

Sizwe chuckled softly. "It must be a challenge. I'm surprised you don't flinch every time you're approached by anyone."

"Oh, believe me I do. I'm just getting good at hiding it till the last second."

"I offered to be your personal guardsman," Vasiliv said, throwing up his arms. "You turned me down. Several times."

"They needed you here more."

"How many assassination attempts?" Vasiliv shot back pointedly.

"I'm not dead yet, am I?" Jackson replied as proof that he was right.

"How are the Elites doing?" Sasha, finally joining the conversation, asked with sudden interest.

"The Elites and Vasiliv have proved quite helpful in our battles," Sizwe said with deep gratitude.

"Soon enough, I hope we'll have formed another elite squad to help with the fight," Sasha said, clearly thinking of the Zhànshì squad.

Sizwe agreed. "Their skills will be immeasurably valuable."

"From the look of things, the General was true to his word," Vasiliv noted. "Now we just need to see if we can hire his garrison for another run on Torro Nus."

"Best secure our hold in Torro Niqa first," Sasha said with wary concern.

"I'm not sure how much we can count on the General's future help," Jackson admitted. "We can't rely on that same bargaining chip, and if he really doesn't have any interest in money, then there's not much else we can offer him."

"But at least today," Sizwe said, pulling them back to the moment, "today is a victory, though there are still a great many more to be won."

Vasiliv nodded in agreement. "It is a victory, and a cause for celebration." He pulled out his flask and took a large gulp before handing it to Jackson, who passed it along to Sasha without taking a draught. Sasha and the other two shared in Vasiliv's victory libation, and although he didn't partake, Jackson enjoyed the celebration of triumph.

After some time, a knock at the door broke them from their celebrations, and Sizwe's closest informant entered. "Sizwe, we have just received a communique. I think you're going to want to hear this."

★ ★ ★ ★ ★

"I think we've had enough of the intense, crazy memories," Ava said to her fellow Zhànshì and Damian as they sat around in the shared room. "Now I want to ask the question we should have gone through when we did the dreamwalk!" She had a wicked smile on her face, which made it clear she thought herself very clever.

Ella scoffed, though in truth, she now appreciated how Ava somehow always managed to be in a good mood, even on her darkest days.

"And what question is that?" Damian asked seriously.

"Well, I can't be the only one who thinks we wasted an opportunity!" she replied, still smiling widely as she picked a snack from the bag and popped it in her mouth. "I mean, who hasn't wanted to relive some of their favorite moments in full color?"

Mikel and Damian seemed to agree, but Ella huffed. "I have no good memories to relive."

"Oh, come on!" Ava disagreed, an exaggerated smile on her face. "Remember when you almost pulled Eli's shoulder from the socket?"

Mikel chuckled, reaching for the crackers and cheese.

"You mean when I was this close to succeeding and you knocked me unconscious?"

Ava scrunched her eyes thoughtfully. "Was that how it ended? Hmm, see, this is why we need to relive it."

Ella rolled her eyes.

"All right, I'll take it on," Mikel said excitedly, matching Ava's playful mood. "I would go back to every match where I beat Kyle in training."

"That never happened," Ella objected.

Ava pointed at Ella as if to say her comment was correct. "That never happened," she agreed.

"Yes, it did!" Mikel shot back defensively. "Look up the scores!"

Ava and Ella shook their heads, for the first time ever being in on the same joke as they teased Mikel.

"Yes, I did!" Mikel said, standing now and looking ready for a fight.

Ella continued to object, but on seeing Mikel's anger, Ava broke character and began laughing out loud.

"You guys suck!" Mikel said, realizing they were just messing with him and sitting back down.

"I will say though," Ava said when she had finished laughing, "if it's that exciting and memorable to you, it probably didn't happen much."

This time Ella pointed at Ava, tickled at her effective taunting of Mikel. They usually were not on the same side of anything. Strangely, Ella found herself liking being on Ava's side for a change.

"Well, at least I had the satisfaction of an actual victory!" Mikel rebutted. "You and Kyle would just go unconscious. Nobody really wins at that point."

"Did you know I faked it once?" Ava said, biting back her smile as if feeling guilty, but finding it hilarious.

"You what?" Ella asked in shock.

Ava giggled in embarrassment before admitting it out loud. "I pretended to go unconscious so I could save my pride and not have to quit against Kyle!"

"You did not!" Mikel said in exasperation.

She nodded emphatically through her laughter. "I've kept that secret for six years! You have to promise not to tell. It can never get back to him!"

"He's dead, Ava," Ella said in pointed annoyance.

"Right. But promise you'll never tell him! Or I'll never live it down."

"Does she know what 'dead' means?" Damian asked Mikel in genuine confusion.

Mikel raised his arms as if to say she was a hopeless cause. Which, she was.

"I can't believe you did that," Ella said, a twist of a smile on her own lips that she masked as disappointment. Ava saw through it, and laughed again.

"I know! It's horrible! I promise, it's the only time I ever cheated in training. He was just so mean and angry and strong, and he was winning, and he was so smug! I couldn't let him have the satisfaction of me quitting, but I had so had it that day!"

"The golden child is not so golden after all," Ella said, but still, Ava only laughed at that.

"All right, golden child," Ella turned it back to Ava. "Since you want to relive your old memories so much, what would you go back to?"

Ava's smile soon changed into a serious expression. "I'd go back to the time before Harrison warped my memories, to see what my relationship with my mom was like. I keep getting these little glimpses. The fact that I relied on her strength during my time in the Russian prison. I know we must have been close, but I don't remember it."

The playful mood grew more somber and serious. It was ultimately Mikel who replied. "You were very close. All of the Zhànshì were jealous of your relationship, and so Kristen tried to show us equal love, but we all knew there was something special between you. I never understood how you drifted apart. I wish I had known. I wish I could have been there for her more through all of that. She was the best woman I ever knew, Ava. I wish you remembered her the way I do."

Ava's smile was somber, but her eyes were alight with a love for her mother. "So do I."

"Ame loved her too," Ella added. "You know Ame, she had a lot of bad things to say about just about every Altman, but she never spoke an ill word about Kristen. I never really knew your mom myself, but I know my mother loved her."

"I met her once myself," Damian said. "Though mostly I just witnessed her from afar. She was a strong woman. And her daughter is no different."

Ava smiled, appreciating his kind words. "What about you, Damian? What memory would you want to relive?"

He was contemplative for several moments before looking up and facing all of them in turn. "I have learned in my life not to long for the past, nor to yearn for the future. The time we are in now, in this very moment, is truly wonderful. We can never know what tomorrow will bring. But right here, in this moment, I am among true warriors, among friends. And there is nowhere I'd rather be."

Ava seemed to internalize his words, as did Mikel, but Ella decided to poke fun at him instead. "Well, thanks for ruining the fun, old man!"

"All right," Ava said, as though Ella had not spoken. "I'll bite. What is it in this moment that you want to hold onto? What is so special about this moment, right now?" Her question was not only directed at Damian, but all of them.

Still, the old man was the one to give an answer. "My homeland in Australia was subjugated by a powerful, dangerous enemy. The nation of my heritage is just as corrupted and broken at this time. Yet here, right now, we are witnessing something wonderful: a continent of people who have been in bondage, yet are rising up, taking a stand and working toward their freedom. I believe it's easy for the three of you to simply do your work, get the job done and go to bed, but do you not realize how much each of you matters? My friends, we are literally changing the course of history. And I cherish the very opportunity to be here and to witness it with my own eyes."

★ ★ ★ ★ ★

Ava lay awake, staring at the ceiling, thoughts of Eli still crowding her mind, even three days later.

Eli had moved in his garrison as promised, keeping his end of the bargain. And rather than remain and fight, it was looking like the Republic was considering a full-on retreat. Maybe it would be a turning point after all.

She and the Zhànshì were slowly being introduced to the culture of the base and its people, and even being included in the war efforts. She could not remember ever being so fully accepted by a group of people so quickly. She decided that Sizwe's screening process had some real merit in saving time and earning trust quickly.

She always took a while to fall asleep, but knew it was still fairly early when she heard a light tapping at the door. Grateful she hadn't yet dozed, she hurried to the door.

Jackson stood outside, looking apologetic. "I'm sorry to wake you," he said in a hurried whisper. "I should have just moved my things out and actually traded rooms."

Ava glanced at the room behind her and to the chair where Jackson's bag sat. She had only used this room to sleep in. During the day she left it alone, so she had convinced him there was no need to change.

"What time is it?" she asked, knowing it couldn't be morning, since she hadn't even fallen asleep yet.

"It's 1 a.m.," he replied, stepping into the room.

"Is everything all right?" she spoke with concern when he hurried to his pack and pulled out his military vest and cargo pants. "If you wanted to see me you could've just asked."

Jackson chuckled, and Ava smiled, though she knew her playful humor was unhelpful at the moment.

"Senior Colonel Yang from the Politburo arrived an hour ago in Torro Nus," Jackson explained. "He has requested immediate audience with the leaders of this rebellion. From the looks of it, he wants to talk about peaceful retreat in the surrounding African territories."

"Why doesn't he just send a broadcast?" she countered, closing the door to the room and moving over closer to the bed.

"This is a big deal for the Republic," Jackson explained, grabbing a few more pieces of clothing and equipment from the pack and setting them on the unmade bed. "They have never surrendered ground before without a serious fight. I assume the formalities are a way to cover for their instability. They'll make it seem like they don't need this ground and are willing to work peacefully with Africa rather than lose to them horribly."

"So...maybe we shouldn't go," Ava replied pointedly.

Jackson turned back toward her then, having collected all the things he needed. "I don't care if they save face, as long as they give us this ground. We can humiliate them later, when we continue to crush their armies and push them out of Africa entirely."

Ava nodded her head to either side in understanding. "I suppose that's fair."

Jackson's expression became suddenly awkward, as if he didn't know how to ask for what he was about to. "I'm sorry...do you mind?" he gestured to his clothing on the bed.

"Oh! Of course! Sorry." She turned away from him then and toward the door, allowing him a bit of privacy while he changed.

"Sorry, it's just, I promised you'd never have to see me shirtless again."

Ava chuckled, remembering their first meeting many years ago. Though she was certainly of a different mind about that now. "We have gone swimming together," she pointed out.

"Remember you made me promise we wouldn't look at each other at all?" he said, teasing her with that awkward reminder. "I kept my promise. Didn't you?"

Ava stifled a laugh, biting her lip through the smile. "Maybe not," she admitted, and she heard him laughing too.

She remained standing there awkwardly, thinking while he changed. But then a new thought occurred to her, and she turned suddenly, forgetting why she had turned around in the first place. "What if it's a trap? What if they don't intend to retreat at all?"

Jackson flinched back in surprise when she turned, but luckily he was mostly dressed by that time and managed to pull his shirt over his arm, covering himself completely in a quick motion.

"Oh. Right. Sorry," Ava said with sudden embarrassment.

Jackson reached for his vest and put it on. "We have considered that possibility," he admitted. "It's possible that they're just looking for an opportunity to nip this rebellion in the bud and take out its leaders before they have any larger victories."

Ava's eyes widened, as the likelihood of that made sense to her. "Of course it's a trap. You shouldn't go, Jackson!"

He fixed his belt, then retrieved his gun and placed it in a holster at his leg. "Regardless, Sizwe is going. He is willing to take the risk. And so am I."

Ava moved closer to him, urgently hoping to change his mind. "But this isn't Eli we're talking about. This isn't a known enemy who is crazy, but predictable. This is the Republic! What if they bomb the entire meeting and take you all out at once?"

"The rebellion in Africa was fragile, even months ago. Sizwe was the only thing that held it together. That's no longer the case. The victory we had in that village eight months ago and the many victories they have secured here since then have reminded the people of this continent what it feels like to fight and to win. Small as those battles were, they have been enough to change things. They have a system in place. And even if Sizwe were to die tonight, the rebellion would continue."

Ava's expression grew serious, and she held his gaze when she admitted, "It's not just Sizwe that I'm worried about."

Jackson watched her with a deeply caring look. It took a long time for him to respond. "This is one of those moments, Ava. Sizwe needs me. And I need to be there."

He stepped forward, a new confidence in his demeanor. "Don't worry. We'll be careful out there. And with any luck, we'll secure the greatest victory against the Republic since the one you started by retaking Australia."

He walked right past her on his way to the door, as if that little statement of confidence would be enough to give her peace when he was about to do something insanely dangerous.

"Wait," Ava pleaded, stopping him a few feet from the door, but when he turned to face her, she couldn't think of anything good enough to say.

"I'm in a hurry," Jackson said apologetically. "I really have to—"

"Just, make sure you come back," she said helplessly.

He watched her and she knew he wanted to say more, but didn't know how—or was afraid to. Eventually, he took a step forward until he was in front of her. He placed his hands on her shoulders, and he leaned in toward her.

She was so certain in that moment that he was going to kiss her, and the mere thought of it took her breath away. But at the last second, it was like he changed his mind. He missed her lips just barely, kissing her partially on the cheek, and partly on the edge of her mouth. Just as she had kissed him in the hallway during the Talks, when she had moved at the last second from kissing his cheek to avoid his beard. And then she was sure that was what he had meant to do all along.

Still, she felt it was a cruel form of payback.

When he pulled away and his bright, confident, and incredibly strong eyes met hers, she didn't mind so much that he hadn't kissed her the right way. His smile was as pure and happy as if he had. "See you in a few hours," he promised.

Then, in a hurry, he left her there alone.

☆ ☆ ☆ ☆ ☆

9

Fracture Point

Eli had been invited to the meeting, not by his supposed allies in Africa, but by the enemy itself, Senior Colonel Yang of the Republic.

Of course, when Jackson Davis heard of this invitation, he requested a private audience with Eli. They now sat alone in a neutral location, and Jackson was the first to speak. "They clearly have something planned," Jackson advised Eli. "I believe this could be an attempt to take out many of their threats in one fell swoop."

Eli didn't altogether see a small leader of a tiny African rebellion and a United Intelligence agent turned rogue as the Republic's greatest threats. But even if this attack was just meant to take out Eli *himself*, the General of the United Kingdoms, it would make sense to sacrifice to do so.

"And what do you propose?" Eli asked in a cool tone.

"We figure out their play. We sabotage it. And we go to the meeting as requested. If they do attempt anything, we stop them. Or if this really is just a peaceful retreat, then we've gained the ground we wanted."

"And you think you'll be able to discover what their grand plan is?"

Jackson was overly confident when he replied. "I'm fairly certain I already have. The meeting tent we'll be going to is separate from their camp, several miles out. It's supposed to be a good middle ground. But I sent out a team to scope the area. I suggested they search for any Tesla markers. And guess what they found?"

"So what? They turn on a Tower-like power source and cause a blackout of your tech? What does that matter?" Deeper though, Eli knew the greater threat.

"They'll overload the Tower core from underneath us. Everything within that five-mile radius will be wasted to smithereens."

"Why not just set off an explosive?"

"This is far less traceable. And much more destructive. We just happen to have someone who can detect it."

Eli didn't know if he could risk going near the Tower. What if he was infected with Counter Intelligence? For some time now, a small part of Eli had hoped that Jackson would be infected and taken out easily because of it. But now, with Ava right there beside Jackson wherever he went, Eli could not risk it.

"There's more you need to know," Eli admitted. "Something that has been quieted for a long time now, something that is a great risk to you, to me, and to anyone else with the chip."

Jackson looked at him with sudden interest. "I'm listening."

And so, Eli gave a brief summary of the events surrounding Counter Intelligence, the greater threat and its risk to those involved.

For some reason, Jackson didn't look as surprised as he should. "Did you already know about this?" Eli could not help asking when he had finished relating the news.

"We have suspected something along these lines from some intel we received a few months back. But it wasn't confirmed."

"And have you taken any precautions?" Eli pressed with sudden distaste.

"Sasha and I disconnected from the link," Jackson admitted hesitatingly.

"And Ava?" Eli insisted.

Jackson was slow to reply. "She was unwilling. But we'll do what we have to in order to keep her from danger."

Eli scoffed. "You are allowing her strong will to put her own life in danger. If she doesn't like the idea, make her do it anyway!"

"We don't operate the way you do," Jackson replied in a cool tone. "With actual facts and intel, I will work harder to convince her."

"Regardless," Eli spoke with frustration at their callous weakness, "it isn't safe for us to attend this meeting."

"I disagree," Jackson replied carefully. "We've already disabled the underground core. I'll have my team check on the signal for Counter Intelligence. We'll ensure we can go in there safely. Still, if you know how, I recommend you disable your connection to the link."

"I don't trust you a lick," Eli declared with suspicion.

"There's one thing we can agree on," Jackson said with a simple, cold smile. "But the only other common ground we have is our desire to cripple the Republic. You know what this could do, for all of us."

Eli considered for a long time. Eventually, he stood. "I'll check on your supposed intel myself. If I find it to my liking, I'll consider your little plan." And with that he exited.

The coordinates were seemingly sound. Eli would not risk Zhànshì Six, but had sent a low-grade Intelligence agent with the chip to the site. He was able to test the results on the man from miles away, and there was no spread of infection.

Eli still didn't like it, but he would go along with it, for now. Still, if there was a chance to watch Jackson Davis and Sizwe killed, alongside Senior Colonel Yang, well, Eli wouldn't be disappointed.

☆ ☆ ☆ ☆ ☆

"We're on?" Mikel asked hopefully when it was just him, Vasiliv and Jackson standing outside the base in the darkness of the night.

"I still don't know how far we can trust the General," Jackson admitted. "But Sizwe is set on this meet. And I think it's worth the risk."

"You sure about not inviting Ava?" Vasiliv asked with concern. "I've seen how that girl can fight."

Mikel shook his head. "Sasha insists she not be involved so long as Eli is. And I agree. But I'll take care of the...technicalities." This with a pointed look at Jackson, who gave a nod in comprehension.

"I have no doubt," Vasiliv muttered.

"We leave in twenty minutes to the coordinates," Jackson directed authoritatively. "I need both of your teams to be in position at that time for whatever they might throw at us."

Vasiliv agreed. "I'll have them ready."

"My team never stops being ready," Mikel said, and there was a touch of arrogance in the comment that caused Vasiliv to scowl.

"Eli can't know you're here," Jackson reminded Mikel.

"Behind the scenes," he agreed.

"And we'll accompany you directly, Jackson," Vasiliv said, "even if they won't allow us into the meet."

Jackson glanced up at the stars and the beaming moon in the sky. This felt like one of those turning points. Either the Republic was serious, and this really would be the greatest possible feat for Africa. Or the Republic intended a double-cross, in which case, they needed to be well prepared for whatever danger might occur.

"This is *yet*, right?" Vasiliv said, as if reading the seriousness in Jackson's thoughts. Jackson and Vasiliv had engaged in that conversation directly. But interestingly, Mikel also smiled, understanding the meaning of the word thanks to new memories from the dreamwalk.

"This is *yet*," Jackson agreed.

"It feels pretty good," Mikel said with a confident intake of breath.

"Feels…cold," Vasiliv said, noting the chill in the air. He had become accustomed to the heat of central Africa, and tonight was particularly chilly.

Jackson smiled, despite himself. "Well, let's do this thing. Let's free Africa."

"Let's just start with Torro Nus," Vasiliv corrected knowingly.

"Nah, let's just save the whole world," Mikel disagreed. "Go big or go home, right?"

☆ ☆ ☆ ☆ ☆

"So, this is the great Agent Jackson Davis?" Senior Colonel Yang gave attempts at pleasantries as he greeted Jackson.

"It's actually Colonel Davis now," Jackson said with much more pleasantness in his tone. "I dropped the 'agent' since I no longer work for the government who gave me that title."

"So the Russians promoted you to colonel in their military," Yang said with a touch of scorn. "Well, Colonel, I have heard much about you. All our attempts to thwart you have, so far, been unsuccessful."

"Were all those assassins from you, then?" Jackson asked, with a strange smile on his face, as if he was entirely at ease with the high member of the Politburo standing right there across from him. Jackson was an arrogant carcass; Eli would give him that.

"We sent four," Yang admitted with a hint of a smile.

"Taint," Jackson said with a sudden shake of his head. "And here I was hoping you were the only ones who wanted me dead."

Senior Colonel Yang gave a laugh. He then turned to face Eli, finally. "You must be the latest version of General Altman?"

That was not exactly the respectful greeting Eli would have liked, and neither did he love the fact that Yang had greeted Jackson first.

"That's right," Eli said coldly.

Next Yang turned to Sizwe. "And you, my friend, have been very lucky to fall in with some powerful allies."

Sizwe grinned. "Some might say they have been lucky enough to fall in with me."

Yang was not amused, but Jackson seemed to appreciate it.

Yang and his five other military leaders took seats around the table, and soon the visitors were invited to do the same.

None of them were allowed weapons, or to bring bodyguards, but Eli did not need either, and he didn't much mind if the other two had anything to protect themselves.

Eli had taken Jackson's advice to disable the chip, at least for the time being, though it was not something he liked to do—taking advice from Jackson Davis. Still, he didn't like the risk of being infected by Counter Intelligence either.

"I'm told that your alliance has secured a great victory over our men," Yang said, moving to the more formal subject. "And while, admittedly, I don't like giving up ground, we don't need this territory. We're here to talk about what you would like to offer in exchange for our peaceful retreat."

✫ ✫ ✫ ✫ ✫

Mikel sat on the outskirts, miles out from the meet, with Ella and Damian standing guard. His mind was entirely focused on that underground Tower core. At the moment, it was still inactive, but Mikel had to be ready if it did turn on, as expected.

"I had no problem shutting down my connection," Ella admitted. "It's not like I have any interest in talking to people, and I certainly have no need to connect to the Towers. All the other uses for the chip are unnecessary for me. I can fight without it. And I don't need its enhancements, either physically, or mentally. My biological enhancements are more than enough."

Mikel tried to tune out her little commentary as he focused on the task at hand. He had met with the great Counter Intelligence once before, for the briefest of moments before the worldwide blackouts. He hadn't been strong enough to take on the entire network as it pulsed its weapon, but he believed he could handle one little Tower core—and of course, he had assured Jackson that he could do so.

"Anything yet?" Ella asked, growing impatient.

"Give him time," Damian urged. "He must focus."

"Who invites you on these operations anyway, old man?" Ella asked harshly. "I don't need your advice and I don't need you to boss me around."

"I am not here for you," Damian informed her softly. "I'm here for Mikel. But you would do well to learn patience, and it would not hurt you to submit to authority once in a while."

"Whatever," Ella grumbled. "You should be in a home. Just try not to complain so much."

"You're one to talk," Mikel muttered to himself, but luckily for everyone, she did not hear him.

✫ ✫ ✫ ✫ ✫

Her mind racing with all the tragic possibilities, Ava couldn't fall asleep again, so eventually she left her room and found Sasha, who was also wide awake, within Sizwe's sitting room. "You okay?" Ava asked, when it was clear Sasha was concerned.

"I'll be fine. It's never easy to sit back while your friends are hard at work."

"Jackson said something similar, a few months ago," Ava admitted, taking a seat beside him. "It's just a simple meet, right? They'll be fine."

Sasha looked at her warily. "Ava, I need you to be prepared for whatever outcome may play out."

She narrowed her eyes in concern. "He lied to my face, didn't he?" Ava said in realization. "This is more dangerous than he made it out to be."

"It's not his place to worry you. And it wouldn't be fair. Let them handle it."

"*Them*...? Where are Mikel and Ella?"

Sasha sighed heavily.

"Sasha, what are you not telling me? What the taint did he leave me out of?"

"It's going to be a long night, love."

★ ★ ★ ★ ★

"That's it. They've turned it on."

"Can you contain it?" Ella asked Mikel as he strained from the pressure.

"Of course I can," he replied confidently, though inwardly he wasn't so sure. The pressure from Counter Intelligence even now was greater than he had anticipated. The Tower was searching for Mikel's link, and attempting to burn him out. Mikel had known this was coming, but this was a lot harder than he had prepared for.

"You don't look so good," Ella noted.

His eyes were clamped shut, and his palms pressed against his temples as he strained with every bit of his strength to keep control.

"What was that?" Damian asked, but Mikel could not break his focus and find out for himself.

"I don't know," Ella whispered hoarsely. "Stay with him, I'm gonna go check it out." She left quickly.

After a measure of time that Mikel had not tracked, Damian touched him gently on the shoulder. "She's been gone too long, Mikel. I'm worried for her safety, and yours. I'm going to find her. Remember your strength. No matter how great Counter Intelligence may be, I believe you are stronger."

Mikel was about to object, but he couldn't manage to speak at all with the pressure that was threatening to crush him.

He had worked for this. He had devoted his life to this. If Harrison could see him now....

Time continued to pass, yet still he had no measure.

Damian was long gone when the sound of Ella's scream from far away shook him. "Mikel! Mikel, run!"

He had trained to be the best, and come to believe that he really was, but in this moment, all he could think was that Jackson had made a mistake in taking a chance on him. They should have brought Ava instead.

Jackson interacted in the negotiations, but mostly, he watched Yang, searching for any sign of...well, anything.

So far there had been no indication of any danger, despite the Republic's unreasonable demands, but there came a moment when Yang glanced at his watch, and cocked his head ever so slightly in surprise.

This was it. The event was supposed to have occurred, but Mikel was managing to stop it.

"Late for something?" Jackson asked, hoping for more indication of a reaction from Yang.

The man faced Jackson, with a stony expression. "No. I just grow tired of these negotiations." Clearly he was lying, and the slight desperation in his eyes proved his disappointment.

Jackson contained his smile, though he was prouder of Mikel than he had realized he would be.

"I hate this part of my job," Vasiliv admitted to Nastia as they stood watch outside the meeting tent. "The waiting. The anticipation. I can't stand it."

"Really?" Nastia asked with a sudden smile. "I live for the anticipation! The actual moments always happen too fast."

He chuckled at that, but another Elite tapped Vasiliv's shoulder, and simply pointed his direction to Yang's personal guard, who were also waiting outside the meeting tent. They were whispering to each other, noting watches and seeming concerned.

Vasiliv smirked. This was a good sign. Or at least, he had assumed it was, right up until Yang's main guardsman met his stare.

There was a new determination. Their original plan had fallen through, but there was always a backup, and in this case, it would not bode well for Vasiliv and his men.

★ ★ ★ ★ ★

Ava had assured Sasha she was not angry with him, though obviously it still infuriated her to be left out of the plans.

"I promise you," he said encouragingly, "this has nothing to do with your mental state at this time. Jackson has complete confidence in you. But he agreed to leave you out, as a personal request to me."

She gave no verbal response, but he could see the anger in her eyes. Or perhaps it was simply concern for her friends. He could not be sure.

"I'm not angry with you, Sasha," she tried to reassure him. "I just wish you had trusted me enough to—" Ava winced suddenly, and then she hunched down with a breathy sound of pain as her hands went to the sides of her head.

"What is it?" Sasha asked in instant concern.

She could not seem to reply for a time, and sat there, trembling in pain before she managed to reply, "Something's wrong."

Feeling utterly helpless, Sasha stood, but there was nowhere to go, no close enemy to fight, no real way to help Ava. It was just like with Kristen's death. Sasha was painfully aware of the danger she was in, and Jackson, and the rest, yet there was nothing he could do to stop it, especially when the pain began pressing on his own mind, even with the chip shut off.

✭ ✭ ✭ ✭ ✭

"That's unacceptable!" Sizwe demanded angrily. "How dare you even suggest it?"

"What did you think? That we were about to hand over the whole of Africa?" Senior Colonel Yang answered proudly. "You want your little territory. Fine. But we keep the remainder of our African territories. Agree to the cease fire, and leave our land alone."

"You and I both know they're never going to agree to this," Jackson said as a sort of mediator.

Truthfully, Eli was not certain why he himself had been invited. He had no real interest either way, and a part of him was tempted to leave and deal with his own matters.

"Besides, they have the firepower right now to win this without your surrender."

"Only with help from the Kingdoms," Yang said, turning to Eli for the first time since the negotiations had begun. "And we have reason to believe that the United Kingdoms may have their own challenges to deal with. You can't maintain this kind of firepower long. And we all know you will not succeed in gaining the whole of Africa. Why not cut your losses?"

"The United Kingdoms have never been stronger!" Eli shot back in quick defense, not allowing that comment to slide. A sudden slight headache began behind his eyes, similar to the start of a migraine. He attempted not to allow the fear to show as he glanced at Jackson and noted that he, too, seemed suddenly uncomfortable.

"Is that so?" Yang asked smugly. "Forgive me, but I have to ask the question. You're not equipped with Intelligence, are you?"

Eli did not waver. His expression remained strong faced. "None of us are afraid of your little weapon," Eli said with a deep glare, even as he faced the inward terror of what might in this very moment be occurring.

"The two hundred thirty-six agents we have so far killed might disagree."

Eli's throat tightened. He felt a sudden disgust in the way this man was clearly so pleased by the death of Eli's good men and women.

"It doesn't matter whether we have help from the Kingdoms or not," Sizwe said assuredly. "We will find a way to be free in the end. And I won't sign any document that assures my own freedom at the cost of someone else's."

Yang's face changed. "Fine," he said. Then strangely, he stood.

Eli assumed that this was the moment where Yang said they had nothing left to talk about, and went on his merry way. But apparently Jackson had read something in him in that split second that no one else sensed. He screamed out and pushed Sizwe out of the way just in time as the first shot was fired.

However, Jackson misjudged one pivotal thing: his own importance. He had moved to protect the African leader, but Yang's bullet rang true on its target: Jackson.

★ ★ ★ ★ ★

Damian had come to help Ella.

In many ways he was weak and feeble, yet the distraction he caused was enough to save her life. She escaped the grip of her foe as soon as Damian approached. Putting distance between herself and this new enemy, she searched for her weapon, but to no avail.

Despite her many claims over the past months that she disliked him, she still screamed out as Damian was killed before her eyes.

"Oh, no need to be scared, Nineteen," the killer said soothingly, using her Zhànshì number. Ella watched Mikel's friend die, clutching the wound at his heart, and only in that moment did it occur to her how much she had come to care for him. He had not only been Mikel's unlikely friend and mentor...he had been hers too.

"I'm an old friend of your mother's. That is, we trained together in our youth. Although, we were never really friends."

"Who the taint are you?"

"My name is Rai. But you would know me as Zhànshì Six."

"What do you want from me?" Ella uttered as Damian took his final gasping breath.

Her instincts told her to attack this enemy, and yet she stood watching in horror, feeling strangely affected by Damian's death. She felt tense and stiff and unable to move or even really breathe.

"Why did you kill him? He didn't have to die, Zhànshì Six!"

"I'm just here to take you home," he offered plainly. "You don't belong here. The old man was in the way."

"This isn't the time!" Ella shot back in anger. "You feel that headache too, don't you?" she spoke, nearly flinching from the intense pain.

His eyes narrowed thoughtfully.

"We can't distract Mikel or we're both dead. We have bigger fish to fry right now."

"On the contrary. This is all I have on my plate. So, let's do this. Are you prepared to fight me? Or would you prefer to surrender?"

Ella gritted her teeth and put her trembling hands up, forming fists. "Never."

★ ★ ★ ★ ★

"Ava," Mikel sent through the link in a last-ditch attempt. *"If you can hear me, please, help. I can't stop this overload on my own. I need your help. I wanted to believe I was strong enough. But I need you to shut it off and save us all, like you did the last time."*

It took swallowing all that was left of his pride to utter those words, but he ultimately managed to do so.

"Last time?" she asked seemingly in confusion. He was too focused on blocking Counter Intelligence from infecting all of them to reply.

"I hear you, Mikel," she answered weakly. It was already affecting her too, though luckily, the others had disconnected from the link and should not be immediately infected. *"I'll do what I can."*

★ ★ ★ ★ ★

Eli fought back against Yang's men, and dodged the man's attempts to shoot him next. But having dealt the quick blow, Yang and his men retreated almost immediately.

Eli seethed in anger, considering chasing them down and making them pay, but reminding himself that this was not his fight. He went to the exit and prepared to leave, with sounds of screams and gunshots, even explosions, outside.

As soon as he was outside, he found what the explosions had been. His truck, and Jackson's, had been thrown up into flames, leaving them with no real escape. And Yang's personal guard would have demolished the tent too, but Colonel Vasiliv and his men fought them off relentlessly.

Eli turned to his radio, frustrated at having to rely on that technology rather than the link. "I need an exit, now!"

"Sir, I almost have her!"

"I don't care about that insolent brat!" Eli shot back. "I want an exit. Now!"

"Yes, sir!"

Eli returned to the tent, where Sizwe crouched down beside Jackson, who was kneeling on the ground, holding his wound and looking deathly pale as blood ran down his abdomen, and even from his mouth.

Sizwe took Jackson by both cheeks, trying to inform him that they would make it out, and all would be well.

But that wound...Jackson would be dead in minutes, and there was no escape. Colonel Vasiliv and one of his men hurried inside the tent and right to Jackson. Vasiliv cursed when he saw the state Jackson was in.

"We need to get him to safety!" Sizwe commanded with intense worry.

"The trucks are up in flames," Vasiliv's man said, but Vasiliv himself was now kneeling on the ground next to Jackson, unable to speak as he realized the seriousness of this situation.

"Sir," another of Vasiliv's women entered the tent. "I got answers out of one of the survivors. They have air support; a drone on its way. They'll be here in minutes. We need to get them out of here!" Only then did the woman notice Jackson. She muttered several curses.

Eli watched from the sidelines. It did not matter to him. He already had another way out. But the seriousness of this situation for them was clearly too painful for any of them to admit.

Jackson was looking more dead every second as he slowly hunched down. He was losing great amounts of blood, on top of a wound that few people survived from, even in the best of circumstances and with immediate help. He was already dead. Eli knew that. Jackson knew that. They all knew it. But none of his friends seemed prepared to admit it.

"Go," Jackson muttered, barely audible.

"No," Vasiliv said, shaking his head in denial. Sizwe, too, looked entirely unprepared to do what was clearly necessary.

Eli almost left then and there, on his way to find Zhànshì Six and leave this whole mess behind, but for some reason, he lingered, wanting to know how this would play out.

"I'm already dead!" Jackson spat, and the scarlet blood from his mouth spattered on the faces of both his friends. "Go!" he tried to command, but neither of them budged. How could someone be so disrespected, or possibly so loved, by his soldiers that they would not even obey such obvious commands?

"I won't leave you," Vasiliv said, and Eli had never known a Russian to be so soft.

"Sir," the woman said, though looking somber, "they'll be here any second! We need to retreat before we're out of time."

"That's an order!" Jackson said, though it sounded more like a pleading now. "Get Sizwe out of here."

"Jackson…" this time it was Sizwe who was hesitant.

"I'm dead," Jackson reiterated, and that seemed truer every second.

"Almost there," Zhànshì Six informed Eli through radio, and once more, he thought to leave and meet him along the way, but he hesitated, and had no earthly understanding of why.

"Go," Jackson pleaded once more. "Please, tell Ava…" he couldn't finish the sentence. It was clear he didn't have just one sentence that would be enough. "Tell her I'm sorry," he spoke through his pain. "I didn't mean to let her down again."

Vasiliv had up until this moment been in denial, but just having a message to take, a last task from Jackson, seemed to wake him out of his denials. "I'll tell her," Vasiliv assured him, "I promise, friend."

Jackson attempted to nod his gratitude, but he couldn't seem to really hold himself up anymore, let alone move.

"Let's go!" Vasiliv ordered, and his men immediately prepared to do so.

Sizwe was pulled along, but forcefully stopped near the exit long enough to turn back to Jackson and say one last piece. "You will not be forgotten, brother. This I swear."

Still, Jackson could not respond. He would likely be dead by the time the air raid arrived, but with the strain on time and the danger of the impending air strike, his friends left him there to die alone.

"Just tell me if there's anything I can do," Sasha pleaded helplessly from beside her, ignoring his headache and seeming to realize her pain was far worse. Ava hardly heard it, being entirely focused on the strain from the Tower. "It wasn't supposed to be strong enough to reach this far. We believed the radius was much smaller. I'm sorry, love. We were supposed to be safe here."

She didn't know details of the plan, or have any real explanation for why this was happening. All she had was Mikel's request and her own connection with the Tower core.

The weight was crushing. She could hardly move, or think, or breathe. All she could do was push back, try and fight against the enemy as it attempted to break her.

Her walls were still in place and that was the worst part. She did not feel she could control the Tower, and yet it had no problem pushing against her.

It didn't matter how much it seemed to be imploding her mind, she had no defense. She could not seem to stop it, could not seem to fight back, could not do anything.

She had all but given up when Mikel's voice stammered through the link once more, and she could feel how weakened he was. "*It's crushing me!*" he said, pleading for help.

Mikel was capable of great things regarding the Tower, but neither he nor Ava had ever faced such an immense, incredible power and force against them as this.

Still, something within that pleading seemed to awaken a new strength within her. She thought of Ame. Of Kyle. Of Breanna. Never again. She would never again be that helpless. No one would die because of her. She had to protect Mikel, whatever it took.

"*You've faced this before, Ava!*" Mikel tried to encourage her. "*Shut it down like last time!*"

"I don't know what you're talking about!" Ava sent a pained reply through the link.

A long silence before he answered. *"The blackouts, Ava. Don't you remember? They turned on the entire global network and released Counter Intelligence. Every man, woman and child with the chip would have been killed in an instant if you hadn't shut it down. Don't you remember?"*

It all came back to her like a heavy kick to the stomach. She did remember. The waves in that hallucination, the ocean that had pushed her under repeatedly and threatened to drown her...it was the same weapon she faced now. Counter Intelligence had attempted to destroy her and everyone else with the chip, but in that same instant, Ava had remembered Breanna's image and learned how to swim.

Eli had tried to blame all the chaos from the blackouts on Ava, but if she had not caused the blackout, he, and countless others, would have been killed in an instant. Her mind had acted instinctually, and apparently Mikel—who had been connected with the Australian Towers at the time—was the only one who knew the truth.

Ava tried to remember the image from Breanna. She must swim with the current, rather than try to impose force against it.

So, with seemingly the weight of the world pressing against her, Ava stopped pushing back. In one instant, the crushing weight overwhelmed her, overtaking her completely. And for that brief instant, Ava stopped. Her heart, her mind, her body, all at once. She fell forward in her own lap, having gone limp. For that one instant, she was truly still.

Had that instant lasted much longer than it did, Sasha might have pronounced her dead.

In that moment, the enemy crept its grasp inside her mind. The moment she stopped pushing, it won.

But with the weight of the world having crushed her entirely, Ava remembered how to swim, and in the very next instant, she moved with the current rather than pushing against it. She sat up again, and her eyes opened.

Sasha gave exclamations of relief.

Ava was aware of the bleeding from her nose, but unfazed by it. Even now, she had absolute control of the Tower core and complete understanding. It did not take every ounce of her focus. Instead, it felt like swimming downstream: simple, easy, relaxing even.

One piece of the Tower was attempting to break, not only Mikel, but all of those in the vicinity with the chip. It was strongest pushing on Mikel, because his access to the link had been open. But it pushed against Eli, Sasha, Ella, Jackson, and several others whom Ava did not know. The only thing that had held it in check was Mikel's attempts to fight it off—otherwise, they all would have been infected, crushed in an instant.

Ava cocked her head, searching for the correct thread.

"Ava, love, are you all right?" Sasha asked helplessly from beside her. "I thought you were…" he trailed off. For a moment, he truly had written her off as dead. And for that moment, she might even have been.

★ ★ ★ ★ ★

Eli left the tent and hurried outside as the truck pulled in. He could see a distant light in the sky that was the drone en route to destroy this location.

Vasiliv and his men were hiking on foot to new terrain, hoping to get to safety before the drone arrived. They had radioed for help, but none of their people had been as close as Zhànshì Six. They were all still several minutes out.

Eli waited outside for the truck, ignoring the overwhelming nudge in his chest telling him to go back.

He did not feel any responsibility for Jackson. He had even wished for the man to die tonight. There was no reason to go back, no reason to sit with his enemy while he died. But he couldn't help thinking of Jackson's last request, those words to be returned to Ava.

Eli gritted his teeth in anger. He did not care for Jackson. If anything, he despised the man. And Jackson certainly felt no good feelings toward him. This was for the best, for everyone involved.

Still, images flashed through his mind. Ava, reading in a tree. Ava, squealing in excitement when she had opened the Jonathan Jordan tickets. Ava, catching Eli smiling in the mirror, and pretending not to have seen it. Ava, over and over again, with him, loving him, trying, even when he gave her every reason not to.

He gritted his teeth, grinding them over and over as his knuckles gripped white. The drone strike grew ever nearer.

Jackson was not worth risking his life for. But Ava...? Ava had always been there for him, and time and time again, he had let her down. He would never be able to repair the damage he had caused by having Hawkins killed. He knew that now. Still, his desire to be worthy of the love she had always offered overwhelmed him in this moment.

Always in the past, he had acted rashly and made the wrong decisions, ignoring the voice that screamed out at him to do good. It would be so easy now to do the same, to ignore that voice and leave Jackson to his fate. He would probably die anyway, no matter what Eli did.

Still, one more image flashed through his mind, of Ava after a terrible fight between them, after Eli had been highly manipulative, and Ava had ultimately accepted his words. He had expected her to run off and brood alone. But instead, Ava had come up to him, leaving all pride behind when she said to him in all honesty, "You know I'll always love you, right?"

Eli had been flabbergasted at the time. She had no reason to love him when he treated her as he did.

Eli turned and ran back to the tent. Whatever else happened, at least he could give her one more reason to love him.

Jackson lay on the ground now, deathly pale and barely breathing. Eli hurried to him, and attempted to pull him up over his shoulders.

But with the seeming last effort of fight left in him, when he saw who it was attempting to grab him, Jackson attempted to stop Eli.

"I'm trying to help you!" Eli growled. "Now stop fighting me and hold still."

Jackson looked surprised but did as commanded.

"I'm outside, sir!" Zhànshì Six informed him, and Eli ran with Jackson over his shoulders, outside of the tent and to the truck. It was still very unlikely that Jackson would survive this. Yet he had made up his mind.

By the time they entered the truck, Jackson was unconscious, near death. Zhànshì Six took off, and Eli attempted a simple medical procedure, doing what he could by providing oxygen and stopping the bleeding.

"Get us to our camp!" Eli ordered. "I want to see if I can't get him in better shape before we send him home. Hurry it up!"

★ ★ ★ ★ ★

Ava found the thread and cut it out. No longer was the Tower core attempting to crush and overload the others. They were all safe.

She found the drone strike headed toward the meeting point, and she shut it down. She found Yang's retreating vehicles, and stopped them in their tracks. She found a vast enemy enclosing in on the surrounding area, prepared to retake this territory. Ava disabled their weapons systems and turned off their power, permanently.

She accounted for everything within the radius of the Tower core. And when she was finished, she searched until she located the thread to disable the Tower itself. Then she shut it off.

★ ★ ★ ★ ★

"What happened?" Sasha demanded when the team returned from the utterly failed mission. He scanned the faces, searching for the one man he most cared to see among them.

"Where is he?" Sasha muttered, not even able to say the boy's name.

No one replied, though all of them looked grave.

"Where is he?" Sasha repeated louder, almost shouting this time.

Vasiliv shook his head, still unable to face Sasha and the reality of what had occurred.

"Answer me!" Sasha shouted, startling everyone in the group. He was painfully aware of the fact that Ava was behind him and was here to witness this.

"We lost four good men," Nastia muttered, making a point of the fact that Sasha's loss was not the only one to be considered. "Jackson was one of them."

The blood drained from Sasha's face, and he moved to the nearest wall in an attempt to stabilize himself.

He was not prepared to accept this. His entire body felt suddenly cold and numb. He attempted to look up to face Ava, but his vision had become suddenly blurry and even his hearing seemed to give out. Sasha had never been faint before, but there could be no other explanation for how his body seemed to collapse, how he fell to the floor, unable to move or deal with the reality.

In truth, he hadn't fully understood how much he had come to care for this boy until that moment.

☆ ☆ ☆ ☆ ☆

Compartmentalization, not of the permanent variety. She would resume her feelings when she was equipped to deal with them. She felt entirely numb to the knowledge of Jackson's death. But she knew if she allowed her feelings to surface, they would crush her as entirely as the Tower had attempted to do, as the enemy still attempted to do from within her mind.

Sasha had been there for her for so long now that it was good for her to care for him for a change. She took him to his room and helped him to his bed. He seemed to be in shock, which she helped him with. He had not been prepared for Jackson's death, no matter how he had warned her to be prepared for any outcome.

"Tomorrow will be better," she attempted to reassure him, but her words came out emotionless and unfeeling.

He was staring at something, and it took a moment before Ava realized it was the bed where Jackson had slept for the past week, with some of his things laid out on it—though most of his belongings were in her room.

For the first time since being pulled off the floor, he looked up to face her. "No," he disagreed strongly. "Tomorrow will be the worst of it. Tomorrow, I'll have to tell myself over and over again that it's real, all the while informing others of the truth. I'll have to speak with the Committee. I'll have to tell Zak. I'll have to admit it to the world, while not really believing it myself."

"I'll tell them if you want," Ava offered, and her voice was as monotone as Valkyrie's.

Sasha's expression grew more somber still as he watched her. When he did speak, his emotions were deafening. "If this is how you need to survive the next few days, weeks, or even months, then so be it. But please Ava, do not allow yourself to ignore your feelings for too long. I can't lose both of you in one night."

His words did not get through to her, not really. She could not deal with this news in any other way. She was too weak, too broken, and losing Jackson…it would be enough to consume her; to truly shatter her.

She did have to do this to survive. Only…she wasn't sure if she would ever be prepared to deal with these emotions. Not really. And maybe this new version of her would be better. Valkyrie never became distracted by her unwilling, human emotions. She got the job done, no matter how hard, and she did it well. Perhaps Ava would be more valuable to the world if she were as emotionless as Valkyrie.

"Please, Ava," Sasha pleaded, gripping her forearm and holding her until she looked him in the eyes. "Promise me. Promise me that you won't leave me too. Not now, not on the same night…. I understand that you're not ready yet…but promise me, you won't shut me out, and everything out, forever."

She could not make any promises, really. Still, she nodded, to humor him. "Goodnight, Sasha," she said, and left the room.

She walked slowly through the corridors. Her mind felt as empty as her emotions in that moment. There were no considerations about what would happen next. All she thought about was the surrounding walls, the hallways before her, and the next step on the floor ahead of her. It was simple, but it kept things in check. It might be better that way, in the end.

Ava made it to the room that had become hers and entered the code Jackson had taught her to get inside. She closed the door behind her and went to the bed. The room was in disorder. She had never fully returned to bed after Jackson had come to the room that night.

She walked slowly to the bed, taking in the room. It might be easier to rest without overthinking everything as she normally did. The best part about these times of erasing her emotions, shoving them to a box in the back of her head, was that she didn't even have to deal with the nightmares. Maybe it would be better that way, for everyone.

She climbed into the bed and pulled the covers over her, but something atop the bed caught her eyes and stopped her. It was the shirt

Jackson had left when he changed into a more suitable uniform before leaving. Now it sat there on the bed, and she was left to stare at it, where he had left it behind when he had shoved his other things back into his pack. She stared for a very long time.

Ava was certain that she would not be able to sleep as long as that shirt remained on the bed. And so, eventually, she climbed out of bed, walked to the edge where the shirt rested, and regarded it for some time more. It was difficult to remove it, and she wasn't sure why.

Eventually, she sat next to it and noticed the duffle bag he hadn't even bothered to zip closed again before he made his quick exit.

It took longer than it ever should have, but eventually Ava was able to pick up the shirt. She was about to carefully toss it across to the duffle bag, but stopped, suddenly pulling it close to her, as if in curiosity. She held the shirt close to her for a time, and then she couldn't help pressing it to her lips. None of this was done with much, if any, feeling, but with the shirt so close, something caught her attention. His scent lingered on the piece of clothing, and it startled her, as if snapping her back into reality.

Ava's eyes suddenly filled with tears that immediately spilled over and were replaced by more. She tried to stop them, to subdue the pain and emotion, but it was too great. There was nothing she could do to subdue the feelings, and she clung to that shirt as she sobbed.

For a long time, she cried, louder and longer than anyone should have.

Even after the tears subsided, she sat there alone on the bed, feeling heavy and pained.

Could she pick up the pieces after this? Could she ever keep going after losing Jackson this way? The very thought of it threatened to break her. She could not do it. She wasn't strong enough.

But suddenly, thoughts of Jackson and how he was always rooting for her gave her pause. He was always so confident in her, even when she had nothing left to give.

She had to find a way to push past it. Jackson would have believed she could, if he were still here. She had to keep going. She could not waver. She had to push through. Just like Sasha did when he lost Kristen. There was so much work to be done, so much that Jackson had left behind, and she could not stop, even if he was no longer there to fight beside her.

Still, the person she was right then and there really would break. She wasn't strong enough to handle this yet.

Ava looked up at the wall before her as a thought occurred to her, the only thing that could truly help her through this. The only thing that could truly make her strong enough to move forward: inner peace.

It took everything within her to set the shirt back down on the bed and stand up to leave the room.

Several hours had passed as she'd sat alone in that room. It was midday now, and Ava walked through the halls, asking every passerby where to find Sizwe.

Eventually, she was directed to his meditation center, which she hadn't previously known existed.

She clenched her fists and her fingernails dug into her palms. Even now, she knew how difficult this would be. She knocked on the door, and after several moments, it opened.

Sizwe stood in the doorway, looking grave. He said nothing, instead watching her for a time.

Her look was one of determination, and he seemed to understand it. "When the student is ready," Sizwe repeated gently, still somber as he mourned his lost brother.

"The teacher appears," Ava finished the sentence weakly.

Another long silence passed before he nodded approvingly and opened the door to her.

She entered the large meditation center, not entirely sure what to expect. It looked more like a fighting gym to her. Ava took in the room, and was surprised when her eyes landed on Mikel, sitting cross legged on the ground. He, too, looked very grave as he mourned his friend and mentor Damian, who had also been lost that night.

"Took you long enough," Mikel said with a pained, knowing smile.

★ ★ ★ ★ ★

"I don't have the patience to deal with your games right now, Eli," Sasha admitted over the radio. "The events of last night were a heavy blow to us."

"I'm not playing games," Eli grumbled. "Believe me, you're going to want to let me in."

"Why?" Sasha replied weakly. "Give me a reason. Why should we open that bay to you? What's to stop you from sending in a bomb to blow us out of existence? We know you sent a Zhànshì to attack Ella and Mikel last night, killing a friend in the process. Damian was a good man, a true soldier for freedom. And that attack on our people is part of the reason things went so poorly at the meet."

Sasha stood in the communications room with several other technicians. Eli had requested him by name for this communique. And on any other day, Sasha might have been equipped to deal with his son. But not today. Not right now.

"Just open the bay, Sasha, and let me show you!"

Sasha was silent for a time. He couldn't help the pang in his heart, wishing Jackson were there to discuss it with him, to weigh the pros and cons, and come to a decision together.

"Have a lovely day, son," Sasha said, hoping to end this now.

"Sasha, open the bay door!" Eli said with sudden frustration. "I'm in the truck myself. If I wished you ill intentions, I could have caused them by now. I sent the garrison and have been true to my word to Jackson. Now please, throw me a bone."

Sasha closed his eyes sadly. Why did everything have to be a game to him? Every interaction had to be a test. Every moment a manipulation.

"I'm not in the mood for this today, Eli," Sasha said in a saddened tone. "I lost my boy last night, as you well know—"

"Open the doors, Sasha! Or I assure you that you'll regret it. I have something that you lost."

Sasha shook his head in annoyance. From the sound of things, and knowing Eli, there really was little danger in obeying. Still, he did not have the patience for this right now.

"Sir?" one of the technicians asked, turning up to face Sasha, who was standing.

Sasha waved his hand with an air of exhaustion. "Let him in," he said helplessly. "But keep the precautions in place that we discussed."

Then he left the communications center and headed with an armed escort toward the bay, feeling emotionally exhausted. The day's work had hardly begun. Already, just hours after news of Jackson's death, the alliance with Russia and Africa was falling apart as the Committee questioned whether to continue or pull back.

For months, Jackson had dealt with the efforts to hold together the fragile alliance. Now there was no one to fill that void. Sasha felt the need to finish the fight Jackson had started. Yet he didn't feel prepared for it as he should have been.

Perhaps, in time, things would get easier. Then again, it never had with the loss of Kristen. Her death was still as painful today as it had been the first day. He was just better at containing it now.

Ava had spent the entire day in prayer and meditation with Sizwe. Sasha hoped it would help her, because in this thing, he did not know how to help her himself, and that only added to his pain and feelings of inadequacy.

"Open it," Sasha said weakly as they made it to the inner entrance to Bay Five.

Eli stood inside, leaning against his truck and looking rather proud of himself. Sasha sighed inwardly. On any other day, he would be overjoyed to see his son and for an opportunity to try and get through to him. But not today.

"I've humored you this far, Eli," Sasha said, feeling the mental, physical and emotional exhaustion as it rang clearly in his tired voice. "Now please, just say what you came here to say."

Eli pulled up from where he leaned against the truck, signaling to the other man sitting in the vehicle, whom Sasha could only assume was the mysterious Zhànshì Six.

The man exited the vehicle and went to open the back hatch. Sasha started to object, demanding that Eli stop being ambiguous and just give him some answers. A ramp was laid out from the truck. They pulled out a gurney on wheels with a man laying on it, connected to various tubes, cords and oxygen.

Instantly curious, Sasha clamped his mouth shut as they wheeled the unconscious man toward Sasha. His beard had been shaved to more easily accommodate the oxygen mask. He was heavily bandaged across his bare abdomen, and he was overlaid with tubes and cords.

He was hardly recognizable. Sasha stared in shock for a time, unable to believe what he was seeing. In the end, it was the boy's full head of dark hair, and the small bandage at his neck from the attack in the

Tower that proved to Sasha it was really him. The sound that escaped Sasha in surprise was not one he was proud of, but he did not mind the embarrassment just now. He ran the few feet of distance to Jackson and took the boy's hand in his. "Eli...how did you...?"

"Your people left him there to die," Eli said with a touch of scorn. "I did what they were unable to do."

Sasha found his own voice choking in his throat as he attempted to speak but was unable. His eyes became blurry with tears of joy.

"He suffered severe abdominal trauma. He has not yet awoken. And although our United Kingdoms equipment, medics and tech were enough to get him this far, there's still little chance he'll actually pull through this."

Sasha shook his head in excited disbelief, not having any idea how to convey his gratitude.

"Most of his equipment and his clothes were done for. But I saved this, thinking it might be of importance." Eli handed the watch to Sasha, the special engraving from him clear on the inside. And only as the boy handed the watch to his father did Sasha notice Eli's own watch, worn proudly on his wrist, a gift Sasha had given many, many years ago.

Sasha had so many reasons to be angry at Eli. And he could never fully forgive him for Ava's abuse. But this humanizing act, and seeing that old watch, touched Sasha in a way he did not realize was possible. He felt a new, overwhelming desire to be there for his son, to help him through his struggles, just as he had of recent times been there for Ava.

Sasha accepted the watch. The gratitude and love he felt overwhelmed him, and he hoped it showed to his son. "Thank you, Eli," Sasha said with a deep bow of his head.

For one instant, Sasha could see how this fatherly love overtook Eli. But soon it was pushed away. "I didn't do it for you," he said coolly. But then his expression softened once more. "I did it for Ava." He struggled for words then as he attempted to ask Sasha for a greater favor. "Could you...tell her...?"

Sasha considered that for a brief moment. Ultimately, he nodded. "I will."

Eli smiled, ever so slightly. Then nodded his gratitude. "He still might not pull through this," Eli reminded him. "He's stable for now, but...."

"We'll take it from here," Sasha assured him. "You have done more than enough, my son."

Eli smiled awkwardly. "Good luck, Sasha." With that, he signaled to his Zhànshì. The two of them closed up the truck and left without another word.

"Let's get him to the infirmary!" Sasha ordered immediately, and as they pushed the gurney from the bay, a greater new hope filled Sasha for both of his boys.

★ ★ ★ ★ ★

Inner peace would indeed be a great feat. She desperately searched for the answers that Sizwe assured her were there. Mikel had left hours ago. Apparently, he had been working with Sizwe since the first day of their arrival. Ava had not been ready then, but she was now.

Sizwe spoke to her of many religions: Buddhism, Christianity, Hinduism, Islam, Judaism, and many more. He said he had found and clung to the truths he believed, but that perhaps the answer could be different for her.

Spirituality was only one step toward inner peace, but it was the step Sizwe had decided to start with. He said there were many pieces to finding inner enlightenment, but to realize the grander scheme of the universe, and one's place within it, was a deeper part of understanding oneself than most people ever realized.

Ava was so intent on the meditation he had told her to continue that she hardly noticed when a light tapping sounded on the door and Sizwe answered it. She never would have opened her eyes either, but Sizwe urgently commanded, "Get up!"

Even without seeing him, she knew he was talking to her. Ava did as ordered.

"Come. Quickly."

She followed him.

"We need to get him back to Russia," Sasha explained. "They have been working on a sort of chamber that assesses the needed vital organs and can synthetically create the perfect match. He's experiencing multisystem organ injury. He's only alive due to these machines at this time, but I think, if we can get him there soon enough—"

"Well what are you waiting for?" Mikel asked urgently. "Just take him and go!"

Sasha smiled, obviously pleased by that reaction and how Mikel now clearly cared as much for Jackson as the others did. The dreamwalk had changed all of them.

"I can't believe he's okay!" Ella said, and the look of actual, pure joy on her face was one Ava had not seen on Ella since before her testing. She, too, had changed her feelings about Jackson, though they had never stopped their teasing digs at one another.

Ava could not take her eyes from the gurney where he lay. There was a new hope, a new possibility, and she clung to it. Even so, there was a real chance that he would not survive, even now. But she already knew, whatever happened, she would learn to be okay. She had to find inner peace. She had to be able to go on living her mission, even without Jackson, if it came to that.

"They're preparing a medical escort as we speak," Sasha explained. "I've already spoken with the top medical minds in Russia. They're preparing every possible asset to save him. We'll get him through this, if God wills it."

Ava looked up at that comment. Sasha had always believed in a higher power. He had always known his role in the greater picture of the universe. Perhaps that was a portion of his strength.

She thought of Lionel. He had once told her that if she truly knew herself, no one could have power over her. And in truth, she did not know herself the way Sasha did, or the way Jackson had, or even Mikel. But she would learn to. She would find herself. She had to.

Unconsciously, she neared the gurney until she was at Jackson's side. She seemed to forget the others entirely as she slowly reached out and put Jackson's hand in hers. There was no movement. *"Jackson,"* she spoke through the link, but there was no reply.

The others continued to speak, but Ava no longer heard them. Eli had done this, had saved Jackson, for her. Whatever ulterior motives he may have, she could only feel gratitude. *"Thank you, Eli,"* she sent to her brother this time.

It was nearly a minute before he replied, *"I guess now we're even."*

She considered that comment, racking her mind to understand the meaning. Was this Eli admitting to Hawkins' death? As grateful as Ava was, and always would be for this, if Eli thought that rescuing a wounded man in battle made up for murder...? Well, he was sorely mistaken. Still, she gave no reply. Eli had hurt her in more ways than she could ever understand or explain. And yet, there was a part of her that agreed. She would have faced all of that again if it meant Eli would save Jackson in this moment when no one else could.

Sasha came and stood before Ava, resting his hands on her shoulders as he looked her in the eyes. "Ava, my love, I know I promised you that I would be here for you, for as long as you needed me. And I truly meant those words. But—"

"You don't even have to ask," Ava shot back seriously. "Go with Jackson! Get him through this. Never leave his side! I don't want any Russian assassins taking advantage of this. He needs you right now, far more than I do."

Sasha nodded soberly, but seemed to be looking deeper in attempt to assure himself that it was true.

"I'm fine, Sasha!" she said earnestly. "Take care of him. Please."

"She will not be alone," Sizwe assured Sasha from the other end of the room.

"That's right," Mikel agreed.

"She's got a team now," Ella finished, as if wanting to prove that they were all there for her now.

Ava smiled gratefully, and Sasha looked around the room at every face there. Eventually, he ended on Sizwe. "You changed us, you know," he said with somber gratitude.

Sizwe offered a half smile. "No. I did not change you. I simply united you."

★ ★ ★ ★ ★

Kyle watched the horses as they munched on the last bit of hay from their evening feed. The snow on the ground and the chill of the evening air caused a crisp, toasty sensation as he leaned into the warmth of his coat and wool socks.

For three days he had enjoyed this barn outside of one of Darya's estates within Russia. For the time being, it was run completely by her household staff, and there was no indication that she had any intentions of returning soon. But at night, he was able to easily search the household, and already had vast amounts of information that were well worth sleeping in a barn filled with animals. Besides, the barn held a sense of simplicity that was enjoyable in the midst of his relentless, careening lifestyle.

He watched the horses feed for a long time with thoughts of the future of the world on his mind. A nearly silent crunch just outside the barn caused him to hop off the fence and creep farther into the barn where he would stay carefully hidden. Still, he drew his weapon just in case.

The crunching grew louder until it was clear that the intruder was just outside the barn. "I made my entrance known on purpose," the male voice spoke, and Kyle was startled by the American accent speaking English. "It is unwise to sneak up on someone like yourself," the man continued in his husky voice. "I know that firsthand."

Kyle did not budge, but he moved his finger to the trigger in preparation.

"I know you're in there. And I am not going to go in, but I think you'll decide to come out here and join me and the horses."

Kyle slowed and quieted his breathing, not taking any chances.

"I know who you are, Kyle," the man said. "And believe me, I'm not with Darya."

He would not give up his location, no matter how curious he became.

"I'm a friend of Ava's. And you need to hear what I came to tell you."

For a long time, Kyle hesitated. All the signs pointed to the fact that this man might be telling the truth. Still, Kyle could not be certain.

"You and I are a lot alike, Kyle," the man continued. "We like to work behind the scenes. We don't care about praise, acknowledgement or recognition. We just want to get the job done. I've been getting the job done now for longer than you've been alive. But I must admit, I have been impressed by your skills and your dedication."

His curiosity was so strong it caused beads of sweat to run down his temples. But curiosity was a good way to get yourself killed.

"I know you don't want to give up your location, when you have no real reason to trust me. If I was with Darya, I would have used that remote-controller on you. If I was with Eli…I would be an idiot."

Kyle stifled a sudden laugh.

"But I'm not. I am like you. And I'm here because your skills, and mine, are greatly needed."

"Who are you?" Kyle finally asked. At this point, there was really no point in avoiding this except to be stubborn.

"Remington. You wouldn't have heard my name, but you've seen my face before."

Of course, the man was just trying to goad Kyle into stepping out into the open. Well, it worked. He left the barn, his gun steadily trained on the face of the large man before him, who stood weaponless. Kyle did not immediately recognize him, however.

"Why are you here?" Kyle asked seriously.

"Yes, let's get to the point," Remington agreed. "No use in wasting either of our time. Four months ago, Ava left Eli and ran to Russia."

Kyle almost caught his breath in surprise. "You're kidding me."

"No, Kyle, I'm not. After you left, things grew much worse. And eventually, she had little choice. But Jackson and Sasha still fight with the ideals of freedom in mind. Ava was accepted with open arms. A few weeks ago, Mikel and Ella joined them."

Kyle's jaw dropped open. The news was shocking, and he almost found himself regretting faking his death and leaving, right before things apparently got interesting. Then again, if he hadn't left, he never would have come to know Valkyrie, and their times of working together these past months were worth every other boring day alone.

"Eli has become a tyrant. Council is being overrun—not that they had much integrity themselves. Soon, the United Kingdoms will be entirely under the General's command. And I don't need to tell you how dangerous that could be. However, I assume you have heard news of the recent victories in Africa."

"Of course," Kyle agreed.

"Your fellow Zhànshì have found a path to fight for freedom beside Jackson Davis. And already they have had incredible success. However, there are things that they cannot do, things that require men like you and me to accomplish."

"What are you suggesting?" Kyle asked with narrowed eyes.

"The fight you are taking on against the Jiānhùrén is necessary and important," Remington said as if to reassure Kyle. Strangely, it did. "And in the end, I think you will be needed to return to it. However, there is something that you and I need to help with first."

Finally, Kyle lowered his weapon, though only slightly. "I'm listening."

Remington was silent for a time, and it occurred to Kyle that this was a very soft-spoken man, and yet, he held a demeanor of incredible strength and power.

"It's time to cripple the Republic," Remington stated. "Once and for all."

PART TWO

Forces of Nature

CHOOSE TO STAND.

10

Embers

"There's only one rule," Nastia briefed the thirty-man team. She pointed to the screen and the picture of the two Zhànshì as they neared the miniature Tower. "Keep these two alive. Any questions?"

One hand went up, and Nastia called on the man. "Can you tell me why we're using tranquilizer guns rather than lethal force?"

"This is what the leader Sizwe likes to call a 'peaceful revolution.' Because of the abilities of our two Zhànshì friends, the enemy's weapons will be rendered useless, opening up the opportunity to take prisoners and avoid casualties. We have taken two Towers in this manner now, which is where this picture came from. Both times, the enemy soldiers eventually moved in to fight using close quarter combat and weapons. That's where the Elites will come in. All of you will focus on long-range, and we'll take care of the close-up combatants."

"As you mentioned, we've done this twice now," another soldier noted. "Don't we think the enemy will find a counterattack eventually?"

"That's why we're doing as much damage as quickly as possible. The other two attacks have both been in the past few days. And we have four more on the roster. The enemy will certainly find a counterattack.

312

But we hope to have liberated the entire continent of Africa by then, causing full retreat by the Republic."

"This may be a stupid question," a third soldier asked, attempting to sound respectful but obviously looking a bit lost. "How exactly are they going to shut off the Tower? Are they just skilled technicians? What exactly are we talking about?"

Nastia smiled. In truth, that was not exactly a question she had a direct answer to. All she could really do was glance back at the picture on the screen. "You'll see."

"Sir, it's happening. Just like the other Towers warned it would."

First Lieutenant Park's eyes widened in sudden fear. "Pull it up, on screen."

Within moments, he was watching the frightening footage. A young man and woman walked along at either side of the Tower, with a team surrounding them in clear defense. His soldier's weapons were immediately rendered useless.

The first soldier, the boy, walked with an air of confidence, his eyes open as he seemed to observe the chaos around him and managed to be completely unfazed by it. Not a flinch, not even a blink. The woman, on the other hand, had her eyes closed, and earbuds in her ears as she walked along, somehow managing to keep her footing and never trip.

They were surrounded by elite soldiers who fended off all attacks and a long-range team took out his officers from the background.

"Counter Intelligence is running?" Park asked in horror.

"Yes, sir, to maximum capacity. It's having no impact on them!"

Park sat down in his seat as the gravity of the situation settled in his mind.

"Sir what do we do?" the informant asked in fear.

The first lieutenant closed his eyes in defeat. "There's nothing to do. It's too late."

Five months had passed, yet the entire world was different now.

Mikel and Ava had spent every waking moment in work with Sizwe. They had learned to overcome their weaknesses, and both of them had come a long way.

For years, Ava had struggled with panic attacks, intense fear and anxiety. But in five months, her healing had been more real and complete than in the close to eleven years since being held captive in Russia.

Through dreamwalking, she had gained a sense of the altered memories from Harrison. She finally had a clear picture in her mind of the things that were true memories, versus those that had been manufactured. She remembered now in vivid color every moment of those horrendous six months in Russia. But she had found real and actual healing to turn those injuries into scars, rather than attempting to cover up a bullet wound with a band aid and wonder why it didn't seem to heal correctly.

She had worked through the emotional abuse from Eli. It was another scar, and one that would remain on her heart forever. But no longer was the wound fresh, threatening to overtake her at any moment. The panic attacks had almost entirely ceased now. And when they did come, she was well-equipped to cope with them and overcome them on her own.

The one wound that had been hardest to overcome was her confidence and how it affected her block with the Tower. She could not, for many of those months, manage even a small connection. And Mikel, too, had struggled with his own walls with his power, though their problem areas were very different.

Mikel had no trouble connecting to and controlling the Towers, but Counter Intelligence was too powerful for him, and no matter how he tried in simulations, he could not combat its effects.

And so, for a time, Sizwe had worked with them on what they could do. Countless hours of meditation, sitting in that room, working with the Towers. Ava had assumed for a long time that she could never overcome her block, and Mikel had decided he would never again work with the Towers, or at least not until Counter Intelligence was eliminated.

The changes didn't come in some swift, groundbreaking moment that changed everything. It wasn't like Breanna's vision, where Ava had tried and tried with no success, then been handed all the answers at once in a hallucinogenic state to the point of controlling all the Towers in the world simultaneously. It was nothing like that this time. This time it was slow, steady, and consistent. It felt like the process of building strength and muscle. One perfect, intense workout did not make any real change. But measured, consistent progress caused immeasurable success. And with one or two or three percent changes every day, eventually she overcame the walls.

Sizwe said it was likely that Ava's walls came undone themselves, as she worked through the many other unhealed wounds, and Ava believed that was true. Just like overcoming those walls, her healing had been slow, steady, but consistent. She felt whole once more.

She would never again be the person she had been during the Talks, not really. But that person was a part of her. Just like the broken version of herself from five months ago would always be a piece of Ava Altman.

Perhaps she wasn't as beautiful, sociable and elegant as she had been during those months mentoring with Lionel, but Ava felt more grounded and more confident than ever. This was the real Ava. This was who she was born to be. It was even who she wanted to be.

She had found her inner peace in those silent hours of meditation, in the painful dreamwalking sessions, and in the countless stories, teachings, and adjustments from Sizwe.

Mikel was more powerful than ever in his connection with the Tower. But he was still unable to stop the effects of Counter Intelligence in simulations. And so, they had decided to utilize the skills they did have. Ava trained relentlessly to be able to master the threads that she had only recently come to understand, the threads of the weapon, Counter Intelligence, which every day threatened to destroy her. And Mikel trained relentlessly in his connection with the Tower. He was already worlds ahead of Ava in that regard. She still had to be conscious and focused when connecting with the Tower. He now did it almost effortlessly, without thought, like moving his fingers or taking a step forward. The Tower had become an extension of him. And although it certainly didn't feel like that when Ava fought the weapon, Counter Intelligence, she was getting better. She felt she understood it better. And she felt that she could account for the instability, the shifting waves, to protect all those whom it threatened. She was prepared to deal with it, as she would any other opponent in a battle.

Weeks previously, Sizwe had recommended Ava listen to music while she fought the simulation. He said that she was too easily distracted, that every sound and movement from around her seemed to break her focus. When he gave her music to focus on, her mind would settle. She had to keep her eyes closed and focus on the task entirely, or even in the simulations, her opponent would best her—though it still had not managed to do so in the real fight against her mind.

Mikel was very confident in his incredible abilities, and he used them with eyes wide open during simulations, standing in the gym as the Elites and others trained, using the distractions to fuel his focus. It worked for him, but not for Ava.

So, with months of planning, and tireless work in uniting the African colonies to a decision to rise up against the Republic, they made their first strike.

The miniature Tower at Cascai was a success. The enemies were captured, with very few casualties.

The second Tower had not gone quite as well. It would have been better if they could have made the attacks simultaneously, but with only the two-man team to deal with the Towers, and without the continued help of the United Kingdoms, who had long since pulled their garrisons and no longer offered aid, the team could only take one Tower at a time. With a day of warning and extra preparation by the enemy, the second strike had afforded quite a few more casualties. They had been prepared with knives and staves and whatever close-quarter weapons they could collect in a day's notice. More than ten people had been killed. But still, it could have been so much worse, and ultimately the Ukombozi, as Sizwe had decided to call them, had obtained another miniature Tower and major city in Africa.

Only four left in the entire continent. If they could manage to accomplish all of these strikes in the next few days, then perhaps the Republic wouldn't have time to implement a counterattack before the Elites won it all.

Ava's eyes remained closed as the Ukombozi began their liberation. She listened to the elaborate music as the complex harmonies and percussion kept her full attention, keeping her completely focused on the combat with the most formidable opponent she had ever faced. When the weapon was targeted, not just at her, but Mikel, Ella and any others close with the chip, it was an extremely difficult battle.

Its power was vast, and its determination was astonishing. There was no reasoning with an enemy such as this, any more than there was reasoning with a gun after its holder had pulled the trigger. Counter Intelligence was a weapon, and the trigger had been pulled. Yet Ava fought the weapon with a formidable strength, holding this opponent at bay. Just as she had once searched for the thread of Counter Intelligence within the Tower, this weapon attempted to locate and cling to whatever threads it could find in her, and the others' minds, in order to crush them.

This wasn't her usual flavor of music. She enjoyed witty lyrics and playful beats. This composition, which she listened to on repeat, was bombastic, even frenetic, with no lyrics and an ostinato rhythm and bass motif—but it maintained her focus, and it felt more like battle music than a witty Jonathan Jordan ballad.

Every time the two-beat melody played its lower base, she tapped her two fists together, one atop the other along with the beat. It gave her a physical connection to the music, which kept her focus even more complete.

Ava felt a slight nudge and was tempted to open her eyes for the briefest of moments. She managed to refrain. Even a millisecond of split focus could allow Counter Intelligence through.

She continued walking at a steady pace. Suddenly a hand clung tightly to hers, pulling her along and walking at a bit faster pace. It was Mikel's hand. She had come to recognize it in simulations where it became necessary for him to pull her along.

She kept her eyes closed, thinking of Remington in her escape from the Korean Tower and the complete trust she had placed in him. From the outside looking on, this battle would have been frighteningly eventful, but Ava, focused entirely on the most powerful adversary there, witnessed none of it.

From the outside, the enemy had become even more prepared. They used crossbows initially, though all the bowmen had been eliminated quickly. Now their officers were attempting to fight off the Ukombozi with knives, swords and spears.

Mikel found his focus wavering slightly at the venom with which these officers fought. With each Tower had come greater casualties and greater fight from the enemy. A part of him envied Ava for the fact that she could not see what was going on around her. If he hadn't boldly told everyone he was just fine to do it this way, he might have changed his decision.

Of course, he *didn't* need the distraction for the same reasons she did. His connection with the Tower was effortless. But the fact that he could not fight, when the ten people surrounding him and Ava were involved in heavy battle to keep all danger away from him and his partner, was a bit frustrating. Maybe he'd work more on that in training. It would be great if he could deal with the Tower in the background, and focus on physical combat at the forefront.

Still, he couldn't do any of this without Ava, who fought the one opponent that terrified Mikel. He had battled countless foes. But Counter Intelligence was stronger than him. And no matter how much he trained for it, he could never come anywhere close to doing what Ava did.

She was humble and claimed that his immense power with the Tower was beyond hers. And maybe there was truth in that. Still, she could do what he was doing right now on any day of the week. And the fact that she was actually irreplaceable was not something he took lightly.

Nastia and Ella remained right up near Mikel and Ava, closer than all the others. The two of them were the last line of defense. Their job was to keep the Zhànshì safe, if all other soldiers failed to do so, and the two of them did nothing but watch their marks—Ella for Mikel, and Nastia for Ava.

Mikel did not flinch when a spear was thrown from a higher vantage within the Tower, and came directly towards him, but Ella nudged him out of the way in time, bumping him into Ava. Nastia aimed her weapon at the one who had thrown the spear, and the officer fell from the upper story to the ground. That was a painful way to go. Hopefully the tranq had knocked him unconscious before he hit the ground.

Ava continued walking beside Mikel without a care in the world, beyond fighting off the most terrifying threat that Mikel had ever encountered. He wasn't entirely sure how she managed to walk along this battlefield without ever even stumbling.

The third Tower was taken, and although the leader of the base had been under strict orders not to surrender, to fight to the death, ultimately, he had given the order for surrender, not wanting to see this end in a bloodbath when the battle had clearly already been lost.

Ava, Mikel and Vasiliv stood together in the Tower core, going over the footage from the event.

"I'm glad you keep the cameras on," Vasiliv said with satisfaction. "It's pretty amazing, watching the two of you walking along with that swagger while there's chaos and destruction all around you."

"Mikel swaggers," Ava corrected, watching the footage for herself. "Mine looks more like a..."

"Dancing meditation," Mikel offered.

She hit him on the side of the arm. "It does not!" she objected.

"No, for real!" Mikel said with a grin. "Just watch for a minute. See? You know I'm right."

"I'm not dancing, I'm walking gracefully."

"He's right," Vasiliv teased, "you're really getting into a groove."

"Would you both shut up?" she objected, yet it was clear she enjoyed it as she could not help smiling.

"You love that music I suggested," Vasiliv said, putting his arms up as if to say it were obvious.

"It's freaky and too much," Ava disagreed.

"Yet she always listens to it," Mikel said with a pointed look at Vasiliv.

"It just has the right vibe, okay? But I would never listen to it any other time."

"See, right there!" Vasiliv pointed to the screen. "You keep doing that with your fists."

"Right to the beat," Mikel agreed.

"Maybe we should talk about how this victory went," Ava replied with pointed frustration. "Or the next battle we have to face."

"She's just embarrassed," Mikel gave in an aside to Vasiliv.

Ava huffed and started out of the room. "I'm gonna get some breakfast. You guys keep watching my dance meditation and tell me how cool my groove is later."

"It could use some work," Vasiliv teased once more as Ava left.

★ ★ ★ ★ ★

"I want to ask you something," Ella directed her comment to Ava when Nastia left the table, and it was just the two of them left to finish their meal alone.

"Okay," Ava replied pleasantly. They hadn't exactly become close over the past months. And truthfully, Ava wasn't certain if they ever would. Yet, there was a change in their relationship. At least now they were surface level friends, rather than enemies.

"It's kind of a doozy," Ella warned.

Ava chuckled. "Have you ever directed a thought to me that wasn't?"

Ella rolled her eyes exaggeratedly, though she, too, was smiling. "Yes, I have. Before the age of ten I offered many. But this is a different type of intense."

"Go for it," Ava offered. "I'm interested."

"You never loved Kyle romantically, did you?" Ella asked seriously.

That *was* a different type of intense for Ella, and it took Ava off guard. She hadn't had "girl talk" with anyone since Hawkins. She didn't even really think Ella was capable of it. But neither did this question seem rooted in her past anger at Ava, or her anger surrounding Kyle's death. She genuinely seemed curious about the simple question.

"No," Ava admitted. "I guess I didn't love him that way."

Ella's eyes narrowed as she considered that. Eventually, she spoke her thoughts in barely more than a whisper. "Well, you're crazier than I thought."

Ava couldn't help laughing in surprise, but then she grew serious again. "You remember from the dreamwalk about the trauma I faced. The memory tampering from Harrison made for some confusion around Kyle. I just felt sick and afraid when I was around him, with no understanding of why. I guess, I was too terrified of that feeling to ever get close enough to fall in love."

"What about when you knew the truth?" Ella pressed. "When you knew why he was a part of the trauma and how he protected you?"

Ava shrugged. "I admit that when I eventually let my guard down with him, there was a moment..." She didn't know exactly how to explain it, so she left it hanging there. "But we agreed it wasn't right, and then...he was gone the next day."

Ella breathed out sadly. "I suppose it's understandable. But Ava... you missed out."

This time it was Ava's eyes that narrowed as she attempted to understand.

"Kyle was the best person that's ever lived," Ella explained soberly. "If Harrison hadn't messed you up, maybe you would have seen what I did."

Even after all these months, Ava had not fully accepted the fact that Kyle might be dead, but listening to Ella's caring words now made it seem more real than it ever had before.

"I was in love with him," Ella admitted carefully. Then she looked up at Ava as if ready for a challenge. "I know what you're gonna say, that thirteen-year-olds can't comprehend love, that it wasn't real. Well, I'm a bit older now. And you still might think I'm too young to know what love is, but I've never stopped being in love with Kyle."

Ava watched her for a time before responding caringly. "I think, if you're old enough to fight this battle, if you're old enough to kill people...then you're old enough to love them too."

Ella offered a half smile, grateful for that. "I know he never saw me that way," she admitted. "He was too focused on you, and his mission. And I was just a little girl in his eyes. Actually, if I'm being honest, I don't know if it ever occurred to Kyle that I'm a girl."

Ava laughed out loud at that. Obviously, Kyle knew Ella was female, but a "girl" was something Kyle may have not really considered in Ella.

Ava's heart suddenly seemed to warm in love for her friend as the two of them shared a bit of laughter together—the first in many years. Suddenly, she wished everything had been different, and that these two could have been friends.

"If he saw me today, he would probably still miss it," Ella admitted sadly. "I've never been all that pretty, and I'm certainly not 'sweet' or 'gentle,' like you. I know he just saw me as his friend and co-worker, but I saw who *he* was. And anyone who did couldn't have helped but fall in love with him."

Ava let out a deep sigh, feeling the pain of Ella's unrequited love as if it were her own.

"I guess that's part of why I resented you so much for everything," Ella admitted. "And I'm sorry I was so horrible to you for so long. You and I have lost all the same people...we could have been so much better as friends."

Ava offered a sad smile. "I think that's true."

"But it's probably a bit late for that," Ella said, leaning back in her seat then.

"Why do you say that?" Ava objected. "We're not dead yet."

Ella was silent for a time as she considered. Eventually, she explained. "I don't know how to be friends with you, Ava. Just like there was something in the way of you loving Kyle. 'Altman' is in the way of you and me. And don't get me wrong, I know you're not on Eli's side anymore. But you're also...well, you're an Altman. And as long as I live, I don't think I'll ever be ready to be your friend."

Ava couldn't comprehend why that hurt so much. All the years and all the painful jabs from Ella, none of them had hurt as much as this one.

She was suddenly defensive of her family, wanting to fight back and tell Ella that she was wrong. But what proof to the contrary did Ava have, when Ella had countless deaths and pains as evidence?

Ava could not reply, instead sitting there and feeling as if she was recovering from a blow to the gut with Ella's painful jab.

"I don't blame you for Kyle anymore," Ella offered. "But Ame... and Breanna...? And even myself. I'm sorry, Ava, I'm not ready to be friend to an Altman. And I don't think I ever will be."

Unable to respond verbally, Ava offered a pained nod of understanding.

Then the silence became uncomfortable, and both of them felt it. In the end, it was Ella who stood. "Well, on to the next battle. See you on the drive."

Vasiliv drove with Ava in the front seat at navigation as the two of them talked, Vasiliv always trying to win Ava over as Jackson's best friend.

Mikel was just lucky enough to be squished into the back seat between Nastia and Ella. If it were any other two women, this might be a pleasant experience. But these two were just rough enough around the edges that Mikel couldn't even have a pleasant conversation with them, let alone a pleasant experience.

Still, after hours of boredom and wondering why they hadn't jumped into a normal military truck and joined the rest of the team, at some point he got ambitious and decided it was worth a try, so he reached for Nastia's hand and put it in his.

She pulled it away forcefully and gave him a look that showed just how disinterested she was in that idea.

Mikel laughed out loud, nodding in acceptance. "All right, fair enough," he said with a laugh. "I guess I misread that scenario."

"I guess so," Nastia replied dryly, then turned to face the window.

After a moment he was sure that Ella was staring at him, and he decided to risk looking in her direction.

The look she gave of "are you kidding me?" only caused him to laugh further.

"Hey, it was worth a try."

"We just have two more Towers," Vasiliv noted as they stood within the core of the newest conquered miniature Tower.

"It was worse today," Nastia replied, and the large cut along the front of her face was a disturbing reminder of that.

"You should get yourself to the infirmary," Vasiliv ordered. "Soon, or it might leave a scar."

"I hope it does," she said with an intense grin. Ava couldn't help thinking of her old training sergeant, Breslin, and the intimidating scar along his face.

"It would look pretty awesome on you," Mikel said approvingly as he looked at her, and it was clear he really meant it. "Very fitting."

"It is getting harder," Ella confessed.

"We lost several men today," Ava agreed.

"They were relentless," Vasiliv added. "They would not give in, and they didn't surrender until the last moment. There were too many casualties today."

"It's going to get worse," Mikel realized with a deep sigh. "Every time we go in using this same power play, the enemy is adjusting, attempting to find a way to beat us."

"But they haven't yet," Vasiliv said in deep consideration. "Is it really worth changing our strategy while we're still winning? Particularly when we don't have any better ideas?"

They were all concerned. In the end, Ava was the one to respond. "The entire point of a power play is finding a maneuver that your team can execute perfectly, so that it almost doesn't matter what the other team does. This play has been that so far. And we all know that at some point the enemy is going to come up with something to counter our play. We have to be prepared with backups, sure. But I agree, Vasiliv, it makes no sense for us to change our strategy when it's still doing so well."

"Except that they're expecting it and each one has had more time to prepare," Ella replied. "Like you said, Ava, they will adjust. Shouldn't we change things up before they do?"

"Eventually, maybe," Mikel offered. "But if we can conquer these last few Towers first...."

"Then we will have effectively liberated the whole of Africa from the overt oppression of the Republic," Ava finished seriously.

A long silence passed as they all considered that.

"What do you think?" Vasiliv asked Ava.

She had apparently proved herself to him that first time, when she had helped Jackson and Vas pick the Elites. Now he often asked for her opinion before making any final decisions, though a part of her almost felt it was out of respect for Jackson.

"I think we go to the next Tower, we take the risk, and then we reassess."

Vasiliv nodded. "Then we keep moving. I don't want to give them any sort of schedule to expect. Do you think you're ready to take a second Tower in one day?"

Everyone looked around as they considered. Battling with Counter Intelligence until they could manually disable it from within the core was exhausting, mentally and physically. But the trip to the next Tower was several hours, and she could rest on the way.

"Let's do it," Mikel replied with that ever-confident air.

Nastia stood then with a sudden new determination. "I better get a few band aids."

★ ★ ★ ★ ★

"So, this is what victory feels like," Ella said from the side of the room, holding tightly to her wounded shoulder, her feet in an ice bath, and several bandages all over. "Kind of...painful, but also good."

"We did it," Mikel said proudly. "We actually won."

"We're far from winning the war," Vasiliv disagreed. "But Africa is liberated."

"It's time to tell the world," Ava said proudly, looking to Sizwe. "Are you ready for that?"

Sizwe stood, looking humbled. He nodded seriously.

"Mandatory updates from the Politburo were the Republic's forte," Vasiliv said with sudden pride. "Let's give them a taste of their own medicine."

"They'll attempt to shut us down, no doubt," Nastia noted. "They'll do everything in their power to keep this news from broadcasting to the whole of the Republic."

"We'll keep it under control," Mikel replied with satisfaction.

"I only wish Jackson were here to give this speech," Sizwe said somberly.

"No," Ava disagreed firmly, and everyone looked at her in surprise, assuming that she wished for that most of all of them. "The message that the citizens of the Republic need to hear is not that Africa was saved by a foreign party, but that you rose up and found a way to save yourselves. Besides, I think it's clear that the speech he wrote was intended for you."

Sizwe nodded slowly. "Then I will deliver it with all the power, enthusiasm, confidence and passion that I know he would have."

Ava gave her mentor a look of pride. "You have fought valiantly for your people, and the cause of freedom, Sizwe. There is no one better to be heard by the people of the Republic."

★ ★ ★ ★ ★

"Brothers and sisters," Sizwe began, and Mikel and Ava focused on maintaining the broadcast so it made it into the homes of every family and individual within the Republic, and anywhere else with Towers.

The technician gave a thumbs up, indicating that everything was going well, but neither Ava nor Mikel needed his signal to know that. They felt the connection in their minds.

"As we speak, the Republic is attempting to stop this communication. They may succeed, our time may be cut short, and I may not be able to deliver the entire message that I hope to. If you hear nothing else from me, I wish you to know that there is one thing they will never succeed in doing. They will never succeed in crushing the spirit of freedom within the heart of man."

"They're fighting it," Mikel noted, and Ava nodded as she strained from the pressure. "And they're good."

Sizwe was in an office room recording, as Mikel, Ava, Ella, Vasiliv and the technician sat in Sizwe's meditation center, where they felt most comfortable.

Both Mikel and Ava sat cross-legged on the floor, though Vas, Ella and the tech man had chairs and laptops.

"I am but a humble servant of freedom. I am just a man. But my cause is great, and I speak for all of mankind when I present it. Over the past months, the people of Africa have fought for liberation against the oppression of the Republic. We have faced immense pain, immeasurable loss, and deep sacrifice. But we have fought on, through every loss, through every sacrifice, because the cause of freedom is far greater than any one man or woman. It is a cause worth fighting for, and if necessary, it is even a cause worth dying for."

Knowing how far Jackson had been willing to go for freedom, Ava felt that line in particular.

"For over a decade, my people have held onto the cause, with a hope for eventual freedom. No matter the oppression, no matter the subjugation, the Republic has never fully managed to quench the fire within us. All that our people needed was a chance, a spark to ignite the flame that was never fully quenched. And after years of painful oppression, we were given that chance."

"They're getting desperate," Mikel said with a slight tremble in his voice. He didn't really need to give her a play by play, since she felt it all too, but Ava didn't bother to mention that to him.

"The Republic will never allow the truth of this into the everyday lives of its people, but I stand here today to tell you that my people have succeeded. We have fought, sacrificed, and ultimately, we have gained our freedom. The Republic has pulled its final remaining officers and armies from our land in an act of total surrender. As they pull back to fortify the lands they do hold, the oppression you face may be more than you have ever seen, and for this, I am sorry.

"Today, I ask no great sacrifices or bold moves on the part of every man, woman and child who watches this communication. Today may not be the day to rise up against them. Instead, I ask you to look deeply into your hearts and minds. For decades, the Republic has used oppression and subjugation to try and beat out that ember of hope within you, that desire for freedom. And they may have succeeded for some. But not all.

"No government power, no matter how strong, can conquer the true heart of man. And today, I ask you to look inside yourselves, search for that ember of hope."

A sudden intense pressure overwhelmed both of them, and at the same time, Mikel and Ava put their hands to their temples as if to help temper the pressure.

"What's happening?" Vasiliv spoke with urgent concern.

Mikel and Ava were too focused on fighting the attempts by the Tower techs to respond, but the single technician with his laptop monitored the data. "They're attempting to cause a blackout!" he said in surprise. "They can't shut off the transmission, so they're trying to shut everything down."

"Well don't let them!" Vasiliv urged the two Zhànshì.

"Yeah, thanks for that," Mikel muttered, and his momentary lack of concentration put more pressure on Ava. She'd have to remind him of that later. He was always so distractible, and normally she didn't mind, but at moments like this....

"Perhaps you feel that ember of hope when you attempt to strive to follow your passions and ambitions and are beaten down time and again. Perhaps you feel that ember of hope when you hear stories of revolution in Russia, Africa and Australia, as you hear of a greater world, where people fight and sacrifice for freedom and achieve the right of all mankind for their people. Perhaps you feel that hope when you look into the eyes of your children, and find yourself wishing for a better future for them."

"They're relentless," Mikel said in exasperation.

"Shut up, would you?" Ava nudged, not meaning to be rude, but not wanting to break focus long enough to think of a nicer way to say it.

The Republic technicians knew everything there was to know about the Towers. Every loophole, every backroad. They attempted to fight off the enemy airwaves using all that knowledge, and they were dang good at it! But one thing they could never understand, unless they had this connection themselves, was how it felt to be one with the Tower and to flow with its current in order to move it where you wanted it to go. No matter how many attempts, how many backroads the technicians took, they could not beat the power of the Tower itself, even in their attempts to shut it off completely. The Republic used force to command their will; Mikel and Ava used connection.

"Whatever ember of hope still lives within you, I plead with you, to hold onto it. Remember it. Never let go of it. A time is coming, very soon, when, just as happened for Russia, Australia and my people, you will be offered a chance, a spark to ignite the flame. I implore you, when that call comes, cling to it, let it ignite the flame of desire for freedom within you."

The pushing subsided and was replaced by something that caught her off guard at first. "They're launching a counterstrike," Ava muttered when of a sudden, all dormant Towers still under Republic control were turned on at once. The weight of controlling increased a hundred percent, and Mikel and Ava both hunched lower as it hit them.

"Why would they turn on the global Tower Network when they no longer have a third of the needed Towers to control it?" Ella asked.

A heavy weight crashed against them, and then they both had the answer as the all too familiar signal of Counter Intelligence began pushing against them fully. The virus was incredible, and all-consuming.

"They're trying to use this signal to infect everyone with the link at once! We have to stop the connection!" Ava was the one to announce the obvious this time.

Still, even as she said it, she was trying to do just that. She could not break focus in fighting Counter Intelligence, even for a millisecond. "You're on your own, Mikel," she breathed in a hoarse whisper as she shifted her focus entirely to the enemy's counterstrike.

"You got this," Mikel tried to reassure her, but the ever-weakening tremble in his voice made her question whether or not *he* did. Still, it was so Mikel to be reassuring her, all while he was on the brink of failure.

"Remember, as you face the horrors of oppression in the following weeks and months from a power that attempts to control you, and quench the embers of hope, that freedom is the right and duty of every man and woman."

So many agents, so many Zhànshì, so many soldiers and countless Jiānhùrén with the link. So many people in the vastness of the earth who would be obliterated, crushed in moments by this virus if she did not stop it.

"Shut it off, Mikel," Ava pleaded in a barely audible whisper. "Shut it off!"

"I'm...trying," he said through gritted teeth. "It's the whole network... all...all at once. I can barely—"

"Just shut it off!" she pressed, though logically she knew that he was doing everything he could. If she wavered, even for the tiniest moment, then countless thousands of people would be killed in an instant.

She found her body physically weakening, and leaned forward in a slump, just like the last time she had faced this foe. Back then, she had only been attempting to protect a handful of people within range of the virus. Now...the virus's reach was the very ends of the earth, and the power from the unified network amplified its strength a million-fold.

"The time is coming, very soon, when a spark will be offered. And I promise you, we will sacrifice, fight, and if necessary, die by your side. Because, brothers and sisters, freedom always wins out over oppression in the end. It has for the people of Australia. It has for the people of Russia. It has for my people. And soon enough, the spark will ignite an opportunity for you too. I implore you, stand up and fight when the opportunity is presented. And I promise, you will not stand alone."

"Mikel!" Ava's terrified voice came out in a shrill scream.

"I'm...I'm trying...."

"What do we do?" Vasiliv asked in terror.

"Trust them," Ella said helplessly. After dozens of times being told the same thing by Damian, apparently she had finally taken it to heart. "There's nothing else we can do."

The crushing weight was worse than anything Ava had ever faced. The enemy had perfected this weapon. The Ava from the bathtub in Russia would have been destroyed. The Ava in the hallucinogenic dream from a dangerous narcotic wouldn't have stood a chance. The Ava who pushed against Darya's remote-control device wouldn't have known what hit her. And even the Ava from that night five months ago would have been swept away by this storm. But that night had changed her. Something had happened, in that brief moment between life and death, Ava had been changed. Ever since that moment, Ava had been fighting this virus. She was getting stronger. She was coming to understand it. At moments, it overcame her. But then she hit back. Five months of training with Sizwe had strengthened her confidence and resolve, but that one instant between life and death had changed her power.

The Ava of today did not crumble under the pressure. Instead, she found the elusive thread of Counter Intelligence, and briefly shoved it into a tiny box in the back of her mind—as she had been trained to do with painful emotions. There it remained while Ava reconnected with the Tower network, pulling the vast power away from Mikel.

She shut it down, and the weight from the network mingled with the pain from the virus both vanished in an instant—the only thing left was that little bit of the enemy that had infected her that night five months ago.

No matter how powerful she had become, her physical body could only handle so much, and Ava collapsed unconscious as soon as the danger was neutralized.

Mikel sat next to the hospital bed, watching Ava as her chest rose and fell. She had managed to do, once again, what he had been unable to. And he was grateful for that. He felt no resentment towards her. But he did feel resentment.

It didn't make sense to him, not really. Ava had never asked for this, and had never really wanted any of it. Having experienced much of her life and her desires in the dreamwalk, he knew firsthand that what Ava wanted was to be like her mother, to be Lionel's protégé. She didn't want to be the powerful force of nature to deal with the Towers. She wanted to be a leader of a nation.

But Mikel; Mikel wanted *this*. More than anything in the world. He wanted to be this hero. He wanted to be the powerful force to work with the Towers. Yet, every time their wills were put up next to each other, she won out. She was more powerful. She was stronger. No matter how hard he worked, how hard he tried, she always won out. And he was not angry at her for that. But he was angry.

Eventually, Ava's eyes slowly opened, and after taking in the medical room, she turned to see him. Mikel was smiling widely when she turned to him.

"Well, good morning, our fearless hero."

"We're alive..." Ava muttered, as if that realization was shocking.

"Thanks to you!" he said proudly. "And beyond that, the entire transmission made it through. Millions of people were watching it. And between Sizwe's powerful presence, and Jackson's passionate words, I think we made an impression."

Ava smiled, but her eyes closed once more. "I think I'll keep sleeping for a few more days." There was a touch of sarcasm in her words, but he sensed that there was some truth in it too.

"You deserve it," he replied with a grin. "Ava, you are the *man!*"

His encouragement was real. He was proud of her. He was in awe of her. And she deserved to be praised, even if he was angry at the situation as a whole.

"The woman," Ava corrected. "Let's change that vernacular forever."

Mikel chuckled. "I think you might have just done it, sweetheart! Now get some sleep. There's a lot to be done yet. And we're gonna need you for it."

He stood up to leave her there, but Ava turned again, saying his name and stopping him. "Mikel. You were incredible."

So many comebacks, so many ill words for himself, reprimands for how poorly he had done. But he did not let them show, not for a second. "Psh! Girl, don't think I doubt it! That taint was crazy. And we rocked it!"

She smiled, but from the deeper expression in her eyes, he almost wondered if she saw right through him.

"Get some sleep," Mikel ordered. "Didn't you hear the news? Jackson's coming back this week. You're going to need your beauty rest."

He expected her to deflect that comment, or shrug it off. Instead, the sweet smile that touched her lips showed, as always, how much she cared for that man. "I'll do my best," she said sweetly, and Mikel left her there to rest alone.

★ ★ ★ ★ ★

"It's done then?" Viktoriya asked, staring at the brain scans on the screen. "It's really over?"

"For him it is," Zak offered. "The chip has been removed. But more than that..."

"The flaw has been cured," Sasha said with a long, relieved sigh. "I can't believe it. What you did, Zak...what you accomplished here..." he shook his head repeatedly, unable to even utter what was on his mind.

"You were there every step of the way," Zak reminded him. "Or at least, for most of the steps. We also wouldn't have had anything without the scientific research Sizwe gave me."

"And we wouldn't have Sizwe without Jackson," Sasha said with a sudden smile, returning to stare at those scans. "So, I guess it all comes full circle. It's only right that he's the first one we would cure with it."

"You two are next," Zak said, and Sasha agreed.

"I'm not doing any sort of surgery and radiation therapy until this baby is done nursing," Viktoriya said assuredly.

"You better not," Zak agreed. "That's my little guy too. But Sasha, your years of exposure to the link are vast. I don't know if things will go as smoothly as they did with Jackson. But—"

"We'll have to take the risk," Sasha offered. "I'll be dead in a couple more years if we don't. I may as well take a chance, and hopefully help the research along."

"Are you sure we shouldn't also wait to treat Sasha?" Viktorya asked hesitantly. "I mean, with how quickly the victories in Africa happened, we could be looking at ending this thing in the next year or so."

"I think my mind will be much more useful in a new, founding era than it is in wartime anyway," Sasha replied pleasantly.

"We don't know how much longer we can wait," Zak explained, then turned to pull up Sasha's scans. The small tumor showed how far he had progressed in the flaw. "He's already worse by miles than any of the other scans we've attained. It might already be too late...."

The look Viktoriya gave him caused Zak to stop in his scientific mutterings to remember they were talking about a human being, who happened to be sitting right there. He attempted to apologize, but Sasha raised his hand to stop him.

"I have been more than ready to go since my wife died. Whenever the good Lord takes me, I will be prepared. Still, I'd rather not die by Harrison's hand, if I can manage. So yes, I would like to be next. I want this so-called 'flaw' removed. That being said, I will not move forward with the surgery until Ava has returned. Another few weeks, then we'll take the risk."

"She's okay with it?" Zak asked curiously.

Sasha nodded. "She understands, and she supports my decision. My hope is, even if I don't survive, that the research will help find answers for her."

"We haven't...that is, she hasn't been willing to let us take her scan yet," Zak explained to Viktoriya. "She says it will make no difference in her choice to keep the link."

"But I'm hopeful I can change her mind, when we're reunited," Sasha said.

Viktoriya was the one to tighten her eyebrows in consideration, though she said nothing. Still, Zak had come to understand her expressions and the meanings behind them. Sasha still held out hope of convincing Ava. But in Viktoriya's estimation, there was no chance of that.

★ ★ ★ ★ ★

"Well, don't you look...busy," Zak observed when he entered Jackson's study. Jackson was feverishly working away at his laptop, deeply involved in his work.

"As always," Jackson agreed.

"How are you feeling? Any headaches? Nausea? Vomiting?"

"Not since a few days ago. I feel...good. I feel like myself. Scars on my abdomen, scars on my brain, but I'm me."

"I think you should be fine to travel to Africa this week, as planned," Zak said optimistically. "If you can manage not to push yourself too hard before then."

"I've been healing in medical centers for the past five months while the fight of my life is going on around me."

It didn't exactly seem like a response to Zak's comment. Jackson turned, for the first time since Zak had entered, to face him. "I'll do whatever you tell me, Zak, if it means I get to go back out there."

Zak pushed a few papers aside on the desk, making room to sit on the edge of it. "It's not exactly as if you've been sitting around or anything," Zak spoke reassuringly. "When you're not working on rehabilitation, you're writing speeches for our great world powers. When you're not meeting with the Committee to keep our alliances on track, you're studying the enemies' weaknesses and finding strategies of where and when to move, sending that information and instructions to Remington and to the Ukombozi to move on the enemy. When you're not healing from a collapsed lung and a gunshot wound, you're undergoing brain surgery and radiation therapy."

"Hmm, I think I need to fill my schedule more," Jackson said sardonically, since having it all said out loud made it sound as extreme as it clearly was. Of course, Jackson had never been anything less than extreme.

"Sasha's going to stay here and keep things under control with the Committee while I'm gone," Jackson said. "I'm just making sure everything's in place to make it as easy for him as possible."

Zak turned Jackson's laptop so he could see exactly what Jackson was working on. It seemed to be character profiles with summaries about each person on the Committee. Zak scanned it for a bit before looking up with a questioning glance. "You're gonna have to explain this one."

"It's information on each of the Russian leadership members, all their ambitions, weak points and strengths. All the taint I've dealt with from them before and how to handle each one if it comes to it."

"Don't you think Sasha could figure it out? He handled things all right during those first few weeks of your recovery."

Jackson shrugged, glancing back at the three-hundred-page document. "Possibly. But without me here, I think a lot of these guys will push for the things that I've been fighting against or try and dismantle the stuff I worked so hard on. I feel like I'm holding this entire country together and in one minute it could all collapse."

Zak waited until Jackson eventually looked up at him again before offering a knowing smile. "I think you might want to consider letting go of some of that pressure, brotha. I know you like to be thorough, and you do a better job than anyone else, but at some point, this nation is going to have to learn how to function without you."

Jackson sighed heavily. "I know, I know. And I realize that the length of this document makes it seem like I'm pouring a lot of wasted energy into the wrong places. But you have no idea how many times this thing has helped me. You have to know both your friends and your enemies in and out when it comes to politics. Minister Tevlov says he wants to pass a bill limiting powers of government to upper class citizens, and if you don't realize that what he actually wants is support on his agricultural bill, then you're fighting the wrong battle for two weeks before you realize that you were wasting your time. Even Russians aren't above sneaky, bureaucratic politics."

Zak smiled warmly, admiring his friend for the work he did that, not only did no one else want to do, but probably no one else ever really could do at his level. "All I'm saying is, Sasha might be okay for a day or two while you go experience the fruits of your labors in Africa."

Jackson breathed in deeply, staring at the document before him. He was about to give in and close it, but a thought about Major General Mikilov's hockey addiction reminded him he had forgotten a few more important things. He found the man's profile and started writing his thoughts quickly, almost forgetting that Zak was still there until his friend chuckled and stood.

"All right, Jackson. You win. Make sure you don't miss anything important."

Her blonde hair was worn down and had grown several inches below her shoulders again. It was touched with waves, pulled out of braids just minutes before she headed to the event. She wore the beautiful, tribal robe that had been prepared for her, and although it was vastly different from the gorgeous dresses Lionel had once had made for her, she found herself loving the attire just as much. There was great beauty in every culture, with different fashions and focus, and incredible colors and styles.

Growing up, she had only been issued black shirts, green cargo pants and black combat boots. But there were many different kinds of uniforms, and Ava felt as important wearing these robes, and as valuable wearing the lavish dresses, as she did wearing her military uniform. Today, she had the opportunity to participate in the celebration of freedom for a people who had been long oppressed. And though her thoughts were solemn, she was in awe of the joy that filled the faces all around.

The celebration was being held in the middle of a village square, though they now had control of the tall, powerful buildings. To this people, the celebration of their freedom could not take place in the buildings that had been constructed by the enemy to oppress them. Instead, they celebrated in the simple villages where, for nearly two decades now, these people had fought and hoped in silence until a chance came, a spark to light the embers, and they had enflamed in purpose and freedom.

The village square was decorated with bright colors and designs, as distinct as the robes she had been given.

She searched the crowd for her friends, but didn't see them. So, she continued to walk through the square. The celebration would begin in just minutes, and even before the official ceremonies started the people were already celebrating.

Ava unconsciously picked at the dirt underneath one fingernail with another. She looked down at them and noticed how, even after a shower, her nails still had dirt under each one. She smiled. It was different from the special manicures before formal events with Lionel's wife Astelle, but there was a sort of beauty in this too, a different type of hard work and accomplishment, and she was proud of both of them.

She made it to the middle of Town Square, and her eyes were immediately drawn to the dais. A man stood there in his own formal robes, being instructed by an older woman—the leader of ceremonies—about his role in the event and where he should be and what he should do.

Ava watched them for several minutes. The man was witty and his smile was contagious as he joked and laughed with the leader of ceremonies and her assistants, speaking their language. He fit right in. He could have been a member of the village, a part of this culture, though he was from a million worlds away.

After several moments, the man seemed to feel Ava's eyes on him, even from such a distance. He looked across the square with the hundreds of other people walking along and his eyes landed directly on her. Before it registered in his mind who she was, he almost looked away. But then apparently he realized who was watching him and he turned back, doing a sort of double take.

He looked so handsome up there, with a clean-shaven face that bore a few ceremonial designs. His hair was messy and unkempt, and he wore the robes of another culture, but he had never looked so good to her.

He smiled, and she smiled, as their eyes locked from afar. Obviously, he could not leave his current post. Much of this event revolved around him and a ceremony of official initiation. Still, Ava could sense that he wanted to, and that was good enough for the time being.

He put his hand up, and waved at her simply, unable to do anything else for the time being. Ava waved a hello in response. Although it was an informal greeting, and less physical than a good hug might have been, she felt her body relax with a sense of peace. There could have been no better way to see him again, after all this time.

The director of ceremonies hit him hard in the chest when it was clear he was no longer paying attention, and Jackson was forced to turn back to the woman. Ava laughed at the scene, and realized she could have been content to stand there watching this man for the rest of the night. Her friends found her then, however, and she was invited to join them at the seats they had saved.

"There's our guy!" Mikel said proudly, looking up at the platform.

"I really don't see why he gets some tribal initiation when it's all of us who did the dirty work to fight the Republic away." The comment could have come from none other than the ever-pleasant Ella herself.

Ava didn't even think to contradict the girl on that, but some of the others immediately had Jackson's back. "He took a bullet in defense of their leader," Mikel was the first to respond.

"He's been holding together the alliance with Russia," Nastia added.

"None of us would be here if it weren't for him," Vasiliv said with an admiring nod toward his friend. "Ever since that first battle in this very village." Vasiliv indicated the square and the significance of the ceremony being held here. "The rest of us had written them off as dead. But he wouldn't give it up. He wouldn't leave it alone. He wouldn't leave *them* alone. *None* of us would be here if it weren't for him. And that's what he does. He finds potential, he finds that little ember, that little bit of hope and desire for freedom, and he lights it up until you can't help but live up to the potential he sees in you."

Vasiliv was usually either inappropriately sarcastic or hardened and rough around the edges. She had never seen him so passionate, so serious. And it was true. Ava resonated with those words more than Vasiliv could have known. That was exactly what Jackson had done for her all those years ago in the library. He had found that tiny ember of hope and lit it, until she could not be content with anything less than greatness. He had done the same thing for Zak, for Vasiliv, and apparently for the country of Russia as a whole.

He had done it here too. It was no wonder that he had been accepted as a Russian citizen and would now be officially inducted as a member of this tribal community.

"I know all that," Ella conceded with a genuine smile. "I just like to make fun of him."

It was during the event, watching the proceedings as a humbled Jackson accepted the honor that was presented to him by Sizwe and his people, watching as Jackson fit in as much in these tribal robes as he had in an officer's uniform in Russia and a soldier's garb in the United Kingdoms, that it truly occurred to Ava that Jackson had never been in this for the United Kingdoms, any more than for Russia, or for the African countries alone. He was not in this for a land, a government, or politicians. He had always fought for and with the people.

When the ceremony was completed, Jackson was allowed to return to the audience with the rest as they began an official celebration of freedom. Vasiliv got Jackson's attention from the side of the stage by whistling obnoxiously, and he happily made his way to them while the celebrations began.

The five of them all stood, excited to greet him. Ava wasn't sure exactly why, but initially she had assumed that he would greet her first. But he went immediately to Vasiliv with a bear hug, and admittedly, that did hurt her slightly, but she pushed it aside, telling herself that they were close friends, and it made perfect sense.

But as they stood there in a half circle around him, Jackson went next to Mikel and greeted him with clasped arms and a caring hug. She found herself suddenly holding her breath as this all pained her. She had no real reason to be offended. She just...wanted to be the most important one to him, even if that was a selfish thought.

When he let go of Mikel, he turned to Ella, of all people. "What was all that hoo-hah?" she said rudely before he could say anything.

Unfazed by her attitude, he replied automatically, "Honestly, I think they did all of that just to bother you."

It was the perfect thing to say, and Ella broke into a grin. "Good to see you again," she admitted, putting her hand out for him to shake, which he did.

Ava didn't exactly like being after Ella, but she was willing to accept it. It was only when, once more, Jackson turned to the last person in the group—who had initially wanted to kill him—that Ava really found herself confused.

"I must say, Nastia," Jackson spoke pleasantly to her, "I am in awe of your accomplishments. The Committee has been raving about you in almost every session. You're making your country proud."

She smiled. She no longer hated him, though she did not yet know him as the others did. Still, it was obvious that she strangely desired to be noticed by this man. "Thank you, sir," she said happily, and it was clear how much she now respected Jackson, given her use of the word "sir." He offered a hand, and she shook it.

Well, that was it, there was nowhere else to turn now but to Ava, and so he went to her. But he didn't seem smug, or angry, or really anything but just happy to see her.

"Hey, you," he said in a softer tone, and that look on his face made it hard to be mad at him. He opened his arms to her, and she accepted the embrace. He held her tightly, and she shivered slightly as his breath ran from her cheek to her neck. He leaned in a little closer so his lips rested by her ear, and he whispered, "You look beautiful tonight."

No, she could not be mad. She did not understand why she had been the last one in the lineup to greet, not until he let go of her, and then remained close by her. Staying there. With her. Ava's heart seemed to melt in comprehension when she realized that his reason for greeting the others first was because all he had to offer them was a greeting. But he had waited to greet her because by her side he intended to remain, for the rest of the night.

And once more, Ava was overwhelmed by a feeling of peace and serenity that she had never felt before.

"Did you happen to save me a seat?" he asked the group at large, and although it was Vasiliv who had a spot beside him for his friend, when they returned to the chairs, Jackson sat beside Ava, and the others automatically adjusted to the other available places.

No, she could not be mad. She could not feel cheated or underappreciated. On the contrary, she felt in that moment like the luckiest woman in the world; for all of these people were honored to be known by this man, even just to be in his presence. And yet it was Ava who was lucky enough to be accompanied by him.

They watched the ceremonies, and Jackson was so entranced by it all that he barely looked away. But it was difficult for Ava to focus on the event when he was sitting there beside her, after all this time, and all she wanted was to watch him.

Still, eventually, she managed to center herself again, focusing on the unique and beautiful ceremonies of freedom.

Of course, it was then it seemed that Jackson could not look away from her. He tried to pay attention, but his eyes always returned to her, and consciously aware of his eyes on her, she could not help but smile.

How could she have gotten so lucky? What made her so special that this man clearly wanted to be beside her? She loved herself more than she ever had before and was confident, and proud of the woman she was. And yet, she knew that she was lucky to even be seen by this man, let alone admired by him.

"You look amazing," he whispered at one point, causing her to turn to him. She was about to object that he'd already mentioned that, but it was clear there was deeper meaning behind his words than just her outward appearance. "At first, I thought it was the robes. Maybe just that I hadn't seen you in so long. But it's not that. You look…confident. You look like yourself. You look stronger than I think I've ever seen you." His serious eyes meant those words, and she appreciated every one.

"I am," she replied in a whisper, and she was truly proud of herself for how far she had come. "I found my inner peace."

His eyes deepened even more as he considered that. Then he nodded, and she could see in his smile how happy those words made him. "I'm glad to hear that. You have no idea how happy that makes me."

"What about you?" she asked hopefully.

And he nodded proudly. "I'm good. I have a couple of gnarly scars. But I'm better. And I'm me too."

She smiled, and leaned in closer with a sudden desire to be near him once more. He seemed to feel it too, and he scooted over just so, allowing their knees to touch, even if that was all it was for the time being. But it was a start.

"I do like the robes though," Jackson suddenly whispered. "They suit you well."

"You too," Ava replied genuinely. "You've never looked so handsome."

He considered that for a second. A part of him seemed to like it, another part seemed to object. Finally, he leaned in closer so he could whisper without causing disruption. "You know, I think I'm okay with that word now."

She watched him as she attempted to understand, but then remembered a time long ago, when he had called her "beautiful" and objected to being called "handsome" in return, because it sounded too much like an old man.

"It's fitting," she offered with a smug little smile on her face as she teased him.

He chuckled at that. But then his thoughts grew serious. Once more, he leaned in close and whispered. "You hated my beard, didn't you?"

11

The Troops

Jackson was up the next morning hours before anyone had a right to be. Of course, for him it felt like an hour later than it was, but even so, he was awake at four in the morning to start his day. He would meet with Sizwe at the half hour mark, and his brother would do a morning meditation with him before they spoke of the war and deliberated the next steps in the cause.

Today, Jackson and the Zhànshì would return to Russia. They had proven themselves trustworthy and were no longer as personae non grata in Russia.

His trip to Africa consisted of two half days and one short night, and he wished he could stay longer. But times were desperate, and they must continue forward. Still, as he walked down the hallway to meet with his brother, he could not help smiling. His consolation for this short trip was the fact that he would not return to Russia alone.

He was set to meet Sizwe in his meditation room, so it surprised him when, passing Sizwe's study, he noticed the light was on under the door. Expecting to meet his brother there, he stepped inside the study and was surprised when it was another face he found there reading on the sofa.

"Ava. What are you doing up so early?"

She squinted her eyes as if trying to understand. Then she glanced at the clock on the wall. "I think you mean what am I doing up so late," she offered through a tired sounding whisper, but she, too, was smiling. "You're not awake for the morning are you?"

He stepped farther into the room and joined her on the sofa. "You're not still awake for the night, are you?" he countered teasingly.

She glanced at the book in her hands. Her feet were pulled up under her on the sofa and she had a throw blanket on. A solitary lamp lit the room enough for her to read. "I was in a really intense part," she explained, though looking a bit guilty for staying up so late. The book was a firsthand account of the shift from aristocracy to communism in China, *Wild Swans.*

"The whole book is intense," Jackson said energetically. "If you're waiting for a calm part to set it down, you might not sleep until you finish."

"Then I guess it's gonna be a long night," she teased with a playful smile. "So, what are you doing up this deathly early?"

"I have a morning meditation and meeting with Sizwe."

She nodded before changing the subject. "The ceremony last night was really special. It occurred to me as I watched you up there with them, just how amazing you actually are."

He raised one eyebrow and considered making a snarky comment about how long it had taken her to notice, but he didn't want to shift the tone too much when it was clear she had something more to say. He didn't have to wait long for her to continue.

"You could fit in with any people, any culture. When we danced at the Talks, I realized then how very Russian you had become. I thought that maybe you had found the people who were your own and that you were meant to stay there. But then, tonight, I realized you could live out the rest of your life with these people and fit in just as much."

He nodded in consideration. "I could," he realized. "Both of these places have become a sort of home to me."

"And I'm sure by the end of this," Ava continued, "you'll be just as loved and welcomed in the rest of the Republic. You could go anywhere, do anything. The people will love you as their own. And you'll love them as yours."

A long silence passed as he considered the truth of that.

"So where will you end up?" she asked curiously. "When all this is over, will you stay in Russia? Will you live with these people in central Africa? Or will you settle down in China?" she gestured to the book in her hands.

Jackson considered for a time. He had pondered on this question many times, truth be told, but it was a difficult decision. "Honestly? If I could, if they would ever accept me back, I would go home to the Kingdoms. It's funny, you say I'm welcomed in every culture. That is, every one but my own. My people think of me as a traitor. And I doubt I could ever really make a place back home. But if I could...I would run for Council."

She cocked her head in surprise. "Really?"

He shrugged. "Yeah. I mean, our nations need freedom as much as any other. And we have a lot to change before we've accomplished that. But obviously, I would never be elected to a government position as a traitor to the state. If I could though, if they ever let me back, that's what I would do."

She smiled sadly. "I hope they do. Council could use a man like you."

Jackson's smile was just as doleful as hers. "They could have used a General like you too."

Ava looked down at her lap, and it was clear his comment was painful to hear. "See, that's the difference between you and me," she related somberly. "You could go anywhere you want, live anywhere you choose. I have nowhere to go. I have nowhere that would really be home. Sure, Sizwe would let me stick around, but it wouldn't be home. I would never fit in. The people would never really understand or accept me—as welcoming as they are. Not really. I can't go back to the Kingdoms. I have no place in Russia. I was never intended to live out a life in real civilization. I was just supposed to finish the mission, be a weapon of the government, then return and report for the next operation."

He glanced leftward thoughtfully. "Wasn't there ever a time in your life when you felt like you fit? Wasn't there anywhere that felt like home?"

She was silent for a long time before she spoke. "Three months of my life. There were three months when I felt like I belonged, when I wasn't playing a part or following orders under cover. Those three months working with Lionel...that was the only time in my life I ever felt like

I actually belonged in the world, outside of orders and operations. But he's gone now. And Eli and Council would never accept me back like that. Besides, I'm told the whole thing was all a sham anyway. Some big joke they were playing on me and Lionel."

He considered that thoughtfully. "Do you believe that?"

She looked up to face him once more as she responded just as seriously. "No. I don't. I know that they believed in me. For however short a time, I know they supported Lionel and me. They wanted us to succeed. They were all sitting back, watching, hoping. And I know they wanted us to make it work. But that tainted blackout ruined everything. The Jiānhùrén ruined everything."

Jackson's chest tightened at the remembrance of Yuri and the loss of so much good in the world. "Yes," he agreed ruefully. "They did."

Another long silence passed as he watched her, as if in mourning for those three months of her life, the only time in her twenty years that had been her own, that had actually felt *real*.

"Don't worry, kid," Jackson offered gently. "If I make it to Council, I'll make sure there's a place for you in the Kingdoms too."

Ava seemed grateful at first, but her expression soon turned to a sarcastic smile. "Well, that sounds like a politician's promise, if I've ever heard one. Don't worry, Councilman! You have my vote!"

Jackson found himself laughing out loud for close to half a minute. Ava laughed too, and as the seconds dragged on that way, it occurred to him that he and Ava had not truly, really laughed together since that drive home to Sasha's mansion, before they presented the plan, before she rejected them, and before everything had fallen apart.

It had taken a long time for them to work through their struggles with each other, slowly placing the pieces back together. But even after they had forgiven each other for the pains and betrayals, Ava had still been struggling. She hadn't had the heart to truly laugh before. But now...she was herself again, stronger and more confident than ever, and Jackson realized once more how much he had truly missed her.

He knew he had spent several minutes here and Sizwe would already be in the meditation room waiting, but he felt there was still something that needed to be said or done before he left. Not knowing what exactly that was, he simply watched her through a long silence as neither of them knew what was still lingering in the air between them.

There had been one thought on his mind the evening before at the ceremony, one that he hadn't been able to shake, and it occurred to him now that it might be what he was unconsciously waiting for. So, he took a careful step in that direction.

"What's this?" Jackson asked, reaching for her hand and holding it as if to get a better view of the ring on her finger. Of course, that was not his reason for taking her hand, and the feel of her hand in his sent shivers through him, but he concealed it well.

"Sizwe gave it to me," she replied, seeming to like the feel of his strong hand holding hers.

Jackson looked up, giving a suspicious glance that caused her to laugh heartily. "Not like that!" Ava replied assuredly. "It was like a mentor gift thing." She used her other hand suddenly, pointing at the ring as she explained. "See, this small crystal represents me. However beautiful—or powerful—I may be, I am small, inconsequential in the grand scheme of things. I am merely human, merely mortal."

Jackson could almost see Sizwe explaining this to Ava, using the same wording in his powerful, soft-spoken voice.

"The ruby in the middle, the medium-sized gem, is a representation of my challenges, my fears, my enemy. They seem so much bigger than me. It seems impossible that I should have any chance against them. But see," she pointed to the last gem, a gorgeous blue sapphire. "The biggest one on the other side represents my mission, my dreams, and the higher power who gave me the call. Sizwe gave the ring to me as a reminder that my dream will always overcome my challenges, if I can just remember to focus on it above my fears, and trust in a higher power who is greater than any enemy I may face."

Jackson smiled meditatively. He hadn't expected the ring to be something so special, when it was simply meant as a segue to holding her hand. "I like that," he said soberly. "I really like that."

"You can ask him for one too if you..." she trailed off as he shifted his hand, entangling his fingers with hers. He was happy to note how perfectly her hand fit in his. She watched him carefully, but there was no fear or hesitation like there had been five months ago. She was clearly more ready to be in a relationship than she had been in the height of her recovery, and he was glad he had never acted on the impulse to pursue her during that difficult time.

"I've been wanting to do that all night," Jackson admitted, gently rubbing his thumb across the side of her thumb. He watched her then, waiting to see if she would shy away or show any sign of fear. He would pull back if she was not ready yet. But she showed no indication of that. In fact, she smiled challengingly.

"Then why didn't you?" she teased.

"I'm a coward," he shot back almost as soon as she finished, and it caused her to laugh out loud once more. He smiled from his soul. "I was worried you wouldn't want me to be so forward. I was worried you weren't ready, or weren't interested, and all those other excuses you have when you're being a coward."

She smiled deeply before saying softly, "Next time you want to do something like that, don't worry so much."

Her words sent a thrill of excitement coursing through him, making it difficult to breathe. It was her way of saying that she was ready, that she was interested. He leaned closer to her, moving in mere inches from her before stopping. "What about this?" he asked softly, still wanting to be certain that he wasn't pushing her into anything before she was ready.

Their eyes locked onto each other. "I've been wanting you to do that all night," she admitted in a whisper, in obvious hopeful anticipation of what came next.

That was all the invitation he needed. But a sudden desire to tease her first held him back a little longer. "And of course, you couldn't just kiss me, because it's against all your dreams of the man being the one who—"

Jackson wasn't able to finish the sentence as she leaned in the last few inches, acting on his challenge and kissing him this time.

He forgot all else in that moment, and unconsciously he pulled his hand from hers, placing it on the smooth hair behind her head so he could pull her even closer.

Every time before there had been hesitation. Every time before there had been confusion. Every time before there had been overwhelming fear. But not this time. This time was perfect. He knew how he felt about her, he knew how much he wanted this. He believed she felt the same for him and that she was actually ready.

Whatever past trauma he had from watching the failed relationships of his mother didn't matter right now. He had long since decided that he would take a chance on Ava, whatever risk there was of being hurt.

He kissed her gently, and held her tightly, and nothing else in that moment mattered but the fact that she was worth the risk. He should have given her a chance to prove herself so many times, when Eli did everything to break them apart. But he *had* been a coward then. He wasn't about to make that mistake now.

The perfect moment ended too soon, and he wished they could remain like that forever. "You're late for your meeting," Ava noted breathily. "He'll have your hide. Believe me, he doesn't like tardiness."

Jackson moved back, despite his desire to hold her in his arms forever, knowing that all that needed to be said and done at this time had been. There would be time for all else in the days to come. Jackson smiled deeply, forcing himself to stand. "Goodnight, Ava."

The look she gave him was so sweet, and so pure, he would never forget it. It was as if she no longer feared or worried anymore. It was as if she was as certain in her affection for him, that she had decided he, too, was worth any risk. She had no idea how much that meant to him, after everything she had been through.

"Good morning, Jackson," she said sweetly.

Once more, his smile grew beyond what he knew it was capable of doing. And although he forced himself to leave the room, it was with a new hope of all the good that lay before them.

This was only the start. But it was a downed good one.

Ava followed just behind Jackson as they neared the jet, with Mikel and Ella behind her. She was excited for what lay ahead, yet there was also a latent mourning of what she was leaving behind.

Jackson was halfway up the ladder when he stopped, looking off into the distance past the others. He nodded past Ava as if indicating her to look that way. She turned around to see what he had.

Sizwe stood below the ladder and back some ten feet, watching them prepare to go. They'd already said their goodbyes, yet he seemed eager for one final word with her as he signaled her to return to the ground.

Awkwardly, Ava pushed past Mikel and Ella and made her way back down to ground.

"Did I forget something?" Ava asked seriously. "I thought you didn't like hugs."

Sizwe actually chuckled at that, causing Ava to smile too.

"You did not forget anything," Sizwe informed her.

Ava glanced behind her and noted the fact that the three others all stood on the ladder, watching the exchange with interest. She was tempted to feel annoyed at that, but found herself laughing instead.

"It is I who forgot something," Sizwe informed her.

She turned back to face him with sudden new interest.

"When the student is ready," Sizwe began their quote of old, the little saying that had gotten them started in this mentorship.

"The teacher appears," Ava added.

Sizwe nodded, then his deep eyes became moist with deep sentiment. She had never seen Sizwe emotional before, and it threatened to move her as well. "When the student is truly ready," Sizwe continued the quote, though they had never related that part before.

The emotion overwhelmed her suddenly as she understood, and her words came out in almost a whisper. "The teacher disappears," she finished the quote.

Through his pained eyes, Sizwe smiled. He put his hand out for her to shake. She gripped his forearm as tears began to stream down her cheeks.

"Goodbye, Ava Altman. I wish you well on your journey."

"And you on yours," Ava said hoarsely. "Goodbye, Sizwe Jelani. I can never thank you enough for how you've changed me."

"There is no need to thank me when you have changed me in equal measure. It was an honor being your teacher."

"It was an honor being your student."

Sizwe let go his grip and signaled her to go. She followed his final prompt as her mentor.

The others still stood, watching from the ladder, but with the loud engines reverberating in the air, they wouldn't have been able to overhear.

They made their way inside the jet as Ava started up the ladder. When she was seated next to Jackson, she wiped at the tears with the back of her sleeve.

"What was that about?" Jackson asked softly. "Is everything okay?"

"We don't always get to thank our mentors for helping us, or say goodbye when it's time." She couldn't help thinking of Lionel, Ame, Kristen, Harrison and even Eric. "I'm glad I had the chance this time."

"Does anyone want to hold him?" Zak asked the three Zhànshì who stood stiffly watching the new baby as if they had never seen one before...which, they hadn't.

"Doesn't it need its mom?" Ella asked with a touch of disgust.

They all stood by the fireplace, while Zak sat on the sofa holding his boy proudly. "He'll need to eat in about an hour. But the other boys needed mommy time, so this is the perfect chance! Anyone?"

Mikel shook his head vigorously. "I'm good."

"Ava?" Zak asked.

She hesitated, mumbling over words before uttering with deep concern, "I probably shouldn't. He might catch something from one of us."

"Doc already cleared you or we wouldn't be in the same room right now."

"Why are you so insistent on one of us holding it?" Ella asked in an accusatory way.

Zak, immediately defensive, replied, "It's not that! It's just, when you really love something, sometimes you want to share it with others."

"You're just going to have to get used to the fact that not everyone shares your love for miniature humans with no personality."

"Are we talking about you, Ella? Or the baby?" Jackson said, walking into the room suddenly.

Of course, it wasn't entirely fair. Ella was taller and bulkier now even than Ava, Still, it caused several laughs around the room, though he only got the obligatory eye roll from Ella.

The others had all clearly been afraid, or uninterested in holding the infant, but Jackson went right up to Zak. "Can I hold him?" he asked hopefully, and Zak was visibly pleased.

"Come to Uncle Jackson, little guy!"

"Good," Zak said proudly. "At least he has *some* love from his relatives."

"Don't you have a real family to shower him with love?" Mikel replied with a touch of disgust. "We are not loving, baby-cuddling types."

"Want to hold him, Ava?" Jackson asked, having missed when she said she didn't. Still, the way he looked at her as if this were the greatest offer in the world, that sweet little smile on his face, made her want to, despite her many concerns.

"Um...sure! I guess."

"Come on," he said, taking a seat on the couch. "I'll help you."

"I'm going to the washroom," Zak said. "I haven't showered in days."

"So that's why you wanted to get rid of him!" Ella declared, proud of the discovery.

He raised his hands to either side before exiting rather smugly.

Ava awkwardly took a seat beside Jackson. "How old is he?"

"Three months," Jackson said. "He's gotten so big already! Here, hold out your arms like this, and I'll put him in."

She could not explain how uneasy this all made her. It was bad enough that Viktoriya once had put a baby in her arms, but that child had been quite a bit older. This little thing would surely break by her rough touch. How did Jackson do it so well?

"You can use the crook of your elbow to support his head," he offered.

Ava was conscious of Mikel and Ella watching the whole exchange with wide eyes. Only Jackson could get Ava to do something so horribly disagreeable and foreign to her.

"Babies don't have strong necks, so you always have to support it here," Jackson explained further as he carefully placed the child in Ava's arms. Several times she almost blurted out that she couldn't do it, but Jackson's confidence kept her strong, despite the obvious look of terror on her face.

She knew she had been right about how worried she looked when Jackson glanced at her face and laughed out loud. "It's okay," he promised. "You're not gonna break him."

She had broken a lot of people's bones in the past, people much bigger and stronger, and she knew just how easy it was. This thing was fragile beyond compare, and she wasn't so sure she could keep it intact.

"There you go. See, not so bad, is it?"

She held her breath, and tried not to move. Jackson had placed the child exactly right, so if she didn't move a muscle, it would be fine.

"You can relax," he said gently. "He's okay."

One careful shake of her head was all she would allow. The child was so tiny, so weightless, so fragile.

"Looks like a rubber chicken to me," Ella observed with deep interest as she watched.

"Totally," Mikel agreed, his face screwed into a grimace as he watched with concern.

"I was never that weak and fragile," Ella said, scrunching her nose in disgust.

The baby squirmed slightly and Ava panicked as it moved itself from its safe position.

"It's okay," Jackson assured her, feeling her tension and fear. He placed his hand on her forearm, straightening it and offering a gentle touch, as if reminding her to relax.

After a few seconds, his touch on her forearm was enough to help her breathe again. "He's so little!" Ava said, and was surprised by how adoring her tone sounded. "So tiny and so cute!"

"Eh..." Mikel disagreed about the second part. But Ava was fully convinced. It was the sweetest, cutest, tiniest little thing she'd ever seen in her life.

She had been so afraid before that she didn't realize how she was beaming until she turned to see Jackson and found him smiling just as brightly. For a split second, the image felt different. She imagined herself right there with him, holding a baby with him holding her just the same. Only, it wasn't Zak and Viktoriya's little one in that mental snapshot.

She was brought back to reality and the moment of imagination was enough to spook her. "I'm done," she said, and apparently her gentle concern for the child disappeared as she practically dropped the thing back into Jackson's arms.

"Whoa," he exclaimed, carefully catching the child as Ava stood and walked back to join the other Zhànshì.

"Yep," Mikel said, "and just like that, you ruined the moment."

"This is why you should have said no in the first place," Ella reprimanded.

Jackson was focused entirely on the baby, and maybe she imagined this too, but she almost thought there was a look of disappointment in his expression. Luckily, she didn't have to acknowledge it because Zak reentered the room, changing the tone of things.

"So much for my shower," he said with deep regret. "Sasha is back. And he didn't come alone. I'm gonna take this guy back to his momma and meet you all in the library. Sasha says not to keep him waiting."

"What," Mikel spoke sarcastically, "like we've been waiting on *him* since we got here last night?"

Jackson returned the baby to his dad, and they all started toward the library.

Sasha was outside the library door waiting for them, looking intent. Ava hadn't seen her father in person in five months, and she had hoped they could have a normal greeting and some time together. But in the thick of this mess, normal wasn't likely.

"Hey sweetie," he said, pulling her close for a brief moment. It almost seemed like he was guarding the library, and she had to wonder who could be inside. When Sasha pulled away, he and Jackson caught each other's glance, and Sasha nodded. Something was exchanged, and it was clear Jackson knew what to expect.

"I don't want to take anyone off guard," Sasha explained to the group, other than Jackson. "We've found a lost friend of yours that I don't think any of you expected to see again. He's here to join us. In fact, he's been fighting on our side for the past five months."

They all waited for an explanation, but Sasha gave none. He often preferred mysterious surprises in these things. Even the little warning he had given was a stretch for him.

He opened the door. "Please join us inside."

They all did as asked. The Zhànshì in Ava focused her attention to the shadows first, before fully taking in the one who sat there in the open. Remington stood in the slightly shadowed part of the room, attempting to remain out of sight. At the table was seated the person Sasha had cryptically warned of.

Jackson seemed pleased, but without surprise, and it was clear he somehow already knew about this. "Kyle," he said happily.

Only after his name was spoken out loud did it seem to register as real to Ella and Mikel, and both of them ran to greet their old comrade. Kyle stood and hugged his friends at once. Soon Jackson stepped up for a proper greeting.

Ava stood there by the door, not moving at all. Remington caught her glance, and when their eyes met, he offered her a caring, understanding look as if to say, "I know what you're feeling. It's okay."

"Are you sure?" she attempted to ask him, not even considering using the link when they clearly understood each other completely.

He nodded deeply, and it was enough to reassure her.

Kyle had finished a long, joyful greeting with the others, and realizing Ava had no intention of running the distance across the room and jumping into his arms, he slowly, carefully crossed the room to her, while everyone else watched awkwardly from the sidelines.

She didn't even know how to properly voice all that she felt. Of course she was relieved. Of course she was happy to see him. But the mixture of painful emotions within was hard to comprehend.

"Hi, Ava," Kyle said when he was standing before her.

She struggled to look him in the eyes, and in the end, she stopped trying.

Kyle seemed somber. Ava wished she knew how to voice what she felt, but she hadn't the slightest idea how.

"I-I'm sorry, Ava. For leaving you there with Eli. I knew what he was becoming—it's the reason I got out. I saw what he did to you in Brazil, and yet I left you there to further focus on my own agenda. I never should have abandoned you to him."

Suddenly, her feelings made sense, and she looked up at him with a sudden fierce anger. "I'm not mad that you left me, Kyle!" she said with a similar fierce tone. "I never wanted you to save me. Remember? You agreed you would stop trying to protect me. I'm not mad that you left me with Eli. I'm angry that you used me! Just like Harrison or Eli would have. You used me to fake your death. I would have lied for you. I would have protected you. But you manipulated me to your little plan. Do you have any idea what I went through? Everyone blamed me. They said it was my fault. They said you did it because of me. And I almost believed them, Kyle! You used me. You should have just told me!"

His regretful expression deepened as he and everyone else understood what she was feeling. All of them knew well what it felt like to be manipulated, and they were all tired of it, particularly from their closest friends.

"I'm sorry, Ava," he said, and she could see he meant it. "I shouldn't have used you like that."

She wanted to rant more about all the pain Eli put her through over Kyle's death, but that wasn't really Kyle's fault. And she could see he was sorry for the suffering he had caused. So she simply swallowed the pain, and chose to forgive him. "Just...promise you won't ever use me again."

Solemnly, he nodded. Then after a moment, he put his hand out for her to accept. "I promise. Friends?"

She hesitated momentarily, calling on her new skills and strength to let go of all the pain and hurt she felt from Kyle before she agreed to this. She glanced at Remington once more, and he smiled, as if to say, "It's okay now. You can let go."

And so, she did.

Ava put her hand out and shook Kyle's. Then he pulled her into a hug, and although she tensed at the strange closeness to him at first, she appreciated the gesture and soon hugged him back.

She had forgotten how intently the others watched her until everyone was happily laughing and smiling in relief when the tension cleared. The others surrounded Kyle again, and she had never seen him so happy as now, surrounded by his friends, free of his oppressors, prepared to fight for his mission.

Zak soon joined them, and they gathered around the library table.

When they were all seated, Jackson addressed them. "Remington, Sasha and I have been in communication for the past few months. We have a plan to rival the General's. Remington and Kyle have been weakening the Republic from within, even as you all focused on the fight in Africa. And now that we have all the right people in place, it's time to take down the Republic."

☆ ☆ ☆ ☆ ☆

"We can't actually be that close to defeating the Republic," Mikel said in awe as Jackson completed his presentation to the crew.

Kyle listened with interest as Jackson took that question head on.

"Absolutely, we are," Jackson countered. "You have to realize that the Republic has been crippled more in the past five years than ever before. Harrison ruined their original attempt to conquer Australia and gained the Kingdoms another ally to start it off. A few years later, the Brazil Tower Massacre left them with serious defeat when they lost Brazil. And sure, they gained Australia at that time, but at a great cost."

"Not to mention the fact," Sasha added, "that their gaining of Australia left them spread thinner than ever. A good third of their armada went to deal with the constant battling there. And as long as they were in Australia, they faced daily losses elsewhere that cost them greatly."

"Thanks to yours truly," Mikel said proudly.

Kyle widened his eyes blankly, slightly embarrassed for his friend and his overt arrogance, before turning back to Jackson as the man continued his explanation.

"When Lionel and Ava retook Australia once and for all, it was at an even greater cost as the Republic attempted to defend the territory. They lost thousands of good officers. Ava's attack timed perfectly with Russia defecting," Jackson continued. "And when they lost another third of their armada—including the main defensive armies within Africa, as the Russians retreated to their homeland—the Republic was more weakened than ever before."

"They tried to fight us," Zak explained further. "But in holding off Russia at the border, they had to pull many of their remaining troops from their African territories."

"Leaving Sizwe and our Ukombozi team the perfect opportunity to free Africa from Republic oppression, once and for all," Sasha spoke proudly.

"Their Korean army was seriously crippled from the losses in Australia," Jackson explained it more simply. "They lost their Russian army completely when the country defected. That leaves them with only a third of their greatest armies intact. The Chinese army has suffered serious losses as they've been spread thin throughout the remainder of the Republic, attempting to keep their forces intact."

"All they really have left is their Chinese army," Sasha added, "and conscripted men from the remainder of the Republic countries. Add to that all the damage from the calculated attacks that Remington and Kyle have operated in the past five months."

"In short," Jackson concluded, "we really are that close. If we can manage uprisings by the people in the remaining Republic countries, if we can take the Towers, and if we can remove the Politburo members, the Republic will be no more. Those three final steps. That's all that's left."

Everyone else seemed right on board with these men, but Kyle wasn't as certain. "This whole thing sounds pretty insane to me," he submitted darkly.

"Maybe. But we're going to manage it anyway," Jackson replied confidently.

Kyle was tempted to call Jackson the idealist and say there was "no way in the General's name."

But strangely, Mikel was now on board. "Alrighty then."

Ella sat back looking suddenly as confident as the others. "Good enough for me."

It still sounded crazy to Kyle, but one unequivocal word from Jackson and they were all suddenly convinced.

Kyle watched Jackson for the remainder of the meeting, searching for answers to what was apparently common understanding between the rest. It was as if they all trusted Jackson so much that a simple assurance was enough to persuade them.

Sure enough, Kyle was persuaded, again, of something else entirely: Jackson Davis was a dangerous man.

He pondered for some time on why they all trusted Jackson's overconfidence when if it were Mikel, they would all tell him to be more cautious when dealing with people's lives. But there was something about Jackson. He was overconfident, yes. He was an idealist, one hundred percent. And yet, as much as Kyle thought about it, he had to admit that Jackson always somehow managed to back up his promises.

He had convinced Sasha to leave behind his decades of devotion for a promise of a new third side, and guess what: here it was! He somehow managed to get the whole of Russia to defect from the Republic with idealistic promises of success and freedom, and they achieved it like it was nothing! He offered some insane idea to Valkyrie for defeating the Jiānhùrén convoy in Africa. Won and done! He convinced Mikel and Ava that they could take over all the Towers in Africa in a crazy run over a few short days. No problemo! And those were just the few small instances Kyle knew about.

Jackson was an idealist, yet he somehow bridged the gap between reality and the ideal that he envisioned. When he looked the members of this room in the eye and said with confidence that they were going to win this, every one of them believed him. And upon closely considering his record, Kyle did too.

A dangerous man indeed. But he might just do it. He might just defeat the Republic.

After a long day of meeting and discussing, one would expect all of them to be tired of each other; but it was a different feeling in the room tonight—a sort of relaxed, enchanting gathering. It felt like the old days in the mansion, when Zak, Sasha and Jackson would gather in this dining room as friends, not just coworkers. And yet, it was even deeper than that. Everyone in this room, they were closer than friends; it felt like a big family reunion. There was so much love and respect around this table that even Jackson couldn't leave, though it caused his work to take three times as long when he finally got back to it.

Jackson tapped away on his laptop at the end of the long dining table. Remington had a seat at the side of the room, in the shadows, where he merely observed. Ella was seated by the others, but she would not join in. Sasha, Zak, Viktoriya, Mikel, Ava and Kyle were all deeply immersed in a parlor game and looked to be having fun. Jackson would join them eventually, but first he had to finish the next speech he was working on for President Volvakov.

Unconsciously, he watched the game, smiling now and then at the dynamics in relationships around the table.

The game involved a point system where a question was read out loud, such as, "who in the group has traveled the most," and all the players assigned their vote to another player. Only, one didn't *want* to receive points. It was a curse to be given votes, and the participants were energetic and persuasive in trying to get other players off their backs.

"Hands down, Remington has traveled the most," Mikel joked.

"He's not playing, dweebob," Ella said with an exaggerated roll of her eyes. "Oh, and by the way, neither am I."

"Well, I know it's not me," Zak said pleasantly. "I've only ever been to Russia. Oh, and Africa. And Brazil and..." he trailed off, remembering just how many places he had been.

"And a tour of the Republic," Sasha reminded him pointedly. "As an early member of my crew."

"And the United Kingdoms," Kyle added. "To meet the General."

"Okay, fine. I've been around the block. But Sasha has been around six times as much as me!"

They started a list of where each of them had been until ultimately the votes were all generously cast on Sasha.

Any time a question was posed on experience, there were long debates on who it might go to. But whenever it came to a question of lack of experience, such as "who has never consumed alcohol" or the like, it was always pointed at Ava and Kyle. Yet, each time, Kyle talked himself out of it by speaking of the past months on his own and the many things he had experienced in that time.

"Oh, here's a good one," Viktoriya read the next question out loud with a mysterious smile. "Who in the group has yet to experience their first kiss?"

"Kyle," Ella blurted immediately.

Kyle scoffed. "Oh, you have no idea. I've had the first, and many more to follow."

"I can back that up," Mikel said proudly. "He caught me up on his adventures today. He's quite the cowboy, our friend here."

"Fine, then Ava," Ella said, though of course, she was certainly *not* playing.

"Yes, I have," Ava said simply. But the silence that followed didn't speak well for her.

"Oh, have you now?" Sasha asked suspiciously.

"Yes," Ava said defensively.

"Kyle?" Ella accused him.

"Don't look at me," he said with a shrug. "I didn't have the pleasure."

"Who then?" Mikel pressed Ava with equal suspicion.

Jackson would have gladly raised his hand and made himself known, but Ava immediately deflected the question in a way that made it clear she didn't want it out in the open. "Doesn't matter. It just matters that I have kissed someone. Several times in fact."

Sasha glanced at Jackson for a sign, and he wasn't the only one. Jackson would have defended her honor here, but instead felt she wanted him to stay out of it, so he pretended to be innocently focused on his work, and did it well apparently, because the glances turned away from him and suspiciously back to Ava.

"You're gonna have to give us something if you don't want the votes," Viktoriya said, slowly sliding her vote card toward Ava as if to press her to answer the truth.

"I won't take these cards!" Ava said in frustration. "You've given me twenty points for dumb things I've never done. But I'm not taking a point when it doesn't apply!"

"She's telling the truth," Zak offered, and everyone turned to face him. Even Ava seemed surprised by his backing her up.

"Oh?" Viktoriya asked with even more suspicion now. "And how would you know?"

"The other party told me," he said plainly. "I didn't know it happened more than once, but I heard about the first time."

Once more, a couple of heads turned to Jackson, but he continued with a straight face and focused well enough on his work to deflect suspicion.

"Let's see," Viktoriya said with sudden interest. "Let's just try and imagine who would have told Zak...."

"Let's not," Ava spoke up quickly. "Let's just agree that I'm not taking that card."

"I know how to settle this," Ella said with a sudden smugness. "Remington? Give us the scoop."

Remington smiled, but shook his head. "I would not betray her trust."

"It's not betrayal!" Ava disagreed. "If you know, then tell 'em!"

Still, Remington shook his head.

"All right, sweety," Mikel said, standing from his seat and walking toward Ava. "No need to make a fool of yourself over this. If you didn't want the card, all you had to do was ask."

The entire room watched in surprise as Mikel slid her seat out a few feet from the table, sat down on her lap, then leaned in and kissed her.

Jackson wasn't looking at his paperwork at that moment. He had no right to feel jealous, but.... Everyone else either laughed or cheered in surprise. But Jackson watched as if he had been punched in the gut. He should have just admitted to being the one she had kissed and avoided this horrible scene.

It wasn't exactly that she kissed Mikel back, but it was several seconds before she punched him in the ribs and pushed him away, and those few seconds—whether they were of shock or just enjoyment— were not Jackson's favorite.

"Mikel, you carc, get off me," she said, but she, too, was laughing and obviously strangely enjoyed it as much as the rest of them.

Still, Jackson watched, unable now to even look away. He wasn't frustrated at her or anything. In fact, a part of him wanted to laugh along with the others at the surprising incident. But he could not deny his jealousy at the same time.

When Mikel stood up he boldly spoke, "See, now, wasn't I much better than the other guy?"

She thought about that for only a second before responding, "Not by a long shot."

Mikel acted as if the words wounded him directly like a bullet, flinching back and falling into Kyle's lap now. His friend caught him, laughing to tears. Kyle had seemingly enjoyed the whole thing as much as, or more than, anyone.

Jackson smiled. He couldn't help it. That was a good response from her.

In the background Mikel spoke, "See, now that'll be the last time I kiss a girl out of pity!"

"Probably shouldn't have been a first time, buddy," Zak responded.

But Jackson wasn't listening now, and neither was Ava. She must have felt his eyes on her, or maybe she just wondered what he thought of all this, because she seemed to drown out the noise and looked across the room at him. Their eyes met. His smile deepened with his eyes, and she matched his smile from across the room.

No woman had ever looked so perfectly beautiful to him before. He didn't want to look away, and she didn't seem to either. They just stared like that for too long before Jackson became conscious of Sasha's observant eyes, having noticed them.

At that point he forced himself to look down, but nothing in the speech draft made sense anymore. It all looked like jumbled words, and all he could think about was that woman across the table.

The next card was dealt, and Kyle read out loud, "Name the person in the group who has never been on a date."

"Ava," Sasha spoke first, but he was immediately followed by Mikel and Zak answering the same way. "Ava."

Then Viktoriya, "Yup, Ava."

At that point Ava glared at them and sank sulkily back in her seat. "I hate this game."

☆ ☆ ☆ ☆ ☆

After the longest, worst game ever, they played a respectable game of poker, which Jackson joined. And of course, in Jackson fashion, he cleared everyone out.

Zak was first out, followed by Viktoriya, then Mikel, Ava and Kyle. It came down to Sasha, Ella and Jackson, and admittedly, Ava was rooting for Ella. But that was mostly because cocky Jackson always seemed to win when he was playing anything these days, and it just wasn't right. She would like to see the young girl smear him. But alas, Sasha was next to go, and Ella was quick to follow.

Everyone else said they were in for another round, but Jackson glanced at his watch and regretfully said he needed to go to bed. He had ridiculously early meetings in the morning and needed a clear head to get the Russian leadership on his side of the issue in question.

Jackson got up to go, but as he stopped at the door, he glanced at Ava. He said nothing. If he still had the link, maybe he could have. But instead, he just looked at her. She sensed some sort of hesitation or longing, and she felt it too. They hadn't had any time alone together, and it was doubtful that the following days would be any different. Of course, it was wonderful to have everyone there in the same place this way, though she wished for time alone with him.

He left, saying nothing, but she couldn't forget that longing look in his eyes, not for anything.

So, after a while, she went all in on a hand that Kyle clearly had in the bag. She lost everything, and didn't mind. What was she going to do with the money the countries of Africa had awarded her anyway?

Once she had been cleared out, she pretended to be tired and said she was done for the night. She didn't bother to glance back and check for suspicion. At this point, maybe she didn't mind if the others knew she was going after Jackson.

She stopped at his door. She didn't see any light coming underneath it, and it had been a good fifteen minutes. It was possible he was already asleep by now.

As much as she wanted to see him, she didn't have the guts to simply knock on the door. So, she left, returning to the kitchens and joining the others for an hour before everyone else went to bed. At that point she should have done the same, but all she could think about was Jackson, and, glancing at the clock when she entered her room, it occurred to her that it was only another couple of hours before he would wake up and start his morning.

It was a terrible idea, but she did it anyway. She sat down on her bed to read, leaving her door cracked open so she would hear when he left his room.

☆ ☆ ☆ ☆ ☆

"What's all this about you being a cowboy?" Ella asked Kyle as the three Zhànshì walked toward the north wing and the guest rooms they all held for the week. "And having a girlfriend?"

"Or two," Mikel piped in with a seeming pride for his friend. "After all those years pining over Ava."

Kyle chuckled, and the fact that he didn't immediately react in defense to Mikel's comment made Ella think he really might have moved on from Ava. "I grew up," he offered. "I'll never stop loving Ava. But I definitely have stopped pining over her. And I only have *one* girlfriend. The first insisted we not label anything, and wait until I returned to see if we had anything between us. I found someone else in the meantime."

Since that moment, seeing Kyle sitting there alive in the library, all of Ella's past hopes had risen once more that maybe now he would see her. He didn't. And it was fine. She had dealt with the pain of those feelings this long; she could handle it now just as well. She was just glad he was alive.

"Cowboy," Mikel muttered the teasing name.

"To be a cowboy requires cattle!" Kyle objected. "I'm not seeing any bovine, are you?"

"Unless you count Mikel and I," Ella offered, and both of the guys laughed at that.

"I don't, to be clear," Kyle said when the laughter had let off.

"It's the archetype of the cowboy," Mikel explained.

"Oh, and that little kiss tonight of yours?" Kyle shot back. "What would you call that?"

"There was nothing little about it!" Mikel objected. "Greatest smooch of my life. I know you've always wanted to kiss her. Now you're living vicariously through me."

Kyle laughed even as he shook his head. But still, the way he was so carefree regarding Mikel's comments about Ava proved to Ella more than anything that he really had moved on. In the past, he had always been so uptight about such teasing and really anything having to do with Ava.

So, who was this incredible other woman who had taken Ava's place in Kyle's heart? Ella couldn't help wondering what was so special about her.

"I couldn't help noticing that she kissed you back," Ella noted in the same teasing humor as the guys.

"She totally did!" Mikel said excitedly, as if it were the best and funniest thing in the world. "I caught her off guard, but her muscle memory must have kicked in, because she went for it!"

"Proving she was telling the truth after all," Ella noted laughingly.

"Or that she's actually been madly in love with *you* all these years," Kyle teased. "And was just waiting for you to make your move."

"Psh! In his dreams," Ella declared as they entered the hallway toward their rooms.

Mikel laughed suddenly. "Wouldn't that be ironic! If *I* won her over *you*?"

"I could've gotten her if I tried," Kyle said confidently.

"Mmhmm," Mikel said in a mock disbelieving tone. "Goodnight, Kyle." With that Mikel entered his room leaving Kyle and Ella alone in the hall.

Kyle turned to face her. "I really could have!"

And Ella had no doubt of that. If Ava knew Kyle as Ella did, there was no way she wouldn't love him.

Still, Ella turned up her brows and approached her own door. "Mmhmm," she mimicked. "Goodnight, Kyle."

✯ ✯ ✯ ✯ ✯

Ava didn't know she had even fallen asleep until she heard her door squeak. She opened her eyes quickly to see Jackson there, attempting to close her door.

"Sorry," he whispered. "I saw the door open and the light on and thought you were awake. I was just going to close it when I saw you sleeping."

She jumped from her bed and walked across the room to where he stood. "I wasn't sleeping. I was reading. I just closed my eyes for a second."

He smiled, but his look said he didn't believe her. "You should get to bed," he chastised, though sweetly. "It's really, really late."

"Or really, really early," she countered, "depending on which end of the clock you live on."

He did not reply, but that look in his eyes was so perfect, all she wanted to do was hold him close and never let go.

"Last night was crazy," he said with a hint of hidden meaning.

"You mean Mikel is crazy!" Ava replied with a dramatic huff, sensing exactly what he meant.

"Well, he had us all laughing. And you didn't seem to hate it all that much." There was no criticism in his words, but a measure of teasing that she enjoyed.

"You weren't..." she trailed off, not wanting to make a fool of herself if the words proved inaccurate.

"Jealous?" he offered, knowing where she was headed with it. She didn't reply verbally, but her eyes confirmed the question. "Oh, beyond belief!"

They both laughed at that, and although it was clearly funny, she almost thought he meant it. After a moment to enjoy his comment, she grew more serious. "You don't have to be though," she assured him, and his eyes shifted to a look just as serious. "You can kiss me anytime you want to."

He observed her seriously for a long time, as if testing the truthfulness of those words. Then, when he was apparently sure she meant that, he leaned in and kissed her. Her mind cleared and all she could do was feel him close to her, enjoying every second of it.

When he did eventually pull away, his smile matched her feelings. "Wow," Ava teased him exaggeratedly.

He chuckled. "Still got it?"

"Oh yeah. Still got it."

He laughed, and she smiled deeply.

Then he stepped back and put his hand on the door to close it. "Goodnight, Ava."

"Good morning, Jackson," she replied softly.

He turned to leave, but then stopped. "Hey," he said, turning back around. "A proverbial little birdy told me you've never been on a date."

She shook her head in aggravation at that stupid game, causing him to laugh once more.

"Well, I was wondering if you'd like to have lunch with me tomorrow?"

She stared at him for a long time. Too long. She probably should have given an answer by now. It was definitely getting awkward. And now there was some tension.

"Uh, I mean, you don't have to—" he offered when she hesitated for way, way too long.

"What? Oh no, I mean, yes! I would love to. But...aren't you too busy? I mean, and we can't leave the mansion, right?"

"Yeah, right. I was thinking maybe we could meet in the library? After my morning meetings I have an hour free, if you're able to come then? I can have Maxim put together something. I mean, I know it's not the most glamorous of first dates or anything but—"

"It's perfect. I'll be there." She reached for the door and closed it in his face, then immediately regretted it. But now it was too late to open it without another awkward encounter. Oh man, she was so bad at this.

Ava closed her eyes tightly, feeling the awkward tension, wishing she had her mother, or Breanna, or Ame or even Hawkins to help her know what to do to prepare for a date. She couldn't very well turn to Ella, and she and Viktoriya just weren't close that way.

She found herself suddenly stressed and overwhelmed by the prospect of something so official, and so foreign.

So much for going to sleep now.

"The success we've had is incredible!" Zak explained as the crew sat around the library table the next morning. "Assuming you're all willing, we'd like to run the scan on each of you, gauge where you're at with the flaw and if any treatment is needed."

Eyes slowly turned to Ava as the other Zhànshì questioned what she thought of it. When it was clear that they were waiting for approval from her, she nodded vigorously. "Of course! I've seen the research myself; this could save a lot of lives. If you're asking me, I think you should all do it!"

Mikel seemed pleased enough by it, and Kyle nodded with acceptance. Only Ella watched her suspiciously. "We should do it. But you're not going to?"

Ava hesitated momentarily. Sasha was the one to respond to the room at large. "Ava has decided not to undergo the scan and treatments herself."

"What?" Jackson asked with sudden surprise. "Why not?"

"She has decided that her specific position and opportunity cost is such that undergoing the scan would be pointless, when treatments would inhibit the abilities we need from her."

"Then I'm not doing it either," Mikel replied stubbornly.

"Yes you are," Kyle said sternly before anyone else could object. "You and I and Ella all should."

"But not her?" Mikel objected.

"It's different for her," Remington replied soberly, the first words he had spoken in this meeting. "I support her decision. Though I hope you'll make a different choice than she has to."

Mikel was clearly frustrated, though Kyle sensed the frustration was more that the others were underestimating *his* value with Intelligence and less of worry specifically for Ava.

"You've made up your mind?" Jackson spoke directly to Ava, clearly not liking the thought at all.

She simply nodded, and Kyle wondered why she had opted to have Sasha represent her in this matter, rather than speak up for herself. She didn't usually have a hard time speaking her mind.

"She is certain of her choice," Sasha reiterated firmly. "If anyone has questions regarding it, you may ask me."

"But I do hope the rest of you will do it and hopefully understand why I'm choosing not to," Ava said with evident yearning.

Many of them accepted it. Only Jackson and Mikel still seemed unable to let go, though neither of them voiced additional concerns.

Conversation eventually moved to other topics. Mikel was the one to bring up his dislike for the name "The Third Side."

"I think we should find something more eloquent. Like, 'The Coalition for Freedom,' or something."

"I don't want to give our alliance any name," was Jackson's rejoinder.

"Well, it already has one!" Mikel shot back. "People refer to us as 'The Third Side' whether you want them to or not. And I really think we could pick a better name than that! It just sounds so…I don't know—juvenile?"

Jackson nodded in agreement. "Maybe so. But I'm not the one spreading that name. We are not a name; we are a cause."

"Causes with catchy names and taglines usually make it further in life," Zak said, offering agreement to Mikel's suggestion.

"Fine," Jackson offered. "Then come up with something and we'll consider it. But that is not what this cause is about. The United Kingdoms, the Republic, even the Jiānhùrén are so fond of their smart names and the meaning behind them. That's just not what we're about. I don't want to give any title to this cause. If people want to call us 'The Third Side,' I'm fine with that, because we are not one singular entity like those other institutions. This fifty-year war has always consisted of two sides: the Kingdoms and the Republic. Up until now, you were on either one of these sides, or you weren't on any side at all. I want to show people that there is another option now. That there is a third side, a real cause, that is greater than catchy names and institutions. We are a united cause for freedom and independence. I don't want the peoples of Africa and Russia having to share some title, because they are not *one*. They are separate, distinct entities who happen to believe in the same cause, and will fight and die for it if necessary."

"What about, 'The Cause?'" Sasha suggested.

There was a moment of deliberation as they all considered that.

"It's not great…" Mikel fussed. "But it's better than 'The Third Side.'"

"Sure," Jackson said after a moment of considering. "All right then, 'The Cause.' I'm still not interested in having posters and billboards. But if you want to start calling us by that, then I'm fine with it."

Mikel sighed heavily, but seemed to accept the rationale, and then the meeting moved along to other, more important matters.

At the conclusion of the meeting, Jackson addressed them once more with a closing statement. "In one week, things will shift forever.

Let's spend these coming days preparing, but also enjoying ourselves, investing in relationships, reminding ourselves what we're fighting for.

"The next battle has the potential to be unlike any other we've faced, for better or worse. And while I remain optimistic about our chances of victory, it will only be achieved at great cost.

"Take these few days. Relax. Breathe. Ponder. And laugh. In one short week, we fight."

"So, is it officially a date?" Mikel asked for a clarification. "Not just like a meeting over lunch to discuss war efforts?"

"I don't know!" Ava said in a panic. "He just said, 'will you have lunch with me?'"

"That does sound like official date language," Kyle said thoughtfully.

"Yeah, but Jackson is a classy guy," Mikel disagreed. "He wouldn't have been afraid to say, 'will you go on a date with me?' and save the confusion."

"He did mention something about a date," Ava replied, pacing her bedroom while the boys sat comfortably on her bed. "Like 'a birdy mentioned you've never been on one' or something."

Mikel and Kyle shared a nod. "Definitely a real date," Kyle said, and Mikel replied a "yes" in agreement.

"Did he mention anything about it being formal?" Kyle offered. "Like, formal or casual dining?"

She watched them blankly for a long time. "We're just meeting in the library over his lunch break."

"Taint," Mikel said.

"Rough," Kyle added.

"What's wrong with that?" Ava asked with urgent concern.

"Well, you have no clues. He might mean a fairytale ballroom date—" Mikel began.

"Or a casual friendly gathering over snacks and conversation."

"The normal world is so confusing," Mikel said with sudden disdain.

"True," Kyle agreed. "My first girlfriend was so unpredictable, and I never knew what she wanted. I had to guess every minute what she was thinking, and I was basically never right."

"They overthink everything," Mikel added. "Like, can't we just have a normal, no expectations date and not have you constantly waiting for me to say or do the right thing?!"

"Exactly!" Kyle exclaimed.

They ranted back and forth for another minute or two before Ava sat down helplessly in the armchair. "You two are no help at all."

"Of course, we are thinking of girls," Kyle noted suddenly.

"Good point! Maybe *he's* just expecting a normal, no confusion date."

They both suddenly looked at Ava suspiciously. "Maybe *you're* the one who's overthinking this," Kyle accused.

"Are you kidding me?" Ava said, throwing her hands in the air. "You two are the ones freaking me out about every possible angle in this! *Of course* I'm overthinking it now!"

"Excuse me," Mikel corrected, "you were freaking out before we came. You asked us here, remember?"

Ava put her face in her hands. "I can't do this day on no sleep."

"Mistake number one," Kyle agreed with a nodding head. "Always get a good night's sleep before attempting to deal with your girlfriend—or guy, in your case. It never goes well if you're tired. Believe me."

"Might be best to reschedule," Mikel said thoughtfully.

"What?" Ava blurted. "Are you guys crazy? Won't that make him overthink, if anything?"

"Nah," Mikel assured her. "You can't take risks with your health when it comes to dating. That is, if you're not at your best, you won't be emotionally prepared to handle your date. Reschedule."

"Don't," Kyle disagreed. "Just nap right now and go refreshed."

"I can't sleep when I'm stressed out of my mind! And by the way, it has gotten exponentially worse since you two came to 'help' me!"

"I don't know what to say," Mikel said, shrugging back into his seat. "Just get dressed like every other day. Go on this lunch outing with no expectations and try not to be disappointed."

Kyle clicked his tongue. "It will be fine. He likes you. Get dressed up if you want. Don't if you don't. Just go and have fun! If you don't overthink it, everything will be fine. You are definitely the one in the relationship who overthinks things."

"Will you stop with that characterization, please?"

"Jackson does think rather like a woman at times..." Mikel noted thoughtfully.

"He didn't have a dad, brothers or male peers growing up," Kyle nodded in agreement. "He was raised by girls."

"This could be an issue," Mikel said thoughtfully. "You might be in trouble."

"Oh, will you both just go? You've been no help at all!"

"Heck no, we're invested in this now! We're gonna see this through!" Kyle said sternly.

"Get up and show us your wardrobe," Mikel ordered. "We'll help you pick a nice outfit."

☆ ☆ ☆ ☆ ☆

"Whoa!" Jackson's first exclamation startled Ava as much as her appearance startled him.

"What's wrong?" she asked in concern.

He looked her up and down, shaking his head and having to convince himself it was Ava he was looking at. High ponytail, black leather jacket, black pants and boots. She looked the spitting image of Valkyrie.

"Nothing! You look...awesome."

Her face deflated and she suddenly looked like she would cry. "I don't want to talk about it," she said, pulling out the ponytail and ridding herself of the black leather jacket for the black t-shirt underneath.

"No, you're fine! Seriously, you just, you look a lot like Valkyrie."

"I don't want to talk about it," she said again weakly, walking into the room and taking a seat at the library table.

"I won't say a word then," he offered, gesturing a lip-zip to keep from doing so.

He joined her at the table and was silent while she worked through her obvious frustration about the outfit.

She immediately started picking at her plate, and he decided not to present it in the fancy four course meal that Maxim had prepared. She had started with course three, and that was just fine.

"So...how are things since coming back to Russia?" he asked, offering simple conversation.

She had to finish chewing her bite before she responded. "Good. You?"

This was going to be difficult. She didn't really seem like she was in the mood for small talk. "We have a week left here," Jackson tried to go deeper. "A week before everything goes crazy again. What do you want to do with it?"

She considered for a time but was still invested in her plate, which was fair. He decided to focus on eating, and they could talk more after.

"If you had one week to live," Ava finally said, when she had finished chewing her bite, "what would you do with it?"

He considered that for a time before responding. "Honestly? I would do what I did this morning. I'd keep with my schedule for the day and for the next day," he motioned to the planner that sat open on the table which showed his ridiculously full schedule for the week. "I would do everything I can to further our plan and get things closer to freedom. And then, if I died at the end of that week, I would know I went out doing everything I possibly could to better the world before I went."

She watched him with a look of admiration, and he was glad she didn't accuse him of being a workaholic like everyone else did. Suddenly she became thoughtful. "What about that whole speech you gave everyone this morning about enjoying this week and remembering why it's all worth fighting for?"

He chuckled as he considered that. "I guess I sort of meant it for everyone else. I have way too much to do behind the scenes to get us ready for next week."

She gave a half smile in understanding.

"What about you? What would you do?" he asked, turning it to her.

"Well, I don't feel like I can go after that! Mine is not nearly as selfless."

"Go ahead," he urged. "Mine was overdramatic anyway. What would you do with one week?"

374

She took a moment to consider, then leaned back in her seat before she answered. "I would go on long walks with Sasha—like we did every day during my recovery. I would meditate with Mikel. Spar with Kyle. Discover new, delicious foods with Ella. I would play silly games and do sports with Zak and Viktoriya. I would sit quietly and say nothing, but everything, with Remington. I would read all my favorite parts in my favorite books by myself. And I would do all of these things with you."

He had been watching her admiringly as she talked, but in that last comment he was overwhelmed by a feeling of love for this woman. He suddenly longed for a perfect week like that with her, with long walks, games, sparring, delicious foods, meditations, quiet moments and the best parts in books shared together. Suddenly, his answer felt so silly compared to hers.

"But obviously," she said, glancing once more at his open calendar, "you probably wouldn't have time for that."

Of course, he was entirely devoted to his mission and his purpose. But in reality, he had become so focused on the mission that he didn't always keep the "what's it all for" present in his mind—even if he preached the flowery words to everyone else. He was about to say he would change his answer, and include many of those things where he could in his busy schedule, but she spoke first.

"So instead, I'll have lunch with you in the cracks of time, say good morning to you when it's night for me, and appreciate every little thing you have done and continue to do to move this whole thing forward. I'm just the one they send into battle. It's easy to forget how much planning and preparation it takes before the leaders make that kind of order."

He watched her thoughtfully for a moment. He almost thought to invite her to join on the backend, but she changed the subject too quickly.

"So...anyway. I guess from the meeting this morning that you'll be pretty involved in Jun's extraction."

He turned back to his plate before answering. "She won't be comfortable with anyone else," he explained. "I think it's best that I help her, both in extraction and as she settles in."

Ava nodded in understanding, but there was something in her expression that showed concern.

"What?" he asked.

She shook her head. "Nothing," she said, and took another bite. But the expression and her demeanor clearly spoke concern.

"What?" Jackson pressed.

Still, she shook her head. "Nothing. It doesn't matter."

"Maybe. But will you tell me anyway? I care if you have any reservations about this plan."

It took several more times of pushing before finally she opened up on her concern. "It's nothing. It just makes sense, I guess. You are always so good at finding the wounded or broken girl and attempting to put her back together. It's that hero complex that you have. It's fine. You'll save her life, and she'll fall madly in love with you in the process, whether you're interested or not."

He jutted his chin forward incredulously, not liking how bad she made it sound. "It's not like I go out in search of girls to save and make them fall in love with me."

Once again, she hesitated before speaking her mind. "Not intentionally."

"What's that supposed to mean?"

She shrugged her shoulders, pushing her plate away as an indication she was no longer hungry. "Nothing. It just means you have a hero complex."

"And is that such a bad thing?"

"No! Not at all, from your perspective. But while you're helping this girl pick up the pieces and put her life back together, inevitably, she will fall in love with you. And when you're done 'saving her,' you'll be done with her, but she will spend the rest of her sorry life trying to get over you. Eli did the same thing with Katia when he 'rescued' her from Russia."

"Well, I'm not Eli," Jackson objected.

Still, she didn't seem to buy it. "And how is what you did with me any different?"

Maybe she didn't mean it as an attack. He tried as hard as he could not to take it personally. But how did she intend for him to take that?

"Well, for one thing, I haven't abandoned you to the wayside now that you're through your rough patch, have I? I was never involved with you just to 'save' you. I care about you."

She scoffed at that, and then his attempts to not let it get to him went out the window.

"Maybe you're still searching for something to fix in me." This she muttered, but it was clear she intended him to hear it.

He paused, forcing himself not to act rashly. "Ava...I have no idea what's happening right now. If you're mad at me for something, I don't know what it is. If you feel like I'm trying to change you or fix you then I'm sorry. I honestly—"

"Can we just drop it?" she interrupted.

"Gladly!" he said, with a touch of frustration.

Unfortunately, it wasn't that easy for either of them to let go of the tense feeling.

"So..." she awkwardly attempted to change the subject, but didn't seem to have any idea where to go.

Jackson had one thing in particular he'd been hoping to discuss with her, although he didn't know if this was the right time after that disagreement. Still, knowing they only had so much time before his next meeting, he decided to try. "I wanted to talk to you about your decision regarding the flaw."

Her guard went up, sending all kinds of warning signs. It was clear he should back off, especially when both of them were already feeling tense. But in a moment of weakness, he moved forward anyway.

"I guess you somehow convinced Sasha and Remington not to push it, and in fact to defend your stance. I just want to know why you won't do the screening."

"I just decided it wasn't right for me," she said, pulling her plate closer again as if in hopes of moving on from this question and to something else.

"It's not like I'm asking you to do the procedure. Just to see if there's a problem in the first place."

"I don't want to," she said, attempting to remain nonchalant.

"Why?"

"Because! What's the point? It's not gonna change anything! I won't do the treatments, or the procedure, even if they find out I need it. The only thing it will do is give a little bit of peace of mind if I don't have a problem and make people sad if I do."

"Peace of mind isn't such a bad thing," he argued, trying not to be too forceful. "And if you are affected, at least we can look at our options then."

"No! There are no other options, all right? I'm not going to do anything that has any chance of weakening my connection with the link or my ability to fight off Counter Intelligence. It's already hard enough as it is! And we both know that, as much as your plan 'rival's the General's,' it still requires my ability to control the Towers and fight off our new enemy. This screening won't change anything, so it's pointless."

Everything in him wanted to act out in rash anger, but he controlled it and gave a careful answer. "I'm not trying to use you like Harrison, Ava."

"I know that," she said assuredly, but he wasn't so sure.

"There's a difference between using, and utilizing. If you don't want to be involved, I'll find another way."

"I'm not asking you to, Jackson! I'm more than happy to be utilized. But there's no point in being screened for something that I won't be able to fix either way. I'd rather just live in ignorant bliss about my health problems for as long as I have."

"But what if there was something we could do to help you and we won't know because you won't do a simple screening?"

"There's nothing! What's the solution? Remove the chip like they did for you? Give me the treatments that make it dormant like they're doing for Sasha? If Zak and Sasha can come up with something that doesn't weaken my ability with the link then sure, maybe I'll consider trying it out. Until then...."

"What if it's your brain scans that help them come up with the solution? They can't fix a problem without knowing what it is in the first place."

She started to object once more, but Jackson's buzzer rang loudly, and even in this tense moment he glanced at it out of habit. He wished he hadn't.

"Taint it!" he cursed, reaching for the mobile.

"What's wrong?" she said, forcing herself to take a breath and relax.

"My meeting with the president and chief advisor got moved ahead of schedule." He cursed silently and stood. "I'm really sorry about this, I need to go."

This was horrible timing. If it were a meeting with just about anyone else, he would have ignored it. But he had to fight to get into Volvakov's schedule at all today. This meeting was imperative.

"It's fine," Ava said, standing and leaving the table for the door. "I have stuff to do anyway."

"Ava..." he pleaded, following her to the door. "Please don't be mad at me. This meeting is really, really important."

"I know!" she assured him, and he thought she meant it, though still, she definitely looked angry. "Go to your meeting. We'll catch up some other time."

She started to open the door, but he put his hand on it, stopping her. "Ava, I'm not trying to pressure you or force you into anything. I'm just worried about you. And if there's anything wrong, I'd like to know it. Especially if it's something we can fix."

"It's not something we can fix!" she shot back in frustration. "There's nothing that can be done! Will you just let it go?"

There was something deeper in that response, in the emotion behind her words. He watched her for a time, wondering if he was right or not. "You're sick, aren't you?" he asked quietly. "That's why you don't want to do the screening. You already know what the results will be."

She gave no verbal response, but her eyes said everything. It was several long beats before she looked down, taking a breath and containing her feelings. "I'm not doing that screening, Jackson. What would be the point? If I'm fine, then it doesn't matter. But even if I'm not, too many people have sacrificed to bring about this opportunity. And even if Harrison was wrong to do it, I will not let all of those sacrifices be in vain. It won't change what I do. So, there's no point. It will just make my only choice harder. Please, can you just support me, like everyone else has?"

Though she denied any knowledge of the flaw within her, he now knew for certain. And as much as he wanted to support her, he could only think now that he was going to lose her, when it was entirely possible they could find a way to fix this if she would just quit being so stubborn.

"Maybe I can't," he spoke helplessly.

She huffed in frustration. "Everyone else has let it go! Why won't you?"

He felt weak and cold suddenly. She was sick. He knew it. And so did she. Maybe even Sasha and Remington too. "Because I care about you," he replied just as helplessly as before.

"Oh, don't give me that!" she spat back. "You won't give it up because you're stubborn. Are you really going to claim you care more for me than my fellow Zhànshì or even Sasha?"

She had stepped forward to be directly in front of Jackson, and now he looked down at her. His eyes were filled with that same challenge. He didn't respond, but the look he gave her probably said what words couldn't, suggesting that, in fact, he did love her more. She wavered under that glance, taking a step back and suddenly looking less certain of herself.

Her expression returned to one of determination. "When you left for that meeting five months ago, I asked you not to go, because I knew in my gut that it might get you killed. And I was right."

He started to object, but she put her fist on his chest in anger and spoke emphatically. "By all accounts you should be dead! For everything *you* did to save yourself, you would be! It's only because Eli felt he owed me a debt that you're standing here now. And you know what? I think you knew the danger. I think you felt it too. But you went anyway. Because it was your job. Someone needed to go to that meet. It had to be you. Well guess what, this is *my* job. And knowing with one hundred percent certainty that you were going to get shot that day, you still would have gone!"

"I would have found another way," he argued.

"You would have done your job," Ava continued as if he hadn't. "You wouldn't have let your friends die fighting your battles. Well, there's no magical other way out of this! Countless people have sacrificed their lives to make it so I can live my mission. I always knew it would mean sacrificing my life. So what if I have to die for it too?"

She argued her point well, using his mission and his choices as an example. In the end, he could not deny the truth of her words, though it was excruciating. He wanted to argue, but in bringing up this instance, he could not deny that she had proved her point to him. He had known that day that he was walking into an ambush and that he might not make it out alive. But he had gone because it was his duty. And no, he would not have let anyone else die fighting his battle. Maybe she was right. Maybe this was hers.

Still, he wanted her to try...to at least see if there was another way. But in this moment, he knew he would not change her mind.

Eventually, he conceded. He closed his eyes in anguish. When he opened them again, he nodded in acceptance. Looking down at her with pain in his eyes, he swallowed hard. "Then I will stop trying to change your mind. I'll respect your decision."

"Thank you," she said, looking relieved, though still ready for a fight.

Though he said nothing, still apparently he offended her.

"Don't look at me that way."

He shook his head helplessly, quietly responding, "What way?"

"Like that! Just don't. It makes me think you care even half as much about me as I do for you. But I know that you don't, because—"

"How do you know that?" he objected. Then his look became even more serious. "Because I've never told you otherwise?"

Her stare affirmed that.

"Ava, I don't know the first thing about healthy relationships. The only example I ever had growing up was a mother who got it all wrong. All I ever wanted in the past was to find love and do it better. I don't even know if the relationships from the books are real, let alone attainable for someone like me. But I see Sasha and your mom. I hear the way he talks about her. The small moments we got to witness in the dreamwalk. Ava, I think I could be a good man like your dad."

The tone and his glance mixed with these words became too overwhelming for her apparently. She backed away, closer to the door, putting her face in her hands. "What is happening right now?" she muttered under her breath.

"You said you cared about me," Jackson explained, once again not taking offense at her strange reaction. "And I'm not going to let you be the only one who says it."

Her hands suddenly came down and her glare pierced through him. "I know an angle when I see one, Jackson!" she shot back in sudden anger. "You don't think I see what you're doing? You couldn't convince me to take the screening, so you're finding another way to confuse me into it."

"That's not what I'm doing, Ava," he replied in a helpless, pained tone. Could she ever believe a word he said without twisting it?

"No! This is exactly what Eli would do. He would manipulate me with whatever means necessary. And if nothing worked, he'd dig deep into his feelings of love for me and guilt me into doing what he wanted. Manipulation after manipulation. This is exactly what he did!"

"I'm not Eli!" Jackson replied quickly. Then, softly. "I'm not Eli. I would never manipulate you. I would never intentionally hurt you. You asked me to respect your decision, and I'm going to try. This has nothing to do with that."

At first, she seemed to believe him. But then she seemed to overthink everything again as she attempted to comprehend what he *was* saying. "So, I'm supposed to believe that you, what? 'Care about' me?" She mockingly quoted the words he had used.

"Is that so hard to believe?" he asked in a soft, serious tone.

"No, Jackson! It isn't!" she replied, intentionally misunderstanding him when she continued, "You care about everyone! Especially the broken ones."

"That's not what I mean. That's not what I'm saying!"

"What are you saying then?" Her frustration flustered him. He realized soon that he couldn't use fanciful words to scoot around the meaning if he wanted her to understand this one. He had to use words that she would understand plainly, words he had never uttered to anyone before. And where he might easily have said it at the beginning of this little date, he felt terrified to do so now.

He froze, his mouth opening and closing, but no words being said.

She waited expectantly, even hopefully, but he could not say the words out loud, no matter how many times they repeated in his mind— so strongly, she'd probably hear him if he still had the link.

An eternity passed with her there waiting, watching, giving him the opportunity to say what he needed to, but he couldn't seem to. Not now. Not when she would certainly misinterpret something so special and vulnerable from him as manipulation. He couldn't say those words now.

Eventually, she lost hope. She put her head down, sighing. "That's what I thought," she muttered, as if his silence had proven he wasn't genuine in his claims.

She looked up at him again, and the ice in her eyes seemed to freeze his heart even further. "You know, at least when Eli was manipulating me he had the guts to say what I wanted to hear."

With that, she left him standing there in the library like a stunned fool.

And if that wasn't hard enough, he had to shake himself out of it, enter the library office and open the video call.

A whole new battle began as he attempted to convince the leaders of Russia that he was, not only sane, but also right.

He wanted nothing more than to chase Ava down and fix things. Instead, he went to the office and did his job, hoping there would be a chance to fix things later.

"How's our Jackson today?" Volvakov asked pleasantly from the computer screen.

"Another day in the life!" Jackson offered with exaggerated enthusiasm. "How are you today, sir?"

"Never better, son! My wife is pregnant again!"

Jackson chuckled. "Aren't you getting a little old to keep having kids, sir?"

"Careful," Volvakov said, though he, too, was laughing now. "This will probably be the last one. We'll see. Anyway, I spoke with Elyia this week."

"Oh yeah? How's she doing?"

"Great! She was asking about you. She actually had me convinced to let the two of you be married for a moment. But then I thought of how many of my people want you dead, and I worried that might be a bad idea."

Jackson smiled pleasantly. "Well, listen, sir. I know you're on a tight schedule today. I appreciate you taking the time for this meeting."

"If I didn't already know you were going to be pitching some insane new idea for Russia's resources, I would clear my schedule for a social call. As it is, you have ten minutes."

Jackson chuckled appreciatively. "Yes, sir. Thank you. As always, you have me figured out. But believe me, President Volvakov, you're going to like this one—at least as much as you hate it."

★ ★ ★ ★ ★

"I'm so tired of being second-best," Mikel fumed as he got in a good hit on Kyle. "I'm sick of everyone thinking of me as an afterthought. I'm sick of everyone taking pity on me when I finish the race a few seconds behind!"

Kyle went for a smooth chain punch while Mikel fumed, and got in several good hits on his friend before Mikel blocked and went for a counterattack.

"I don't know what you want me to say," Kyle replied honestly. "You're not good enough? Get better! You lack the skills you want to win the race? Train harder!"

"I train twice as hard as my competitor!" Mikel hissed. "She was born of talent. She doesn't have to try. Meanwhile I work my tail off ten hours a day training to be able to withstand Counter Intelligence, and I have barely scratched the surface! I am so freaking tired of all of this!"

"Then maybe you made the wrong goal," Kyle offered, then went in for another attack. When he had backed up again, he continued his thought. "Maybe you should stop comparing yourself to your competitor, and start working on beating your own score."

"This isn't preschool, Kyle!" Mikel shot in anger. "This isn't some game where all the competitors get a prize at the end."

"No, it's not," Kyle agreed, and then had to refocus when Mikel came in with several heavy blows. "This is a tainted war, Mikel!" Kyle said as he fought off his friend. "And you're still so obsessed with this naive goal you made at the age of ten, that you've forgotten who you're fighting! Are you trying to beat Ava's scores? Or are you trying to beat the Republic?"

"Neither," Mikel said with a glare. "And both," this with a grin. "Depends on how you look at it."

"Well whatever it is you want, maybe stop brooding to me and get out there and earn it!"

"I'm trying!" Mikel yelled, then went in for his fiercest attack. Kyle kept him at bay, expending only about eighty percent of his energy on the fight.

"You two fight like ninnies," Ella said, jumping onto the mat. "Let me show you how the big kids like to fight!"

"Give me a break," Mikel replied peevishly.

"You're on," Kyle challenged.

It was every man for himself, and they fought like the old days in training, but without any referees to tell them to tone it down.

Kyle was impressed with the skills of both of his fellow Zhànshì as they gave the fight their all. But he didn't have the heart to tell them that he was the only one not going at one hundred and ten percent. Even with the two opponents, he found himself keeping up easily and keeping both of them in place, where they likely thought he was just barely hanging above them by a thread. They were good, both of them. But Kyle was better.

Mikel got a good hit on Ella and Kyle went right after, knocking her off the mat and into a huddle of dummies. She was apparently so infuriated by their teamwork to get her out, that she grabbed one of the life-size dummies and shoved it onto the mat full force at Kyle.

He was impressed by her strength as the dummy crashed into him and sent pain shooting through his knee and stomach where it had made impact. In the heat of the moment, he decided to continue the attack onto the next foe and shifted the dummy across at Mikel, who was unprepared for the ambush, and it hit him even more forcefully than it had Kyle.

"Poor Mikel," Ella teased rudely. "Always coming in second," her comment proving she had been listening in on them. "Can't even beat a dummy!"

Mikel hissed, pulling a real knife and flinging it across so it just missed Ella's face and pegged into the dummy behind her.

Kyle and Ella both made surprised, challenging sounds. "Oh, it's on now, twerp!" Ella called out, removing her own knife.

It was probably irresponsible to join instead of stopping them. But they were all adults—well, most of them—and they knew how to handle tools. Kyle pulled out his own knife. Mikel retrieved his and they all returned to the mat, prepared to escalate the intensity. They were seconds from starting when a fatherly voice objected, "I'd really prefer you didn't stain my mat with meaningless blood."

They all turned to Sasha who had entered the room, accompanied by Remington.

Kyle was the first to put his knife away, and the others followed suit. "We were just upping the stakes," Mikel offered innocently.

"Certain stakes should be saved for the battlefield, friends," Sasha spoke wisely.

"You old farts are no fun at all," Ella said with a huff.

"Who won?" Sasha asked, changing the subject.

The three of them looked around at one another. "It was a three-way tie," Ella lied to save face.

Kyle chuckled but Mikel objected strongly to that.

"Fine, then Kyle won," Ella revised when Mikel wouldn't let her have it. "And once again, Mikel came in second."

Mikel glared menacingly at her.

"Why don't you join us?" Kyle asked, his interest piquing to see these two men spar.

Remington chuckled, and Sasha shook his head. "I am very out of practice!" he objected.

"I'll go easy on you," Kyle spoke smugly.

Remington and Sasha shared a laugh. "This new generation," Sasha lamented, "they're always eager to challenge one another!"

"You in or out?" Kyle pressed.

"If Remington got on that mat," Sasha spoke for his friend, "you would all be wiped clean without knowing what hit you."

Remington clearly had no desire to join the sparring session.

"But sure, I will take you on, Kyle." Sasha stepped on the mat, and Mikel and Ella made challenge cheers as they stepped down.

"I'm not a Zhànshì or anything," Sasha said as he stretched his muscles in preparation. "But I have won a sparring match or two."

Kyle took position as Sasha got into a fighting stance. "Besides," Sasha offered as Mikel counted them down, "I've been utilizing my Intelligence Quotient in fights longer than you've been alive."

"Go!" Mikel shouted.

And the fight began.

Ava stood at the dining window, watching Jackson play in the yard with Boris, Kai and Jon. For a man who was relentless in his work, he sure knew how to have fun too. Of course, their date had been an exception, but she was willing to admit that was mostly her fault.

She had started accusing him of things; she had been a real jerk. And when he asked valid questions about her decision, she was defensive and, once again, accusatory. And lastly, when he had opened up to her about his feelings, she had shut him down, accusing him again of being like Eli.

He had every right to be done with her. She wouldn't blame him if, after that, he had decided she was just too much, and didn't want to deal with her anymore.

She had realized even in the moment that she was being unfair. And yet, she couldn't seem to push away those reactions. It was like something had been triggered within her, putting her in defense mode, so that no matter what he said or did, all she could think about was how Eli used to manipulate her.

So she had found her inner peace, sure. But that didn't mean she wasn't still a real piece of work.

Ava sensed the presence as it entered the room, and she didn't have to look behind her to know who it was.

"Were you listening? During that whole 'date?'" she asked, still watching through the window.

Remington walked and hovered just behind her. "Old habits," he admitted.

"I don't mind," she assured him. "There's a part of me that always hopes you're there in the background, wherever I am."

He did not respond, but in the reflection on the window, she saw him smile. She watched his likeness for a time before noting that he was now paying attention to what she previously had been. She returned her attention to Jackson and the boys.

"He's a good man, you know," Remington spoke softly.

Ava sighed. "I know."

"He'll never forgive himself for leaving you there with Eli," Remington said somberly. "But you probably can't imagine how much it hurts him every time you compare him to your brother."

Ava closed her eyes sadly. "I know," she admitted. "I don't mean to. I know he's different. But when I feel like I have to defend myself, I attack."

"And you hit your enemy where it hurts," Remington added.

Ava nodded.

"But it isn't just that," Remington said. "It will be a long time before you forget the way your brother hurt you. Whether you want to or not, unconsciously you are always comparing every interaction to him. And whether you mean to or not, you're always sort of wondering if the people you're talking to are just like him and will hurt you the same way."

She closed her eyes sadly. How did he understand everything so completely? How did he know what no one else could have?

"It will be a long time before you fully heal the wounds he inflicted," Remington told her seriously. "I'm sorry to tell you that healing doesn't happen overnight. You will be in recovery for a long time. But with Jackson, you won't have to go through it alone. If you allow him to, he can help you learn to trust again. He's a good man. He cares for you deeply. And Ava, while you will have to remind yourself of it day in and out: *he isn't Eli.*"

She nodded in understanding, resonating with the truth of every word.

"Give it time. I promise, it will get better. It will be easier one day."

"What if I'm not worth it to him? What if he gives up on me? What if I'm just too messed up and he decides to find someone less…broken?"

Remington placed his hand on her shoulder lovingly. "Trust, Ava. Give it time. And allow Jackson to do the same. I hope he'll decide to stick it through, for both of you."

He removed his hand, and Ava turned to face him. "You're leaving, aren't you?" she realized suddenly. Somehow, she simply knew it.

He nodded. "I'm needed elsewhere. But don't worry. I never really leave you either." He winked at her, and Ava smiled.

Whether he meant hidden cameras and bugs, or simply remaining in her heart, she didn't know. Whichever, it was true. In one way or another, he would always be there.

"Goodbye, Remington."

"See you soon, Ava."

She waited a long time by the front door for Jackson and the boys to return. When he did walk through with the two kids and Boris, he was obviously surprised to see her there. But he didn't seem angry, like she had expected. He actually seemed glad to see her.

"Uh…I'm gonna turn a movie on for them real quick," he said, pulling the boys into the parlor. "Give me a minute?"

She nodded, waiting outside the parlor by the front door.

A minute or two later he returned. "Hey…" he said, standing before her.

"Hi..."

"I wanted to—"

"I feel like I should—" they both started speaking at the same time, then stopped, and smiled. "Um...I'll go first," Ava said. Though generally it was polite to let others speak first, when it came to apologizing, she felt like she should go. "I wanted to tell you I'm sorry for acting so crazy at lunch. I know I'm still a wreck in so many ways. You didn't do anything wrong. I just misunderstood, and I always overthink everything and I shouldn't have said what I did and I'm such a wreck sometimes and—"

"Hey," he stopped her. "It's okay. Come here."

She accepted as he pulled her into a hug. For some reason, she teared up once she was in his arms. She had been so sure he would say he didn't have the time to deal with her craziness. The last thing she expected was for him to hold her so tightly and lovingly as this.

"I'm so sorry, Ava," he whispered, his lips an inch from her ear. "I promise, I didn't just want you because you were broken. I've wanted you the whole time."

She fought the urge to tell him that she had been broken the whole time, and still was, and that maybe his only attraction to her was what a mess she was.

He held her tightly, saying nothing else, and she couldn't think of anything good enough to say in response to him. They pulled apart when a little human tapped on each of their legs until they moved.

They looked down to see Kai looking up at them impatiently. "Yes?" Jackson asked.

"The movie isn't working," Kai said in disappointment.

"Okay. Go back in there. I'll come fix it."

"Come now," Kai ordered.

"Go on," Jackson persisted.

Kai sighed deeply, like a little teenager, but did as his uncle told him.

Ava was smiling when Jackson turned back to her. "Sorry about that. Since my meeting got moved to earlier I had a free hour, and of course Viktoriya dumped the kids on me so they could nap."

"It's all good! I should...um..." she couldn't think of any excuses to leave.

"Do you want to watch a show with us?" Jackson offered hopefully. "It's Kai's favorite! It's about a potato who lives at the circus."

She narrowed her eyes suspiciously. "Sounds horrible."

"Yeah, pretty much," Jackson agreed.

Through her smile, she nodded. "I'd love to watch with you."

"And if we get bored, we can probably think of something else to do while we sit there." This he said with an innocent shrug.

Ava offered an awkward smile before Jackson explained, "I'm kidding. Totally kidding. I love this show."

Ava chuckled as she followed him into the parlor. She laughed again pleasantly when she saw the three boys sitting on the couch waiting for their movie. Jon and Kai, and big old Boris, looking like an excited three-year-old.

Boris glared when he saw her laughing, as if to say, "Don't mock me."

Ava shook her head and mouthed, "I wouldn't dare!"

12

The Cause

"All right everyone, gather round, gather round," Zak ordered as the team filed into the parlor and found a place to sit. "Everyone take a seat. Mikel and Ella, don't make me separate you two."

When everyone was seated and somewhat quiet, Zak called for their attention. He didn't have the same amazing mind talents of Mikel or Ava. He didn't have the incredible fighting skills of Kyle or Ella. He didn't have the miraculous leadership abilities of Sasha or Jackson. And he certainly didn't have the myriad talents to compare with his perfect wife Viktoriya. But Zak had learned that his place on the team was just as special and important as everyone else's. He would bring to the table what was his to do, and it would be more than enough.

"On this, the night before execution of our outrageous plan," Zak began, and many chuckles sounded around the room, "it is important that we remember what we're fighting for. Sasha once told Jackson and me, early on in our journey, that we would be shocked by the people who ultimately joined our team. And just as disturbed by those who didn't make it. Well, ladies and gentlemen, look around. This is us. This is our crew. These are the faces of the team that will finish what a lot of great men and women started."

They all looked around and took in the faces in the room.

"But I think it's important that we remember some of the many wonderful people who got us here. We have all left behind amazing people who we miss terribly. We have all given some. But these people gave their all.

"With my outrageously incredible hacking skills," again, more laughter, "and a bit of help from Sasha, I have compiled this special tribute that I'd like to share with you. I should warn you, it's a possible trigger hazard, so if there's anyone who doesn't feel ready to face it, no shame in leaving now."

No one moved.

"Ella?" Zak singled her out. She glared at him. "You good? Promise you won't kill me?"

"No promises, carcface."

"Good enough! Now, if you'll excuse my imperfect guitar skills, I haven't had much practice since Jackson uprooted me from my perfectly normal life."

More laughter. If that was all he could bring to this crew, that was enough. Every one of them could use a bit more of it. Sasha nodded approvingly, and although Zak sensed that many people considered his gesture a bit cheesy, he intended to run with it.

"I wrote this song for all the ones who got us here."

He started playing the guitar, and Sasha pressed start on the video montage. Okay, they were right; it was cheesy. But it was too late to back out now.

The video started with pictures of the crew as they were now. Zak had snapped a few fun photos in the past week, and figured it was good to start on a happy note. Sparring. Game night. Meals and more.

Next it showed pictures of Sasha's original crew: Elyia, Zak, Alexia, Demitri, Albert and Marco. Work on the Towers. Arm wrestles. Fun in the pub, and so on.

Soon, he sang of the ones who hadn't made it all the way. It showed a bit more of Marco, their silly old friend.

Then things shifted and the video showed Yuri.

Yuri with Zak, bantering. Yuri with Sasha, arguing. Yuri with Jackson, laughing. And even Yuri with Ava, working during the Talks.

Looking around the room as he sang, he saw the sober looks of all those who had known Yuri.

From there, it moved to Ava's friend Hawkins, and even those who hadn't known her personally watched with tender understanding of she who had been lost.

From there to Lionel, at which point, Ava teared up right there in front of everyone. And if Zak could manage to make them laugh and cry in the same night, he had indeed done enough.

From Lionel, it moved to Kristen Altman. Here was one person all of them could relate to losing. And in fact, Sasha had given Zak pictures of each of the Zhànshì with her, which apparently Kristen had kept in a safe file that only Sasha had access to. It was actually this file that inspired Zak to write the song in the first place.

Ava smiled sweetly as a photo showed her eight-year-old self hugging her mother tightly.

Kyle looked fondly when an eleven-year-old Kyle and the Colonel saluted each other, with her salute looking as straight and respectful as his.

Mikel looked most touched by the picture of Kristen doing push-ups beside him. He had been given a punishment for disobedience and charged with several extra hours of training. But Kristen stayed beside him the entire time and did everything with him. It was clear he remembered it well.

Lastly, the video showed Kristen standing close to Ame, and both of them holding tightly to a three-year-old Ella.

Zak watched the girl carefully, in case it became prudent for him to run for his life. She watched the video intently as pictures shifted to Ame.

There were many photos of Ella with her mother in training that Kristen had kept for her friend. Even some of Ame with the other Zhànshì. Finally, they stopped on one of Ella, Ame, and Breanna. And there it shifted to another friend.

Breanna with all of the other Zhànshì. Fighting Kyle on the mat. Standing beside Mikel, both with rifles in their hands. Breanna and Ava running on the track.

The Zhànshì all seemed taken aback and in awe of these photos, which they hadn't known existed. An entire hidden cache that Kristen had apparently kept close to her heart, of all the kids she considered her own.

Zak had thrown in a picture of Kristen and Valkyrie for good measure, and he was surprised when, of all people, Kyle seemed to appreciate that one the most.

The pictures shifted again to these Zhànshì in training, the ones who had made it.

A young Kyle, Mikel, Ella and Ava in every combination.

Things shifted, and everyone made exclamations and laughs when it showed Jackson and Viktoriya—or Lauren—in the Academy together. Zak had decided to include that one simply for nostalgia, but everyone seemed to like it.

The next were of Viktoriya's husband and family in Korea—a reminder to everyone that the enemy they would fight come tomorrow were good people, just on the other end of things.

It showed Sasha with some of his close friends on the Politburo. Pictures of the crew at the gala in Korea—even Luka, who was gone now.

Soon it shifted again, once more surprising everyone with pictures of Jackson and his talked about, but never met, family. His mother, who looked so much like her son, and his sister Maelyn; the real Alexia.

Jackson watched the pictures soberly, then turned to Ava and whispered something about the photos that made her smile. When he turned around, he, too, was somewhat teary eyed.

Pictures of Sasha and Kristen ended things, and a quoted picture of the words that had become a motto for so many, "Let the Colonel win."

With that, the song and the video ended.

The feeling in the room was emotional, but in a good way. He could tell that every member of the team had been touched by it, and once again, he decided that was enough.

No one clapped or cheered or anything, and in fact, it was awkwardly silent for a time. Finally, Jackson was the one to break the silence. "Thank you, Zak," he said seriously. "That was really special."

"Good as J.J." Kyle agreed with a needling directed at Ava, though he had obviously greatly enjoyed it too.

"Better," Viktoriya corrected.

"Ella?" Zak asked the girl who still seemed very focused on her own thoughts.

She looked up at him, and her perpetual frown remained, but her eyes were touched by a meaningful twinkle. "I'll kill you later," she offered simply.

"I'll take it!" Zak answered with a laugh.

☆ ☆ ☆ ☆ ☆

Ava watched their interaction from beside Jackson.

"They're here," Jackson informed Kyle. "You ready?"

"As I'll ever be," Kyle said, putting out his arm. Jackson clasped it and held tightly.

"It's good to have you with us, friend," he said seriously. "And to have you alive."

"Let's keep it that way, yeah?" Kyle gibed.

"Agreed," Jackson said with a chuckle.

Ava would have moved then to say goodbye, but Mikel beat her to it. "You off, man?" Mikel asked, moving up to greet his friend.

"Oh yeah!" Kyle said emphatically.

"You still owe me a hundred if she kicks your carcass for even asking," Mikel teased.

"You got it. Ella, pay off my debt if I fail. I won't make it out alive if I do!"

Several people laughed, and one by one they made their goodbyes.

"Are we a team?" Ava asked, repeating the phrase that had in the past week become common among all of them again. "Or are we a bunch of lone wolves?"

He smiled, clearly thinking of Valkyrie, of Ava, and of all of them who were now members of that special squad. "We're a team," Kyle answered, reaching for her hand to clasp.

She moved in for a hug instead. "Good luck," she said. "I wish I were going with."

"I know they need you somewhere else," Kyle noted. "Still, you've already done half the work of getting her on our side. Thanks for that."

Ella pushed Ava away and stole the spotlight then. "My turn. Come here, you big carcass."

Kyle moved in to hug Ella tightly next. "I know you're a cowboy now," Ella said quietly, though Ava heard, "but you'll always be my first—and only best friend. Bye, Kyle."

He pulled away and faced her seriously. "Goodbye, Ella. See you soon."

When everyone had said their goodbyes, Kyle went out to the helicopter pad where his ride awaited. "Good luck, guys!" he shouted over the thundering sound of the helo. "I'm gonna go get us a Valkyrie."

☆ ☆ ☆ ☆ ☆

"All packed?" Sasha asked.

"Yes, sir," Jackson affirmed. "Though we don't leave until tonight."

"Our team is the next to head out," Sasha replied.

Jackson knew that very well. Ava was on it.

He suddenly had the desire to ask Sasha all the things he wished he knew about how to build a relationship with Ava. But he had long since stopped talking to Sasha about Ava, and it was hard to go back now.

Sasha started to leave the room when Jackson spoke. "Sasha, when you and Kristen would split up, every time after a brief time together..." he trailed off, not exactly sure what he was asking.

"One rule I made for myself," Sasha offered, as if knowing exactly where Jackson had been going with his question, "was that no matter what happened in our brief time together, I would never leave anything unsaid. I never knew when our goodbye would be the last one. And I couldn't imagine regretting what I forgot to say for the rest of my life. My last words to my wife were, 'I love you more than life itself.' And whatever else I might regret, I never have regretted that." With this, Sasha nodded seriously and smiling, he left the room.

Although his friend and mentor had already left, Jackson smiled, and spoke as if to him. "Thanks, Sasha."

He found her alone at the kitchen island, and she was slicing strawberries when he entered. She used to work these kitchens with Maxim and was therefore very comfortable here.

"You're leaving today," Jackson said, awkwardly standing on the other side of the island.

She was clearly deep in thought as she focused on her slicing. Jackson couldn't help remembering that he was the one who had taught her how. "Yeah," she replied. "We leave in an hour. I'm just getting a bit of a snack before I finish getting ready."

Jackson fought the urge to mention that strawberries were quite delicious when eaten whole, and it saved a lot of time to eat them that way. This would give him the chance to say what he needed to.

"Do you mind if I talk to you for a minute?" he asked, again more awkwardly than he intended. It didn't matter if he made a complete fool of himself, he would say what needed to be said, and he would do so now.

She gave a confused smile. "I'd be sad if you didn't, Jackson."

He chuckled, taking the hint. Only, she didn't quite understand that he meant a more serious talk than usual.

"We've, uh...we've said goodbye a lot of times," he related, hoping this would be a good segue into the words he'd been trying to get off his chest for over about two years now.

Ava watched him with that same confused smile, clearly wondering why he was being so awkward with her. "I suppose we have."

"You know that letter you wrote me? The one you sent with Yuri."

Now it was her who took on an awkward expression. "Oh, no. Did you read it?"

He laughed out loud. "Yeah."

"Yikes..." she trailed off awkwardly. "Embarrassing, wasn't it?"

He watched her, uncomprehending at first. Then suddenly overthinking everything, he wondered if her new discomfort was because her feelings had changed since what she wrote in the letter. But knowing it was too late to back down at this point, he continued forward—though even more nervously now.

"You-uh, know how in that letter, you talked about each time we came together and said goodbye again, and what it meant to you?"

She nodded, returning to the strawberries and seeming uncomfortable. "Vaguely."

His eyes narrowed. What did she mean by that?

"I-um, I probably should have just written you a letter back. But do you mind if I tell you my side?"

She grew even more uncomfortable now, and that made him second-guess everything. Still, hesitatingly, she agreed, and he knew he had to just say it, fear of rejection and all.

"Sorry if this comes off a bit like a prepared speech. I've been gathering my thoughts for a while now. It probably is somewhat of a speech." He shook his head, trying to get to the point.

"I like your speeches," Ava offered, though still looking uncomfortable.

He bit his lip and carefully started. "So...after we first met at the training compound, our first goodbye was pretty casual. Even then, I struggled to leave, but I somehow knew I'd see you again. Maybe that was the whole 'part of something' thing you talked about in your letter. I don't know. I just somehow knew it wasn't over. Still, I never expected that I'd see you again while I was undercover in Russia. And I can't tell you how much of a relief it was when you came."

She smiled genuinely now, and he appreciated the look of encouragement from her.

"I always knew insertion would be difficult, but starting it off with the incident of Natasha's death made for a painful beginning. Before that, I used to love my job. Like, I really, really loved it. But I lost a lot of my passion for my work after that. When you came though, I genuinely started having fun again."

Ava focused back on the strawberries as he spoke, as if feeling how hard it was for him to speak when she was looking at him.

"Saying goodbye to you when I left for Brazil was too easy, because so much of me naively assumed I'd come back to you three days later. If I'd had any clue at that point what would actually happen...I don't think I ever could have left you."

She had continued slicing until this point, but on those last words, she risked looking up at him. It was only for a second, and as soon as she met his keen eyes, she looked down again. But he felt the connection for what it was. She was listening, and hearing every word.

"I had to, though. What I faced in Brazil changed me. It got me started on this journey," he gestured to the room before them, indicating Russia itself. "Still, those months after you went back to the Kingdoms were excruciating. I hated my work more than ever. I missed you more than I knew was possible. And every day it just got worse. When you came back to me in Korea..." he trailed off, not knowing exactly how to explain the feeling.

"Everything fell into place again," he continued. "Somehow, even with the painful work we did by day...you helped me have fun again, every day after hours. I started to be happy again. But during that time, I lied to you about my inner struggle, about my future plans. I drove a wedge between us over your family. And all of that I did foolishly because I wanted you to pick me over them. I know now how stupid my actions were, and I'm sorry for all of that. But then, in the midst of all of that...you kissed me...."

Her face tightened into embarrassment, and she was clearly glad not to be facing him just then. She had sliced an entire plate of strawberries by this point, and Jackson wondered if she had intended to, or if she just needed the distraction as long as he was talking, so she wouldn't have to face him while he spoke.

"You kissed me, and it changed things. It brought me to a place I'd never allowed myself to go before. And no matter how much I tried— and believe me, I tried—but I've never been able to go back. Saying goodbye to you then was difficult, but not because I knew it would end tragically. Only because there was so much I wanted to tell you, but I couldn't form the words, and so I left them unsaid, and I can't tell you how many times I've regretted that."

Again, she risked looking up at him, and he wished she hadn't, because it caused his voice to crack on the last word. This time he was the one to look down uncomfortably, wondering what he was doing, if he was crazy, and if he could actually go through with this dramatic speech.

She was still watching him searchingly when he looked up again, and having to face her striking eyes as he spoke was much harder than he had anticipated.

"Over the next months, after my cover was blown, everything changed for me—and for you too, I suspect. When you and Eli showed up here.... Well, you remember what a mess I was. Seeing you there with him was painful, to say the least. It felt like circumstances, more than anything, had forced you to pick him over me, and I felt like I wasn't even given a chance to plead my case with you. But I had plenty of chances. I was just too afraid of rejection to take them."

Sensing how hard it was for him now, she looked down again, and resumed slicing the strawberries.

"Even then, you somehow managed to make me smile again. Comments about my beard and whatnot."

She smiled at that. It was an indication of pleasantness on her side at all of these memories they shared, and it fueled him enough to keep going.

"That night was the first time since Korea that I felt genuinely happy again. You helped me forget about my worries and focus on the good things about life. But it all ended too soon. And when you came to say goodbye to me early the next morning, I had almost formed the words. As you were leaving, I knew what I needed to say to you, but I was too much of a coward and chose not to say it. If I had just been honest with you then. If I had told you about the revolution...."

Unable to utter the words very loudly still, he almost seemed to whisper the next sentence. "If I had told you how I felt about you, maybe things would have gone better the next time. I have wondered and regretted my silence more times than I know how to admit."

He struggled to continue, with things getting so...real. Would she react like she had on their date? Would she push him away and then come running back? Or would this be the time she stayed away and decided not to come back?

Ava had now taken to slicing the strawberries smaller, having finished the entire two pounds from the package. He wondered how to wrap this whole thing up more quickly, marveling that in such a public area, they hadn't yet been interrupted.

"You came back. We presented our plans. And you left without saying goodbye. I understand why it went down that way. But it still hurt." He shook his head, trying to keep a brave face—even if she wasn't looking. "It felt like you picked Eli over me...." He wanted to curse at how weak he sounded.

She seemed to notice it too, and always choosing to look at the worst moments, she glanced up at him again. They watched each other for a long time. He felt strangely weak and emotional, as if all the feelings he had kept inside all these years were now surfacing at once. It occurred to him that perhaps he should have opened up to Sasha, or anyone, before now. He might not look so helpless when speaking to her.

Was this a good time to say, "That's all," and head out? Or did he really have to say more with her watching him that way?

He looked away and stared at the wall to his right. His speech didn't seem to go so eloquently after that, with her looking at him.

"Anyway, our meetings from then on were painful. And the goodbyes were worse. It didn't help when you kissed me after the gala. It was sort of a kiss. I guess I don't know what that was."

She still hadn't looked away, and he was mumbling through his whole speech at this point. He continued to look around the room as he spoke, anywhere but at her. If he hadn't already said so much, hadn't already shown so many of his cards, he was sure he would've changed his mind at this point and stopped talking.

"I struggled the night of the Talks because I was scared to be vulnerable, when so much of me knew you would still pick Eli over me. That same night, Yuri started convincing me that you were using me. And the next day Eli destroyed a base that I had mentioned to you in passing the night before."

He paused, swallowing hard. "I should have given you the benefit of the doubt, but at the time, I was convinced that I couldn't give you the chance to convince me of anything other than what I believed to be true. I believed that my feelings for you were clouding my judgment. So, I didn't take the chance."

He looked back to meet her gaze then. This goodbye was the one he felt he needed to explain to her the most. It was amazingly difficult to face her when he spoke, but he held on to her glance and spoke strongly as he could manage.

"Ava, you can say I was mistrusting, disloyal, you can say that I was blind. You can even say that I was a fool. But you can't say that I didn't love you." He gave a simple shake of his head that emphasized his seriousness.

She closed her lips tightly, looking suddenly pale. She picked up the knife again and began dicing the strawberries nervously. Before, it seemed to be more for his sake that she looked away. Now it was clearly for her own. His emotions were so involved in his words now, he didn't know how much longer he could speak, or how soon till they were interrupted, so he tried to get to the point.

"Because I did love you."

For some reason, those words seemed to hurt her, rather than soothe. She did not look pleased, she looked sad. It didn't occur to him in the moment that he had referred to his love in the past tense, causing her to think that meant it was over.

Not realizing his mistake and *why* it had hurt her, he hesitated, wondering if he could continue if it hurt her to hear this, but he had already come this far.

"That was the thing that I wanted to say at every goodbye. Sometimes I didn't know the words. Sometimes I was too scared to say them. But what I should have said in Korea, what I should have said that night on the balcony, or the next morning when you left, or when I went willingly into an ambush and left you for five months, was that I did love you."

She took a pained breath, biting her lip and trying to continue dicing, but her movements were now awkward and clumsy.

He couldn't understand, why did she look so sad? Why did it look like she was the one expecting rejection?

"And now, I don't know if the trip after this goodbye is going to be long and painful, or if we'll meet up as planned in just a few days. But I can't let you go without telling you this time that, Ava, I do love you."

She tensed, holding her breath, looking partially relieved, partially uncertain.

He stopped, shaking his head. "No, that's not it exactly. It's not that I love you."

Now her expression became truly pained.

"What I meant is that...I'm in love with you."

She looked up as if in shock. Hadn't she known that was where he was going with all of this?

His expression was serious and uncertain, but he managed to finish. "I've loved a lot of people in my life. But I've only ever been in love with you."

Her eyes filled with tears and strangely, he noticed, his did too, almost as if in reaction to seeing hers.

They watched each other for a long time, with her looking in shock and him feeling uncertain of her feelings. He couldn't tell how much time passed before she looked as if she was about to say something—at least she was working up to it. But the sound of talking in the next room, getting closer, stopped her. Ava looked down at the cutting board as Zak entered the room.

Jackson couldn't decide if he hated the man for his poor timing, or if he was just relieved he had been able to say everything he needed to before anyone interrupted. Perhaps there was a bit of both.

Zak walked right beside Ava and spoke excitedly. "Ooh, strawberries! Can I have one?" he reached over and took a small piece, even as he asked.

Jackson hoped they could both remain quietly until Zak left again.

"You can have all of them," Ava responded pleasantly, then hurriedly she left the room.

Jackson's heart sank.

"I don't...need that many..." Zak said, looking around in surprise. "There are a lot," he explained when he noticed Jackson looking at him.

Jackson didn't respond.

Zak shrugged, taking a handful of the strawberries and placing them in a bowl. As he left the kitchen Jackson heard him mutter to himself, "I've never seen *diced* strawberries as a snack before. Still good though."

Jackson remained in the kitchen for a long time. He'd said everything he knew how to say. She'd run away. Again.

It could mean many things. Perhaps she just needed time to process. Maybe she had just been embarrassed by Zak coming in at that time. Or maybe she wanted nothing more to do with Jackson. None of these scenarios seemed altogether unlikely.

Not having an answer, and having done everything he knew to do, Jackson left the kitchen, not exactly defeated, but not really happy either.

An hour later, Ava left with the others. She gave him not even a word of goodbye. Not even a glance. She wouldn't even look at him.

Realistically, he knew that he had uncovered deep wounds. He knew it would take time for her to get her bearings, to navigate how to deal with this. Most of the time, he didn't allow himself to get too hurt by her jabs. But for some reason, this silence stabbed at him.

He had his own wounds, whether he liked to admit it or not. After years of being too afraid of this vulnerability, he had laid it all on the line. She had given him absolutely nothing in return.

It turned out, this goodbye hurt enough to rival any other.

★ ★ ★ ★ ★

"Good ol' Brazil," Mikel said pleasantly. "It's nice to have a bit of respite from the storm."

"For you it will be respite," Sasha said pointedly, placing the dinner napkin on his lap. "Ava and I have to enter into an intense bout of politics, which is generally worse than any storm I've ever weathered."

"Weren't you on the Politburo? And then the Russian Leadership Committee?" Mikel replied just as pointedly. "Maybe that was a mistake, for someone who hates politics."

Sasha clicked his tongue. "Well, we do what we must."

"You good?" Mikel asked, pointing the attention to Ava.

She looked up as if pulled from a daze. "What? Oh, yeah. Fine. I actually enjoy politics. If anything, I'm kind of looking forward to it."

"Miss Altman," the waiter said, stepping forward, "we're so delighted to have you at our restaurant!"

Sasha and Mikel shared a glance, not expecting to have been noticed when they were attempting to remain low-key.

Even Ava was surprised by the recognition, since Council had worked so tirelessly to erase her from the public's eye.

"We would like to offer your meal, and those of your friends, on the house!"

"Oh, you really don't have to do that," Ava replied quickly.

"Please, it would be our honor!"

She was about to object, but Sasha spoke up first. "And it is our honor to accept your kindness, sir." The look he gave her was one of his reminders that it was okay to accept help. She gave a tight-lipped smile and attempted not to object.

"If there's anything else we can offer, please, just say the word! I've already spoken to the hotel kiosk, and they've prepared the grand suite and two adjoining rooms for you and your friends."

He left then, and when Ava turned to meet the others, their eyes were wide with surprise.

"Maybe we should have gotten take-out after all," Sasha said awkwardly.

"Your expensive taste might get us all in trouble," Mikel agreed.

"At least we don't have to pay for it!" Sasha said with a chuckle, sitting back in his seat.

"How does he know me?" Ava muttered in confusion. "It's been over a year. Council would have stopped at nothing to erase me...."

"I'm sure he was a fan during your short reign," Sasha said with a shrug. "Nothing to worry about."

"Although, you do look rather underdressed for such an occasion," Mikel said, nodding to her casual shirt and sweatpants with tennis shoes. "You should have let Kyle and I get you ready."

"I will never forgive you for that, you little twerp!" she growled in sudden anger. "You should have told me I looked like Valkyrie!"

"Kyle said you looked hot. I agreed. I didn't think about Valkyrie at the time."

Her glare deepened, causing him to back as far away from her in his seat as he could.

"What's all this?" Sasha asked, wanting to be let in on the secret.

Mikel would have explained, but Ava stopped him. "Nothing. Let's just get ready to order."

"We both already decided what we want," Mikel said. "We've turned the waiter down twice because you were still lost in your menu."

"...Oh." She looked down, but the menu which she had apparently been staring at looked brand new. It hadn't exactly been the object of her thoughts. "Well, what should I order?"

"Stop being so indecisive all the time," Mikel said teasingly.

"I bet you'll like this one," Sasha said in a much more helpful way, pointing to a chicken dish on the menu.

"Sounds good," Ava said, putting the menu down. "I'm ready."

The waiter returned, and took their orders, all the while looking like he had something he wanted to say. Only when they had finished did he awkwardly address Ava. "I'm sorry, Miss Altman, would you mind if I took a picture with you? My wife is the biggest fan. She would hate me if I didn't get a picture!"

Ava looked around with a sort of question for a moment before it occurred to her what she was looking for: Eli. She was looking to see if he would give her permission, but Eli wasn't here, and she didn't need his permission for things anymore.

"Uh...sure, of course! Sasha, will you take it?"

Sasha and Mikel both seemed a bit taken aback, but Sasha agreed, and when the waiter had the photo, he left to get their orders to the kitchen.

"Maybe we should pick a small motel..." Mikel said with a hint of concern.

Sasha nodded his agreement. "Probably best not to draw too much attention to ourselves." Then he sighed regretfully. "Such a shame to miss out on such wonderful meals though."

"Especially when they're free!" Mikel added teasingly to Sasha.

"Ah well, it can't be avoided. Let's go before he notices us exiting."

They tried to walk out without being seen, but apparently that was impossible. All eyes in the restaurant now seemed to be on her. It was as if she had a target on her back that said, "Don't look away or you'll miss something big!"

The hotel manager stopped them as they neared the exit. "I'm sorry, Miss Altman! Was everything not to your liking? Or is there something we can get for you?"

She shook her head vigorously. "Everything is great! We just left something in the car."

"I'll have someone sent out immediately to—"

"No, it's fine! It's kind of a special item that we don't want anyone else handling."

They pressed on to the exit and were about to open the doors.

"I understand. Only, I wouldn't go out that way, ma'am!"

It was too late. Sasha and Mikel had opened the door and practically dragged Ava through, only to be bombarded by a flash mob of media.

Cameras flashing and people shouting for her to look at them had her wide-eyed and frozen in fear for a moment before Mikel and Sasha grabbed her by either hand and pulled her back inside.

"As I was saying, ma'am," the manager explained, "our security won't allow them inside the building, but they've flooded the outside to get a glimpse of your departure."

"Would you be so kind as to take us to that suite now?" Sasha asked, dragging Ava along as she found herself strangely in shock.

"Of course. Right this way!"

This didn't make any sense. This shouldn't be happening. How did these people know who she was?

As they walked down the hall and to the elevator, Mikel made conversation with the manager while Sasha helped Ava along.

"You all right, dear?" he asked in a soft whisper.

For some reason, she was handling this altogether worse than she should. She had been so good at all this, with King Lionel and Queen Astelle by her side teaching her every angle of the spotlight. But without them, and with everything that had happened, the last thing she wanted in the world was to be noticed.

"So, I guess Miss Altman is pretty famous around here," Mikel observed awkwardly, hoping for some explanation.

The manager chuckled. "You could say that. Right this way."

They entered the elevator and Ava's breath caught. Propaganda posters lined the elevator, just like the old ones of her mother. Only, this time it wasn't Kristen's face she saw.

Written in large letters were little lines like "join the fight" and "let the Colonel win." But instead of Kristen, it was images of Ava.

Mikel whistled slowly.

"That sly dog," Sasha muttered almost to himself.

"We'll get to the room ourselves from here," Mikel thanked the manager.

"Of course, sir! And if there's anything else you need—" his query was cut off as the elevator door closed.

"I don't understand," Ava said in confusion, staring at photos that she didn't remember having taken.

"You said that Lionel brought you to Brazil to get them on board," Sasha said, though it sounded more a question.

Ava nodded. "The leadership of Brazil, yes."

"Eli couldn't erase you without breaking things off with them," Sasha explained. "Especially once Lionel was out of the picture."

"So, he pretended you were still the General," Mikel said with wide eyes.

"Or at least, the face of the Kingdoms," Sasha added in agreement.

"What do we do now?" Mikel asked in sudden concern.

Ava smiled abruptly in a sad sort of understanding.

"Well," Sasha said, "in short...."

Ava nodded as things suddenly made sense to her. "Eli just handed us Brazil."

Sasha hung up his mobile and entered the large suite where the others sat waiting. "I just got off a secure line with Jackson," he explained.

Ava almost flinched at the mention of his name, which was cause for concern, but Sasha overlooked it for the time being.

"We have agreed that we can't play into Eli's little facade here. We need to present ourselves truthfully, which won't be as easy when we're offering Russia rather than the Kingdoms to these people. Still, I hope that we can get them on our side. We knew it was a longshot coming in the first place. But Eli has increased our chances by keeping you in their hearts and minds as he has. The other thing we might want to consider is that media coverage might not be such a bad thing. It could be useful to get the people excited about you for at least a day or two, before we try and convince the government to change alliances."

"So, to the people we play into the facade?" Mikel asked with suspicion.

Sasha shrugged. "Not necessarily. We'll go about our business as we will. If people recognize Ava Altman in the lobby or the streets, well, that is her name, isn't it?"

"I mean, as long as Jackson's conscience isn't hurt by it," Mikel said, putting his arms in the air to either side.

"He suggested it," Sasha replied. "Australia didn't join the Kingdoms until the people were on board. The government and the people of Brazil are already loyal to Ava. Offering a bit of love in return, before we ask for something, isn't such a bad thing."

"What if Eli sees it? In the media?" Ava asked with a touch of concern.

"Oh, I'm sure he already has," Sasha replied. "I wouldn't be surprised if he's already boarded a plane on his way."

"Doesn't that worry us at all?" Mikel asked with wide eyes.

"Tremendously," Sasha replied. "But both Jackson and I think, given a choice between Eli and Ava, our girl will win Brazil over. It's too late to protect ourselves from Eli here or do this thing quietly, so the bigger a production we can make it, the better. Just keep in mind, there's a reason Ava's face is posted on the elevators and shuttle cars, and not Eli's."

"Because she's way prettier," Mikel teased.

"Jackson still believes Eli has served us Brazil on a platter," Sasha continued. "It will just take a bit of maneuvering to get the platter out of his strong grasp."

"What do we do tonight?" Mikel asked.

Sasha turned on the television to a local news station. "Ava Altman is currently lodging at the Grand Am Hotel," the newscaster said from just outside.

"I assume this means we've got enough media coverage for the night?" Mikel asked.

Sasha nodded his agreement. "The entire nation is talking about it. Local law enforcement has been called in as extra security for the hotel. The government officials are handling everything. And they've asked for an audience with Ava tomorrow. Let's give them some time to gather the best and brightest media and officials to the city while we rest. In the morning, we'll pick things up where we left off."

"We should probably trade off keeping watch," Mikel suggested, glancing at the door. "I don't know if the two guards they gave us outside are enough, if things do get crazy, or if Eli gets any insane ideas."

"I'll go first," Ava said. "I can't sleep now anyway."

"Then I'm gonna hit the sack!" Mikel replied happily, exiting into one of the adjoining rooms.

Ava looked down at her lap as she sat on the large bed, still looking sad and thoughtful.

"You worried about Eli?" Sasha asked with loving concern.

She shook her head. "No, it's not that."

"This whole thing is a lot," he offered.

She shook her head. "It's not that either."

He tried to consider what else might be wrong when it occurred to him she had been in her own thoughts all day, since leaving Russia.

"Jackson?" he asked carefully.

She nodded, still not looking up at him.

He sat beside her on the luxurious bed. "Anything you'd like to talk about?"

She thought about it for a time before responding. "Jackson talked to me before we left. He said...and...." She couldn't seem to finish, or really start either.

"And what?"

"He said he, umm, he said that he.... I don't know how to explain it."

"He said that he forgives you?" Sasha shot in the dark.

"No, it's not that. We're past that already. He said that he...." She cleared her throat. "That he has, umm...."

"That he has feelings for you?" Sasha ventured to ask, clenching his fists at the risk of being wrong, though the conversation he'd had with Jackson before made him think it might be possible.

She nodded nonchalantly, trying to hide how it must make her feel. "Yeah, that. And umm." She broke off, biting her lip as her eyes flooded with tears. "*Really*? *This* again?" As bothered as she was, the tears didn't go away.

"And you're not sure if you believe him?" Sasha offered, confused by her sadness.

"No, it's not that. I mean, he was really convincing. I think I believe him."

"Then might I ask why you're crying?" Sasha asked gently, worried what the answer must be. After everything, did Ava really not love him back?

"Well, when he told me, he had this whole prepared speech, and the whole time, I kept expecting him to break up with me. I don't know why. I was just so sure. I just knew that everything he said was leading up to him saying he wanted to be done." The tears increased though she fought them off.

"When he finally finished, I was so shocked...I was so surprised that he didn't end things, that I froze. I don't know why exactly, but I couldn't say anything. I guess I had been preparing the whole time to handle a breakup, I didn't know what to do with anything else, especially something so...beautiful. And then Zak came and I was embarrassed, and I didn't know how to respond, so I ran away."

"I see..." Sasha offered, though still not understanding her concern. In truth, he hadn't known they were officially together in the first place.

"I think he meant what he said," Ava reiterated. "But the problem is, I responded so stupidly, and then I left without saying anything. And after everything this week...? All day I've been worried, umm," her eyes filled even more, and her expression became pained. "I was so dumb that he probably changed his mind."

Sasha had to stop from laughing out loud at first at how silly that was. But his heart softened when he saw how deeply that fear pained her. His sweet little girl. All he wanted was to reassure her, but he thought it would be better coming from Jackson himself.

"Well, I doubt very much that he changed his mind that quickly," Sasha offered. "But... you could always call him and ask."

Her wet eyes widened. "No way."

"Why not?"

She shrugged shyly. "I don't want to like, you know, he's so busy. I don't want to bother him."

Again, his heart softened at the silly sweetness of it all. She had never been in a relationship before, clearly.

"Ava dear, he just told you that he loves you, yes? Is that the word he used?"

Ava nodded, and Sasha was relieved the man hadn't used words like "I'm interested in you" or "I think I might like you." It seemed Ava had a hard time even comprehending the strongest of meanings.

"Right, well he said he loves you. I doubt very much he would be bothered to receive a call from you."

"Yeah, but if he *has* changed his mind...?"

Sasha smiled gently. After a moment he reached for her mobile off the nightstand and tried handing it to her.

"Will *you* call him?" she asked hopefully.

With a chuckle he responded, "Absolutely not!"

She seemed to sink at his reply. "I can't...I can't do it. I can't...."

He stared at her for a long time, unsure how to help her. If it were anyone else in the world, he would tell them to buck up and grow a spine. But Ava was strong in so many areas. This weakness may have more to do with the scars of her past than of simple cowardice. The manipulation she had faced particularly in the past two years could easily cause her to fear this situation now.

His heart clenched at the thought of Eli using the word "love" against her, giving it in full one day just to rip it away the next—but that was exactly the type of thing he had done.

"I'll tell you what, dear," Sasha offered. "I'll dial the number for you. Then you can either do the talking or simply hang up."

"That doesn't seem like a good plan," Ava said, wiping away at the fresh tears on her face. "Maybe I'll just forget about it, assume he's changed his mind and never talk to him about it again. That feels like a better option right now."

Sasha fought the urge to laugh outright at how resolute she seemed to be. He was already dialing the number, but she was too preoccupied in her thoughts to notice.

"Besides, he probably doesn't even have my number saved in his phone, so he would think I'm some salesman or stalker or assassin. I guess an assassin wouldn't want to call him, but still."

"He does actually have your number," Sasha said, smiling even more that she seemed to be explaining all sorts of reasons not to call. "Besides, you could always announce yourself by saying 'this is Ava.' Though I'm sure he would recognize your voice."

"No, I don't think he would recognize it. We don't talk much or anything so he would probably think I'm some random girl he's never met who—"

"Hello?" Jackson's voice came over the phone as Sasha turned on the speakerphone. Jackson sounded surprised, tired, even sad, but trying to come off upbeat.

Ava's eyes widened as she looked at the phone. Sasha was glad to see she didn't look betrayed by him, just unsure what to do now.

Sasha used his hands to make a talking gesture as he mouthed the words, "Just say something!"

She took the phone hesitantly. She looked like a scared girl holding a tarantula, yet trying to be brave.

"Hello?" Jackson's voice came through again.

"Umm, ...hi," Ava said.

"Hi, Ava."

"This is Ava. Oh, you already knew that."

Sasha put his hand over his mouth, trying to stifle any laughter. His dear girl was too adorable for words.

Jackson chuckled slightly from the other end, though still sounding a bit off. "Yeah, I knew it was you."

"Okay," Ava said, trying to sit up straighter and be brave as she got the next words out. She didn't say anything for a long time.

"What's up?" Jackson finally asked. Though he, too, was trying to hide it, Sasha could hear in his voice that Jackson was just as nervous.

"Umm...so, you know that thing you said earlier," Ava finally got out, and Sasha was proud to see that she had completely stopped crying.

A long pause before Jackson replied. "That I love you?" he finally responded carefully. His nerves must be just as crazy. She had run away from his confession, which knowing Jackson, would have been extremely hard to share in the first place. Was she calling now to offer the greater rejection? Yet, he was bold enough to say the words again, and Sasha had been waiting so long to hear Jackson admit to that, it almost made him, too, want to cry.

"Yeah, that," Ava responded, still struggling to say the words. "Well, umm, so I was wondering if, if you umm..." her eyes filled with tears again as she moved the phone far away from her momentarily. Sasha worried she meant to hang up.

She didn't. She just worked to collect herself again before finishing, "if you still meant that...?"

Then her eyes closed tightly as she waited for an answer. It occurred to Sasha only now that she genuinely believed Jackson had changed his mind, not just in wanting to be with her, but in loving her at all, and she was waiting for the blow to the gut rejection to come over the phone.

Jackson hesitated for a long time. Momentarily Sasha wished he were there, able to cheer Jackson on this time and say, "Don't worry. It sounds bad. But have hope. Give her a minute. She doesn't have the words like you do, but she'll form them eventually. She loves you too."

Of course, Jackson wouldn't accept Sasha's presence the way Ava did. In fact, it was best if he never found out about Sasha's being here at all.

Finally, Jackson responded. "Yes, Ava. I still mean what I said."

Ava's eyes opened and she looked hopefully, happily at Sasha. He couldn't help smiling just as happily in return.

Nearly a minute passed without Ava responding, so Sasha gestured to the mobile to remind her that the conversation wasn't quite finished.

"Oh! Okay. Umm. All right, bye."

Sasha's eyes widened in panic. He managed to gesture again pointedly before Ava hung up the mobile.

Luckily, Ava understood. "Oh! I love you too."

After a piercing silence on the other end, Jackson let out a breath that could easily be heard. Poor guy. That was a suspenseful moment indeed.

The silence lingered again until finally Jackson spoke. "Goodnight, Ava."

"Good morning, Jackson. Oh, I mean, goodnight."

She was smiling now, staring at the phone, seeming to have forgotten Sasha and her tears.

"I love you," Ava said again, as if in fear that he would hang up.

Sasha could almost hear Jackson's smile through the line. "I love you too, kid."

Ava clapped her hand to her mouth happily, seeming to not want the moment to end, not knowing how to say goodbye.

Eventually, she hung up the phone and set it down. Only then did she remember that Sasha was still there. She couldn't seem to stop smiling from ear to ear.

"I guess one of us should get some rest," Sasha offered, standing up.

"But what do I do now?"

Sasha shrugged. "What do you want to do?"

"I want to talk to him forever," Ava admitted happily.

"Then call him back."

"No, I can't do that! I already called him once today! At least, he thinks I did."

"Well then, wait, we'll get some rest and see how things go tomorrow."

"Okay. Thanks for your help, Sasha. Goodnight." She got up to hug him tightly.

When they let go she asked, "If I did call him...what else would I say?"

"Just talk to him. I think you'll pick it up easily enough. A good place to start is to simply ask him what he's up to tonight, or how his day was, or something like that."

Ava nodded, considering. "All right, maybe I'll try that sometime."

"He won't be bothered if you call him again," Sasha reassured her. "In fact, I think he might really appreciate you making the extra effort, after how you almost hung up without giving him anything."

Ava giggled. "Whoops."

"You'll figure it out, love. You'll do just fine."

With that he left, but he couldn't help remaining outside the door in hopes that she'd dial the number. She did, and he heard Jackson's voice on the other end, as Ava chose speakerphone even when Sasha was gone.

"Hi again," Jackson said. He sounded genuinely happy.

"Hi. I'm not bothering you, am I? You can hang up whenever you want!"

Jackson chuckled from the other end. "No, I want to talk to you."

Ava didn't respond. Sasha considered going back in and reminding her of some good conversation starters when the silence lingered, but luckily Jackson at least knew what he was doing.

"How did your trip go? Are you settled in over there?" Jackson asked.

Ava replied, and so much of Sasha yearned to stay there and listen forever. But, knowing he should leave them be, he sighed and headed to his room.

He couldn't help thinking about Kristen, about their courtship and the many sweet conversations. Of course, he and Kristen had started phone conversations long before saying the words "I love you." But, though Jackson and Ava's romance was not in the least traditional, it was just as beautiful.

★ ★ ★ ★ ★

"Good morning, Miss Altman," the man said from outside her suite. Mikel and Sasha both stood nearby in case they were needed.

"I hope I'm not disturbing you this morning. We had a delivery sent here for you. We have thoroughly checked them to ensure your safety and privacy, though you may of course have your bodyguards do the same. He indicated Sasha and Mikel.

Mikel seemed to like that title. He walked out into the hall, rifling through the packaging. Pulling a scanner from his side pocket, he ran it over the packages. "Yes, we'll take it from here. Thank you."

"It was delivered with this note." The concierge handed it to Ava as Mikel grabbed the packages and pulled them inside.

"What is it?" Sasha asked, when the door was closed.

"Looks like a bunch of clothes?" Mikel replied helplessly.

Ava opened the note and read it out loud, smiling.

Let the Colonel, and the rightful General, win.
—Queen Astelle.

☆ ☆ ☆ ☆ ☆

"Ava," every voice called out at her at once as Sasha and Mikel walked her through the crowd on the way back to the hotel that afternoon. "Ava, look over here!"

So many voices, so many flashes. She tried to be friendly, tried to fit the beautiful white pantsuit that was among the many things Astelle had sent to help her play this part. Still, it felt like a portrayal, an affectation. She felt like an imposter. In the past, wearing these clothes and speaking to her people, she had never felt more like herself. But Eli had taken all of that away from her, and even her own name felt strange to her now.

"Ava! Here!"

"Over here!"

One voice stuck out to her. "General Altman," she said, unlike the rest, who simply called her by her first name, or sometimes "Miss Altman."

Ava searched the crowd for who had called her something different.

"General Altman. I'm a friend of Hawkins," the reporter continued.

Ava looked up suddenly, still searching the crowd of reporters until she found the only one who wasn't holding up a camera or a microphone. The woman stood resolute, almost morose. Ava stared directly at the woman, and her serious expression was a stark contrast to the rest. She nodded, matching her demeanor. "I need a few minutes of your time, ma'am. For Hawkins."

"I would prefer to meet with the General alone," the woman said to Sasha, who requested to remain in the hotel briefing room with them.

"Oh, I don't know about that," Sasha objected.

"I know this reporter," Mikel, who had previously remained quietly in the background, spoke up.

The reporter looked up and met his eyes. "You!" she said in surprise. "How do you...you know her?" she indicated Ava.

Mikel grinned. "Any enemy of Eli's is a friend of mine." Then he turned to Sasha. "We're good," he assured him. "We can wait outside."

Sasha looked at Ava to be certain. Ava looked the reporter up and down. *"I mean, short of her being some insane, newly invented weapon, I'm pretty certain I can take her."*

Sasha smiled, enjoying the comment she had shared with him through the link. Although Sasha had been undergoing treatments to the flaw, his chip had not yet been removed, and he still had access to the link.

"All right, we'll be outside."

Ava and the reporter sat down across from each other at the large briefing table. The hotel manager had reserved this briefing room for her stay.

"My name is Hailey Ramirez."

"Nice to meet you. I'm..." she trailed off. It was still strange introducing herself by her true name.

"You're General Altman," Hailey completed the introduction confidently.

Ava gave a pained laugh. "Not anymore."

Hailey observed her with interest before muttering under her breath. "Gosh, you look so much like Shannon."

Ava perked up in surprise. "What?"

"Sorry, my boyfriend's coworker. She looks a lot like you, only older. And scarier."

Ava's eyes narrowed. "And her name is Shannon?"

"Yeah."

"What's your *boyfriend's* name?"

Hailey suddenly looked concerned, and she changed the subject. "Ex-boyfriend. He died a few months back. Anyway, I don't want to take up too much of your time." She reached into her briefcase and pulled out a file, placing it on the table in front of her. Then she retrieved a photo from inside and slid it in front of Ava.

"This is Harvey Caldwell. He was the top journalist in the Kingdoms for the past ten years."

Ava nodded. "I'm familiar with his work. I used to follow his journalism, when I was still in the Kingdoms."

"Well, ten months ago, he suffered a severe stroke that left him practically braindead. And a few weeks later, he died of complications from the stroke."

"I'm sorry," Ava said, when it was clear how much this journalist had meant to Hailey.

She slid another picture forward, one Ava recognized well. "This is Lionel Prichette the Second, of Pallsbury."

Ava's eyebrows pulled together in confusion. "What does this have to do with—"

"Two years ago, he was diagnosed with Alzheimer's; late stage. There was no history of the disease in his family. As the king, he received top medical care on a daily basis. Yet, somehow, they didn't catch this until it was in the late stages, when it was too late to do anything."

Ava remained still, not comprehending.

"Five months ago," Hailey continued confidently, "he died of complications from the disease."

"I'm not sure what you're suggesting," Ava muttered, though in truth, she was starting to.

Hailey pushed another photo forward. "This is Sergeant Kathleen Hawkins. Ten months ago, she was killed in a hit and run by a vehicle not registered in the system."

"What are you trying to say?" Ava suddenly asked in an accusatory tone.

"Hawkins was killed two days before Harvey Caldwell suffered his stroke. He renamed the story he was working on in her honor, the night he suffered that stroke, entitling his story 'Hawkins.'"

"Miss Ramirez," Ava said helplessly.

But she wasn't done. She pushed another photo forward. "This is Councilman Warren Green. He was incriminated with treason one year ago and put on death row. Two months ago, they carried out that sentence." The disdain in her face was extreme. "I have firsthand knowledge of his innocence. But I was told, by him, not to share the story too soon. He died, knowing full well that he could have been saved, but that it wasn't time."

After a moment to let that set in, she pressed another photo forward. "This is General Harrison Altman."

"Don't," Ava pleaded, knowing for sure now where this was headed.

"Nine years ago, he was shot and killed on stage. An investigation lasted for years, but there was never enough evidence to incriminate anyone." She pressed forward a ballistics report. "This was the weapon he was killed with. Registered to one Eli Altman."

"That's not enough proof to—"

"No, it's not, which is why Lionel never came forward with the ballistics report. It wasn't until a total freak accident caused a worldwide blackout—" Hailey spoke this pointedly, indicating she knew far more about that than she'd let on. "—and Eli somehow managed to worm his way permanently to the seat of the General, all the while seeming like the humble leader when he didn't even cast a vote for himself, that Lionel recognized the pattern and decided it was time to come forward before it was too late."

"What do you mean he came forward?"

"This story isn't just Harvey's, or Hawkins's, or even Councilman Green's. First, and foremost, this is Lionel's story. These are the decades of secrets he was forced to keep. The horrendous acts he was forced to accept. The corruption he was forced to turn a blind eye to. In his dying days, he was done being forced, done being silenced. He decided it was time to break free of that pretty little birdcage that had held him captive."

Ava thought of her last visit with Lionel, how he had used that same analogy to describe *her* position. How could Hailey know what she did? Was this the truth, or were these just more twisted lies?

"You can't really think that Eli killed the General, the King, and countless others in search of power, can you?"

Hailey seemed to find that comment funny, but chose to answer as seriously as Ava had asked. "Power has corrupted countless politicians, princes, dukes and noblemen to pillage, kill and destroy the lives of people much closer to them—in Britain's history alone. Why not Eli?"

Ava shook her head. "It's just not him. I don't buy it. He never wanted to be the General. He cursed Eric for leaving him as regent General!"

"Who's to say Eric's heart attack wasn't just as timely?" Hailey replied pointedly. "I haven't found any proof of foul play here, and so I don't yet include his name in my story. But who's to say he didn't curse Eric for leaving him as 'regent' General, rather than offering him what he already believed was rightfully his?"

Ava shook her head stubbornly. "No. I don't believe that. I know he's done horrible, unforgivable things, but I can't believe that he planned this from the beginning!"

"Believe what you want, General Altman," Hailey said, and Ava flinched at the title she used. "I'm not here to convince you that Eli is corrupt. You already know that much, and I believe it's why you left him. I'm here to warn you.

"Ma'am, my source in Brazil is just a little bit better than Eli's, and I got tipped off about your arrival sooner. But I'm certain he won't be much longer than I was. When he gets here, Eli will do whatever he can to work this out peaceably, to get you back on his side, because he can't afford to lose Brazil, or you. But ma'am, this story is bigger than all of us. There are backups in place that I don't even know about. Even if Eli kills me, this story will ultimately be released. And when it is, Eli and everyone connected with him will be incriminated. I still believe, as did Harvey, Lionel and Hawkins, that you are just a victim of Eli's power grab. Please, General Altman, don't make yourself one of the villains by making the same mistake as Lionel and aligning yourself with the bad guys. You can't change them. And in the end, you will be brought down and corrupted with them."

She pulled together her things and stood. "Thank you for your time, General Altman." Then she smiled. "Let the Colonel, and the rightful General, win."

☆ ☆ ☆ ☆ ☆

Mikel related how he knew this reporter as they waited outside, but her meeting with Ava was short and sweet, and Mikel had hardly told Sasha the half of it when the girl exited.

"Wanna tell me how you aligned yourself as General Altman's bodyguard, from a simple waiter at King Richard's palace?" she spoke to Mikel with a challenge in her eyes.

"I'm the best, what can I say?" He grinned his pretty little grin, and Sasha had to look away. That boy was trouble. No doubt about it.

"How did your meeting go?" he asked in his flirtatious, charming voice.

"It went well, thank you."

"How long are you in town?" Mikel pressed. "We should grab a bite to eat while you're here."

At first, the girl looked like she would spit in his face, but Sasha sensed a sudden curiosity in her eyes. "I'm free at one. Meet me at the lobby, back exit?"

"You got it."

She walked away from them and down the hall. Sasha gave Mikel a pointed look.

"What?" Mikel asked. "Can't I have an hour of personal time while you guys do your thing?"

Sasha sighed, turning away and looking back down the hall. The girl was still making her exit, but she caught sight of someone, and turned awkwardly to the right, entering an "Employees Only" room.

Sasha narrowed his eyes in concern, but he didn't have to wonder for long.

"Where is she?" a voice boomed in the lobby.

"Right this way, General Altman," the clerk offered.

"Here comes trouble," Mikel said as both of them stood up straighter, prepared for a fight. "You think Ava's ready?" Mikel asked carefully.

"I'm ready," she replied for herself, exiting the briefing room and joining them in the hall. "Let's do this."

13

The People

Eli knew very well who he would find when he made his way down the hall toward Ava. He walked with a procession behind him—bodyguards, fiancé, and the media following to get this story out far and wide.

So, they wanted to bombard his territory and turn it into their own? They would face a fearsome fight on the way.

The General did well to avoid Sasha's stare as well as Mikel's, looking only at his sister. He put on his best smile, and it would rival his mother's. Ava wavered under that perfect look he gave her. She had seemed stern and confident at first, as if prepared for a fight, but when he offered a look of delight and love, it was like she didn't know what to do.

He'd known this about her for a long time and had used it to his advantage many times. Still, she had never seen him this bright, this happy, this delighted. Of course, it was all for show. Yet, she fell for it completely.

When he was but a few feet away, he opened his arms to her. "Come here, Ava!" he said with exaggerated joy that came off loving and genuine.

423

Once again, she seemed to cave under that pressure, and not knowing what else to do, she stepped forward. He pulled her into his arms. Eli was just glad Jackson wasn't there. He was the only one worrisome enough to keep a distance between them. Even Sasha seemed overcome by Eli's delight and looked just as taken aback.

When she was in his arms, he held her tightly, lovingly. Then, when it was clear she was flabbergasted and overcome, he turned and brought her, still under his arm, into the cameras. He smiled happily for the media, and after a moment, not knowing what else to do, Ava did the same.

The image of Ava that Brazil had fallen in love with no longer existed. At this point, it was a figment of imagination—or at least, a figment of the past.

Council had ordered Eli to destroy that ambition and talent in Ava. And he had done it flawlessly.

If Jackson wanted to use Ava to try and steal Brazil, Eli would turn it against him, even if it meant destroying the image of Ava Altman in the process. Of course, it started with a bit of pleasantries for the people to enjoy.

When he was sure they had gotten a few good shots, he turned to her, and reaching out for his fiancé, invited her forward.

"Ava, this is Isabella, my fiancé."

Isabella put out her hand, looking regal. She, too, was good at playing a part. All this ambitious woman cared about was status and power. And in marrying the General, she gained both, but if she managed to make Eli more popular among the general populace, that was enough for him.

Ava looked at the woman in shock. *"What about Katia?"* Ava asked him through the link.

Eli's smile never wavered. *"Katia is Russian. You understand why we couldn't go through with that. Not when our Kingdoms are at stake."*

"You mean not when your image is at stake," she disagreed.

"If there's anything you learned from Mom, it's that those are the same exact thing."

"It's so nice to see you again, sweetie!" Isabella said, inserting dominance with that one demeaning word. Atta girl.

"We've never met," Ava disagreed.

"Oh, I was at your birthday party," Isabella answered. "It was captivating."

Ava just stared, looking confused and taken aback.

"Captive..." Ava muttered. "That's exactly what it was."

With Eli and Isabella there looking like the height of the aristocracy, and Ava standing there like an utter fool, Eli hoped the cameras would catch a bit of the glory.

"Come stay with us at the Tower, won't you?" Isabella pleaded.

"Yes, come!" Eli agreed, reaching his hand to her arm and pulling her gently along.

Sasha and Mikel both stepped forward at that point. "She'll stay with us," Sasha objected.

"Of course! You can come too," Eli said as if it were obvious. Still, he avoided looking Sasha in the eyes, as if the man's station had him below Eli's notice or consideration.

"Come on," Eli urged, grabbing her arm and moving forward. "We have so much to talk about!"

"Don't pull her!" Sasha said, forcefully moving Eli's hand.

Eli didn't even have to react. His guards all drew weapons and trained them on Sasha and Mikel at once.

"You really don't want to turn this into a battle, do you?" Eli addressed Sasha, though still avoiding his gaze.

"Don't do this Eli," Sasha pleaded.

"*Because we both know I'll win,*" Eli finished through the link, and for the first time, he looked into Sasha's eyes with a challenging stare.

Sasha did not seem to waver, though he should have. Most people were crippled by Eli in such times, knowing the power he possessed as General.

"*I have faced stronger men than you, Eli,*" Sasha challenged through the link.

"*Oh, was it you who killed Harrison then?*" Eli mocked him. "*Oh, that's right. Try as you might, you could never get close enough. What makes you think you have any chance against me?*"

Sasha gritted his teeth.

"Yes, let's go," Ava said, walking forward and pulling Eli along.

Clearly, she noticed the guard force with guns on Sasha, even if the lunatic himself didn't.

★ ★ ★ ★ ★

"Well, score is at Eli two. Ava zero."

"Thanks for that, Mikel," Ava said dryly. "What are his two points anyway?"

"One, winning the media. Two, getting us to move from our safe hotel into his turf. Now we're stuck in the Tower."

Ava gave him a "seriously" look. "Stuck in the Tower?" she replied pointedly. "You and I?"

Mikel looked to the side thoughtfully as her comment made sense to him. "Yeah, that may have been a misstep on his part."

"You shouldn't have done what he asked," Sasha said in frustration.

"Would it have been better to get in a gunfight right then?" Ava disagreed.

Sasha shook his head in frustration. "He's just like him. He's become the General, through and through."

"Yeah," Mikel agreed. "Did anyone else get deja vu when you tried to pull Ava away and all the guards stepped up?"

Ava nodded. "The moment on the training ground, when Sasha and Kristen went to confront Harrison about me."

"That look in his eyes," Sasha said through gritted teeth.

"I thought it was Harrison we were looking at," Mikel said with a shiver. "That kid's gotten scary!"

"That wasn't when he reminded me of him," Ava said, remembering the whole scene. "It was when he first started down the hall. That loving, confident smile on his face. That air and demeanor. He looked just like Harrison."

"He's gotten much better at this," Mikel agreed.

"And I've gotten much worse," Ava realized helplessly. "I don't know if I can do this…. I don't know if I can actually beat him. And that Isabella girl."

"Gorgeous," Mikel agreed with exaggerated wide eyes. "And very graceful. The perfect Spanish aristo for the General's wife."

"Maybe we should call Jackson and change the plan," Ava admitted sadly.

Sasha was suddenly on high alert. "You don't mean that?" he asked, seeming not to believe it himself.

"I mean, you saw how that went down! I lost my Altman smile. And his could *be* the General's! How am I supposed to win the people—let alone the government officials—when I'm facing against the General reincarnate?"

Sasha stood, thoughtful and silent for almost a minute before he turned to face them. When he did, there was a new light and passion in his eyes.

"There was one person who could have rivaled, and even beaten Harrison, if she had tried. It was your mother." He said that with such surety, Ava had to wonder if it were true, even though it seemed unlikely.

"She would never do it, because she had too much to lose. She was worried for her children. For Eli..." he trailed off sadly as the irony of how it had happened registered. "She worried about you," to Ava, "and you," to Mikel, who seemed pleased to be included when it came to Kristen.

"But Harrison forced her into an image she never asked for, and never wanted. In so doing, by making her the image and the face of the war, he gave her the power to overthrow him. But she had too much to lose."

Sasha looked Ava in the eyes as his passion spilled over. "Ava, Eli has already taken everything from you. What more do you have to lose that's within his power to take?"

She went through a list of names in her mind, but each of these people were already at risk. And anyway, Eli was unlikely to be able to get to them.

"Nothing," Ava agreed.

"He gave you the means to overthrow him," Mikel noted in realization. "At least in Brazil."

"What did that letter say this morning?" Sasha reminded her. "What was it you told us that reporter said when she left?"

"They said," Mikel offered when Ava didn't answer, "'Let the Colonel, and the rightful General, win.'"

Sasha nodded as his passion brimmed over the edge. "Ava Altman, you are the General's rival."

★ ★ ★ ★ ★

"If you think you've got it," Jackson told them over the web camera, "I have complete faith in all of you."

"We've got this," Mikel said confidently, and the others added their agreement.

"I wouldn't discount Eli yet either," Jackson warned. "It doesn't make sense to invite you right into the Tower. He has to have something up his sleeve."

"I agree," Sasha replied. "Though I haven't been able to figure it out yet."

"Parliament meets in the Tower now," Mikel offered. "Maybe it's just a show of power, to prove he's not afraid of us?"

"Oh, he's terrified of us," Sasha disagreed.

"When do you meet with Parliament?" Jackson directed this question to Ava.

"We meet in roughly one hour," Ava replied, looking beautiful, even over a computer screen.

He smiled at her unconsciously.

"Focus," Mikel teased, apparently having noticed Jackson's look.

Jackson turned back to the others, feeling suddenly embarrassed. "I think the draft you sent was brilliant. I mean, there were a few word choice suggestions I added, but overall, it's really well done. Who wrote all that?"

"I did," Ava replied shyly.

"Wow. Really? Where did you learn..." he trailed off. "Lionel?"

She nodded.

"Well, he's a good teacher. I wouldn't change a thing."

"You literally just said you would change several things," Mikel teased. "Word choice suggestions?"

"Semantics," Jackson waved away, and Ava smiled at his use of the word.

Sasha and Jackson began discussing a few specific scenarios to be wary of. Maybe he was just always unconsciously watching her, but Jackson easily noticed when Ava blinked her eyes closed for a bit too long, then leaned farther back in her seat.

She was probably just tired, and he ignored it at first. It wasn't until she let out a subtle gasp that he was sure something was wrong.

"I think it should work as long as—" Sasha was saying.

"Are you okay, Ava?" Jackson cut him off.

Mikel and Sasha looked at Ava, who was sitting in the room beside them. Her hands went to her head, and she suddenly hunched lower. Jackson was immediately filled with dread. It was the flaw, the sickness she denied. It was affecting her. He could lose her at any moment.

The pain seemed to intensify, and Ava gasped louder, holding her head fiercely.

"What's wrong?" Sasha pressed. "The flaw?"

She shook her head as if to deny it.

"Counter Intelligence," Mikel said as if it were obvious.

"No!" she practically shouted between her clenched teeth. "No. It's not that. It's Eli!"

They all watched in confusion as she struggled through the pain. "What does that mean?" Sasha pressed for more information.

"The device...like Darya. He used this on me when he put me in the Brazil Tower before!"

"How do we stop it?" Mikel asked with instant concern.

Every second she hunched lower as the pain intensified. So, this was Eli's grand plan to cripple her. Well, it was working.

"I'll stop him!" Sasha said through gritted teeth.

"No!" Ava reached for Sasha, holding him there. "You won't stop him. He'll just do the same thing to you."

"Then what do we do?" Jackson asked, as if he had any chance of actually helping from Moscow. "Can we turn it off?"

Mikel shook his head. "Not unless we can get to the device."

"What do we do?" Sasha asked, seeming just as helpless as Jackson felt.

"Maybe we can switch it," Mikel offered urgently. "Like a wireless connection, move it from one signal to the next."

"Won't they notice the switch?" Jackson asked worriedly, watching as Ava got worse every moment.

"We're in a Tower!" Mikel insisted. "I'll mask the data!"

Ava screamed out suddenly. "He's killing me!" she cried. "He doesn't even mean to. He doesn't know he's doing it. But it's going to kill me!" She seemed so pained, and so certain that it would lead to her death, that all of them believed it to be true.

"Sasha, do something!" Jackson said helplessly, having no idea what the man would even attempt.

Sasha helped his shaking daughter to the floor.

"Why is it killing you?" Mikel asked seriously. "They've done this to you before. Why is it going to kill you now?"

Jackson desperately just wanted someone to fix this, though he knew they were trying.

"It's not the device that will kill me," she said, shaking her head over and over. "It's Counter Intelligence."

"We're in Brazil!" Mikel objected. "Do they have access to it here?"

"It's always here!" Ava screamed in pain. "Ever since that night. It's always here. I can't fight it when he's hurting me. If I stop fighting, even for a second...gah! He's killing me! He has to stop."

"Find Eli!" Jackson shouted. "Tell him to stop!"

Rather than following orders, Mikel closed his eyes and seemed to go into his own head. "Turn off your connection with the link, Ava," he ordered her. "I'll switch it to me."

"No, Mikel, you can't," she said through the pain.

"Yes, he can," Sasha disagreed. "Shut it off for just a second."

She shook her head repeatedly. "I've already been infected," she said between breaths. "If I stop fighting...."

None of them had any idea what she meant by any of this, and Jackson could barely understand her through her gasping breaths. It was clear that she had been dealing with whatever this fight was entirely on her own.

"I can't stop. I can't stop. He's killing me!"

"Sasha, get to Eli!" Jackson ordered.

Sasha stood and ran to the door, then cursed. "It's locked and sealed! Mikel, open the door!"

Mikel didn't seem to hear, as he was completely in his mind now.

"Don't take it, Mikel," Ava pleaded. "You don't know how much it hurts."

"Long as it doesn't kill me," he replied absently.

"Mikel, no! I don't want to risk you getting infected too. You can't fight it like me."

"I can handle it!" Mikel shot back.

Jackson sat there watching helplessly. He suddenly reached for his mobile as an idea entered, and he started dialing a secure line to his enemy. "Pick up, Eli!" he cursed, but no answer.

"Almost there," Mikel said, scanning through his mind in search of the connection. "Just got to make a quick jump."

"You can't take the chance!" Ava pleaded.

"I'm not gonna let you die right now, Ava!" he spat through gritted teeth.

"Better than if we both die in thirty seconds!" she replied in similar anger.

Sasha was now banging on the door and screaming for release. "He won't answer! Not even through the link!"

Mikel suddenly grinned. "There she is." He cocked his head momentarily, and then the pain and desperation that had just been on Ava's face transferred to his. He grabbed his head as the pain overtook him.

"Sasha!" Jackson shouted. "Check on Mikel!"

Sasha was there in a second. "Are you infected?" he asked worriedly.

Mikel shook his head through the pain. "Don't think so. It just hurts. Gah. Really bad. But I don't think I'm dying."

By then, Ava had managed to pull herself to a sitting position and she crawled to where Mikel was. With the little strength she could muster, she punched him heavily in the gut. "You idiot! You could have gotten us both killed!"

Sasha pulled her back. "Let's not beat a man while he's down, dear."

"We're both alive, aren't we?" Mikel offered, somehow managing that grin of his through the pain. "Now, you go meet with Parliament. Eli doesn't know this is possible. He doesn't know about me. Let's play the bluff. He'll think you're stronger than ever!"

"You won't last long like this," Ava disagreed. "And he'll increase it every second when I don't conform."

"I can handle it!" he said, as if he had something to prove. "Just go out and get us Brazil."

Sasha looked once more to the screen as if hoping Jackson had some insight.

"You heard the man!" was all Jackson could think to answer.

Sasha helped Ava to her feet, and Mikel buckled under the impending pressure and pain. The next words he muttered regretfully under his breath, "So much for my date."

★ ★ ★ ★ ★

Eli happily entered the Parliament meeting at a few minutes after the hour. He had once been very punctual, but in this instance, it would prove his superior status to arrive a minute or two late. Not long enough to make them really wait, but enough to be the last one to arrive.

The large room was filled with Brazilian officials. He walked inside and took the seat that was always set aside for him, the visiting ambassador's chair. "I'm sorry to announce that my sister wasn't feeling well," Eli said, taking his seat. "She will be unable to attend after all."

Several people looked at him strangely.

"Is that so?" Prime Minister dos Santos asked with a hint of sarcasm.

Eli glanced at the prime minister's seat and almost flinched when, sitting beside the man in the seat only ever used by visiting royalty, was Ava. She smiled mockingly at him.

That was impossible. She should be in excruciating pain. She should be totally incapacitated. There was no way she could be sitting there, that mocking look in her eyes, as if nothing was wrong. No, it couldn't be.

"Oh, Ava!" he said, attempting to save face and using her first name to neglect any sign of respect. "I'm glad to see you're feeling better!"

"You must have been misinformed, Eli."

He almost hissed as she used his first name, ignoring the titles he was owed.

"I've been feeling perfectly well all day. In fact, the Prime Minister and I just shared a wonderful lunch before the meeting was set to begin."

It took everything he had to smile, rather than glare deeply at her. "Oh, how nice," he replied with a mocking air.

"It was," the prime minister agreed. "Your sister certainly has a way about her! It is an honor to have her back in our homeland again."

"I'm sure," Eli offered carefully. "Well, it's several minutes after the hour, perhaps we should get started?"

"Indeed," dos Santos agreed. "Although, General Altman, we would appreciate punctuality in the future. We're all busy people. I'm sure you understand."

The silence lingered as Eli considered how he would like to address that insolent comment. "Of course! I'll be sure and make more of an effort to do so in the future," he managed, despite his fury.

"We have set aside the majority of our meeting time for Miss Altman," the timekeeper announced. "But if the General has anything he would like to start with, he may have opening remarks."

Eli did not appreciate how that whole sentence was worded. But yes, he would take a moment to speak.

"My sister Ava and I are excited to be here together in your country again," Eli spoke warmly. "Obviously, she has been preoccupied with poor health for the past year and a half, and regrets that she hasn't been able to come more often. However, we would love to discuss war efforts within Brazil and how recruitment and retention are going. Ava would love to hear more about Brazil's efforts to support our cause."

The room went blank and silent for a moment until a member offered to give the reports.

"*Zhànshì Six,*" Eli spoke through the link. "*Have them check Ava's signal. She should be in excruciating pain! Have them up the intensity. Keep going by increments of one every minute until I tell you to stop.*"

"*Yes, sir.*"

Ava sat quietly and gracefully, seeming pleased as they read her the reports. She made not the slightest reaction as they intensified the push on her signal. It was impossible. How could she withstand it completely? This had been his last hope in controlling her, and now he didn't even have that. Eli was infuriated.

"The time is now yours, Miss Altman," a member turned it to her.

"Actually," Eli interrupted, "before she speaks, I just want to thank Ava for making the trip. As I said, her ill health has kept her from a lot of things, and will probably keep her from future visits to Brazil. That being the case, she wanted to officially explain that all future dealings will be done through me."

No one replied.

"You have mentioned her poor health, several times now," Prime Minister dos Santos noted.

"Miss Altman, the time is now yours," a member turned it to her again.

Ava thanked him. "Before I begin. Eli, is there anything else you would like to say?"

He wasn't sure if that was a challenge.

"I just want to make sure you've had a chance to say what you need," she replied sweetly, as if she wasn't clearly mocking him again.

It took everything in him to return to a smile over a glare. "Just how sorry I am that your health prevents you from doing Brazil the service they deserve."

Prime Minister dos Santos actually rolled his eyes, and then Eli's glare broke through.

"Anything else?" Ava offered.

He almost snarled at her, but managed to mask it with another careful smile. "No, there is not at this time." What else could he say? He was not prepared for her to be at this meeting.

"Zhànshì Six, report!"

"We're at maximum capacity, sir. We can't stay here long without risking permanent damage."

Eli's knuckles pulled together, forming rock solid fists. *"Turn it down. But only enough to maintain long-term safety."*

"Yes, sir."

"You may address the Parliament, Miss Altman," a member turned it back to her.

"Thank you," she said, standing and literally taking the floor as she walked to the front of the room.

"And thank you, Eli, for that wonderful introduction. Unfortunately, General Altman has been lying to you for the past year."

Everyone looked down at her in surprise, and Eli's eyes widened in panic. She wouldn't dare. Would she?

"I am no longer aligned with the United Kingdoms. I, and everyone else who believed in actual freedom of the people, was either killed, silenced, or like myself, defamed and removed from any position of power. In the rest of the United Kingdoms, I have been removed from the media, and censored from the people's view.

"As you know, King Lionel died from supposedly natural causes some months ago. Only, that wasn't really an accident either, was it?" She looked at Eli with a challenge he had never seen in her before. Then she turned back to the others.

"Eli has been lying to Brazil. He used my image to continue inspiring loyalty with your people, because he knew, rightly, that you weren't foolish enough to align with him or the many other corrupt Council members. Brazil only joined, after decades of persuasion, because you were promised real change and real hope. But the General and his lapdogs have eliminated any chance of either of those within the Kingdoms.

"The symbol he spreads in propaganda around your nation is a lie. I do not support the United Kingdoms or Council. And I certainly don't support this despot.

"Instead, I have found, and aligned myself with, the only people— other than yourselves—who still seem to be fighting for the ideal—for the freedom of the people. I have aligned myself with those you know as 'The Third Side.'"

There were gasps of surprise and awe around the hall. Eli racked his mind for an answer of how to save this. "*Turn it on to full capacity!*" he ordered. "*Tell them to do whatever they have to!*"

"I'm sure you've all heard of this infamous 'Third Side,'" Ava continued. "Or, as we're more accurately coming to be known, 'The Cause.' A United Intelligence agent was abandoned in the Republic and ultimately defected from his homeland, helping Russia, and now Africa, achieve actual freedom from the Republic. There are rumors that this agent still works for and under Council, but I assure you, that isn't true either.

"You saw the speech three weeks ago from the African leader who has helped his people to freedom. You heard his call. Unfortunately, without Towers in their homeland, most of the United Kingdoms haven't had any real knowledge about The Cause and the success we're having. And believe me, Eli would have done anything to keep you in the dark too.

"My friends of Brazil, General Eli Altman will do everything in his power to convince you that I'm sick, that I'm unwell, and that everything I see is the figment of some wild imaginings. He's lied to you about me for the past year, and he's not about to stop now.

"Almost two years ago, Lionel came to meet you himself, and even introduced me to you. Together we promised you that we would help take Brazil to freedom, prosperity, and peace. Eli never pulled my image because he knew that, now that Lionel is gone, I'm the last one who still cares to keep that promise.

"I'm here to deliver, but it isn't through the United Kingdoms. You always had that much right. You refused to join them for decades. Not until Lionel and I convinced you of a greater opportunity, a new chance. The government of the Republic is corrupt and must be stopped. But the government of Council is no better. When the leader from Africa, Sizwe Jelani, spoke to you, he said there would be a call to stand and join the new, third side. That time is right now."

Eli cursed. Not at Ava's nice little speech, but at the gleam in the eye of the prime minister. Whatever she had said to him during their pleasant little lunch had persuaded him. Looking around the room, Eli couldn't believe it. These people couldn't already be convinced. What, were they just going to take her word for it?

Ava continued on, even using a statement piece from President Volvakov and the tribal leader Sizwe as little recruitment videos. Eli was disturbed how effective these seemed to be. Had these people no pride? They couldn't be this easy to convince!

What had Lionel said in that first introduction? What was it that had these people on Ava's side without her even really having to try? This was ridiculous!

When she had finished and sat down, someone in the Parliament began clapping, and soon they all roared into applause.

Eli gritted his teeth in anger.

He stood up and screamed to be heard. They were all too busy clapping over nothing. It wasn't like she was the General. Her speech hadn't been that eloquent. It did not deserve so much applause!

He tried to think of a way to make her pay, some way to make her feel his wrath and regret ever crossing him. But he couldn't think of anything to do, short of bombing Russia and killing Jackson, which wasn't exactly in his power to do anymore.

He screamed out for them to stop until the applause died out. "I have plenty of proof to show that you're insane!" Eli spat.

"I need no more proof to know that *you* are," dos Santos replied quickly.

Eli turned a snarl to the man. "You must be forgetting the terms of our alliance. You can't just jump ship and join these deserters! Our alliance is hard pressed and binding. If you leave, you will pay dearly for it!"

"You're forgetting that Lionel formed the alliance himself," Ava explained with that irritating confidence of hers. "Lionel was my mentor. And a smart man. Look into section B7 of the alliance contract. Brazil is well within their rights to leave."

The prime minister grinned proudly. This must have been one of the many things she'd already shared with him.

"If you leave our alliance it will be as our enemy! We will stop at nothing to burn your nation to the ground!"

The prime minister stood up with a sudden light in his eyes. "I don't appreciate being threatened in my own home, General Altman. But if the Kingdoms want to start a fight with Brazil, and our alliance with the free nations of Russia and Africa, then so be it. You have one day to remove yourself, and any of your people, from our nation, before they are held as prisoners of war. Fortunately, our people weren't allowed travel to your mainland, so we have no one to recall. You may go. We'd like to put our decision to a vote. Though I can't imagine any of us are rooting for you."

Eli growled once more. This couldn't actually be happening. Had she really just stolen Brazil?

"I'll make you and Jackson pay for this!" Eli snarled through the link.

"I'm sure you will, Eli. Oh, and by the way, you can save the energy on that device by turning it off now. Or should I just break it like I did Darya's?"

He could not comprehend how easily she had swooped in and taken everything. He hadn't stood a chance. The second she entered that room, they were on her side. He still blamed Lionel for that.

★ ★ ★ ★ ★

"How is he?" Ava asked, joining Sasha in the room adjoining the suite.

Mikel lay on his bed, looking faint and ill.

"He passed out from the pain at one point," Sasha noted with concern. "He only just came to, and still, he looks unwell, but I think the pain has stopped. How did it go?"

Ava's prior excitement was gravely dampened with Mikel there looking so bad, but she gave a satisfied nod. "We got 'em. Jackson was right. That meeting ahead of time with Prime Minister dos Santos made all the difference. I showed him everything that Eli might possibly use against me. I shared that speech I had prepared, and he was on board before we ever entered the hall. Not to mention, he had already spoken personally to half the Parliament by the time it started and said basically, 'We're switching sides again! Still with Ava though.'" She chuckled. "They were convinced before I even started speaking!"

Sasha couldn't seem to stifle his laugh, before remembering poor Mikel. "How did Eli take it?"

"He wants us all dead," Ava related honestly. "But he was helpless to do anything. It's so funny, I was terrified to face him in that room, but from the moment he saw me, it was like all his cards went out the window. He didn't even put up a fight."

"Men like Eli assume they have accounted for every possible scenario. In reality, they're used to things going their way. When it doesn't, they're generally out of aces."

"Well don't just stand there," Mikel spoke weakly from the bed. "Nurse me back to health!"

Ava laughed sweetly, walking to him. Then, seriously she asked, "Be honest. Is Counter Intelligence trying to crush you right now? Were you infected?"

"I...I'm not sure."

She smiled sadly. "Then you haven't been infected," she assured him.

"It sounds like you have something you need to tell us," Sasha spoke in a concerned tone.

"Later," Ava said, thinking still of Mikel.

"No," Mikel disagreed, still as weak as she'd ever seen him. "Now."

Sasha added his agreement. Then he motioned her to the chair beside Mikel. "Sit. And talk."

She sighed heavily, but obeyed. It took her a long time to work up to speaking, though eventually she managed. "Five months ago, the night of the ambush on the African camp, they released Counter Intelligence on us."

Both Mikel and Sasha agreed, saying that was common knowledge. "I couldn't handle it on my own," Mikel related, "and you saved the day. So what?"

"I haven't..." Ava started carefully, then stopped again. "I haven't been the same since that night. Something changed in me. When you couldn't hold off the virus," she turned to Mikel as she spoke, "before I knew what hit me, my brain was already attempting to fight it off. If I had been only trying to protect myself, I think I could have. But I looked further, and there were so many signals, so many of you that would have been infected too."

"What did you do, love?" Sasha asked in a pained tone.

She took a heavy breath. She hadn't wanted to admit this to anyone, not even really herself. This was far worse than the flaw. "I had automatically put a barrier between Counter Intelligence and my neural link. But when I sensed how many others would be affected if I didn't stop it, I dropped my defenses for a brief moment. Just long enough to increase my range and change the flow from pushing to swimming. I didn't realize how quickly it would take a hold of me."

Sasha put his head down as the truth of it struck him. "That moment," he whispered as if to himself. "That moment when I thought you had died on me. You had." His words were so quiet, she almost didn't know if she'd heard him right, but when he looked up to face her again, there were tears in his eyes.

"You were infected," Mikel said the words that none of them wanted to say out loud.

Ava gave a painful nod of affirmation.

"Shouldn't you be dead right now?" Mikel shot back in confusion, sitting up on the bed and strangely looking far less ill than before.

"I've been fighting it, ever since. Day and night. All the time. It's harder to sleep now, and some nights I'm terrified to sleep because I worry my brain will stop fighting, and it'll be the end. That I'll never wake up."

"Oh, Ava," Sasha said, and a tear spilled down his cheek.

"Are you telling me that your brain has been trying to overload itself for the past five months?" Mikel asked in shock. "Ava, I faced Counter Intelligence for less than ten minutes, and the push was so great I knew it would crush me in another instant. How have you managed to fight it for so long?"

She shook her head, raising her shoulders. "I guess, you adapt to whatever challenges are there? I don't know. All I know is that it takes a bit of my focus, at all times. I think that was why it was so difficult to learn to control the Towers again."

"But when we took Africa, when you had the full force of Counter Intelligence on you, didn't that break your focus?" Mikel objected.

Again, she shrugged. "It was the same enemy and therefore the same fight? I don't know. But this morning, when that intense pain from Eli overwhelmed me, it almost caused me to stop pushing back. I wouldn't have made it as long as you did, Mikel. Counter Intelligence would have crushed me—overloaded my brain, electrocuted me, burned me out, whatever you want to call it."

Sasha put his face in his hands as he tried to come to terms with this. "That's why you insisted against the brain scans," he noted with regret. Then his scientific side came out as he explained it to Mikel. "The flaw of Intelligence is a gradual shadow it casts on areas of your brain until it eventually forms a tumor. Most people don't develop a tumor until decades after receiving the chip. Counter Intelligence, on the other hand, is an instant overload of too many electrons being flooded into the brain, as the Tower connects to the chip. Normally it kills its victims instantly by overt electrocution. But if one was to fight the flooding of electrons with the chip, it could be tempered. Still, prolonged exposure would also increase the affected areas from the flaw, forming the tumor more rapidly than ever."

She nodded sadly. "We don't have a cure for Counter Intelligence. The work you and Zak have done is to stop the flaw from casting those shadows and forming those tumors. Removing the tumor usually means removing the chip—like you did with Jackson. You can't reverse the damage that's already been done without removing the chip. And removing the chip takes away my only defense against Counter Intelligence."

"So," Mikel tried to explain it to himself in simpler terms, "essentially, you have a tumor in your brain that is getting bigger every day—especially because of Counter Intelligence. But removing that tumor, or if you stop fighting the virus for even a moment...."

"Then my brain will overload," Ava agreed. "And I will die instantly."

"That doesn't make sense," Mikel disagreed. "The chip is where the virus is. So, removing it should mean it can no longer overload your brain."

Sasha shook his head. "Not if she's already infected. The energy would have already spread to her entire brain like a biological virus. The chip is only the conduit to spreading the virus to the brain. The only thing keeping it from killing her is the chip, which gives her an ability to fight back. But the virus won't just magically disappear when the chip does."

"There has to be something we can do!" Mikel said, looking urgently at Sasha. "Isn't there any way to shrink it, or stop it, or have it removed?"

Sasha shook his head sadly. "Nothing we have found has been able to reverse Counter Intelligence, though admittedly, we've never seen anyone infected who survived longer than two minutes. The small tumor from the flaw in my brain has responded well to treatments and may not need to be removed, but with the treatments has come a weakening in my access to the chip. It's a miracle Ava can fight off the virus as it is. If we do anything to weaken the chip, she may not have the strength to fight the virus."

"It's just a computer virus, right? Well, let's find a way to change its coding!" Mikel replied hopefully.

Sasha raised his hand. "Be my guest," he pleaded. "Right now, we have no idea how they created it. It's highly doubtful we can change its coding at this point, when she's already been infected with the original. We know of no way to remove Counter Intelligence. And the flaw will affect her more every day because of it. Basically, it's only a matter of time before, either Counter Intelligence overloads her brain, or the flaw kills her first."

Ava swallowed hard. She knew it was bad. She had known for a long time. Yet, hearing Sasha explain it so indelicately was the first time she realized just *how* bad it was. And suddenly, all she could think of was Jackson. She should never have gotten him into this. She should never have become involved in a relationship when she knew there was a great risk to her life. Still, she hadn't realized how dire it was until this moment.

"Why can't we change it?" Mikel blurted, grasping at straws without understanding them. "The chip is a highly advanced piece of technology. The virus is simple coding, right? Let's just erase that virus. Or add to it, or something! I don't know, guys. You're the techy!" he threw a gesture at Sasha. "Think of something."

"You don't think I have been working on a way to change Counter Intelligence for the past five months?" Sasha replied pointedly, looking bereft of hope. "Until we get a copy of the specific coding..." he trailed off in consideration.

"What?" Ava asked with a sudden new hope.

He began tapping his finger on the edge of his chin. "This could work," he said to himself.

"What?" Ava pressed again.

"We would need to get into their mainframe, but we already have a plan in place that would allow us to. Of course, that would deter us from the other mission, but if we—"

"Sasha!" Mikel practically yelled at him. "You're rambling incoherently. Please, do share!"

Sasha looked up to face him. "It's risky," Sasha warned. "But at this point...."

"What have we got to lose?" Mikel offered, a reminder of their motto in the fight against Eli.

Sasha nodded. "I think the three of us can do this."

"The three of us?" Ava asked with sudden suspicion.

Sasha pursed his lips. "This may be a very bad idea. It is very risky, but if we do it right, it will only be my life at risk."

"No, Sasha," Ava objected. "I won't let you—"

"You don't have a choice!" Sasha raised his finger and spoke sternly at her.

Still, Ava would have objected, but Sasha spoke from a place of pain, frustration, fear and resolve, never wavering his hold on her eyes. "I sat and watched helplessly over a television screen as my wife was murdered before my eyes. Ava, you will not stop me in trying to protect you. The two of you can either help me, or stay the taint out of my way."

Ava almost flinched at the intensity of his tone. She had never seen him speak so fiercely, nor had Mikel.

After a moment to let that sink in, he softened his tone. "Now, I do believe my odds of success are much greater with your help."

"Then we're in," Mikel spoke for them both. "What's the plan?"

Sasha looked suddenly guilty. "We can't tell the others."

"What? Why?" Ava objected.

"Ava, I'm a man who believes in truth. I believe in trust, and I believe in honesty. However, there is something I value more, and that is doing what is mine to do, and allowing others to do the same. I have used deception in my mission for a lot of years. It's part of my work. Sometimes, I've even had to lie to those closest to me, to protect them and others."

"What does this have to do with telling our team some new addition to the plan?"

"If Jackson knows you're infected, do you really think he'll let you infiltrate the Towers with us? When you came this close to being crushed by that virus only a few hours ago?"

She didn't have an answer for that. Still, she didn't like this.

"More to the point, he would never let me be the one to risk myself the way I'm going to have to. He would take on the role himself. You both know that to be the truth. He will risk himself at every turn. He is so afraid to lose those he cares for, he won't allow them to do the same."

He sighed deeply as he considered. "We can't afford to lose Jackson right now. And the world most certainly can't. Me, on the other hand...."

"Sasha, don't say that!" Ava objected. "I won't let you go into this either. You're crazy!"

He raised his hand to hush her. "My love, please don't make the same mistake as Jackson in being unwilling to let others take risks with their own lives." He looked her in the eyes then, and the tears filled his once more. "Ava, your mother and I made the choice to fight, and if necessary, die for our missions. And I hate to ask this of you, and of you Mikel, but will you support me? And will you join me when it's yours to do?"

It didn't make sense. Everything he said sounded absolutely ludicrous—particularly the idea of keeping it all from their team leader. Wasn't this the type of cliché in all those dramas she had read that lead to utter catastrophe? Logically, it sounded insane and like a horrible idea. And yet, she could not deny how *right* it felt.

Maybe it was her utter trust in Sasha. Maybe it was his confidence that this was the right solution, even with deception. She didn't know for sure, but glancing at Mikel, she could sense in his demeanor that he felt the same way she did.

"If you die, Jackson will never forgive me," Ava muttered emotionally.

"But could you learn to forgive yourself?"

This she considered for a long time before agreeing. "If you ask me to support you, then I will."

"Me too," Mikel agreed. "But you better not die over this."

Sasha smiled. "If I have it my way, we'll all make it out alive."

She had already given her word, and she knew she would go through with it, but the pain in her heart was overwhelming at the thought that this might be the foolhardy plan that would lead to Sasha's death.

★ ★ ★ ★ ★

Eli loved his sister, but he hated Ava Altman.

He struggled to open the door to his quarters, shaking and in a stunned daze as he finally faced the truth of emotions he had never allowed himself to dwell on before: his rage toward Ava.

"How did it go?" Isabella asked absently from the side of the room. Eli waved his hand in the air to silence her, and she took the message.

He struggled to walk to the washroom door, and his hand was shaking slightly as he pulled the door closed. Eli made it to the mirror, and set his hands on the sink to stabilize himself. He stared at the man in the mirror, but the mask of Harrison had fallen. He looked weak, pale, and as broken as he felt. Ava had taken everything from him, once again.

These people would follow her without a second thought. She had swooped in and won them over in an instant, without really even having to try. Whereas Eli's unflagging months of labor and dedication to win them over were now meaningless.

Like every other time, Eli did the work, and came up empty. And all Ava had to do was flash her winning smile and she captivated them.

Eli gritted his teeth, staring at the man in the reflection, and hating what he saw.

For years, he had made it his calling to find the weakness in others and to rip it out of them. He had been successful in most every case he attempted. All but one.

No matter what he did to Ava, he could not get to her weakness. She wore her pains and struggles on her sleeve for him in a way that made her untouchable. He had done everything in his power to humble her—even to break her—for her own sake. All his attempts had come up empty.

Eli watched the mirror as his cheeks began trembling in anger.

Ava had never earned a tainted thing in her life. It was all handed to her. Where Eli worked his blistering carcass off day in and out to earn his place, Ava was handed titles and power and money simply because she entered the room, and fit nicely in it.

Eric had always been a placeholder after Harrison's death—everyone knew that. But what really got to Eli was the fact that Eric, and everyone else, had assumed the same thing of Eli.

He was the General's protégé! He was meant to be the General's successor! He had enacted Harrison's plan. This was *his* role! Yet, Eric handed over his title and wealth to Eli with an expiration date: Ava's coming of age. Eric, and Council, and everyone had seen Eli as another placeholder—for *Ava*, of all people!

She had never earned anything! She didn't deserve any of this. Eli had worked relentlessly. Ava didn't even have to try.

Eli's anger boiled into an intense fury.

He had done all that Harrison asked. He had carried out the General's final orders, at risk to his own freedom and very life! And yet, Ava, the perfect little golden child, had ruined everything by covering Harrison that day. Eli had to spend the rest of his life hiding his choice—the actions that Harrison had directly ordered! Whereas Ava got to be remembered as the hero. Eli had to pull the trigger, yet Ava received all the acclaim.

He let out a breath of hot fury.

Who was this child who swooped in and took everything away without thought?

She had stolen everything from him! Yet, *he* was made out to be the villain?

Eli didn't care about the money. But it was not right or fair that Eric would will it all to this insolent girl when Eli had worked beside Eric for seven years, guiding the Kingdoms and Eric through everything following Harrison's death!

He did not care about the title. But what right did Ava, naive little Ava, have to wear the General's name on her chest? What right did she have to be considered the hero?

His fury turned to a seething rage until his temples pulsed and his entire body trembled.

So many feelings, so much pain and betrayal and anger that he had kept inside himself for all of these years. It all seemed to erupt now.

When Kristen had uncovered the truth of Eli's involvement in Harrison's death, she had tried to get him to open up, to answer the painful questions—but he would not do so.

"You killed the General, Eli," she had finally said, "and you shot my baby girl. What do you want me to think? How do you want me to deal with this information? You need help, Eli. Or you need to tell me why you did it! I won't let this go."

She had chosen Ava.

He had no other choice. Leaking her whereabouts to Republic officers had been the only possibility. One little helpful tip that they would like what they found there, and they had bitten. He could not get her blood on his own hands—he could never have pulled the trigger on his mother. Yet, hadn't he done just that by telling them where to look for her?

He had almost immediately regretted his actions and had radioed a warning to the squadron, but apparently it was too late.

Kristen was dead because of her devotion to Ava. They all picked her. And for what reason? Ava had turned away from her mother, practically abandoned all love and relationship with her after the memory tampering. Eli had been there for Kristen every day of his life. Yet she, too, chose this worthless, insolent child?

Eli gripped the countertop until his knuckles went white. So much anger. So much hatred. So much fury.

Worst of all, Eli could not forget those final days with Harrison.

Eli was the General's hands. Harrison would say "make it so," and Eli would. Years of devotion and trust and work for this man. He had done everything for Harrison, without question, even so far as committing murder for him.

Ava had been nothing more than a child. She had never done anything for Harrison. Yet, in one moment the little golden child had won his heart and become his pride and joy.

Harrison loved and believed in Ava more than anyone in the world. All of Eli's years of devotion had ultimately meant nothing to the General. He still chose Ava. They all did. And that enraged him more than anything.

Sasha, Kristen, Harrison, Eric, Council, Lionel. Everyone. And now, even Brazil! They all picked Ava, every time, without fail. And she had never done anything to deserve it.

Yet, no matter how long or hard he worked, no one ever recognized Eli. No one picked him. No one cared about him. Not with golden little Ava around.

Eli did not remember pulling the trigger that day, but he felt that same intense rage he must have felt at the time, and he had no doubt that, even all those years ago, he had wanted to hurt her.

His white-knuckle grip increased till he thought he might break the tiling.

She had stolen his very birthright. She had taken everything and everyone that should have been his! Yet, he was supposedly the bad guy?

No. The story would not end like this. It was Eli's turn.

She had taken everything from him. Before this was all over, he would repay the favor.

Eli loved his sister. But he hated Ava Altman. And soon, she would know it.

Valkyrie raided the camp in the dead of night. No one knew she was coming. No one knew to fight or run or hide.

Australia was still not free of the invaders from the Republic, even after all this time. There were pockets of the enemy within their homeland, and Eli had sent her here to eliminate them.

No one in the camp was prepared. None of them knew what was about to hit them. No one except for Kyle.

He had been following her for over a day now. After returning to London, hacking into United Intelligence servers and discovering Valkyrie's whereabouts in the form of her current orders, he had gone quickly to Australia. It had taken him several days to find her. It wasn't all that difficult. He just had to go where the danger was. Valkyrie was likely to be there.

She entered the camp like a thief in the night, and he watched from behind the scenes. Valkyrie was a force of nature. Few stood a chance when facing her in battle, and this camp of officers was no different.

She could have taken them out like a wave, before anyone knew what hit them, but Kyle watched in surprise and confusion when she did the very unexpected.

After preparing a line of explosives on the only escape to the side of the beach where they camped, she snuck into the commanding officer's tent. Kyle listened with the ears of the Chameleon, happy to have his old friend back. That was the other thing he had done while in London. This suit was built for his body, so what use was it to the Kingdoms in storage anyway?

Of course, it provided Eli with a clue that he might not be so dead as assumed. But at this point, Kyle wasn't so sure he cared. What could Eli do to him now?

"Wake up," Valkyrie said, and Kyle's mouth dropped open in surprise.

She wasn't the type to arm a man before killing him. Honor and chivalry weren't necessarily tools on Valkyrie's tool belt. Mostly, she went in and did things quickly and quietly. Apparently, not tonight.

"Wake up," she commanded more forcefully.

Kyle narrowed the Chameleon's eyes, and it showed a thermal scan of the heat signatures in the room, though unfortunately, Valkyrie's nanites made her undetectable through the tent.

"Wake up," she commanded once more.

The officer shot up in his bed, clumsily retrieving a weapon which was now trained on Valkyrie. The man cursed.

"I want to give you and your men a chance to leave this place," Valkyrie said, and now it was Kyle who found himself cursing. What was she doing?

"I have orders to eliminate you as a threat. However, your location at the beach would make for an easy escape to your homeland."

"Your ships will shoot us down in the water!" the man shot back. "Why do you think we're still here?"

Kyle slowly moved forward, wishing he had a better view of Valkyrie in there.

"These are coordinates to a lane of safe passage," she said, and once more, Kyle cursed. That was not the type of thing to give one's enemy.

"You must think me mad!" the officer growled, but Kyle noted it was after several long moments of consideration. "What sort of twisted game are you playing?"

"No game," Valkyrie replied in monotone. "I am offering a way out for you and your men. Enough blood has been shed. Your government has already pulled the majority of their troops. Your brigade was just unlucky enough to be left behind."

"We tried to get out! But your soldiers blocked the only exit." The man spoke desperately, but still had a hint of anger, even through what sounded like pleading. "We've been waiting for an extraction, but my commanders said no help is coming."

"I know," Valkyrie replied, and there was almost a touch of understanding in her tone. Kyle neared the tent, close enough that he could hear their voices, almost without the Chameleon's ears. "That's why I'm trying to give it to you."

The man hesitated for a long time. "Why?"

"As I said, enough blood has been shed. Our people have retaken our land. We have exchanged prisoners of war. There is no need for you and your men to be massacred."

"You would give me safe passage, for nothing in return?" he asked in pure shock, which Kyle was just as overwhelmed with in that moment.

"Yes," Valkyrie replied simply.

"Why? Who are you?"

She said nothing.

"What assurance do I have that your ships won't destroy us as soon as we're within range?"

"None."

"I'm sorry, that's not good enough for me." He raised his weapon higher.

"Then my friend will stop you before you have the chance to fire," she replied.

Just then, the man prepared to fire, and Kyle jumped inside the tent, retrieving the weapon before the bullet left the gun, and putting the man in a chokehold until he went unconscious. All the while Valkyrie stood there casually, as if she had been expecting it. Only when Kyle let the drooping man to the floor and stood up to face Valkyrie did it register what she had said.

"Wait," Kyle suddenly said as he uncamouflaged himself with the Chameleon. "Did you just say, 'Your friend?' You knew I was here?"

"You've been trailing me for over a day now," she replied in monotone.

"Huh...I never can deceive you, can I?"

She didn't answer, instead looking down at the unconscious man and seeming strangely sad.

"So, um, what the taint was all that?" Kyle asked, gesturing to the unconscious man as well as to her.

Valkyrie turned. "I was giving him a chance," she replied, that similar sad tone coloring her words as it had her expression.

"Yeah; why, exactly?"

"Maybe I'm tired of killing people," she muttered.

"What?" Kyle pressed, walking up closer to her. He had heard her just fine, but he couldn't believe she had said it.

"Maybe I'm tired of killing people," Valkyrie replied, putting slow emphasis on every word for him.

He watched her for a long time before responding. "Are you?"

She watched him before admitting, "This is your fault."

"What? How is it my fault?"

"Because before you, I just did my job. I didn't have to think about whether it was wrong or right—whether Eli was wrong or right. I just did my job. But now...." She trailed off, and Kyle watched her in shock.

"Did you know that several of these officers have their children with them?" Valkyrie said, gesturing to the camp outside. "Things were so secure in Australia that some officers brought their families to live as they occupied. Then we drove them out, and continue to do so, without considering the casualties."

"They invaded our homeland," Kyle replied pointedly. "They killed thousands of men, women and children. They drove people from their homes. They subjugated millions."

"Yes, they did," Valkyrie agreed. "But him?" she pointed at the officer on the ground. "He was just doing his job. They were all just following orders. Just like I have been."

It wasn't that Kyle didn't agree with her. It wasn't that he didn't often have deeper thoughts about such horrors within war. But to hear this from Valkyrie? It was shocking enough to have him on defense, even if she was right.

He considered for a long time before asking frankly, "So what was your plan? How were you going to get them safely home? You really think the naval fleet will let them pass just because you say please? And if you did give them real coordinates to safety, and it got back to Eli, then what?"

"I don't know," Valkyrie admitted. "I don't have my entire life planned out. I was just thinking about this one move."

"Well, you can't do that!" Kyle said, a bit too forcefully. "You can't just think one move ahead in something like this."

"Why not?" she challenged. "Why can't I just make one decision, and then the next?"

"Because! It's all well and good to save these people tonight, but if they get captured or killed in the waters anyway, and word gets back to Eli, you could be in serious trouble!"

"That's my choice," Valkyrie replied defensively. "I get to have at least that, don't I?"

He stared at her without comprehension. "What are you talking about?"

"Everyone else gets to make decisions. Why not me?"

"Listen, Valkyrie, following orders is a decision. And if Eli gives you the wrong orders, then that's on him!"

"Then why did you leave?"

Kyle watched her helplessly. Of course, what she was saying had merit. But it was like a child trying to comprehend something so much bigger than them. "It's complicated," Kyle muttered, when he had no better answers.

"Too complicated for me?" Valkyrie asked, and the look in her eyes was of hurt.

Kyle sighed, not knowing how to solve this, particularly right now with an entire camp of enemy officers surrounding them. "Are you going to wreck this camp tonight?" he asked, mostly just to know what their next steps should be.

"No," she replied sternly.

"Then let's put some distance between ourselves and it, and we'll talk about this moral dilemma when we can breathe properly."

"Is the elevation affecting you?" she asked, and though she meant it sincerely, he was just a bit offended by the insinuation.

"What? No! I just mean, we're surrounded by enemies! It's easier to breathe away from them."

"Did the officer knock the air out of you?"

"What? No! Would you stop?"

"My breathing is fine," Valkyrie replied seriously.

Kyle huffed in annoyance before being taken in by how cute and innocent she looked, standing there uncomprehending. He walked closer, and closer still until his mouth was an inch from hers. "How about now?" he whispered through a loving smile.

"Harder now," she admitted, and it was clear she was indeed struggling to breathe normally.

"Then let's get out of here."

She nodded her agreement and they carefully made their exit.

★ ★ ★ ★ ★

"From Brazil to Russia, Africa to Korea to France, there are some things all of us as people share. We all feel pain. We all experience love. We have the inner desire to be free, an inner hope that cannot be truly defeated. We're united by these commonalities.

"Whatever governments and officials rule, we cannot judge an entire people by the few. Humanity is within us all. I have been to all of these nations and more. I have seen that same desire, that same pain, that same hope, in the faces of the children in the bitterest pits of the Republic, and the brightest homes of the Kingdoms.

"This war has been long, painful, and brutal. It has touched every man, woman and child in the world. We have all felt that suffering. We have all felt that hope. We have all felt that desire. For sixty years, governments have waged war in hopes of gaining power—some in the name of peace, others in the name of prosperity. I have seen the leaders of many nations corrupted by power. Corrupted by violence. Corrupted by this war.

"Until now, I had not ever seen anyone who fought in the name of the people. The success that the new third side has been having is not because of stronger battalions or more powerful technology alone. The success is the people's.

"The nation of Russia has become a free state. The countries of Africa have become independent of their oppressors. And today, Brazil joins the success of the people. We are a free state. We are independent of our oppressors. And as we continue to fight for the rights of the people, our success will be immeasurable.

"For, try as they might, oppressors may succeed for a time. But the fight for freedom will always win in the end."

"She's good," Volvakov noted, watching the passionate woman on the screen as she united yet another nation to The Cause.

"She had a good teacher," Jackson agreed, thinking of Lionel, and wishing he'd had a chance to truly get to know the man.

"She has the same vigor and passion as the General—the first one," Minister Stepanov of foreign affairs said as he watched the large screen.

"Still young, and inexperienced," President Volvakov agreed, "but she'll get there."

Jackson's attention turned back to Ava as she neared the end of the speech. Her face became somber and serious, and she spoke more reverently, speaking now in Mandarin. "For those of you still racked by your oppressors, do not lose heart. Your time is coming. Your moment is nearing. We fight for the people. And should they choose to fight with us, the people will be free."

"Well done, Jackson," Zukov congratulated. "Another well-written speech."

"Wasn't mine," he replied proudly. "She wrote it."

The others seemed impressed as the speech ended. "Did we broadcast it to the whole of the Republic?" Volvakov asked to be certain.

Jackson nodded. "Yes, sir. We're preparing them with every announcement of more success."

"Then, come tomorrow..." Volvakov trailed off.

"Come tomorrow," Jackson continued where the president had left off, "the Republic will begin an inner revolution with the help of The Cause. For better or worse, everything changes and begins tomorrow."

"Well, you've done it, Jackson," Stepanov declared with a deep sigh. "You have Russia on your side, even in this insane attempt. But if you don't make good on your promises...I'll kill you myself."

Jackson smiled. "I would expect nothing less, Minister."

★ ★ ★ ★ ★

"Do you believe I should have massacred that camp?" Valkyrie asked with a bit of accusation.

Kyle glanced at the fire, warming his hands by holding them out in front of the flames. "Not exactly," he admitted. "I don't necessarily think your hands would be dirty if you *did*. That camp is filled with enemy soldiers who invaded our land and murdered our people. You're right that they were just following orders and doing their jobs. But our job is to protect our people, and follow our orders. If that means we have to purge enemy soldiers from our land, then so be it."

"What orders do you follow now?" she asked. He knew she didn't mean to challenge him; she genuinely wanted to know. But it felt all too much like his inner turmoil, wondering often if he had done the right thing, or if he was a traitor to his homeland and nation.

Kyle looked down at the fire, not having an answer for her.

"Jackson's?" Valkyrie offered.

"Sort of," he replied. "I mean, yes, I guess so."

"Jackson is no longer on Eli's side," Valkyrie observed.

He found himself suddenly frustrated by her again, wishing she understood everything the way he did. "No, he's not."

"But The Cause that he commands has gained a lot of ground in the past months."

Kyle looked up at her in surprise. "You know about that?"

"Doesn't everyone know?" she replied as if it were obvious. "The leader Sizwe Jelani's speech, a recent speech from the president of Russia, and now Ava's speech in Brazil today."

Kyle nodded. "I mean, yeah, I know about it. I just didn't know you would."

"Are you a part of The Cause?" Valkyrie asked with genuine interest.

"Yeah," Kyle admitted gruffly, though even admitting that was difficult to do. "I guess I am."

"Then why are you ashamed?" she asked, once more surprising him with how much she understood, even if it didn't always come out in her words.

"I don't know exactly. I'm proud. I really believe in the leaders and The Cause. I really believe in what they're doing. But...I still can't help but feeling like...." He couldn't finish.

"Like a traitor," Valkyrie finished for him, and eventually Kyle nodded.

A long silence passed before Valkyrie asked, "Why did you come here, Kyle?"

He didn't have a response, not for a long time. "I don't know really," he lied.

He had been so certain before finding Valkyrie, of what he needed to do, and of his ability to get her on their side. But now...for some reason, he could not seem to do it.

"Is it possible that the answer could be different for some of us than it is for others?" she asked, once again surprising him with her depth, when so often her language came off like a child.

He looked up to face her.

"You came to get me," Valkyrie said, as if somehow she had known all along.

Kyle nodded shamefully.

"Then why haven't you asked me?"

He stared at her for a long time, with no response.

Eventually, she stood from her place in the dirt on the other side of the fire, sat beside him and looked up into his eyes. Well, if it had been hard to face her before....

"Why haven't you asked me?" she pressed with care.

He shook his head, unable to reply.

"Because you already know the answer?" she offered in almost a whisper.

He finally managed to face her. "Why is that the answer?" he asked with sudden frustration. "If you're questioning Eli. If you believe in The Cause. You believe in both Jackson and Ava. Why is this your answer?"

"I haven't given it yet," she replied somberly.

"Yes, you have," he huffed. "I knew it the moment I saw you!"

"Why?" she pressed. It was clear she was simply attempting to get the words out of him, since she already knew the answers for herself.

"Because!" he shot in anger. "Because you're too busy making a mess of your orders. Because you're stuck doing the General's bidding! Because you're a robot assassin!"

She cocked her head. He could see the slight hurt, though she managed not to take it personally. "Why, Kyle?" she pressed.

He looked down and gritted his teeth. "Because of Eli," he said through his clenching jaw.

Valkyrie smiled softly, looking as sad as he was angry. "He would never let me go," she said regretfully.

"He wouldn't have a choice!" Kyle growled. "We'll take him down! He will have no power over you. We'll get you away from him, and he can never hurt you again!"

She shook her head sadly. "My chip, the things they did to me, it's not like the rest of you," she explained. "You know that, deep down, don't you?"

He swallowed hard. "Ava got out."

"She had Jackson, and Russia."

He looked at her helplessly. "You have me."

She smiled tenderly. He could feel her love for him, but still, her answer would not change. He knew that much.

"You don't know the power they have over me, Kyle. You don't know what would happen if I tried to disobey him."

"You're twisting his orders right now!" he replied, indicating the camp far out in the distance.

"It's not the same," Valkyrie replied, "and you know that. He expects obedience of me, and so he offers me some extent of freedom. But if I were to challenge him...or leave him..." she shook her head.

Kyle cursed in frustration, and when she offered her comforting hand on his arm, he pushed it off. He stood up and paced by the fire.

"Kyle," Valkyrie spoke softly. "Please, don't be angry with me."

"I'm not!" he nearly screamed. Then his anger fumed. "It's him. I hate him! I hate the power he has. I hate that he won't hesitate to use it. I hate him!"

Valkyrie stood and walked to where he stood. Gently she reached her hands out and placed them on his. "There's too much hatred in the world," she spoke sweetly, even in her monotone voice.

His anger subsided as he looked into her eyes, replaced by a deep sadness that he didn't know how to handle as his eyes flooded with tears. Kyle was not one to cry, and this feeling was awkward and uncomfortable, but he forgot it in the look she gave him.

"I think," he started, and had to stop as his voice cracked with emotion, "I think I might love you, Valkyrie."

Her eyes were just as touched by sadness at first, but then it melted into a peaceful acceptance and she smiled, sweetly, though just as pained. "That's better," she said softly. "That's what we need more of."

The tears spilled down his cheeks, and he could no longer find that anger that had fueled him to be strong before. All he felt now was a deep love, and an overwhelming sadness that left him feeling weak and helpless. "I don't want to lose you, Valkyrie," he whispered in pain.

"Then don't," she replied, still managing to smile when he was there, a total mess. She placed her hand on his chest, as if to touch his beating heart. "That's the good thing about love. You don't have to lose anyone. They can stay right there with you forever."

He wanted to tell her that in her innocence, she had misunderstood him again. But it was clear from her expression that she understood perfectly.

"If he does..." Valkyrie began, but struggled to say the words that both of them dreaded. Then she pulled his hand to hers and placed them both on her heart this time. "Just know, I haven't lost you either. Even if he makes me forget myself."

He watched her sadly for a long time before muttering a promise to remember. Then he leaned in and kissed her, knowing that they had so little time now, and desperately wishing for more.

She allowed him to kiss her for several seconds before she pushed him away. She looked breathless and a bit starry eyed, but also intent. "We'll get to that," she promised. "But first...." The look in her eyes was one of intense concentration.

Kyle leaned back and narrowed his eyes suspiciously. When he was sure he had figured her out, he chuckled. "We're going to go rescue that camp, aren't we?"

Valkyrie grinned.

14

Waves

"Listen up, people," Nastia commanded the crew as if it was her squadron. "No one touches her. No one talks to her. No one even looks at her. You got it? Our safety requires her complete focus. She loses that for even a second, we're all dead. Understood?"

The squadron all responded in the affirmative. Nastia looked directly at Jackson. "You got that, squad leader?"

He raised his eyebrows at the challenge, glancing behind Nastia to the vehicle where Ava stood. She had her hair down and curled, which was vastly different from her usual fighting style. Her eyes were closed tightly, her ear buds were in and already playing music loudly. Jackson had seen the videos of Ava and Mikel conquering the Towers, with Nastia and her people as protection. Still, seeing this woman, his woman, so close, and yet entirely in her own world, was strange. They hadn't even had a chance to say hello again. Even here at the designated point, Ava was already practicing, working on her connection with the Beijing Tower an hour from here.

"Yup," Jackson replied, still watching Ava.

"Good," Nastia said coolly. Then she turned to the others. "If I'm killed, you people better not let my work be for nothing! Take over her protection. We have to win this thing." She spoke intensely, then stepped back and approached Ava.

Gently, she touched Ava's arm, then, when she had her attention, she reached up and pulled out the earbud. "You good to go?" Nastia whispered.

Ava didn't open her eyes or reply verbally. All her concentration was already on the enemy. She simply nodded.

Nastia put the earbud back and walked to Jackson's position. "Listen," she said quietly, so as not to be heard by the rest of the squad. "My job is to protect her. I'm good at it. She trusts me beside her in battle. I'll keep her safe. So, you need to focus one hundred percent on your part. Got it?"

Jackson smiled at the serious intensity of this woman as she commanded him. "Yup," Jackson replied again.

"Good," Nastia replied, then looked a bit awkward as she stepped down from being so fully in his face.

"You still remember who's leading this squad, right?" Jackson asked, honestly not sure if she did.

She softened her intensity and looked more subdued suddenly. "Yeah, I know."

"Good. Then you do your job and I'll do mine. Yeah?"

Nastia raised her chin and resumed that arrogant air. He didn't mind so much if that arrogance kept Ava safe today. "Yes, sir."

Jackson offered a salute, and she returned it. "They're all yours," she said, backing down and resuming her position by Ava.

"All right, squad," Jackson addressed them now. "This has to be as close to flawless as possible. There are too many moving parts to screw this one up. Everyone, remember your job and do it well. Let's move out!"

Nastia helped Ava into their vehicle, and the squad piled into the other two.

At the four major Towers in the Republic, at rendezvous points like this, squadrons just like this one were gathering and preparing for the fight of their life.

★ ★ ★ ★ ★

Sasha waited at the rendezvous point for their final squad members to show. Generally, such high-tech operations were performed at night, for maximum efficiency. However, part of Jackson's plan was the hype and media coverage they would undoubtedly receive from doing it in the daylight hours. The people had to know about this attack, and no better way to show them than conducting it in broad daylight. It was nearing noon now, and the operation was on schedule.

Ava and Mikel had been sent separately into the two most powerful Towers, so their connection against the greater enemy would be better; but each of them also connected long distance with the other Towers.

The simultaneous attack would target the four main Towers of the Republic at once. One in China, where Jackson commanded a squad, one in Korea, where Kyle led a team, one in India, where Sasha was in charge, and one in Kazakhstan, where Vasiliv led a squad. Each force was also equipped with at least one Tower specialist to do the reprogramming. Sasha, Jackson and Kyle doubled as team leader and Tower specialist, where Zak was a member of Vasiliv's team to do the programming.

Mikel and Ava had personal protectors, and along with that, each squad was composed of elite ops specialists to form a small army at the four attack points.

There were so many details, so many moving parts, but if they could pull this off...the Republic would never recover from such a crippling blow.

There was only one small problem. Along with the overall plan, which was complicated enough as it was, Sasha had his own agenda, and it mattered just as much to him as the ultimate, greater plan.

They had to find a way to stop Counter Intelligence—*permanently*. He would complete the mission and the reprogramming before he remained there in search of answers; but he would not leave the Tower without them. Even if it killed him to accomplish it.

Mikel scanned his connection with the Towers, preparing for the battle that would ensue. Ava would personally fend off Counter Intelligence at all of the four Towers and focus on some simple commands within Beijing where needed. Mikel would keep the basic threat level down from the four Towers, close off enemy soldiers, turn off weaponry, and whatever else he could to keep the squadrons safe, as well as opening doors and offering safe passage in the remaining three Towers—other than Ava's.

They had their work cut out for them, to say the least. Of course, it didn't help that they were two minutes away from deployment, and their team leader hadn't arrived.

"Anything?" Mikel pressed the scouting officer.

"Nothing, sir."

Mikel huffed in annoyance. "Kyle, you better show!"

Mikel believed he could lead this squad while controlling the Towers, but he most certainly couldn't do the techy stuff that Kyle needed to— although some of the others here were trained to handle it, if nothing else.

Another minute passed, and Mikel stared at his wristwatch. At the thirty second mark, he moved to address the now impatient squadron. "All right, guys," he offered confidently. "Change of plans. I'll take lead—"

"Second," a gruff voice stopped him mid-sentence. "You mean you'll take second, as always."

Mikel grinned as Kyle pulled into the group. "You always did like to take your time," Mikel teased. Then, noticing the solemn look on his face, Mikel sobered. "No Valkyrie?"

Kyle simply shook his head.

Mikel offered a sympathetic expression before turning to the link. *"Ava, relay to Jackson. Valkyrie is a no go. Tell him to pull in the secondary drones for you guys. You're going to need them there."*

"Understood."

"Well...?" Mikel said, turning things over to Kyle for a little pep talk.

"You know what to do," Kyle spoke to the squad. "Let's move!"

★ ★ ★ ★ ★

"Valkyrie's not coming," Ava muttered.

"What?" Nastia asked, moving in closer.

It took every ounce of focus to keep Counter Intelligence at bay and stop it from infecting the several Zhànshì and Sasha as they neared the Towers. She kept her eyes closed. She allowed her mind to move with the rhythm of the song playing in her ears.

She had been fighting this enemy a long time, in the back of her mind, and she had gotten good at it. But fighting against the push of Counter Intelligence as it actively fought against the minds of, not one, but four other people, was another story entirely.

She wasn't so sure of her ability to keep it at bay and still get them safely into the Beijing Tower. Even these months of training, even the constant fight against her greatest foe, had not fully prepared her for how powerful the Beijing Tower was compared to any other she had been to. Suddenly, she wondered if it shouldn't be Mikel here instead. He was so much better at swimming with the current of the Tower than she was.

"Tell Squad Leader," Ava muttered, still attempting to focus fully on the greater threat, "Valkyrie is not coming. We need the backup drones."

"Understood," Nastia said, and moved to her radio.

Ava was conscious of the fact that Jackson was here, in the vehicle ahead, but that was not something she could allow her mind to give any attention to. It was too consumed in the battle that had already begun for her, even if the others sat in anticipation of what lay ahead.

She was aware of the risks in Sasha's secondary plan and the fact that she might lose him today, but this, too, was not something she could risk thinking about. Anything that broke her focus was unacceptable right now. Too many other lives were at stake—not just her own, like it used to be when her mind wandered in the fight.

Eli would be proud. She had finally learned the lesson he wanted her to. Only, it wasn't he who had taught her. It was an enemy more powerful than she could imagine, more incredible than she could describe. An enemy that had already infected her with its venom. One moment of breaking focus, and four others would be immediately killed by the venom too. Her one consolation was that Jackson no longer had the chip, and that he, at least, was safe from Counter Intelligence.

This enemy may yet succeed in killing her. But not today. Not if she had anything to do with it.

★ ★ ★ ★ ★

"One minute to game time," Jackson said through his earpiece. At times like this, there was a part of him that really missed the link. The others could talk easily, communicate during the entire operation with nothing but a thought. He still believed it was necessary that he be the one to take the step of chip removal. The others had to know it was an option. Viktoriya had been afraid to do it, and only after Jackson's success had she been willing to undergo the surgery. He wouldn't change his choice, but a small part of him envied the others and the conversations they would surely have today, where he must rely on the earpiece.

"Are all squadrons in position?" he asked the team leaders.

"Affirmative," Vasiliv replied first. "Squad four is in position."

"Squadron two is on target," Kyle replied next.

"Squadron three is in position," Sasha replied.

"Tech support is on task," came the last response from HQ.

The seconds passed. The vehicles pulled in closer to the vicinity of the Beijing Tower.

"On my mark," Jackson said as the vehicles raced closer still. "Three. Two. One. Mark!"

The vehicles skidded to a stop at the entrance at the same time that the previously smoke screened drones began an attack on the Tower—another thing Mikel had managed to do, by hiding the drones from each Tower's radar until it was too late.

Jackson and his team piled from the vehicles, using them for cover as they began a rain of fire on the gates.

Nastia hovered close beside Ava, protecting her from any outside threat, though Ava's greater enemy would be in her mind.

The officers at the gates immediately began to return fire, but the drones had the gates cleared even before Ava had them open.

"Move in!" Jackson ordered, and the team piled past the vehicles through the first gate.

"Anti-aircraft is powering up again," one of the officers declared urgently. "They got it back online!"

Jackson glanced at Ava, hoping she knew it too.

Nastia made a nasty face at him, a reminder not to say a word. He refrained.

A few seconds later, the Tower's anti-aircraft system powered down.

"Move, move, move!" Jackson ordered, and they ran through the entrance. By that time, the next gate had opened, and again before the team entered the secondary gate, the drones had cleared the area.

Five outer gates before they made it to the main entrance of the Tower, and by then, backup for the enemy officers was flooding in from behind. Ava closed and sealed the gates, keeping anyone else from following them.

They made it to the main entrance, and Jackson pushed past the sea of fallen Republic officers who had been taken down by the drones, regretting the long list of casualties. This operation would, unfortunately, not be painless. However, to cripple the oppressive government, this move was necessary. He was just glad that, thanks to the chip, this attack would be far less horrific than it might have been otherwise, for both sides.

They waited longer at the final gate as Ava attempted to command the Tower doors open, while the lockdown instigated by their attack fought her commands.

"Move to the sides," Jackson urged. "Let the drones clear our path as much as possible before we move in. Be prepared for an army waiting for us inside."

Within another five seconds, the door opened. Shots fired from within, but the guards were unable to stop the drones as they entered. Ava closed the door once the drones were inside.

That hadn't exactly been his plan. He didn't like the image of the massacre inside. Then again, without Valkyrie's help on this, perhaps it was necessary.

The doors opened again, leaving a path that had been cleared by the drones for the team through the lobby.

Jackson led the squad through the foyer, and signaled for the teams to split. There would be five teams of four at this Tower. Each of the other four teams would go in for an extraction of a Politburo member within the Tower.

They had intel on the whereabouts of all thirteen Politburo members throughout the Republic. Ten of them were within Towers, the other three at their homes or abroad. All of them would be captured today.

Ava and Nastia remained with Jackson and two other officers as the rest of the squad peeled off. They arrived at the stairwell, and Jackson was about to lead them in when Nastia shouted, "Hold!"

He looked back. Ava had her arm up in the hold position, and Nastia translated. Jackson and the others took defensive positions until Ava's signal gave them the go ahead.

Priority one of this operation was the thirteen extractions. But priority two was almost as important. They would upload an untraceable program into the Tower interface at each of the secondary command centers. With the Towers on lockdown in this state of panic, there was little to no chance they would make it into the core, but if they could flood enough of the secondary command centers with this new program, then the Tower would follow the command coding on the reboot.

While the other four teams in Beijing focused fully on extractions, Jackson's small team would move to the secondary command centers and upload the program.

This same two-point operation was being run at each of the other three Towers. Small crews would focus on extractions, while the team with a Tower specialist would upload the program at each of the secondary command points.

Jackson's team made it to the first control center, and Jackson began the upload. Zak had created a compressed file that managed to upload the entire program in a matter of seconds. The first one went smoothly.

"All right," Jackson said, turning to the others. One down, fourteen more to go."

★ ★ ★ ★ ★

Open this door. Close that one. Shut off that light. Seal that entrance. Shut off that system. Open that door again.

The input and output were going a hundred miles a minute in his mind. In the past, Mikel had been able to work with the Towers easily, eyes wide open as he walked through the battle scene. But very quickly in this one, he had to close his eyes and use the earbud he carried in his vest just in case in one ear. The other ear held an earpiece radio for communication with the other squads.

One of Vasiliv's Elites, Pierre, whom Mikel knew well, led him just like Ava's bodyguard did for her. Still, it wasn't necessary. He knew where he was. He knew what he was doing. It just required every ounce of his focus to sway three Towers in literally sixteen different directions at once.

Kyle and his team grew frustrated again at the long wait as Mikel focused on clearing a path for Sasha and Vasiliv's teams.

"*Let's go, Mikel!*" Kyle pressed through the link, though he was standing right beside him.

"*Working on it.*"

Another door opened. Another closed. Another weapons system shut off. Another pathway blocked from advancing enemy soldiers. Those months of training could not have prepared him for how involved this fight was.

"Man down! Man down! Taking heavy fire!" a Russian officer yelled through the earpiece.

Mikel cursed and removed the radio from his ear, quickly closing the door for the men under fire. He had missed a team, for a split second. Someone was dead because of it.

"Move faster," Kyle urged in a hoarse whisper.

"I have a lot of people to focus on!" Mikel rebutted. "We're safe right now. Some of them aren't! Shut up and let me work!"

He replaced the earpiece back into his ear, and turned the music louder on the earbud on the other side.

"We need cover!" an officer shouted. Mikel turned off the weapons system that threatened them, and they were able to move freely once more.

"*How's it going on your end?*" Mikel reached out to Ava through the link, hoping for better news.

There was a long pause before a response came. "*Don't talk to me unless it's absolutely necessary.*"

"*That bad?*"

"*What did I just say?*" she pressed.

Mikel's mood lightened in response to her testiness, despite his frustration at the three lives lost already.

The door opened and Kyle led the team forward to the station right on the other side.

Mikel was grateful for a moment's respite from this team to focus on the others while the upload took place.

"Done," Kyle said as another upload completed. "Get us to the next one."

Mikel cursed.

Block off the enemy here. Close them in there. Make a path for the allies here. Clear a line of safety there.

Close this door. Shut off that system. Protect those men. Close off those ones.

This was the battle of his life, but as always, he was up for the challenge.

And it had all started with a flickering wall light.

☆ ☆ ☆ ☆ ☆

Pushing. Pulling. One moment she was sinking. The next she was floating. Spinning in circles. Being crushed by a wave. Pushing it aside. Swimming through the deep. Drowning in the surf.

Counter Intelligence was a force to be reckoned with, and every second that force seemed to grow stronger. The constant distraction in the Tower, having to get her teams to the next section and the next, broke her focus on an enemy that would crush them all if it could.

One moment she was drowning. Then she was gasping for breath. She was only ever hanging on by a thread. She never had the upper hand against this foe.

In a normal fight, she got in as many good hits as her enemy. But there was no hitting this one. There was no weakening this adversary. It had a never-ending supply of strength and endurance, and every second she was growing weaker.

No training could have prepared her for this. Nothing could have.

She heard Jackson's voice in a lull in her music. "We've been here too long. They're right outside."

"She'll get it!" Nastia rebuked.

"Or I will," Jackson said, letting his weapon hang on its sling and going to the door.

"What are you doing?" Nastia questioned in anger.

"Opening the door," he replied.

"And what if the enemy's on the other side?"

"Then we'll eliminate them. They're gonna break down the door behind us any second, and we're running out of time before the entire Tower is overrun by their defense teams."

Ava turned up her music.

The water threatened to crush her. Threatened to sweep her underneath, wave after wave until her lungs collapsed.

She swam to the top, gasping once more for breath as she was relieved from the water. But there was no attacking a vast ocean in return. She could fight all she wanted. But ultimately, she would be drowned. The ocean would win out. There was no way to defeat an enemy that was a very force of nature.

She felt Nastia pull her forward, which must have meant that Jackson opened the door. Or had she done that? She could not remember.

They had a whole eleven minutes from start to finish until the Republic backup forces would overrun the Towers, and there would be no escape.

They were closing in on that deadline, though she could not say how much longer they had.

Ava stopped in her tracks, literally gasping for breath now as Counter Intelligence sent a heavy wave that shook her.

However much time was left on the clock, it didn't matter. They had to hurry. She would not survive much more of this.

☆ ☆ ☆ ☆ ☆

"How many is that again?" Sasha asked, losing track, even though it was him who had been doing the uploading.

"Five," Ella answered, and there was no impatience in her tone, which he appreciated.

"Great. Only two more."

"We should have sent more Zhànshì to Beijing," Ella said regretfully as they hurried to the next section, waiting for Mikel to open the door for them. "You haven't needed me here, but I have a feeling that things are worse at a Tower where they have fifteen program points. Not to mention the extractions!"

"They'll be fine," Sasha replied confidently. "Besides, you'll need to take leadership of this team if anything happens to me."

Ella's face lit up with suspicion. "What's that supposed to mean?"

The next door opened, and the team rushed through. "It means...I'm getting old."

"He's taking way too long on this," Vasiliv growled in anger.

"He's kind of got a lot on his plate," Zak responded defensively.

"We're running out of time," Vasiliv replied. "We should never have trusted an entire plan to a couple of twenty-year-olds who have to do it all at four different Towers!"

Zak glanced at his watch in sudden agreement. "We didn't," he replied, moving to the door and working on opening it. "There's a reason he put a Tower specialist on every team." He got into the wires and moved them around while Vasiliv watched in confusion. "We may not be as fast or efficient as Mikel or Ava, but fortunately for you," the door opened, and Zak smiled, "I am very good at this."

★ ★ ★ ★ ★

"Three more," Kyle spoke as another program finished its upload. "And five minutes to go. We're doing great! Now, hurry it up, Mikel."

"You just said we were doing great!" Mikel argued.

"No thanks to you," Kyle replied sarcastically. "Let's go!"

"Working on it," Mikel replied dryly. "There's for Sasha. There's Vasiliv's, and there's yours."

The door opened.

"Move!" Kyle commanded them all through.

"A thank you once in a while would be nice."

★ ★ ★ ★ ★

"It's too much," Ava muttered as they pulled to another stop. "No, I can't. It's too much."

470

Jackson went to the door and tried to work on it quickly. He had so far had little success in getting the doors opened before Ava eventually got around to it, but there was no point in sitting there waiting.

"It's too strong," she muttered again to herself.

Jackson glanced to where she stood, a sudden concern forming in his mind.

She was shaking her head slowly, muttering to herself. "It's too much. No. I can't do it." Her hands went to her head and she held it tightly. Everyone in the team watched her unconsciously. Up until now she had completely kept to herself, but these sudden mutterings and gaspings were a bit frightening, especially for Jackson.

He turned away from the door and took a step closer to Ava.

"Don't!" Nastia commanded him. "Stay back."

He didn't ever really like being bossed by this woman, but it was particularly bothersome to him at that moment.

"I can't…it's winning. It's winning. I can't. I can't."

He took another step closer, and Nastia moved her body in front of him to stop him. He glared down at her, but her scowl was just as strong. "She will be fine," Nastia spoke sternly. "Don't mess with her, or you'll make it worse."

He looked across at Ava again, and watched her for a time. Soon enough, her hands lowered again, and the door opened.

Jackson took point once more, leaving Nastia to watch over Ava, but hating every second of it.

"Let's move!"

"So that's it?" Ella asked in surprise. "We're done? That was way too easy."

"You should never say that, my dear," Sasha warned as the backup team followed their lead. "It's an invitation for disaster."

Ella rolled her eyes. "That's an old wives' tale, if I've ever heard one."

"Old wives usually knew what they were talking about," Sasha replied with a chuckle. He turned down a hall, but the wrong one.

"It's this way," Ella corrected him.

Sasha stopped and faced the team. "We have finished our objective several minutes ahead of time, which was my hope. Our other team members have already left the building with the Politburo members. Now I need to use these final few minutes to gain access to the core."

"What, are you insane?" Ella spat.

"Possibly," Sasha affirmed. "However, I am very serious about this. You may take the team and exit. I need to do this first." He turned to leave.

"*What?*" Ella demanded. "*What* are you doing?"

He stopped, facing her once more, looking very serious as he considered whether to tell the truth or not. "I'm going to find a cure for Counter Intelligence," he blurted, and she could tell it was the truth.

"Why now?" Ella asked forcefully. "Why in the middle of this?"

"We may never have another chance," he offered.

"That's a load of taint!" Ella called him on it. "When they turn on the full global Tower Network and we gain complete access to Tower servers, you could acquire it then."

Sasha's face sobered. "When the reboot occurs, their previous systems and information will be erased. There is a chance, in the long run, that we may acquire the answers. However, it may be too late for Ava by then."

Ella involuntarily gasped. Her words were soft and somber, "She's been infected?"

Sasha nodded painfully. "And I'm running out of time."

Ella looked up and faced him. "You're right, Sasha. We are." Then she turned to the squadron. "Move out! We'll meet you at the rendezvous point."

"Yes, ma'am."

Ella expected Sasha to object. Most people would. Most of her friends all wanted to play the hero, without letting anyone else risk themselves, but not Sasha. He looked her in the eyes somberly when she returned to face him. "Are you sure?" he asked simply, giving her an out if she wanted one.

"You're getting old, remember? You're gonna need me if you have any hope of success."

He smiled. "Honestly, Ella, I think that you are right about that."

✯ ✯ ✯ ✯ ✯

They broke into the psychiatric ward and doctors and workers screamed, flooding to the walls with their hands up.

Ava pointed her finger in the right direction, and they ran toward the closed door that opened just in time for them. Several more doors, and a few orderlies and security guards to get through before they made it to the right place.

Two doctors from within screamed and got down on the floor on Jackson's frightening command.

Jun was wearing a straitjacket, and struggled to get up and run to the side of the room. She screamed in terror as Jackson approached, but he lowered his weapon.

Ava opened her eyes as Jackson neared the terror-stricken woman, trembling in fear at the side of the rubber walls.

"It's okay, Jun," he spoke in that gentle, loving way that only he could do so well. "It's okay. It's Jackson. It's me."

The terror remained as she mouthed that name over and over again, as if trying to remember where she'd heard it before. Then the realization touched her eyes, and she looked up at him with a new light. "Jackson?" she said weakly. "My Jackson?"

"It's me," he said, reaching his hands out to her. She pulled forward and into his arms, and he held her for a second before relating to her the need to hurry. "We need to go, but we're going to get you to safety. I promise."

She believed him wholly and started forward as he directed.

Ava swallowed her pain. It was clear that this woman needed Jackson and him alone. Jun needed someone she could trust completely. Someone who truly had her best interests in mind and would do anything to help her. She needed "her" Jackson.

Ava let go of any jealousy. She let go of her own desire for this man. He wasn't hers. Not really. He would be there for Jun, just as he had helped Ava. She had known it would be the case. She had been preparing for it. And as much as it threatened to, she wouldn't let it hurt her. She had a mission to complete.

Ava had fully expected Jackson to hold Jun close while they exited the Tower, as if keeping her under his wing. It shocked Ava when, after removing the straitjacket he brought Jun right up to her instead.

"Jun, this is Ava," he said, as if this girl should know that name.

Apparently, she did. Jun's eyes flooded with tears. She looked at Ava with an understanding that only Remington had shown before, and it almost made Ava flinch.

"Ava," Jun said sweetly. She reached out her hand. "My dear Ava."

Ava glanced at Jackson for answers, for anything to explain what she should do now. Jackson looked at her as if to tell Ava she already knew.

Ava clasped Jun's hand tightly. "You're safe now," Ava told her weakly, so many other things threatening to break her focus right now.

"Don't look at me," Jun's voice sounded through the link *"It's all right. You can close your eyes. I know the enemy you face. I'm sorry that I helped them create it."*

Ava's eyebrows narrowed, but before she could respond, a heavy push from Counter Intelligence knocked against her, like a gust of heavy wind making her lose her footing.

Ava closed her eyes out of self-preservation alone, her hands going back to her head.

Nastia slipped the missing earbud back into Ava's ear, and Jackson led them out.

☆ ☆ ☆ ☆ ☆

The outside of the core was flooded with close to fifty men, protecting it from the threat of the attackers. Sasha cursed as the mirror showed them what they would face around the corner. "It's too much."

"Where are those drones?" Ella asked.

"With our squads, to get them safe passage out."

"And *our* safe passage out?" Ella asked pointedly.

Sasha smiled. "You're a Zhànshì, and I'm a highly skilled specialist. We'll find our way."

She didn't exactly buy that, but now was not the time to question his foolhardy plan which she had freely chosen to join.

"Distraction?" Ella offered.

Sasha nodded. "Mikel?" he replied in response.

Ella shrugged. "Let's ask."

★ ★ ★ ★ ★

"Three more," Kyle said proudly. "Let's finish this!"

Mikel stopped in his tracks, despite a clear path and people pressing him forward. "Tell Zak he's on his own."

"I'm sorry, what?" Kyle pressed in confusion.

"Zak is doing just fine without me!" Mikel explained. "I'm needed elsewhere. Tell Vasiliv they are on their own."

"We can't just abandon them—"

"They're practically done. Their extraction teams have already exited the building. And Zak is nearly as fast as me anyway. Just prepare them to expect it. I'll give additional help when I can."

Kyle growled in frustration, but relayed the information through the radio.

"What does he mean he's needed elsewhere?" Jackson asked, clearly not liking the sound of that either. "Where the taint else could he be sending his help right now? He's needed here in this battle!"

Kyle looked at Mikel, prepared to relay that message, but he stopped. There was a sudden seriousness in Mikel's expression, even with his closed eyes, that Kyle had never seen in him before. A concentration, even unlike he had held in the rest of this attack. Kyle did not know what it was Mikel was doing, but he had a feeling it might be best not to distract or interfere.

★ ★ ★ ★ ★

"We're down to twenty," Sasha noted. "You think we can take them?"

Ella smiled, which Sasha had never seen from her before. "You and me? Absolutely!"

They moved in.

She was good. Very good. He hadn't expected so much from the girl after seeing her sparring match with the boys, but it was clear she was the type who performed better under real pressure. And between them, they managed to quickly eliminate the threat outside the core.

475

Sasha began working on the door while Ella watched for backup officers.

"*Mikel,*" Sasha reached out to him, "*it's time. We need to get into the core. And to do so quickly.*"

"Why does it feel like we're just dragging this loser along now?" the Russian Elite Pierre asked, pulling Mikel along, who was now completely in his own world.

Kyle worked on the door, cursing how difficult it was. "Because we are," he admitted. "Wherever he is in his head, it's not with us."

The Elite muttered an oath.

"Don't worry, friend," Kyle offered. "We have three minutes and one program left. We'll be fine."

Exiting the Tower felt impossible. Ava was weakened to a state of exhaustion. She had little to nothing left to give, yet the enemy remained as unwavering and powerful as ever. She had to be able to do this, yet every second her abilities were closer to failing her.

"*I don't know if I can do it alone, Ava,*" Mikel told her honestly. "*I've never broken into a Tower on lockdown before. Little help?*"

"I can't..." Ava muttered out loud. "I can't...do this."

Still, she pressed forward, attempting to help Sasha, Mikel and the rest.

The pressure was excruciating. She felt weaker than ever in her life. And yet she was unable to fold, unable to bend, unable to break. She had to press forward through the pain, through the exhaustion, through the torment. She could not stop paddling forward, not even for a second.

★ ★ ★ ★ ★

The core opened, and Ella made a quick entrance before Sasha could even move forward. Together, they swept through the small room and the unprepared officers.

"We're in!" Sasha announced to Mikel when the enemy were all incapacitated.

"I'll guard the door," Ella said, standing watch.

"There's a lot of data to sort through," Sasha spoke out loud, "but if I can isolate the topic, and download anything in that subgenre—"

"No idea what you're talking about," Ella replied, "but good luck with that."

Sasha chuckled, working quickly on the download process. The same compressed file type that Zak had used to upload the program onto Tower servers would be useful in downloading the information onto Sasha's drive now.

"How long?" Ella pressed. "We might have company soon."

"Almost there," Sasha spoke as he worked. "Just a little more time."

"I'll be back then, because we don't have any."

She left the room, and the sound of heavy gunfire outside broke his focus momentarily as it occurred to Sasha that there was no way he could have done this without the girl. He breathed deeply in gratitude. They might just manage this.

"I can't," Ava muttered. "It's too much, it's too much!"

Jackson tried not to listen too closely to her mutterings. The overwhelming desire to hold her and help her through this took hold any time he did. But even if he tried, he'd probably be murdered on the spot by her bodyguard. And he knew that she could not risk breaking focus. Still, every time she muttered the words, "I can't" or "I'm not strong enough" he wanted to look her in the eyes and tell her, "Yes you can! You *are* strong enough. You can do this!"

One of the other squad members led Jun on, and Jackson unconsciously watched how Jun paid attention to Ava's every move. The look of understanding on her face made Jackson wonder if the girl knew what Ava was up against.

☆ ☆ ☆ ☆ ☆

There was a sudden flicker in the lights, and it gave Kyle pause. Had that been Mikel, or...?

Mikel's eyes shot open, and a look of panic overtook him. "We need to get out! We need to get out of here. Now!"

It was too late. Almost as soon as the words were uttered, an intense pain crippled Kyle, a pain he thought maybe he had faced before. But it didn't make sense. The Jiānhùrén were enemies to every government and nation. Why would they want to stop The Cause in this attempt to cripple such a powerful world leader?

He had no time to consider or answer that question before he and Mikel were on the floor, screaming and holding their heads in pain. No, this was worse than the Jiānhùrén. That intense pain had crippled him. But this? This was killing him.

"It's not the Jiānhùrén," Mikel spoke through the link, almost as if he had heard Kyle's thoughts. Come to think of it, maybe Kyle had projected them to his friend. *"It's far worse than that. It's Counter Intelligence."*

☆ ☆ ☆ ☆ ☆

Ava screamed at the top of her lungs, her hands going to her head.

"They released the backup wave!" Jun urgently told Jackson. "She will not be able to protect everyone. It will kill her. And all of them!"

Jackson certainly didn't like the sound of that.

"What do we do?" Nastia asked Jun in sudden fear.

Jun shook her head, a look of regret and deep sadness. "There is nothing to do. It's too late. They are all dead."

☆ ☆ ☆ ☆ ☆

Sasha wavered and hunched on the floor. The pain was immeasurable, and more terrifying than any he had felt before. He heard Ella gasping for breath outside and knew she felt it too.

He struggled to finish the download when every inch of his body felt like it was on fire, and that at any moment he would be no more. But the download completed, and he practically dragged himself from the room and to Ella's side outside the core. She had taken care of the enemy officers, but in this state they were no match for even one rogue who might meet them on their exit. That was, of course, if this force within didn't kill them first.

✫ ✫ ✫ ✫ ✫

Ava hunched to the ground, leaning her head on the wall and desperately screaming out loud. That shriek of pain felt like a bullet to his heart, and he felt frozen stiff in fear when he saw the blood drip from her nose and ears.

"It is too late," Jun muttered regretfully as tears stained her cheeks. "They are all dead. All of my friends. They are all dead because of me!"

His moment of fear-stricken terror was replaced with determination. This wasn't going to happen. He wasn't going to lose Ava, and Sasha, and all of them, just like that.

Nastia didn't attempt to stop him when he went to the screaming Ava, kneeling down and placing his hands on her cheeks. Maybe it was a distraction of focus, but at this point, what was there to lose?

She startled at his touch, but her eyes remained closed, and she continued gasping and screaming as the pain overwhelmed her. "Ava, baby, it's me."

Her eyes opened suddenly, but it took them a moment to find his. She looked terrified. "Ava, you can do this!" he said urgently. "You're stronger than this. You're stronger than Counter Intelligence. You are Harrison's secret weapon. He believed in you, Ava. He knew you could do it! And I do too."

The blood dripped from her ears down his hands. She was shaking, but she did not break his gaze.

"Kristen would be so proud, Ava, if she could see you now! If she knew how strong you are. You're just like your mother. And Eric?" He laughed, through his tears. "He would be proud too. Can you imagine if Lionel were here? You're everything Harrison imagined and more. You can do this, Ava. I know you can do this. And they did too!"

She trembled from the pain, and he felt the movement as if he were trembling too. Maybe he was. Her words were so muffled and quiet, he struggled to understand when she spoke. "Th–think they would—proud of—of me?"

He nodded, over and over, and tears streamed down his cheeks. "Yes, Ava. I know they would. Now, you listen to me. This fight is not over. Show your mother how strong you are. Show Harrison that he was right. Show Lionel he picked the right girl. And show Eli who is boss."

She laughed, one simple laugh through the pain.

His words were an attempt at a pep talk, but the longer he held her, the more certain he was that Jun was right, that Ava was already dead—that they all were.

His face streamed with tears unlike any he'd ever shed before. He would tell her to fight until her last breath. But every second, that last breath drew nearer. She was not going to survive this. He was certain of that now. And it broke his heart, but in these last moments, all he thought of was being there for her, and making sure she knew how much she was loved.

"I love you, baby," he whispered, moving in and kissing her through his tears, past the blood dripping from her nostrils. "I love you, Ava."

☆ ☆ ☆ ☆ ☆

Kyle managed to crawl across the floor to Mikel. He had ordered the squad to finish the job and get out of here. Mikel and Kyle were useless now, but this operation still had to be completed.

Weakly, Kyle made it to his friend's side. Mikel was shaking, and looked helpless there on the floor. "We should be dead by now," Mikel muttered between gasps. "She's still fighting it...we haven't been fully infected...but it's winning."

"What are you doing?" Kyle asked his friend gruffly. "What the taint are you doing?"

Mikel looked at him in frustration, but had no immediate response to that. "What do you think I'm doing?" Mikel shot back. "I'm dying!"

Kyle growled. "Get up!" he yelled.

Mikel looked shocked. "You're on the floor too, carcass!" Mikel reminded him.

"Get the taint up!" Kyle screamed, despite the excruciating pain.

Mikel watched him with a look of horror.

"You want to be the best?" Kyle said through gritted teeth.

It was several seconds before Mikel nodded.

"You want to be the best?" Kyle repeated, this time in a scream.

"Yes!" Mikel screamed in response.

"Then get up!" Kyle shouted. "Get your carcass up off the ground and earn it!"

A look of determination overtook Mikel, and slowly he pulled himself up and to a sitting position.

"Get up!" Kyle screamed. "Get up and earn it!"

Mikel pulled himself up farther until he was standing.

"You want to be the best?" Kyle shouted.

"Yes!" Mikel said through the intense pain that showed plainly on his face.

"Then earn it, Mikel! Earn it!"

Mikel screamed, closing his eyes as his hands went to his head.

"Earn it!" Kyle shouted once more.

☆ ☆ ☆ ☆ ☆

Jackson pulled away, and his heart stopped in his chest. Her eyes were closed, and she was still.

He couldn't believe it at first. He couldn't accept it at first. She couldn't be dead.

Nastia slowly moved forward and put her hand on Ava's neck, checking her pulse. She moved away, saying nothing, but Jackson knew what that meant.

Jackson knelt there on the ground before Ava, only half conscious of his knees and the shooting pain.

"We need to get out," Nastia said from behind him, though she was directing her words to the others.

"How much time?" one of the others asked.

"Less than a minute."

"Squad leader," a voice spoke through Jackson's earpiece. "We lost General Li. Repeat, General Li was not extracted. He and his armed guards have safely exited the Tower and are no longer in targetable position."

"This is squadron two. We missed a member as well," another voice sounded. "Our team leader and operations specialist are down. We were ordered to complete the mission without them. We lost three more men. Extraction failed and we are attempting to escape the Tower."

"There's no way we get out that quick," an officer growled from the room behind Jackson. "Certainly not without her help."

"Then we'll face their defense squads."

"Taint no! I'd rather they take us in alive. If we surrender now—"

Jackson stood then, determined. "We're not giving up," he spoke, though the words didn't sound like his own. "We're not going to surrender." His words and passion felt so disconnected from reality, almost as if he were watching someone else. Perhaps his body was reacting from training, perhaps his disconnected emotions just couldn't comprehend that he was the same man as the leader of this squadron. Either way, Jackson Davis was not about to quit.

"We will take on their defense squad if we have to. And we will win."

"We've made it this far, haven't we?" another officer tried to encourage the others.

"And we will make it out of—" Jackson's comment was cut off as the lights went out and everything went dark.

"What the?" Nastia gasped.

"Blackout?" an officer guessed.

"Squad leader," a voice came through the earpiece. "This is tech support at HQ. All Towers have gone dark. Repeat, we are experiencing a full-scale blackout."

"Why would they—" Jackson started to ask, but he was interrupted by a gasping breath from behind him.

Jackson almost collapsed on the ground by her as Ava sat now clutching her beating heart and sucking in more air to her lungs.

"You did it!" Jackson said, pulling her into his arms in the darkened room. "You did it, Ava. You beat it!"

She shook her head, over and over, but was unable to speak. "Wasn't—me," she finally managed.

Honestly, he didn't care who it was right now. She was alive! He had never been so relieved in his life.

"Let's get out of here!" Nastia screamed with sudden passion.

Nastia and Jackson moved to help Ava to a standing position. She was so weak and fragile then that he wanted to carry her himself. Jackson felt in a state of literal shock as he walked forward, holding her.

"Take point," Nastia ordered him. "I've got her."

He was tempted to let her have it then, but as shaky and confused as he was, as the blood drained from his hands leaving them numb, he realized he might not be the best help to Ava now anyway. Still, it was the hardest thing he had ever done in that moment to let her go and resume leadership. But his training and discipline took over. The numbness disappeared, and the shock slowly vanished.

Jackson was a soldier. And this was a war.

"They did it!" Sasha said excitedly, getting to his feet.

"Who?" Ella asked.

"Who cares? Let's get out of here!"

Little, angry Ella actually chuckled at that. "Fair enough."

They had only just gotten to their feet when the sound of a gunshot rang, a fatal shot. The moment seemed to happen in slow motion as Sasha screamed.

He had known the risks. He had known that he might be killed. But he had not planned for this.

Ella collapsed. Before Sasha went to her side, he drew his weapon and took out the shooter.

Then he fell to his knees before the girl. The wound was precise, and deadly. She would not last more than a minute—probably not even that.

Sasha's eyes flooded with tears, and they dripped onto the girl's shocked face. "Ella, sweet girl. I am so sorry. I never should have dragged you into this."

She clearly could not feel the pain as she chuckled. "Ironic, isn't it?" she said with a touch of her dry humor.

Sasha choked on his own words and could not reply. This poor girl should have had nothing to do with this.

Ella stared at the ceiling as she considered the irony of it all, which Sasha did not yet understand. "Tell Ava, in the end, I didn't mind so much dying for her. I guess...when it's right, it's right."

Those were the last words Ella ever spoke.

15

Tyrant

"She always said this was how she wanted to be put in the ground," Kyle spoke somberly as he watched the flames in the darkened night. "She couldn't stand the thought of being buried. She wanted her ending to be an ending. She said there was no better way than to end in flames."

Jackson watched the fire as he listened, conscious of Ava at his side. "She and I never exactly hit it off," Jackson admitted. "Right up until the end, I'm not sure either of us actually said a kind word to one another. But there was something deeper than words. Even through our sarcasm, through all the teasing, she knew I loved her—like an annoying little sister. And I think she felt the same."

The silence lingered until Mikel was the one to speak. "She certainly liked to poke at my insecurities and flaws. But from the moment she joined me on my mission in Australia, she was a sort of grounding presence in my life. Even in her menacing jabs, I felt her pushing me always to be better. And I know I am because of her."

Another long silence. "She was my first real friend," Kyle spoke somberly. "She taught me how to be a friend—beyond fighting in the arena. She taught me how to open up, and let myself be heard." He chuckled. "She may not have been the warmest or most comforting of

485

friends. But she was my first real one. And without what she taught me, I may not have found any others. I'll never forget her for that."

"I'll give her this," Zak said, in his sarcastic, but also clearly loving way, "she never did end up killing me. Which was honestly more than I could have asked for."

Jackson was not the only one to smile at that, and he once more appreciated Zak's ability to bring joy, even in moments of pain.

"She was relentless in the battlefield," Nastia spoke with pride. "And I always felt more confident with her at my side."

"I learned a lot of fighting techniques from that little fireball," Vasiliv agreed. "She was really something."

After another long silence, Jackson unconsciously found himself glancing at Sasha, and at Ava by his side—the only two who hadn't said anything yet.

Ava must have felt his eyes, and a few other eyes on her, because she opened up her mouth to speak next.

"Ella was a soldier, a hero. It's easy to second-guess every move, to wonder if we might have done something to save her. Maybe we could have. But her death wasn't any of our fault. And to think it was would not do her heroism justice. She said she died for me. Maybe that's true. But it's more than that. Ella spent her entire life rebelling in anger against those who had hurt her. Even in joining our cause, she was upfront that her reasoning wasn't noble. She wanted revenge. But Ella didn't die in vengeance. She didn't die in anger. She died in heroism. She died for a greater cause. She died protecting. She died for freedom. And after everything she suffered, everything she was put through, her heroic death is more a testament to our cause than any other."

Jackson thought of Natasha, and Ava's reprimand when he claimed the woman's death was his fault. She had said much the same thing to him, that to blame himself would not pay tribute to the sacrifice Natasha deserved. Jackson found himself awed, that even now, even when Ava might have every reason to blame herself, she practiced what she preached, though he knew for certain that was not easy to do.

Jackson couldn't help looking at Sasha at that moment. His friend watched the fire, long after the others were prepared to move on.

Even after Ella was killed, even at risk to himself, Sasha had carried the girl's body out of the Tower, and brought her safely back to Russia.

TYRANT

When he was asked why he put himself at such great risk for someone who was no longer living, he soberly replied, "I wasn't going to let the enemy hurt her. Not even now. She deserves a proper burial. And she will receive one."

Everyone seemed to be waiting now for Sasha to say something profound. He had been there in Ella's final moments. He had attested to that heroism that Ava spoke of. And as the wise, scholar and mentor to the group, everyone hushed in anticipation of the final words that would pull it together, leaving them all inspired by the memory of this girl.

Sasha's expression was more somber than the others—even those who had been her closest friends. It was clear he felt her death on an entirely different level than the others. And the longer they watched, the longer he stood there in sober silence, Jackson almost wondered if he should speak the final words instead, and let poor Sasha be.

Before he had the chance to do so, Sasha cleared his throat to speak. Even then the words were slow in coming as he took a deep breath. When he finally began, his tone was just as pained, but there was an anger masked behind his words that shocked everyone, coming from this generally kind and gentle man.

"She was a fifteen-year-old girl," Sasha said, half mourning, half with a controlled rage. "She was a traumatized child. She shouldn't have had to be a hero. I will never forgive Harrison for that. It's time to end this sick war."

With that, he turned, and just as somberly, just as angrily, he left the fire.

☆ ☆ ☆ ☆ ☆

Zak entered the Tower infirmary with a careful expression, trying not to give away too much before they had the opportunity to see for themselves.

Ava sat, with Jackson standing beside her, and Sasha stood somberly on the other end of the room. He hadn't had the heart to look over the scans with Zak. He didn't have the stomach to watch another traumatized child receive a death sentence. Zak understood

487

where he was coming from, especially as Ava's father. But a part of him resented the fact that he had to play the part of the sage medic offering a diagnosis like this alone.

Zak moved a table and placed it before Ava and Jackson. Then he laid the papers down one at a time. "This is a healthy, normal person's brain scan—mine, to be exact." He laid down the next scan. "This was Jackson's scan, before we performed the chip removal operation. You can see in this section here, where the prefrontal cortex has a bit of shadowing. This shows how the flaw affected Jackson's brain in a matter of about ten years."

The next scan was placed on the table. "This was Sasha's scan before we started the flaw stunting treatments. As you can see, the shadow on his prefrontal cortex is much darker, there's a small tumor. The damage is much worse than Jackson's. Still, it was minor enough that he probably has another good ten years before it causes any severe damage, especially with the shunt we've put in to stop it from progressing."

Zak reached for the last scan in his file, hesitating momentarily before he placed it before them.

"Taint," Jackson cursed when he saw the scan.

Sasha turned away, putting his face in his hands.

"This is your scan," Zak explained, and it took everything in him to remain strong faced as he saw their reactions, and felt a similar pain.

The shadowing in the prefrontal cortex was much darker than Sasha's. But it wasn't isolated to that area of her brain. There were shadowy, or affected areas, scattered in little patches all over her brain. And the tumor around the chip was the size of a large grape.

"Putting it lightly, Ava," Zak said carefully, "I'm not certain how you're alive right now. I don't know how or why your heart restarted in the Tower when it did. I don't know how you're able to talk, and walk, and move the way you are. Everything I know about neurology tells me, and the other experts who have seen this, that you should be dead."

"Well, that's reassuring," Ava said, attempting to remain strong, clearly for the others.

Zak offered a half smile. "From what I have been able to discern in the past months, the flaw targets the prefrontal cortex of the brain, affecting it and ultimately causing a sort of tumor in the brain. The flaw can cause heart attacks, paralysis, and many other damaging symptoms before the tumor becomes noticeable, because of its slow development. It is usually a few decades before the tumor develops and there's any real danger.

"Counter Intelligence, on the other hand, is a fast-acting computer virus, a sort of wave of energy that floods and overwhelms the brain. You shouldn't have had to deal with the prolonged exposure from the flaw for a few more years yet. The scans we have of your brain from when you arrived in Russia initially came back clean, but in the past five months, your mind has been fighting the wave of energy, and it's progressed the development of the flaw by years. Beyond just this one tumor, it seems like the prolonged exposure to Counter Intelligence is affecting several pockets of your brain. There's just one tumor for now, but another week, month or year, and it will be much worse."

Sasha was still turned away, unable to face the group. He knew what these scans meant. They all did, but Sasha particularly was coming to the realization that there might not be any saving Ava, even with the coding of Counter Intelligence.

"From what I can tell," Zak continued, "you are suffering severely from both the effects of the flaw and that of Counter Intelligence. It's attacked you from both angles. The last five months that you've been fighting Counter Intelligence, you've essentially been stopping the weapon from fully forming and ultimately overpowering your brain. But it hasn't given up so quickly in its fight either. And as it has continued to work on destroying your brain, the flaw has essentially sped up its pace, and like a virus, or a cancer, it's spread to many other areas in your brain and began forming similar tumor-like shadows."

"So, what's the verdict?" Ava asked, still attempting strength as she received the death sentence.

Zak's mouth opened, but he struggled to respond. "I haven't the faintest idea. You could have seconds. You could have weeks. You could have a year."

"That's the most?" she asked weakly. "The longest I have is a year?"

He pursed his lips. "That's being generous. Luckily, Counter Intelligence left your body in your miraculous fight in the Tower. Maybe it left when your heart stopped. Maybe Mikel managed to remove the virus when he began blocking it for everyone else somehow. I don't know. The damage will spread much more slowly now. But I am afraid I don't know of any way to reverse what has been done here. It was a miracle you came back to us in the Tower. But I'm sorry to say that it will be short-lived."

Jackson swallowed hard, and Ava looked down at her lap. They all remained there as if in stunned silence. Zak wished he knew a way to comfort them, or give them hope, but with everything he and the other experts knew, she shouldn't be alive now.

"You have to understand," Zak added, though really it felt like adding insult to injury at this point, "that you are at serious risk for those other symptoms we discussed—paralysis like Liam. Heart failure. Seizures. You are in a state of severe fragility right now." He was about to add more to the list of things to be wary of, but it was clear that all of them had had enough at this point.

"I'm sorry," Zak said somberly. "I really wish I had better news."

Sasha finally turned, and it was clear that he had been fighting back the tears in his eyes. Jackson squeezed Ava's shoulder. They were both clearly trying to be strong for her, but Zak knew them both well enough to know how much this was hurting them.

"One year," Ava muttered.

"At most," Zak corrected, but immediately regretted it.

Ava took a deep breath, smiling first at Jackson, then at Sasha. "I guess you were right," she said to her father, strangely looking perfectly fine, even though she definitely shouldn't be, "we better win this war quickly!"

She stood then, and the others attempted to go with her, but she requested an hour to go back to her room and rest before she had to think about it all again. They both agreed, and let her leave alone.

Zak wondered once more if he should give Ava or Jackson the list of symptoms to be watchful of and all the many things to avoid. But almost as soon as Ava left, Jackson went in the other direction, getting out of there quickly.

Sasha stayed a moment longer, and seemed to understand Zak's awkward air. "I'll take it," he said softly, reaching his hand for the list.

Zak carefully handed it to his mentor. "I—I'm sorry, Sasha."

Sasha nodded, not able to look Zak in the eyes just then. "So am I," he agreed. "So am I."

Mikel spent almost every moment in his room now, trying to understand and cope with Counter Intelligence. He couldn't understand how Ava had ever slept. He couldn't comprehend how she had ever managed to laugh or play or have fun. How could she do anything but fight this powerful, terrible enemy?

The only time since the Tower that Mikel had left his quarters was to attend Ella's memorial, and even then, he had been so distracted in his fight that it was hard to concentrate on the girl who had been a true friend.

He was terrified to close his eyes, no matter how tired he became. This enemy would kill him, he knew that. If he let his guard down, even for a second, he would be crushed by the weight that was pressing down on him.

Kyle told him he had earned it, that he was the best. But Mikel knew that wasn't true. Ava had fought this thing, day and night, for five months. Ultimately, it had weakened her enough to overcome her, and she had practically died in the Tower.

Mikel's good timing in taking the beast from Ava's mind just seconds before her brain exploded was the only reason she was alive now. But he had been fighting for three days, and already he felt himself weakening to a breakable level.

If it took Counter Intelligence five months to weaken Ava enough to destroy her, Mikel couldn't comprehend how powerful she was. He already felt like he was on the verge of giving up. He was constantly fighting the temptation to just let go, and let it be. This battle, it was pointless. He was going to die anyway. It was going to beat him in a matter of days, or weeks, or at most, months, anyway—why not just save himself the trouble and let go now?

There was only one thing that kept him going. Ringing in his mind over and over was that intense reprimand from Kyle. "Do you want to be the best? Then get up and earn it!"

Ava had lasted five months, two weeks and four days. If Mikel could simply last five months, two weeks and five days, then, *then* he could let go. And not a moment before it.

He wanted to be the best, more than anything in the world. He wanted this. And it would be the fight of his life—it already had been—but he was determined. He would *not* let go. He had five months, two weeks and two days left. Then he could stop fighting. Then he could give up. Then he could go knowing that he would be remembered as someone who didn't quit before the game was finished.

If it meant these five months were full of constant, horrible pain and terror, if it meant he did not sleep, then so be it. He would not let go. He would not quit. He would not give up. Not until he earned it. Not until he was the best.

★ ★ ★ ★ ★

Jackson watched the rain as it crashed down on the windshield. His hands rested on the steering wheel, his foot sat limp by the peddle, and his entire body ached with a desire to move, to run, to drive, to go somewhere, to get out of here and clear his mind.

But he couldn't leave the Northeastern Tower without an armed escort, not when ninety percent of Russians still wanted him dead, and Sasha had put limits on his ability to leave the Tower alone. So, he simply sat there in the parking lot, watching the rain, feeling stuck.

The passenger side door opened, and he didn't have to look to know who it was. "I don't want to talk right now, Sasha."

Sasha sat and closed the door. It was a long time before he responded with choked up emotion. "I don't want to talk right now either," he replied weakly.

Jackson looked across the cab at the grieving man with tear-streaked cheeks. Jackson had assumed he was here for some sort of pep talk. But when he saw the broken demeanor of his hero, it occurred to Jackson that in fact Sasha was the one in need of comfort this time.

The only other time Jackson had seen Sasha in pain like this was when Kristen died. The last thing this man had wanted then was Jackson's presence. But now...after everything, perhaps Jackson had something to offer Sasha for a change.

He wasn't sure if his friend just wanted a moment of silence together, a pep talk or a hug. Jackson wasn't sure what he wanted himself either.

"I just got her back," Sasha said through his tears. "I just got her back from him..." he trailed off, and Jackson was sure he once again felt intense hatred for Harrison in that moment. "And now I'm going to lose her again."

Jackson had nothing. No words of wisdom. No inspirational pep talk. Sasha's description was exactly what Jackson was feeling himself—only with Eli as the focal point of his anger.

"I'm going to lose her..." Sasha repeated helplessly.

Jackson had come in feeling angry, and sad, and terrified. He still felt those things. He really did. But maybe it was because he had just been through this—he had just experienced losing Ava in those brief moments in the Tower. It had broken him. It really had. But at the same time, he had gotten back up, he had kept going, even when he thought he had lost her forever. There had been a numbness, a sort of disconnectedness from emotions, mind and body. But he had managed to keep going.

Losing Ava would crush him. It would break him. He might never find a connection with his emotions and body again. But he would keep going. He might never be happy again. But he would keep fighting. He had been preparing himself to lose Ava since the moment he thought he had. And although he still mourned the loss that was ahead, not only of Ava, but of a piece of himself, still he felt he was going to be okay.

Sasha looked like he would never recover from this. And in truth, he may not.

Jackson reached his arm out to his friend for comfort, and Sasha collapsed into Jackson's side as he broke down in tears.

For the first time there were no words to be said between the two of them. Jackson comforted his mentor as he cried, already promising himself that no matter what happened, he could not stop fighting. He could never be worthy of Ava if he did.

Kyle sat alone at the cafeteria. Mikel was at war with the enemy in his room. Ava was facing her impending doom. Jackson and Sasha were mourning. And Zak was working on decoding the information on Counter Intelligence. Ella was gone. Shannon couldn't join them. So, Kyle ate alone.

It wasn't so bad. He had eaten many meals alone. Most of his life he had eaten alone. But in the past weeks he had grown so close to these friends of his that he was almost never alone, particularly at supper time.

It was nearing time for Kyle to leave again. He still had a greater enemy to eliminate. He had spoken to Jackson about the Jiānhùrén, and they had worked on plans together to destroy them. Ultimately, Kyle still felt his place was not here. He needed to go on and get back to his work. Still, he wanted to rest and mourn a few days more.

Someone entered the cafeteria with an armed escort. He had never seen the Asian woman before, but guessed it must be the girl Jun that Jackson had spoken of. He looked back to his food, an almost empty plate, and decided to get up and go back for more.

"Kyle," a voice said from behind him in line. He turned to face her.

"Yes," he said gruffly.

"I knew it was you," Jun said almost to herself.

He didn't know how to make small talk when he felt tired and sad, so he said nothing.

"I am so sorry for the loss of Ella," she said, seeming to mean it as if she had been her friend.

"You didn't know her," Kyle replied with the tiniest bit of contempt. Of course, it was not really this woman's fault that Counter Intelligence had come about. Yet he had a hard time distinguishing her involvement from the death of all his friends at this point. Ava was as good as gone now, and Mikel would likely soon follow.

"I did know her," Jun disagreed. "In my way, I did."

Still, he didn't have a response, so he turned around to face the line before him.

"Can you ever forgive me?" she pleaded in her trembling tone.

He turned back around prepared to tell her there was no way in the General's name. But the look of innocence and regret in her eyes was so familiar, and he could not help but think of Valkyrie.

"It's not your fault," he muttered, almost before he knew what he had said. "You were their slave. You can't be held accountable for what they made you do."

He could see in her eyes how much that meant to her. "They used medication to confuse me," she explained. "Truth serums and hallucinogens. And then they would ask me questions, and I wouldn't realize I was giving answers to your enemy. I never meant to hurt you or any of your friends."

"I know," he said, and as he spoke, he realized that was true. "Your government used you, just like ours did to us. Both sides got their hands dirty in this fight. And we're the results of that."

"We are their weapons," Jun replied in a pained agreement. "We no longer count as their people, or their family. We are only tools, fashioned to do their will."

Of course, Kyle had always known that there were good guys among the Republic. He had always known deep down that their true enemy was the government, not the people. But when Ava spoke of fighting for the innocents in the Republic, and when Valkyrie decided to save a camp of enemy soldiers, he could not deny that he had disagreed, lumping these people right in with the enemy that he sought to destroy. But seeing this girl now, hearing her speak, and realizing that she was just like him, just like the other Zhànshì...it was sobering, and he wondered why he had allowed himself to be blind to that before.

"Who are the bad guys, Kyle?" Jun asked, and once more, he could not help seeing Valkyrie in those innocent, uncomprehending eyes.

"Corrupted, power-hungry tyrants," Kyle replied, feeling all of his past prejudices crumble as he watched this girl and finally understood what Jackson said when he spoke of fighting for freedom for all, and not just a nation. Or when Ava spoke of fighting for the people, and not just for the United Kingdoms.

"Are they only among my people?" she asked, and suddenly it occurred to him that, just like Valkyrie, this girl understood far more than she seemed to, that she was pressing him to face biases he hadn't even realized he had. "Are those evil men only in the Republic?"

"Not even close," Kyle admitted.

"And the people who used you as their weapons?" she asked innocently, though he could tell she was pushing him, just as Valkyrie would have.

"Yes," he said gruffly. "They were power-hungry and tyrannical too."

"And what about The Cause?" she asked hopefully. "Are these people any better?"

Kyle considered that thoughtfully. There were probably some among the leadership of these nations that were gathering who fit that description. Still, overall, they were different. Jackson, Sasha and Ava were different.

"This third side is different," he finally admitted confidently. "You can trust them."

"Then why will you leave them again?" she asked, and once more, he found himself astounded by how much she reminded him of Valkyrie.

"Because I have my own path," he offered. "I have my own enemy to fight."

She seemed to accept this, but looked saddened. "I understand."

Suddenly not feeling so hungry anymore, Kyle left the line and started toward the door. *"Would it be okay,"* her voice sounded to him through the link, *"if I spoke to you sometimes?"*

He stopped, turning to face her once more.

I always hear you," she explained, *"but you never hear me. No one listens anymore, now that Jackson no longer has the link."*

No one could hear, or understand Valkyrie either, Kyle realized. They all saw a robot assassin, and that was what they got. But Valkyrie was there, sweeter and truer and deeper than anyone had ever realized. This woman was just as invisible, just as overlooked. She saw and heard and understood more than anyone realized. But no one seemed to notice her.

"Yeah, you can talk to me sometimes," he offered in response, realizing that he might have more to learn from this woman than she could ever hope to receive from him in return.

"I hope I will see you again, Zhànshì Kyle," she said with a deep sadness that touched her eyes.

"I'm sure you will, Jun."

★ ★ ★ ★ ★

Jackson prepared himself, once more pushing aside his pain in order to help Ava through hers. It had been a long time since he thought about the supposedly fake Altman smile, since he had judged Kristen for using it in a time of such horror, after the General's shooting. It only now occurred to him, as he swallowed his pain, that Kristen using that smile had protected millions from overwhelming fear in a time of great turmoil. At the time, she had managed to see past her own pain and fear, and focused on the many who looked to her, who needed her to be strong even when she shouldn't have to be. If that was what was required of Jackson now, he would gladly play the part.

He stood in the empty Tower hallway and lightly tapped on the door to her room. It was a moment before a faint voice answered from within, inviting him to come inside.

She was not in the main room, but with the washroom door sitting open, he knew where to find her. She sat inside, holding a pillow to her chest on the edge of the large jetted tub, though he had expected her to be hiding inside. Perhaps she had climbed to the edge when she heard him knocking.

She looked somber and thoughtful, which was unsurprising given the kind of day she'd had. "How you doing?" he asked softly, caringly.

She didn't look up. Clearly, she had a lot on her mind.

"Do you want more time? Or do you want company?"

She shook her head, though he had given her two options, leaving him unsure of what to do. He stood there awkwardly in the doorway for a moment. Eventually, she swallowed and prepared to speak. "I've been thinking," she said seriously. "I've been thinking a lot. I guess I don't have much time left, and I think we need to spend it wisely."

He narrowed his eyes, not liking how professional she sounded as she addressed him. "We need to focus on getting the Tower network up and turned over. We need to overthrow Eli. We need to take down the Jiānhùrén."

Jackson stepped closer to her and would have sat down, but she seemed to pull away from him, indicating she did not want him close. "Yes," Jackson agreed warily, "we do need to do those things."

She was pleased by his agreement. "You have so much to do," Ava continued. "So many things that need your attention. And I need to focus on staying alive, and preparing to be there when I'm needed."

"Yes. You do," Jackson agreed, but every minute he grew more concerned about where she was going with this.

"We don't have time to play fairytale," she said suddenly, and now he was certain he didn't like where she was going.

"Oh, is that what our relationship has been?" Jackson asked challengingly.

"It's been fun," Ava moved forward as though she had not heard him. "But I think it's time for us to let go."

He watched her for a long time, searching for some sign that she didn't really mean what she was saying. It was clear that she had made up her mind.

"This is you breaking up with me," Jackson said flatly, not sure he should believe it.

She didn't respond verbally, but her expression confirmed it.

Jackson let out a surprised laugh. "Well, that's a horrible plan!" he said, attempting to lighten the mood. It fell just as flat.

"You asked me once what I would do if I had a week left to live," Ava said seriously. "And my answer was a childish dream of all the things I enjoy the most. I don't know how long I have. Possibly months. Possibly less than a week. But I won't waste it living out a childish fantasy when I need to spend every breath working on taking down the enemy. Too many people have died for me to do this. I won't let their deaths be for nothing."

It occurred to Jackson suddenly that he might not be able to change her mind. Not when Ella, and so many others, had died for Ava already. Not when her grief at Ella's loss was so fresh. And for the first time, it occurred to Jackson that she might actually be right.

How could they live out some self-indulgent dream in the final moments of her life, rather than work tirelessly to fight the enemy that was theirs to fight? So many had given their lives to help Ava win this. How could they do anything but work toward that end?

Still, he didn't want her to be right. He didn't want this to be the answer.

"So, what?" Jackson asked helplessly. "We end things now, we focus on the fight, and we settle for longing looks across the briefing room table? We pass each other helplessly in the halls? We try and pretend that we haven't lived through what we have? You think we should just let that all go, and pretend it never happened?"

"I owe it to these people to fight," Ava demanded.

"We have been fighting!" Jackson argued. "Relentlessly! We've done nothing but fight! And sure, we got in a kiss here and an 'I love you' there, but don't try and tell me we've been too distracted in our love to give everything to this battle. What about what we just went through? What about every moment I have spent building up this cause?" His passion made him seem angrier than he was, and he attempted to soften some.

"You've been fighting," Ava said. "And you've done well. But I've been distracted. I have been too lenient. I have let myself grow complacent towards my mission. I've been too unfocused, thinking about you. Even in the Tower, I broke my focus because of jealousy about Jun. What if that's why I couldn't withstand Counter Intelligence? What if that's the reason Ella is dead?"

"Don't," Jackson pleaded. "Don't do that. Don't diminish everything we've been through in the past month and label it 'a distraction.'"

"What else should I call it?"

"So, you're going to push me away," Jackson said, the realization that he had no chance against this stubborn woman causing him sudden infuriation. "Like you always do. You're going to push me away and abandon me to the wayside while you focus on your inner peace?"

Clearly, those words hurt her. Maybe he had meant them to.

"You think I'm doing this for myself?" she asked, and her eyes touched with deep sadness. "Jackson, I have never felt so happy, I have never felt so loved as I have by you. I'm not doing this selfishly. I'm doing this for them. And for you!"

"Don't do that either," he spat, once more sounding too angry and gruff, but struggling to control his intense emotions. "Don't you pretend this has anything to do with me! This isn't for me."

"Yes, it is," Ava disagreed. "Every day that we're together, I increase the loss you'll feel when I'm gone."

He laughed out loud in shock, though his expression remained one of anger and utter helplessness. "That's the stupidest thing I've ever heard."

"Jackson—"

"No! No, you know what? You can push me away. You can make this choice. But don't you for a second pretend to yourself that it's for me."

She gave no response, but the determination in her expression was the last thing he needed to be certain. There was no changing her mind. He had already lost her. And there was no use pretending otherwise.

He let out a breath of pain and surprise that sounded more like a huff of anger. Then, not knowing what else to do, he stood and walked slowly to the door. He ran through the entire conversation in his mind, wondering where he had gone wrong, racking his brain for the moment when he could have repaired this. But it did not exist. She had made up her mind before he ever entered that room. And nothing he said or did would change it.

He left the washroom and walked in a daze through the bedroom, stopping at the door and staring at it for a long time. He was infuriated. He was angry. He was hurt. But at the same time, he couldn't help returning to the thought that perhaps she was right.

His hand went to the doorknob and lingered there. He was overwhelmed by so many conflicting emotions, it was hard to discern what was keeping him there, why he hadn't left yet.

It was that word that seemed to stabilize him. Yet.

Suddenly, he was overcome by a new passion and determination. He thought of himself at a village in central Africa. Everything and everyone said it was time to give up. To let go. To move on. But Jackson would not give up that easily.

He thought of the first dreamwalk with Sizwe, and a million moments flashed through Jackson's mind when all odds were against him, and it seemed like there was no other option but retreat. He thought of himself at the Tower, when he had just lost the love of his life, and his body seemed disconnected from himself. Yet, even then, he would not give up, when all odds were against them.

Jackson had never given up anything so easily in his life. He was not about to give up on Ava.

He turned, and marched with determination to the washroom. Ava remained exactly as she had been before, but she was crying silently now.

"No, Ava," Jackson said, as stubbornly as her. "You don't get to make this decision for both of us. You don't get to push me out without a fight." He walked toward her, and she flinched away, so he gave her space, but sat beside her on the side of the large tub. "You're right that we need to win this war and spend our last breaths focusing on winning. But do you really think we're giving you more time in life by taking away everything that makes you want to live?" Maybe that was a bit of a cocky sentiment, assuming he was that for her, but the look she gave him seemed to affirm the truth of his words, though she still looked determined to push him away.

"I'm sorry I've distracted you. I'm sorry I haven't spent enough time lifting you up and reminding you what we're in this for. I'll do better."

She shook her head. "Jackson—"

"No!" he replied, this time being the insanely stubborn one. "It's my turn. We don't know how long you have. Are we going to spend the rest of your life being depressed and brokenhearted? Or are we going to do it living out our dreams? All of them."

She couldn't seem to respond.

"Marry me," Jackson said, and then the expression on her face turned to shock.

"Marry me," he repeated, "and we'll spend the rest of your life saving the world together."

This time it was her turn to huff in surprise. "You're crazy," she said, seeming to really believe that.

"I've been told that a time or two," Jackson agreed.

Only then did she truly seem to consider what he had suggested.

"Marry me," Jackson pleaded this time. "I will help you fight the enemy. You and I both know we're better together. You want to push me away? Well, I want to pull you closer."

She smiled at that, despite the pain in her expression and her tear-stained cheeks.

"Well?" he asked, not sure how many times he had to propose before she would at least say something.

She considered his offer for a long time before clearly thinking herself out of it. Then she shook her head over and over again. "No, Jackson. No. I won't do that to you. I won't hurt you that way."

"And what do you think breaking up with me does?" he replied pointedly.

"At least then you can let go before I die."

"No, Ava!" he said, louder than intended. "I can't! Don't you get that by now? This isn't a little teenage fling for me. I told you; I am in love with you. It crushed me in pieces when I thought I lost you in the Tower, and it will again when I lose you for real. But it won't help me to let you go by suffering the next months until I lose you for good. It'll just make it worse."

She shook her head as if in disagreement.

He put his hands on her cheeks then, and at least this time she didn't pull away. "Listen to me, Ava. Please, just listen to me. I am going to lose you either way. And that will be the hardest thing I ever face. Now, if you're trying to save me somehow, then marrying me is the only option."

She looked up at him, and this time it was clear she was certain he was crazy.

"Think about it," he said, somehow managing to chuckle at that moment. "If I'm going to spend the rest of my life in mourning and pining over my loss of you, would it be better if I was mourning my wife, and the love of my life? Or a two week 'fantasy' that according to you doesn't even count as a real relationship?"

She laughed, and he smiled. "I mean, come on," he pressed it further, "what will other people think of me?"

"They'll think you're crazy," she said through sudden laughter that seemed genuine.

He smiled deeper. "Right. But people will understand if I'm mourning my wife. Won't they?"

She didn't reply. Instead, she looked up at him with what could only be described as puppy dog eyes, a new hope gleaming as she watched him. The stubbornness was gone, the determination was gone. And

Jackson was awed. He had never seen her change her mind once she had made it up so strongly.

Still, she hadn't said yes.

Yet.

Jackson pulled off from the side of the tub to a kneeling position on the floor before Ava. She still held tightly to her pillow, but she allowed him to pull her hands into his as he spoke.

"Ava Altman," he said seriously, lovingly now, letting go of all the anger and determination. "Will you marry me?"

She watched him for a long time before slowly, carefully, she nodded. She couldn't seem to make a verbal response, but he accepted that for now. "That's a yes?" he asked to be certain.

She didn't trust her voice yet, but she smiled. Then nodded again. "Yes," she said in a barely audible whisper.

He leaned up closer to her. "You sure?" he teased. "Because there's always time to back out until the papers are signed."

Her jaw dropped open and she pushed him away teasingly. But then he moved forward and pulled her closer.

☆ ☆ ☆ ☆ ☆

Sasha entered the lab, in a state of dismal acceptance. It was too late for Ava; he knew that now. But perhaps he could find answers for the future. For Mikel.

He was taken aback to see Zak there at his worktable, burning the midnight oil as he tapped away on his laptop intently.

"What are you doing?" Sasha asked in surprise.

Zak didn't even look up. "I'm working."

Sasha pulled a chair beside the boy. "That part was obvious," Sasha said pointedly. "I mean, what are you doing working at this hour?"

Finally, Zak looked away from his work, long enough to look Sasha in the eyes. Sasha almost flinched at the look of determination. He had never seen such fierce passion in Zak before. "Jackson has given countless hours, and several times risked his very life, never stopping for a moment as he relentlessly worked to save my people. This is my chance to repay the favor."

Sasha sighed deeply. "You're trying to find a way to save Ava. We both saw those scans, my boy. This is one answer we will not find. There is no saving her."

Zak turned away from Sasha, back to his work. "Maybe, but after every relentless hour Jackson spent racking his brain and searching for solutions for a problem that wasn't really his own, but my people's...I can do this one thing."

"It's a waste of time," Sasha disagreed.

Zak looked up and faced him sharply. "Then get out!" he said, pointing at the door just as resolutely.

This time Sasha did flinch in surprise. Zak had only ever been the humble mentee. He had never addressed Sasha this way.

"After everything he has done for me," Zak said with an ambitious determination that suited him better than Sasha could have imagined, "I owe this to him. I will find a way. Or die trying."

Sasha watched him for a long time. It was a while before he managed to place why that passion was so familiar. It was exactly like Jackson's. And when Jackson made a determined decision, he followed through.

Sasha nodded somberly, pulling his chair in closer. "All right, Zak. All right. How can I help?"

★ ★ ★ ★ ★

Mikel was losing this fight. He was exhausted, but he could get no relief, he could get no rest. This enemy was going to conquer him. It was only a matter of time, and that time was growing ever shorter.

The door to his room swung open, and he managed to open his eyes long enough to see the blurry image before him. Kristen.

No, wait, that didn't make any sense. Kristen was dead. He blinked again, and thought he saw Damian this time. But then he blinked once more, and it became the Colonel.

He closed his eyes tightly suddenly, focused on the enemy as it sent another wave in attempts to crush him.

Kristen walked closer to him, determined. He was taken aback when she grabbed him on either side of his face and spoke passionately. "Listen to me, Mikel. Listen to my words. This enemy is stronger than you've ever faced. But you're the strongest enemy it has ever faced, too. Mikel, this foe will search for your weak points. It will find your doubts and fears, and it will prey on them. It will tempt you to give up, to stop fighting, and it will give downed compelling reasons. But you cannot obey."

He did not respond as he struggled for breath with the crushing weight of his enemy bearing against him.

Any other day, he would be in awe. Any other moment, he would be happily cheering to see the closest thing to a mother that he'd ever known. But right now, he could do little else but focus on his enemy.

"Open your eyes, Mikel," Damian pushed in his stern, yet somehow encouraging voice.

"I can't!" Mikel objected, shaking his head and wondering that now the closest thing he'd ever had to a father was here too. "It will win. It will crush me. I can't!"

"Yes, you can," Damian pressed. "It's lying to you. It makes you feel like you're losing—even when you're not. But your mind knows what it's doing. Trust me, Mikel. Open your eyes."

Slowly, he obeyed, and a part of him was expecting to be killed in the process. He was instead relieved to find that he was still alive. Damian was the one before him now.

"You need sleep," he told Mikel gravely.

Mikel blinked his eyes in confusion. How was Damian here? How could this be possible? Was he hallucinating? He hadn't slept in days. Perhaps his mind was playing tricks on him.

"You need rest," Damian repeated.

"No!" Mikel spoke in terror. "I can't sleep. I can't stop fighting." His eyes closed, then reopened again, and there was Kristen instead.

"You won't stop fighting," she urged. "You have been fighting this thing on no sleep for several days now. Your mind knows what it's doing. Ava stayed awake for the first five days," she explained somberly. "She was able to peg it off as grieving and fear for Jackson. But she was terrified to fall asleep. We've left you alone until now because you had to train your mind with complete focus to fight this enemy. But you're prepared now. Trust yourself. Trust your strength. Trust your training."

"No," he objected weakly, again shaking his head in fear. He closed his eyes again and gasped at the crushing weight.

She waited patiently as he fought the terrifying battle. When the next wave had passed, he opened his eyes. His perceptions were distorted as his view switched between Damian and the Colonel.

"Remember your old Zhànshì lessons about compartmentalization?" Kristen asked.

He nodded, unsure if he was able to respond or if it would kill him to do so.

"Right now, this battle feels like it's raging in every area of your mind. Do you feel that?"

He nodded.

"Close your eyes now," she ordered, and he did so.

"Do you feel the enemy?" Damian asked. "Do you feel the battle?"

Mikel nodded once more.

"Good," Damian spoke. "Now, isolate it."

"I can't—" Mikel started to object.

"Yes, you can," Kristen spoke surely. "Find the enemy, and isolate it. Imagine you're stuffing it into a box, like we trained you to do with your feelings during battle. Stuff the enemy into the box." She waited several minutes in silence before asking, "Did you do it?"

He swallowed hard. "I think so."

"Good," Damian spoke. "Now, don't close the box yet. Before you lock the enemy inside, you need to put one more thing in it. You also need to put in the fiercest, strongest parts of the Zhànshì Mikel. Find those pieces. Find your strength. Find your ferocity. Find your determination. Summon your anger. And most importantly, your Mikel confidence. Now, put them in the box."

Several more minutes until he responded through gritted teeth. "They're—inside."

"Good. Now close the box, tightly. Seal it shut like you would seal a door in the Tower."

Another long silence.

"It's closed."

"Now, here's the important part. Move the box to the back recesses of your mind. And leave it there."

Several more minutes before he replied, "Done."

"Open your eyes, Mikel."

He did so, only this time it didn't feel like it would break him to obey.

Kristen watched him seriously for a time before she spoke with that same confidence in him. "Those things you locked in that box? They're just as powerful as the foe inside. And they will be the rival of his life! But you cannot put every ounce of focus on fighting that enemy, or you will lose before you've even had a chance to hit him back. This fight is not like your old sparring matches. It's not like a quick operation in the Tower where you have a ticking clock until it ends. You are in this for the long haul. And in order to fight this enemy, you will need sleep. You will need nourishment. You will even need a bit of laughter and joy."

He blinked and in the second his eyes were closed, she shifted once more, and it was Damian before him.

"You are stronger than that enemy, Mikel, because it is using every ounce of energy to fight you. But right now, it's a little battle in a box at the back of your mind. Sometimes the box will break open, and you will have to push him back inside and seal him in there again. As long as you lock your greatest fighting spirit in that box with him, you will not stop fighting—even in your sleep. Even when you're weak. Even when outside distractions come along."

He blinked. Kristen stood before him.

"You are stronger than Counter Intelligence, Mikel. You are the strongest enemy it has ever faced. And guess what? You are going to beat it!"

✮ ✮ ✮ ✮ ✮

Kyle sat in the Tower cafeteria, but this time he was not alone. Mikel was there, and Jackson—though Sasha and Zak had locked themselves in the lab like recluses who would never come out of it again.

Ava was with Jun, helping her through her recovery and her withdrawals coming off the heavy narcotics.

The meal was about as silent as if he were eating alone. Kyle was the first to speak. "I'm going to leave as soon as we turn on the Global Tower Network," he admitted.

The others didn't seem all that surprised. "I need to focus on the Jiānhùrén. And I know you guys have a lot to do before you can turn your attention there, but I can't let them get any more out of hand."

Neither responded, though both of them seemed approving.

"I'm beating it," Mikel was the next to speak, some minutes later. "I'm going to destroy Counter Intelligence. I'm getting stronger every minute. And it's losing ground."

Jackson smiled proudly, and Kyle nodded his approval, though he suspected Mikel's arrogance led him to the lie more than anything. It was unlikely Kyle would see his friend again, when he left in two days, and that broke his heart, but there was nothing he could do for Mikel.

"I got married this morning," Jackson was the last to speak his piece, and both of their heads shot up in surprise.

"You what?" Mikel asked.

"To who?" Kyle said almost at the same time.

Jackson looked at Kyle with a funny expression, addressing his comment first. "Who do you think?"

"Oh, right. But...how did that happen?"

He shrugged. "I'm not sure. A part of me still can't believe it did. But Sasha left his work long enough to join us for the ceremony, and the Tower chaplain met us in the main hall."

"You didn't invite us?" Mikel said, seeming truly hurt by that.

"She didn't want to make a deal of it. We just wanted to be married, so we were."

A long silence passed awkwardly, and they focused on their food again. "Congratulations, by the way," Kyle offered after a long time.

"Thanks."

The silence lingered.

"The burritos are really good today," Mikel noted.

"Yeah, they are." Kyle agreed.

"Yup," Jackson added his two cents.

☆ ☆ ☆ ☆ ☆

It was certainly not a traditional wedding night. Although they had chosen to be married quickly, there were certain things that would take time—and that was just as it should be.

"What do I do about this?" Jackson spoke helplessly as he showed her the intelligence report about the Republic over the past several days.

"You want my help?" she asked in surprise. "I'm not a great world leader! I don't have a vast education on politics or how to promote freedom in chaos—" she was about to continue with her list of disqualifications, but Jackson stopped her.

"You're my wife," he offered. "That's often more qualification to help a man than that of the greatest political advisors."

She smiled sweetly at first, and he could see how much that meant to her before she shifted her tone to one of sarcasm. "I have a feeling it's gonna be a much harder job than theirs too."

He scoffed good-naturedly, and joined her on the couch as she read over the file.

"This is bad," she muttered as her eyes scanned the documents. "This is really bad."

He nodded grimly. "I have a meeting with the Committee tomorrow morning. Somehow, I think they're going to have a different opinion. But I agree with you. It changes things."

She shook her head as she tried to take it all in, but gave no answer; so he voiced his opinion on it. "We attacked the Towers with the intention of extracting all the Politburo members and helping the people of the Republic to hold a trial for them."

"But now..." she trailed off. "How can you?"

He gave a deep sigh. "Exactly."

She placed her hand on his and held it lovingly. "Let's figure it out."

For several hours they talked, debated, and argued on again and off again. They spoke of far more than the trials, but of the future of the Republic, and their role in it. They spoke of how involved they should be in putting things back together. They spoke of the danger of the Towers, and how to cripple its horrific power of control without taking away the electrical grid for the entire continent of Asia—if it were even possible, or right, to do so.

They talked of politics, government, tyranny, communism, the problems with each, and the possibilities of governing with freedom at the core.

All the while, in the back of his mind, he knew this night must eventually end, and he resented that fact. Always in his life, he dreamed of being married and of not having to say goodbye at the end of the night to the woman he loved. But that wasn't realistic with Ava, not yet. For now, she would continue with her own sleeping quarters, and he his.

Still, as the hours dragged on, he many times offered to walk her to her room, but she was never ready to end their conversation, and he didn't want her to go, so he never pushed it—forgetting his generally regimented sleep schedule.

They spoke of the United Kingdoms, of Council, of General Altman—they spoke of all of it the way they did the Republic, more as an idea than as real people who were so close to them. They spoke of the ideal. They spoke of what would need to change and how they could do it.

He really did want to run for Council. And although she shied from the topic whenever he turned it to her, he sensed that she missed all that had been taken from her. She missed working with Lionel. She missed being in Council, she missed speaking to the public and inspiring hope and strength within them. She missed the pressure and the struggle and the intensity. And he almost thought she would give up active military duty to be in that room again, if she could.

As the minutes moved to hours, they grew tired, and once more he offered to take her to her room. Instead, she laid her head on his shoulder, and he wrapped his arms around her where they sat together on the couch.

"What is the greatest flaw with the Kingdoms' current governmental structure?" she asked drowsily.

And of course, that was exactly the right question to ask to get him passionately talking again. He went on and on for a long time with her lying in his arms before he realized she wasn't responding much.

He smiled. He would get up in a minute and take her to her room. For now, he couldn't help closing his eyes for just a moment and feeling the weight of his own exhaustion.

It wasn't until she woke up screaming in his arms hours later that he wished he had chosen differently.

Apparently waking up from a nightmare and finding his arm around her was the worst possible scenario for her. She ran from him and huddled in the corner of the room, panting for breath.

Likewise, it was frightening on his end to be woken up at four in the morning by a deathly scream like that, and he, too, was panting and on edge at first, though it was easier for him to calm down than her.

He stood slowly, and carefully attempted to approach her, reassuring her that it was just him, but she screamed further, and flinched away. He waited, offering words of comfort until she seemed fully awake. She eventually recognized him.

"It's okay, Ava," he spoke gently. "It's just me, baby."

She nodded repeatedly, as if to tell him she knew that now. The terror left as she realized where she was, who was there, and what was happening. Then he knew it was safe to approach.

"I'm sorry," he whispered. "I should have taken you to your room."

She shook her head, as if to tell him she didn't blame him. She wasn't afraid of him now, and he expected her breathing to grow steady, but when she rubbed her fingers against her numbing palms, he knew that wasn't going to happen.

Sasha had always helped her through this in the past. Jackson hadn't the slightest idea what to do to help her...and yet, he wanted to be the one to do so.

As her breathing increased in frequency, as she realized that the panic attack was not going to go away easily, she stood and prepared to leave—running to Sasha like she always had before.

Jackson meant to reach his hand out, but stopped it halfway, realizing that physical touch was not welcome in that moment. Maybe it was a selfish thing, but he couldn't stand the thought of her running to Sasha because of a panic attack caused in part by Jackson, by her husband. He wanted to be the one she ran to now. He had to learn how to help her through this.

"Wait," he pleaded, holding his hand out carefully as an offering for her to take. "Will you stay?" he asked softly. "Please, let me be the one to help you?"

She still struggled for breath, and now seemed to be choking in attempts to fill her lungs with air. But even so, he saw the understanding in her eyes. He saw how she considered his request—however selfish it might have been. And though she said no words, she sat down once more into his arms.

Still, he had no idea what he was doing. Maybe she was better off going to Sasha, but her father had to have learned it at some point too, and Jackson wanted to do the same.

"It's going to be okay," Jackson offered, trying to be helpful. "You can breathe, love. It's okay."

☆ ☆ ☆ ☆ ☆

"He has never been late before..." Volvakov said from the large screen. "Perhaps his work has been catching up to him. He should have taken at least a day off after that operation like I told him to."

Sasha smiled. "I'm sure he'll be here any minute, Andre. If you don't mind waiting, I'll check in on him, to be certain."

"Of course. We'll begin the meeting with the basics."

Sasha excused himself from the briefing and went to Jackson's room, not bothering to knock before entering.

Jackson lay in his room asleep, but he was not alone. Of course, Sasha had known that they were married and that they would ultimately share a room. But Jackson had insisted that Ava needed her own space and that it would be a long time before she was ready to room with him. Sasha had agreed and hence was shocked to find them there. He could not help smiling at the surprise, having suddenly more hope that the two of them would have a normal, happy marriage—however short-lived.

With that in mind, he decided not to wake them. Jackson could miss one meeting, on the morning after his wedding day.

He reentered the briefing room, and they waited for an explanation. "I see you came alone," Volvakov noted discontentedly.

Sasha decided to cut to the chase. "Jackson was married yesterday. He might want a day off, though I realize, in light of recent events, it is terrible timing."

The entire Defense Committee made exclamations of surprise. "That dog!" Zukov said in frustration. "He was supposed to marry *my* daughter!"

"I should have told Elyia yes," Volvakov suddenly replied in consideration. "It may have been worth the risk."

"I wouldn't let him near my daughters," Stepanov disagreed. "And Yuri was always glad he never had a girl to have to keep Jackson away from."

"Well, tell him congratulations, I suppose," Volvakov offered, though still looking somewhat disappointed in his past decision, which caused Sasha to laugh out loud.

"Who is she?" Zukov asked with clear resentment. He had on many occasions attempted to pair Jackson with his own daughter, after all.

"*My* daughter," Sasha replied with a sudden chuckle.

Volvakov cursed. "Sasha, you..." he trailed off, taking a breath. "You are smarter than I am."

"I, for one, am glad the viper is off the market," Stepanov said, though even he seemed impressed by Sasha's accomplishment.

"Shall we continue the meeting?" Sasha asked, getting back on track.

Just then, the briefing room door swung open and Jackson entered quickly, taking a seat. "I am so sorry, everyone," he apologized, looking a bit frazzled. "I must have missed my alarm."

"Oh, is that what you did?" Zukov said with a deep glare.

Jackson watched the defense minister with a strange attempt at understanding. "...*Yes*," Jackson said, obviously confused by the random attack.

Everyone watched Jackson with a knowing comprehension that he did not understand, and he stared at them all in search of answers to their strange expressions. "What?" he asked, when no one else said anything.

"Let's get down to business," General Genrich said.

"I'm glad you decided to join us, Jackson," Stepanov added. "You've got some explaining to do."

★ ★ ★ ★ ★

A man was tardy for one meeting, and everyone acted like the world was ending. Of course, it was a rather important meeting. And sure, Jackson was usually the one there ten to twenty minutes early. But still. The strange behavior from the rest of the Committee was bad enough, but Sasha gave him several long stares throughout that had

Jackson shifting nervously in his seat. What was he looking for? Why was everyone making such a big deal of it? Every one of these men had been late before. Why couldn't Jackson have a turn?

Eventually, the meeting moved along, though never with any clarity as to why they were all so mad at him.

"We couldn't have seen this coming," Jackson said somberly. "I was sick to my stomach as I received the reports. Of course, there was nothing we could have done. The leadership of the Republic crippled us immediately with their counterstrike, and we had no one left to send in when they were the ones who needed aid."

Sasha shook his head in similar disbelief. "We managed to extract eight of the thirteen Politburo members before the blackout. Including the presidents of China and Korea. General Li was not so fortunate."

"I'm not too torn up about it," General Genrich muttered. "He got what was coming to him."

Although a part of Jackson agreed, knowing how stern and hard these Russians could be, he had to act the part of mercy. Luckily, Sasha was the one to appeal for mercy first. "Those men deserved a fair trial. What happened after we left was a massacre."

"By the people," Minister Stepanov argued. "These people have been enslaved by the Republic government for the past sixty years. They deserved no less than the opportunity to receive justice for all that was lost."

"I agree," Jackson clarified. "But we need to make sure that justice doesn't become a cry for blood. We don't need another French Revolution on our hands."

"General Li was a tyrant and a murderer," Stepanov spoke coldly. "He and the other four men who were killed in the Tower raids after the blackout are the lucky ones. Their deaths were quick and merciful. Those who stand to face trial will not have it so easy."

"That's exactly the problem I have," Jackson cut in. "Before the raids on the Tower, we had every intention of bringing the Politburo members to face trial by the people of the Republic. I fought for that outcome instead of a neutralizing operation. And to be perfectly honest with you, I don't mind that General Li is dead. I think the people had every right to carry out justice. And when he fought back, as anyone would, it was only natural that the hundreds of civilians would carry out their version of justice. I need to clarify; I'm not losing any sleep over what happened to Li. This isn't about him."

"It's about the other eight men in our prisons," President Volvakov said as if in realization.

"No," Jackson disagreed. Finally, he had their interest and attention now as they all struggled to comprehend what he *was* saying.

"Those eight men will be downed, one way or another," Jackson spoke coldly. "They chose their fate when they killed and enslaved millions for power. My concern is not for them. But if we give those eight men back to the people of the Republic right now, when their bloodlust and call for revenge is at an all-time high, when they're still dealing with the effects of the withdrawals from the blackout, we will have an endless cry for blood that will leave the Republic as ravaged and horrific as before. The Republic used force and control over its people, both physical force and the suppression from the Towers. For sixty years they have enslaved their people. They were built on communism, war and hunger for power. And it needed to change. We broke their governmental system. We targeted a number of their leaders, then ran for cover before we could finish the job, or help them find what was next. My point is, they are in a state of destructive anarchy right now. And the last thing they need is more heads to roll."

"So, what do we do with our eight tyrants?" General Genrich asked in concern.

"I don't know yet," Jackson said seriously. "Although we can't return them at this time, it isn't right for me, or even for Russia to try them." Jackson chewed on his lower lip, the inner conflict showing outwardly as the others watched him, expecting answers. He and Ava had spent hours on this topic. He still didn't know what to do.

A long silence passed before President Volvakov was the one to respond. "Well, Jackson, I'm sorry you feel so conflicted about this. I, however, feel no conflict."

Jackson narrowed his eyes in concern, not liking the sound of that. "I'm sorry, sir, what does that mean?"

"That's right. You need not concern yourself with it. Nor need anyone else. Those Politburo members are held in a *Russian* prison, guarded by *Russian* military. Where they will remain. For a very long time." He emphasized each word proudly, and it was clear he had no intention of changing his mind on this one.

In truth, Jackson didn't have any better answers for the time being. This decision from Volvakov was the definition of executive prerogative. He was not constitutionally allowed to make this choice, but if no one stopped him, he would get away with it. He may not have the constitutional power to make this call, but he had done it. No one would stop him, and it was one of those times where it might just be worth it, though a part of Jackson could never get behind breaches in constitutional checks and balances. Jackson wouldn't be able to change his mind without a better option, and he wasn't sure he even wanted to.

Jackson could not help thinking of the Louisiana Purchase and the Emancipation Proclamation—two executive decisions made by American presidents that Jackson found to be worth the executive overreach—and the legislature of the time had apparently agreed.

Eventually, when the Republic was ready to face the difficult decisions surrounding Politburo members, Jackson hoped to be right there to watch them receive a fair trial, and probably die for their crimes.

Jackson moved along, knowing there was little else to be done for the time being. "I would like to request that we send in extraction teams to procure the families of the Politburo members—those who are left, that is."

"You want to play the part of the Scarlet Pimpernel, do you?" Stepanov asked with a hint of annoyance.

Jackson looked up to face him boldly. "Better him than Chauvelin."

None of them seemed to buy that.

"Look, we got them into this mess," Jackson insisted. "The least we can do is—"

"We did not get them into this mess," Genrich disagreed. "They chose to be a part of the Republic."

"What? Like all of you?" Jackson pointed out sternly. He allowed the painful silence to pass as the others took that jab from him. "Your people got out less than a year ago," Jackson reminded them soberly. "One year. If this operation had been run one year sooner, it would be your own lives, and your families being considered right now."

Another silence passed. Jackson allowed for it.

"We'll get them out," Volvakov decided.

Jackson nodded. "Thank you."

"Now," Sasha said, changing the tone and topic of conversation. "The leadership of the Republic is gone. The people have overrun the Towers and remain in a state of chaos throughout the many countries of the Republic. What do we do now?"

The meeting soon adjourned, and Jackson gathered his things, painfully aware of Sasha's eyes on him again.

Jackson tried to avoid his gaze, but ultimately that proved impossible. So, he looked up to face him, not sure exactly what to expect. "I'll make sure not to be late to any meetings in the future," Jackson said, hoping to nip this whole reprimand in the bud.

Apparently, that was not the source of Sasha's thoughts. Finally, he gave Jackson something to explain his strange looks. "I went to check on you, this morning, when you didn't show."

Several beats passed before Jackson responded. "...Oh."

"Needless to say, I found you were not alone."

"Nothing happened!" Jackson replied defensively, as if feeling a need to explain himself to an angry father.

Sasha raised his hand. "That's none of my business," he said, though it was clear that had been the reason he had stared at Jackson on and off as he searched for an answer to that question. "Your marriage is between the two of you. I'll be sure to knock, from now on."

Jackson watched him awkwardly for a time, not sure how he was supposed to respond to this entire conversation that was growing more uncomfortable with every passing second.

Sasha smiled. "If anything, I was happy to see your wife with you. Though I admit it did shake me a bit. She can't sleep in the same room as anyone...and her nightmares. I would have expected it to cause a panic attack."

Jackson looked seriously at Sasha. "It did."

Sasha's eyes tightened in confusion. "But she never...."

"Went to you?" Jackson offered. "No. I helped her through it."

"I...I see."

Jackson could see how Sasha tried not to let that hurt him.

"Sasha—" Jackson tried to explain, but once again, Sasha raised his hand.

"You have no need to explain yourself. It is your right and your duty. I'm just...surprised. I guess..." he trailed off sadly for a moment. "I guess I'll just have to accept that she might not need me anymore, at least as much as she used to. No, don't apologize, son! It is as it should be." He managed a smile. "I am truly happy for you, Jackson. And for her. I only wish that..." he trailed off before resuming. "I only wish that you had more time, and could manage to live out all the dreams you had with my daughter."

Jackson's smile was somber and pained. "Me too."

Sasha perked up then. "But no use dwelling on what is not. Life is short, whoever you are and whatever your circumstances. Just know, Jackson, that I considered you my son long before you married my daughter. And I will be there as your father, long after she is gone."

He could not tell Sasha how much that meant to him. But fortunately, he did not have to. Sasha stood and gathered his things. "Well, I suppose I should allow you to move on with your work, and I'll resume mine. The world doesn't stop for us, even when we want it to. And if we don't keep up, it will get away from us."

Jackson chuckled. "Married one day. The next day, we defeat the Republic."

★ ★ ★ ★ ★

"You better make this quick," Eli hissed as he entered the fully attended Council meeting. "You know I don't have time for your silly, meaningless politics anymore." And that was true. He had not attended one of these ridiculous meetings since that day ten months ago when they told him they would not attack Russia no matter what he thought was best.

The entire room watched Eli, as if looking to him for answers amidst this new chaos. Finally, it was King Richard who addressed him. "General Altman," he spoke in a tone of deep respect. "In light of recent events—"

"You mean how Russia used our Zhànshì to perform a calculated, head-on attack against the Towers of the Republic?" Eli asked, not hiding his tone of accusation. "Or was it that they stole Brazil from under our noses?"

"In light of these events," Richard went on awkwardly, seeming an ignorant child as he spoke for this group of naive men and women just the same. "We have come to the unanimous realization—I'm sorry, that is, the unanimous *decision*, to move forward against Russia, as you have previously suggested. And more particularly, to eliminate Sasha Ivanov and Jackson Davis, as our former General, Eric Altman suggested. We believe, given the new information, that it would be prudent to eliminate these threats, as well as the rogue Zhànshì they recruited. We also believe it is time, as you previously suggested, to extract Zhànshì Fourteen and hand her over to your discretion in turning her by whatever means necessary."

Eli watched the room as a whole for an uncomfortably long time and allowed the silence to linger before he laughed out loud, mockingly, as if in all of their faces. "You mean you want me to clean up your messes?"

A long silence passed. "General Altman," Richard spoke carefully, "as our Kingdoms are still run by democratic vote among our Council members, it is not fair to say that one man's voice should be put above the rule of the majority—"

"Cut the taint, will you?" Eli spat vehemently. "Call a spade a spade. Do you or do you not want me to clean up the mess you people made?"

An even longer, tense silence passed before finally the king responded. "Yes, General Altman, we do."

Eli nodded appreciatively, continuing the vicious, wild-eyed look that terrified so many with its ferocity. "And are you prepared to return higher government authority to the seat of the General as we enter wartime ruling?"

Silence. Then, a word from Richard. "Yes, General Altman, we are prepared to turn temporary power over to the seat of the General during our state of emergency."

Eli smiled inwardly, though not a hint of it touched his face. He nodded gravely. "Then let's move forward, and make whatever official changes are necessary to make this happen."

"I—if I may, sir," Richard interjected. "What exactly do you intend to do about Russia?"

Eli grinned a chilling smile. "What do we always do when facing our greatest enemies? We're going to send them the wrath of the General."

★ ★ ★ ★ ★

Ava watched Jackson from across the table. He usually led these meetings and did it well. But this morning he was racked with thoughts and concerns, and Sasha must have noticed that, because he led the proceedings for the first half hour.

Everyone had an opinion, and today Ava spoke as much as the others, though she was conscious of Jackson's silence every time she, or one of the others, suggested something.

"So now it's just a simple matter of finding the leaders in each country," Mikel offered, "and empowering them to leadership."

"As Jackson did with Russia and Africa," Zak agreed.

"And as Ava did in Brazil with Prime Minister dos Santos," Mikel added.

"Still seems like a good plan to me," Kyle said with a shrug. "As long as I'm not the one who's supposed to find the leaders."

"Of course not," Mikel said harshly. "Jackson will do that."

Jackson closed his eyes sadly, and Ava noticed the movement. He had decided. They had talked over breakfast, and she had seen then how conflicted he had become about their next steps in regard to the Republic. She knew his thoughts had changed, yet he hadn't been able to express in words how he felt. Every time she had urged him to speak, he had only been able to repeat that same phrase. "What if we're not supposed to...?" and then he would curse and mutter to himself incoherently once more, never fully expressing his new thought.

She could see it in his eyes now though. Something had changed. He had decided. She only hoped that whatever he had planned, he would be able to express it now better than he had to her earlier, otherwise there was little chance of anyone following him, let alone knowing what it was he wanted.

"Jackson does have a knack for that, after all," Sasha chuckled. "In fact, he has made many contacts over the past months to possible leaders in the Republic. I think we have found people for just about every country. He will be very busy the next little while. Now we simply need to help them set up a structure that will—"

Jackson shook his head sternly, suddenly attracting all eyes to him as he spoke. "No. No, I don't think we're going to do that."

Several eyes narrowed in confusion. "It's your plan..." Vasiliv pointed out. "You've been working on this for years."

"I'm not sure I understand you, son," Sasha said carefully, and Ava could see a greater concern from Sasha, who recognized Jackson's resolute posture. "Are you not certain anymore of the contacts you've made?"

Jackson shook his head. "It's not that. It's all of this. I don't know that we should be trying to fix things in the Republic."

That took Ava by surprise. She wanted to support him, but first she had to understand what in the General's name he was talking about. How did this make any sense? "We just destroyed the only governmental system these people have known for half a century!" Ava objected. "You want to just abandon them when they're most vulnerable?"

"You can't really mean to abandon the Republic now," Sasha tried to get to Jackson's meaning.

Jackson pushed his lips out pensively as he often did when he was conflicted. He considered for a long time before he looked up at them. When he did, his face was determined. "This is going to sound counterintuitive, but after what happened when we left the Towers vulnerable, after what the people did taking the Towers, I have been reconsidering everything."

"You can't blame them for what they did," Ava said in quick defense of the people.

"Not at all!" Jackson replied assuredly. "Not for a second. As gruesome as those attacks were, it is justice. That was justice. And it was justice by the people."

"So why do you want to abandon them then?" Ava asked, still having no comprehension of what he was thinking.

"It would have been wrong for me to order those executions, or to make it happen myself. It would not have been our right as foreign powers to move in and kill their leaders one by one. But I'm not losing any sleep over the fact that it happened. As terrible as that was and as horrific to think that it could happen, not only was it not necessarily wrong for the people to do it—though of course, perhaps they could have done better—but it is their right and responsibility to take out that kind of an oppressive government."

"Still not following," Kyle objected. Jackson kept talking as if Kyle hadn't.

"At the end of the day, as gruesome, as horrible as it was, and as fast as it happened, it made me realize that maybe fixing the Republic isn't mine to do."

A long silence followed as none of them had an answer for that bold statement.

"I think you're going to have to explain more than that, bud," Zak pressed in shock.

Jackson took a breath and prepared for what would hopefully be a more articulate explanation. "If you are walking down a darkened alley one night and you see a man or a group of men beating a pregnant woman on the street, you stop them, yes?"

Everyone agreed assuredly.

"You do whatever it takes to stop them from hurting her," Jackson continued emphatically. "But just because you save this woman from those who would abuse her, that doesn't mean then that it's your job to dictate to her what hospital she has to have her baby in, who her midwife will be, what kind of diet that baby will be on, and what university that baby will go to when it grows up. It doesn't mean you should fund their future. And saving her from her abusers certainly doesn't give you the right to control her from then on."

"There's a difference between controlling and helping," Mikel disagreed.

Jackson bit his lip again before he replied sternly, "Not this time."

Another long silence followed as no one quite understood what he meant by that.

Then, out of nowhere, Kyle stood, an absent look on his face, and left the room. Everyone watched him go in surprise until the door was closed.

"See?" Mikel spoke harshly. "Kyle hates your new plan so much that he's leaving!"

Still, Jackson did not seem fazed by Mikel's sarcastic comment as he continued. "There is a certain duty when witnessing a wrong, and acting to protect that pregnant woman—even if you have no stewardship over her, and even if you don't know her. There is a duty to step in at certain places where you can stop atrocious injustices from happening. But that doesn't make you the father of that woman or the father of her child. It doesn't give you the right to control her or the baby from that time forward.

"Now, that's not to say that there's never a place to help, and to mentor and to give more, but it is to say that as we're looking at this, it is imperative that we separate the duty and the calling to stop wrongs, from the do-gooder social engineer idea that says 'because I know better than others, I have the right then to control them, and put my will on them.' None of us knows everything we need to truly help these people move forward. And even if we did, it doesn't give us the right to do it."

Sasha was the one to object now. "But we just destroyed the only governmental system they had—"

"We took out an oppressor on the street," Jackson said, referring back to his analogy. "An oppressor who, not only attacked this pregnant woman, but had plans laid out to attack each of our families too, and were already in the process of doing so."

"All right," Sasha said, prepared now to take him on. "But if you put it in those terms, that oppressor was the woman's father, or husband, or the one who had a stewardship to help provide for her. And yes, he was oppressive and abusive. And yes, we had a duty to stop that wrong. But if we eliminate her only source of income and care, we have a duty to provide her with something."

"I felt the same way," Jackson explained. "All along, I have intended to be directly involved in rebuilding the countries of the Republic after their current system was taken out. But we did not kill the oppressors. We extracted eight men and prepared to put them on fair trial. They killed those who remained. We did not order that pregnant woman to eliminate those oppressors who we missed. We did not tell the people of the Republic to ravage the Tower and take out the remaining Politburo members. We had no right to give them that order. It was their right, and their duty to do so. And I have been reconsidering everything since then.

"It may sound absurd coming from the American in the room. Because of my opportunities, because of my ability, everything that I have, the blessings and the knowledge, I, and all of us, have a responsibility to stop these evils from happening. But despite my opportunity, despite my freedom and my knowledge, I will not become a tyrant just because I think I know better."

"Jackson," Ava spoke in disagreement, "we're not going to take over their countries and form another Politburo. We just want to find the right leaders and empower them to victory. Then help them set up a secure, free government."

"How can you, or I, or anyone know exactly who should stand up and lead those people? I've spent the last months trying to build leaders from the ground up. But who gave me the power or the right to pick the new leaders of the Republic countries?

"I love spreading the manifest destiny of freedom and opportunity for everyone, of being willing to fight for those who desperately need us to fight for them. But we need to be willing to fight for them in a way where we realize we are not their god. And I will not make myself that, despite my American upbringing and everything that means.

"Yes, we have opportunity, and yes, it comes with responsibility. But it does not come with omniscience, or omnipotence. And it certainly doesn't come with the right to play God just because we think we'd be good at it. Or even because they need it. Neither of those things give us the right to control and force, and make everybody in our perfect image."

"None of us is suggesting that we fully write out their new governmental system and enforce it," Sasha clarified. "But we owe it to them to help them find peace in the coming chaos."

"I appreciate your sentiment, Sasha. And I even agree with it. But with all of that said, and with everything I've studied, I feel like the real answer is that sometimes it's our job to stop the wrong but not our job to fix or to set up and control everything. It was right for us to come in and give them a chance. To step in and stop the oppressors from beating that pregnant woman. But we are not the ones who drove those people into the Towers. The people took the chance when they had it.

"My intention was to be highly involved in what happened next in the Republic. But seeing the people stand up and fight for their own rights...? What an impressive reminder that this governmental power should be in the hands of the people. And I hope and pray that they figure it out. And I'm absolutely going to be here to share principles, forms, history and experience when they ask, and I'm absolutely going to be here to build relationships where I feel appropriate in trying to make the process as easy as possible for them. We will absolutely offer aid and wisdom and help where we can, and where they want it. But what right do I have to walk into their countries and tell them who gets to rule, and how they should do it?"

No one had an answer, and the silence lingered until Jackson continued. "Again: I know it feels counterintuitive, and I know so much that I want desperately to be the one to go in there and show them these forms, show them these principles, help them know every book to read, help them find the leaders who are ready, and help mentor and instruct those leaders to set up everything because I know so much and I'm so prepared." He took a deep breath before he stared the room down. "But who gave me the right to lead them? And if I force my leadership, however great, upon them, what makes me different from the tyrants who do the same?"

No response.

"We stopped the wrongs. We have given them a chance. And I will offer myself as much as I can to assist those who stand up and lead. I will offer what wisdom and knowledge and aid I can. But you're all talking about how it's my job to go into those countries and build a government for them. I'm sorry. I won't do that. I will not play God. I will not pretend that I have all the answers for a people with a sacred history, culture and background that has nothing to do with me. I will not pretend because I'm well-read that I have all the answers to their problems. I know without a doubt I do have answers that would help. And inasmuch as they want it, I will offer that knowledge and wisdom. If they ask for my advice, I'll happily share it. But I will not make myself their tyrant just because I think I could do a good job of it. I am not God. And I will never pretend to be."

Ava didn't like it. A part of her wanted to object, to say he was wrong and that they owed these people more. And yet, she could not deny the truthfulness of his words. None of them could.

Sizwe had found *Jackson*. He had self-selected himself to be a great leader and to align himself with those who could make a difference.

Prime Minister dos Santos was already an elected leader by the people, and had been ready to stand up and fight for his country. And even in Russia, where Jackson, Sasha and Zak had met with the Russian leadership and persuaded them to stand up and fight, there had been a different understanding, and a different stewardship there. She couldn't exactly put into words why it was different, and yet, she knew it was.

What gave Jackson, or any of them, the right to waltz into India or China or Korea and dictate to the people what they must do next? What gave them the right, as foreign leaders, to move into their nations and tell them how they must live, and govern and work?

Of course, they would help. Of course, they would offer whatever support they could. But Jackson was right. They could not just go in and force their ideals on this people, any more than General Li had a right to conquer the countries of Africa and subjugate them to his will.

"So...what do we do now?" Sasha asked seriously. "None of us likes the idea of standing back and watching the people burn."

"They're not going to," Ava surprised herself by responding with confidence. All eyes turned to her. But it was the confident, proud look that Jackson gave her that really empowered her to speak what had been on her mind since she was a simple Zhànshì in training, watching the world powers fight *for* the people. Never *with* them.

"We underestimate them. They've been through hell and back again. And they may struggle for a time. They *will* struggle for a time. But they're better prepared than any of us realize. These people deserve the opportunity to stand up and fight for themselves, just as they did during the blackout.

"Will new tyrants rise up in some countries and usurp power and authority? Probably. As they have throughout history. But the people will rise. And mark my words when I say that we will be surprised by those countries who are ready for change, who are prepared to abandon tyranny and communism for a better way. Heaven knows many were surprised by Russia! Some may turn to us, and we will help how we can. The Politburo threatened freedom worldwide, and it was our duty to stop them. But we have no more right to control these people than Zhang did."

"Leaders will rise," Jackson added. "And they'll lead their people to better life."

"Tyrants will rise," Ava continued. "And they'll take their nations by storm. We will offer the support that we can to those who oppose the tyrants and seek for freedom."

"But we will not infringe upon the rights of the people who deserve the opportunity to be free," Jackson demanded.

"We have to be better than that," Ava spoke with similar passion.

Jackson kept her glance and offered an appreciative nod. She nodded respectfully, as if to affirm that she was beside him to the end.

Another long silence passed as everyone around the table accepted the clear change in direction. This hadn't been the plan. And yet, it felt more right than their previous objective ever had.

It was easy for them to want to do everything. But not everything was theirs to do.

"So, that's it?" Mikel asked. "We just let them figure it out for themselves?"

Zak sighed heavily, yet seemed to agree with their new plan. "Have you already told the Committee you have no intention of gaining the rest of the Republic?"

Jackson smiled. "No. But I'll convince them." Although he said it as though it were nothing, Ava knew well it would be the most difficult battle he had faced yet—convincing the Committee to stand down and let the world be rather than conquer it all for themselves.

"So, what now?" Vasiliv urged in slight frustration. "We just wait for them to reach out?"

"I have many contacts within the Republic," Jackson explained. "People who I expect will rise and move forward in the next weeks. Many in the Committee have similar contacts. We'll actively reach out and offer support. For those who want it, we will be prepared to—"

He was cut off as the door slammed open. Everyone looked to where Kyle was holding on to a frantic Jun, attempting to keep her calm. "I'm sorry to interrupt, Jackson," Kyle spoke urgently, "but she's insistent!"

"It's okay," Jackson said warily, standing and walking to her. "What's wrong, Jun? What's going on?"

She had been muttering to herself, and only now looked up to face him. "They're coming!" she said with a terror that couldn't help striking fear into Ava's heart.

"Who's coming, Jun?" Jackson asked carefully. "The Republic?"

"No! No! They're coming!" she shouted.

"Who's coming?" he repeated. "I need to know who it is, Jun."

She shook her head, and pulled away from Kyle until he let her go. Then her hands went to her head and she sat on the floor, trembling as she worked through her terror. "So many voices. So many orders. They're coming, Jackson! They're all coming!"

Ava had a sneaking suspicion she might understand what Jun was saying, but Jackson got down to her level and asked once more just to be certain. "Please, Jun, I need to know who it is."

She finally looked him in the eyes. "He's recalled all his weapons," Jun said urgently. "He's even recalled Valkyrie. They're coming for us. The chip-enhanced army, Valkyrie—all of them, they're coming for us."

PART THREE

The General vs. The Altman Girl

THIS IS OUR LEGACY.

16

Orders

"Zak," Jackson said urgently, "raise our homeland defense to high alert!"

Zak jumped from his seat and left the room quickly.

"Vasiliv," Jackson shouted the next order, "get the Northeastern Tower on stage one alert immediately and have Moscow do the same."

"Yes, sir!"

Jackson turned back to Jun, still kneeling on the ground with her. "Is there anything else you can give me, Jun? Is there anything else you know that could help us?"

She shook her head repeatedly, giving no reply. Jackson looked up to where Kyle stood. "Get her somewhere quiet. Stay with her, talk to her. I need to know of any intel she gets that might help us."

"Understood," Kyle said, helping Jun to her feet and walking her from the room.

"Sasha, get me the president on the phone. And send my assistant," Jackson sent the next order as Ava waited, standing in the back of the room for her own orders.

Sasha hurried quickly from the room, acting immediately on his orders.

"Mikel, send a message to Sizwe and our other allies. Tell them to hold strong. We need the Elites recalled ASAP."

Soon, Jackson's assistant entered the room, the young male officer looking intent. "Sir!" he said, hurrying to his commanding officer.

Jackson barked out several more hurried orders to the man before other officers came in and went to Jackson to receive their own orders.

He hurriedly commanded each one to separate needs, and still Ava remained standing there uncertainly. Everyone else had a task. She stood there feeling useless.

Sasha reentered the room and handed Jackson a mobile.

"How sure are you about this intel?" President Volvakov asked from the video call when Jackson had finished his hurried explanation.

"I'm one hundred percent certain that it's not worth taking the chance of ignoring it and being wrong," Jackson replied confidently.

Volvakov cursed, but then agreed. From the other end, he began barking out his own commands to his men in preparation for what was to come.

And still, Ava stood, useless and uncertain.

Jackson handed the mobile back to Sasha, and moved to one of his officers, snapping out the next commands. Sasha left in a rush, apparently knowing what was needed from him already.

It was nearly five intense, harried minutes before Jackson finally glanced at Ava. He smiled, sweetly, even amidst his stress and myriad concerns. But then he turned back to his work, and she had never been so frustrated at him in their entire married life as in that moment. Not that it had been that long.

"Begin a mandatory evacuation of the Towers," Jackson ordered Zak when he returned. "All non-essential personnel are to evacuate immediately. And call in reinforcements to defend against a full-scale attack."

A line of three men vied for Jackson's attention as he continually gave out commands to the others. Realizing he wasn't about to notice her any other way, Ava joined the three men.

Jackson addressed one, barking out orders. Then the next. Then the next. Then he looked at her, and realizing it was just her, was ready to write her off, but she wasn't about to allow that.

"What do you need me to do?" she demanded.

He stopped, biting his lip carefully before he admitted softly, even in front of the others, "I didn't exactly want to get into the habit of giving you orders."

Ava's frustration softened as she understood. He wasn't trying to lock her in the fridge. But after all her abuse from Eli, Jackson was attempting not to do anything that Eli might have. Still, it wasn't going to fly, and she confidently told him so. "That's the dumbest thing I've ever heard! We're in a crisis, and you're in charge. Tell me what you need me to do."

He smiled appreciatively before seriously considering her words. "All right. If you're sure. I need someone to direct the officers in preparation for battle. They have no clue what they're in for. They'll need direction from someone who does."

"Yes, sir!" she said, and didn't bother to acknowledge how he flinched at that title as she quickly left the room.

There was no doubt they were equals in their relationship and marriage. He would never attempt to act superior and would always elevate her, if anything. But this wasn't a time to battle about rank. He was unequivocally the commanding officer in this scenario, and it didn't hurt her pride or her confidence in the slightest to follow whatever order he gave when they were working.

She would rather follow her commanding officer's direction—even if he also happened to be her husband—than stand there uselessly in the corner. And if Eli was about to send in that long-anticipated attack he had promised, they had a lot to do to get ready.

It was nearly six hours later when Jackson called the others back in for a strategic planning meeting. Sasha, Vasiliv, Zak, Jackson and the three Zhànshì gathered once more around the briefing table.

Ava hadn't had even a few seconds with him since this morning. And after only one day of marriage, she decided it was a crying shame that Eli had chosen this time to attack. Would Jackson and Ava ever have even one normal day? Would they ever have just a moment to imagine things were fine, that they were okay, and that they could really be happy? Or would their greatest enemies always be just a moment away, prepared to attack the mere second that these two stood any chance of happiness together?

"What we've accomplished in the last few hours was just preliminary preparations," Jackson explained. "There's a lot to be done in preparing a nation for war. Now let's talk strategy. You four know Council better than anyone here." This referring to the Zhànshì, as well as Sasha. "What are they planning? What do we need to prepare for? And how do we win this?"

Mikel was the first to respond. "They want Ava. They'll move heaven and earth to get her back. We all stand in the way, and so to them we're collateral damage."

"There's more to it than that," Kyle disagreed. "Their number one priority is to extract Ava, no doubt. But I think Council has finally realized their mistake."

Everyone watched him, waiting for more explanation. "The day Eric died he gave me one final order. He said it was against the wishes of Council, but that he was certain it had to be done. He ordered me to neutralize Jackson and Sasha."

Ava was taken aback. They all were. But surprisingly, Sasha smiled as if he was loving the comment. "That old mongrel," he chuckled. "At least he finally tried to do something on his own two feet. Would've been a smart move for him too."

Kyle nodded. "Apparently, Lionel convinced Council that you were more useful alive, and insisted that eventually they would be able to secure an alliance with Russia through Sasha. When Eric died, I wrestled long with the decision before ultimately giving it up."

"That's why you wanted to kill me," Jackson said in sudden revelation. "That day during the attack on the African village."

Kyle affirmed that. "General Altman believed you were the greatest threat to the United Kingdoms as it stood. I suppose in the end, he was right. But the United Kingdoms as it stood was an enemy to freedom."

Jackson and Kyle shared a respectful glance, and Ava couldn't explain why it meant so much to her that these two were finally true friends.

"So, yes," Kyle reiterated. "I agree that their first priority is Ava, but a close second will be eliminating you two."

Jackson was about to move along and strategize with this knowledge, but Ava raised her hand. Jackson smiled. "You don't need to raise your hand, Ava. What is it?"

"Oh, sorry," she said with sudden embarrassment. A moment passed as she watched the others and considered. "You're both right, to some degree, but I think it goes even a step further."

She straightened in her seat and awkwardly cleared her throat. She used to be good at speaking in leadership meetings with Lionel—or at the very least, she had been confident. Now, in a room with her closest friends, she struggled for the right words, but everyone watched and waited patiently until she was ready to elaborate.

"You're all talking about Council. But you don't know Council like I do. Council doesn't do things. Council doesn't take risks. Council doesn't move forward. They sit back and wait for stuff to happen. They get involved in gridlocks and argue away their time to pretend they're doing something useful. They are quite literally forty-nine elected aristocrats who use money, fame and power to act the role of the greatest free coalition of nations in the world. The United Kingdoms is not ruled by Council. It was moved by Harrison. By Lionel. And now that they're gone, if anyone, it will be ruled and moved by the General. So that's the piece that we have to understand right now. Council isn't coming for us. Eli is."

The room went cold and silent as they all considered the repercussions that might have on all of them.

"Well, now I'm actually terrified," Zak said with a hint of sarcasm.

Ava looked him in the eyes with a deep, serious pain. "You should be."

Sarcasm soon turned to soberness as Zak caught a glimpse of how terrified Ava actually was.

Still, not everyone seemed to understand just how serious this was. Ava swallowed hard, then tried another way. "Raise your hand if Eli was ever your superior officer, or if you ever took any orders directly from him."

Mikel was the first to raise his hand, followed by Kyle, and then even, though reluctantly, Jackson raised his hand. Ava was the last to do so. "Now, keep your hand up if at any point, you deserted or betrayed him."

All hands remained up. Ava let the silence linger for emphasis before she explained, "This is not just a practical extraction, or even a neutralizing mission. In his mind, every one of us betrayed him, and it cost him Russia, Brazil, the Republic, and quite possibly the United Kingdoms too. This mission isn't about my extraction or your assassination. This is about revenge.

"He will hit every single one of us where it hurts. He wants to make us pay. And believe me when I say, he's good at it. He has spent the last nine years of his life in an obsessive search to find and understand other people's weaknesses. He'll find our weak spots, and he'll stomp them hard."

No one in the room liked the idea of that, and yet she could see as she related these words that every one of them resonated with the truthfulness of it. They all knew Eli. They knew what he was capable of. Worst of all, *he* knew *them* too.

"Well, as disturbing as the thought is," Mikel offered dryly, "maybe it can give us a leg up. Everyone just think, what's the worst thing that anyone could do to me? Then we'll keep that from happening and all is well."

Sasha shook his head bitterly. "Unfortunately, he's too smart for that. He'll hit us, and hit us hard, and if we try to protect one weak point, he'll reveal the hidden weakness we didn't even know was there."

"Eli is tough to have on your side," Ava noted sadly. "But he is an absolute horror to his enemies."

"How do we defend against this?" Zak asked with concern. "I don't like the sound of this. At all. I mean, I never took orders from him, but—"

"He knows you," Ava disagreed. "He knows your involvement in all of this. You're on his hit list, I assure you."

Zak's jaw tightened, and Jackson and Ava's eyes met. She tried to convey her concern to him, and was grateful when he clearly understood. "Go to Viktoriya," Jackson ordered his friend. "Get your family to safety. We'll take care of things here."

Zak stood and quickly left the room, not needing to be told twice.

Jackson looked around the room then, as if to see who else might need to receive the same order. "Vas?" he asked his friend, but Vasiliv shook his head.

"My ex-wife isn't a part of my life. She won't even speak to me anymore."

Jackson was about to move on, but Ava spoke urgently. "Send a team for her. He *will* go after her."

Vasiliv's eyes sobered as he watched Ava. An eerie feeling filled the room as everyone realized how certain Ava was. And of all of them, she had been the closest to him. She knew him the best. She knew all too well what he was capable of.

Vasiliv turned a questioning, hopeful glance to Jackson, who agreed. "Go. Send someone to get her to safety. And anyone else who might be used against you."

It was just Sasha, Jackson and the Zhànshì left in the room after that.

"Now that Damian is gone, the only people he could use against me are in this room," Mikel noted. "And I have a feeling that we're all gonna get trampled by the end of this."

"How much could he know?" Kyle asked with deep concern. "Does he even know I'm alive? Does he know who I was involved with before I died?" Clearly, there was someone he was worried about.

Ava shook her head uncertainly. "I don't know, Kyle. If there's someone you're worried about...best be safe. But then, what if making the call is what reveals it to Eli?"

Kyle gritted his teeth in frustration.

"She's in the Kingdoms, yes?" Jackson asked, and Ava's eyes narrowed. How did Jackson know Kyle's deep dark secrets?

Kyle nodded simply in response.

"I'll send Remington."

Relieved, Kyle was finally able to sit back in his seat. "Thank you."

"What about you, Sasha?" Jackson asked, turning it to him now.

Sasha sighed heavily. "I have hundreds of close friends who I would be heartbroken to lose. But I wouldn't even know where to begin." He closed his eyes sadly in consideration. When he opened them again, he sighed once more. "No, don't worry about me. He already knows the greatest weapon against me is himself."

"That's not really comforting," Mikel said sarcastically.

"What about you, Ava?" Jackson asked, and she had been hoping to avoid the question and attention from everyone.

Her heart clenched within her chest. A list of names ran through her mind.

Harrison. Ame. Kristen. Breanna. Liam. Eric. Yuri. Hawkins. Ella.

All of the people she had lost. All of the people who Eli had some hand in ripping away from her. At least, if Hailey was right, Ava could pretty much blame every loss on Eli. From Harrison to Ella—other than Kristen's death, for which she could only blame the Republic.

She had lost so much already. And yet...there was still so much to lose.

Jackson.

Sasha.

Kyle.

Mikel.

Zak, Viktoriya and the kids.

Remington.

Even Valkyrie.

Just one more of these losses felt like it would crush her. But she had a feeling Eli intended far more than a simple victory. He would play for a grand slam. He wanted revenge on all of them. But her most of all. And when he made all the rest of them pay, he would rip everything away from her. Everyone she loved. It felt imminent. There was probably nothing she could do to stop it from happening.

Unable to respond to the question at first, she shook her head, then managed a hoarse response. "There's no one to collect. Just...just you guys."

Jackson gave her a tender look from across the table, and she wished they were seated next to one another, so that at the very least he could offer a comforting hand in that moment.

"What about you, Jackson?" Mikel turned it to him.

Jackson struggled to answer for a long time. "There are a lot of people I'm worried about," he admitted. "I...I don't know where to start either." He chewed his lip in consideration. "Yuri's wife and sons," he said with sudden clarity. "I have an aunt and uncle in Australia. My sister Maelyn in Brazil. I'll send help for all of them."

He looked up then, and his eyes met Ava's. "You think he wants to hurt you most," Jackson said to her, though all the others were there to witness it. "But he promised me ten months ago that he would send his wrath to destroy Russia, and me. It's taken him this long to gain the power, I guess. But he's not just coming to hurt you. We've all made an enemy of him."

"He made an enemy of us," Mikel clarified.

"I still don't know how we're supposed to come up with a defense against this," Kyle said in frustration. "He's sending in the fiercest soldiers and Zhànshì after us."

"No," Mikel disagreed with sudden confidence that emanated in his demeanor. "He's sending the best of what he has left. He already lost the greatest soldiers and Zhànshì he had. And if he wants to send us hell, then we'll give it right on back to him."

★ ★ ★ ★ ★

Jackson lay awake in his bed, unable to sleep, though the hour was late and he was exhausted.

There were still so many things to do and prepare. New thoughts continually popped into his mind, and he would reach for his mobile again and make the contact or send the order. Then he would lay his head down once more and attempt to sleep, before starting the process all over again.

It was half past three when the door cracked open and someone entered, shuffling in quietly.

"Ava?" Jackson asked the figure as she entered. "Is that you?"

"Are you asleep?" Ava replied in a careful whisper.

He chuckled to himself before responding sarcastically, "Yup."

She clicked her tongue and made her way over, joining him under the covers. He accepted her into his arms.

"You couldn't sleep either, huh?" he asked, adjusting this time to using his full voice, rather than a whisper.

Ava shook her head. "I can never sleep."

"See, you say that, but you always fall asleep just fine in my arms."

She gave a loving smile. "Maybe that's why I'm here."

He returned the look of adoration before noticing the shirt she had on. It was his shirt—one she must have taken from his dresser.

"Nice outfit," he teased.

"I stole your shirt because it smells like you. I used to wear the one you left in Africa to help me fall asleep and it worked until it stopped smelling like you. So now I have this one."

Jackson made a sound of mock frustration. "You could always just come for the real deal."

"I didn't want to bother you. But I guess…I did do that eventually, didn't I?"

Laughing, he playfully grabbed her and tickled her before saying, "You realize I love you. That means all I do is sit here alone and pine over you and wish you were here."

She giggled sweetly, pushing his hand away to stop him from tickling her. "No you don't."

"I literally do," Jackson said challengingly, and he kissed her cheek lovingly as if to reiterate his feelings.

After a moment, he pulled back and glanced seriously at her. Apparently, his look was too full of longing because she sat up, pulling away from him slightly.

He couldn't help the fact that he sometimes looked at her that way. Still, this was him trying.

"It's only been two days," Ava noted softly. "How different do you think it would have been if we actually broke up?"

"Not all that different, honestly," Jackson said wistfully. "Longing looks from across the briefing table, as I suggested. Working my carcass off, wishing that instead I was with you. Wondering in the tiniest solitary moments if you were going through the same thing, or if you're too busy and involved in your own work to ever think of me."

"I'm always thinking about you," Ava retorted with a sweet smile. "And no, we don't get too much time together. But I wouldn't be here now if we had broken up."

"Oh, I don't know. I think it would be right around night three where you realized you made a mistake and came running back to me."

She hit him hard in the arm, and he laughed, though he moved his hand to rub the tender spot.

Ava leaned her head on his shoulder and lingered there as he held her close, hanging on to every moment with her. "I wish we had more time," she muttered, and she had no idea how often that thought crossed his mind.

"So do I," he admitted in a pained whisper.

"I thought we'd have at least a few weeks...maybe even months together before we'd have to worry."

"Eli only just recalled his troops," Jackson offered hopefully. "It could be a couple of weeks before they attack. And Jun is listening to every word. We'll be ready when they come for us."

Another silence passed, and he held her tighter still, not wanting it to end. A new thought occurred to him, about the weak state of her mind and the fact that this next fight could be what pushed it to the edge. "I don't want you to die from this battle," Jackson whispered hoarsely. "If Eli is the one that causes your death..." he trailed off as his teeth ground together and his nostrils flared in anger.

Ava sat up again slowly, then watched him for a moment before her soft temperament managed to change the whole feel and tone of the conversation. "You know what's crazy?" she said with enthusiasm.

"Huh?" Jackson said, still not fully past his sudden anger.

"For fifty years, Harrison fought relentlessly for a way to defeat the Republic. When the chip came along, he spent countless money, hundreds of lives, and endless hours of research on a way to use it to beat them. And it worked. We did it. We actually defeated the Republic. I mean, there were a few adjustments along the way from his original plan. But Harrison got Sasha, me, you, Kyle, and in a way, he even got Mikel and Ella in place too! And of course, we couldn't have done it without Breanna and Liam. He made a plan, and he made it happen. And it worked." A silence passed before she said soberly, "Who would have realized that, in the end, the Republic wasn't even the greatest enemy we had to face?"

Jackson watched her seriously. Holding her in his arms like this, having simple pillow talk with his wife, was a dream come true—one he thought would never be fulfilled. It was a tragedy that it would be so short-lived. But he still managed to cherish this moment for all it was worth.

Ava's expression became even more serious, if that was possible. When she spoke, it was in almost a whisper. "I think Eli killed Harrison."

Silence lingered, and Jackson didn't attempt to respond before she spoke again. "I don't know if it was to gain power, or for revenge or out of anger, or something else entirely. But I think he really did it."

"I'm sorry, Ava," Jackson offered, not knowing how else to respond to that.

She offered a saddened smile. "Me too. I wanted so badly for him to choose to be good. I tried so hard to help him. I did everything I could. But I guess—just like Mikel teaches us—you can't underestimate someone who really wants to be great. I guess Eli shows us that you can't make someone be good, no matter how much you want them to, when they continually make the wrong choices."

"We can only control ourselves," Jackson replied sadly. "And hope that through our extreme discipline, passion and example we can inspire others to follow where we lead."

Ava smiled, and at least there was a bit of light in her eyes. "Did I ever mention how much you have inspired me?" she asked him earnestly. "You changed my whole world, Jackson."

His eyes blurred with sudden tears as that touched him deeply, but he blinked it away with a loving smile. "You changed my world too."

Her face suddenly grew serious as she seemed to have another thought. When she spoke, it was with such depth and emotion that he felt every word. "I would live out your dreams with you now, Jackson, if we could. I would have a family with you. I would have your kids. If we had time. You can't imagine how much I want that now. For me, as much as you. If we had time...I would have a family with you. I promise, I would."

He knew she meant that. And although they unfortunately didn't have time to live out those dreams, the fact that she would have meant more to him than anything in the world. He loved this woman. And he now had a greater understanding and desire for a family than he ever had before. He had always wanted to be a husband and a dad. But suddenly his dreams were so much bigger than that. His dreams were no longer just about him but about her. He longed for her to have the opportunity to be a wife, to be a mother, to be an amazing leader in the United Kingdoms. To grow and heal and change the world like only she could.

And only now, as he looked at Ava, did he truly understand what it meant to love someone, and what it meant to have a dream. He would give anything in the world to watch her accomplish everything she wanted. The fact that she had chosen him, of all people, was an honor he couldn't even attempt to describe.

His dream of a family was stronger and purer in that moment than it ever had been. Yet he also felt that, even in the short amount of time they had been allotted, they were already living it. This *was* a family. And even if they never had the kids that both of them now wanted, the fact that she *would* have...that was enough.

Jackson placed his hand on her cheek. Strands of her long hair fell around his hand to frame her face as he gently caressed her cheek with his thumb. He didn't have the words to say how much it meant to him, so he didn't attempt to. Instead, he softly, slowly pulled her closer toward him, and kissed her gently.

★ ★ ★ ★ ★

"Anything?" Mikel asked as Kyle exited the room and walked into the main hall.

"Nothing," Kyle replied disappointedly. "It's been three days, and she hasn't heard a thing."

"Makes you wonder if they're playing a trick on us," Mikel replied sourly as they walked the hall together.

"Eli doesn't know about Jun. He doesn't know we have this resource. So how would he know to play that game?"

Mikel shrugged. "Who's to say he doesn't know about Jun? He has eyes and ears everywhere. He has agents inserted in the whole of the Republic. Taint! He probably has an agent or two inserted in this Tower that we don't even know about."

Kyle scoffed in frustration. "I need to get out of here. I have a bigger enemy to fight. I have the Jiānhùrén to take on. I can't afford to waste my time here, waiting around for a fight that may never come."

"Then why are you still here?" Mikel said pointedly. "If you feel you need to go, then go."

It was a long time before Kyle worked up a response. "I can't leave. Not if Valkyrie is coming."

Mikel stopped walking, and in a moment or two Kyle did the same, having to turn now to face him.

"Is it us you want to protect from her? Or are you trying to protect her from us?"

Kyle faced him seriously for a long time, but said nothing.

"That thing you told everyone in the meeting," Mikel spoke when it was clear Kyle wouldn't, "that we have no way of reaching Valkyrie, that Eli has a way to control her that none of us can stop."

"What about it?" Kyle pressed gruffly.

"What makes you think you're any different? Come on, Kyle. You had a fling with a girl. Good for you. But Valkyrie is still a robot assassin."

Kyle stepped in warningly. "Careful," he said with a touch of anger.

"That's what I'm worried about," Mikel spoke with sudden, intense passion. "When Valkyrie comes and attempts to sweep through us, I'm starting to wonder if you'll be prepared to do what is necessary. We don't have time for your conflicted feelings about a girl, Kyle. This is war. And you and your girlfriend are on different sides. When she gets here, she won't be conflicted. Don't you make that mistake yourself."

Kyle shook his head in frustration, turning away.

"Don't walk away from me," Mikel growled.

Kyle did not listen as he walked resolutely.

Mikel hurried forward, grabbing Kyle by the shoulder to stop him. Either Kyle's pent-up energy and anxiety was getting to him, or he had been really vexed by Mikel's comments about Valkyrie, because in that moment, he turned and punched Mikel directly in the side of his face, a crashing blow that sent Mikel stumbling back a few feet.

He regretted his action immediately. This was Mikel. This was his best friend! But in that moment, all he could think was to defend Valkyrie. Even if...no, even *though* Mikel was right.

When Mikel had recovered from the pain of the blow, he looked up to face Kyle, and the serious look on his face said whatever he didn't. "Maybe you do need to leave, Kyle," he said intently, warningly. "Your feelings here are too involved. Either pull yourself together, or you need to leave before this battle happens."

Kyle shook his head.

"I'm not kidding," Mikel shot back immediately. "We have enough to deal with when they come without having to worry about your conflicted loyalties. Just go. Let us handle this. We'll try not to kill her, and try not to be killed by her. But if it comes to it...I'm sorry, friend, you know the decision I'll have to make—one I don't think you're prepared for."

Kyle laughed in sudden frustration. "I'm not just gonna run away, Mikel! You think I'll head for the hills and let you all fight this battle alone?"

"I don't want you here," Mikel said genuinely. "None of us wants you here. Not when you're like this. So, go. Get out of here. Go fight the great battle you have to deal with alone. We'll do what we have to. We're better off in this fight without you."

Kyle gritted his teeth in anger, but it was clear that Mikel meant every word, and that he would not back down.

"I'll report to the others," Mikel warned. "I'll tell them you're not fit for this. I'll tell them why—"

Kyle huffed warningly.

"You won't scare me off, Kyle. I've known you a long time. And I know when your head isn't in the game. I also know what you look like when you're questioning loyalties."

"You don't know what you're talking about," Kyle hissed.

"Please, Kyle," Mikel said pleadingly. "Please, just get out of here. We can't afford this right now. Go fight the Jiānhùrén. Come back when this has all blown over."

There was no changing Mikel's mind. Kyle knew he would indeed report his concerns to the others, and that they would be uncertain of him after that. He couldn't afford that either.

"Just go, all right?" Mikel pleaded.

It didn't make sense to leave them. But at the same time...he knew he could never pull the trigger on Valkyrie either, no matter what the cost. Perhaps it was better if he left. Perhaps it was better that they deal with her without him.

The moment he thought perhaps he must leave was the moment he realized that a part of him hoped Valkyrie would win, even against these, his friends.

"Shake it off, Kyle," Mikel repeated once more. "Or get out of here!"

Kyle swallowed hard, and without another word, he walked down the hallway alone.

Eli glanced again at the list of targets before handing it to Valkyrie. She stared at the pictures and the names—a simple hit list, which was all Valkyrie required.

Though generally she received orders through the link, recent intelligence informed Eli that they couldn't afford to use the link right now without giving away their plans to the enemy. All orders must be given in person.

"We'll hit them before they know to expect it," Eli said confidently, though there was no reason to explain plans to her. "Then, when they are crippled from the first blow, I'll send you and the others in."

Generally, Valkyrie followed orders with no complaint. But Eli understood that, if anything, this mission would have the power to become painful or personal. Valkyrie didn't have the luxury of running away, or disobeying orders as some of the other insolent Zhànshì had done. Still, he wasn't about to take any risks with her.

She cocked her head in surprise at the list. "All in the same Tower in Russia?" she asked, which was unusual for her.

"Yes," he replied simply. "When we go in, you'll take out that list. When you are done, we will send a second wave of orders to finish off the job. You may go."

She turned and left the room, and the hit list, behind her. She would not need it anymore. She had memorized the names and faces, and she would deal with them easily.

Eli turned to where Zhànshì Six lurked in the corner of the room. "Here's yours," Eli said, handing him the file.

Zhànshì Six scanned the list carefully. Jackson's sister, Zak's family, all of these traitors' loved ones. Eli had no remorse for any of them. They would get what was coming to them. But Zhànshì Six stopped on one name, looking up to face Eli. "Toby O'Del, sir?"

Eli nodded absently. "Breanna's father."

"Yes, sir. I'm not certain I understand the connection with this fight."

Eli snickered, but then met Zhànshì Six's face with a cold expression. "The connection? Breanna was the first of these rebellious Zhànshì to run. She received no punishment, and in fact was celebrated among the other Zhànshì as a hero for her actions. She paved the way for this tainted Zhànshì revolution. Besides, the others still care for her. This man's death will deal a blow they must feel."

"I understand, sir, but I worked with Breanna myself. She was a great girl, and an excellent Zhànshì—"

"She was a traitor!" Eli hissed. "They all are! And they have to learn that they cannot get away with it! Eric was weak. He was a coward. He didn't do the job that needed to be done. He thought he would offer mercy with a simple brain wipe. The General should have killed Toby the second Breanna disobeyed Zhànshì conduct to meet with her father. I will not make the same mistakes. Our people have to be held to a greater standard."

"Sir, Breanna is already dead—" Zhànshì Six argued further, though attempting a respectful tone. "I don't understand how this man's death teaches anyone a lesson. It just seems like kicking Breanna when she's already in her grave."

"Disciplining," Eli argued through gritted teeth. "And they *should* have done it while she was still alive. Because they didn't, I have to."

"But, sir—"

"This is not up for discussion, Zhànshì Six! You have your orders. You'll take care of Toby and the others on the list. The rest of us will handle the real battle."

Once more Zhànshì Six attempted to object, but Eli raised his hand and hushed him. "Go!" he shouted.

Fortunately for Zhànshì Six, he followed orders at that point.

Eli went down the names on the list before him. It wasn't entirely about discipline. He also had a battle to win. And the only way to defeat an enemy with seemingly more strength was to find their weakness and pinpoint it. He had to hit them where it hurt.

Ava was immensely powerful. And Jackson commanded full armies now. But they would be no match for the fight Eli had planned. And certainly not after the events that would take place before the battle even started.

"Try the burritos," Kyle suggested. "They make them really well here!" Remington looked over in surprise. "The *burritos*...in *Russia*?"

"No, he's right," Jackson agreed. "They're really good."

"Anything else I should include on my plate?" Remington asked with a sort of caring smile.

Jackson, Mikel and Kyle each offered their suggestions as they waited in line behind him.

When they had all filled their plates, they went to the commissary tables and sat down with the others. Jackson moved to take a seat beside Ava, but Remington beat him to it. Jackson stood there awkwardly for a moment. Sasha was already seated on the other side of Ava, so instead Jackson sat down beside Remington.

Jackson hadn't realized Remington meant anything by it until he noticed the teasing smile on the man's face when Jackson was finally seated. "Oh, I'm sorry," he said quietly, "did the two of you want to sit together?"

"It's okay," Ava assured him, just as Jackson was about to say he would like to sit with his wife.

"All right then," Jackson muttered to himself sarcastically. "I'll just sit...here." Still, even as he joked about it, he didn't truly mind. There was a bond between Ava and Remington almost as a father and daughter, and she didn't get to see him very often.

"Thanks for taking care of that thing for me," Kyle said ambiguously to Remington, who just nodded in return.

He was usually a man of very few words. He was not one for light or meaningless conversation. He only said enough to get the job done.

It was strange, really. For a man who did not open up verbally, he had somehow made it into the hearts of each of them. Jackson watched with interest as everyone at the table was overly conscious of Remington, of every word and every move. But it wasn't out of discomfort. It was a sort of love, a sort of respect, a bond that Jackson couldn't explain. They all wanted to be known, to be noticed by Remington. They wanted to be his friend, even though none of them knew much, if anything, about him.

Mikel had encountered Remington only once before joining The Cause. And yet, Remington had been enough to recruit and inspire Mikel and Ella to leave Eli and to join the others.

A similar encounter with Kyle had been enough for him too, and the two of them had worked closely together for months to cripple the Republic.

Even though Jackson had a bit of communication and time with Remington over the five months of retaking Africa, still, Jackson wasn't sure Remington had ever spoken more than ten full words together at a time to him. And certainly, he had never opened up about his own life. Yet Jackson felt it too. A sort of bond, a brotherhood, a desire to be known and loved and respected by this great man.

It was easy to understand why Sasha and Ava felt so close to him, but it was just the same with the rest, and Jackson didn't exactly have answers as to why this man was so loved and respected. He just was.

"The burritos *are* quite good," Remington offered as they ate.

"Thanks for joining us to eat," Ava said with a loving smile.

"For you, my dear," he said sweetly in his gruff voice.

"You're American," Jackson noted for the first time, wondering why he hadn't thought of that before.

Remington did not bother to look up from his food.

"With a name like Remington," Sasha laughed, "of course he is."

"Well, we share that in common," Jackson noted pleasantly, quite enjoying that he could relate with Remington at any level.

"If you could compare your personality with anyone here," Mikel asked Remington thoughtfully, "who would you say you're most like?"

Remington did not look up. "Kyle," he answered simply.

Kyle grinned, leaning farther back in his seat, and Mikel groaned. "Please, don't inflate his ego any more than it already is!" Mikel teased.

"*My* ego?" Kyle replied pointedly. "Says the most arrogant man alive."

"Long as I back it up," Mikel countered for all to hear.

Almost everyone laughed. Even Remington offered a comical smile, though he was clearly somewhat uncomfortable in the open commissary with so many eyes on him. He almost seemed to have a sort of social anxiety at times, as he never looked anyone in the eyes—other than Ava. But then, perhaps that was more out of habit. A man who did not want to be noticed rarely looked other people directly in the eyes.

"Do we have any word from the enemy?" Jackson asked Jun, mercifully turning the conversation away from Remington. Jun had been quietly seated and said nothing up to this point. A security guard watched her from the side of the room as an extra precaution.

"I have heard nothing," she replied seriously.

Jackson clicked his tongue in disappointment.

"We will be ready," Sasha said assuredly. "We have everyone and everything we need to accomplish this."

"Eli doesn't stand a chance," Mikel agreed proudly.

"I didn't say that," Sasha disagreed.

"There are a lot of good Zhànshì, agents and soldiers still on his side," Remington added, and Jackson suddenly attempted counting the words of that sentence. Fourteen. Remington had done it! He'd beaten his record.

Ava nodded seriously in agreement. "Overconfidence could be our downfall. We are prepared, and we will fight with whatever we have; but we can't forget the strength of our enemy—or underestimate them either."

Mikel rolled his eyes. "Overconfidence has gotten me this far," he muttered more for Kyle than anyone.

"Must be a difficult thing," Sasha said, turning back to Jun. "All the different orders and directions you hear. I'm sure it's hard to make sense of it all."

She shook her head as if to disagree. "I know each voice, each signal as their own." She paused, and then gave Sasha a sort of knowing look. "I knew Kristen too. All the years you were apart, when your link was activated, I knew how much you cared for one another when you spoke so often to each other."

Sasha became suddenly tense. He grew stiff and uncomfortable in his seat, as he often was when speaking of his wife. He still had not managed to overcome his grief—if ever he could. Unconsciously, Jackson glanced at Ava on the other side of Remington, wondering if he would ever overcome his own grief when she was gone, or if he, too, would struggle with the pain for the remainder of his life.

Sasha couldn't seem to respond, and turned back to his plate.

"Did you and Liam ever notice each other?" Ava asked with a touch of curiosity.

Jun shook her head. "I knew of him. But until Jackson spoke directly to me, I did not know how to respond. He did not know of me."

A silence passed as the conversations trailed off. Mikel was ultimately the one to break it, turning to Jackson and Ava. "Well, guys, it's been three weeks. How is marriage treating you?"

The two of them glanced at each other, and Jackson smiled deeply, though Ava blushed from the sudden attention on such an intimate matter. "Quite well," Jackson answered for them both. "I highly recommend it."

Mikel sighed. "I don't have a lot of options these days. Although, there was that one girl."

"The reporter," Ava said with excitement.

"There was definitely something between you two," Sasha agreed happily.

"Reporter," Kyle muttered under his breath, but it was Remington's reaction that took everyone by surprise. He who hardly reacted to anything, laughed out loud suddenly, as if this was the funniest thing in the world. Everyone at the table stopped and watched him until he gave off laughing.

He cleared his throat awkwardly. "Sorry."

"Can I ask what's so funny?" Ava pleaded, clearly delighted just to see Remington that way.

He shook his head. "Nothing." He stood, grabbing his now empty plate. "You were right though. The burritos are excellent. I'll be back with more in a moment."

Once again, he had beat his record. This dinner was some real progress!

Remington pulled his chair back and began to turn.

The shocking gunfire sounded before the man even turned around.

Ava screamed, and for an instant Jackson almost thought it was she who had been hit as she went after Remington.

Jackson pulled out his sidearm and was up in less than a second, but Kyle had already fired on the enemy before them.

A passerby in the cafeteria had walked behind Remington at the same instant he stood to go. And before he was even able to face him, the Russian officer had fired on Remington, a fatal shot to the head.

Almost at the same time another officer walked just steps behind the first. His concealed weapon he pointed at Sasha, and would have fired, but didn't have the chance before Ava shoved the man, and he was filled with bullets from the rest of the team before he had any chance to readjust.

Ava fell to her knees on the ground above Remington, empty palms facing helplessly upward, scanning the whole of him in stunned silence.

The rest of them stood with weapons drawn, with no enemy to fight. That was until Mikel noticed Jun's security guard on the side of the room as the woman drew her weapon and aimed across the room.

Mikel fired on her at the same instant, but the officer's aim rang true as another body fell to the ground in a lifeless heap. Jun.

The whole thing happened in a matter of less than ten seconds. Yet already five casualties. And two of them of immeasurable loss.

"Clear the room!" Jackson screamed.

At this moment, any one of the nearly twenty officers in the cafeteria could be part of the enemy. This wasn't the usual assassination attempts on Jackson from Russians. This was a surgical attack by Eli.

Mikel, Jackson and Kyle took offensive positions, brandishing their weapons out menacingly.

"Everyone on the ground!" Jackson screamed. "Hands in the air!"

"Call for backup!" Mikel urged an officer as the other terrified people obeyed orders and got on the ground.

"No!" Jackson shot back. "We don't know who's on our side. Get our people out of here. Then we'll send in a team. Go!"

Out of the corner of his eye as Jackson watched the room filled with officers, he saw Ava on the ground above Remington's body.

Eli always won. But never in the ways they anticipated. They had prepared for so many things, but Jackson knew she had not been prepared for this. *He* certainly hadn't been.

Sasha yanked Ava away from Remington as she mourned her fallen friend. "We have to get out of here," he pleaded hurriedly. "Come on, Ava. Come with me."

Reluctantly, she obeyed, though still, she couldn't seem to take her eyes from Remington.

Jackson couldn't ignore the body of poor, innocent, helpless Jun. It had been his job to protect her, and he had failed miserably.

Sasha pulled Ava across the room as Mikel, Kyle and Jackson held cover, though the officers were all submissive now on the floor. "Go!" Jackson ordered the others.

Only then did Ava look back to face him as she made it to the doorway. Her look of horror expressed how much she wanted him to come with them. If he, too, died right now....

"Vasiliv," Jackson called from his earpiece. "I need backup in the cafeteria ASAP. We have two friendly casualties and at least three enemy attackers."

"Jackson," Ava pleaded, not prepared to leave him there alone.

"Go!" Jackson ordered Sasha.

Sasha pulled Ava from the room. "Help cover them," Jackson ordered the others. "We could have as many spies out there. I have a handle here. Get out of here!"

Reluctantly Kyle and Mikel obeyed. Almost as soon as they were gone, Vasiliv and his men arrived.

Jackson went to the bodies when his men were in place, but they were both dead. No suffering. No prolonged death. Just one fatal bullet to the head. Remington, Ava's protector. And Jun, The Cause's ears. Not only had these people been highly valuable to this team—they had been friends.

A plate lay shattered on the floor beside Remington, and Jackson cursed at the thought of him getting up for a stupid burrito when he was killed. Jackson closed the man's eyes respectfully, and reached for tags, but Remington wore none. There was no one to call. No family to tell. None of them knew anything of his past. Remington was a lone soldier.

And Jun...? The only family she had, General Li, had been killed by the people during the raids on the Towers.

Jackson left somberly to follow the others, and was taken aback to find Kyle just outside waiting for him. "I thought I told you—"

"You did," Kyle agreed. "But the three of them can handle themselves. You had a room of twenty people to fend off alone."

He didn't object, and they silently made their way on high alert. He should never have let his guard down for a second, not when he had been warned that Eli was coming for him. He should have known, and he could not forgive himself for that.

Ava sat alone on the floor against the wall of Mikel's apartment room. Mikel stood by the door when the others entered, as if to guard it. Sasha stood a few feet from Ava. He attempted to lean down and speak to her when the others entered, but she raised her hand.

"Don't," she pleaded. Her cheeks were streaked with the tears she had shed, though she was no longer crying.

"Ava," he spoke softly.

"Don't!" she repeated, more harshly this time.

"Give her a minute," Jackson urged when Sasha looked up to face him.

"What the taint happened out there?" Mikel demanded when they were all safely inside with the door closed. "We can't even trust our own people?"

"They weren't Russians," Jackson clarified. "They were Intelligence agents."

"That's what I'm saying!" Mikel spat in anger. "Are we supposed to stand beside these people when Eli attacks? How do we know they won't turn on us in the middle of the battle? Shoot us in the back? We're supposed to watch our front, and our back, and our sides, at every moment in the middle of a fight?"

"You're a Zhànshì!" Jackson replied with a similar intensity. "Suck it up!" He was suddenly bothered by how Mikel seemed to push this on Jackson as if it was his fault and his responsibility to make the battlefield safer. He already felt responsibility for these deaths, but he didn't need Mikel's indignation on top of that.

Mikel steadied, backing down.

Sasha looked deeply pained and even dazed. "He killed Remington."

"And he killed Jun," Kyle muttered bitterly, as though in reminder that her name must be remembered and mourned for too.

Everyone looked beaten. Everyone looked broken. And the battle hadn't even started yet.

Jackson was just as defeated. He felt like a fool, and a failure, and a blistering carcass for every reason. He should have been smarter. This was his responsibility, and he was to blame. But the three weeks with not a sign had put his guard down. Such a meaningless moment to lose two key players, and two true warriors. Such a waste. He was furious at himself.

Yet, with everyone else here looking like it was all over, with every other face mirroring the defeat that Jackson felt, he knew it was his job to move past it. Things were not over. Far from it. And it would get much worse before it got better.

"Yes, he killed Jun," Jackson said with sudden intensity that took all of them by surprise. "And he killed Remington. He tried to kill Sasha. And guess what, he's gonna kill a lot of other people before this is over. We are talking about a full-scale war! And this is just the beginning."

All the training, all the preparation, yet now none of them looked prepared for what that cost might mean.

"Why did he kill Jun?" Jackson asked seriously, intently. "Because somehow he knew about her abilities, and that it would help us? Yes. But also because she's an innocent. Because she's sweet, and gentle and helpless. He killed her to prove some power over us, that every one of us failed to protect her.

"Why did he kill Remington?" Jackson continued, stepping farther into the room and raising his voice a touch higher. Even Ava turned to face him then, her tear-streaked face looking shattered and desperate for an answer to that question. "Because Remington is the greatest warrior any of us has ever known. Because he has abilities that we could only wish to match. But also because every one of us loved him. Because that loss hurt all of us. Because none of us saw it coming. Because every one of us is now falling apart over it.

"He attempted to kill Sasha too. Why Sasha? Because it would have crushed us to lose him.

"Why did Eli kill those two people, when those gunshots could have just as easily taken out any other two of us? They weren't the face of the revolution. They weren't the power behind our victory. Why did he kill them?" Jackson urged, growing louder and more intense every second. "To break us!" This he shouted fiercely, and the others flinched from his intense scream.

Silence passed as he let that sink in. And when he spoke again, it was almost a whisper. "Are we going to let him win?"

The room remained silent. Seconds passed, dragging into minutes.

No reply. Nothing. Still, they looked shattered. Still, they looked defeated.

Jackson almost thought it was over, time to throw in the towel.

Finally, Ava pulled herself to her feet and walked farther into the room where all could now see the grief on her horrified face. Every one of them saw it when that horror turned into determination. She spoke each exaggerated word through gritted teeth in her fury.

"I will *never* yield to him again."

Jackson and the others had their eyes trained on Ava. This fight would be all of theirs. But it was clear in that moment, *she* would defeat Eli. There was no other way this could go down. She was determined, and she would not back down.

The enemy had no idea what was coming for him.

Eli had lost his sister when he killed Hawkins. But the General's greatest mistake of all was killing Remington. Ava Altman was coming for him.

"It sounds like a good opportunity," Nassar said as he looked over the plans.

Darya clicked her tongue discontentedly. "It is more than a good opportunity," she corrected. "It's the opportunity we've been waiting for. The Republic has been demolished. There are only two superpowers left. And the tyrants of both will be crushed all at once."

"You intend to take them all down together," he clarified.

"One fell swoop," she said proudly. "There is no better way. Prepare an upload and we'll give the orders."

"Consider it done." With that, Nassar left to make the necessary preparations regarding the chip.

Darya looked down at the plans laid before her. "One more battle, Harrison," she promised her enemy, even past the grave. "One more fight, and you will be destroyed. An eye for an eye. A tooth for a tooth. My precious little angel, for yours."

★ ★ ★ ★ ★

Ava sat alone on the bed when Jackson entered the room. She was quiet, and angry. She hadn't spoken a word to Jackson since the evening before, since losing Remington.

Everything remained on high alert. They would have no warning now when Eli and his armies would come, and so at every moment they were ready. As they should have been yesterday.

Ava tried not to look directly at Jackson as he closed the door, went to his dresser and changed from his gear.

They shared a room now. She was glad of that. And yet, at this moment, she was angry with him. She wanted him to address it, but as much as she avoided speaking to him, he did the same with her. Clearly, he knew she was angry, but instead of taking her into his arms and trying to fix things as he normally might have, neither one had anything to say.

Jackson continued to prepare for bed and ignored her as if she wasn't even there. He knew why she was angry, but he believed he was right, and so neither of them was prepared to let go or say they were sorry. When he had changed, he simply moved to his side of the bed, climbed in under the covers and turned off the lamp. He lay turned away from her and that hurt most of all.

She sat there in bitter silence, holding her breath in pain until he spoke one simple word, as if unable to go to bed without saying it.

"Goodnight," he whispered gently.

Suddenly overwhelmed by the pain of all of this, Ava climbed from the bed and started toward the door.

She assumed he would ignore that as he had everything, but he sat up in the bed and turned the lamp on once more. "Where are you going?" he asked in a tone of concern. "I don't want you wandering the Tower alone right now."

She stopped, swallowing her anger but finding herself unable to let it go. Then she turned to face him, still standing by the door. "What about you?" she asked forcefully.

He watched her, confused. "What about me?" he repeated as if clueless.

"You wander the halls alone, night or day. You take on a room of twenty possible hostiles alone and send me a guard of Zhànshì. Do you honestly think I'm weak? That I can't handle myself?" She clenched her jaw in sudden anger. "The last thing I need is for you to treat me like *I'm* fragile—while you risk your life like you're untouchable!"

"I don't have a tumor in my head that could kill me any second," Jackson countered, attempting to remain calm though she could see that he, too, was angry. "I'm not months or weeks or seconds away from dying."

"Is that what this is about?" she shot back. "You're trying to get yourself killed before I die first?"

He let out a breath of surprise and frustration. "No, Ava. I'm just doing my job."

"It could have been you that Eli targeted, Jackson. Don't you realize that? It could have just as easily been you as the others. He hates you. Strategically he could have crippled The Cause by neutralizing you. And the only reason you're still alive is because he wants you to suffer first. But at any moment he might change his mind, and realize how naive he's being. And when he does, what's to stop him from targeting you next?"

"He could just as easily take you out too," Jackson argued.

Ava shook her head repeatedly, stepping in farther. "No he wouldn't. I'll be the last person he kills. He wants you to hurt. But he wants me to break. And he'll keep me alive to watch every other person I love die before he'll ever take the shot in my direction."

"He won't have to," Jackson muttered bitterly.

Ava huffed in frustration, then spoke in a pained tone. "You asked for this. I said we should let go and focus on the mission. You're the one who wanted this!" She turned back to the door and opened it.

"Don't leave," Jackson pleaded, climbing off the bed and walking toward her.

"You knew what you were getting into," Ava reminded him in anger. "Yes, I'm gonna die. But you said you wanted me anyway!"

She tried to leave then, but he moved himself in front of her path to stop her. "I do," he said reassuringly, but it wasn't all that convincing.

"Just let me go," she said, not looking up to meet his gaze.

"Ava," he pleaded.

"Move out of my way," she spoke coolly.

He hesitated a moment before doing as she asked.

She looked into the hall and checked to ensure it was empty before exiting the room.

"Ava," he pleaded once more. "Don't do this. Where are you even going to go?"

She gave no answer, walking with determination down the hallway.

It took him a moment to catch up because he retrieved his weapon before following.

"Would you stop?" he said, sounding suddenly angry as he followed her through the hall.

She continued walking. "Go back to the room," she urged.

"No," he answered sharply. "Ava, just stop."

"What do you want from me?" she asked, turning suddenly to face him. "You want me to not die? Well, I'm sorry, Jackson. I can't give you that. *But you told me you wanted me anyway!*"

"I do!" he repeated insistently. Then he cursed. "Gah! Can't you at least attempt to understand where I'm coming from? I have been calm and patient and loving through everything. But any time anything at all gets hard you try and run for the hills. Any time I have even a moment of weakness, you act like I've betrayed you and that you have every right to leave me!"

Jackson stopped, hovering a hand on the side of his pants where he held his weapon as an officer passed them in the adjoining hallway. He looked wary and concerned. He was on edge. Even those officers who had been closest to him before were now suspected as Eli's men.

Ava felt a sudden touch of sympathy for him. This whole thing had been painful and horrific for her, but clearly it had affected him too.

When the threat was gone, he looked back at her, yet his hand remained by his gun. "Can we please just go back in there and talk about this?" he pleaded in a whisper.

Until that moment she had no intention of returning with him. She wanted him to apologize, to take her in his arms and say he was sorry for staying in that room while ordering Sasha to take her away. That he was sorry for treating her like a child while he took insane risks with his own life. She was still angry at him. Yet now, seeing the fear, seeing the turmoil, seeing his own pain, her feelings suddenly changed, and all she could think now was to take *him* in *her* arms and promise it would be okay.

"Please?" he pleaded further, and the way his hand flexed beside his weapon as he warily watched the halls made her feel even more deeply for him.

She simply nodded, and went with him back to their room.

Ava still felt hurt, and anger, and incredible grief over the loss of Remington. She felt like screaming and crying and lashing out all at once, but she didn't know how or where to start.

When they were in the room with the door closed and locked, Jackson finally turned back to her, prepared for a fight. "You don't get to be the only one who has off moments," he said angrily. "I do everything I can to make sure you know that you're loved and you're safe. So maybe I go too far sometimes. But I didn't just order them out for your protection. Eli targeted Sasha. And I wanted you all to protect *him*! So maybe I take risks with my life. But how is that any different than what you do every time you risk yourself with the Towers? You are a ticking time bomb. And yet you never hesitate to do what is necessary. Neither can I!"

Ava watched him and his anger. So much of her wanted to fight back. To have her way and tell him where he, too, was wrong. Yet another part just wanted to cry and be held by him and grieve over her lost friend.

Instead, she simply watched him with uncertainty, unable to react in either direction.

"I chose you, all right?" he pressed with continued frustration. "And I still do. But that doesn't mean I can't ever have even a moment of anger at the realization that I could lose you any second! And believe me, I try to keep that to myself. You have enough to deal with, and I knew what I was getting into. I know you're hurting over Remington. I know you loved him more than any of us could have. But it hurt me too, all right? That meaningless attack hurt me too. Maybe I made the wrong call. But I made a call. And it was my job to do so!"

He seemed to grow angrier with every second as he spoke quickly, his pain and emotion overwhelming him.

Still, her conflicting desires confused her, and she did not know how or which way to react.

Seeing him there, listening as he passionately continued with his argument, she saw a glimpse of that Jackson in the hall, during the Talks, wearing a tuxedo and looking as handsome as ever, so close, yet miles from her. She remembered that feeling of wanting to repair everything, yet having no clue where to start.

She acted on impulse, even before she knew what she was doing, moving in closer and breaking Jackson's comment off mid-sentence as she kissed him.

"The taint!?" he pulled back in shock, still clearly angry and not expecting that. But as he watched her then, his anger shifted until it was entirely replaced with something else. Then he leaned in and kissed her passionately.

Neither of them said sorry, or even attempted to fix things at all. It was almost as if they both decided in that moment to let it go, and they managed to entirely.

By the time she was close to falling asleep in his arms some time later, she felt nothing of that anger, though still there was the pain of losing Remington.

"He's coming," Jackson whispered sadly as they lay there. "And it's going to get so much worse."

She sensed his fear in that moment. He was so good at hiding it, so good at pretending to have it all together for everyone else's sake. He never seemed to fall apart, even when everyone else did. When Remington and Jun had been killed, Ava had assumed it didn't mean as much to Jackson, because he so easily moved into inspiring the others and being the strong one. But she felt his pain now. He was hurt; he was scared. He just didn't let the others see it.

"You're as good as my mom, you know," she whispered a response that had nothing to do with his comment.

His eyes met hers with a question in them. "You remain strong for everyone else's sake. But you're as scared as the rest of us."

He kept her gaze, and in his eyes she saw everything that he would never say to the rest of the team. "I'm not scared," he said in a tortured whisper. "I'm terrified."

☆ ☆ ☆ ☆ ☆

"This is it," Zak spoke assuredly. "The radars have them a few miles out."

Jackson and the others walked together in a sort of procession, like the king used to have, though these were all men and women of equal standing in most ways.

"You sure you want to be here for this?" Jackson asked, giving Zak one final out before the battle.

"Viktoriya and the kids are safe. And we both agree, I couldn't leave you all alone. You're gonna need me on this one."

"Thank you, Zak," Ava said with a caring look as she squeezed his shoulder.

"They made it past the frontline defenses," Vasiliv said in frustration. "I was hoping they were weaker than expected, that we could take them out on the spot."

"We will," Mikel replied confidently. "Just not that one."

Jackson was about to send everyone to their stations, but he stopped, turning to face them all at once. Usually this was the time for one last inspiring speech. But he had nothing. He attempted to think of something, anything to give them one last hope as they entered the battle. All he could do was look at each face in turn, studying them, burning this moment into his mind.

Sasha, Mikel, Kyle, Zak, Vasiliv, Nastia, and Ava. These were more than just friends. More than just brothers in arms. These had become his family.

"We have everything we need," Sasha said, and the team turned their attention to him instead. "We have all the right people in place. And this is the time. It's the time for our confidence. It is time for our strength. It is time for our tenacity. We must honor and remember those who didn't make it this far. But remember, their sacrifices are what got us to this point. We would not be here without Kristen. And I know, none of us would be here without Remington either. So many gave their lives for the battle we face tonight. We have everything and everyone we need. Now it is time to finish this. It is time to win."

Jackson breathed out deeply, more grateful than ever for Sasha in that moment.

"Team cheer?" Mikel asked, putting his hand in the middle of them.

Kyle groaned, Ava laughed, and Vasiliv snickered. But Jackson humored him, placing his hand in the middle.

Slowly the others followed suit.

"High school cheer squad," Kyle muttered, the last one to put his hand in.

"Go team!" This Zak said in a high-pitched voice, attempting to sound like a teenage girl.

Several people laughed out loud. Through his laughter, Jackson repeated the sentence, "Go team."

They pulled their hands down. "We are never doing that again," Kyle clarified.

Still, several of them continued to laugh, enjoying this last jovial moment together before the battle would rage.

Once more, he looked at them, and noticed that Ava was doing the same; they all were.

When the moment ended, Jackson turned to commands. "Get to the core," Jackson ordered Zak. "Whatever happens, you and your team do not let them take the Tower."

Zak nodded and left to follow orders.

"Mikel and Ava," Jackson said, "you're the first line of defense. Here and in Moscow. Do what you can."

"You got it," Mikel said proudly.

"Understood," Ava replied at the same time.

"Nastia, you and your team of Elites do what you do best. Protect our people." This nodding at Mikel and Ava.

"Yes, sir!" Nastia served a little attitude by responding with exaggerated deference. But then, quieter and with earnestness: "You know we will."

"Vasiliv, Kyle, Sasha," he addressed the rest of them, "let's get to our stations. We're going to hold this Tower."

☆ ☆ ☆ ☆ ☆

"Your Majesty," another voice called from the crowd of people during her lengthy interview before the gala. "May we ask what designer you're wearing?"

Astelle smiled and gave a response. She had never gotten the really good questions like Lionel did. Most everything the public wanted to know about her pertained to fashion choices and event plans. She missed the times when they would ask Lionel a question, a really good one, like, "What are your plans for helping homeless veterans through the upcoming economic challenges as we are receiving so many wounded from the frontlines?" They would direct those questions to Lionel, and proudly, he would invite her to answer instead.

Now there was no one to direct queries to her. There were no exciting questions. Her son had gone the way of the rest of Council's corruption and would proudly keep her quietly, ornamentally, in the public's eye.

"Well, you look beautiful, your Majesty," the young male reporter complimented kindly.

"Thank you, love," she teased, "but I think you're a bit young for me."

The response got laughter from the crowd and her publicist announced that there would be no more questions. Astelle rose from her seat and started from the stand, but a confident young voice stood out to her suddenly when the reporter called, "Queen Astelle, I have a message from Lionel."

Of course, Lionel had been several months gone, passed away from his illness. Everyone knew that—Astelle most of all. But for some reason, the confidence of the tone caused Astelle to stop, and turn once more to face the crowd. She could not spot who had spoken until the young reporter continued.

"Queen Astelle, the message from the throne is that it's time."

Astelle met the eyes of the young woman. This couldn't really be the reporter they had chosen to replace Harvey Caldwell, could it? She was so young. She couldn't have had much experience. But there was a surety, a confidence and a strength about her that reassured the queen.

Astelle stood up straighter and proud. Then she addressed the young woman, and the entire crowd when she spoke. "Then let the Colonel, and the rightful General win."

She left the stand as the audience roared with surprise. This little call had been used by revolutionaries for the past few months. But certainly never from the mouth of someone as highly esteemed as the queen.

She hoped enough people would see the live footage before Council attempted to erase it. But in the end, it would not matter. Lionel had done enough to ensure that.

If it truly was time for the release of this story, then indeed, it was also time for the Colonel, and the rightful General's victory.

17

Siege

"Do you want to handle the lights? I'll deal with the aircraft?" Mikel asked as they walked toward the core.

"Dude," Ava replied absently, "I'm in Moscow right now."

"Right. Have the armies arrived there too?"

She nodded. "But with most of Russia defending it, and with Eli sending most of the enemy our way, I think we'll hold all right."

Mikel sighed. "Fine. I'll take care of both. I'm just grateful we don't have to deal with Counter Intelligence simultaneously."

She opened her eyes briefly to give him a searching look.

"I mean, the rest of you," he clarified. "I'm getting good at this whole battle with it. I think I'll win any day now."

She smiled softly to herself. "You go, Mikel." She closed her eyes and continued walking. Nastia and the other Elites surrounded them, but Nastia was distractedly speaking through her earpiece.

"Whoops," Mikel said, attempting to pull Ava out of the way, but not in time as she collided with an oncoming crew of hurried officers.

Ava winced and opened her eyes as they passed. She turned, attempting to see who it was who had run into her. It wasn't the impact, but a sort of stinging in her arm that had happened at the same time that bothered her. But the officers were hurriedly along the next hall, unfazed by the disruption.

"You good?" Mikel asked, noting the concern on her face.

She looked down at her arm, but the stinging was gone, and no mark to explain it. "Yeah. Probably just hit a pin on his uniform," she offered, closing her eyes once more as Nastia urged them forward again.

"They don't wear pins," Mikel noted absently. "Just badges. All right, hold on, it's go time."

"Pick up your speed," Nastia commanded. "We need to get the core sealed immediately, with you two in it. If we hadn't taken time for that little girl scout meeting...."

Mikel chuckled, and Ava smiled. "Worth it," she whispered to Mikel, and he laughingly agreed.

☆ ☆ ☆ ☆ ☆

The Tower was beautiful in the night sky, even from the tallest viewing area where Kyle stood. The large building lit up the clouds.

"Going dark now," Mikel said, and in an instant, the Tower went dark. Everything turned to pitch black, and Kyle shifted the Chameleon's eyes to night mode.

The surrounding cities had been evacuated, and the people settled safely within bunkers. Only the armies of The Cause remained to fight this battle.

He heard the slight hum of the enemy's aircraft before they came fully into the line of sight. Kyle was the first to see them through the Chameleon's eyes as he stood in the viewing room at the highest point in the Tower.

"They're almost in range," he said through his earpiece. "They'll be able to see us any minute."

"Understood," Jackson replied. "I want word the second Valkyrie is in. Our ground troops have no idea what's coming, but let's give them as much warning as possible."

Reluctantly, Kyle agreed. No ground troop would manage to get to Valkyrie anyway.

☆ ☆ ☆ ☆ ☆

"This is gonna be a heck of a fight," Vasiliv said through their personal channel, watching the skies for anything as he aimed his artillery cannon from a balcony on the level below. Jackson could see a clear view of Vasiliv down and to the right from where he manned his own cannon.

"I never really thought I would be a ground soldier in a battlefield like this," Jackson agreed. "I'm used to smaller tactical operations. And of course, I'm used to being the attacker, not the defender."

"It's fun, in a way," Vasiliv said. "Being the aggressor in an operation makes you feel more in control. But being on defense has its charms."

"Such as?"

Vasiliv tilted up the end of his artillery cannon pointedly. "You don't get to use a gun like this when you're on offense."

Jackson chuckled. "Fair enough."

"Would you two quit chattering?" Sasha said from another balcony. "You're making me nervous."

"Small talk helps with nerves," Vasiliv disagreed. "By the way, how's that abscess on Boris' leg doing?"

Sasha groaned.

"Looks like a volcano erupting," Jackson replied honestly. "Not pretty. But the doc says it's getting better."

"Boris should be out here with us," Sasha said with a hint of sarcasm. "He's invincible."

"And I'm sure he knows his way around an artillery cannon," Vasiliv added.

"That's why we need him to protect Viktoriya and the boys," Jackson replied.

"Taint, he could take on the whole army himself!" Sasha replied facetiously.

The sound of the aircraft buzzed louder every second, warning the arrival of Harrison's secret army from America.

Remington had told them who was coming. Dozens of agents, all active Zhànshì, and hundreds of Harrison's private army, who had been reserved for emergencies and trained on the American continent. All of the army had the physical and mental enhancements from the chip, and the martial training of the highest caliber.

Vasiliv was right about at least one thing. This would be one heck of a fight.

☆ ☆ ☆ ☆ ☆

"We have a signal incoming, requesting we open a channel."

Zak looked at the signal in surprise. "It's coming from the enemy."

"Weird time to have a chat," his secondary specialist noted.

Zak nodded an agreement. "Jackson," he said, turning to his earpiece. "What should I do about a request of audience from the enemy?"

There was a momentary silence as Jackson considered. "Have Ava answer it securely. Don't let them send any virus or anything in it. But have her take the call."

"Yes, sir."

Zak rolled his office chair away from the controls and to face the two meditating Zhànshì. They sat cross legged on the floor, eyes closed, hands on their knees, and looked in perfect meditation as they controlled the Towers.

"Someone wants to talk," Mikel muttered out loud as he, too, caught the incoming signal.

"Ava," Zak said carefully. It felt weird to interrupt her then.

"Hmm?" she asked, focused entirely on her own objective.

"Incoming call for you."

She opened her eyes in surprise. "Answer it? I guess?" she asked more than ordered.

Zak securely answered the transmission and a video feed came on screen. It was the General, looking fierce and ready for battle from the cabin of his jet.

"Hello, Ava."

She stood, and walked toward the screen. There was no friendliness or love in the look she gave him in return. "What do you want, Eli?"

"I want to end this peacefully," he lied. At least, it was probably a lie. Though he looked quite serious.

Ava scoffed. "Stop playing games. We both know you're here for revenge. All you want is a bloodbath."

"On the contrary," he countered. "Jackson Davis is the one who turned this into a battle. All I ever wanted was my sister back."

Ava leaned into the camera menacingly. "You. Can't. Have. Her." Each word she said with overt fury.

"Haven't enough people died for you?" he said in what seemed a pained tone. He was good. Here he was, a terrible aggressor, yet he played the victim, he played the hero, and he played it well. "Hasn't enough blood been spilled?"

"Not yours," she growled.

Eli's eyes touched with deep sadness. "And I'm the one out for revenge? Ava, think about what you're doing. You can't come back from this. None of you can."

"What do you want, Eli?"

"Stand down. Surrender. Let's begin peaceful negotiations."

"Never going to happen."

"You want this bloodbath to ensue?" he accused, as if it were her doing the attacking.

"Standing down," Ava called him on it, "surrendering, will not save these people. It will just provide you with the tools you need to massacre them."

"I would do no such thing," he disagreed. "I have no vendetta."

"That's a load of taint," Ava hissed.

"I have no agenda," he continued as he ignored her interjection. "I am simply representing my nation. You are aligned with an enemy superpower who has grown too strong, and has become a threat to the security of every free nation left. We will not allow you to trample us."

"Stop pretending to be the good guy, Eli," Ava returned. "I know exactly who and what you are. And if this little show is for your people, if this is to make them believe in your cause, then make sure you include in this transmission to all of them that you're a mass murderer. And that you killed General Harrison Altman for power."

Zak and the other technicians checked to be certain after her clue—though this broadcast was not transmitting to their own people, it was transmitting to Eli's. So, that was his game. He had to look like the good guy, for them. And she had to look like the insane, power-hungry traitor.

Eli's eyes tightened with disdain. "Turn it off," he ordered one of the men on his end. But it only stopped the transmission to his people. The feed continued for just Ava and Eli now.

"Surrender peacefully," Eli urged, "or your past dead friends' won't be the only blood on your hands." He signaled, and a soldier pulled a young woman into view. She was gagged, tied up, and terrified. Zak did not recognize her, but clearly Ava did.

Eli signaled once more, and the soldier dragging the woman pointed a gun to her head. "Surrender, or I kill her."

Ava's eyes softened as she watched the poor girl. "I'm sorry I got you involved in this mess, Katia," Ava spoke directly to the girl. "But I gave you a chance to get out. I wish I could help you now. But you made your choice." Then she looked once more at Eli, determined. "And I have to make mine."

Eli hissed. Then, he hesitated. It almost looked as if he didn't want to kill the girl. It was as if he had been so certain it would work that he had played a bluff he was unwilling to follow through on. But as he watched Ava, Zak could see the same intense determination. He also saw the moment when Eli decided to do it.

One more signal to his soldier, and the shot fired.

Ava did not flinch, but her eyes touched with pain as her friend was killed. Zak thought back to Sasha's words, Eli got his revenge, yet "never in the ways they expected."

Eli looked intensely angry now as his eyes peeled open and his nostrils flared. He hadn't wanted to play that card. And he blamed Ava for forcing his hand. The maniac actually blamed her for the girl's death, when he was the one who gave the order.

It was then that Zak was sure Eli was insane, and that there would be no reasoning with him, no ending this by one side defeating the other as in normal warfare. This would not end until Eli, or Ava, was dead.

"*You* did this!" Eli shouted in anger.

"No," Ava disagreed, a gentleness to her demeanor that paid respect to the fallen girl but would not give in to Eli's lies either. "You did."

"They're all dead because of you!" Eli seethed. "How many more people have to die before you realize that you're in the wrong?" he demanded.

Ava watched him, a look of painful mourning for the brother she had lost. "I jumped in front of Harrison to save him while you pulled the trigger. Right now, I'm jumping in front of the United Kingdoms and the freedom of her people, and you are still pulling the trigger. How many more people will you kill before you realize what you've become?"

He was shaking with anger now. "I will make you pay for this," he growled. "You, and Jackson, and all of you! I will make you pay for what you've done."

Ava was about to respond, but she wasn't given the chance as Eli ended the transmission.

Ava stayed there momentarily, staring at the now dark screen. Eventually, she moved, and Zak caught her glance. "I'm sorry, Ava," he offered caringly.

She had no response, but she placed her hand on his shoulder as she walked away, as if to say thank you.

She returned to the floor with Mikel.

"Now," she said to all who could hear her. "Now, the battle begins."

☆ ☆ ☆ ☆ ☆

King Richard watched in terror for only a moment or two before he yelled for his secretary. The middle-aged man entered. "Yes, sir?"

"Get me the Gen—" he cut off, remembering where Eli was right now. "Taint! Get me Councilman Holden. Now!"

The man left in a hurry, and Richard reached for his mobile, dialing a number in a frenzy.

"Hello?"

"Where is my mother?" Richard spoke immediately when the man answered. "I need her immediately."

"She has retreated to her personal safe house with your brothers and sister. I'm sorry, sir, but your wife and daughters have retired there as well. They will be unreachable."

Richard cursed and hung up the phone before dialing another number.

"Sir," his publicist said from the other end, sounding alert.

"Are you seeing this?" Richard asked in a wavering tone, glancing once more at the news broadcast.

There was a long pause before a response came. "Yes, sir, I am."

"Well, it's all a load of taint! I need this thing taken care of. Now!"

Another long pause before a response. "Yes, sir. I'll do my best."

"Get it done!" Richard ordered, not liking the tone of his publicist on this.

"I will try my best, sir," the reply came, and Richard knew then the scope of this story.

This man didn't "try." He got the job done, every time. His lack of confidence assured Richard that this was, indeed, as bad as he had suspected.

✫ ✫ ✫ ✫ ✫

The humming grew nearer every second, and Jackson had his eyes peeled as his heart began beating rapidly. He took a deep breath, calming the effects of the adrenaline. He counted the seconds with a controlled exhale.

He made it to six before the first aircraft came into view, but the fleet looked so much vaster and deadlier with his own eyes than on the radar.

He aimed the artillery cannon and got a lock on target. Before he fired, the buzzing sound grew even louder still, and the scope of the enemy ahead finally registered as he witnessed it with his own eyes in that moment.

"Holy car—" Jackson started, but didn't have the chance to finish the curse as he fired on the first of many aircraft.

"You can say that again," Vasiliv's response came through the earpiece, and then all Jackson could hear was the loud buzzing, with the sound of weapons fire on both sides.

✫ ✫ ✫ ✫ ✫

"My legs are tired," Mikel said to Ava as they sat fighting the enemy from within the core.

"Shut up," she pleaded.

"No, really. I should have asked for a cushion or something. This floor is incredibly uncomfortable!"

He opened his eyes then to see Zak watching him pointedly, as if to say, "we're here safe in the core while the soldiers are fighting on that battlefield, and you're complaining about comfort?"

Mikel looked away. It was a good point. He'd stop complaining now.

He glanced at Ava before closing his eyes. But the state she had been in registered and he quickly opened his eyes again. "Are you okay?" he asked with sudden concern.

She didn't respond, but her face was pale, and she was sweating profusely. She did not look well.

"Hey," he turned to Zak, "can you turn down the heat in here?"

"I'm a little busy," Zak replied pointedly again.

"It's not for my comfort this time," Mikel explained, a nod toward Ava.

Zak's eyes narrowed in concern when he noticed Ava. "Malya, can you turn down the heat?"

The girl stood and did as they requested.

"Are you feeling all right?" Mikel asked Ava again.

"Stop talking to me, Mikel," she pleaded, opening her eyes to face him. But her look was absent, almost as if she didn't know where to look to find him.

She let out a breath of confusion, and looked around the room as if worried. "Are the lights on?" she asked, and Mikel's stomach dropped.

"It's bright as day in here, Ava," he said in a worried whisper. "Can't you see anything?"

She blinked her eyes open and shut, with apparently no success, as sweat beaded and dripped from her face and arms.

Dizzy from confusion, she got to her knees, and attempted to stand, but was unable to. Mikel moved to try and help her, but it was no use.

"Something's wrong," she muttered. She tried to take a step, then she fell unconscious in his arms.

★ ★ ★ ★ ★

"We've got a problem in here!" Zak said to Jackson through his earpiece, but the intensity of the battle before him was such that it was nearly a minute before he was physically able to respond as explosions blasted above, below and nearly on him. He continued firing on the enemy, as the ships flew into, around and past the Tower, strafing it from every angle.

"Handle it!" Jackson said urgently. "We've got some problems of our own out here!"

A long silence came through the radio before Zak replied somberly, "Jackson...it's Ava."

Kyle was the eyes and the ears. He watched from the greatest vantage point, invisible to the enemy with the Chameleon suit. That didn't stop it from being a highly dangerous job. A blast from the aircraft hit not a few feet from him, the force of the impact knocking him to the ground in pain. That wasn't good.

Being on the highest point of the Tower gave him the ability to see everything. But it was also an easily targetable position for the myriad aircraft flying at the Tower.

He heard over radio about Ava collapsing into a coma. He heard Jackson respond bravely, "Do your best to take care of her. And send word to Moscow that they're on their own."

"I'll handle their Tower too," Mikel disagreed. "I swayed three enemy Towers simultaneously. I can handle it."

"Is she all right, Zak?" Sasha said worriedly.

Once more, Zak was slow to answer. "I don't think so. I'm sorry."

Kyle felt for Jackson in that moment. The woman he loved, his wife, was dying, yet he could not abandon his men in the middle of this battle.

It almost didn't seem possible to Kyle. Could Ava really ever die? He couldn't imagine it. He couldn't believe it. Somehow, some way, she had to pull through. The world just didn't make sense without Ava Altman in it.

Kyle watched for a drop carefully. He thought back to the moment he had been given this position and his choice to take it.

"Kyle," Jackson had said from the briefing table, "with your stealth suit and your experience working with her, I'd like for you to take lookout and warn us when Valkyrie arrives."

"Uh, sir," Mikel objected immediately, "I'm not so sure that's a good idea."

Kyle shot Mikel an angry glance, yet inwardly he felt a similar panic. It was bad enough to be in a battle against Valkyrie. But to be the one to report her to the enemy?

Jackson locked eyes with Kyle. The look he gave Kyle then seemed to be some sort of invitation. "Is there any reason you shouldn't take that role?" Jackson asked seriously.

And, of course, there was. But at the same time, he wasn't fully ready for anyone to take Valkyrie out. This gave him an opportunity to make that call when it came to it.

"No, sir. I am prepared for the job."

Mikel was about to object, but the conversation moved on, and Kyle gave him a confident look that said it would be fine. Maybe it would. He wasn't sure yet.

Kyle was pulled back to reality as an enemy aircraft flew in a little closer than the rest, and apparently in the frenzy Mikel and the Tower specialists had missed it as the anti-aircraft mechanisms on the Tower failed to eliminate it.

But perhaps this one ship had particular jamming frequencies. Watching it closely, Kyle noticed as the aircraft flew in as close as possible, slower than was wise. He tuned in his eyes, and saw as a package was dropped on an empty balcony on one of the lower sections of the Tower. The package would not have been noticed by anyone else. Kyle watched as the dark figure stood.

A woman dressed all in black, and prepared for battle.

Valkyrie.

★ ★ ★ ★ ★

His mind and body were completely disconnected as he continued to fight. He couldn't think of Ava. He couldn't think of his loss. He could not be overwhelmed by his grief. He had to act the part of the soldier, of the leader.

Jackson was grateful suddenly for that moment in the Tower in Beijing when he had nearly lost Ava. That moment had proved to him that he could continue to fight, despite his pain. That he would not give up, even if he lost her. And that was the truth. He did not give up. He did not cease fighting. He would finish this battle. But after this was over... he would never be the same.

"Jackson," Kyle spoke carefully. "Valkyrie is here."

Jackson breathed a sigh of relief. Not that Valkyrie had arrived—that was a bad thing. But that Kyle had ultimately chosen a side. He understood how painful that choice must have been. But he hoped they could save many lives with this knowledge.

"What level is she on?" Jackson asked, firing on another aircraft and clipping its wing.

"She's on level thirteen."

Jackson's gut clenched and he glanced down at the sign on the balcony that indicated the level he was on. Thirteen.

He whipped around at a sound behind him, and there stood Agent Valkyrie.

★ ★ ★ ★ ★

Jackson Davis stood before Valkyrie. She watched him. He watched her. He looked afraid. He had every reason to be. It was within Valkyrie's orders to eliminate him. But not at this time. There were others who were meant to come first.

He wisely remained staring at her with wide eyes. The large artillery cannon behind him was of little use against Valkyrie, as it aimed the wrong direction and would be difficult to turn her way. The rifle on the ground was just as useless, and clearly he knew that. If she intended to kill him, he would be dead before he reached the rifle.

Valkyrie stepped forward.

"I'm assuming it's a waste of time to reach for my sidearm," Jackson Davis said, backing away from her as his hand hovered at his holster.

She simply nodded. "I will not kill you yet," she explained.

"Yet...such a comforting word," he replied sardonically.

She could sense his fear of her. And yet, he also managed to joke in her presence. She liked this man. It would be a shame to kill him.

Her orders for this mission were unkind. They always were. Valkyrie was not sent in to do kind things to others. But these orders were not just unkind to others. They were unkind to herself.

Valkyrie had very few friends in the world. They resided within this Tower. And her orders were to hurt, or to kill, all of them.

She stepped forward once more, and an explosion from an aircraft lit up the balcony as it hit the Tower beside them.

Jackson stood still. "I'm not gonna lie," he said, almost to himself. "There's a part of me that's relieved."

She cocked her head in surprise. "You wish to die."

He watched her. "No. Not really. But I'm not sure how to learn to live again without Ava."

Valkyrie's heart became heavy. "Ava? She is dead?"

He breathed out painfully. "She's dying. And this battle...Eli...there's no way she'll survive this."

Valkyrie gave a genuine look of concern that seemed to surprise Jackson. "Eli would not hurt his own sister."

Jackson's pain became unmistakable. "You have no idea how much he already has. And how much more he intends. Valkyrie...if there's any part of you that still cares about Ava—"

She cut him off, walking closer, menacingly. He steeled himself in preparation for what she intended to do to him.

Valkyrie held something out to him. He took a long pause before he accepted it.

"My watch?" he asked in surprise.

"Yes," Valkyrie replied. "It is not fair that I keep this watch after what I will do to your people this night. You may have it."

He watched her with deep understanding. Eventually, he handed it back to her. "No, Valkyrie. It's yours. Whatever you do. You helped me once, and I gave it to you willingly. But Valkyrie...if there's any part of you that is able to resist—"

"There is not," Valkyrie replied simply.

Jackson swallowed sadly. "I always hoped you'd be on our side in the end."

Her eyes became sorrowful. "So did I."

Another moment passed before he forced her to accept the watch. "Whatever happens now, this is yours."

He could not understand how much this meant, and at the same time, how deeply it hurt her. She accepted the watch gratefully. Jackson was a friend. But she would kill him before daylight.

Still, first, Eli intended to hurt him in every way possible, and it was Valkyrie who was intended to carry out those orders.

She rushed past him, and Jackson almost flinched, expecting to die in that moment. Instead, Valkyrie jumped, as if flying, to the balcony just below and to the side where a Russian officer continually fired on the aircraft.

Jackson apparently realized what was about to happen moments before it did, and he screamed out the name of his friend. "Vasiliv!"

But too late. Valkyrie had finished the job.

☆ ☆ ☆ ☆ ☆

Mikel tried to focus on the task at hand. He opened a spotlight to the sky, highlighting the aircraft for the artillery soldiers. He fired weapons from the Tower. He tried to block Valkyrie's path as best he could—although she was resilient and somehow always managed her way around.

He handled the fight in Moscow the best he could too. They were doing well there, holding their defenses.

He still had high hopes and optimism that they could win this. But he was also conscious of Ava, now laying on the side of the room, near death.

Zak's assistant—who also happened to be his cousin, Malya, did her best to keep Ava cared for and comfortable, but Zak said there was little they could do for her now.

Mikel opened his eyes briefly, looking at her. She was shaking slightly now, as if shivering from the cold.

Malya noticed Mikel's concern. "I can't get her enough blankets, and I already turned up the heat again. But one second she's burning hot, the next she's ice cold. I have no idea what's happening to her. And I'm not sure how to help her."

Mikel watched her sadly, even as he fought the battle on many different fronts within his mind.

"Hang in there, Ava," he pleaded through the link. *"Don't you give up yet. You've come through worse. We can get you through this too."*

The infection in his mind from Counter Intelligence took advantage of his many focused distractions, and sent a crushing wave in attempts to drown him.

His hands shot to the side of his head, and he closed his eyes, completely focused once more on his greatest enemy, while in the back of his mind, he led the Towers of Russia in defense of their land.

★ ★ ★ ★ ★

Valkyrie would go to every one of Jackson's friends within the Tower. His assistant, his closest counselors, his staff. Her list was long, and Zhànshì Six was dealing with a similar list outside of the Tower, destroying all those whom Jackson Davis loved.

First, she was to defeat the enemy from the balconies, particularly those closest to Jackson.

Eli was angry with Jackson. Valkyrie did not fully know why. More and more it was clear to her that she was on the wrong side. But Valkyrie did not have the luxury of running. She did not have the choice to switch sides, like the others had.

Harrison had ensured long ago that Valkyrie would be the General's lapdog, and like a shock collar that punished her for disobedience, her chip had been programmed to keep her on track. She could not disobey orders without great pain. And if she attempted anything so audacious as switching sides…Eli would kill her in an instant.

Valkyrie found herself on another balcony, prepared to eliminate the next target.

The man turned to face her quickly, and the scene was similar to her interaction with Jackson previously.

"Shannon," the man said, and she almost thought she saw something for her in those eyes. The way he looked at her, it was the way Kristen used to.

"You are Kristen's husband," Valkyrie noted out loud.

He nodded sadly. "Yes, Shannon, I was your sister's husband."

She watched him. "And you are Ava's father," she added.

"Yes, I am."

"Ava is dying," Valkyrie said, wondering if he knew.

Painfully, he nodded once more. "She is."

"Why?"

"She was infected with a virus, a weapon."

"Counter Intelligence," Valkyrie said.

"Yes. This weapon, and her exposure to the chip, was too much for her."

"She will not survive," Valkyrie asked, but it sounded a statement.

He shook his head. "No, she won't."

Valkyrie closed her eyes sadly, for the briefest of moments. Jacob Harris did not notice. Kyle would have.

"I am here to eliminate you," Valkyrie explained.

"I know, Shannon," he said. Why did he speak to her this way? He sounded loving. He sounded caring. He sounded like Kristen used to.

"I am here to kill you, because your death will hurt Jackson."

He agreed sadly. "It will. After Ava is gone, I would be all he has left."

"It will not matter," Valkyrie assured him. "I will kill him too, before the night is through."

He watched her caringly for a time. "What would happen if you didn't?"

She did not reply.

He watched her, lovingly. Why?

Harrison had never given Shannon such a fatherly look. And Valkyrie had known Jacob Harris very little in his life. It was almost as though he loved her for Kristen's sake alone.

"Kristen was the only one who still loved me," Valkyrie related sadly, though it came out in monotone. "After I changed. The others only cared to use me for my abilities. But Kristen always treated me as a sister."

"She loved you very much. She would have done anything to protect you, Shannon. She loved you like her own daughter."

"Ava is her own daughter," Valkyrie said pointedly. "Perhaps that is why we are twins."

He smiled. "You do look an awful lot alike," he agreed.

A long silence passed, and ultimately, Valkyrie made her decision. "I must eliminate you, before the night has ended. But I will wait. For

Kristen's sake. And for Ava's. Because they were the only ones who ever still saw me. For them, you may live some time longer."

He tried to make another plea, likely for Jackson's life, but it was too late. Valkyrie was gone.

✦ ✦ ✦ ✦ ✦

The garden was vast and fragrant. Everything was covered with trees, bushes, flowers and plants she had never seen before. It was beautiful.

As long as she walked down the cobblestone pave way, it never seemed to end.

The scent of the garden was overwhelming and delightful. Lavender, Russian Olive trees and lilacs were some of the fragrances she could put a name to, yet so many other scents filled the paved garden.

She couldn't place where she was, or how she had gotten here, or really much of anything that had happened before being in this place. But as lost as she might have been, she didn't feel lost. It was peaceful and safe here.

From around the oncoming hedge, she noticed a bright figure, and she continued down the path until she could place who it was.

"Hello, Ava," the beautiful woman said kindly.

And then Ava remembered who she was, and all that had happened before this moment came back to her. "Mom," she said in realization. "Am...am I dead?"

Kristen smiled gently. "Not yet."

✦ ✦ ✦ ✦ ✦

"They're sending in the ground troops," Kyle said through the earpiece, leaving his vantage point and descending into the Tower. "The aircraft aren't pulling out, but they'll use it as a distraction to send the ground soldiers in."

"Everyone pull from the balconies," Jackson ordered. "Then we'll have Mikel seal the doors."

"We can't afford to let the aircraft continue firing on us," Kyle disagreed. "We've been in this fight less than ten minutes and have already suffered extensive damage. They'll blow the Tower to pieces. The ships have already hit our primary anti-aircraft guns."

"Valkyrie is picking off the artillery men one by one!" Jackson explained in a calm anger. "We need to seal those doors with her on the outside."

"Too late," Sasha replied quickly. "She just entered from the next level up. Valkyrie is within the Tower walls."

Jackson cursed audibly on the intercom. "All right, plan B it is. Mikel, when you manage to locate her, seal her in."

"I'll try," Mikel replied. "But as Kyle warned, the Tower sensors aren't picking up anything."

"Seal off the entire level nine," Sasha urged.

"She'll get through," Kyle warned. "She has high tech training and gear to make it through those walls easily."

"Gas the level," Jackson ordered.

"There are over twenty officers on that level," Mikel warned.

Jackson cursed once more. "They're dead anyway," he muttered as he tried to make the right call.

Kyle panicked initially at the thought of them killing Valkyrie so quickly, but decided to offer an alternative. "I've seen her withstand any gassing you could throw at her," he spoke quickly. "She'll break through any door. You can't stop her with enough soldiers."

"Then what do you suggest?" Jackson replied in frustration.

"Let me go after her."

"No. We need you on the ground. Your stealth suit and your skills in taking on armies alone is imperative."

"She'll kill every one of your officers from inside the building. She'll win this battle in less than an hour if you let her go at it!"

"Then gas the level," Jackson ordered, though it was clear he was still conflicted.

"She might not even be on that level anymore!" Kyle answered quickly. He was already making his way through the Tower, toward level nine, toward Valkyrie.

In the past, he would have gone off on his own without concern for Jackson's plan. But a thought kept running through his mind, a memory of Ava yelling at Valkyrie and Kyle after a failed mission and repeatedly asking them, "Are we a bunch of lone wolves? Or are we a team?" This had become their motto on the crew ever since.

He could not deny that this crew was better as a team. Still, he wasn't ready to write off Valkyrie either.

"Please, Jackson, I'm asking you to let me do this. We owe it to Valkyrie, and to all of your men on that level, to at least try."

Jackson hesitated momentarily. "You won't get through to her."

"Then I'll do what I have to. With the Chameleon suit, I have an advantage over her. If I can't reach her, then I'll kill her myself."

"I can't ask you to do that, Kyle," Jackson wavered.

"You're not asking me to. I'm asking you. Let me do this."

One more moment of hesitation before Jackson answered. "Do it. All other troops, join me on the base level. We'll have taint to face when the army makes it inside."

☆ ☆ ☆ ☆ ☆

Ava looked around the place in confusion. "Where are we?"

"This is Lionel's garden," Kristen explained. "I spent a lot of time here as a kid, playing in the stream with Eric while Lionel and Harrison conversed."

She motioned down the path beyond her, and Ava moved to see what she was gesturing to.

Harrison and Lionel sat together on a wooden bench near the bridge crossing the stream. They looked younger than she remembered either of them. And they discussed passionately, debating back and forth, though she couldn't make out what they were saying.

"Admittedly," Kristen spoke again, "I spent a lot of time here later on in life too. Lionel always opened up this space for me to find peace in the hardest moments of my life. He was by my side through everything. The father I never had in Harrison. And I'm delighted that you found him in your life too."

Ava watched Lionel and Harrison for a long time, uncomprehending before she turned back to Kristen. "I guess this is that moment they talk about then, where I see a light at the end of a long tunnel, and have to decide whether or not to walk toward it."

Kristen smiled softly. "Not exactly, love. You're not going to die tonight. Your mission isn't complete yet."

Ava scoffed. "A lot of people die before completing their missions."

Kristen shook her head. "I don't think that's true."

Ava squinted her eyes in disagreement, but didn't respond.

"So many of you say that Harrison died too soon," Kristen explained further, "that none of this horrific chaos would have happened if he had lived. And that may be true. But he had completed what was his to do. He might not have made it worse, the way his replacements have, but he couldn't have brought on the end of the war either. He didn't have the simplistic power that it took."

"The connection with the Towers?" Ava asked, though it sounded more a statement.

Kristen laughed once softly. "No. Not that. He thought that was what he lacked. But it was something much simpler even than that."

Ava looked around, suddenly frustrated by this place and the lack of answers. "If I'm not dying, then why am I here?"

"I didn't say you weren't dying. I said you weren't going to die. And I'm not the one who brought you here. When you wake up, you might wonder if I was ever even here at all. You can call it a dream, a hallucination, or conversing with angels. It doesn't matter too much, whether it's your mind creating this scenario to solve the problem before you, or whether I really am here. The result will be the same."

"The result? All right then, let's get to it! My friends are dying out there. I need to get back and help them. How do I go back?"

"How did you get back last time?" Kristen asked seriously.

Ava found herself racking her memory, trying to understand what Kristen meant by this. Finally, she found an answer.

"The Jiānhùrén," she muttered. Then she looked up to face her mother again. "That pinprick in the halls. They injected me with something?"

Kristen did not respond, but it was clear Ava had it right.

"Well, what's that cure that Remington gave me?" Ava said excitedly. "I need them to inject me with whatever he found."

"Possibly," Kristen offered. "But is that really how you got out last time?"

Ava huffed in frustration. "Wasn't it?" she pressed back.

Kristen raised her hands to either side. "I don't know. You tell me."

☆ ☆ ☆ ☆ ☆

"It won't hold much longer," Mikel warned. "They're cutting through the doors with great success."

"Understood," Jackson replied, holding position in the Tower lobby.

This lobby, a hotel-like floor would become a battleground. The officers beside him remained strong and resolute. The enemy that was coming would remain just as determined. A commander such as Jackson didn't always fight on the front with his men. It was dangerous to lose a leader, the man who made the calls. And he remained in a secure position compared to some of his men. But without Kyle's presence here, Jackson had a feeling that these men needed expert help in facing soldiers with the chip.

Sasha was prepared to take command if Jackson was shot down. Of course he, too, was securely positioned in the lobby. If both of these men were lost, Zak would take charge. Jackson hoped it wouldn't come to that, but Zak was just as prepared to do what was necessary, if the others were killed in this battle.

The lobby was dark, nearly pitch black. The only light came from the laser as it cut through the large metal door. All eyes watched the entrance. They were almost through. Just moments more.

Jackson looked across the way to where Sasha was positioned, checking to see if he could spot his friend.

"A few more seconds," Mikel said. "I'm sorry, there's nothing I can do."

"We're ready," Sasha replied through the earpiece. "Good luck, everyone."

The laser pinpointed the last inches of space needed to cause a large opening in the door. Jackson breathed in and out. The soldiers brought another anxiety, but after facing the aircraft, a number of ground soldiers seemed minimal in comparison.

The hatch that had been cut through the door was kicked in, and all of his men remained at ready. But nothing happened. No soldiers filed in. They were waiting for something. Jackson unconsciously held his breath in anticipation. Why weren't they filing inside?

A sudden blur at the opening caught his eyes, and made him squint in closer. He thought he had seen something, but it had disappeared almost as soon as he saw it. He had seen an image like that before. Where?

It hit him in a sudden realization, but by then it was too late.

"They have stealth suits!" he tried to warn through his earpiece, but dozens of enemy soldiers had already entered, practically invisible to their eyes, and by the time Jackson gave warning to his men, they were already under fire from the invisible threat.

Ava let out a sigh of anger. "Well, you're no help at all."

Kristen smiled deeply. "You've said that to me before, love, when you chose Harrison over me, time and again."

Ava's expression changed to one of regret. "I'm sorry, Mom. I didn't know then what I do now."

"I know that. And I never blamed you."

"You blamed Harrison," Ava replied carefully.

Kristen's smile faded into a look of pain. "He had his blind spots. He had his shortcomings, as we all do. But his weaknesses happened to affect those closest to him on a greater level than anyone should have to suffer through."

"As hard as I try," Ava admitted, "I still can't find it in myself to hate him."

"Maybe that's okay. Do you hate Eli?"

Ava considered that for a long time before admitting, "No. I hate what he's done. I even hate who he's become. But I don't think I can find it in myself to hate him either."

"Neither can I," Kristen agreed. "But just because we don't hate someone doesn't mean we can allow them to cause harm to ourselves, or to those we care about."

Ava nodded in agreement. "Did you ever fight Harrison?"

Kristen watched Ava for a time before responding. "Every day."

"Then why didn't you beat him? You were stronger than him in so many ways. You could have won the people over. You could have had a chance, a real shot at least!"

Kristen smiled. "I could. And I did. But beating Harrison was sadly never in the cards for me."

"And me? Do I have any chance of beating Eli? Or is my cause just as hopeless as yours?"

Kristen's expression became serious and resolute. "Not only do you stand a chance, Ava, it is imperative that you succeed. You have to beat Eli. Or everything that all of us have worked for will be for nothing."

☆ ☆ ☆ ☆ ☆

Attacked from every angle by unseen foes, Sasha and his officers were no match for what was happening to them.

Within less than a minute, they no longer thought at all about attacking the enemy—instead, simply trying to evade it. He saw the fear in his men's eyes as guns fired in the darkened room. Sasha had been at this a long time, but he didn't have the slightest idea how to train his men to fight an invisible enemy in the blink of an eye.

"Turn on the lights!" Jackson ordered Mikel through the intercom.

Sasha immediately agreed with the idea. Clearly, all of these stealth suits were enhanced with night vision. But perhaps the blurry figures would be easier to spot in full light.

No such luck.

Mikel did as ordered, and the lights went on. Everything went still. The enemy stopped their attacks, but no matter which way Sasha whipped around, aiming his gun at the ready, he couldn't see anything.

"Why have they stopped firing?" Sasha whispered through the intercom.

"They have to be careful in broad light," Kyle explained. "They will have to remain in one location at such a close distance, or they'll be easily spotted."

"Keep your eyes open," Jackson ordered the officers on the main channel. "They'll slip up. And we'll get them."

Still, as peeled as his eyes were, as much as he continued to whip around and look for any sign, Sasha saw nothing.

"I'm coming," Kyle said through the intercom. "I'll help you fight this first."

"Personally, I'm still worried about Valkyrie," Mikel disagreed. "Taint. I wish Ava were here! Maybe she and I could have taken Valkyrie on together."

Sasha swallowed carefully, his eyes fixed on his surroundings. The officers around him were just as scared, and showed it more visibly than him.

"Our people don't have much time down there!" Kyle explained urgently.

"Neither do the rest of the officers that Valkyrie will pummel through. And what if she gets to the core?"

"Stay on Valkyrie," Jackson ordered. "We have to take out that threat. We'll think of something."

Sasha had never disliked Jackson's confidence so much. They were certainly going to die. Then again, how much help could Kyle, only one man in a stealth suit, present against an entire army of similarly equipped soldiers? At least, if he focused on Valkyrie, he could take out one threat and be of some real use.

Someone screamed, a shot was fired, and an officer was down. Another officer shot in the general direction where the hidden foe had attacked his friend, but his rapid fire amounted to nothing.

Seconds passed. Another scream, another shot, another man down.

"They're slowly picking us off one by one," Sasha whispered into the intercom. "Jackson, you better think of something quick, or I'll tear your carcass apart myself!"

Another scream. Another man down.

Jackson cursed through the intercom.

A shot, a scream, and another man down.

Sasha looked in every direction, trying to see something, any clue, but finding none.

An officer not ten feet from Sasha gasped and attempted to fire his weapon but wasn't given the chance before his neck was snapped.

Sasha fired in every direction around the dead officer, but got nothing. "Taint it, Jackson!" he shouted this time. That image...the poor man's neck snapped seemingly by nothing at all, was a disturbing sight that Sasha would not soon forget.

"Smoke bomb!" Jackson said suddenly as if it would make sense to everyone. "Mikel! Smoke up the room through the ventilation system!"

★ ★ ★ ★ ★

"My friends are probably out there dying right now," Ava said in frustration, "and I'm stuck in this fantasy world until I remember some grand moment from the last time the Jiānhùrén tried to kill me?"

Kristen shrugged. "I didn't design this."

Ava sighed deeply, feeling tired and overwhelmed. She sat down cross-legged on the cobblestone pave way.

"Looks...comfortable," Kristen teased as Ava pulled a loose pebble from underneath her.

"I'm exhausted," Ava admitted.

"You have had a rough couple of months," Kristen agreed.

"Rough year, more like," Ava added in a grumble.

Kristen cocked her head and considered. "'Rough life' might be the better explanation."

Ava chuckled. "Yeah. Maybe. But it was finally getting good." This she said with a tone of regret.

"You and Jackson," Kristen said in understanding. She took a seat on the pave way, across from Ava. "You're good together."

Ava shook her head. "He's too good for me. I'm a mess. I wish I could be better for him. I try. But I'll never deserve him."

Kristen smiled gently. "I used to think that about Sasha too. In many ways, it was true, his temperament and outlook on life was so much better than mine. I dealt with extreme anxiety and depression..." she nodded her head to one shoulder, then the next. "And mood swings."

Ava laughed. "I can relate to that."

Kristen chuckled, then her expression became serious. "Eventually, it occurred to me that as good as my husband was, he deserved to have everything he wanted. For whatever reason, he chose me. And so, I did the best I could to give him all that he deserved."

Ava nodded as she considered. "Jackson made me promise not to leave anymore. Evidently, every time we disagree, he expects us to have a normal, sane conversation. But apparently I always jump straight to taking off." She huffed in sarcastic exaggeration, and Kristen laughed heartily at that. "But after the last time, I promised I wouldn't leave anymore. I guess, every time we disagree, there's a part of me that's expecting him to say we're done. And so, I guess, I try and save myself from the heartbreak by being the one to leave first."

"But he doesn't see it that way," Kristen noted.

Ava shook her head. "No. Despite all his own trauma and baggage from childhood, he's so...good. So strong. And I'm a wreck, on a regular basis."

"And yet," Kristen said with a knowing smile, "for whatever reason, he chose you."

Ava smiled softly. "Yeah. I guess he did." The silence lingered as she considered that. Then, suddenly she remembered where he was right now, and the battle that was raging that Ava had abandoned too soon. "I don't mean to sound cocky or anything, but I think they need me out there."

Kristen gave a deep nod. "I think that's true."

"So how do I get out of here?" Ava repeated.

Kristen gave another knowing look. "You tell me."

Ava closed her eyes in frustration. This was not going to be easy.

The room filled with artificial smoke and Mikel had adjusted the heat temperatures to cover the heat signatures of their people, so the stealth suits could not locate them automatically. Jackson could not even see ten feet in front of him. If this didn't work as he hoped it would, at the very least, it would make it more difficult for the enemy to spot his men. Of course, he was hoping for much more than that.

Seconds passed, turning to minutes. Nothing yet, but the fact that there hadn't been another officer killed in nearly two minutes was victory in itself.

"Zak," Jackson whispered into his earpiece, hoping it would not alert the enemy to his position. "Check the Tower sensors. See if you can pick them off from the upper guns in the lobby."

"I'm sorry to say," Zak's voice came through the radio, "I already thought of that. There are no extra heat signatures being detected on the sensors."

"The stealth suit will mask it," Kyle explained. "The only way to detect them is to see the blurry figures with your own eyes."

Jackson had suspected as much, but figured it was worth checking.

Of course, the stealth suits were also enhanced with greater hearing ability. Even while whispering, he had been heard by the enemy. He was certain of that much when the smoke moved awkwardly in several directions coming toward him. Not one, but four different figures approached slowly.

On the one hand, his plan had worked. He could see the figures nearing in the smoke. On the other hand, it looked an awful lot like he was about to die.

18

Smoke Screen

Kyle searched level after level for her. Nothing. He could not find Valkyrie. And now the others were being attacked by a serious foe. He felt torn, whether to disobey Jackson's orders on this one to go help him, or whether to continue to search for Valkyrie.

"Zak," he asked through the radio channel. "Have you had any sign or warning of Valkyrie? Any glimpse on a camera? Any sensor being tripped? Any heat signatures rapidly disappearing as she picks them off?"

"Nothing," Zak said apologetically. "I'm searching. But I haven't found anything. We sealed that level. Either she's still there with you, or she had already moved on before we sealed it."

Kyle scoffed. "She's gone all right," he said in realization. "She's probably swept through several floors by now!" He hurried to the nearest stairwell. "I'm at stairwell nine three. Open it up. I need to get to her quickly!"

"Understood."

The door opened and Kyle hurried through. Something shoved past him almost as soon as he was through the door, knocking him forward several feet. He cursed, glancing in that direction, and only saw a flash of Valkyrie as she ran down the stairs and into the next floor.

"Seal off level ten!" Kyle ordered, running after her rapidly.

He had been wrong. Valkyrie was stuck on level nine until he gave the order that let her out.

"The entrance to level ten was right next to the lift access shaft," Zak observed. "If she got into it...."

Kyle cursed again, running back partly the way he had come and picking the other fork that he had skipped before.

The door to the lift was now sealed shut, but what if she had gotten inside before Zak had finished the job?

Kyle clenched his jaw. Or what if she was using him to clear the path for her?

★ ★ ★ ★ ★

"A part of me wouldn't mind staying right here with you forever," Ava admitted as they walked toward the cobblestone bridge. They stopped then, to look at the stream.

"I wouldn't mind that either," Kristen agreed softly. She pulled from her pocket a few pebbles, and began throwing them into the stream. After a time, she handed some to Ava.

"But as you said, you're still needed there."

"To defeat Eli," Ava replied sadly.

Kristen nodded. "Sasha and Jackson and my Zhànshì boys may yet beat Eli's armies. They may even be able to win against Valkyrie. But none of them will be able to take on Eli's power and dominion, and this won't end until someone does."

There was always a deep pain for Ava when she spoke of Eli as an enemy, but she sensed that the pain ran so much deeper for Kristen. This boy was her son. And if Ava felt as if she had failed him, there was no telling how much that plagued his own mother.

"Why did he change?" Ava asked. "Why did he choose this? Why did he leave all of us for this?"

Kristen was silent and somber for a long time. "There could be many answers to that question. There was always a bit of hunger for power in his nature. But that's usually what we call healthy ambition. At some point, it changed. Little by little it became tainted in the literal sense;

corrupted. He shifted greatly when Harrison died, but I suspect that it had started, at least in some ways, before that.

"Still, he did not fully decide until a lot later. That time you spent with him was not wasted. You gave him the chance to choose better. And he could have. But so many things compelled him in the wrong direction. I couldn't tell you why he became what he did, but I know *how* it happened. Day by day. One choice, one decision at a time. Here a little, and there a little. The opportunities for him to choose good or bad were many. And there were moments when he chose good. But far too many times he chose otherwise. And the more he did so, the easier it became. And the easier it became, the more he did so."

Ava passively watched the flowing stream as she listened.

"Harrison followed a similar path," Kristen explained further. "For so long, all he cared about was making a difference. He had his heart in the right place. But I guess at some point he made the decision to go below his standards and choose, what he referred to as 'necessary evil.' And then, decision after decision, it became easier, until it was harder not to."

"It's that easy," Ava said somberly, "to become a tyrant."

Kristen smiled sadly. "It wasn't just Eli," Kristen admitted. "There were outside pressures too. Harrison, Eric, Council, and even those who meant to help him at times got it wrong. But ultimately, the decision was his. That is to say, each of those decisions were his."

They watched the stream for several minutes. It suddenly occurred to Ava that she hoped time passed faster here than in reality. Already it had been too long. She was needed elsewhere. She was stuck here.

Yet, even so, she found herself cherishing every moment. A part of her wished she could remain here, by her mother's side in this peaceful place, forever.

☆ ☆ ☆ ☆ ☆

The figures moved in closer. Five of them now.

Jackson took in a breath, expecting the worst. He unconsciously crawled farther back to the railing he was rammed up against for cover as they came from every other direction. His automatic rifle would only get him so far before one of these soldiers got him, especially if they were all armed. But if he was dead anyway, best take out as many as possible.

Jackson pulled a grenade from his vest, holding it momentarily to the count of three before throwing it directly at the middle figure. Before it made impact, he launched himself over the railing and fell down a full flight to the lobby floor. The explosion went off before he impacted the ground. The impact might have injured or killed him, but he was insanely lucky enough to land directly on another invisible figure. Still, it hurt like the tainted General.

The super soldier attempted to get a grip on his neck as they grappled with each other on the ground. The man was already weakened by Jackson landing on him, and he was sure that helped against the physically and mentally enhanced super soldier. Even so, this guy was tough. Neither of them could get a weapon pointed at the other, though they continually attempted to do so. They got in close jabs and knees to as many sensitive areas as possible. The soldier wanted to end it with a cracking neck, and Jackson wasn't about to go out that way.

He heard the sound of gunfire throughout the lobby, and hoped his men were having as much luck in spotting the enemy as he was, rather than being snuffed out by the soldiers.

Jackson and his invisible enemy grunted and gasped in pain, each in their turn as the other got in a good hit. Jackson was grateful for his months of practice with Ava. She was excellent in her grappling skills, and he was the better for what she had taught him. Even so, he could not deny that, without the chip, and compared to this soldier, he might not be much of a match in the end.

The soldier pushed Jackson onto his side, then got his arm around Jackson's neck, putting it in the crook of his arm. He moved to a chokehold when breaking Jackson's neck proved impossible.

Jackson fought with every gasping second to break free, but with his airway compressed his seconds were nearing an end. He needed to get out of this quickly, or he really was a goner.

A sudden figure came lurking through the fog, and when Jackson was certain it wasn't one of his own, he fired at the soldier with his arm still at an awkward, twisted angle.

The gunshot only clipped the man in the side. Jackson once more attempted to point the weapon at the man holding him, but the guy kicked his weapon away.

Taint. Not good.

The figure in the smoke came closer, angry at being shot. The fog moved about where his midriff should be, rising up, and although Jackson was unable to place the actual body parts, the smoke moved to show him the stance.

Jackson used his full force to roll his first attacker onto himself just in time as the other soldier fired his weapon.

Jackson gasped for breath as the arm around his neck went limp. But forcing this new soldier to kill his ally in friendly fire only made the man angrier. These guys liked hand to hand combat over long-range weapons— or possibly, they limited gunfire to hide their position. Either way, the man moved in on Jackson and the smoke around him drifted quickly to the side.

Jackson followed the smoke signals, pushing the first man off him in time and using his right leg to kick with full force at the attacker before he made it to the ground after him.

The man screamed out in pain, and Jackson guessed he had judged right in kicking the man's wound, which he had surmised due to the blood patterns on the floor.

Jackson reached for his fallen weapon and fired on the enemy before the man had time to recover.

But the exchange and the gunfire only brought more foes. As two more lurking, shadowy figures came after him, it occurred to Jackson that if he wanted to win against this army, he had to fight as covertly and fiercely as they.

Jackson fired on the last two figures, then holstered his gun and moved quickly away from that position.

He may not have a stealth suit of his own, but he would make do.

☆ ☆ ☆ ☆ ☆

"I hate this," one of Nastia's men muttered in frustration. "Standing here uselessly guarding a closed door while our people are out there being pummeled!"

"It comes with the job," Nastia said patiently, walking the perimeter of level one, outside the core.

"We are the best that Russia has!" the man argued.

"That's why we're here, Matvey," she replied absently. "We guard this core. No one gets in. The enemy makes it inside that room, and the battle is over."

Nastia glanced down the hallway to where two of the others had taken to playing cards on the floor.

"Get up!" she ordered. "Idiots! Get up and be alert. The enemy could come through that door any second."

"The enemy are in the lobby, Nastia," Pierre replied pointedly, though he gathered the cards and stood.

"Just do your job," she demanded.

Pierre was still bitter that Vasiliv had given her command over him, and he did whatever he could to make her work to keep the job.

Nastia walked away, muttering to herself.

"I'll be ready," Pierre called out to her. "Some of us don't have to be on edge to be on guard."

"All teams," came a transmission from Zak Chekov, "all teams be advised. Agent Valkyrie has gained access to the lift and may appear on any level."

Nastia had never seen Pierre get up and on his guard so quickly.

Several of the others muttered curses.

"You wanted the fight, Matvey!" she said to the now concerned man.

"I didn't mean *that* fight!" he replied in terror.

"Well, congratulations," she said, though inside she, too, found herself suffering a terrible new anxiety.

"Does she really look just like Ava?" Matvey muttered to Nastia.

"That's what I'm told," she offered. "I've never seen her myself."

"Ava's not all that scary," Pierre said hopefully. "And I've been wanting a rematch since our last fight. But Jackson won't let me near her."

"That's because you're a pig," Nastia said, jutting out her chin at the man. "But if you'd like to fight Valkyrie alone, I'll stand aside and watch."

Pierre looked suddenly petrified, and Nastia laughed out loud. Served him right.

"She won't really come here, will she?" Matvey whispered furtively.

SMOKE SCREEN

Nastia considered that for a long time before turning slowly to face each of her team in turn. "I think we should be prepared for the fact that there's nowhere else in the Tower more important for her to go. We are Russia's best. We'll hold this place."

"Russia hasn't conducted scientific advancements on our soldiers!" Pierre disagreed with deep concern.

Nastia huffed. "Only because the Republic wouldn't let us," she muttered. "Now all of you pull yourselves together. We'll probably face Valkyrie today. And we'll have one riveting story to tell our grandkids because of it!"

☆ ☆ ☆ ☆ ☆

"I'll give you a clue," Kristen offered as they absently threw rocks into the stream.

Ava waited expectantly.

"What happened before you woke up last time?"

Ava tried to remember. The whole thing was hazy in her mind. She wasn't sure how much had been memory, how much had been hallucination, and how much had been reality. She also wasn't sure how much she remembered now.

"A lot of things?" Ava replied helplessly. "I talked to you, and Breanna, and Liam—"

"What did he say?"

"Who? Liam?"

Kristen nodded.

Ava struggled for the answer, scanning her foggy recollections of the strange experience. "I don't know. A lot of people said a lot of things."

"But what did Liam say?"

Ava let out a long breath as she racked her brain. "He said...he said the same thing he told me before he died."

Kristen nodded vigorously. "And what was that?"

"Mom, if you have the answer, will you just give it to me?"

"I don't have the answer."

"Then how do you know you're even leading me in the right direction?"

Kristen smiled. "I think subconsciously, you already know these answers. It's my job to help guide you there. What did Liam say? What were his last words to you? What were his final words to anyone?"

Ava sobered as she replied. "He told me that Harrison, and that everyone, had it wrong. He said there was one person who had it figured out, and I needed to find him."

"And have you?"

Ava shrugged. "I mean, I think so. I've assumed since I ran into Mikel that he was the one who figured it out."

Kristen nodded in consideration. "What else did he say before he died?"

"He said, 'you need to remember what Breanna was trying to tell you.'"

"And have you?"

"Yes! I mean, I think so. The image she sent, the picture she saw before she died. Somehow, she saw a visual interpretation of the energy field as I fought the Tower. She saw me pushing against the field as I consciously fought it. But she saw a different energy pattern being transmitted at the same time. A softer, subtler pattern."

"Like fractured light allowing us to see colorful rainbows," Kristen said thoughtfully.

Ava nodded her agreement. "She realized that we had been doing it all wrong. It was too late to change anything then. But she sent an image, and eventually, when the time was right, I was able to interpret it."

"Is that all?"

"What do you mean?"

"Was that all she wanted to tell you? Was that all that Liam meant when he said that the rest of us got it wrong?"

"Yes. I mean, I thought it was."

"Is it?" Kristen pressed.

"I'm guessing from the fact that you're annoyingly repeating that question that maybe it wasn't."

Kristen laughed out loud. "I have missed that dry sense of humor of yours."

Ava smiled despite herself.

Then the moment grew serious again, and Kristen spoke soberly. "What else could Liam have meant? What did the rest of us miss? What did Harrison get wrong, Ava?"

"I don't know…" Ava said helplessly.

"Neither do I," Kristen offered.

A long silence passed before Kristen spoke again. "I have a feeling that you'll have to answer that question before you leave here. But there's more you need to take with you than just that answer."

"Oh yeah? And what is that? Let me guess: you don't know."

Kristen smiled. "Actually, this one I do know."

Ava waited, but Kristen said nothing more until Ava raised her hands pointedly.

"Would you like me to tell you?"

"I mean, duh."

Kristen laughed out loud again. "I never got to enjoy you in your teenage years, love. Harrison had taken you from me by then. But I'm glad to see you're still as charming and youthful as ever."

"I'm twenty now," Ava replied stubbornly. "And you bring out the immaturity in me."

"What are mothers for?" she said sweetly, but then she became serious. "The second thing you need to consider is your Intelligence Quotient."

"My I.Q.?" Ava asked in confusion.

"Yes. But I'm not talking about how smart you are. I'm talking about the link here. Your Intelligence Quotient is the degree or amount that you are able to connect to the link, and your incredible skills in accessing it.

"You have an ability Ava, beyond connecting with the Towers. Mikel has surpassed you in many ways. But there are things that you are capable of that even he cannot do."

Ava considered that. "If anything, I'd say his Intelligence Quotient is much higher than mine," she disagreed. "He's taking on Counter Intelligence better than I ever did."

"He is," Kristen agreed. "And in some areas, I would agree his Intelligence Quotient is higher than yours. But I didn't mean that either. Ava, there have been a few times in your life when you did something that no one else has, something that shouldn't even really be possible.

You've done it three times now, if my count is correct. Once to Eric. Once to Darya and her men. And once to the Zhànshì team who attempted to extract you from Russia."

Ava looked up at her mother in realization. "You mean pushing on their link."

Kristen nodded. "To Eric, you simply caused a nudge of pain. But to the others who truly threatened your safety, you managed to completely incapacitate them."

"What does that mean?"

"You tell me."

Ava groaned. "I don't have time for this. My people are fighting right now! If I can help them—"

"You can."

"Then tell me how."

"What could Liam have meant? What was Breanna trying to tell you? And what did you learn from Eric's pomposity about your Intelligence Quotient? You answer those three questions, and you will have won the war."

☆ ☆ ☆ ☆ ☆

Sasha and the four officers nearest faced a full army, it seemed, as more and more blurry figures moved toward them through the smoke.

They managed to keep the army back, picking off the soldiers every time they neared, but more and more kept coming. There seemed no end to this battle, and as they increased in numbers, Sasha wondered if he weren't doing this all wrong. Still, he didn't have time to think of an alternative. He was too busy fending off the continual stream of soldiers.

Things grew more tense as the numbers of oncoming soldiers increased.

It couldn't have been more than five minutes since they had smoked the room, but he had been very busy almost the entire time.

An influx of soldiers suddenly came from up the stairwell, and Sasha watched in awe as the smoke seemed to move completely out of the way. That must be a lot of bodies pushing toward them.

"We need to fall back!" he yelled to his men. He stood from his crouching position and carefully moved through the smoke toward a section of large pillars for better cover. His men followed, firing on the sea of soldiers as they went.

Sasha bumped into something, but looking urgently behind him, he saw nothing. Which meant he had walked right into a hidden soldier.

The foggy figure got in a good blow to the side of his face before Sasha had time to react, and it knocked him from his firm footing, pushing him back slightly. He fired in the direction it had come, but the man was beside him now and attempted to disarm him in a smooth motion.

Sasha fought it, pushing his wrist against the pain and firing again. He heard a scream as another shadowy figure was hit by the bullet.

The man attempting to disarm him made a crashing kick to the side of Sasha's knee, and this time it was him who screamed out in pain as his kneecap was pushed from its socket.

Three men attempted to help Sasha, but shadowy figures were on them just as quickly, so that each of them was now fighting for their lives against a much more powerful enemy.

Sasha collapsed to his knees, which intensified the pain of his broken kneecap. He shifted weight to his right side and had little time to defend himself as the enemy sent another crashing blow to the side of his face.

Soon the enemy had him on his back. Sasha attempted to reach for a knife at his belt, but unsuccessfully as the heavy man moved in closer, placing a blade on Sasha's neck and pressing it into his skin.

Sasha moved his hands to the shadowy arm in an attempt to push it back, but this soldier was much stronger than he. So, he held off the heavy arm with his left hand, and used his right to explore the nearly invisible form above him. When he had located the eye sockets, he made a calculated decision. Sasha reached for his dog tags at the side of his chest, pulling them free and stabbing it at the spot of air where he remembered the man's eye to be. The figure screamed out in horrific pain and rolled off Sasha to tend to his own wounds.

Kristen had saved his life with the memento he wore near his heart always.

Sasha retrieved his weapon and fired on the next several figures as they came close, but there were too many of them, and there was nowhere to retreat to. His leg was throbbing, and he had to limp to get anywhere.

It couldn't have been another minute, yet it felt an eternity as he fought off the invisible army. Only two of his men remained, and they were surrounded by the soldiers.

Cornered, Sasha stood beside his men as they butted up against the wall. Shadowy figures moved in at every angle. These three men would not be able to take them. Sasha was not one to contemplate surrender, though he must admit that the thought crossed his mind in that moment.

He pushed it aside. "If we must die, we die with honor and dignity," he said for his men, who knew it was the end as much as he did.

They fired their weapons to eliminate as many of the enemy as possible before their time was up. The enemy drew in ever nearer, and where soldiers fell, more moved in to take their place.

As the line of dark soldiers closed in, Sasha gasped at the realization of how close to death he was now. He couldn't remember it ever being so inevitable.

Through the fog, he saw something. Not the same shadowy figure. Something more visible, and yet, just as determined, and just as deadly.

Two arms went around the neck of one of the figures and moved in a snapping motion, though Sasha could not see the victim.

The new, more visible attacker then used a large blade against the next two enemy soldiers.

Sasha let out a breath of relief when he finally recognized the figure as it quickly moved from one soldier to the next, taking them out as fiercely and swiftly as the soldiers had been doing to them.

Sasha and his men fired on the enemy more rapidly, and between them, and their new help, they eliminated the small army in a matter of thirty seconds.

"Colonel!" one of the young Russian officers said in relief when the enemy was down.

"Sir!" the other said, with similar excitement.

"Thanks," Sasha said simply.

"Any time," Jackson whispered pleasantly.

"You were rather terrifying over there."

"Put those down," Jackson urged, pointing to their weapons.

"But, Colonel!" the young officer disagreed.

"They alert them right to you. We have to fight this quietly. And fiercely. It's not that hard," Jackson said, this directed at Sasha who watched him with uncertainty, thinking of his broken leg. "Just channel your inner Kyle."

☆ ☆ ☆ ☆ ☆

"Let's take it one at a time," Ava suggested. "I'll make guesses, and you tell me if I'm hot or cold."

Kristen giggled. They sat together under a large shade tree now, and the clover was much more comfortable than the cobblestone pathway had been.

"All right, go ahead," Kristen agreed.

Ava was surprised, but didn't waste any time asking if she was serious. "That thing that Eric taught me, the ability I can use on other people's chip. I'm supposed to use that on Eli?"

"It's not a matter of 'supposed' to," Kristen corrected. "There's no one perfect way for this to go down, no preconceived plan."

Ava raised her eyebrows. "Isn't that all Harrison ever did?"

"But this is not about Harrison, love. This is about you. Harrison certainly didn't account for Eli becoming a tyrant. It is not a matter of what you are supposed to do. Instead, it is what you decide to do."

"So, if I decide to use the chip against Eli, then I'll win the war?"

She shrugged noncommittally. "Possibly. I suppose it would depend on how you decided to do it."

"Ugh..." Ava complained. "All right, fine. Let's move to the next thing."

"We only just started," Kristen disagreed.

"You won't give me anything!"

"No," she said honestly. "I won't. But what will you think of?"

The conversation was interrupted as storm clouds began to gather. "I hope it will rain," Kristen said more to herself than anyone. "I love the rain."

Ava watched her with raised eyebrows, trying to decide whether this was real or not. Ultimately, it did not matter. Whether it was really

Kristen, a hallucination, or even the chip attempting to communicate with her, it didn't matter. One way or another, Kristen was here to help her—though it seemed Ava would have to find the answers herself.

"What more did you want to discuss about topic number one?"

Kristen smiled. "Your Intelligence Quotient, that is, your ability with the chip."

"What about it?"

"Well, it is interesting that with Eric, a small threat, all you managed was a little nudge of pain. With the Jiānhùrén, the threat was much greater. You knocked out several men in an instant. And a similar threat level from the Zhànshì, you incapacitated four at once."

"Why does that matter?"

"I didn't say it did. Just that it was interesting. Although, I have to wonder what greater threat you could possibly face than what is invading the Tower as we speak."

Ava squinted her eyes in attempts to understand, but Kristen changed the subject too soon. "How about topic two? What was Breanna trying to tell you?"

"I already figured that out," Ava said in frustration.

"Yes, you did. The thing she was trying to tell you was that there was a better way to access the power of the link to control the Tower. But what did she manage to tell you, quite by accident, as she conveyed that message?"

Ava pondered for several minutes. "I don't know...that Harrison wasn't always right?"

Kristen looked up to face the sky again. She watched it thoughtfully for some time as the clouds continued to gather. "This place, in your mind, is so vivid, it almost seems real."

"Hallucinations can be very convincing," Ava said dryly.

Kristen smiled. "How vivid was the picture she sent you?"

"Clear as day," Ava responded, then curiously she tried to understand why that was important. Clearly, from the look Kristen was giving her, it was.

"What did your friend manage to tell you, in conveying the picture of the Tower?"

Thoughtfully, Ava pondered that before responding. "That we have the ability to project images through the link."

Kristen smiled. "Let's talk about issue number three."

Ava didn't exactly feel settled on the other two topics, but it was obvious she wasn't in charge here. "Okay," Ava offered. "You start."

"What did Harrison get wrong?" Kristen asked seriously.

Ava let out a deep sigh. This would be the hardest question of all. Where to even start?

☆ ☆ ☆ ☆ ☆

"General Altman, sir. Our radar is picking up an oncoming convoy. Hundreds of military vessels, headed right for us."

"Backup?" Eli asked in frustration. "How? We're keeping them just as busy in Moscow and at the frontlines. They don't have any more help to come!"

"I don't think it's Russia, sir. Our long-range cameras picked this up." The soldier held up the image for the General to see. A symbol, marking every truck, every jeep, and every tank.

Eli cursed. "Alert all our men to a new, greater threat. The Jiānhùrén are here."

☆ ☆ ☆ ☆ ☆

Nastia stood ready with her men at the elevator shaft. They had been warned once more, this time by Kyle, that it was very likely Valkyrie might appear.

Nastia only hoped that the five of them against the one woman alone would be enough.

"I think I heard something," Matvey whispered.

"Hold," Nastia ordered, though it was more for herself than the others.

Seconds passed, and sweat beaded on Nastia's forehead.

The lift door began cracking open as a metal object pulled it apart. The hall was silent aside from the screeching sound as the enemy broke through, and Nastia watched as she and her men quivered from the pressure. They would not stand down, though it had never been so hard to remain strong.

The door was soon pulled open enough for a grenade to be thrown through, and on command from Nastia, Pierre did so. It had two seconds to detonation when a hand caught it in the air from behind the shaft.

The grenade was thrown back out, and everyone screamed in horror, ducking for cover.

They were unprepared to meet the enemy as they writhed on the ground—those who had survived the explosion.

Valkyrie went to each of the team quickly. They attempted to get up and face her, and some even managed to do so, but she was quicker and stronger than any of them—especially wounded as they were. Several times from her spot on the ground, Nastia attempted to fire on Valkyrie, but the woman miraculously always moved before the shots could reach her.

Nastia attempted to get to her feet as Valkyrie finished off the last of her men. Screaming in fear, Nastia stood and limping, she ran at her foe, rapid firing as she charged directly at Valkyrie.

She was relieved of her gun before she even knew what happened, and then she was on her back, with Valkyrie's hands around her neck.

Nastia screamed and gasped in fear, trying to fight back, but with no success. If Valkyrie had been trying to kill her immediately, she would have died as quickly as her men, but apparently the robot assassin wanted to talk first.

"Please!" Nastia screamed despite herself. She cut off mid-sentence, not wanting to end in shame by begging for her life. Instead, she screamed in terror as Valkyrie moved in closer.

"You are Ava's friend," the robot said in monotone.

"No!" Nastia said, almost pleadingly. "I was her bodyguard. I was just doing my job! We were never friends!"

The robot had no expression as she moved in closer. "I am sorry. But Eli believes otherwise."

Nastia let out one final scream before her world went dark.

★ ★ ★ ★ ★

"*Send in the troops,*" Darya ordered. "*And while they're distracted with each other, we'll take over the Tower.*"

"*Yes, ma'am!*" Bashir said through the link.

Darya turned to the driver of her truck. "Get me to the General's jet. We have some other business to conclude."

☆ ☆ ☆ ☆ ☆

"She's getting worse!" Malya warned. "Her pulse is thready. She doesn't have long."

Zak looked up from his work to where Ava was. "Keep working," he ordered his two-man team, standing and walking across the room. "You can go help," he told Malya. "I'll do what I can for her."

Somehow, it just didn't seem right for Ava to fade away in the arms of a stranger. She and Zak had never been all that close, but they were friends, and through Jackson, they cared for each other. He knelt down on the floor beside her, wishing he had cushions or a bed, or some amount of comfort to offer her in her final moments.

"I wish you would stay a little longer," Zak said to the dying woman. "I wish you would wait for Jackson to be here. I wish you would stay long enough for him to say goodbye."

He grabbed her hand in his, and it was warmer than it had a right to be. She was sweating profusely, and her pulse was, indeed, weak.

Something caught Zak's attention, however. He noticed her eyes moving from underneath her eyelids. She was not entirely still. Something was going on in there. He turned to Mikel, who had been concentrating previously, but now watched Zak with a hopeful look. "You should try talking to her through the link," Zak suggested.

"I have. Repeatedly. No response."

Zak sighed in sad understanding, turning back to face her. She wore a simple ring on her left hand, a wedding band from Jackson. Seeing the unadorned band sent a pang through Zak's heart. Jackson was planning on getting her something more special, more beautiful, more lasting. Only Zak knew that. Jackson would never have the chance.

"You were a good friend, Lex," Zak said lovingly. "All those months we worked together. I would have asked you out, if Demitri hadn't scared me off." He chuckled. "I guess it worked out in the end. I got Viktoriya and he got you." He rubbed her hand lovingly.

"I still blame myself for what happened in Korea. I shouldn't have guilted you into letting me take Boris for his walk. Viktoriya really wanted to get to know you. She's not great at making friends—especially with other women. But she really tried with you. And when she heard you and Jackson were married...man, she was so happy. She *really* wanted to be your friend."

He watched her sadly for a time. "You were a good auntie to my kids. They'll miss you too. And Boris? I don't think he'll ever recover. But don't worry. We'll take care of Jackson. He'll be okay. We'll help him be okay."

Her hand gripped his tightly, and his eyes widened in surprise. "Do you hear me, Ava? Are you still in there?"

The hand loosened its grip, and Zak sighed.

"Uh-oh," Mikel said with sudden concern.

"We have a problem!" Zak's secondary tech said, almost at the same time.

"What's wrong?" Zak asked. "What's happening?"

"Something's gripping the door," Malya replied in confusion. "There's some sort of magnetic mechanism attempting to break the seal."

"She's here," Mikel muttered.

Zak stood, carefully setting Ava's hand beside her and running back to the control center. He tried for several minutes, but there was nothing he could do. He turned to the meditating Zhànshì. "Mikel?"

"I'm trying," Mikel answered absently. "I'm blocking it. They must have some new tech. They were probably tired of not being able to break into Tower cores. Don't worry, I won't let her—" his eyes shot open, a sudden look of panic. Without a word he stood and ran to the entrance as the door was ripped open.

"Get back!" Zak ordered his team as the agent Valkyrie appeared in the room.

Mikel ran for her, and he put up more of a fight than probably most could. Zak used his sidearm, hoping to get in a hit while she distractedly fought Mikel.

Valkyrie dodged his bullets as easily as Mikel's hits. Soon enough, she had Mikel, gripped on either shoulder, and banged his head so hard against the wall that he was knocked immediately unconscious.

Zak stood in front of his team protectively, but Valkyrie was not there for them. She scanned the room before her eyes fell on Ava. She started toward her.

Ava was dead anyway, and Zak knew that consciously. He had a wife and a family to think about. But in that moment, all he could think about was Jackson and the debt he owed his friend. He had not managed to save Ava from the flaw—though he was so close to having a solution, if she'd just lived a little longer—but he would not let Jackson's wife be taken so easily for Eli.

Zak ran, while Valkyrie only walked, and he put himself in front of Ava's unconscious body. The plan ended there, and it occurred to him then that it made no sense for both of them to be killed when she was dying anyway, yet he did not budge.

"You are Ava's friend?" Valkyrie asked in monotone.

"Yes," Zak said seriously, and surprisingly, he was unafraid. If this was his time to go, then so be it.

"You would protect her with your life?"

Zak nodded. "Yes. I would."

Valkyrie's face showed expression—the first he had ever seen from her: relief. She pulled something from her pocket, holding it out to him. "Then you must administer this."

He watched her, uncomprehending.

"You are on my hitlist," Valkyrie said once again in monotone. "And I am ordered to clear this room completely."

Zak glanced at his terrified team. None of them liked the sound of that. "I will follow my orders eventually," she said, and he saw a sort of strain, as if the decision to wait was physically painful to make. "But first, you must save Ava."

Zak looked at the vial in her hands, not certain he could trust her. "How do I know it won't hurt her?"

She cocked her head, as if that was a strange question. "This is medicine."

"No medicine can fix what's wrong with her."

She stepped in closer, holding the hand out firmly. "Remington once told me that Ava might need this. She is dying. She needs the medicine from Remington."

It was all so absurd, so confusing. There was no miracle cure for the flaw, as far as Zak knew, but Ava was probably dead either way. It didn't seem as if Valkyrie intended harm. And if administering this drug bought his team even a few minutes more, maybe it was worth the try.

"All right," he said, carefully reaching his hand out and retrieving the vial. He watched her absently as he knelt once more beside Ava. "Did he say where to administer it?"

Valkyrie gave an ever so slight shake of her head, and Zak made a safe guess by jabbing the needle into her thigh.

As soon as the drug was administered, he stood to face Valkyrie again.

"Thank you," she said in monotone.

"Can I ask," Zak risked, "why couldn't you have done that yourself?"

She struggled, a seeming strain or pain in her head and her eyes closed briefly before reopening. "I am pushing my orders as it is. I am unable to go that far." Her look almost showed a touch of sorrow when she spoke again. "Now, I must clear the room."

"Wait," he pleaded, raising his hands, "my team has nothing to do with Eli. Let them go. I know I'm on your hitlist, but they're not. Please?"

She looked around the room, straining in intense pain. Slowly, she nodded, but then she winced as if that decision, too, was painful.

"Get out!" he told the team hurriedly. "Go!"

And they did, as quickly as possible, though Malya hesitated momentarily.

Zak hadn't even been able to report to Jackson that Valkyrie was here, but he was relieved when that news was sent through his earpiece by Malya as soon as she and the team were out of the core.

"I'm on my way!" Kyle replied. "Hold on, Zak!"

"Your team is gone," Valkyrie said, still straining from the pain. "The core is clear. But you are on my hitlist."

"I know and that will be great when it comes, but before we get to that, I wanted to ask about you and Kyle."

She looked up at him in shock.

"I heard you worked together, briefly. I kinda got the vibe that he might have a crush."

Valkyrie stared at him, the most expression on her face that he had ever witnessed. She seemed disturbed.

"You're not into him too, are you?"

Valkyrie winced. "I must kill you now."

"By all means, we'll get to that, like I said. But first—"

She shook her head, straining in pain and walking in toward him. "No. Now."

Zak flinched, and closed his eyes as she hurriedly approached him, going in for the kill.

☆ ☆ ☆ ☆ ☆

"Valkyrie!" Kyle spoke her name loudly, stopping her in her tracks.

She was less than a foot from Zak and had a look of determination on her face. He had seen that look on her in battle many times.

"Kyle," she said, not bothering to turn toward him. She winced suddenly in pain, and then gasped. "I have to...gah!" Her hands went to her head, and she shrunk lower as the pain overwhelmed her.

Kyle glanced at Ava's unconscious body lying on the ground beside the other two. "Get her out of here!" he ordered Zak by mouthing the words, so as not to warn Valkyrie.

Zak moved to the ground and picked Ava up, hurrying from the room quickly.

Kyle moved in, past Mikel's unconscious body, moving closer to Valkyrie and hoping that unconsciousness would not cause Mikel to lose his battle with Counter Intelligence.

Shannon winced and worked through the pain, before managing to open her eyes and face him. "Please," she begged, "do not be near me."

He stepped in closer, placing a gentle hand on her forearm. She flinched away, putting distance between them in the room. She looked at him now that he had turned off the Chameleon to interact with her. She stared at him for several seconds, struggling through something that Kyle did not understand.

"I said, do not be near me." She said each word slowly and painfully.

"Why?" he asked, adding a touch of loving sarcasm. "Are you having trouble breathing?"

She laughed at that, for the briefest of moments, then her hands went to her head, and she winced once more.

Kyle stepped in closer. "What's he doing to you? Is he hurting you right now?"

She shook her head. "No. I am hurting myself. The pain always comes. If I stray from my orders, the pain comes. And it is unbearable! I have let too many live today. I have strayed too far. And it hurts more than it ever has before!"

Kyle stepped in closer still, until he was before her, and he placed his loving hands on top of hers gently, where they rested on her temples.

She seemed to appreciate the touch at first, but then she gasped in pain, and pulled away. "Leave me alone!" she pleaded. "Do not be near me!"

"What's wrong, Valkyrie?" he asked weakly. "You've never been hurt to be around me before!"

"You are the top of my hitlist, above even Jackson. I am to eliminate you at whatever cost. And there was no waiting to ensure you felt the pain of the lives lost as I am to do with Jackson. I'm ordered to kill you on sight."

"Then why haven't you?" he urged, hoping her power to resist these orders was above Eli's power to enforce them.

She shook her head over and over, and her eyes tightening further. "Please! Leave. I cannot kill you. Please, Kyle! I cannot kill you!"

"Then don't," he whispered in a pained tone. "Don't follow Eli's tainted orders! You can conquer this pain. You can win against him, Valkyrie. I know you can!"

Again, she shook her head over and over until apparently the pain became too much. Then she screamed, and when her eyes opened and looked at him with that heated anger, he almost thought she had decided to kill him.

Instead, she bolted and ran from the room.

☆ ☆ ☆ ☆ ☆

Private Smirnoff had previously believed all hope was lost, and would have proudly died beside General Sasha Ivanov, although he was terrified to do so. However, things had shifted since that time. Colonel Jackson Davis had aided them in the nick of time, and since then Smirnoff had seen the ferocity of these two warriors as he and the sergeant fought side by side with them.

Smirnoff was one of many Russians who had before this time wished Jackson Davis dead. But he changed his mind when the man came to his rescue against the United Kingdoms' army.

They should not have stood any real chance against a practically invisible enemy, but the determination and confidence of his leaders kept the private going, even when he was ordered to drop his weapon— his main line of defense—and use a simple fixed blade against a highly powerful foe.

The four-man team made their way to every sound of gunshot, aiding their fellow officers before it was too late. And each time, they would add another Russian soldier to their group, simultaneously eliminating more and more of the enemy soldiers. The small team continued to grow.

Soon, however, the smoke began to dissipate, and it became harder and harder to see the shadowy figures without help from the smoke.

"Zak," Jackson whispered on the main line. "Is there any way you can get back into the core?"

"I was trying to hide myself and Ava from Valkyrie, who definitely wants me dead now. I think she's hunting me. But sure, yeah, I'll do my best."

Jackson grimaced. "Never mind. We'll manage."

Smirnoff had heard such comments from the colonel before, and didn't necessarily like the thought of them being on their own, yet he could not deny that Jackson Davis had always thought of something and had resourcefully managed every time.

Their team had grown to over a dozen men now. An easier crew for the enemy to spot, but also more difficult to eliminate.

"We have a problem," a weary voice sounded through the common radio. "This is Malya. I made it to a secondary command center. Another army is entering the vicinity. The Jiānhùrén apparently want a taste of the conflict."

Gunfire sounded, and Jackson Davis once more led the team right toward the sound.

Smirnoff should have been more afraid, but the fact that neither Colonel Davis nor even the wounded General Ivanov seemed at all afraid, led the private forward with confidence.

★ ★ ★ ★ ★

Bashir and his men surrounded the opening of the Tower. The small burned-through hatch was enough to allow his men access, but he paused before entering and took a careful look inside. The room was lit up and artificial smoke filled the air. It would be difficult to spot the enemy in this state, but it would also be difficult to be seen.

He and his men were able to file into the room completely unnoticed. The specific programming on their chips would allow them to see the shadow figures in Eli's army—and the Russian officers would be no problem at all.

Bashir followed his team through the fog until they spotted enemy soldiers. Then they picked them off one by one in the smoky area, Russians and Kingdoms' men alike. They would have this lobby, and this Tower, cleared in no time.

Of course, it took Bashir off guard when several figures stepped suddenly through the shadows and attacked him and his men, armed with little more than five-inch blades. While this small, elite team attacked Bashir and his men, the gunfire had apparently alerted the stealth officers to Bashir's location as well.

As the smoke dissipated further, Bashir caught a clear image of the scene before them. The center of the Tower lobby had become a battlefield with three fronts.

Jackson Davis fought with his elite squad, and the General's army fought just as ferociously. Bashir's men were likewise merciless.

The three-way battle raged, and although Bashir had more men, with the other two sides seeming to take on the Jiānhùrén together, there was no clear advantage. Yet, one way or another, Bashir and his team would finish things.

★ ★ ★ ★ ★

The pain was unbearable. Valkyrie had gone too far against her orders, and she paid dearly for it now. The pain had never been this bad. There was only one way to stop it. She had to end this, all of this. And yet, Valkyrie was not certain she could face Jackson Davis again, and do what was necessary. Ava's father had been left alive, and he, too, must be eliminated. The technician Zak Chekov and his team must die. The Zhànshì Mikel, whom she had left unconscious in the core. Kyle.

Each time she had chosen to let them live a little longer. She had always intended to return and finish the job eventually. And yet, somewhere in the back of her mind, she had always sort of hoped that this battle would end somehow before she had to complete her orders. The battle had not ended, and she had gone too far. The pain was too much, and it was time to complete the mission.

Even now, in the way she would finish the job, she was straying some from the orders she was given, and as Valkyrie set explosive charges in the Tower generator room, the pain increased. Eli wanted every individual to see her face and to know his wrath before their end, but Valkyrie did not have the strength anymore to do this. She had little left to give. And so, in order to survive this pain, there was only one solution: a quick, simultaneous ending for them all.

She set another explosive charge. No one had easy access to this room. It was nearly impossible for enemy soldiers to make it inside, but Valkyrie had done so. And now she would finish this fight once and for all.

She set another charge, with a timer for three minutes. It may give her enough time to exit the Tower. Or she might be caught in the blast. Neither possibility seemed preferable at this point.

Until the job was done, and the charges were set, she had been sure she would at least attempt to escape—but what would she be returning to? The General, who would use, hurt and control her for power? The General, who would force her to attack her own friends for revenge? The General, who no longer cared for her except as a weapon for his will?

Valkyrie closed her eyes sadly as the pain overwhelmed every sense. She made a decision. She would not wait the three minutes in hopes of escape. She would set the charge automatically.

Valkyrie opened her eyes and returned to the last charge she had set. She opened the button protector, and stared at the red switch for a long time. It had to be done. There was no other way to end this. She moved her thumb forward.

"Shannon, wait!"

Valkyrie whipped around at Kyle's pleading voice. "No," she said weakly. "You cannot be near me. Please, Kyle. Go!"

He shook his head. She could see in his eyes how much he cared for her, even now, even after all the wrong she had done in Eli's name. "No, I'm not leaving you," he said lovingly.

"I will kill you!" she said, though not threateningly, simply as an inevitability.

He stepped in closer. "Then go ahead," he said, setting his pistol on the floor and raising his hands up as if to offer himself freely.

The pain was incredible, terrible, and worsening every moment. Every instinct told her to make the kill, and the pain would stop. She knew it would help. She knew it would fix the worsening pain, and yet, she also somehow instinctively knew that it would create a new pain, a worse pain, and one that would never subside no matter how many of the General's orders she followed perfectly.

Valkyrie looked back at the red switch on the explosive charge. "I am going to end this!" she said determinedly.

Kyle stepped in closer as if to stop her. "Not like that, you aren't."

She nodded her head emphatically. "I have to, Kyle! There's no other way to stop the pain."

Kyle shook his head sadly, taking yet another step toward her. "I'm sorry, Valkyrie, I can't let you do that."

She growled. How would he stop her? Kyle was strong, but Valkyrie was much quicker. He would be dead before he stood a chance. He walked closer, circling around as if to put himself between Valkyrie and the explosive charge. Strangely, she allowed him to do it, shifting as he did until they had completely changed places.

"I'm going to disarm this weapon," Kyle said in monotone, stating the fact so she would understand.

She hissed. "No!"

He nodded slowly, carefully. "Yes, Shannon. I am."

"I will not let you! I will set off that charge!"

"Then you will have to go through me, Valkyrie," he said gently. "Because I will not let you kill all of my friends, and help Eli win this war, in one fell swoop."

"He has already won!" Valkyrie shot back, almost in a sob.

Kyle shook his head. "No, Valkyrie, he hasn't. And we can't allow him to."

A sudden burst of pain came, and acting entirely on instinct, Valkyrie retrieved his pistol from the floor and aimed it at him, intending the kill.

Only at the instant before she pulled the trigger did she remember who this was, and then she could not do it. She could not kill Kyle.

She struggled through the pain, and tears streamed down her face. Valkyrie could not remember crying since she was a child in Harrison's lap, yet she cried now.

Kyle seemed to feel her pain as if he carried the weight himself. His face seemed just as tortured, and tears welled in his eyes, though they did not stream down his cheeks.

Valkyrie strained, holding the gun at him. She did not normally use weapons such as this, but she could not get close to Kyle without affecting her breath, and then she would not be able to best him.

"I will set off that charge!" she said, though even she did not believe it anymore.

"No, Valkyrie," Kyle said sedately. "You won't."

The pain was too much, and every second worse. All she wanted was to scream and hold to the sides of her throbbing head, yet she remained there, aiming the weapon at Kyle, at a man whom she loved, and who somehow loved her too, despite everything she was and all that she had done.

"Put the gun down," Kyle pleaded.

She shook her head. "I cannot," and these words she meant, for she was sure that disobeying that kill order now would cause her own immediate death.

"Then pull the trigger."

She cried audibly. "No! I cannot!"

"Valkyrie," Kyle pleaded, "Shannon, look at me!"

Her eyes were now clamped tightly closed. She shook her head over and over. "No!" she screamed through the pain.

The instinct and the orders repeated over and over again in her mind. "*Kill. Kill. Kill.*" She fought it with everything in her, and with every passing second the General's safeguard against her grew stronger still.

Valkyrie opened her eyes suddenly. It occurred to her in an instant that there was still one way to fix this. One way to save all of the good guys and give them a fighting chance. One way to cripple Eli and ruin his plans. Most of all...one way to stop the pain.

Valkyrie's expression became accepting as she knew what she must do.

"I guess my father's safeguard came with a failsafe," Valkyrie said in realization.

Kyle looked suddenly confused, and worried.

"I should have realized it long ago. All these years...all this time, it was always there, though I never recognized it."

"What are you talking about?" Kyle asked in caring concern.

Valkyrie took a breath, and then smiled. There was a way to be free, but only one that she alone could see.

"All these years, I never noticed, but I could have used the failsafe. I could have long ago. Though I am glad I did not, or I would never have come to know you, Kyle."

"What are you doing, Valkyrie?" Kyle said with sudden fear in his expression as it became clearer what she was saying.

"Every time I followed orders, it was always there, ready in case I wanted to use it. I don't know that I ever could have until now. For all these years, all this time, the orders only ever said..." Valkyrie smiled, one last real smile for him, "kill."

Valkyrie changed the direction of the pistol.

Kyle cried out in horror, but too late.

Valkyrie pulled the trigger.

☆ ☆ ☆ ☆ ☆

Jackson's men were forced to retreat farther back into the Tower as the lobby was overwhelmed by the Jiānhùrén. Countless soldiers from the General's army still filled the Tower, and the number of Russian officers was dwindling.

Fighting enemies on not one, but two fronts, and both of them much more powerful, well-equipped and greater in numbers, the small team of now thirty Russian officers still followed their leaders confidently;

but Sasha and Jackson shared a look as they retreated farther into the Tower. There would be no victory this day—not for them.

Still, they would fight until their dying breath, because there could be no victory in surrender to either the Jiānhùrén or to Eli either. And so, as the night dragged on, and the battle raged, Jackson and Sasha alike accepted that this night they would die together in battle.

"I wouldn't have it any other way," Sasha whispered, as Jackson helped the limping man up an empty stairwell, "than to die fighting by your side, my son."

Jackson's expression became solemn, but proud. "We die well, my friend. We die fighting for the cause of truth, of freedom, of right. Even if we drop the torch tonight, others will rise to pick it up and carry it onward."

Sasha gripped Jackson's arm, and Jackson returned the strong grip. "We die, fighting for freedom."

"There is no greater way to go."

Sasha smiled. "No, there isn't. Not for men like you and me."

Shots fired from above, indicating that the enemy had already made it to the higher levels. They stopped, prepared to turn back around again, but from below came shadowy figures, barely visible.

This was it. They were surrounded, this would be the end.

Jackson let go of Sasha, and the man took to firing on the Jiānhùrén on the upper levels, while Jackson moved to train fire on the General's army below. The small team of thirty officers split fire between the two sides, and they fought valiantly with what would inevitably be their final breaths.

☆ ☆ ☆ ☆ ☆

The General and his men fought off the attacking Jiānhùrén, but too much of his army had been sent into the Tower. He had few soldiers left to defend him, and Darya was equipped with countless men. Eventually, she broke through.

Eli fought her desperately alone, when all of his personal guard had been killed. But of course, Darya had a weapon against those with the chip, and when she entered the room and turned the device on, Eli fell to the cabin floor, writhing in intense pain.

"Nice to see you like this again, Eli," Darya said in her arrogant, sneering tone. "We have so much to catch up on."

★ ★ ★ ★ ★

"Do you have what you need?" Kristen asked as they stood near the main entrance of the garden. Ava nodded somberly. "I think so."

Kristen reached her hand out and lovingly touched Ava's cheek. "I think so too, love."

Ava smiled, despite her fear and concern. "I'll miss you," Ava said, not caring anymore whether this was hallucination or reality. She *would* miss this. That much she knew.

"I have never left you, Ava. Just as Remington told you once. You will never be alone. We're always right here, right with you. That's the whole point, isn't it?"

Ava smilingly nodded. "Yes, I guess it is."

"Now go, love. You're needed elsewhere. It's time to win this battle. It's time to end the half-a-century's war."

"Thank you, Mom."

"Thank *you*, Ava," Kristen countered with a deep pride in her daughter. "Thank you for finishing what so many started, but were unable to complete. Thank you for all that has already been done, and for what is still to come."

Reluctantly, Ava left her mother and the peaceful garden behind for a horrific war that seemed already lost.

19

The General's Rival

The sound of gunfire from every direction flooded Jackson's ears, and they rang in pain from the crashing sounds. Every second the enemy grew closer. Obviously, he was afraid. Yet he also felt a strange sort of peace. He only wished he had the link and a way to send a final message to Ava in this moment. She would probably die today as well, but if by some miracle she survived, he hoped she knew how much he loved her.

"Give up your weapons and surrender!" the Jiānhùrén ordered. "You're all as good as dead!"

It occurred to Jackson that the blurry figures of the General's army stopped moving because they, too, were surrounded.

One of the indistinct forms nearest Jackson came out of stealth mode to face him. He was an enemy soldier, and yet the look he gave Jackson was a sort of invitation.

"Give up your weapons!" the Jiānhùrén ordered.

The stealth soldier shrugged as if to tell Jackson he didn't mind either way. Jackson smiled. He liked this man.

"Give up your guns and surrender!"

"Nah," Jackson said to the soldier. The man smiled, and evanesced into stealth mode. They resumed firing from both sides, though this time Jackson took the risk of trusting the stealth soldiers to the bottom steps, and he helped his men focus above.

There was no winning in giving up to Darya. She was a terrorist, and would just as likely kill them on their knees as soon as they surrendered their guns. He would rather go out fighting than helpless, especially with the perfunctory alliance with the General's army.

The battle raged for minutes more, but every second became more dire. Despite the momentary hope, there would be no winning this. The Jiānhùrén were too many, and Jackson's men and the General's remaining army too few.

When it became clear to Jackson that this really was the end, he strangely found himself smiling. He still could not deny: this was a fine way to go.

Then, out of nowhere, things shifted entirely.

Sasha collapsed from beside Jackson, and at first he thought Sasha had been hit. But the attacking fire stopped suddenly, when one of the Jiānhùrén who had also seemingly gone unconscious, fell down the middle of the stairwell and hit the ground with heavy impact. The room went still and quiet.

"Hold fire!" Jackson ordered with sudden uncertainty. He checked Sasha's pulse, and found him still alive, as suspected, yet fully unconscious.

The room was deathly silent as moments dragged on, and his officers waited in fear.

"What's happening, sir?" one of the young officers whispered in confusion.

"I have no idea," Jackson admitted as the unconscious stealth soldiers became visible on the stairs where they lay.

The neural connection between the chip and the suit was how they accomplished invisibility, and as soon as any of them were killed that connection broke and they became visible.

These men, however, were not dead; he could see them breathing. Jackson assumed that simply being knocked unconscious would not be enough to fully break the neural connection. There had to be safeguards to protect them under such circumstances. Jackson walked slowly down the steps to the stealth soldier who had become his ally, checking his pulse. Definitely alive, and definitely unconscious.

He risked walking farther down, past all the now-visible stealth soldiers. Beyond the General's army, dozens of Jiānhùrén soldiers lay collapsed and likewise unconscious on the ground. The only people who had not been taken down by whatever this sabotage might be were Jackson and the Russian officers.

Jackson returned to his men thoughtfully. What did Sasha, the Jiānhùrén, and the General's army all have in common that Jackson and these officers did not?

The chip.

☆ ☆ ☆ ☆ ☆

Eli opened his eyes. He was standing, looking down, and the first thing he saw was the dirt on the ground beneath his boots. He wore his green cargo pants and a black T, adorned with a black watch—his old military garb. He stood outside, in some sort of dirt field. He looked up. He stood alone in a large, circular arena. He had been here before. It was a Zhànshì training ring.

Suddenly, he was not alone. Outside the ring, Zhànshì appeared, watching him silently. They were joined by countless United Intelligence agents. Soon he recognized the faces of some of his stealth army also standing outside the ring, watching, looking as confused as him as to where they were, and how they had gotten here.

There were many soldiers he had never seen before, of many ethnicities. Only when he spotted Darya standing among them did he understand: they were the Jiānhùrén.

So many faces he recognized, and so many he had never seen before, but all of them surrounded the ring, watching, and attempting to understand.

Closest to him outside the ring, Eli noticed Sergeant Breslin, and the other young Zhànshì in training who had been there that day two years ago, the day that Eli and Ava had first challenged one another. Of course, Breslin was now supposedly suffering late stages of effects from the flaw, and was near death. In actuality, his ill health was Eli's doing.

And then suddenly, he knew why he was here.

He looked across the field. There she was.

Ava wore her old Zhànshì training uniform, her hair braided back, but she was older than she had been when this was her uniform. She looked like the Ava of twenty, the Ava who was his enemy.

Eli scanned once more the faces of the crowd as they watched in confusion. He spotted Sasha, and then Kyle, who looked saddened and unfocused on the fight before him. Eli could not understand how they had been transported here, or why all of these people looked as confused as he did—all but Ava.

He stood there uncomprehending for a time before it occurred to him that everyone was watching him in anticipation of this inevitable fight.

Eli walked forward toward Ava until they were not ten feet away from one another, then he stopped.

"Hi, Ava," he said carefully.

"Eli."

The crowd watched, and Eli half expected them to start placing bets. None of them did so.

"Why are we here, Ava?" Eli asked, discomfited to give away so much power by asking the question.

"I don't know, Eli. Why are we?"

He shrugged. "Rehashing old wounds?" he offered sarcastically.

She did not react. She looked pristine. She looked put together. She looked strong.

She looked like her mother.

Eli hoped he looked like a hardened, strong, brilliant General like Harrison, and not a floundering fool like Eric.

"*Old* wounds?" Ava said pointedly.

"Is this about Remington then?"

"Remington? Yes. And Katia. Vasiliv. Nastia—"

"All your little Russian friends," he said coldly.

"—and Valkyrie," she continued as though he hadn't.

Eli's eyes pulled together. Had Valkyrie been killed in the fight? He had been too busy dealing with Darya to pay attention.

"Sergeant Hawkins, and all the rest."

"So, this is about revenge?" he spoke in a demeaning tone, practically mocking her.

Ava shook her head once. "No, Eli. I don't work that way."

Eli unconsciously glanced once more at the audience. It was clear they were sizing the opponents up, trying to decide who had the better chance of winning. He had to make an impression if he was to keep their support.

Eventually, he turned back to Ava. She had not taken her eyes off him, almost as if she didn't even know the others were there watching, and she thought it was just the two of them. A ridiculous mistake, and she would pay for it. If she wanted support, she would have to vie for it.

"You always do this," Eli said, adding a touch of condescension. "You always feel the need to compete with me for power. You lost the seat of the General on your own. I was elected to this place freely, and you ran away like a sore loser, switching sides because you didn't like how it went down."

He glanced at the crowd, noting that his soldiers and agents mostly seemed to agree with that, though he didn't like the number of them who didn't seem entirely positive.

He scanned the faces further. Not just the armies he had brought to Russia. Every person with the chip seemed to be here. How had they all gotten here? What had happened?

"I'm not here to fight you for the seat of the General," Ava replied confidently.

Eli snickered. "That's right. As the Zhànshì will recall," he said pointing to the large group who had been there last time, "you were scared to fight me then, and it will be no different now."

Eli glanced at Breslin, but almost flinched to see the scorn in the man's face. The other Zhànshì looked similar. Apparently, they had seen Ava's surrender differently.

Still, Ava seemed completely focused on Eli alone. "I'm not here to back down either," she explained with that same confidence.

It was all one big joke, and she was making a fool of herself. Eli took a fighting stance. "All right, Ava. I'll play your game—though usually you accuse me of being the one to play games with you. Let's do this."

She offered a half smile. "Not like that," she said, remaining strong, proud and resolute.

Awkwardly, Eli dropped his fists and returned to a normal stance. "Then why are we here?"

For the first time, Ava broke her glance from Eli. She scanned the crowd, as if taking stock of who was there, pausing on a few specific faces that she apparently recognized.

"Why are we here?" Eli demanded.

Her eyes met his again. Something in that look sent shivers down his spine, though he could not place why.

Eli kept the fear from his face, standing up straighter and attempting to look more assured as he once more glanced at the crowd. He didn't like the looks they gave him, or the way they looked at Ava. They hadn't even begun the fight yet, and somehow, it almost looked as if, in the minds of these people, Ava Altman had already won.

☆ ☆ ☆ ☆ ☆

It came down to this. Somehow, it always did. Ava versus Eli.

In a way, this was the same battle that had raged between Harrison and Kristen in their time.

Ava versus Eli. Harrison versus Kristen. The General versus the Altman girl.

Today the battle would end.

Kristen had fought hard. And, in finding meaning and choice where there seemed to be none, she always managed to…not lose. Yet, she had never been able to win—she had never beat Harrison, let alone achieved full freedom and victory for what she believed.

Today would be different.

Ava looked across the arena at her brother and finally she understood all of it. The battle was suddenly clear, and with that clarity, the victory— the only possible outcome—was just as obvious. All that was left was for Ava to do her part.

And so, the Altman girl smiled. And then she spoke.

"Harrison wasn't what I thought he was. I see that now. Yet, whether it's manipulation, mind control, or simply that I can't ignore the good he really *did* do for the world, I still have to think of him as a great leader—a hero, even. But not the one the world needs now. Not the one to win this battle or this war.

"Harrison always talked about moral relativism—like it was his best friend or his greatest strength. Ironically, it was actually his main— possibly his only—failing. And also *your* greatest blind spot."

Eli glared, not liking the way Ava commanded the floor as she spoke, but seemingly having no idea how to stop her now.

"You want this battle to be a fight between you and me. Countless times you have tried to convince me that I have to forget my friends, my mentors, my allies—even many of my own greatest strengths and talents. You've defined this battle—even to yourself—as you and me fighting one-on-one, on your terms, and in your arena. That's how you want to test for superiority, strength or greatness.

"Truthfully, I actually think I'd have a pretty good shot at beating you even in that—and there are people in those stands who'd put money on me."

She pointed directly at Sergeant Breslin, and he and the Zhànshì wore proud looks as they nodded emphatically.

"But your version of the 'real battle' misses the whole point. *You* miss the whole point."

Eli growled.

"It's not about whether I can best you in this arena, or out-maneuver you in strategy or politics, or outshine you in the media. Or any of the other all-important tasks you've concocted to prove to yourself that you're better than me.

"You see, Eli, it's not about you versus me. It never was about that— it couldn't be about that."

"Stop messing around and let's do this!" Eli hissed.

Ava continued, unwavering. "I'm not supposed to fight you one-on-one—I'm not *supposed* to win that battle. That might be your battle, but it's never been mine."

"Then we both know who the stronger one is!" he spat in anger.

Ava did not react. "When I fight you, Eli—and I *will* fight you— I'm not fighting alone. I'm not some great champion *for* the world. I'm fighting *with the people*. I'm not just a great warrior, I'm on a huge team of great warriors and missionaries for freedom."

Eli snarled, glancing again at the crowd. Apparently, he did not like what he saw, because he turned back to her again in fear. He quickly replaced it with anger.

"Those minds you try to poison against me, they're not blindly following or wisely turning away from me, they're fighting *their* piece of this same battle. Those names you like to throw in my face to tear me down or prove my failures, they didn't die *for* me, because they didn't *fight for me*, but *with* me."

Ava looked at the crowd. Some of them, the Jiānhùrén, still looked uncertain. But Ava felt a swelling in her heart as she realized how many of the General's soldiers and agents were now intently listening to her, and seemed to offer support in the way they watched her.

"Beating you here today isn't about finding that one grand gesture that trumps whatever you could concoct—although I think I've got you there. It's not about the great Ava Altman finally taking down the puny General. It's so much bigger and so much smaller than that.

"Harrison got close sometimes—he figured out he could do much more if he used other people for his purposes. But even as he got so close, he missed the whole point. Semantics."

Ava smiled, thinking of Lionel, and of Yuri, and the lessons these great leaders had taught her in their time.

"The key is not to use everyone for your own purposes but to learn to help them in *their* purpose, to simply do what's yours to do and trust that enough brave and inspired men and women will do the same. And, Eli, they always *do*."

He began shaking with anger now, looking further embarrassed and lost every time he looked at those in the crowd who were supposedly on his side.

"Don't you get it?" Ava asked, a touch of sadness as she addressed him. "You will never be strong enough, smart enough, manipulative enough, or powerful enough to beat me when I stand *with* them—all of them." She pointed to the crowd.

Eli attempted an arrogant chuckle, but it sounded more uncertain than anything.

"It's the ultimate guerilla warfare!" Ava continued proudly. "As powerful and well-armed as you are, in this battle there will always be another ragtag militiaman hidden in a thicket or behind a ruined wall ready to take out your training and your equipment. And this time *he's* in the right, willing to put everything on the line to defend his home, his freedom, and what matters most—to throw his lot in against your perfectly manicured despotism."

Eli gritted his teeth in overwhelming fury.

"This isn't a fight between you and me," Ava spoke softly, sadly. "It's you against me *and* Russia. *And* Africa. *And* Brazil. You're fighting against me *and* Jackson. *And* Kyle and Mikel. *And* Sasha. But the battle is even bigger than that. It's not just you against me, Eli. It's you against me *and* Hawkins and Lionel. *And* Kristen and Ame. *And* Ella and Breanna."

Eli panted deeply and tensed from head to toe. He looked again at the crowd; at apparently the one friendly face he had left there: Zhànshì Six. Eli flinched. The mention of Breanna had been enough to change Zhànshì Six's supportive glance. He now looked angry.

"It really does come down to semantics," Ava said softly. "I will utilize the power of individuals who live their missions, compounding upon each other to change the world, and in so doing, we will defeat you every single time."

"You stand no chance against me!" Eli growled, but all the while looking less confident.

Again, Ava went on as though he had not spoken. "I will defeat you because it's not up to me to make everything right in some huge way or one fell swoop that makes everyone else's lives, sacrifices or heroism a moot point. No. It's up to me to stand up in *my* purpose and do my small and unique role. Just like each and every one of them." Again, she pointed at the crowd, and many of them seemed to feel the words as they were specifically directed to them.

"That's what it means to live your mission. That's what it means to change the world. And that's what it takes to beat a tyrant like you."

Again, Eli snickered, but he had no verbal response to that.

"So, I'm not the culmination of Harrison's dream by right of some simplistic or literal power. Rather, I'm another drop in the ocean of Kristen's—another single, small person doing what's mine to do. Because good men and women doing what's theirs to do, and linking arms with others to make the world more ideal will always, *always* win.

"Harrison liked to brag that if it didn't further his cause, it didn't matter. But he was wrong. This idea simply isn't a true principle, and like all false ideals, when it comes right down to it, it doesn't even work. It will always fall apart eventually.

"No one person could ever be smart enough, prepared enough, great enough to rule the world with their own two hands better than the countless hands of freedom and mission combined across all places and times. Not Harrison; not you."

Eli was trembling in anger, but was unable to speak.

"Your social-engineering, grand-designing plan, however complex and genius, will never replace the ingenuity, initiative, and sheer force of nature that comes from generations of individuals designing, planning, and *acting.*

"Brother, I don't fight alone. I fight with them—each and every one of them who chooses to place their name and their mission on the side of freedom, goodness, and right. I combine my purpose and all my strength with *all of theirs.* And we're not here to yield.

"We're here to win."

Ava shifted the images around them. Everything changed, until it was just Eli and Ava in Eric's townhome. The entire house was a wreck, following the battle between Eli and Ava.

Eli knelt on the ground, trembling in anger and looking a mess from the cuts and bruises.

Ava stood a few feet back, looking just as physically horrible, and holding her limp, broken arm with her left hand.

"You're forgetting, Eli," Ava told him softly, kindly, "we already fought each other in your version of battle."

He looked up to face her, and they locked eyes.

"We already fought. And I already won," she said.

He trembled, and she watched as his feigned confidence broke.

"I forgive you, Eli," Ava said in a soft whisper.

The images shifted. They were back on the training arena once more, both of them still looking bruised and battered, and Ava still with her broken arm. All eyes were on them once more. Ava opened her mouth and spoke, finishing the sentence from before. "But I will never again yield."

Ava took a step forward, toward her brother, toward her greatest enemy.

"Go ahead, Eli," she said kindly as the arena gates opened, allowing entrance for the crowd. "Call on your soldiers, and I'll call on mine."

Still, despite everything, Eli laughed condescendingly. "You think you stand any chance against my armies?" he said in snide laughter. "I command all of those soldiers and agents! Who do you have? Sasha and Kyle? Breslin and his puny Zhànshì? You really think you stand a chance?"

Ava gave a half smile. "In fact, Eli, I have more than a chance. I've already won the battle."

Eli laughed out loud, but in an instant, the images shifted. One place after the other, all the significant moments, all of the battles between these two, all of the memories that showed who these soldiers had been following, and the corruption. The trail of bodies. The endless pain he had caused so many. The meaningless battles he waged in search of revenge.

Mere seconds passed in the real world, but like in the dreamwalk, the crowd witnessed a lifetime or two of compelling evidence. For it was not just Ava's biased memories that she shared in those seconds. She accessed Eli's own memories and pinpointed the moments that could not be ignored.

In a courtroom, perhaps it would not be fair to use such evidence against a defendant. But in a battle, in defeating this tyrant, Ava utilized her abilities to show the truth to the hundreds of soldiers and agents who blindly followed the General, as well as to all others who had the chip.

And when it was done, when she had shown all they needed to understand the difference between the General and the Altman girl, the images faded.

"Goodbye, Eli," she said one final word as she let go her hold on the minds of those she had gripped. They all woke up at once.

All but Ava herself.

☆ ☆ ☆ ☆ ☆

The remaining officers could only zip tie so many of the nearly hundred soldiers before time ran out, but Jackson and his men worked as quickly as possible, removing weapons and restraining hands and feet.

Soon the stairs and the lobby were cleared. "Split into teams of three," Jackson ordered, "and sweep the Tower a level at a time." He handed each team another full box of zip ties. "Get as many as you can. Let's hope they don't wake up any time soon."

"Yes, sir," the officers replied, heading out to follow orders.

Although these were all enemy soldiers, and although the Russian officers pointed out that if it were Jackson and his team who had gone unconscious, the enemy would not have hesitated to take advantage of the moment and kill them all, Jackson wasn't going to massacre over a hundred sleeping men. That just didn't sit right. They would deal with prisoners of war, although he would have to find a way to prevent the Jiānhùrén from activating their cyanide as soon as they woke. There were a lot of considerations to be made, and he didn't know how much time he had.

"Jackson," Zak called outside the core as Jackson neared.

"Hey, man!" Jackson said, clapping Zak on the shoulder. "Good to see you alive."

Zak chuckled. "Barely. By many a miracle."

Jackson smiled his agreement, and they entered the core together. Jackson noted in awe the door that had been completely ripped from the wall. That was impressive.

Mikel was inside and had been laid beside Ava—both of them were unconscious.

There were a lot of things to do, but Jackson had thought he'd never see Ava again. Even with her unconscious on the ground, he could not help going to her, and pulling her hand into his. "Thank you, Ava," he muttered for only her to hear. "Whatever you did, whatever you're doing, thank you. I love you, kid."

"Tower sensors are back online," Zak said from the control center, and Jackson got up to meet him. "I'm picking up heat signatures all throughout. Your men better work quickly. There are a lot of these guys."

"I better get back out there then," Jackson said, walking back to the door. Someone grunted from behind, and Jackson noticed Mikel waking up beside Ava.

He met eyes with Zak in sudden worry.

"Sir!" a voice sounded through the radio. "They're waking up. All of them!"

Jackson watched Ava hopefully, wanting her to wake up too. Mikel was fully up and holding his wounded, throbbing head before it became clear that Ava would not wake up.

"I'm sorry," Zak whispered, apparently knowing what Jackson had hoped for.

Jackson smiled, despite himself. "I'll be back. Good luck in here."

★ ★ ★ ★ ★

Kyle rose from the generator room where he had collapsed unconscious.

Ava had won the battle. The fight was over, yet Kyle's work was not finished. There was still more that only he could do. He looked longingly once more at the body of Valkyrie, the woman he loved, before retrieving the gun from her hand.

Despite losing Valkyrie, despite his pain and tremendous heartbreak, Kyle found that he was still whole. He would mourn her. He would miss her, probably for the rest of his life, but he would go on, and ultimately, he would be all right.

Perhaps it was those words Valkyrie had shared with him around the campfire some weeks ago, when she said that there was too much hatred in the world, and not enough love, for Kyle was not angry.

He would not let Darya and the Jiānhùrén, or even the General and his armies, move forward in attacking and hurting the world as they had, but he did not hate them. He did not, even as he hunted down his enemies, find a need for revenge.

Valkyrie was gone, and he would mourn her, but it was not the reason that Kyle would do this job. No, it was simply that it was his job to do.

Perhaps there was a sort of poetic justice in him being the one to fulfill this, but it was as Jackson had said in referring to the people raiding the Towers. It *was* justice, nonetheless.

Kyle mourned Valkyrie and would love her to his dying breath. And yet, he felt no need to avenge her. Harrison, the man who had done this to Valkyrie, was long dead, and those who had hurt her or taken advantage of her since that time had chosen wrong, and it was horrific of them to do as they had. But that was not why Kyle did this job. No, it was simply his to do.

And so, he would do it without question.

☆ ☆ ☆ ☆ ☆

Eli gasped, and sat up quickly, but his timing was seconds behind Darya. She held her weapon, and she was ready to fire.

"Well that was a sweet little encounter," she said in a demeaning tone. "Little sister and yourself? What a loving embrace."

Eli snarled, but could not respond. All he saw was the barrel of the gun pointed at his face.

"It's a shame, Eli. It really is, how misguided you are. You, and Harrison, and all others like you. How many times did you both claim you were fighting for freedom? All the while, Harrison just wanted to hurt me and his other enemies, while both of you chose to hurt those closest to you."

"What makes you any better?" Eli shot back between gritted teeth.

"Don't worry, General, I make no magnanimous claims. I don't pretend to fight for any great cause. I don't pretend to be anything other than what I am. I want but one thing, and I will achieve it. Revenge. An eye for an eye. Ava will die because of me, and so will you."

She laughed bitterly. "But before I kill you, there is one thing you really must know. This way that you chose, this path that you followed, it was all in the name of honoring Harrison. But I don't think you would ever have crossed the line as you have if you didn't already think it was too late."

Eli's teeth gritted further. She had in the past used her knowledge of Harrison's death against Eli. That was the day he changed. That was the moment he crossed the line. And Darya was the only one who knew the truth.

"Everything you've done in the name of following Harrison, all the lives you took, all the lines you crossed, you did because of the assumption that you had already killed the General and there was only one possible way to move forward from there."

The "assumption"? Eli's eyes narrowed in an attempt to understand her use of that one very specific word.

"You never chose to be better, because you always believed it was too late for you." She laughed menacingly, and Eli sat still, frozen in fear and defeat, wondering where she could possibly be going with this.

"You did all that you did based on the assumption that you had killed the General, and therefore must complete his plan as he had directed. But you were wrong about one thing."

Eli watched her uncomprehendingly. What did she mean? What was she suggesting? And why did Eli's gut wrench as the feeling overcame him that he had made a terrible, horrifying mistake?

Darya grinned, a chilling expression. "You didn't kill Harrison. *I* did."

Eli's stomach dropped as images flashed through his mind—the images Ava had just thrown out for all of the Intelligence world to see. All of Eli's decisions since that day.

The week surrounding Harrison's death was all so blurry and confused. But one thing was certain. He had changed after that day. He had committed fully to Harrison's plan and to doing whatever it took to accomplish it.

He had already crossed the line in killing the General, and it had changed him.

But what if he had been wrong all along? What if he had become this man, the General's tyrant, for nothing...?

★ ★ ★ ★ ★

Kyle's resolution failed as he thought of what came next. Could he really go through with this? Could he return to look Jackson in the eyes and presume any sort of trust between them after this? Could he face Ava and admit to her that he was responsible for Eli's death?

His quick pace slowed through the halls as his certainty wavered. Suddenly he had to ask the question: could he really be the one to kill Eli and have his hands clean of guilt for the remainder of his life? Or would this action of necessity be one of revenge because of Valkyrie's loss?

Kyle turned down a fork in the hall, heavy with thought. He caught his breath when he found Sasha there, leaning against a wall and attempting to hobble down the hallway.

"Kyle!" Sasha said in sudden relief. "Come and help me get somewhere of use!"

Kyle said nothing. His eyes became mournful with that same heaviness. Could he be the one to take the life of Sasha's son?

Sasha's expression changed from relief to sudden understanding. "Where are you going?" he asked, though it was clear he already knew the answer to that question.

Kyle clenched his jaw. He knew of a certainty that this must be done. But could he really be the one to do it?

Sasha's eyes closed momentarily in sudden pained understanding. He took a heavy breath that seemed to last for an eternity. Finally, he opened his eyes to face Kyle once more.

"Do it," he said, and it was not permission. Instead, it seemed to be an order.

Kyle's resolve returned. He nodded resolutely before quickening his pace and heading down the hallway.

"Kyle!" Sasha called back to him before he had disappeared. Kyle turned back to face the injured Sasha once more.

Sasha's pain was evident, yet he was just as certain of this action as Kyle had been. "Don't make him suffer, if you can help it. He doesn't deserve any more pain. Just a quick ending. It's what he would want if he still had it in him to ask for it."

Kyle nodded once more, comprehending the merciful complexity of this grave undertaking. "Yes, sir."

With that Kyle left to do the job that was his to do, the job only he could do and remain whole. This was not an act of revenge. This had nothing to do with Valkyrie. Instead, Kyle ran toward his mark with a new sense of purpose. He was doing this for Sasha, who was unable to do it himself.

No, this was not an act of revenge. It was an act of compassion.

☆ ☆ ☆ ☆ ☆

"How are you feeling?" Zak asked Sasha. Having found him in the hallway, Zak had then helped him to the core where he was now seated.

Sasha's pain at this time was deeper than any physical wound, knowing the mission Kyle was on and what it would mean, yet he looked up at Zak pointedly and gestured to his kneecap. "How do you think I feel?"

Zak looked down at the kneecap, but was unable to see anything through the cargo pants. "Relieved?" Zak offered positively. "We won, didn't we?"

Sasha chuckled softly, his eyes turning to see Ava there on the ground. "Yes," he agreed proudly, "we did."

Darya pointed her weapon as if for the kill, and Eli faced it unwavering. The gunshot sounded, but he felt no pain, and instead it was Darya who fell to the ground.

Eli's eyes shot up to the entrance of the jet where a blurry figure walked in closer. It was one of his soldiers! He had been saved in the nick of time.

The blurry vision faded and changed into a distinct person standing before him. Eli caught his breath. It was not one of his own.

"Kyle!" Eli croaked. "You saved me! Thank you!" He attempted to seem friendly, but he sensed that Kyle did not share that feeling.

Having eliminated Darya, Kyle inspected his pistol thoughtfully. It was some time before the man spoke. "This is the weapon that ended Valkyrie's life. It only seems right that it is used to end those who hurt her most."

Eli's eyes widened and he pulled further to the corner of the jet's cabin, away from the sullen Zhànshì.

"Don't do this, Kyle," Eli pleaded, once again, thoughts of Darya's last words haunting him with the man he had become. "This isn't how your people fight! At the very least, I deserve a fair trial! I deserve to plead my case!"

"Maybe," Kyle admitted, still inspecting the bloodstained pistol. "And despite everything you've cruelly done to him, if Jackson were the one here, I think he might even give it to you." Determinedly, Kyle pointed the weapon at Eli.

"But I am not Jackson Davis."

There was a look of certainty in Kyle's eyes that terrified him, but Eli would not go down without a fight.

Jackson entered the Tower cells, walking until he met with the stealth soldier who had become his friend in the fight. "I was told you wanted to see me," Jackson said pleasantly.

The man stood quickly at attention, catching Jackson off guard. "I did, sir."

Jackson's eyebrows pulled together. He didn't think their little battle moment had been *that* unifying. "What's your name, soldier?" Jackson asked.

"I'm Lincoln."

Jackson's lips pulled into a grin. "Good name. Very American."

Lincoln grinned in return. "Yes, sir, I am."

"How can I help you, Lincoln?"

"I speak for myself and my stealth team. We have all spoken extensively and have made a decision."

Jackson was about to object—there was no way they could have conversed since waking up in the Tower cells—but he immediately remembered that all of these soldiers were equipped with the chip, and therefore, the link. "And what decision is that?" Jackson asked carefully.

"Sir, we want to inform you that our allegiance has shifted. We now report directly to the General."

Jackson gave the man a look of confusion, as if to object, "Didn't you always?"

"Sir," the man explained, seeming to understand Jackson's look of uncertainty. "That is, we report to the *rightful* General."

☆ ☆ ☆ ☆ ☆

The corrupt members of Council did everything within their power to cover things up, but too many people had seen it. There was no covering this up. There was no erasing the truth. Too much evidence, too much proof, and too many of the good guys incriminating the bad.

The story stuck.

A series of arrests were made, removing all corrupt Council members and military officers from positions of power and replacing them with secondary leadership, people Lionel had approved of when he outlined this story.

Within minutes of the story dropping, Jonathan Jordan released a new single that was clearly written about Ava, about Eli, and about Council. He could have been in on the Hawkins Files for how flawlessly the song went along with it. Of course, Hailey knew he'd had no knowledge of any of it, but had simply taken advantage of the Hawkins Files release to share the story he, too, had been working on.

Hailey watched the news from the safe house that had been provided for her. She couldn't help thinking of Kyle. Wherever he was, off fighting his bad guy, she hoped he would see this and realize that Hailey's role had been different, but just as integral.

He had claimed they stood no chance of real justice in the Kingdoms. And in truth, his version of justice was not necessary here. He could not have fought or killed enough people to bring true change to the Kingdoms. But King Lionel, and Harvey Caldwell, Sergeant Kathleen Hawkins, Councilman Warren Green, and even Hailey in a small way, had spoken the words, and fought the fight that could win in the Kingdoms. A fight for freedom and justice that mattered just as much as the fight Kyle was waging out in the world somewhere.

The part that really got to Hailey was the news broadcasts showing the peaceful protests on the streets. No rioting, no mobbing like had happened in the Republic. The people of the United Kingdoms were prepared to act peacefully for their freedom. To demand change. To demand greater leadership.

She could not help getting teary-eyed as she watched the news show hundreds of people gathering across the nations of the United Kingdoms, signs held high in support of the Colonel's dream, signs that demanded Ava Altman be reinstated to power. And best of all, signs that said the last words Lionel had left for this peaceful revolution.

"Let the Colonel, and the rightful General win."

Wherever General Ava Altman was in the world, Hailey hoped that she, too, was witnessing this, and that she was smiling.

20

The Best

"I was so distracted," Zak explained in frustration. "I was so concentrated on the core and the battle. I didn't focus enough on the brain scans that the Tower sensors picked up from the core."

They were gathered around the infirmary. Jackson and Kyle were finally being treated for the minor injuries they had received in the battle, whereas Sasha had a full cast on his leg, and Mikel's entire skull was bandaged. Kyle teased him relentlessly, calling it the wrap of shame. Mikel was not impressed.

"I should have been paying more attention to her needs at the time," Zak said apologetically, clearly angry with himself.

"No one blames you," Jackson assured him. "What did you miss?"

Mikel watched anxiously as Zak pulled up the scans from the time while they were all stuck in the core, before Valkyrie had arrived.

"As you can see, she was unconscious, in a sort of hallucinogenic state—"

"Like the time when the Jiānhùrén drugged her," Kyle offered. "When she caused the blackout."

"Right," Zak agreed, pulling up the scans they had stolen from Intelligence servers. "In fact, the brain activity for the majority of that time is almost identical."

"Show them the thing," Mikel pushed. He had seen all of this. He had helped Zak figure it out.

"Getting to that," Zak said, pulling up the video feed. The film showed Mikel and Ava walking, pre-battle, protected by Nastia and her men. A group of oncoming soldiers passed by, and one of them ran into Ava, not veering his course though it would have been easy to do so.

Then Ava stopped, holding up her arm, and looking at the passing officers as if trying to find something.

"She said she felt a pinprick," Mikel said, beating himself up now. "I should have trusted that something was wrong, but I brushed it off."

Zak pushed "rewind" on the video feed, pulling into the officer's face. "This man later joined the Jiānhùrén against us. He was killed in the battle, but he was one of their people."

Sasha cursed sadly to himself.

"They drugged her," Jackson said the words out loud.

Zak nodded. "Just like they did before. And it would have killed her that time if Remington had not shown up."

"Which is where Valkyrie comes in," Mikel added, conscious of Kyle, and hoping the mention of Valkyrie did not pain his friend too much.

Zak pulled up a later feed, Valkyrie giving Zak the drug and him administering it to Ava. "Within minutes of this," Zak explained, "the Tower sensors show a different sort of brain activity. She could have woken up just fine, after sleeping it off."

"So, why didn't she?" Kyle asked pointedly.

Zak gave a sad shake of his head.

"Her brain scans were similar to that of all of us," Mikel explained, since it was difficult for Zak to, "while we were all under the effect from Intelligence. It only changed in the instant we all woke up."

Everyone watched, uncomprehending, waiting for an explanation.

Zak was ultimately the one to give it. "In the instant that you all awoke from that state of dreaming, Ava slipped into a coma." He pulled up another scan. "This is the Zhànshì Liam. He spent over a decade in a similar coma, only able to communicate through the link."

"Has anyone tried talking to her?" Jackson asked hopefully.

Almost everyone nodded their heads—that is, all those who had the chip. "No response," Sasha related sadly.

Jackson deflated.

"So, she could live for years this way?" Sasha asked, looking still as if he was waking up from the surgery on his knee. Normally, he would have been right by Zak's side in conducting this research, but given his unfortunate circumstances, he had been unable.

"I don't think so," Zak said sadly. "She seems to be fading quickly. Possibly, the stimulation that it took to conduct that dream state for everyone with the chip was too much. Maybe it was just her time. I don't know."

"What are you saying?" Kyle asked in frustration. "Are we here for you to tell us that all hope is lost?"

Zak hesitated. "Actually...no. There is a chance for her."

Jackson looked up with a sudden hope. If he knew what Mikel did, he would not be so hopeful.

"It is very unlikely that it would work," Zak explained carefully. "However, I am cautiously optimistic. In the past, we were hesitant to remove the tumor because it had formed around the chip. She went into that first brain scan, only with the understanding that if it would affect her ability to connect with the chip, then she would not do the surgery. She said too many lives were at stake, and she would not give up the one chance we had against the enemy."

"But we won," Viktoriya said hopefully. She had mostly kept to herself in the corner of the room until then. She had arrived an hour or so previously and was helping in the cleanup efforts and treating wounded soldiers. "I mean, you guys did. I wasn't really a part of it."

"Your part mattered just as much," Jackson said automatically, though it almost felt disconnected, as if his mind said it out of habit, though his heart wasn't really in it.

Sasha nodded agreement. "Raising the future generation is arguably more important."

"Yes, yes, I know I matter," she interjected impatiently. "Can we save her?"

Zak offered a loving smile for his wife. "I'm hopeful. I've been working for the past weeks on a way to decrease the affected areas in her brain and I've had a lot of success. There's about a twenty percent chance that removing the tumor wouldn't kill her. Then the other shadowy spots on her brain might still become tumorous later on in life, although I hope that the research Sasha and I have done will be enough to help treat that. If we can even get her strong enough to attempt some of the treatments, I think we can ultimately find a way to reverse the affected areas. She would no longer have access to the link. She would no longer be able to help with the Towers."

"But she would be alive," Jackson said, still seeming almost as if his heart were not in this room while he dealt with this situation.

"If she survived," Zak agreed.

"I don't like those odds," Kyle objected.

"That's not the only problem," Zak added. "We still don't know what to do with the Towers. That resource is too powerful and dangerous. The ability to control and the weapon that it is...."

"Not that it makes any difference in what we do with Ava," Mikel observed. "It's not like we can really ask for help right—"

"Mikel."

Mikel stopped mid-sentence, his mouth dropping open. He recognized that signal.

"What?" Zak asked in concern.

Mikel looked behind him, but the curtains were drawn. He stood, despite the throbbing in his head, and pulled the curtains aside.

"Ava?"

"Mikel, I need your help."

"She's talking to me!" Mikel uttered in exasperated excitement. The others hurriedly ran across the room—all but Sasha, who was unable to walk—in order to see if she might wake up, or at least to witness whatever happened next.

"What is it?" Mikel asked through the link. *"What's wrong?"*

"Over a hundred Tower cell doors opened. I'm trying to fight back, but there are too many of them, and I'm too weak."

Mikel got right to work, connecting quickly to the Towers.

"What's happening?" Jackson asked, and this time there seemed real emotion behind his words.

Mikel scanned the cells, locating those that had been opened. He attempted to block the level doors, but they had been opened too. "Taint!"

"Mikel!" Kyle shouted.

"The Jiānhùrén!" he blurted in reply. "They're escaping!"

Several more curses as Jackson and Kyle pushed through the room to face the threat.

Mikel attempted to locate the enemy, but so many Tower systems were disabled and still offline. Valkyrie, the stealth soldiers, and particularly the Jiānhùrén had done a real number on the control centers and the Tower systems during the battle.

"I-I...I can't stop them," Mikel stuttered. "I can't even find them!"

Jackson sat looking frustrated at the briefing table. Kyle watched him with commiseration. They had faced a great many defeats, and even with the overarching victory, this was a serious blow.

How many times had Kyle attempted to warn everyone about the threat of the Jiānhùrén? No one ever listened. He wasn't bitter, really, but he did wish he had managed to be more convincing when it mattered.

"The Jiānhùrén are resourceful, and they're incredibly talented, fast learners," he explained. "They all opted into the chip for the physical and mental enhancements. I assume that, while the rest of us were caught up in watching the battle between Ava and Eli, the Jiānhùrén were observing, and learning from, Ava."

"If they simply learned to work with the Tower like I did..." Mikel said pointedly.

Jackson nodded in consideration. "They've taken the remaining Towers of the Republic," he said, announcing the fact that all of them knew. "In three days, they have overwhelmed the systems. We left one ridiculous loose end, and we'll pay dearly for it."

"We were kind of busy," Mikel pointed out.

Jackson shook his head stubbornly. "We don't get to be too busy to catch something so important!" He closed his eyes, pounding his fist in frustration. When he opened his eyes he thankfully looked a bit more optimistic. He even managed to smile. "An anarchist terrorist organization now has control of twelve major Tower systems. Any good ideas?"

"Send Kyle after them!" Mikel said sarcastically. "He's always claimed it was his job to handle them. Well then, go ahead, Kyle."

Kyle glared at his friend, and Mikel chuckled.

"We'll call that 'option B,'" Jackson said, his attempt to deal with Mikel's annoying habit of joking around in serious moments. "Any other ideas?"

"Worldwide blackout," Kyle offered. "For good this time. Knock out the entire global Tower network for good."

Jackson genuinely considered that one. "I don't know," he muttered uncertainly. "It's hard to imagine that causing a long-term blackout can be a good thing. So many people rely on this technology."

"Then maybe it's time they learn a new way," Sasha offered. "There is other technology. There are other ways. This weapon may be too great, particularly when it gets into the wrong hands, as it has."

"And what?" Jackson argued. "We just let Russia keep theirs? I'm not liking this lesson in ethics right now."

"Maybe Russia relearns a way to power our world too," Zak offered with a shrug. "I mean, don't get me wrong, it sounds terrible! Having to find alternative ways to charge and power various technology, I mean, it sounds like an utter waste of time and resources. But maybe the Towers *are* too powerful."

Jackson shook his head. "I just can't wrap my head around the right answer being to become a sort of luddite anarchist group of our own, bent on destroying technology. Is it really the answer to force the world back half a century?"

"Sometimes there is no right answer," Kyle disagreed. "Perhaps there is just the answer we choose."

Jackson listened, and considered. It was clear to Kyle now that he had earned Jackson's respect. He no longer spoke to Kyle as if he were an inferior—if ever he had. He spoke to him as an equal, and as a friend.

"You may be right," Jackson offered. "Still, I don't know if I'm ready to make that call."

"If we did," Sasha said, exploring the idea further, "just for argument's sake, if we did decide to do it. How would we accomplish it? The Jiānhùrén have apparently discovered immunity to Counter Intelligence, but they have the system up and running for all others with the chip who would oppose them. They've powered it on stronger than the Republic ever did."

Mikel agreed. "Attempting to connect with the Towers now would probably be suicide. I'd like to believe that Ava and I could split it up as we have in the past, but it might just as easily kill us both."

"Who knew that there could be something worse than the Republic?" Viktoriya muttered. She was generally quiet, but now and then she added her thoughts to the mix.

"Well, there was Eli, for one," Mikel said. "And we fixed that problem."

"There is some real truth to that statement," Sasha said in response to Viktoriya. "In some ways, this group is far worse than the Republic. They do not believe in organized government, and would destroy all such organizations, whereas the Republic hoped to expand, and bring others along. This group is unafraid to die for their cause, and in fact, the only way they managed to overtake the Towers was at great loss to their group. And yet, worst of all, they seem to have never-ending numbers. Not all within their organization are equipped with Intelligence, but enough of them are to add to that threat level."

"And we just left those Towers for them," Jackson said, still attempting to remain optimistic, though he was clearly frustrated with himself. "While we fought off Eli and a handful of the Jiānhùrén, the rest of them overturned the Republic. And we have no idea the damage they intend."

"Maybe they'll destroy the Towers for us," Zak said hopefully.

"Maybe," Sasha agreed. "Though not before doing irreparable damage to the rest of us, and the Republic, first."

"All right," Jackson said, moving along, "let's label this current idea of destroying all the Towers and risking Ava and Mikel 'option C.' Now, anyone got a good plan A?"

Jackson entered the room alone. He stared at the dresser that held Ava's clothes, and the chair where she was usually reading when he came home. He stared at the bed they had shared for such a short time. Their marriage had been so rushed, and had come to this tragic ending far too quickly. Yet he still cherished those memories, as painful as it was now to be alone.

It didn't help that anyone with the chip was now able to communicate with her, but Jackson had removed his. *Go figure.*

He took off his boots, and set them on the floor.

Then for a long time he lay in bed, trying to sleep with little success. It felt as if the world was on his shoulders. He had made one stupid mistake, preoccupied in the heat of war, and everyone was paying dearly for it. He had to fix this, but he hadn't the slightest idea how.

"I wish you were here, Ava," he said as if through the link, wishing she could hear him.

A long silence passed. Then, suddenly, *"Who said I'm not?"*

He sat bolt upright in his bed. There was no way. He had to have imagined it. *"Ava, is that you? Please, tell me I'm not imagining this!"*

There was no reply.

Jackson rolled out of his bed, replacing his boots, grabbing his sidearm and returning to the infirmary. He tried to speak with her from her bedside, through the link and verbally, but there was never any response, and after a while he was sure he had imagined it.

Still, he did not want to go back to their room alone, so he pulled the chair close to her bedside, holding her hand in his, and lay his head down beside her. He quickly fell asleep after that.

☆ ☆ ☆ ☆ ☆

"Why did you kill Eli and Darya?" Mikel asked as the two of them walked the perimeter of the Tower, searching for damages.

Kyle was slow to reply. "They killed each other," he reiterated that story, but Mikel knew it was a load of carc.

"Don't lie to me," Mikel said benignly. "I know what really happened. So why? For revenge? To make them pay?"

Again, he was slow to answer. Apparently, Mikel had touched on the right guesses to get Kyle to open up, because he soon replied. "I have said many times that I felt it was my job to fight the Jiānhùrén. I had hoped that their cause would end with Darya. I guess I was wrong."

"What about Eli?" Mikel pressed, not accusingly, but curiously.

"Honestly? Eli was literally insane. And our justice system isn't perfect. I worried he would get off easy. Eli is too powerful, too dangerous, and too vengeful. He would have found a way out. And he would have hurt many more people. But mostly, I did it because I felt as if it was something I needed to do."

Mikel nodded in understanding. "And if there's something that I felt I needed to do, what would you think?"

Kyle watched him as they walked, scanning for any sign of what Mikel might mean. "What do you feel you need to do?"

Mikel shrugged, looking back at the grounds ahead. "I'm just saying, if there was something, what would you suggest?"

Kyle considered for a time. "Jackson says it isn't our right to play God. He is right."

"And yet," Mikel argued, "you killed Eli."

Kyle nodded. "I guess I figured, maybe there was some hope for Eli because of his insanity, but if so, God can figure that out in the next life. In this life, Eli is too evil and too dangerous to be left in some United Kingdoms prison."

Mikel considered for a long time, and ultimately it was up to Kyle to speak again. "Have you shared your supposed calling with Jackson?"

Mikel shook his head. "I already know what he would say."

"That it's not our job to play God," Kyle repeated.

Mikel nodded. "And yeah, I mean, I'm sure he's right. He's usually right about all this stuff."

"And yet," Kyle said knowingly, but left it hanging.

"And yet...maybe I feel like doing it anyway."

Kyle shook his head warningly. "I don't know, Mikel."

"You don't even know what it is I want to do!" Mikel objected.

"But I know you," Kyle countered.

Mikel huffed in annoyance. "So what? You're allowed to break the rules but somehow I'm bound to them?"

"Some people should stick to the rules," Kyle answered. "You've always been a rebel. I have always been strict in my obedience. When I disobey an order, it's different. Half the time, you just do it to cause a scene."

"Those who know the rules can break them, right?" Mikel said condescendingly.

Kyle replied pointedly. "Yes. To some extent. But it's bigger than that. When I made that decision, I knew fully well the extent of what I was doing. I knew the effect it would have. I knew the cost I might have to pay for that choice. I considered every angle. I'm sorry, Mikel, but your arrogance has gotten you into trouble too many times. I'm worried that, whatever this is, you haven't thought it through—"

"I have," Mikel disagreed firmly.

"Then share it with me. Let me see what I think."

"You didn't tell the rest of us you were going after them," Mikel huffed in annoyance.

"I'm not an arrogant blistering carc."

Mikel growled, stopped and hit Kyle as hard as he could in the stomach. Kyle didn't even attempt to block it and seemed completely unfazed by the blow.

"I'm sorry, Mikel," Kyle said firmly. "I don't think you've thought it through."

Mikel ground his teeth, hitting Kyle on the jaw this time. Still, Kyle did not flinch, though the blow had hit him very hard, and blood dripped from his mouth. Kyle didn't even attempt to wipe it away.

"Did you think that through?" Kyle asked pointedly, and Mikel growled again.

"I'm not trying to offend you, Mikel," Kyle explained. "I just know you. Don't get me wrong, your arrogance is a powerful thing. That confidence and determination helped you to accomplish something that no one in the world before you has. And every day since that time, you have continually worked to earn the place you wanted, as the best. You've done well. And even now, you fight an enemy that I was certain would have killed you by now. I don't think that anyone less arrogant or less determined could have done what you did. But I also think you're exactly the type of person who *would* play God. You always think you know best. You act on impulsive desires, just because you like the feel of glory. I don't think you should make any world-changing decisions without talking to Jackson first."

Mikel gritted his teeth. "So, you don't trust me?"

Kyle's expression became somber. "I trust you with a lot of things, Mikel, including my life. But I don't know if I trust you with this."

"So, the three things," Sasha asked her as they sat within her dreamworld. He liked it here. It was peaceful and pleasant. From within this dream, his leg did not throb and in fact, he could walk perfectly fine.

"She walked me through each question in its turn," Ava explained, sitting on the little bench from within the garden, though Sasha preferred to stand when it was so easy to do here.

"First, what did Breanna tell me by sharing that image about the Towers?" Ava signaled to the world around them as if in explanation. "She showed me that we have the ability to project images through the link. With that in mind, I was able to create the scenario for our final meeting and share those images, like in the dreamwalk."

"Which you have managed to do flawlessly," Sasha told her proudly. "This place is so real."

"It is. And so was that image of my mother. I know realistically that it was probably all a projection from the link, and yet, I haven't been able to bring *her* back since it all ended."

Sasha smiled painfully. The scientist in him knew it to be nothing but a projection from the link. But the believer in him was willing to consider the possibility of something more. "She was there for you when you needed her most. It doesn't really matter how or why or what caused it. It was your mother's spirit, in one form or another."

Ava seemed appreciative of Sasha's supportive words.

"What were the other two things?" he asked, still eager to hear how all this had transpired.

"The second question was about my Intelligence Quotient, if you will. I learned that I have the ability to reach out and push on other minds with the link. So, not only could I project these images on a small scale, but I found a way to access the minds of every individual with the link at once and bring them into this world."

"Incredible," Sasha muttered, still disbelieving. "You are unlike any other, Ava."

Not seeming to want the attention on her any more, she shifted to the final point. "What was it that Harrison got wrong? Whatever Liam originally meant by his statement, my mother took me in a very specific direction with it. That was what my entire conversation with Eli was about. Harrison was a moral relativist who believed that any and all means were necessary to accomplish his will. He believed it was his duty to use and manipulate those around him to further his plan. But that's not how freedom is won. That's not what The Cause is about. With Kristen's help, I realized that the whole point is to stand up and do what is ours alone to do, and trust that enough others will do the same."

"With that in mind," Sasha said in realization, "all you had to do was take them through it, show them the truth, and trust that they would make the right choices for themselves."

Ava nodded her affirmation. "I don't think that what I did was any sort of great feat. It was just *mine to do*, and so I did it. But the things that you and all the others did were just as integral." She smiled soberly. "That's the whole point."

"I suppose it is," Sasha agreed genuinely.

Ava's expression became serious suddenly. "And on that note, there's a reason I asked you here."

Sasha sighed heavily. He had known this was coming but had hoped to enjoy a simple, pleasant moment with his daughter without any pressure of having to figure out how to save the world. Of course, for these two individuals, that was too much to ask for.

"What is it, Ava?" he asked in a pained tone. "What is it that will be required of us next?"

She smiled somberly. "Possibly everything."

☆ ☆ ☆ ☆ ☆

Ava had been moved to a more private, long-term room within the infirmary. And though Jackson still worked tirelessly through most of the day, he always set aside his lunch hour to spend with her, as they had before.

The bed she had been moved to was larger, large enough that he was able to lay beside her with plenty of space. He generally attempted to talk to her, both verbally and through the link—yes, he was not ready to write off that moment of hearing her as insanity just yet.

The lunch hour came to a close, but today's work he could accomplish from his scanner, so he remained there beside her on the bed as he worked.

A light tap sounded at the door, and Jackson assumed one of the nurses had come to check on Ava again. "Come in," he said absently as he continued his work.

The door opened, but it was Sasha who entered, wheeling himself inside. Sasha smiled when he saw Jackson's positioning beside his wife.

"Oh, hi," Jackson said, setting his scanner aside, when he realized who it was.

Sasha moved inside and closed the door.

"I have been thinking," Sasha admitted somberly.

Jackson sat up on the bed. "All right."

"Ava and I have been thinking of a possible plan A." There was a sort of gravity to the way Sasha spoke that Jackson understood. This plan would not be without great sacrifice.

"Go on," Jackson said carefully.

"We believe it would be possible to remotely target the Jiānhùrén within the Tower, without causing any blackout, permanent or otherwise. From there, it would be a simple matter of sending in teams to turn off Counter Intelligence, and hold the Towers until we can turn them over to legitimate governments as they are formed. We could even disable the systems that gave the Tower any ability over transcranial stimulation."

"All right, that sounds promising," Jackson said hopefully. "How do we target them remotely?"

Sasha's expression became more somber still. His eyes turned to the girl who lay beside Jackson.

"Through Ava," Jackson realized helplessly.

Sasha nodded. "We would not move forward with any plans to remove the chip. Instead, we would utilize whatever power and energy she has left to finish this war once and for all."

Jackson chewed his lip, painfully considering.

"She would not run the risk of Counter Intelligence by targeting their chips remotely. But I fear that as weak as she already is, she may not survive—if she managed to accomplish it at all."

Jackson nodded in understanding. "Have you...asked her about it?" he asked, once more hating the fact that he couldn't do so himself.

Sasha nodded somberly. "I have. We believe that it's the best possibility, but she wanted me to convince you, since she is unable to do so." Sasha softened, becoming even more somber as he spoke once more, "She said she had promised never to voluntarily leave you again. She says she will only do it if you agree."

Jackson's jaw clenched as the pain overwhelmed him. He looked away from Sasha to hide his eyes as they blurred with tears.

"Believe me, Jackson. I don't like this. When there is even the slightest chance that we could save her, I don't want to let her go." His voice cracked on that last word, and he, too, shied away from Jackson, overwhelmed by his own pain. "I'll leave you to think it through," Sasha said, and slowly, he left the room, closing the door behind him.

Jackson sat there for a long time, watching her, fighting the tears that he did not want to deal with right now.

"*Please,*" Jackson pleaded helplessly. "*Just say something to* me, Ava, *if you can hear me. Please, just say something to* me."

He waited, for a long time, but she said nothing.

Jackson closed his eyes sadly, giving in. He had chosen to give up that power, to give up the chip. And he had never regretted anything more.

★ ★ ★ ★ ★

"We're sure she wants this?" Kyle asked, clearly not liking it.

"You can ask her," Jackson said, and for some reason, Mikel sensed a slight bitterness in that comment.

"She believes it's our best chance," Sasha explained. "And I agree."

"But this is Ava!" Mikel argued. "We have a chance to save her, and we're just gonna ask her to sacrifice yet again?"

"There was little chance for survival anyway," Zak offered sadly, though clearly he, too, didn't like it.

No one did! So why was everyone else giving in, rather than searching for another solution?

"I'll learn how to do it," Mikel offered confidently. "Ava can teach me how."

Sasha shook his head. "No one else with the chip has had any success in this."

"No one else has tried!" Mikel argued.

"Go ahead then," Kyle said hopefully. "If anyone could figure it out, you could. Do it."

Mikel accepted the challenge, reaching into the deepest recesses of his mind and searching for the confidence and the determination that had gotten him this far in life. Then he reached out with all the power he could muster, and he felt the physical power that he was accessing as he attempted to push against Kyle's chip. He had felt it, and it should have worked.

Nothing happened.

"It will take me time," Mikel explained. "Sizwe and I could figure it out."

"We don't have time, unfortunately," Jackson said sadly. "The Jiānhùrén have already done too much. They have caused horrific damage in a matter of days. We don't have the weeks or months that it might take for you to learn this, though believe me, I wish we did."

"So, we're essentially electing to kill Ava?" Mikel retorted confrontationally.

"Don't say it that way to him!" Zak replied just as harshly. "This is his wife we're talking about. He knows the weight of what he's suggesting."

Mikel met Zak's stare. He knew he was being unreasonable, and even rude, but he wasn't ready to write Ava off yet. Apparently, everyone else had already decided.

Mikel gritted his teeth in anger.

"I know how hard this is for you, Mikel," Sasha said with a tone of understanding. "You're the only other one who actually has any power to stop the Jiānhùrén. But this is the right way to do this. We have thought through every angle. This is what must be done. Besides, it's what Ava wants. We're not doing this. She is."

Mikel kept his mouth shut for the remainder of the meeting. He understood why they thought this was the only option, but frankly, he disagreed.

"Even after we eliminate the Jiānhùrén," Jackson admitted, "there will be a lot of regulation and care necessary to keep the Towers from falling into the hands of those who would abuse their power. For a time, we may have to control and regulate in ways I was really hoping to avoid."

"Still, we may be able to disrupt many of the most dangerous and threatening systems," Sasha added hopefully. "And then turn it back to the people."

Once more, Mikel found himself in disagreement. It seemed that this plan had as many flaws as the one he wanted to follow. There was only one difference, and it would make *all* the difference to Mikel.

When the meeting adjourned, Mikel made his way to Ava. Everyone else was ready to let her die, and make her be the hero, yet again. But not Mikel.

Mikel stood by the hospital bed, and asked the nurses for a minute alone. *"Ava,"* he asked through the link, *"can we talk?"*

Mikel closed his eyes, and when they reopened, he was standing in a large, beautiful gazebo filled with myriad flowers of every type and color.

Ava stood, misting the flowers with a spray bottle. She looked her normal self, lively and beautiful and strong. She had learned this new skill, and any time someone wanted to talk to her, she would pull them into a world of her own.

"What are you doing?" Mikel asked in frustration.

"I'm watering Lionel's flowers," she said as though it were obvious.

"No, I mean what are you doing in this imaginary world?"

She looked over at him, her brows knit together in surprise. "You sure look ready to pick a fight."

"That's right," he replied sternly. "Someone's got to."

Ava sighed, turning back to the flowers. "So, have you all decided yet? Do I have a go on taking down the Jiānhùrén within the Towers?"

Mikel's pursed his lips to contain an impulsive response. He watched her for a long time. She was completely entranced in this little fantasy. She was enjoying the flowers and the peaceful garden gazebo. She was wasting her life away in this dream.

Mikel walked forward until he was before her. "Wake up, Ava!" he ordered.

"I can't," she said, attempting to sound regretful of the fact. Mikel saw right through her. Why hadn't anyone else?

"Oh, please," Mikel spat a challenge to her. "You can access the minds of everyone in the world with the chip and transport them to whatever world you can imagine, but you can't wake up from a simple coma?"

She turned to face him, annoyed now. "No, I can't," she insisted. Then, turning back to the flowers, "I've tried."

"What? Like once? You said, 'maybe I'll try and wake uh—ah, never mind, too hard,' and gave up?"

Ava gritted her teeth. "Shut up, Mikel."

He moved in closer, knocking the spray bottle from her hands and to the cobblestone below. "No! Not this time. Everyone else has moved on," he said with extreme intensity. Ava had turned to face him just as intensely. "Everyone else has written you off. Taint, you've even written off yourself! Well, guess what, I don't buy it."

At first, Ava looked like she would take him on, but soon she backed down, retrieving the water bottle and returning to her chore.

"You know what I think?" Mikel said challengingly.

"I'm not sure I care what you think," Ava muttered.

Mikel stepped in closer still. "I think you're scared. I think you're afraid to wake up."

Ava shook her head in annoyance. "You don't know what you're talking about."

"Actually, I think I do," Mikel disagreed. He chuckled as it suddenly made sense to him. "That's right, you're scared to wake up. You're scared to have the chip removed. Who is Ava Altman without the chip? You're scared to face the world without that power, without that title."

She returned to looking at him, a challenge in her eyes. Then of all things, she sprayed him with the water bottle, then returned to her work.

Mikel wiped the mist from his bare forearm, moving in closer until his head was inches from hers, and he spoke in that same challenging tone. "You're afraid to go back. Your marriage with Jackson always had a deadline, and you always knew you'd be the one to go first, so you were willing to move forward with him. But if you wake up, if you go back, you'll have to face what marriage really is. You'll have to face questions about family and sticking through the hard times. You'll have to face the possibility of him dying before you do and trying to go on without him."

"Back up off me, Mikel!" she said through gritted teeth, pushing him away several feet.

"You've heard that the American armies have committed loyalty to you, and that the United Kingdoms have opted to reinstate you as the General. And you're terrified to go back. When you were the General before, it was with Lionel's help. But you're afraid you're not good enough to go it alone!"

Ava ground her teeth together in frustration. Then, she made a decision. "You can get out of my head now, Mikel." She attempted to push him out. She would have managed to do so, to anyone else, but not Mikel.

He pushed back. "Oh, no, sweetheart, I'm not leaving yet."

Again, her eyes met his, and she looked ready to challenge him with all her strength. "I can't wake up," she insisted. "And there's no point anyway. They need the last of my strength to fight the Jiānhùrén. I won't fail them now."

Mikel chuckled fiercely. "And they say I'm the arrogant one."

Ava shook her head in frustration, pretending she didn't care what he thought, but it was clear she did.

"That's it, isn't it?" Mikel pressed further. "You've been told you were the hero, the chosen one, for so many years now, you can't imagine a world where you're not. You'd rather go out now, die in a blaze of glory, than have to face what the real world is like for an ordinary person."

"I said shut up, Mikel!" she snarled.

"No. Not this time. They have a way to save you. They have an actual chance of letting you live out a long, normal life. But you would rather live in this fantasy world, and die as a martyr than go back and face the real world!"

"I don't want to die!" Ava shot back.

"Maybe not," he offered. "But you don't really know how to live either, do you?"

Ava growled. "Get out of my mind, Mikel! Or I'll make you go!"

"Oh no, love. I'm not leaving. If you want me to get out of this little dreamworld, well then, you first."

In a moment of anger, she ran at him, attempting to push him to the ground. He moved in time, and she fell to the paved floor alone. From the ground, she turned and hissed. "Get out of my head!"

"Wake up, Ava," he insisted. "You want to be a hero? Then wake up. Go back to your responsibilities. Learn to face the world like the everyday heroes have to. Learn what it means to actually be married and committed to the man you love in a way that means building a life together. Go back and learn what it takes to be a leader. Those people are counting on you to help rebuild and change things. Wake up and take responsibility."

"I can't!" Ava screamed, standing once more and clearly angrier than ever.

"No," Mikel disagreed, "you *won't*, because you're not ready to go back into a world and face the loss of Eli and everyone else who won't be there anymore."

She ground her teeth, looking ready to attack again, but she remained there.

"You don't want to go back," he said, softly, caringly this time, "you don't want to wake up, because it's hard to face reality. It would be so much easier to die as the hero. Well, I'm sorry, you don't get to be the hero this time." Mikel grinned. "I do."

☆ ☆ ☆ ☆ ☆

Ava sat up. She could not stop him, but she had to try. She quickly began removing the cords and tubes that restrained her to the bed.

Mikel stood in the room before her hospital bed. His hands were on his temples, his eyes closed as he made connection with the Towers of the Republic.

"Stop, Mikel!" she shrieked, climbing from the bed. Her legs had not moved in days, and were weak and wobbly at first, but she made it to him, grabbing his hands and now leaning on him for support. *"Don't do this, Mikel!"* she pleaded through the link. *"It'll kill you!"*

Ava heard the sound of gasps and excitement as the nurses reentered the room and found her standing there.

"Get Colonel Davis and General Ivanov!" one of the nurses ordered.

"Mikel, it'll kill you," Ava warned.

Mikel gasped from the pain. *"It already is, love."*

Ava tried to access the Towers, to help, to stop him, to do anything. But she could not find them. It was almost as if he was blocking her. How was he doing this?

"You carc!" she hissed. "You did what the Jiānhùrén did. You were just in my head to try and learn from me!"

"No, not just that," he grinned. "Also, to wake you up. Seems I accomplish everything I try, huh?"

"Don't do this, Mikel!" she ordered, but she knew it was too late.

"Ava!" Jackson gasped, entering the room with Sasha right behind him.

"He's connecting with the Towers!" Ava warned, not even looking at them. "He's going to do something stupid!"

Jackson moved in closer, attempting to help stabilize Ava as she struggled to stand, still holding on to Mikel's arms to hold her up. *"Mikel!"* Ava shouted through the link. *"Don't do this."*

Kyle entered the room, looking just as surprised and awed.

"We can't do this, Mikel," Jackson said seriously. "We don't have the right to make this decision for the entire world."

"You haven't thought this through!" Kyle said hurriedly, rushing to the side of his friend.

"Oh, yes I have," Mikel disagreed. "The Tower technology is powerful and impressive. And in the right hands, it may even be good. But in the wrong hands, it is a weapon of control and mass destruction. If we don't have the right to control who comes to leadership in the countries of the Republic, then neither do we have the right to leave this weapon sitting there, to be taken up by anyone who might get their hands on it."

"The Towers are more than just a weapon," Jackson disagreed, "they power the entire technology of the Republic. You would destroy their entire economic infrastructure."

"Then teach them a new way," Mikel said, straining now from the pain.

Ava's entire body became hot and shaky, and her head especially felt light. Jackson seemed to notice how she grew weak, and he helped her to a sitting position on the bed.

"Please, Mikel," Ava pleaded weakly.

Kyle moved to his friend, placing his hands on Mikel's shoulders. "Look at me, Mikel," Kyle ordered.

Mikel opened his eyes, facing his friend, though he was straining and sweating profusely now. "I'm not trying to play God here," Mikel promised through the pain, and Ava saw the fear in his eyes. He was already dead. "But this is *mine to do.*"

"Are you sure?" Kyle asked carefully. "Mikel, are you sure?"

Mikel struggled for breath. Ava could almost see the waves of Counter Intelligence beating against him as he strained. "Yes, I'm sure."

Kyle's expression became serious, his words were spoken in a whisper for just Mikel. "Then I support you, friend. Kick their blistering carcasses!"

Mikel grinned, and Kyle shared the smile, though there was a sort of sad mourning in Kyle's demeanor. He would lose his friend; he knew that now.

Mikel shared the grin with Kyle for several seconds before he turned his glance to Ava. "*You never wanted this,*" he said through the link for only her to hear. "*You never wanted to be the one to control the Towers, or save the world with the link. Harrison forced you into that role, and you submitted, because there was no one else. But there is someone else now, Ava.*"

Her eyes filled with tears, but she held his gaze with a demeanor of strength and pride in him.

"*I always wanted this,*" he assured her. "*All I ever wanted was to prove Harrison wrong, and to be the best. At this. So, you go out and be the General that Lionel taught you to be. Become the wife that Jackson deserves and that you wanted to be for him. You go out and live your dream. And let me die, living mine.*"

Ava's eyes blurred with tears, and Jackson held her, relieved that she was awake, yet also shocked by what was happening with Mikel.

"You are the best, Mikel," Ava said out loud as tears streamed down her cheeks. "You *are* the best."

Mikel grinned. "I know."

☆ ☆ ☆ ☆ ☆

Mikel's connection with the Towers caused a system overload. In a few minutes, he destroyed twelve separate Towers within the Republic, leaving only the Tower in Brazil, and two in Russia.

The Jiānhùrén within the Towers were killed from the explosions, and they could only hope the civilian casualties were minimal.

The team sat around the briefing table.

The day following Mikel's destructive action, Ava had undergone the tumor and chip removal surgery. She was recovering well, and everything had gone better than expected.

With further treatments, she might even survive this.

Jackson found the conflicting emotions overwhelming. He was grateful to Mikel for bringing Ava back, yet mad at him for disobeying orders. He was grateful to Mikel for doing what was necessary, so that Ava didn't have to. But he was angry at Mikel for doing something so destructive, making that choice unilaterally for the rest of the world in a way he had no right to do. Jackson was glad to have his wife back. Yet, he also mourned the Zhànshì Mikel, who had become a sort of brother.

The only geopolitical consolation in all of this was that, following the attacks from the Kingdoms, Russia was so fragile, needing all their energy and resources to focus on repair, that they no longer had any inclination to conquer the whole of the Republic. Jackson needed to do very little to tame their ambition in this, since they had been so heavily hurt by the attacks from Eli.

They looked at each other around the briefing table once more. Jackson was the leader. It was his job to say something inspiring or profound, to talk about what was next, and where they were headed, but he had no words to offer.

The room remained silent and somber as they mourned Mikel, while also being grateful for Ava's successful surgery. Twenty minutes passed, and no one said a word.

It was not until the door opened that everyone looked up from their silent, somber thoughts. Ava was there. She should not be walking around yet, and Jackson got up to help her into a seat.

"I'm fine," she said assuredly, taking a seat with his help. She did look fine. In fact, in a certain way, she looked better than ever.

Ava looked around the table, stopping on every face. Jackson, Kyle, Sasha, Zak, Viktoriya. This was what was left of the team. So many others had been lost along the way.

Harrison, Ame, Kristen, Breanna.

Liam, Eric, Yuri, Hawkins.

Lionel, Damian, Ella, Remington, Jun.

Vasiliv, Nastia, Shannon.

Eli.

Mikel.

So many of their friends, gone. So many who should be here. Who *could* have been here. Mikel's death seemed the culmination. Jackson hadn't ever even realized how special Mikel's charms were until they sat in this silent room. He would have made them laugh. He would have made them curse. He would have made them happy. He would have made them angry. He had a special way about him. He had always been special, but Jackson hadn't ever appreciated just how special and amazing Mikel had been, until now, when he was gone.

Jackson glanced at Ava, at Kyle, at Zak and Sasha and Viktoriya. These were who remained.

Jackson had always known that the cost would be great, but this was so much greater than anticipated.

No one spoke. Everyone mourned, everyone considered the losses.

In the end, it was Zak who broke the silence. "What are we supposed to do now?"

Jackson resonated with that question, yet he hadn't the slightest idea how to answer it. Jackson looked at Sasha, but he looked just as lost and uncertain. Kyle had no answers, nor did Viktoriya.

It was Ava, though, who offered a true grin, looking almost like Mikel.

"See, now, *that's* the fun part," she spoke gently.

All eyes slowly turned up to face her, wondering how anything could really be "fun" after what they had just lived through.

Everyone watched Ava, but she looked across the large table and met Jackson's eyes directly when she spoke. "We saved the world. Now we get to change it."

Epilogue

"General Altman!" the gathering crowd all seemed to yell at once.

"Councilman Davis!" others yelled just as enthusiastically.

Jackson and Ava walked past the noisy crowd toward their vehicle, and Jackson reached for Ava's hand as they went.

"General Altman, how does it feel to have your husband on Council with you?"

The election had ended the day previously, and Jackson was in.

Ava smiled widely, apparently deciding she would take that question. "It feels great," Ava said proudly. Then she turned to Jackson, who was watching her with a look of admiration that only showed a small part of what he felt for this woman. "I can't get enough of this guy."

"General Altman, will there be any conflict of interest on the upcoming resolution?"

"Councilman Davis, will you support the bill for an upcoming general election?"

"General Altman, will you take maternity leave when the baby is born?"

Jackson and Ava made it to the vehicle and the door was closed behind them. "That's gonna get old," Jackson said as the vehicle pulled away.

"Hey, at least they're not all trying to assassinate you," Ava teased.

He tilted his head toward one shoulder and then the other. "Progress."

Jackson placed his hand on Ava's knee and leaned back, breathing in and out as the vehicle moved slowly through the crowd. He was exhausted, and yet it was just one small victory, a beginning to so much more.

"You stressed?" she asked in concern.

He kept his head there, leaning on the back of the seat as he shook his head from side to side drowsily. "Tired."

Ava smiled. "You made it to Council. Now maybe you can sleep!"

He chuckled. "I have a feeling I won't ever have a chance to sleep again."

☆ ☆ ☆ ☆ ☆

"The three of us," Hailey said, disbelieving. "You think the three of us can take on the great Jiānhùrén alone?"

"Why not?" Helio asked with beaming excitement. "I've got the money, you've got the voice, and Kyle here has...well, just about everything else we could possibly need to accomplish this."

Kyle grinned widely.

"Don't inflate his ego," Hailey replied coolly.

"What do you say?" Kyle asked. "Are you in?"

She watched them both for a long time, still skeptical about this.

Eventually, Kyle put his hand out above the middle of the table, as if to start a team shout.

Helio joined, placing his hand in the middle with Kyle's.

Hailey sighed heavily, but followed suit. "Fine. I'm in. But there better be good pay involved. My last major gig was pro bono. And I'm broke."

☆ ☆ ☆ ☆ ☆

"We recalled our troops from the border," Captain Lincoln explained from the defense briefing table. "But we have reason to believe the newly founded leadership doesn't intend to keep the peace we have requested. I believe it would be prudent to have the Councilman join the peace talks." Lincoln nodded toward Jackson.

"I agree," Jackson said. "I have some experience dealing with Cassim. I think we can work it out amicably."

"Of course," Ava agreed. "You should go. If we can keep the peace with them, we should."

"I wouldn't mind having him in the field if things go awry anyway," Lincoln said, though the sound of his comment was a bit fuzzy, as if there were static over the radio — but they were in the same room.

"What was that?" Ava asked him.

Lincoln looked at her strangely. "I didn't say anything, ma'am."

She stared at him with an awkward glance for several seconds before Councilman Rojas changed the subject, something about safe passage through Africa into the enemy territory.

"Lincoln, you out of that meeting yet?" a male voice asked gruffly. *"We want to go out for drinks while we're here. The British know how to pub."*

Ava squinted her eyes in confusion, and Lincoln smiled as if to himself.

Jackson responded to the comment of the other Councilman, though she heard nothing of their conversation. She stared at Lincoln in confusion.

"Everything all right, ma'am?" he asked in concern. *"Why are you staring at me that way?"*

It was unmistakable! She had been watching him that time. She heard the words of the second sentence, but his lips had not moved.

"Are you talking to me?" Ava said, attempting to project her thoughts through the link, though she no longer had the chip.

It was Lincoln who looked taken aback that time. *"General Altman?"* he said in surprise.

"What do you think, General?" Jackson asked, and she was pulled back into the meeting.

"I'm sorry, can you repeat the question?" she asked, trying to shake off her surprise.

Jackson did so, but she didn't hear it any better this time as her thoughts raced with unanswered questions.

"You can hear me?" Lincoln asked. She heard his voice clearly, and yet, his lips did not move. Even when she had the link, she had never heard their voices. It had always translated as her own, although she could recognize signals.

"Can you hear me?" Ava asked through the link that she no longer had access to.

"Clear as day, ma'am," Lincoln replied in surprise.

"Am I missing something?" Jackson asked, noting how the two of them stared at each other in awe.

"*I hear you as if you were speaking aloud,*" Lincoln said through the link. "*I've never heard it sound like someone's real voice before.*"

Ava let out a breath of surprise. "*I have.*"

☆ ☆ ☆ ☆ ☆

Sasha entered the Altman memorial, a slight limp as he walked and relying on the cane to help him. He was getting old all right. His leg would never be the same, yet he did not mind. It was a reminder of the past. It was a reminder of all that had happened, all the sacrifices, all the pain, and of those who had given all.

His offering had been minimal in comparison, and he would give both legs—or even his life—in the blink of an eye to keep the freedom and prosperity that so many were experiencing now.

All his life he had fought to see the world as it was right now, today. And yes, they had a long way to go, but that would not be Sasha's to do.

He had given thirty-some years of service, and fifty years of devotion to the cause of the freedom his people.

Sasha stopped a long time at Harrison's memorial. He remained longer still at Eric's. And as he stood before Kristen's, he managed to smile. Her memory was no longer painful. He would miss her until the day they were reunited, but he no longer felt as if he would break at a mere mention of her name. Living out her dream of freedom had somehow healed the wound of their separation. A familiar scar, fondly met, was left in its place,

Sasha moved to the next memorial, Eli's. His memory would not be honored in the same way, and many would curse his name—the tyrant General, as he was now universally called. Sasha had insisted that his body be brought here and buried beside the rest.

Eli had gotten lost along the way. And yet, at the center of the boy there was an admixture: there was goodness, there was hopelessness, there was love, and there was so much pain. He had hurt many people, and no one could ever hope to repair the damage that had been caused. He would be remembered by the world as a horrific, corrupt tyrant. But he would be remembered by Sasha as a gentle young boy, comforting his mother, and trying to beat Sasha in video games—though of course, Sasha always won.

When Sasha had paid his respects to all the others, he stopped at Shannon's memorial. Her story had been one of tragedy. She had never known the joy, love and kindness that a gentle spirit like hers should have experienced. Yet, in her way, she had fought for freedom and done her part.

Every little drop in the ocean. That's how freedom wins.

"A little more love in the world, just like you wanted," Sasha spoke aloud so Shannon would hear the news directly from him. "Jackson and Ava are going to have a baby. A little girl. And they have decided to name her Shannon."

☆ ☆ ☆ ☆ ☆

...*Sedulous*

—Jonathan Jordan

What a shame they stole your fame
Just when the public remembered your name
A new Altman smile leading us to the fight

A clarion call vowing Freedom and Right

On the back of a child, Council scapegoated all
A sword they could brandish when they lost their control.
With blurred media vision, pain- and fear-ammunition
To force "inspiration," they broadcast condemnation.

I have mused to the masses, lyrics hiding the truth
Now the Symphony shattered, can a Kintsugi sleuth?
They needed a mask, One to be brave
So they cast up a shadow on the wall of the cave

[CHORUS]

They say you've betrayed everything that is good
Done things your mother and The General never would
Something ominous has happened behind Public's Eye
Are you finally the one who will fight by our side?

A disheveled peasant, they say you rebel.
But he called you "New Joan," oppression's death knell.
On the hero's path, toward a martyr's end
A warrior, an icon, a mentor, a friend.

You are Cinderella with the Victoria Cross,
And never a moment to grieve your own loss.
Undaunted you stood as they tore you apart
Like mother, like daughter; please, girl - don't lose heart.

You're our Sedulous now—our main driving force
Who never gives up; it's the true hero's course
But the hero's sore curse is so often the same
Lived by Hercules, Thor and the young Orleans dame

While they tarnish your name on the streets and the screens
"She failed and she never lived up to his dreams...
She's fallen, she's done, she is just one of them,"
They assure as they post and exploit and condemn

[CHORUS]

They still say you're a villain, betrayed all that is good
A charlatan, a criminal—but you're just misunderstood.
Though something ominous happened behind Republic's Eye,
You are finally the one who will fight by our side.

But the crowds know the truth, as they usually do
A phoenix has fallen, Council says, and it's true
Yet the fear of a phoenix is one tricky lie
'Cause the rising is coming, see the smoke in the sky?

I am Music but right now I fear suicide
If you call out Tyrant General there is no place to hide
Speak to Power this way, and your name they'll erase
If I'm jailed or gone...well...then I rest my case

But I'll die for this cause, and I know she will too.
She is MORE than they are—we will win 'cause it's true
A General by Council's choice, whim or decree
Is no path to Greatness or a world for the free

[CRESCENDO]

Another ranked puppet now hangs by a thread
How many lies until freedom is dead?
But if Words can be swallowed, then Orders can sin.
Let the Colonel and Rightful General win

—Written by Abigail DeMille—

ELIZA ROBINSON is really good
at burning broccoli.

Her hobbies include strength training,
amateur construction and
birthday cake sampling.

She and her husband Skot own
a small pizzeria in Cedar City, Utah.

They have two daughters.

....

Made in United States
Troutdale, OR
03/05/2024

18228670R00375